STANDARD OF HONOR

Also by Jack Whyte

A DREAM OF EAGLES

The Skystone

The Singing Sword

The Eagles' Brood

The Saxon Shore

The Sorcerer, Volume I: The Fort at River's Bend

The Sorcerer, Volume II: Metamorphosis

— —

Uther

— —

THE GOLDEN EAGLE

Clothar the Frank

The Eagle

— —

THE TEMPLAR TRILOGY

Knights of the Black and White

STANDARD OF HONOR

BOOK TWO OF THE
TEMPLAR TRILOGY

JACK WHYTE

G. P. Putnam's Sons   New York

G. P. Putnam's Sons
Publishers Since 1838
Published by the Penguin Group
Penguin Group (USA) Inc., 375 Hudson Street, New York, New York 10014, USA • Penguin Group
(Canada), 90 Eglinton Avenue East, Suite 700, Toronto, Ontario M4P 2Y3, Canada (a division of
Pearson Penguin Canada Inc.) • Penguin Books Ltd, 80 Strand, London WC2R 0RL, England •
Penguin Ireland, 25 St Stephen's Green, Dublin 2, Ireland (a division of Penguin Books Ltd) • Penguin
Group (Australia), 250 Camberwell Road, Camberwell, Victoria 3124, Australia (a division of Pearson
Australia Group Pty Ltd) • Penguin Books India Pvt Ltd, 11 Community Centre, Panchsheel Park,
New Delhi–110 017, India • Penguin Group (NZ), 67 Apollo Drive, Rosedale, North Shore 0632,
New Zealand (a division of Pearson New Zealand Ltd) • Penguin Books (South Africa) (Pty) Ltd,
24 Sturdee Avenue, Rosebank, Johannesburg 2196, South Africa

Penguin Books Ltd, Registered Offices: 80 Strand, London WC2R 0RL, England

Library of Congress Cataloging-in-Publication Data
Whyte, Jack.
Standard of honor / Jack Whyte.
p.   cm.—(Templar trilogy ; bk. 2)
ISBN 978-0-399-15429-4
1. Templars—Fiction.   2. Crusades—Fiction.   I. Title.
PR9199.3.W4589S73   2007   2007035757
813'.54—dc22

Printed in the United States of America
1   3   5   7   9   10   8   6   4   2

This is a work of fiction. Names, characters, places, and incidents either are the product of the author's
imagination or are used fictitiously, and any resemblance to actual persons, living or dead, businesses,
companies, events, or locales is entirely coincidental.

While the author has made every effort to provide accurate telephone numbers and Internet addresses at
the time of publication, neither the publisher nor the author assumes any responsibility for errors, or for
changes that occur after publication. Further, the publisher does not have any control over and does not
assume any responsibility for author or third-party websites or their content.

For my wife, Beverley,
Endlessly patient, long-suffering,
encouraging, supportive, and inspiring

Every Frank feels that once we have reconquered the [Syrian] coast, and the veil of their honor is torn off and destroyed, this country will slip from their grasp, and our hand will reach out towards their own countries.

—Abu Shama, Arab historian, 1203–1267 A.D.

The soldier of Christ kills safely: he dies the more safely. He serves his own interest in dying, and Christ's interests in killing!

—St. Bernard of Clairvaux, 1090–1153 A.D.

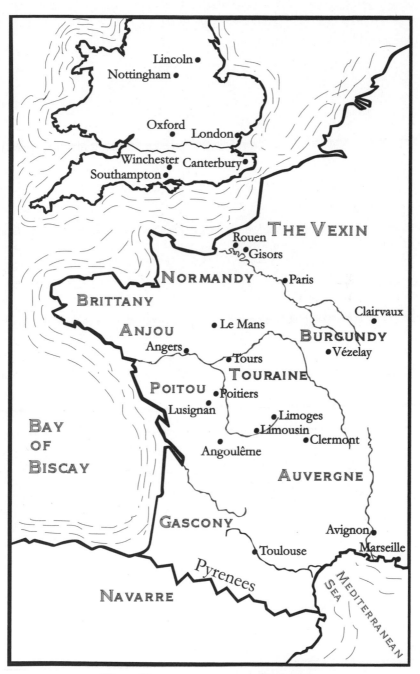

THE PLANTAGENET EMPIRE

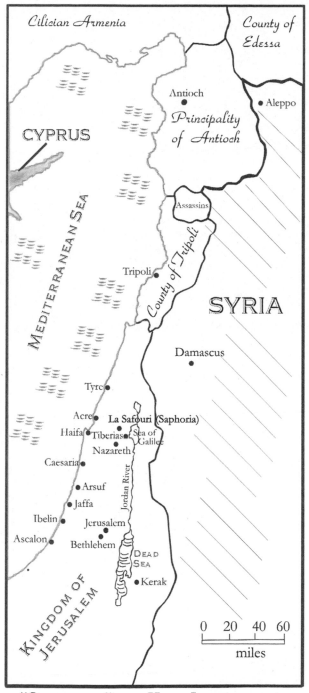

Cilician Armenia

County of Edessa

CYPRUS

Antioch

Aleppo

Principality of Antioch

MEDITERRANEAN SEA

Assassins

County of Tripoli

Tripoli

SYRIA

Damascus

Tyre

Acre

La Safouri (Saphoria)

Haifa

Tiberias

Sea of Galilee

Nazareth

Caesaria

Jordan River

Arsuf

Jaffa

Ibelin

Jerusalem

Ascalon

Bethlehem

DEAD SEA

KINGDOM OF JERUSALEM

Kerak

0   20   40   60
miles

"OUTREMER," THE HOLY LAND IN 1191

AUTHOR'S NOTE

Where is France? If anyone were to ask you that question casually, you would probably wonder at the ignorance that must obviously underlie it, because you, of course, know exactly where France is, having seen it a thousand times on maps of one kind or another, and it has been there forever, or at least since the last Ice Age came to an end, about ten thousand years ago. So clearly, anyone with a lick of education ought to know where it is without having to ask. And yet, as a writer of historical fiction, I have been having trouble with that question ever since I began to deal with it, because I feel an obligation to maintain a standard of accuracy in the background to my stories, and yet, were I to stick faithfully to the historical sources and absolutes in writing about medieval France, Britain, and Europe, I would be bound to perplex most of my readers, whose simple wish, I believe, is to be amused, entertained, and, one hopes, even fascinated for a few hours while absorbing a reasonably accurate tale about what life was like in other, ancient times.

In writing my Arthurian novels, for example, I was forced to accept and then to demonstrate that the French knight Lancelot du Lac could not have been French in fifth-century, post-Roman Europe, and could not possibly have been called Lancelot du Lac (Lancelot of the Lake) because the country was still called Gaul in those days and the French language, the language of the Franks, was the primitive tongue of the migrating tribes who would one day, hundreds of years in the future, give their name to the territories they conquered.

I have had the same difficulty, although admittedly to a lesser degree, in writing this book, because although the country, or more

Author's Note

accurately the geographical territory known as France, existed by the twelfth century, it was a far cry from being the France we know today. The Capet family was the royal house of France, but its holdings were still relatively small, and the French king at the time of this story was Philip Augustus. Philip's kingdom was centered upon Paris and extended westward, in a very narrow belt, to the English Channel, and it had only just begun to develop into the state it would become within the following hundred and fifty years. At the beginning of the twelfth century, it was still tiny, hemmed in by powerful duchies and counties like Burgundy, Anjou, Normandy, Poitou, Aquitaine, Flanders, Brittany, Gascony, and an area called the Vexin, which bordered France's northern border and would soon be absorbed into the French kingdom. The people of all these territories spoke a common language that would become known as French, but only the people who lived in the actual kingdom of France called themselves Frenchmen. The others took great pride in being Angevins (from Anjou), Poitevins, Normans, Gascons, Bretons, and Burgundians. (Richard Plantagenet, the Duke of Aquitaine and Anjou, in many ways was wealthier and far more potent than the French king. Upon the death of his father, King Henry II, Richard would become King of England, the first of his name, the paladin known as Richard the Lionheart, and he would rule an empire built by his father and his mother, Eleanor of Aquitaine, that was far greater than the territories governed by King Philip.)

To all of us today, they are all Frenchmen, but that was not so in their day, and the task of making that clear to modern readers, demonstrating that those differences existed and were crucially important at times to the people concerned, is the main reason why I often have to ask myself the question I began with here: Where is France?

At the time of this story, in the days of Richard Plantagenet and the Third Crusade, the war against the Saracens under the Sultan Saladin, the Knights Templar had not yet achieved the pinnacles of wealth, power, and putative corruption that would so infuriate their contemporaries in later years, engendering envy, malice, and cupidity. But they had nonetheless made unbelievable advances since the time, a mere eighty years earlier, when their membership had numbered nine obscure, penniless knights, living and laboring in the tunnels beneath the Temple Mount in Jerusalem. Within the eight decades since their founding, they had become the standing army of Christianity in Outremer, and their reputation for honor, righteousness, and obedient, unquestioning loyalty to the Catholic Church was sterling and unblemished. From obscurity, the nascent Order had moved directly to celebrity and universal acceptance, and within the same short time, thanks mainly to the enthusiastic and unstinting support of St. Bernard of Clairvaux, the greatest churchman of his day, it had also gone from penury to the possession of incalculable wealth, both in specie and in real property.

From its beginnings, however, the Order had been a secret and secretive society, its rites and ceremonies shrouded in mystery and conducted in darkness, far from the eyes and ears of the uninitiated, and that secrecy, no matter how legitimate its roots might have been, quickly and perhaps inevitably gave rise to the elitism and arrogance that would eventually alienate the rest of the world and contribute greatly to the Order's downfall.

I suspect that if, after reading this book, you were to go and ask the question of your friends and acquaintances, you might experience some difficulty finding someone who could give you, off the cuff, an accurate and adequate definition of honor. Those who do respond will probably offer synonyms, digging into their memories for other words that are seldom used in today's world, like integrity, probity, morality, and self-sufficiency based upon an ethical and moral code. Some might even refine that further to include a conscience, but no one has ever really succeeded in defining honor absolutely, because it is a very personal phenomenon, resonating differently in everyone who is aware of it. We seldom speak of it today, in our post-modern, post-everything society. It is an anachronism, a quaint, mildly amusing concept from a bygone time, and those of us who do speak of it and think of it are regarded benevolently, and condescendingly, as eccentrics. But honor, in every age except, perhaps, our own, has been highly regarded and greatly

respected, and it has always been one of those intangible attributes
that everyone assumes they possess naturally and in abundance. The
standards established for it have always been high, and often artifi-
cially so, and throughout history battle standards have been waved
as symbols of the honor and prowess of their owners. But for men
and women of goodwill, the standard of honor has always been individual, jealously guarded, intensely personal, and uncaring of what
others may think, say, or do.

Jack Whyte
Kelowna, British Columbia, Canada
July 2007

STANDARD
OF
HONOR

THE HORNS OF HATTIN 1187

ONE

"We should never have left La Safouri. In Christ's name, a blind man could see that."

"Is that so? Then why didn't some blind man speak up and say so before we left? I'm sure de Ridefort would have listened and paid heed, especially to a blind man."

"You can shove your sarcasm up your arse, de Belin, I mean what I say. What are we doing here?"

"We're waiting to be told what to do. Waiting to die. That's what soldiers do, is it not?"

Alexander Sinclair, knight of the Temple, listened to the quiet but intense argument behind him, but he took pains to appear oblivious to it, because even though a part of him agreed with what Sir Antoine de Lavisse was complaining about so bitterly, he could not afford to be seen to agree. That might be prejudicial to discipline. He pulled the scarf tighter around his face and stood up in his stirrups to scan the darkened encampment around them, hearing the muffled sounds of unseen movement everywhere and another, distant Arabic voice, part of the litany that had been going on all night, shouting "Allahu Akbar," God is great. At his back, Lavisse was still muttering.

"Why would any sane man leave a strong, secure position, with stone walls and all the fresh water his army might ever need, to march into the desert in the height of summer? And against an enemy who *lives* in that desert, swarms like locusts, and is immune to heat? Tell me, please, de Belin. I need to know the answer to that question."

"Don't ask me, then." De Belin's voice was taut with disgust and frustration. "Go and ask de Ridefort, in God's name. He's the one who talked the idiot King into this and I've no doubt he'll be glad to

3

tell you why. And then he'll likely bind you to your saddle, blind-fold you and send you out alone, bare-arsed, as an amusement offer-ing to the Saracens."

Sinclair sucked his breath sharply. It was unjust to place the blame for their current predicament solely upon the shoulders of Gerard de Ridefort. The Grand Master of the Temple was too easy and too prominent a target. Besides, Guy de Lusignan, King of Jerusalem, *needed* to be goaded if he were ever to achieve anything. The man was a king in name only, crowned at the insistence of his doting wife, Sibylla, sister of the former king and now the legitimate Queen of Jerusalem. He was utterly feckless when it came to wield-ing power, congenitally weak and indecisive. The arguing men at Sinclair's back, however, had no interest in being judicious. They were merely complaining for the sake of complaining.

"Sh! Watch out, here comes Moray."

Sinclair frowned into the darkness and turned his head slightly to where he could see his friend, Sir Lachlan Moray, approaching, mounted and ready for whatever the dawn might bring, even though there must be a full hour of night remaining. Sinclair was unsur-prised, for from what he had already seen, no one had been able to sleep in the course of that awful, nerve-racking night. The sound of coughing was everywhere, the harsh, raw-throated barking of men starved for fresh air and choking in smoke. The Saracens swarming around and above them on the hillsides under the cover of darkness had set the brush up there ablaze in the middle of the night, and the stink of smoldering resinous thorn bushes had been growing ever stronger by the minute. Sinclair felt a threatening tickle in his own throat and forced himself to breathe shallowly, reflecting that ten years earlier, when he had first set foot in the Holy Land, he had never heard of such a creature as a Saracen. Now it was the most common word in use out here, describing all the faithful, zealous warriors of the Prophet Muhammad—and more accurately of the Kurdish Sultan Saladin—irrespective of their race. Saladin's empire was enormous, for he had combined the two great Muslim territories of Syria and Egypt, and his army was composed of all breeds of infidel, from the dark-faced Bedouins of Asia Minor to the mulattos and ebony Nubians of Egypt. But they all spoke Arabic and they were now all Saracens.

"Well, I see I'm not alone in having slept well and dreamlessly." Moray had drawn alongside him and nudged his horse forward until he and Sinclair were sitting knee to knee, and now he stared upward into the darkness, following Sinclair's gaze to where the closer of the twin peaks known as the Horns of Hattin loomed above them. "How long, think you, have we left to live?"

"Not long, I fear, Lachlan. We may all be dead by noon."

"You, too? I needed you to tell me something different there, my friend." Moray sighed. "I would never have believed that so many men could die as the result of one arrogant braggart's folly ... one petty tyrant's folly and a king's gutlessness."

The city of Tiberias, the destination that they could have reached the night before, and the freshwater lake on which it stood, lay less than six miles ahead of them, but the governor of that city was Count Raymond of Tripoli, and Gerard de Ridefort, Master of the Temple, had decided months earlier that he detested Raymond, calling the man a Muslim turncoat, treacherous and untrustworthy.

In defiance of all logic in the matter of reaching safety and protecting his army, de Ridefort had decided the previous afternoon that he had no wish to arrive at Tiberias too soon. It was not born of a reluctance to meet Raymond of Tripoli again, for Raymond was here in camp, with the army, and his citadel in Tiberias was being defended by his wife, the lady Eschiva, in his absence. But whatever his reasons, de Ridefort had made his decision, and no one had dared gainsay him, since the majority of the army's knights were Templars. There was a well in the tiny village of Maskana, close to where they were at that moment, de Ridefort had pointed out to his fellow commanders, and so they would rest there overnight and push down towards Lake Tiberias in the morning.

Of course, Guy de Lusignan, as King of Jerusalem, could have vetoed de Ridefort's suggestion as soon as it was made, but, true to his vacillating nature, he had acceded to de Ridefort's demands, encouraged by Reynald de Chatillon, another formidable Templar and a sometime ally of the Master of the Temple. De Chatillon, a vicious and foresworn law unto himself and even more arrogant and autocratic than de Ridefort, was the castellan of the fortress of Kerak, known as the Crow's Castle, the most formidable fortress in the world, and he held the distinction of being the man whom Saladin, Sultan of Egypt, Syria, and Mesopotamia, hated most in all the Frankish armies.

And so the signal had been passed and the army of Jerusalem, the greatest single army ever assembled by the eighty-year-old kingdom, had stopped and made camp, while the legions of Saladin's vast army—its cavalry alone outnumbered the Franks by ten to one—almost completely encircled them. Hemmed in on all sides even before night fell, the Frankish army of twelve hundred knights, supported by ten thousand foot soldiers and some two thousand light cavalry, made an uncomfortable camp, dismayed and unnerved, alas too late, by the swift-breaking news that the well by which their leaders had chosen to stop was dry. No one had thought to check it in advance.

When a light breeze sprang up at nightfall they were grateful for the coolness it brought, but within the hour they were cursing it for blowing the smoke among them throughout the night.

Now the sky was growing pale with the first light of the approaching day, and Sinclair knew, deep in his gut, that the likelihood of him or any of his companions surviving the coming hours was slim at best. The odds against them were laughable.

The Temple Knights, whose motto was "First to attack; last to retreat," loved to boast that a single Christian sword could rout a hundred enemies. That arrogant belief had led to an incredible slaughter of a large force of Templars and Hospitallers at Cresson, a month and some days earlier. Every man in the Christian force, except for the Master de Ridefort himself and four wounded, nameless knights, had gone down to death that day. But the army surrounding them this day would quickly put the lie to such vaunting nonsense, probably once and for all. Saladin's army was composed almost entirely of versatile, resilient light cavalry. Mounted on superbly agile Yemeni horses and lightly armored for speed, these warriors were armed with weapons of damascened steel and light, lethal lances with shafts made from reeds. Thoroughly trained in the tactics of swift attack and withdrawal, they operated in small, fast, highly mobile squadrons and were well organized, well led and disciplined. There were countless thousands of them, and they all spoke the same language, Arabic, which gave them an enormous advantage over the Franks, many of whom could not speak the language of the Christians fighting next to them.

Sinclair had known for months that the army Saladin had gathered for this Holy War—the host that now surrounded the Frankish army—contained contingents from Asia Minor, Egypt, Syria, and Mesopotamia, and he knew, too, that leadership of the various divisions of the army had been entrusted to Saladin's ferocious Kurdish allies, his elite troops. The mounted cavalry alone, according to rumor, numbered somewhere in the realm of fifteen thousand, and he had seen with his own eyes that the supporting host accompanying them was so vast it filled the horizon as it approached the Frankish camp, stretching as far as the eye could see. Sinclair had clearly heard the number of eighty thousand swords being passed from mouth to mouth among his own ranks. He believed the number to be closer to fifty thousand, but he gained no comfort from that.

"De Ridefort's to blame for this disaster, Sinclair. We both know that, so why won't you admit it?"

Sinclair sighed and rubbed the end of his sleeve across his eyes. "Because I can't, Lachie. I can't. I am a knight of the Temple and he *is* my Master. I am bound to him by vows of obedience. I can say nothing more than that without being disloyal."

Lachlan Moray hawked and spat without looking to see where. "Aye, well, he is not *my* master, so I can say what I want, and I think he's insane … him and all his ilk. The King and the Master of the Temple are two of a kind, and that animal de Chatillon is worse than both of them combined. This is insane and humiliating, to be stuck here in such conditions. I want to go home."

A grin quirked at the corner of Sinclair's mouth. "It's a long way to Inverness, Lachlan, and you might not reach there today. Best you stay here and stick close by me."

"If these heathens kill me today, I'll be there before the sun sets over Ben Wyvis." Moray hesitated, then looked sideways at his friend. "Stick close by you, you say? I'm not of your company, and you are the rearguard."

"No, you are not." Sinclair was gazing eastward, to where the sky was lightening rapidly. "But I have the feeling that before the sun climbs halfway up the sky this day it will be of no concern to any of us who rides with whom, Templars or otherwise. Stick you by me, my friend, and if we are to die and go home to Scotland, then let us go back together, as we left it to come here." His gaze shifted slightly towards the light that had begun to glow within the massive black shadow that was the royal tent. "The King is astir."

"That is a shame," Moray muttered. "On this, of all days, he should remain abed. That way, we might have hope of doing something right and coming out of this alive."

Sinclair shot him a quick grin. "Build not your hopes on that, Lachlan. If we come through this day alive, we will be ta'en and sold as slaves. Better to die a clean, quick death—" He was interrupted by the braying of a trumpet, and his hands dropped automatically to the weapons at his belt. "There, time to assemble. Now remember, stay close by me. The first chance you have—and I swear it will no' be long—head back for our ranks. We won't be hard to find."

Moray punched his friend on the shoulder. "I'll try, so be it I don't have to leave my friends in danger. Be well."

"I will, but we are all in danger this day, more than ever before. All we may do now is sell our lives dearly, and in the doing of that, simply because my brethren are all Templars, you will have more chance to fight on with me than I would have with your companions, brave though they be. Fare ye well."

Both men swung about and headed towards their allocated positions, Sinclair among the Temple Knights at the rear of the knoll behind the King's tents and Moray among the hastily assembled crew of Christian knights and adventurers who had answered the call to arms sent out by Guy de Lusignan after his coronation. It was these men who now surrounded the King's person, and the precious reliquary of the True Cross that loomed above them all.

Glancing up, Sinclair saw that it was already close to daybreak, the sky to the east flushed with pink. And then he shivered, in spite of himself, as he saw the bright, blazing new star in the lightening sky. He was not superstitious, unlike most of his fellows, but he could barely suppress the feelings of unease that sometimes welled up in him nowadays. This star had appeared a mere ten days before, exactly three weeks after the slaughter of the Templar knights at Cresson, and the sight of it stirred dread among the Franks, for it was another in a long string of strange occurrences that they had seen in the skies in recent times. Since the year before this one, there had been six eclipses of the sun and two eclipses of the moon. Eight clear signs, to most people, that God was unhappy with what was happening in His Holy Land. And then had come this blaze in the sky, a star so bright that it could be seen by day. Some said, and the priests said little to discourage them, that this was a reappearance of the Star of Bethlehem, burning again in the sky to remind the Frankish warriors of their duty to their God and His beloved Son.

Sinclair was more inclined to believe what was being said among the French-speaking Arabs of his acquaintance. They believed that the stars moved independently of each other, and that a number of the brightest stars in the firmament had now somehow moved into alignment with each other and combined their light to generate this blazing beacon, so bright it could often be seen even at noon.

When he reached his own squadron, Sinclair settled his flat steel helm more firmly on his brows and scanned his men. All awake and solemn; no badinage or laughter this morning ... not, he reflected, that there ever was much laughter among the knights of the Temple. It was officially discouraged as being frivolous and not conducive to pious behavior. He sought out Louis Chisholm, the sergeant-at-arms, Alexander Sinclair's personal servant since boyhood. Faced with the prospect of life as a free man when his employer joined the brotherhood of the Temple Knights, Chisholm had opted to remain close to the man he knew best in all the world, and had volunteered as a sergeant brother in the Order. Now as Sinclair approached him, he twisted around in his saddle and peered up through the drifting smoke towards the peaks of the Horns of Hattin.

"They say that's where Jesus preached the Sermon on the Mount," he said. "Right up there on the slopes of that mountain. I wonder if anything he could say to that crowd out there today would make any difference to what's going to happen." He turned back and looked Sinclair in the eye, then lapsed into a heavy Scots accent. "We've come a long way from Edinburgh, Sir Alec, and we've changed a bit, the two o' us, since we first set out ... but this is an awfu' grim place to die."

"We had nae choice, Louis," Sinclair replied quietly, pronouncing the other's name in the Scots fashion, as Lewis. "It wasna our doin'."

Chisholm grimaced. "Aye, well, you know what I think about that." He looked about him again. "We're about ready. The Hospitallers are starting to form up, over there on the right. They'll move out soon, so we'd best be ready here. Ye'll have seen how many we're up against out there?" He spat, then ran the tip of his tongue over his teeth, sucking at the grains of sand there before spitting again. "It'll be a short fight, I'm thinking, but we'll try to make it a good one. Good luck to ye, Sir Alec. I'll be right at your back, minding your arse."

Sinclair smiled as he reached out and took the other man's hand. "God bless you, Louis. I'll have an eye for you, too. Now, what's causing the delay?"

As he said the words, the first trumpet call rang out and was answered immediately by others as the army began to move into its battle formations, beginning with the Knights of the Hospital, who formed the army's vanguard. The King's division in the center, his royal standard swaying high above him, moved forward behind the veteran Hospitallers, although, encircled as they were, there was no clearly defined front for the Hospital Knights to face. Nevertheless, the knights of the royal bodyguard formed up at the King's back, as did the Christian prelates and priests, bearing the giant, elaborate reliquary. It was fashioned in the shape of a mother-of-pearl cross and encrusted with jewels and precious stones, and it provided a highly visible rallying point, not only for its protectors but also for their attackers.

Beyond the block formations of the Christian army, surrounding them on all sides, Saladin's great force eddied and moved, visible now although obscured at times by drifting smoke and the dust stirred up by their own movement. They waited patiently, and largely in silence, to see what the Christian army would attempt to do.

The crowd around Sinclair was abnormally quiet. Each man rose in his stirrups and craned to see over the heads of the men directly in front of him in the dawning light. The sounds of the horses were all that was utterly familiar—the stamping hooves and snorting breaths and the creaks and jingle of saddle leathers and harness. Already even the little movement they made was stirring up clouds of choking dust to add to the swirling smoke.

Sinclair loosened his sword in its sheath and bent forward in the saddle slightly to glance across at Louis Chisholm again.

"Bide ye close by me, now, Louis. This is going to be a dour, dirty fight."

The words were barely out of his mouth when a flurry of competing trumpet calls began to sound, and as the army around him stirred in response, preparing to surge forward, Sinclair wondered who could have been responsible for such idiocy, for they had nowhere to go that did not lead directly into the masses of enemy cavalry. That single thought was the last coherent memory he would have of the chaos that followed, for a commotion in the ranks of the Templars at his back announced the arrival of a heavy charge of Saracen cavalry who had approached unseen from the still-dark west, under cover of the drifting smoke.

Sinclair and his fellow Templars of the rearguard, outmaneuvered and outnumbered from the outset, fought grimly to repulse the attack from their rear by Saladin's elite cavalry. They mounted charge after futile charge against an enemy who fell away in front of them each time, only to regroup and encircle the frustrated, heavily armored knights. Enraged by the perfidy of the Muslim archers who concentrated on killing their horses and then picked off the dismounted riders, the Templars were driven inexorably backward into their own forces, only to discover that the King had ordered his followers to erect a barrier of tents between him and the enemy encroaching from the rear. The barrier, flimsy and futile though it was, nevertheless generated chaos among the surviving Templars, forcing them to break their depleted formations as they wheeled and dodged to ride between the useless tents, with the enemy cavalry snapping at their heels. Even when they passed beyond the canvas walls they found neither relief nor support, because the knights of the center were milling helplessly around the King and the True Cross, impeding one another and oblivious to any need to give themselves space in which to fight.

Sinclair, acting purely on instinct, swerved to his right and led his own squadron around the confusion of floundering men and horses, veering hard left in a tight arc, aware that in so doing he was exposing their unshielded right sides to the missiles of the enemy archers. He saw Louis Chisholm go down, struck by at least two arrows, but he himself was under attack at that moment from a warrior who had charged at him out of nowhere on a hardy, agile little mount. By the time Sinclair had deflected the Saracen's sweeping scimitar and brought himself knee to knee with his assailant for long enough to chop him from the saddle with a short, savage slash to the throat, Louis lay far behind him, and Sinclair was too hard pressed to look back for him.

What had become of their twelve thousand infantry? Sinclair could see no sign of them, but by then his world had been reduced to a tiny, trampled arena filled with smoke, dust, chaos, and all the screams of Hell, as man and beast were maimed and killed on every side. He saw and recognized things and events in snatches of vision and incomplete thoughts, forgotten in the urgency of the next eye blink, the next encounter with a savage, bare-toothed face, the next swing of his shield or sword. He felt a heavy blow against his back and saved himself from being unhorsed only by hooking an elbow on the cantle of his saddle. That cost him his shield, but he knew he was a dead man anyway if he was hit again or fell. He managed to right himself, wrenching at his horse's reins to turn the animal away from the threat. Then, for a space of heartbeats, he found himself on the fringes of the melee, at the edge of the high ground, looking down a slope to where the Hospitallers of the vanguard were surrounded, cut off from the main army by a wedge of enemy horsemen who had cut cleanly through the narrow space between van and center.

He had no time to see more than that, for his presence there alone had been noticed and he was being attacked again by two men at once, converging on him from each side. He chose the man on the right, the smaller of the two, and spurred his tiring horse straight for him, his long sword held high until the last moment, when he dropped it to the horizontal and allowed the fellow to impale himself on it, the speed of his passing almost wrenching the weapon from Sinclair's grasp. Panting, he spun the horse around, left-handed, searching for the second man who was now close behind him. His horse reared and shied, taken unawares by the hurtling shadow closing on it. In a feat that he had practiced times beyond counting, Sinclair bent forward in the saddle, then, standing in his stirrups, he dropped the reins on the rearing horse's neck and drew his dagger. A straight sword thrust deflected the enemy's stabbing blade, and as their bodies came together he stabbed upward, hooking desperately with the foot-long, one-edged dirk in his left hand. The point struck a metal boss on the quilted armor of his assailant's chest and glanced off, plunging into the soft flesh beneath his chin, the shock of the impact tumbling him backward from the saddle, heels in the air. Sinclair tightened his grasp instinctively, bracing himself against the falling weight of the dead man, but the dirk slid free easily and he was able to right himself. He reeled helplessly for the few moments it took him to see that he was alone again, in an eddy of comparative stillness.

Sunlight glinted on metal in the morning light above and beyond him and he glanced up to see another distant battle taking place high on the slopes of Mount Hattin. Infantry formations, obviously Christian, appeared to be breaking away from the crest of the high ridge and heading down towards the east, towards Tiberias. But then he heard his name being called and swung away to see a tight knot of his brothers in arms sweeping towards him. He spurred his horse and rode to join them, vaguely aware of arrows filling the air about him like angry wasps, and together they charged back up the hill towards the King's tent, to defend King Guy and the True Cross. Once there, close to the King, they won a brief respite as the enemy withdrew to regroup, and Sinclair, looking towards the distant heights with his companions, saw a tragedy develop.

The infantry—on whose orders it was never known—were attempting to scale the slopes of Mount Hattin. They had almost reached the summit before being blocked by even more of Saladin's inexhaustible supply of cavalry formations. The entire hillside seemed to be ablaze up there, and the entire infantry brigade, ten thousand men supported by two thousand light cavalry, apparently driven insane by thirst and smoke, wheeled away and began a desperate foray down towards the sanctuary offered by the distant sight of the waters of Lake Tiberias, glinting far below them in the morning sunlight. It was evident that they intended to smash through the enemy ranks and win through to the lake, but Sinclair knew exactly, and sickeningly, what was going to happen. There was nothing he could do, and his own duty was clear—he and his fellows had threats of their own to deal with—so he had little time to watch the slaughter that occurred on the lower slopes, where the Saracen cavalry simply withdrew ahead of the charge and left it to their mounted bowmen to exterminate the advancing infantry. Within the hour it was all over, in plain view of the knoll where the King's tent was pitched. There were no survivors, and as hard set as they were while the carnage was carried out below them, there was not a single knight among the ranks surrounding the King who was unaware that twelve thousand of their men had died uselessly down below, beyond the reach of any assistance they might have thought to offer.

The Saracens saw it too, and their response was a frenzied attack on the mounted party atop the knoll. They pressed in hard from all sides, advancing and withdrawing in waves, intent upon wiping out the mounted knights by sheer weight of numbers. Saladin, as Sinclair would later learn, had thought deeply on this attack for months beforehand and had decided that his mounted bowmen would be his strongest asset in the fight against the heavily armored Christian knights. Every archer had gone into the fight with a full quiver of arrows, and seventy camels in their baggage train had been laden with extra arrows to replenish them. The Frankish knights fell quickly, battered and beaten by a hailstorm of missiles shot at them from all sides.

TWO

Lachlan Moray saw Sir Alexander Sinclair fall, but he was unable to tell if his friend was wounded or not, because it was Sinclair's horse that he actually saw topple, its chest and flanks bristling with arrows. Sinclair he merely glimpsed as the white-mantled knight pitched forward behind the animal's rearing bulk, disappearing from view among the rocks as his Templar companions fought to control their terrified mounts and to bring the fight to the elusive enemy.

Moray himself was already bewildered, having suddenly found himself the only survivor of a knot of six knights making their way towards King Guy and his party. They had been isolated for a moment, separated from the King's retreating party by a steep, stony slope, and before they could catch up to the others they had been singled out by the enemy's bowmen. Moray had never seen anything remotely like the volley of arrows that struck them; it had been almost opaque, a sudden darkening of the air as the lethal missiles landed upon them like a swarm of locusts, and before he could grasp what had happened, he had found himself alone, his companions swept from their saddles into death. Miraculously, although he would not think of it that way for some time, both he and his horse remained uninjured. He had been hit by only one arrow, and that had glanced off his shoulder harness, knocking him back in his saddle but doing no damage.

Moray was alone and vulnerable and he knew he would be dead before he could urge his mount up the stony scree above him. Remembering Sinclair's words, he turned to look below for him, just in time to recognize his friend and see him go down. Cursing, the Scots knight spurred his mount hard, looking about him in vain for an enemy to strike as he hurtled down the slope. But no enemy warrior came within reach of his sword, and he flung himself down from the saddle beside Sinclair's dead mount, making no attempt to tether his own and noting that the Temple Knights who had swarmed there moments earlier had moved away.

He scrambled to the first fallen knight he saw and crouched above him, using the bulk of a dead horse for protection. But the corpse was not Alec Sinclair, nor was the man lying beyond him, in a sprawl of armored limbs. Farther away, two more men lay, pierced by many arrows, but he could see they were too far away to be his fallen friend. He could see no sign of Alec Sinclair. In the meantime, his untethered horse, unnerved by the smell of blood, had cavorted away. He considered chasing after it, thinking that Sinclair must somehow have escaped on his own, but he stifled the urge quickly, for an unmanned horse was no target, but a running man was. And so he let the beast go, hoping that it would stop soon and wait for him.

Moray rose to a crouch and looked about him, aware in the back of his mind that he appeared to be in no danger, at least for the moment. He spotted a crevice in the rocks close by, a shadowed cleft between the boulder nearest him and the one directly behind it. He stepped towards it quickly and saw an armored leg thrusting up from a narrow rift that was wider than it had at first appeared. Two more running steps and he was close enough to crouch and peer into the hidden space. The body there was lying face up: it was Sinclair. To Moray's relief, his friend appeared to be uninjured, for there was no blood visible on or about him. He was deeply unconscious, however, and Moray quickly climbed into the crevice and bent over him. His left shoulder was unnaturally twisted, and the limb attached to it had been wrenched up behind his back where nature never intended it to go. Moray dragged him farther into the crevice, to where he could lay him flat in what turned out to be a tiny, cave-like shelter formed by three large, wind-scoured slabs of stone, one of them forming an angled roof above the other two.

The left side of Sinclair's flat steel helmet was scratched and crusted with a residue of gray dust that matched some deep scrapes on the rock he had clearly struck head-first in falling. Thinking quickly now, and gratefully aware that he could hear nothing threatening happening close by, Moray stretched the other man out at full length and attempted to adjust the twisted arm. It moved, but not to its original position, and he knew that the shoulder had been wrenched out of its joint in the fall. He could not tell, however, whether the arm was broken, and so he sat down with his back against one side of their shelter, laid his unblooded and unused sword down by his side, then braced his legs against Sinclair's body and hauled brutally on the injured limb, twisting it hard until he felt it shift and snap back into place. The pain would have been insufferable had Sinclair been conscious, but it failed to penetrate his awareness, and Moray sank back, exhausted.

He began to look about him. They were completely hidden there, he realized; the only thing he could see in any direction was an expanse of sky above the cleft through which he had entered. He listened then, concentrating intently. There were sounds aplenty out there, the noises of battle and the screams of dying men and animals, but they were far away and he suspected they were coming from the hillside high above them, although he knew he might be misinterpreting sounds deflected and distorted by the surrounding stones. Cautiously, after glancing again at the unconscious Sinclair, he crawled back to the entrance and slowly raised himself up, keeping his head in the shadow of the sloping boulder above him, to where he could look out at the surrounding terrain.

There was not a living soul in sight for as far as he could see. He raised himself higher, careful to make no sudden movements, until he could see up the hill, beyond the side of the great stone in front of him. Even then he could see little, because of the boulders littering the ground behind their shelter. All the noise was definitely coming from up there, however, and the silence surrounding their refuge seemed ghostly by comparison. Emboldened, he moved out slowly from his hiding place, keeping his head low and creeping forward between massive stones and around outcrops of rock until he found a vantage spot that allowed him to observe without being seen.

There were people everywhere he looked now, all of them Saracens, and all making their way swiftly up towards the top of the ridge that had drawn King Guy and his supporters, and the crest itself, when he was finally able to see that far, swarmed with mounted warriors. He caught sight of the True Cross in its magnificent jeweled casing, held high above the surging throng, with King Guy's great tent rearing behind it, marking the center of the Christian forces. But at that precise moment the upright Cross swayed alarmingly, then righted itself briefly and finally toppled from sight. Moray shivered with horror as the King's tent collapsed and disappeared from view, its guy ropes evidently cut. The immediate, swelling howl of triumph from the heights above him told its own story: the victory at Hattin had gone to the Followers of the Prophet.

Stunned and sickened, unable to believe how quickly the army of Christendom had been destroyed, or even to begin to imagine what would follow on the heels of such a conquest, Sir Lachlan Moray turned away and looked down at the slopes below the rocks that had sheltered him. Bodies lay everywhere, both men and horses, and few of the dead wore the desert robes of Saladin's warriors. In the distance, where the Frankish infantry had made its futile charge, the corpses lay in overlapping heaps, a long, thick caterpillar of death stretching from where they had begun their doomed advance to the point at which the last of their twelve thousand had fallen. Frowning and dry mouthed, shaking his head yet in disbelief, the thought came to him that he ought to be weeping at such loss. Ten thousand corpses in a single place. His next thought told him he ought not to be alive, and he wondered briefly why he had been spared, but he knew now that it was merely a matter of time before he and Sinclair would be discovered and killed like the others, for the Prophet's faithful seemed to be taking no prisoners. He swallowed hard, his throat parched, and crouched there in his hiding place, staring down the hillside.

Vultures were already spiraling downward, landing in increasing numbers to feast on the dead, and as he watched them, time slipped away from him and he lost all awareness, for a spell, of who and where he was. But he straightened up in shock, vibrantly alive again, when a loud, keening wail of agony told him that his friend Sinclair was no longer oblivious. Moments later he was scrambling back towards their rocky hiding place, keeping his head low and almost whimpering in terror at the thought that the enemy might hear the noise Sinclair was making before he could reach him and stifle his cries. But the noises suddenly stopped, and the silence that followed them, broken only by the scrambling clatter of his own booted feet on the rocks, seemed a blessing.

Moray crouched spread-legged in the entranceway to the shelter, peering in at Sinclair, his heart still pounding with fright. He was relieved to see his friend was still alive, for he had begun to have doubts, so abrupt had the transition been from wailing to stillness. But now he could hear for himself that Sinclair was breathing stertorously, the labored rise and fall of his chest visible even beneath the bulk of his armor. Then, before Moray could move closer to him, Sinclair tossed an arm out violently and began to keen again, his head thrashing from side to side. Moray reached him in a single leap and clamped his hand over the unconscious man's mouth, and the moment he did so, Sinclair's eyes snapped open and he fell silent, staring up at the face that was bent over him.

Moray saw the intelligence and sanity in those eyes, and he removed his hand cautiously. Sinclair lay unmoving for a few moments, still gazing up at his friend, and then he glanced up at the weathered boulder that roofed their hiding place.

"Where are we, Lachie? What happened? How long have we been here?"

Moray sagged back on his heels and grunted with relief. "Three questions. That means your head's still working. I suppose you want one answer?"

Sinclair closed his eyes and lay for a while without responding, but then he opened them again and shook his head. "The last thing

I remember is rallying some of my knights and turning them to ride uphill, towards the others on the slopes above us. Before that, we had watched our infantry being slaughtered." He coughed, and Moray watched the color drain from his cheeks as pain racked him from somewhere, but then he gritted his teeth and continued. "I know, too, that had we fared well in the fighting, you and I would now be surrounded by friends. We are not, so I assume you came seeking me as I bade you. Where's Louis?"

"I've no idea, Alec. I've seen no sign of him since the start of this. He might have made his way up onto the crest with the rest of them ... but there was no safety up there, high ground or no."

Sinclair stared at him. "What are you saying? They lost the high ground?"

Moray pursed his lips, shaking his head. "More than that, Alec. They lost everything. I saw the True Cross captured by the Muslim. I saw the King's tent go down, mere moments later, and I heard the howls of victory. We lost the day, Alec, and I fear we may have lost the kingdom itself."

Shocked into speechlessness, Sinclair made to sit up, but then the breath caught in his throat. The color drained instantly from his face as his eyes turned up into his head, his body twisted, and he lapsed back into unconsciousness.

Moray could do nothing for him, with no certain knowledge of what was causing his friend's pain. But Sinclair recovered quickly this time, and although his face was still gray and haggard when he opened his eyes, his mind was lucid.

"Something's broken. My arm, I think, although it feels like my shoulder. Can you see blood anywhere?"

"No. I looked when I first found you in here, thinking you might have been wounded. You were like a dead man when I found you, and your arm was out of its socket, so I took the opportunity to snap it back, knowing you might not feel the pain." He hesitated, and then grinned. "I didn't really know what I was doing, but I've seen that kind of thing done twice before. I couldn't find any other breaks in your arm ... but evidently you've found one."

"Aye, evidently." Sinclair drew a deep breath. "Here, help me to sit up against the rock there. That should make it easier to find where the pain is coming from. But be careful. Don't kill me simply because *you* can't feel the pain."

Moray, not deigning to recognize his friend's black humor, concentrated on raising Sinclair to where he could sit up in some kind of comfort and look about him, but that was more easily said than done, for in the course of his manipulations he discovered that his friend's left arm hung uselessly and hurt Sinclair unbearably whenever it swung loose. The upper arm bone—he knew it must have a name, but could not begin to guess what it might be—was broken a short distance above the elbow. He lodged his friend upright and leaned into him, holding him in place while he used both hands to undo and remove the belt around the injured man's waist, and when he was done, he worked to immobilize the broken limb, strapping it as tightly as he could against Sinclair's ribs.

It was only when he had finished that task and moved back to seat himself that he realized he could no longer hear any sounds coming from the hillside above, and that he had no recollection of the noises fading away. He looked over to find Sinclair watching him.

"Tell me then, what happened?"

As he listened to his friend relating what he had seen and heard, Sinclair's face grew increasingly strained, but he made no attempt to interrupt until Moray eventually fell silent. Then he sat chewing on his lip, his features pinched.

"Damn them all," he said eventually. "They brought it on themselves, with their jealousies and squabbling. I knew it in my gut, from the moment they decided to stop the advance on Tiberias yesterday. There was no sound reason for doing that. No reason a good commander could justify. We had already marched twelve miles through hellish heat, with less than six remaining. We could have won to safety before nightfall had we but stuck together and continued our advance. To stop was utter folly."

"Folly and spite. And arrogance. Your Master of the Temple, de Ridefort, wanted to spite the Count of Tripoli. And Reynald de

Chatillon backed him, using his influence on the King and bullying Guy into changing his mind."

Sinclair grunted from pain and gripped his broken arm with his other hand. "I cannot speak for de Chatillon," he said between gritted teeth. "I have no truck with him nor ever have. The man is a savage and a disgrace to the Temple and all it stands for. But de Ridefort is a man of principles and he truly believes Raymond of Tripoli to be a traitor to our cause. He had sound reasons for his distrust of him."

"Mayhap, but the Count of Tripoli's was the only voice of sanity among our leaders. He said it would be madness to leave our solid base in La Safouri with Saladin's masses on the move, and he was right."

"Aye, he was, but he had made alliance with Saladin prior to that, and then reneged on it, or so he would have us believe. And that alliance cost us a hundred and thirty Templars and Hospitallers at Cresson last month. De Ridefort was right to distrust him."

"It was de Ridefort who lost those men, Alec. He led them, all of them, in a downhill charge against fourteen thousand mounted men. It was his arrogance and his hotheadedness that are to blame for that. Raymond of Tripoli was nowhere near the place."

"No, but had Raymond of Tripoli not granted Saladin's army the right to cross his territory that day, those fourteen thousand men would not have been there to provoke de Ridefort. The Master of the Temple might have been blameworthy, but the Count of Tripoli was at fault."

Moray shrugged. "Aye, you might be right, but when we were talking about leaving the safety of La Safouri, Raymond's own wife was under siege in Tiberias, and even so he said he would rather lose her than endanger our whole army. That has no smell to me of treachery."

Sinclair said nothing for a while after that, then grimaced again, his teeth clenched in pain. "So be it. There is no point in arguing over it now, when the damage is irretrievable. Right now, we have to find out what's going on up on the crest. Can you do that without being seen?"

"Aye. There's a spot among the rocks. I'll go and look."

Moray was back within minutes, scuttling sideways like a crab in an effort to keep his head down and out of sight from anyone on the hillside above.

"They're on the move," he hissed, pushing Sinclair gently down to lie on his back. "They're coming down. The hillside's alive with them, and they all seem to be heading this way. In five minutes' time they'll be all around us, and if we aren't seen and dragged out of here it will be a miracle. So say your prayers, Alec. Pray as you've never prayed before—but silently."

Somewhere close by a horse nickered and was answered by another. Hooves clattered on stone, as though right above the two motionless men, and then moved away. For the next hour or so they lay still, scarcely breathing and expecting discovery and capture with every heartbeat. But the time came when they could hear nothing, no movement, no voices, no matter how hard they strained to hear, and eventually Moray crawled out of the concealment and looked about him.

"They're gone," he announced from the mouth of the shelter. "They don't appear to have left anyone up above, on the heights, and the mass of them seems to be headed now for Tiberias."

"Aye, that's where they'll go first. The Citadel will surrender, now that the army's destroyed. What else did you see?"

"Columns of dust going down from the ridge up there, towards Saladin's encampment, east of Tiberias. It's bigger than the city. Couldn't see who was going down, because of the slope of the hill, but they're raising a lot of dust. Whoever it is, they're moving in strength."

"Probably prisoners for ransom, and their escorts."

Sir Lachlan Moray sat silent after that, frowning and chewing gently on the inside of his lip for a while, until he said, "Prisoners? Will there be Templars among them, think you?"

"Probably. Why would you think otherwise?"

Moray shook his head slightly. "I thought Templars were forbidden to surrender, but must fight to the death. It has never happened before, because it has always been death or glory. They've never been defeated and left alive, but—"

"Aye, *but*. You are correct. And yet you're wrong, too. The Rule says no surrender in the face of odds less than five to one. Greater than that, there is room for discretion, and the odds today were overwhelming. Better to live and be ransomed to fight again than to be slaughtered to no good purpose. But we have duties to fulfill. We need to find a way back to La Safouri with word of this, and from there to Jerusalem, so we had better start planning our route. If Saladin's force is split in two, to the south and to the east of us, then we will have to make our way back the way we came and hope to avoid their patrols. They will be everywhere, mopping up survivors like us. Here, help me to sit up."

As soon as Moray slipped his arm about the other man's waist and began to raise him up gently, he heard a loud click as Sinclair's teeth snapped together, and he saw the color drain from the man's cheeks again, his lips and forehead beaded with sweat and his teeth gritted together against the pain that had swept up in him. Appalled, and not knowing what to do, Moray was barely able to recognize the urgency with which Sinclair was straining to turn to his right, away from the pain of his broken arm. Only at the last possible moment did he have an inkling of what was happening, and he twisted sideways just in time to let Sinclair vomit on the floor beside him.

Afterwards, Sinclair lay shuddering and fighting for breath, his head lolling weakly from side to side as Lachlan Moray sat beside him, wringing his hands and fretting over what he should do next, for there was nothing he could think of that might help his friend.

Gradually the injured man's laborious breathing eased, and suddenly his eyes were open, staring up into Moray's.

"Splints," he said, his voice weak. "We need to set the arm and splint it so that it can't be moved or jarred again. Is there anything nearby we could use?"

"I don't know. Let me go and look."

Once again Moray crawled out of their hiding place and disappeared, leaving Sinclair alone, but this time Sinclair lost all awareness of how long he had been gone, and when he next opened his eyes, Moray was crouched above him, his face drawn in a mask of concern.

"Did you find splints?"

Moray shook his head. "No, nothing good enough. A few arrow shafts, but they're too light, not enough rigidity."

"Spears. We need a spear shaft."

"I know, but the Saracens appear to have taken all the weapons they could find on their way past. They took the horses, too, which is no surprise. I'll have to look farther uphill to find a spear shaft."

"Then I'll come with you, but after dark. We can't stay here, and it's too dangerous for us to separate. We'll use strips cut from my surcoat to bind my arm immovably against my chest, and then I'll lean on you and use you as a crutch. Fortunately, my sword arm is sound, should we have need of it."

By the time they eventually secured the limb so that it hung comfortably and largely without pain, Moray had been outside several times to gather spent arrows with which to frame and brace the arm before they bound it tightly into place. By then it was growing dark, and as soon as they judged it dark enough to emerge, yet still sufficiently light to see without being seen, they began to make their way up towards the ridge on the skyline behind them. It was slow going, and arduous, and it did not take long for Sinclair's arm, even constrained as it was, to react unfavorably to the constant jarring of walking uphill across uneven terrain. Within the first few hours of setting out on their odyssey, he lost all will to talk and walked grimly on, his eyes unfocused and his mouth twisted in a rictus of pain, his good hand clutching firmly at Lachlan Moray's elbow.

During those first few hours Lachlan discovered that his belief that the Saracens had all gone down the mountain was inaccurate. It was a burst of unrestrained laughter that warned him that he and Sinclair were not alone. He left Sinclair propped up among a clump of boulders and made his way alone to where he could see what was going on at the top of the ridge of Hattin, and what he saw—a collection of several large tents surrounded by a large number of Saracen guards, everyone in high spirits—was sufficient to send him back and lead his friend thereafter in a completely different direction, heading northwest, away from the Saracen presence and directly towards La Safouri and its oasis.

THEY WALKED FROM DUSK until dawn that first night, although they did not make anything like the kind of progress they were used to. With no horses beneath them, they were reduced to the pace of ordinary men. Although the going improved once they had cleared the breast of the hill and started back downward in the direction of La Safouri, some twelve miles distant, Moray estimated that they had not covered half of that distance after more than seven hours of walking. But the stink of the charred, sour underbrush had diminished as soon as they had drawn away from the battlefield, and the battlefield itself had been mercifully veiled by the darkness of the clouded night. They had stumbled only twice over bodies lying directly in their path, and one of those had been a horse, with a full skin of water lying between its stiffened legs. This had slaked their thirst and given them energy to keep moving.

Dawn came too soon, and Moray was faced with making a decision concerning how to proceed, since his glassy-eyed companion was clearly not capable. They were in a stretch of giant dunes, and he knew the sun would broil them there no matter what they did. Was it better to keep moving in search of shelter and a place to rest, secure in the advantage offered them by the skin of water? Or would they be safer simply digging themselves a pit of some kind in the side of a dune and waiting in there for darkness to come around again? Moray decided on the former, purely because they had nothing with which to dig a hole of any kind, and so he kept walking, leading Sinclair, who was now reeling with every step, his glazed eyes staring off towards some distant place that he alone could see.

Several hours later they emerged from the dunes into an entirely different landscape, littered with sparse scrub and sharply broken stones. They soon found a dry streambed, the kind the local residents called a wadi, and Moray made his ailing companion as comfortable as he could in the shade of a slight overhang on one of the banks. He gave Sinclair more to drink and then left him heavily asleep in the meager shelter while he took the single crossbow and the few bolts he had salvaged from the battlefield of Hattin and went hunting for anything he might find that moved and could be eaten. The desert was a deadly place, but he knew, too, that it sustained an astonishing variety of creatures. Alec Sinclair's life depended on him and upon his hunting skills, and so he gave no thought to his own tiredness, which was quickly approaching exhaustion. Moving slowly and with great caution, so as not to alarm the shy desert creatures that might be watching him, Moray armed his crossbow, his eyes and ears on full alert, poised for the sound or sight of movement.

He found more of both than he had bargained for.

It was a dust cloud that first attracted his attention and made his spirits soar, for it was the sign of mounted men, and it came boiling towards him from the direction of La Safouri, the oasis to which he and Sinclair were heading. For a while he stood there in plain sight, watching the dust plume grow as the riders drew closer, but then, just before they would have been close enough to see him, a distant, circular shield flickered in the sun's glare, its shape unmistakable. The sight of it was enough to drive Moray to his knees, and from there to his rump, with his back pressed against the stone closest to him. Circular shields were unknown among the Franks; only Muslims used them, light, flimsy-looking things that nonetheless worked beautifully and efficiently. As he sat there, absorbing that, he saw another plume of dust, this one approaching from the south to meet with the one from La Safouri, and he cursed, estimating that the two paths would converge right where he sat. The riders were coming quickly, and he knew that if he was to hide, he had bare moments in which to do so.

Moray examined the terrain around him, looking for conceal-ment, but saw only one grouping of boulders, and that did not look as though it offered any sanctuary. He had no choice, however, and he saw at a glance that the crossbow he carried would be a liability, impossible to disguise or conceal. Moving quickly, he scooped a shallow hole in the sand beside him and buried the weapon, covering it sufficiently, he hoped, to conceal its shape without hiding it so well that he would not be able to find it again. Then, aware of just how little time he had left before the distant riders arrived, he dropped flat and snaked towards the boulders, using his elbows to propel himself and offering a quick, agonized plea to God to keep his friend Sinclair unconscious and unaware.

There were five large stones in the cluster, and nothing approaching a sheltering roof among them, but he wormed himself among them until he could fold his body into the space on the ground created by their shapes. It was less than perfect, but he told himself that only a direct examination would betray him, and besides, there was nothing else he could do as everything around him, sight and sound, was swept away in the thunder of hooves. He had guessed, from what he had been able to observe, that there must be approximately two score, or perhaps even three, in each of the two groups, and the babble of voices that replaced the drumming of hooves seemed to support his conjecture. He was confident that he was listening to a hundred men in high spirits, exchanging good tidings and information.

Moray did not speak Arabic, but he had been in Outremer long enough to have grown familiar with the sounds and cadences of the language, and it no longer intimidated him as it once had. He could pick out certain spoken combinations, too, common words and phrases such as *Allahu Akbar*, God is great, which seemed to be the single most-used expression among the Muslims. Now he heard a single word, *Suffiriyya*, being spoken over and over again on all sides. Suffiriyya, he knew, was the Arabic name for La Safouri, and he interpreted the excitement surrounding him as a probable indication that Saladin's army had captured the oasis after the departure of the Christian army for Tiberias. He wished Sinclair were with him, for his friend's knowledge of Arabic was wondrous and he would have understood every word of the gibberish that flooded over Moray's head.

Frustrated by his inability to see what was happening, he had no option but to lie still and hope that no part of him was sticking out where it would be visible. As one noisy group approached his hiding place he grew tense, expecting at any moment to hear a howl announcing his discovery. He heard them halt very close to him and knew they must be standing directly above him, almost within arm's length of where he lay. Then there came a series of grunts and indecipherable sounds of movement, followed by a rapid, unintelligible gush of conversation involving three or perhaps four voices. Listening to them, holding his breath and willing himself to shrink into invisibility, Moray felt a surge of despair as his leg muscles began to tighten into what he knew immediately would be savage cramps.

Sure enough, the ensuing five minutes seemed to him to be the longest in his entire life as he lay in agony, unable to move or to make a sound while his tortured limbs objected to the unnatural way they were disposed. He did remain silent, nonetheless, concentrating on willing his leg muscles to relax, and eventually, gradually, the dementing pain began to recede. Shortly after that, just as he was beginning to adjust to the idea that the cramps had gone, the Saracens left, too, in response to a series of commands from a loud but distant voice that rang with authority. At one moment there were men above him speaking in loud voices, and then, without warning, they fell silent and moved away, only the sound of their receding footsteps announcing their departure.

It seemed to him that the individual groups were separating again, returning to the paths they had been following when they first saw each other. The dwindling sounds of their shouted farewells made it simple for him to deduce that the first group was heading southeast again, towards Tiberias, while the other continued north, into the desert wastes. Moray gave the last of them ample time to ride away before he emerged from his cache—and his heart sprang into his mouth when he saw that he was not alone. A single Saracen lay, apparently asleep, on the sand beside the boulders. Moray stood frozen, one hand on the boulder that separated them, before he saw the blood that stained the sand beneath the man's body.

Cautiously, not daring to make a sound, he inched forward until he heard, and then saw, the clouds of flies that swarmed over the recumbent form. The man was dead, his torso pierced by a crossbow bolt, his chain-mail shirt clotted with gore and his face pallid beneath his sun-bronzed skin. He lay between two long spears and had obviously been laid carefully to rest, his arms crossed on his chest, his bow and a quiver of arrows laid beside him, and it became clear, as Moray studied him, that the fellow had been a man of some influence among his people. His clothing and the quality of the inlaid bow and quiver by his side proclaimed both wealth and rank, but his rich green cloak was blackened with blood, and the shimmering tunic of fine chain mail he wore had been insufficient to protect him from the lethal force of the steel bolt that had driven the metal mesh into his wound.

The spears on each side of the body puzzled Moray initially, until he gave them a closer look, and realized instantly that they had formed a kind of bier, their tapered ends separated by a short crossbar made from a broken length from another spear shaft bound firmly in place by tight lashings of rawhide that had been soaked in place and then allowed to dry in the sun. From that junction several long ropes of tightly plaited leather lay piled on the ground. The man, whoever he was, had been strapped onto the bier and obviously pulled behind a horse, for the marks where the ends had been dragged were deep and clearly defined. It was no great feat for Moray to divine that the man on the litter must have been supported on a network of more leather straps, lashed around the two spear shafts. He must have died a short time before his escorts reached this spot, Moray concluded, and his comrades, having left him so decorously laid out, would no doubt return to collect him.

Moray stepped out from behind his rocks and looked all around him now, seeing no signs of movement in any direction. The sun had started its fall towards the west, but it still had a long way to go, and its strength was ferocious, baking the landscape so that the rocks and even the sand itself shimmered and wavered, their surfaces warped by the heat that rose up in palpable waves. He searched the dead man quickly, hoping against hope to find a water bottle, but he found nothing of value, other than the bow and its quiver of arrows. The dead man's sword and dagger were missing, probably taken by his comrades for safekeeping.

He picked up the inlaid bow before slinging the quiver over his shoulder and setting off to find his friend Alec.

Sinclair was still unconscious when Moray returned. Deep lines and creases had settled into his sleeping face, and his forehead was fiery hot to the touch. Moray grew increasingly apprehensive, for he knew that in order to provide the kind of help his friend needed, he would have to either lead Sinclair home safely to their own kind, and quickly, or surrender them both to the mercies of the Saracens. The latter was unthinkable, and so he decided that they would rest for the remainder of the day, then walk again throughout the night. But where could they go, now that La Safouri was closed to them? Back towards Nazareth was the only solution that presented itself to Moray, and it was the last image in his mind as he fell asleep that afternoon, huddled beside Alexander Sinclair.

THREE

When he awoke some time later, Moray was enormously relieved to find that Sinclair was conscious and appeared to be on the mend, but his optimism did not survive the first words Sinclair spoke to him, for the whispery weakness of his friend's voice shocked him profoundly. Sinclair's face was haggard, the blazing eyes dulled and unfocused and the eyeballs sunk deep in their sockets. The Alexander Sinclair in front of him now barely resembled the vital man Moray had spoken with the day before.

Nonetheless, although he could not judge how much of the information was penetrating Sinclair's lethargy, Moray patiently told him about everything that had happened that day, and explained that they would now have to try to make their way southwestward, towards Nazareth, walking through the night again to avoid the roving Saracen patrols. His sole concern, he ended, was that Sinclair might not feel equal to the task of walking all night. At that point, however, Sinclair set his mind greatly at rest by closing his eyes and summoning the ghost of a smile. He could walk all night, he said in that reedy, lusterless voice, providing Moray held him upright and pointed him in the right direction.

That simple assurance, so bravely and so innocently given, was Lachlan Moray's introduction to Hell, for within an hour of giving it, Alexander Sinclair had begun to lose all sense of himself. He remained awake throughout that time and seemed to be lucid, but when Moray carefully raised him to his feet, taking his weight with an arm across his shoulders, all the strength drained from Sinclair in a rush and he slumped in a swoon. From a manageable burden he became a deadweight within a heartbeat, and almost pulled Moray down with him. Gasping and grunting words of useless encouragement, Moray managed to lower him to the ground again without dropping him on his broken arm, and then he knelt over him, peering in consternation at his friend's pain-ravaged face and feeling despair well up inside him as he recognized the finality of their situation.

It was as he was kneeling there, peering at Sinclair's unresponsive face, that a sudden connection occurred in Moray's mind, between the unconscious Sinclair and another old friend, Lachlan's kinsman and former captain, Lord George Moray, who had been generally expected to die two years earlier after being gravely wounded.

That the Scots nobleman had not died, and had recovered fully, had been due to the efforts of a single man, a Syrian physician called Imad Al-Ashraf, and Lachlan Moray remembered Imad Al-Ashraf very clearly, because the man had saved Lord George's life by means of a magical white powder that relieved his lordship's pain and kept him comatose until his broken body had had time and opportunity to heal itself.

Moray dropped his hand to the scrip that hung from his belt, reaching inside the overhanging flap with finger and thumb and pinching the soft kid leather of the tiny pouch that was sewn onto the back of the flap. Called away by some emergency before Lord George had made a full recovery, Al-Ashraf had declared that the worst was over and that his lordship would recover without a physician's help from that time on, providing he did nothing stupid to endanger himself again. Lachlan, who had barely left his lord's side since the incident in which he had been wounded, assured the Syrian physician that he himself would take responsibility for seeing to that. Al-Ashraf bowed his head in respect and acknowledgment of the pledge and then, before he left, provided Moray with a small packet containing eight carefully measured doses of the magical white powder that he called an opiate, warning him seriously of the dangers of using the nostrum carelessly and too often, then going on to instruct the knight concerning the signs and conditions he should look for before feeding any of the drug to the injured man. When

Moray had shown a sufficiently wide-eyed respect for what he was being told, Al-Ashraf went on to teach him how to mix and administer the drug, which both erased pain, or at least the awareness of pain, and enforced sleep upon the recipient.

Moray had no notion how the potions that he mixed went about their work, or how sick a man would have to be to require the use of them, but he used four of the eight doses on Lord George in the latter stages of the nobleman's recovery. And he had marveled each time at the swiftness with which the potions completely overwhelmed his stubborn and intransigent superior, rendering him unconscious, and apparently depriving him even of the power to toss and turn in his sleep.

Moray had carried the four unused doses with him ever since, in a blind but profound belief that he might have need of their magical powers on his own behalf someday. Although he knew that, should the need arise for him to use them himself, he might be physically incapable of doing so, too ill or too badly wounded, still he had told no one about them, suspecting that their value might make possession of them dangerous.

His grasp on the small pouch tightened, but he hesitated to pull it free of the stitching that held it in place. Lachlan was afraid, deep inside himself, that he might endanger his friend Sinclair by forcing him to drink something that might, against all reason and logic, be poisonous, despite the good he had seen it do formerly. And even if it helped Sinclair, the white powder would kill any possibility of their leaving this place that day, since it would plunge Sinclair into a deep sleep for hours on end. But Sinclair was most evidently in agony.

Slowly, reluctant still, he pulled the small package free of its stitching and opened it, gazing down at the four separate doses, individually wrapped in fine white muslin, that lay inside. Now, feeling an excitement welling up in his chest, he opened one of the small, carefully wrapped measures and emptied it into his drinking cup, then mixed it with some of the water. A moment later, he had raised Sinclair's head and helped him to swallow the contents of the cup without spilling a drop.

That done, he laid his friend down again, made him as comfortable as he could, and then sat back on his heels. Within minutes, Sinclair was deeply asleep, his breathing, it seemed to Moray, already steadied and strengthened. Recognizing the change, he felt grateful, but he also grinned wryly, wondering aloud to himself what was to become of them now, helpless as they were, unable to move and dangerously low on water, for he knew that one, at least, of the Muslim patrols would visit this place again, to pick up their dead comrade.

It was then that Moray remembered the device in which the dead man in the desert had been dragged behind a horse for so many miles. The idea was enough to give him strength, and he went scuttling out into the late-afternoon light, crouching low and raising his head with great caution above the rim of the wadi that had sheltered them. He made no move that might betray his presence until he was certain that he was alone and that there was no one out there looking either for him or at him.

It was a quarter of a mile from the wadi that concealed them to the clump of boulders where he had hidden from the Saracens that afternoon, and he crossed it quickly, conscious that he was a very conspicuous target. He went directly to where the dead man lay beside the clump of stones and tried to roll the body off the improvised bier, only to discover that it had stiffened since he last touched it and was now rigid and difficult to handle. But it was soon done and he gathered up the apparatus. The framework of lashed spears felt strong and sturdy, but he was surprised by the unexpected weight of the coiled ropes of braided leather that he slung crosswise over his shoulders, and he had a ludicrously difficult time after that in simply bending down to pick up his crossbow and bolts. He had to make several attempts, fighting to keep his balance beneath the burden he was carrying as he stooped and bent, weaving and groping blindly towards the weapons on the ground.

Within the half hour, he was back at the wadi dragging the apparatus behind him and unsurprised to discover that Sinclair did not appear to have moved a muscle since he had left. He bent over to feel the sleeping man's forehead, noting that his breathing was deep and regular and that the strange rasping rattle in his throat had disappeared. What concerned him most at that moment, however, was the need to make sure that Sinclair was still deeply asleep, for Moray had been thinking furiously, and for the first time since dawn on the slopes of Hattin the previous day, he had a detailed plan in mind, one that he thought he would be able to execute, providing that he could first set and somehow splint Sinclair's broken arm.

Moray had two weapons at his disposal: the crossbow and six foot-long steel bolts, and the inlaid, double-curved bow with its quiver of more than a score of finely fletched arrows. Six crossbow bolts, when compared with twenty-two arrows, made his deliberations simple. He stood up and wearily removed his linen surcoat, armored hauberk and leggings, dropping them carelessly on the sand before leaning over to cut the straps that fastened his friend's heavy mail hauberk. He stripped Sinclair, too, of his hauberk and leggings, removing close to fifty pounds of steel links, knowing that the armor would be useless to them were they captured by Saracens. He piled the discarded chain mail to one side, then patiently worked his own sleeveless leather jerkin over Sinclair's broken arm until, by dint of much pulling, he was able to wrap the garment completely around him and feed the other arm, much more easily, through the arm hole. That done, he cinched Sinclair's belt about the unconscious man's waist and sank wearily to his knees beside his friend, contemplating the task that faced him next: the setting of Sinclair's broken arm.

It was not a task with which Lachlan Moray felt comfortable. Kneeling on the sandy floor, he stared down into the sleeping face, reviewing what he must do within the next short time and cursing himself for not having paid more attention to the procedure when he had seen it done before, by other people. But on those few occasions, he had turned his face away, as squeamish as everyone else about the noises of bone grating upon splintered bone, and hoping blindly that he himself would never have to undergo the pain such manipulations must involve. It had never occurred to him that he might someday have to perform the operation himself. *Sweet Jesus, Alec,* he thought. *Don't wake up while I'm doing this.*

He inhaled deeply, bent forward, and carefully cut away the insubstantial arrow splints he had applied the day before. Then, clenching his teeth and shutting his mind to what he was about, he braced himself and pulled on the broken arm, feeling the loose bones grate as they shifted in response to his manipulations. When he felt sure the arm was as close to naturally straight as he could make it, he cut several lengths from the yards of leather rope that had bound the dead Muslim's conveyance to the horse that pulled it. He tore the remnants of Sinclair's white surcoat into strips and looped four short pieces around the broken limb, above and below the elbow, knotting them with care so that they were loose yet snug enough to remain in place. Then he carefully inserted the six steel bolts, weaving them over and under the loops so that they were all held in place by at least two of the straps, and when he was confident that they were all properly positioned he bound them again, firmly this time, so that they formed a steel cage around the broken limb from wrist to biceps. As soon as he had finished that, he used two longer lengths of the rope to bind the arm itself tightly against Sinclair's body.

He dragged the still unconscious man to the conveyance he had rescued, then pushed and hauled and shifted Sinclair's deadweight bulk until he thought it was evenly distributed across the straps between the two supporting poles, and when he was satisfied that it was, he worked for a time on shortening and adjusting the harness that had originally joined the poles to the horse that pulled them, painstakingly knotting the ropes into a crude harness of netting that bore a very faint resemblance to the salmon nets he had used as a boy in Scotland but would serve, he knew, to distribute the weight of his burden across his chest and shoulders. Only then, when there was nothing more he could do, did he drink sparingly and lie down to sleep for the last remaining hour of the day, knowing he would awaken when the evening chill settled across the cooling sands.

MORAY AWOKE SOON AFTER NIGHTFALL, and still it appeared that Sinclair, deeply in the grip of the Syrian's wondrous powder, had not moved. He bent to listen to the sound of his friend's deep, regular breathing before he rose to his feet and drank again from the water skin. He then placed it securely beside Sinclair on the bier and bound it to the straps there, alongside the Saracen's bow and quiver. Finally he inserted his arms without much difficulty into the harness he had made, tightening the bindings across his chest until they were as comfortable as possible, and set out on his journey. The weight at his back was solid and ponderous, but the harness served its purpose well, and he leaned into it like a draft horse taking the traces, his enormous muscles making relatively light work of pulling the weight at his back. He felt much freer without the burden of his chain mail, and grateful for the bright light of the moon. The only sounds he could hear were his own footfalls on the hard-packed, windblown sand and the steady hiss of the pole ends gouging parallel tracks behind him.

He had lost track of time and distance by the time he heard Sinclair grunt deeply and move suddenly, disturbing the plodding rhythm of his walk and almost throwing him off balance. He was glad to stop and shrug out of the harness, twisting around as he tried to lower his end gently without jarring the injured man.

"Where in God's name are we?"

Moray noted that Sinclair's voice, while still weak, was noticeably stronger. He stood up on his toes and stretched hugely, swinging his arms for a time to loosen his shoulder joints before he made any attempt to answer.

"And why can't I move? What am I tied to?"

Moray ruffled his friend's hair. "Well, God bless you, too, Alec. I'm well, thank you, merely having hauled the solid weight of your large and miserable arse halfway across this desert. But it is a relief to listen to your complaining and know therefore that you are well, too." His voice altered from one word to the next, dropping its tone of raillery and becoming serious. "You can't move because you're trussed up like a pig's carcass, and you're trussed up because it was the only way I could stop you from flailing your arm about. It's badly broken and you were growing sick because of the pain, tossing about and raving. I used crossbow bolts for splints. And you are lashed to the only means I have of moving you in the hope of reaching safety. Saracens are swarming all about us. As for where we are, I have no idea. We're in the desert somewhere, heading southwest towards Nazareth because I can't think of anywhere else to go. I overheard two Saracen patrols exchanging information—Saladin has taken La Safouri, so there's no refuge there. I borrowed this thing that you are lying on from a corpse that was left behind. I've been dragging you across Outremer ever since."

He fell silent and watched his friend absorb everything he had said, noticing as he did so that Sinclair's face appeared to be less haggard than it had been earlier that day, although that might have been the effect of the moonlight, for the moon was now riding high overhead.

Sinclair frowned. "You are dragging me? How?"

"With ropes. A leather harness."

"You mean, like a horse?"

Moray grinned as he untied the bindings of the water skin. "Aye, the same thought had occurred to me. Like a horse. A workhorse. See what you've made of me?"

"You said there are Saracens everywhere. Why is that?"

"I don't know. They're probably looking for fugitives like us, people who escaped from Hattin. You look better than you did earlier, thanks be to God. Here, have some of this."

He knelt and held the water skin to Sinclair's mouth, and when he had finished drinking, the injured man looked around at the moonlit waste surrounding them.

"You have no idea where we are?"

"South and west of Hattin and Tiberias, perhaps four leagues, or five. I must have come five miles at least, pulling you, and we walked all night last night. Do you remember that?"

Sinclair looked almost hurt. "Of course I do." He hesitated. "But I don't recall much else."

"I dosed you with some medication I had in my scrip and you've been asleep for hours. How much pain are you in?"

Sinclair made a movement that might have been a shrug. "Some, not much. There's pain, but it's … distant, somehow."

"Aye, that will be the drug. I'll give you more of it later."

"Be damned if you will. I need no drugs."

Moray shrugged. "Not now, it's plain. But later, if you start raving again, I'll be the one to make that decision." He peered up at the sky again, as though expecting to see clouds. "In the meantime, we have to keep moving. The moon's high, so we'll have light for an hour or two more, but after that, if I can't see the ground underfoot, it might be nasty for both of us."

"Then keep your eyes open for another place to hide during the day that's coming. The loss of an hour or two of darkness won't make much of a difference to our journey if we don't know where we are or where we're going. But what about water? Have we enough?"

Moray hefted the water bag. "We have until we reach the end of this. After that we're in God's hands."

"We're in God's *sands*, Lachlan, and like to die here if He doesn't provide for us."

"Well, we'll find that out tomorrow. For now, I walk and you take your ease."

He fastened the water bag carefully in place, then strapped on the harness again and set off. They did not speak to each other after that, for they both knew how sound can travel in the desert at night and they had no wish to attract company. Moray quickly steadied himself into the plodding gait he had been using for hours, but he was aware from the outset that fatigue was rising in him. He gritted his teeth and willed himself to ignore the shooting pains in his calves and thighs, concentrating solely on the incessant rhythm of placing one foot ahead of the other.

Some time later, much later, he decided afterwards, an agonized groan from Sinclair brought him back to awareness, and he stopped short, surprised to see that the terrain around him had changed completely and that he had walked from one desert zone into another without realizing it.

"Alec? Are you awake?"

Sinclair did not answer him, and Moray stopped on the point of peeling off the harness that felt now as though it had embedded itself into his body. Instead, he straightened up, arching his back and suddenly aware of the pain and stiffness he had blanked out of his mind until then, and looked about him carefully. The moon was low in the sky, but it still threw sufficient light for him to see his surroundings clearly enough to be amazed at what lay before him. The ground beneath his feet now was hard, scoured down to bedrock by the wind, and he was standing on the edge of what he saw as an enormous tilted bowl that loomed above and ahead of him, a broad, almost circular area of flat land, more than half a mile in extent, that was littered with great boulders and surrounded on all sides, except for where he stood, by towering, featureless walls of sand. Mountainous dunes, their gigantic slopes painted silver and black by moonlight and shadows, swept up on both sides of him to shut out the horizon ahead, eclipsing the stars. As he stood there, hearing only the pounding of his own heartbeat, he became aware of the stillness of the night; nothing moved and no smallest sound disturbed the absolute calm.

"Alec, can you hear me?" There was still no response, but he spoke again, quickly, as though he had heard one. "We're in a different kind of place here, but it looks promising, as far as finding shelter goes. There are boulders ahead, within reach, and we should be able to find a spot among them where the sun won't roast us tomorrow. It's late, and the moon's almost gone, and I'm too tired to go much farther, so I'm going to take us there and find a spot to rest. And then I'm going to sleep, perhaps for the entire day tomorrow. But first I'm going to feed you some more of those drugs you don't want. That is if I can force my feet to move again. Hold on, and I'll try."

He bent to the traces again and, after the first few faltering steps, found the plodding rhythm that had enabled him to keep forging ahead for hours. Within another quarter of an hour he was close enough to the largest pile of boulders to see that there was shelter aplenty among them, chinks and crevices that looked large enough to swallow both of them with ease. He lowered Sinclair's bier to the ground and peeled himself agonizingly out of the network of straps and braces that had sunk into his tortured flesh. As he bent to check his friend's breathing, Sinclair opened his eyes.

"Lachlan. It's you. I was dreaming. Where are we?"

"Hazard a guess. You're as likely to be right as I am." Moray was massaging his right arm, moving his elbow in circles and grimacing with pain as his fingers dug into the muscles of his shoulder. "Damnation, but you make a heavy load, Sinclair. I feel as though I've been hauling a dead horse behind me since the day I was born." He saw his friend's quick frown and waved away the apology before it could be uttered. "You would do the same for me. But I'm looking forward to having you back on your feet and walking again. Then you'll be able to pull me." He grunted and switched his ministrations to his other shoulder. "I believe I've found us a place to rest out of the sun tomorrow, but I'm going to leave you here while I make sure of it. In the meantime, you should pray and give thanks to God that I was clever enough to get rid of all our armor before we set out on this little sojourn. I'll be back."

He returned quickly, a strange expression on his face, so that Sinclair, after hawking to clear his throat, asked, "What's wrong? Did you not find a place?"

Moray shook his head. "Did you pray? You must have. I hoped to find a gap between the stones that would shelter us. I found a cave instead—a cave that has been very recently in use as a living place. I found a cache of bread—stale but edible—along with water, dates, dried meat and a bag of dried dung, camel and horse both, for fuel. If I had not been here in this accursed *Holy Land* for so long, I would think it a miracle. As it is, it's a stroke of fortune of the kind a cynic like me can barely contemplate."

Sinclair was frowning. "Who would live out here?"

"Some nomad. There are more than a few of them out here. And who but a nomad would think to hoard dry dung?"

"But—think you he might be still around here?"

Moray stooped and hoisted the bier by the short cross-brace at its head, throwing the mass of straps across Sinclair's legs at the same time. "I doubt it," he said, grunting with the effort of lifting Sinclair's weight again. "Whoever he was, he's probably at La Safouri now, or at Tiberias, celebrating our defeat. Since you appear to be praying effectively, pray then that I am correct. One way or the other, we will know soon. Now lie back, it's not far."

SINCLAIR AWOKE IN THE DAWN LIGHT, his arm on fire, the pain of it a living thing that he could feel somewhere at the back of his throat, or so it seemed to him. He knew immediately what had happened to him, and that his arm was broken, but he had no awareness at first of where he was or how he had come there. Then he heard a soft sound and turned his head to see Moray's shape silhouetted against the morning brightness at the cave's mouth, and everything came back to him. He tried to call Moray's name, but on the first attempt, although his lips moved and he articulated the sounds, nothing emerged. He swallowed, trying to moisten his dry mouth, and tried again, his voice emerging as little more than a croak.

"Lachlan."

Moray did not stir, although Sinclair knew he must have heard him, and his eyes narrowed as he took note of the tension and rigidity of the other man's posture. Moray stood stiffly in the entranceway, one hand braced against the side of the deep cleft in the rock that was their shelter, his entire body inclined slightly forward as he peered at whatever it was in the distance that had caught his attention.

"Lachlan, what is it? What can you see?"

Moray straightened slightly, the tension fading from his stance as he did so, and spun to move purposefully back towards Sinclair. "Vultures," he said, as though the word explained everything. "I saw them circling when I went outside to piss and I've been watching them ever since, until the last of them disappeared."

Sinclair felt as though he were missing something painfully obvious. "I don't understand. There are always vultures in the sky out here in the desert. Always one, at least …"

"Aye, until something dies, and then they gather in flocks as by magic. No one knows how they know, but they always do."

"What are you saying?"

"There were scores of them, Alec, and now they're all gone. They're down and feeding, on dead men, I am sure, for only large carcasses would attract so many of them. And they're not too far from here."

"I still don't understand."

"I can see that, but consider: here we are, in dire straits. We have a small amount of food, thanks to our absent, solitary host, but we ate most of it last night. Our water supply is little better. But if there are bodies lying out there on the sand within reach of us, there might well be food and water lying by them, for the taking. I have to go and find out, and I have to go now, because I mislike the cast of the sky out there. The air is dead calm and sultry and there might be storms about. I'll prop the end of your bier up on that low ledge, so that you'll be above the floor and comfortable, and I'll leave you here for the morning. I should not be gone longer than that. I gauged the distance from the size of the birds, and my guess is that I'll be an hour, perhaps slightly more, in reaching them, and then the same in coming back, so I should return before noon."

"What will you use to fight them off?"

Moray smiled. "What, the vultures, or the dead men? I'll take the Mussulman's bow with me. How is your arm?"

"It feels as though it's afire. Hot, but little pain, unless I jar it."

"I thought as much. I have another packet of the powder I fed you before, and you will please me by taking it without complaining. The first one worked wonders for you, so this next one should do even more, and if you improve as much between now and tonight as you did yesterday, then you'll be able to walk on your own and I will not have to break my back again."

He busied himself then mixing the powder with water while Sinclair watched, and when he was done, the sick man swallowed the potion down obediently, with only the wrinkling of his nose denoting any unpleasantness of thought or taste.

"I'm going out there now, and as I say, it ought not to take me long, but we are in the desert, so it makes sense to take precautions against my being delayed. I might get lost, or have an accident, or even meet some of Allah's faithful servants. You are not strong enough to come looking for me and it would be foolish of you even to try. I'll leave this bag of food above you, hanging from this peg provided by our thoughtful host, and with it will be this bag of water. I'll take some food and the smaller water bag with me, since it is lighter." He tilted his head, smiling down at Sinclair, whose eyes were now dull and unfocused beneath fluttering lashes as he fought against the powerful opiate. "Alec? Can you still hear me? Your eyes are closing. Will you remem …"

FOUR

S inclair woke up to find the cave filled with whirling sand and the pandemonic screaming of a wind such as he had never heard. His mouth and nostrils were clogged, so dry that he was unable even to spit to clear them. The terror he felt at that moment was overwhelming. He tried to move, but he was hampered by his bound arm. Several times he tried to reach the water bag that Moray had hung on the peg above him, but his efforts were wasted against the howling force of the wind. There was light, too, filtering weakly through the depths of the churning dust, so there was still daylight beyond the cave, although it appeared to be more dusk than day out there. Moray had wrapped the sole remaining fragment of his torn surcoat about his shoulders. With one trembling hand Sinclair now wound it around his head, covering his face as completely as he could, worrying that he might not be able to breathe, but fearing the sandstorm more. He struggled with the burden of his tightly trussed arm until he managed to turn onto his right side, his back to the cave's entrance and the calamitous wind that raged through it. The stupefying noise was unrelenting, but lying on his side, with his good hand cupped over the folds of cloth about his face, he found it easier to breathe. With nothing more in his power to help himself, he fell into unconsciousness again, wondering about how Moray might be faring and hoping he had been able to find some kind of shelter before the tempest struck.

Sinclair's next conscious thought was that the silence had awakened him, for it was tomblike after the tumult of the awful dreams that lingered, shapeless yet full of noise and dread, in the deep recesses of his memory. He continued to lie there for some time, motionless, eyes closed, focusing his mind on the absolute stillness around him, and it was only when he finally attempted to open his eyes that he realized that something was seriously amiss, for although his eyelids twitched obediently, there was pressure against them, weighing on them and preventing them from opening. Panic-stricken, he drew in a quick breath and tried to claw at his face with both hands, forgetting that his left arm was tightly bound. His right hand sprang up quickly enough and landed heavily against what felt like a cloth, a cloth covered with sand, enveloping his face. Still deep in the grip of panic, he clutched at the thing and tried to jerk it away from him, only to discover that it was wrapped about his head. His fingers still gripping the bindings that shrouded him, he slowly sagged back against his bracings, knowing with sudden certainty that his nightmares had been real. He had dreamed of a chaos of noise, the demented screaming of a multitude of damned souls, and seething clouds of roiling smoke that threatened to choke the life from him and hurl him into Hell. But it had been no dream.

What was it Lachlan had said? *The air is dead calm and sultry and there might be storms about.* He was right, then. But where was he now? He had not been in the dreams.

"Lachlan? Are you there?"

His voice was muffled by the folds of cloth, but it was loud enough, nonetheless, for Lachlan to have heard and answered, and in the ensuing silence he realized, with great reluctance, that he was not surprised. Lachlan Moray must have been out there when that cataclysm came down, and Sinclair knew that the odds against his having been able to locate their cave under such conditions were incalculable.

Cautiously then, working one-handed, he hunched forward as far he could and unwound the remains of his white linen surcoat from his head.

Now, in the deathly stillness of the cave, he took stock of his condition as best he could. If he was to survive from now on, he knew it must be by his own efforts. He flexed the fingers of his left hand and felt them move, very slightly but blessedly without pain.

The pain had gone, or abated, and he felt clear headed and healthy. But he was lying on his back and he knew he had to get up, and he knew, too, from past experience, that this would not be a simple thing to achieve with his left arm lashed rigidly along his side. He made to swing his legs to the side, to his right, but they would not move and he felt fear flare up in his breast again, wondering what was wrong with him now. He opened his eyes, hugely relieved to discover he could do so without pain, then pushed himself up on his elbow as far as he could, straining against his own lack of mobility until he could look downward, his chin on his breast, to see that his entire lower body, from the waist down, was covered in sand. To his left, a blaze of brilliance announced that there was daylight beyond the cave, but inside, everything was shaded and muted by the carpet of sand that surrounded and half covered him.

He thanked God that Lachlan had thought to prop the top end of his bier against the ledge at his back. Had he not done that, Sinclair knew the sand would have covered him completely, smothering him in his drugged sleep. Calming himself then, he concentrated on moving his legs, one at a time, kicking and flexing his knees with great difficulty until first one, then the other came free and lay atop the sand that had covered them. That done, he twisted slowly to his right, grasping the pole on that side tightly and using the leverage he gained to pull himself up and swing his legs until he was sitting, with his feet on the sand that covered the floor of the cave.

He succeeded in struggling to his feet on the third attempt and stood swaying, clutching the pole that had risen with him as soon as his weight was removed from the bed. The peg lodged in the wall still held the bags of food and water that Lachlan had left for him, but it also supported a belt with a sheathed, single-edged dirk attached, and he looked down immediately at the lashings that bound his arm against his body. Moments later, he lodged the sheath firmly between his body and his bound arm and withdrew the foot-long blade. Three slashes freed the splinted arm, but the weight of it, bound as it was by the solid steel bolts of the splints, dragged immediately at his shoulder, bringing echoes of the pain he had felt the day before. He dropped the dirk at his feet and reached for the water bag, knowing as soon as he felt its sagging, flaccid bulk that it would not be an easy task to drink from it one-handed. But Lachlan's drinking cup was there, too, he knew, and close to hand, somewhere beneath the sand.

He looked about him for the best place to sit, and then slowly lowered himself to the ledge that had supported his bier. He cradled the bag on his knee and reached down and dredged with his fingers until he found the cup, then lodged it securely between his knees. He drew the stopper from the bag with his teeth and very slowly, moving with excruciating care, manipulated the cumbersome, wobbling container until it lay along his forearm. Then, twisting down and sideways with the caution of a tumbler balancing on a rope, he brought the open spout to the rim of the cup and dribbled the precious liquid gently into it as slowly as he could until it was half filled. He barely spilled a drop, but he had to sit up again and replace the stopper with his teeth before he could lay the bag down and take up the cup.

He rinsed his mouth carefully with the first mouthful, then spat it out and rinsed again, and this time he was able to feel more water than sand in his mouth. On the third and last draft, his mouth felt normal and he swallowed gratefully before carefully pouring another half cupful. He sipped at it this time, watching the tiny ripples on the surface, caused by the trembling in his hand, and thinking that nothing in his life had ever tasted so sweet and pure. Then he filled his mouth with it, swished it around and swallowed it with a definite feeling of triumph, feeling the life spring up in him again, even if only faintly.

He sat up straighter, noting everything there was to see in the cave, which was shallow but wide. He could find no sign that Lachlan Moray had ever been there. Sighing, and refusing to think about what that might entail, he opened the bag of food and found several flat, hard disks of unleavened bread, a cloth-wrapped bundle of surprisingly fresh dates, a hard lump of something unidentifiable that he guessed was goat cheese, and several small pieces of dried meat. He did not feel hungry, but he knew he needed to eat, so he tore a piece of meat off with his teeth and spent the next few moments thinking that he might as well have been chewing on dried tree bark. But as his saliva began to moisten the meat its flavor, strong and gamy, began to emerge and with it came his appetite, so that he discovered he was ravenous and he had to restrain himself from eating everything in the bag.

When he had repacked the remnants of his food, he sat back, gritting his teeth against a sudden temptation to feel sorry for himself. He had never been the type to wallow in self-pity and could not abide people who did so, but nonetheless he felt a need to fight against some kind of creeping lethargy that felt very much the same as self-pity, and he wondered if it might be caused by Moray's drug, whatever it might have been. He knew he had to do something to help himself, alone as he was and ludicrously defenseless. He might be hurt, he told himself determinedly, but he was not yet dead or dying, and he had no intention of simply giving up and rolling over simply because he had been left alone. And so he sat up straighter yet and looked about him, searching for inspiration among the scant resources available to him.

He discovered that the bier or litter on which he had lain was made from a pair of spears lashed together to a short cross-piece that had supported his head and given the frail-looking device some rigidity, and he made short work of cutting away the lashings, along with the woven network of straps that had supported his body. Two spears were useless to him, one-armed as he was, but one would serve him well as a walking staff and provide him with a weapon of self-defense, since he had no idea what had happened to his sword. That concerned him for no more than a moment, aware as he was that he would have been incapable of using it to any effect.

Because his useless arm was rigidly splinted, it was utterly inflexible. He studied the ends of the steel shafts encircling his wrist and then, using his good hand and his teeth, he set about fashioning a sling from the longest of the straps from the bed of the litter. By dint of much knotting and adjustment, and muttering to himself as he worked, he eventually created a primitive harness that worked quite effectively, a large loop fitting around his neck while a smaller one was hooked firmly around the ends of two of the crossbow-bolt splints. The device was not comfortable—the strap cut sharply into his neck and shoulder muscles—but it kept the limb from hanging straight down from his shoulder like a leaden weight.

Sinclair could not believe how difficult it was to do even the smallest thing properly with only one hand. The simple effort of removing the belt from its peg and cinching it about his waist, weighted as it was with its sheathed dirk, became the most infuriating task he had ever undertaken, requiring eight attempts and a variety of outlandish contortions, and he achieved it only by clamping the belt in his teeth in the correct place and feeding the other end through the buckle with great care. Three times he lost his grip while transferring the weight, and had to restart each time. After that, seated and with the belt securely buckled, he tried unsuccessfully to shrug his massive shoulders through the loop of the belt, but he had to be content in the end with hanging it diagonally across his chest, and even then he had to undo the sling he had arranged so carefully a short time before, in order to hang the bags containing his food and water comfortably across his chest and beneath his left arm, because his earliest attempt, to make them hang comfortably over the rigid limb, quickly proved futile.

Finally, after one last look around the sand-filled cave, he took up his spear staff and carefully made his way to the cave's mouth. He was forced to stoop lower and lower as he approached because the opening had filled up with blowing sand and was less than one third its former size. Beyond it, however, was where the surprise lay concealed, and Sinclair stood in the doorway, his eyes wrinkled to slits against the severity of the blazing sun as he tried to comprehend what he was seeing.

It had been dark when they arrived, but the moonlight had been strong enough to reveal the scoured earth of the boulder-littered bowl in which they had sheltered beneath the shadows of the giant dunes. He stood gazing now for a long time, feeling apprehension tightening his throat, for he could see nothing that he recognized. The silence was absolute, and the vast expanse of windblown sand before him bore no tracks of any living creature. The sun was halfway up the sky, but even so, he thought, it might be halfway down, because he had no means of identifying direction. He had paid no attention to such details as Lachlan dragged him into the cave, and for a moment the enormity of his own ignorance threatened to overwhelm him. Rather than give in to that feeling, however, he harangued himself in silence. *Come on now*, he thought. *You're alive, you've eaten and drunk, and you have both food and water to keep you going. You're in no more pain than you might be with a bad toothache. You even have a weapon, by God, and it will double as a walking staff, so stop whining to yourself like a lost little boy and get on with it!* But he had no clue which way to go and so he stood there, helpless.

The worst part of his helplessness sprang from not knowing where he could even begin to search for his friend Lachlan, who had done so much for him. Moray could be anywhere out there, sheltering miles away in some rocky hole or in the lee of a dune, or he could be lying dead within paces of this cave, smothered and buried by drifting sand. Frustrated beyond bearing, to the point of not caring who else might hear his shout, he cupped his good hand by the side of his mouth and called Lachlan's name at the top of his voice, then listened carefully for an answer from the silent immensity of the desert. Four times he tried, facing a different direction each time, before accepting the futility of what he was doing. He inhaled deeply then, gritted his teeth, and set out strongly without looking back, trudging ankle deep in sand towards wherever the Fates directed him, and although aware that he was leaving deep and unmistakable tracks as he went, he consoled himself by almost believing that Lachlan Moray might stumble across his trail and follow him.

SINCLAIR SOON DISCOVERED that the sun had been halfway *up* the sky when he set out, because as he walked onward, taking great care

over where he placed each foot, it climbed higher until it was
directly overhead. He thought about stopping to eat and drink at that
point, but he was on a long, level stretch and, remembering the difficulty he had had with the water bag, he decided to wait a little longer
in the hope of finding something to sit on before making the attempt.
And so he moved on, changing his direction slightly towards a low
rise in the sand ahead of him and to his right. Soon after that,
although he could see no incline, the increased strain on his legs told
him that he had begun to climb, and some time later he crested the
high point of a long, low ridge and stopped to stretch and work the
kinks from his hips and shoulders.

Standing straight and eyeing the distant horizon, he caught a
flicker of movement at the edge of his right eye and spun to face it.
But there was nothing to be seen other than bare, smooth sand and
the slowly rising edge of the ridge, curling away from him, back the
way he had come, to form a large dune. He stared for a long time,
his eyes narrowed to slits as he quartered every inch of rising ground
up there, and it came again, a definite flicker of movement, low to
the ground, just as he was about to turn away. But he lost it again
immediately. He flexed his fingers on the shaft of his spear and set
out determinedly, up the length of the low ridge, feeling the pull of
the slope sapping the strength from his tiring legs, and straining for
another sight of whatever it was up there that had moved. It was
small, he knew, but he was also hoping it would be edible and sufficiently accommodating to allow itself to be caught and eaten.

Several minutes later he saw the movement again, but as soon as
he focused on the spot where the movement had been, he also saw
what had confused him: indistinguishable from the sand behind it,
the edge of the spine that formed the ridge was curling back to his
right just at that point, and the space behind it had been scooped
clean by the wind. What he had seen was the twitching ear of a horse
that was hidden by the edge of the spine. Now he could see the
animal's entire head, a pale and unusual golden color, almost the
exact shade of the sand surrounding it, and as he saw it for what it
was, the beast lowered its head out of sight again.

Sinclair had instantly frozen into a crouch, raising his spear defensively and fighting against the rush of tension in his chest, for where there was a horse, so far from any signs of life, there must also be a rider. It was several moments before he decided he was not in imminent danger of attack, and he moved forward slowly, inch by inch, until he could raise his head above the edge of the sandy spine and look down into the place below.

The horse skittered away from him as soon as it saw him, but Sinclair paid it no heed. His entire attention was claimed by an unevenness in the flat, windswept sand beneath the shelter of the ridge, and a small triangle of green-and-white cloth that lay just at the edge of the irregularity. He rose up cautiously and scanned the area around the disturbance for footprints, but the only tracks were those made by the horse, and so he stepped off the crest of the ridge and plowed down the steep slope, leaning far back and bracing himself strongly with the shaft of the spear.

By the time he reached the bottom he was grimacing with pain as his heavily braced broken arm objected to the violence of his lurching descent, but as soon as his feet touched level sand he drew himself up and stood swaying, gritting his teeth until the pain subsided to a tolerable level. He looked about him before crossing to the triangle of cloth, which he grasped and tugged. It moved only very slightly, weighted as it was with sand, but what he had uncovered was enough to confirm his suspicions. He had often seen the desert nomads using large cloth squares to fashion temporary shelters from the sun, and sometimes from the wind, weighting the rear edges with sand and propping up the leading edge with a stout stick, or sometimes two of them, to erect a small, primitive one-man tent. The man this one had been made to protect was probably dead beneath it, but Sinclair barely gave that a thought. That man had been an infidel, perhaps even a Saracen, and Sinclair's sole concern at that moment was for his own welfare. Had the fellow been carrying food and water when he died?

He took note of the right-angled corner and the lines of the triangle's edges, then traced its approximate shape and size with his right heel, digging an outline and gauging the length of the sides from memory. When it was complete, he slowly knelt, taking care not to overbalance, then began to scoop holes for his knees, piling the sand up on his left side as he removed it. By the time he had judged his knee holes deep enough, there was a pyramid beside him, and he braced his useless left arm with his other hand as he lifted it and placed it on top of the small mound, immediately relieving himself and his shoulder joint of the weight of the rigid limb. Only when it was firmly braced did he bend forward again, and, using his good forearm as a shovel to sweep the burden of sand from the cloth beneath, he began working doggedly, one-handed, to uncover the fabric, but making no attempt to raise it in any way.

Before he was halfway done, he had felt the outline of the corpse beneath him and had formed a picture of the dead man, lying on his left side, his legs outstretched stiffly, his right foot pointed as though frozen in the act of kicking someone. But there were other shapes beneath there, too, and as the thirst grew in him, aggravated by the hard work, Sinclair prayed that some of them were vessels containing water.

Finally the green-and-white-striped cloth lay almost completely exposed, the outline of the dead nomad clearly limned beneath it. Sinclair straightened his back and drew in one great, deep breath and held it. He took one corner of the cloth in his hand, counted to three, and then swept the covering away with one great, swooping tug, steeling himself against the possibility of finding a long-dead, rotting corpse. He found nothing of the kind, no rush of foul air, no swarming flies or insects, and he breathed normally again.

The man who lay there, face pillowed on the ground, was newly dead, but his rich clothing and fine armor made it plain he had been no common desert nomad, caught and overwhelmed by the storm. On the sand at his back was a folded pile of white cotton cloth that Sinclair recognized as a kufiya, the large, square scarf that the nomadic people of the Arab races used to shield their heads from the desert sun, and on it the man had carefully positioned a finely made Saracen helmet, its tapering crown rising to a high spike. The edges of the headgear were trimmed with a light, intricately fashioned visor and a shoulder-length canopy of fine mail. Beside it rested a long, curved scimitar, its bone hilt polished by age and its scuffed scabbard attesting to years of use. Whoever he was, the man had bled to death. His entire lower body was blackened and encrusted by a seemingly solid casing of gore-clotted sand. Beneath one outstretched foot, the one Sinclair had noticed as being frozen in a kick, was the stick that had supported his shelter, and Sinclair had no difficulty in imagining what had happened. The dying man's last, agonized kick had brought the shelter down upon him, shutting off his life.

Moved by the solitary tragedy of such a death, Sinclair found himself searching for words to say over the body, before it came to him that anything he might say would be wasted. This was a Muslim warrior, an infidel who would have thanked no man for commending his soul to the Christian God of his enemies. Nevertheless, he bowed his head, looking down at the corpse, and muttered, "Rest in peace, whoever you were. Not even your Allah would object to my wish of that for you."

He turned his head away and looked at the other objects that had been covered by the tent cloth, and the first thing he saw was a water bag, swollen and heavy. Nearby, its position suggesting that the dead man might have used it as a pillow, was a beautifully made saddle, the leather of its seat coated with dried blood, more heavily on the left side than the right, as though the rider had been wounded in the groin. Reins and a bridle lay carefully coiled beside it, and beyond those, within reach of the supine man, lay the water skin and a set of solidly packed saddlebags.

Carefully cradling his injured arm, Sinclair nudged the heavy saddlebags with his foot, pushing and sliding them until they were close to the largest pile of sand he had swept up, and then he lowered himself to sit on the small pyramid and bent forward to seize the bags with his good hand and drag them to rest against his leg. They were heavy, and he sensed that whatever weighed them down might be useful to him.

Sinclair now went about the business of removing his own water bag from about his neck, securing the cup between his knees and settling the bag's sagging, untrustworthy bulk along his bent forearm before he removed the stopper with his teeth. It seemed to take hours, and his lips and mouth were parched and sore throughout, but eventually he was able to set down the bag and drink from the cup. He resisted the temptation to refill it when he had finished, and stuffed the cup firmly inside his leather jerkin. His eyes were fixed on the saddlebags.

Even with only one hand, he had the bags untied in mere moments. The one on the right contained food and the materials for preparing it: a substantial bag of flour, a tiny one of ground salt, and several pieces of dried, heavily spiced meat, all of which he assumed to be goat. There was also a selection of dates, both fresh and dried, along with a handful of olives carefully wrapped in a muslin cloth. In another large square of cloth he found a hinged cooking tripod and a supple, oiled boiling bag of antelope skin to suspend from it, along with a small bowl and a plate, both of burnished metal. Another, smaller bundle held two spoons, one of horn and the other of wood, and a sharp knife.

The second bag contained a bag of grain and a folded nose bag for the horse, along with two packages, one much larger and heavier than the other and both wrapped in the same green-and-white-striped cloth that had formed the tent canopy. Sinclair opened the larger one first, to reveal a chain-mail tunic the likes of which he had never seen. The edges of its square-cut collar and sleeves were woven of some kind of flattened silver metal, too tough to be real silver, and its flat-sided links were of the finest, lightest steel mesh he had ever handled. The entire garment was lined throughout with a soft but immensely strong green fabric that showed no creases or wrinkles. He set the thing aside and opened the second packet to reveal a magnificently ornate sheathed dagger with a hooked blade, its hilt and scabbard chased with silver filigree and studded with polished precious stones in red, green, and blue. He picked the weapon up, conscious that he had never held such a valuable piece before, and hefted it in his hand as he turned to glance at the dead man beside him.

"Well, Infidel," he murmured, "I have no way of knowing who you were, but you took pride in your possessions, so I promise you I will take good care of them and use them gratefully if ever I escape from here."

He repacked the saddlebags and rose to his feet again, then folded the tent that had covered the dead man until he could pick it up and lay it beside the saddle and bags, aware that he would have more need of it in the times ahead than its former owner would. He collected the two supporting sticks and placed them between the folds of the cloth. He buried the Saracen as well as he could then, wrapping him in his blood-drenched cloak and laying his helmet by his head and his scimitar by his side, then dragging sand into place with one foot until he could shape it into a mound over the shallow grave, leaving no trace of the body beneath. The signs of his digging, he knew, would vanish within days, and there was a strong probability that the grave would remain undisturbed thereafter, its occupant safe from the vultures and vulnerable only to the possibility of some wandering beast smelling the decay and unearthing the meat that caused it. His task complete, he wrapped the dead man's kufiya about his head, scrubbed the dried blood off the saddle as well as he could, using handfuls of sand, and set about capturing the horse.

Within the hour he was walking again, leading the animal by the bridle. The effort of saddling it one-handed had almost exhausted him. Luckily, the horse, once captured, had submitted to the procedure and stood patiently as Sinclair struggled to hoist the heavy saddle and wrestle it into place on its back, and then to tighten the girths and extend the stirrup leathers, for its former owner had been a hand's width shorter in the legs than Sinclair. Now, with tent, saddlebags, and water skins securely fastened to the beast's saddle, and the beast itself watered and fed with a handful of grain, he walked at its head, his eyes scanning the middle distance, the reins looped over his good shoulder and his only burden the tall, heavy spear in his hand.

He found what he was looking for within half an hour, a single boulder that thrust its crest above the sand in the lee of the dune that soared above it. He led the horse directly up to the outcrop and climbed up to the top of it. Using the summit as a mounting block and his long spear shaft as a counterbalance, he clambered awkwardly into the saddle, his left arm braced over the animal's shoulders in front of him. Once there, safely settled with his feet in the stirrups, he felt immensely better and permitted himself, for the first time since awakening alone in the cave, to think, even to hope, that he might yet survive this ordeal. Only the twitching of the horse's ears suggested that it was aware of having a new and very large rider on its back. Sinclair grimaced. What would happen if the horse were to rebel when he ordered it to move? One good, head-down heave and he'd be flat on his back on the ground.

And what was he to do, now, with his spear? It had become as useless as his former sword, since he could not hold it and ply the reins at the same time. He looked at the sturdy weapon regretfully, then stabbed the shaft point-first into the sand. He opened the left saddlebag and removed the jeweled dagger. He unwrapped its cloth binding and took a moment to admire it again before slipping the weapon into the front of his jerkin. Then he gritted his teeth, took a firm grip on the reins, and dug in his heels, regretting not having checked the horse's former owner for spurs. The animal uttered a single grunt, then began to walk sedately, and Sinclair offered a silent prayer to whichever deity might be responsible. The gentle walk pleased him well, for he had no wish to do anything precipitate before he had time to judge the horse's mettle against his own, but now that he was riding, he was conscious that his traveling speed had increased at least threefold.

He reached down and patted the horse's neck gratefully, encouragingly.

"Well done, beast," he whispered. "It looks as though it will be thee and me, together, from now on."

FIVE

ulled by the steady, familiar rhythm of the horse's gait, Sinclair had no thought of falling asleep in the saddle, but when the horse halted suddenly, whickering softly, he snapped awake, excitement and fear flaring in his breast. He recognized instantly that he had been asleep, and he was already wondering what his folly might have condemned him to. But there was no danger that he could see, no one close by, and no threat that he could perceive. The only element of the scene that was extraordinary was that his horse was standing stock-still, its ears pointing straight ahead.

There had been no cliffs within sight in any direction the last time Sinclair had looked about him, but now, no more than fifteen paces in front of him, a rocky escarpment towered above him to a height more than four times his own. More wide-awake now than he had been in days, he stared at the rock ahead of him, at the diagonal black slash of the fissure facing him, and at a spear, not unlike the one he had abandoned earlier, that stood in front of it, its point buried in the sand. He knew that if it was similar in length to his own it must be half-buried. He knew, too, that there might well be someone waiting inside the cave mouth to attack him, possibly someone with a bow, and that to remain where he was without moving was inviting attack.

He was on the point of wheeling away when his eyes returned to the upright spear shaft.

Lachlan Moray had found the litter made of two spears, one of which Sinclair had used as a staff; the other he had left behind in the cave where he had sheltered from the storm. What if there had been a third, he wondered now, and Lachlan had taken it with him? Unlikely, yes, but not impossible. He had been unconscious most of the time Lachlan had dragged him on the bier, and he had been behind him all the time. And if that were the case, the half-buried weapon in front of the fissure in the cliff might well be that same spear, thrust into the ground as a signal. Two paces behind it, the fissure rose stark and black from the sand that must surely have filled it, at least partially. Moray might be lying in there, asleep or injured.

Sinclair dismounted, lowering himself as gently as he could. He drew his long-bladed dirk and walked forward cautiously, squinting against the glare reflected from the rock face as he peered towards the black incision of the cave opening. But it took only two paces to reveal that he was looking at a shadow, not an opening in the wall. A bladelike protrusion in the surface jutted towards him; its sharp-edged facade blended perfectly into the stone face behind, and it formed a sheltered corner, its vertical edge casting the hard, dark shadow he had mistaken for an entrance to a cave. Annoyed with himself for having dismounted to no good purpose, Sinclair straightened up from his crouch and was on the point of turning away when something, some nudging of curiosity, urged him to approach more closely and make sure that the sheltered nook was, in fact, as empty as it now appeared to be.

It was not. Wedged into the corner of the shallow cleft, the head and upper torso of a man were clearly discernible beneath a light covering of sand, slumped but apparently sitting upright in the angle made by the two walls. Sinclair's immediate reaction was elation that Moray had found shelter and survived, just as he had wished and hoped. He advanced quickly, dropping to his knees and brushing away the sand from the cloth-wrapped head. The head moved, jerking away in surprise or protest from the unexpected touch, but Sinclair's fingers had already hooked into the edge of one layer of cloth and the sudden movement pulled the covering free, exposing part of the face beneath. Within a heartbeat he was upright again. He brought up the point of his dirk, then stood there, swaying.

The inch or so of skin and hair that he had seen did not belong to Sir Lachlan Moray. Lachy's hair was blond, almost red gold, and his cheeks were fair, constantly burning and peeling and never tanning in the desert sun. Whoever was lying in front of Sinclair now was no friend. The skin of that face was a deep nut brown, and the hairs about the mouth were black and wiry. Sinclair backed away another step, his dirk poised to strike. He knew he was in no danger, because the man in the corner was even more deeply buried than he himself had been, and he remembered how difficult it had been for him to struggle free. As he stood there, looking down at the recumbent form, his eye caught a small, peaked irregularity in the windblown surface of the shroud that masked the man, and without removing his eyes from the still concealed head in front of him, Sinclair sheathed his dirk, then stooped and groped at the protrusion with his fingers, finding the hilt of a sword.

He straightened up slowly, pulling the weapon with him, and found himself holding a Saracen scimitar, its curved, burnished blade worked in the intricate Syrian fashion known as Damascene. It was a fine blade, he knew, and that told him that its owner was a warrior, and therefore doubly dangerous. But Sinclair knew he had no need to kill him. All he need do was walk away, remount his horse and ride off, leaving the infidel to his fate. But even as he thought that, Sinclair knew he would not do it. He too was a warrior, and he lived by a warrior's code. He had never killed anyone who was not attempting, in one fashion or another, to kill him. Already cursing himself for a fool, he thrust the sword point-first into the sand, close to hand, and knelt by the slumped form. As he took hold of the wrapped cloth again, the figure in the sand stirred violently, but Sinclair merely lowered his splinted arm to the area of the man's sternum and pinned him with it while he unwound the multiple loops of cloth from about the head, then backed away to look at what he had uncovered.

The face that looked back at him was, as he had suspected, unmistakably Saracen, thin and high browed, hawk nosed, with prominent, tight-skinned cheekbones beneath deep-set, narrow eyes so dark that they appeared to be uniformly black. Lips and chin were covered in black, wiry, glistening hair, each strand apparently coated with its own covering of sandy dust. The eye whites were discolored and angry looking, irritated probably beyond bearing, he suspected, by the same grit and dust, but the face itself was not angry. The word that sprang into Sinclair's mind, unthought of for years, was *Stoic*, and he thought it apt.

The Saracen, unable to move, gazed at him without expression, clearly waiting to see what he would do next, and for several minutes neither man moved or made a sound.

Finally Sinclair drew in a breath. "Right, laddie," he said in his native Scots. "Let's have you out o' there." He raised a finger to his lips in warning, then drew the dirk from its sheath and held it up for the Saracen to examine before he thrust it into the sand by his right knee. Then, without another word, he bent forward and began to scoop the sand away, starting beneath the man's chin and baring his shoulders before going on to free his left arm, exposing a shirt of fine chain mail that reminded him of the one he had found on the dead man. From that point on the Saracen worked with him, thrusting the accumulated sand away from his own body. Twice Sinclair repositioned himself, throwing the scimitar behind him out of reach the first time but keeping his dirk close to him yet safe from the other man's grasp.

They worked together, the only sounds their heavy breathing as they labored, but when Sinclair finally dug his hand beneath the level of the fellow's waist, to scoop an armful from between his buried legs, the other grunted deeply and jerked his arm into the air in an unmistakable signal to take care. Sinclair sat back and blinked, wondering what he had done wrong, but the Saracen bent forward and indicated where his left leg must be, making vigorous shoveling motions and obviously telling Sinclair to continue. The Frankish knight went back to work, but as he did so, he saw the caution with which the Saracen now worked on freeing his own right leg, and understood that the leg must be injured. He saw, too, how haggard the man had become since first they started digging, and the recognition reminded him of his own thirst. He straightened abruptly and walked back to his horse, on the far side of the sheltering wall, where he retrieved the larger and fuller of the two water bags, and as he returned he could hear the Saracen spitting sand. The sound stopped as soon as Sinclair's shadow came into view, and as he rounded the edge of the blade of rock he found the man he had already begun to think of as Blackbeard staring at him as he had before, stoically, his face expressionless.

Sinclair leaned against the cliff wall and lobbed the heavy water bag towards the other man, who caught it with both hands, his face registering surprise for the first time.

"Go ahead, laddie. Drink." He nodded, and the Saracen nodded in return, his face unreadable again, then began to remove the bag's stopper. Sinclair watched him wryly. "It's a grand thing to have two hands when you need to drink from a bag, is it not?"

The Saracen had stopped before the bag reached his mouth, his eyes on Sinclair and his incomprehension plainly visible. On the point of repeating what he had said in Arabic, Sinclair caught himself and continued in his native tongue. "Go on, drink, but pour some for me." He drew the metal cup from inside his jerkin and tapped it against the splints on his useless arm, then moved forward, his hand outstretched. The Saracen glanced at the arm, then nodded his understanding and filled the cup. Sinclair sipped delicately and rinsed his mouth, spitting before he took a second, proper sip and returned to lean against the wall. The Saracen did the same, rinsing his mouth carefully and deliberately before spitting the resultant mud out with some delicacy. He looked again at Sinclair, clearly asking permission, and when Sinclair nodded, he repeated the sequence, then took a third sip with evident relish, washing it around his mouth but swallowing it this time.

"Go ahead. Take more. And wash your eyes, for I know just how you feel." Sinclair picked up the cloth that had wrapped the fellow's head. He took one end of it and flapped it until it was relatively free of sand, then mimed wetting it and bathing his eyes before handing it to the other man, who watched him cautiously and then did as

Sinclair suggested. When he had finished, he hefted the bag, clearly asking Sinclair if he wished to drink again, and when Sinclair shook his head he corked the bag deftly and set it down beside him. Sinclair stepped forward and retrieved the dirk that was still stuck in the sand, then stood looking down at the other man.

"I have a question here, Master Blackbeard: are you my prisoner, or am I yours? I have the dirk and your sword, but I'm no' certain they'll do me much good, gin it comes to a fight. It will depend, I'm thinking, on that leg o' yours, for if it's in better shape than my arm is, then I might have to pay the piper." He paused, debating with himself on the best course of action, but well aware that he would have to finish the task he had begun. "Come on, then," he said, shrugging, "let's find out."

Several minutes later, he unearthed the Saracen's buried left foot and brushed off the last of the sand from the leg, but the Saracen himself was still proceeding very cautiously with his right, brushing delicately at the sand and clearly concerned about what yet lay beneath it. Soon enough, Sinclair could see for himself what was wrong. The leg was heavily bandaged and splinted, and it had clearly been done by someone who knew how. Sinclair laughed aloud, although there was no humor in the sound.

"Well, we're the fine pair, are we not? Six good limbs between the two o' us and both o' us so useless, we canna even talk to each other, let alone fight." He hoisted his arm and tapped the steel bolts of his splints with the blade of his dirk, and for the first time a hint of what might have been a smile flickered at one corner of the other man's mouth.

"Well, we might as well have another drink, because I canna think what to do next. I doubt I'll be able to climb back onto my horse wi' this damn arm, lacking a mounting block, and even if I could, you couldna get up behind me." He picked up the water bag again and handed it to the Saracen. "Here, you pour better than me, so pour away." Moments later, his cup brimming, he moved away and sat carefully on a heap of sand. As he reached down to balance the cup carefully at his feet, the hilt of the jeweled dagger slipped out from the folds of his jerkin. Before he could push it back in, he heard the Saracen's gasp, and he looked up to see a strange, wide-eyed expression on the man's face.

"What's wrong? Is it this?" He pulled the dagger free and held it up, and as the man looked at it, Sinclair saw something enter his eyes, and then his face went as still as it had been before.

"Where did you obtain that knife?" The question was in Arabic, but Sinclair had anticipated it, and he kept his own face blank as he shook his head and shrugged, as though not understanding a word. He could not have explained to anyone why he was pretending igno-rance, but he knew instinctively that it was the right thing to do. The Saracen frowned, then made another attempt.

"How did you come by that?"

The question was in French this time, and Sinclair's eyes widened with shock, but he answered immediately in the same tongue, genuinely pleased to have a means of communicating with this man without revealing his understanding of Arabic.

"I found it, this morning. On a dead man. Several miles from here."

There was a long pause before the Saracen said, "You killed him?"

Sinclair heard pain in the question and he shook his head, then lifted his rigid arm so that it rested on his upraised knee. "No," he said, adjusting the arm to make it as comfortable as possible. "I told you, I found him dead, buried like you. Who was he? It's plain that you knew him."

The Saracen paused, but then he dipped his head in acceptance. "His name was Arouf. He was youngest brother to my wife. He was sorely wounded when he left here. The bleeding had been stopped for hours by then, and the wound was packed and tightly bound, but it must have opened again while he was riding."

"He took your horse and left you here?"

"There was no other choice. We were three men, with two horses. Arouf rode north in search of help, and Sayeed rode east. They left me here safely in the shade. None of us knew the storm would come."

"So the other man, this Sayeed, may still be alive?"

"Aye, if Allah so wills. If it is written in the Angel's book. If it is not, then it may be written therein that you and I will die here, together." He looked about him. "But we will not die yet. I, too, have water, and a bag of food, buried somewhere here by the wind."

Sinclair ignored that. "What happened to your leg, and who did this?" He waved towards the splinted limb.

"Sayeed saved both of us. He is learned in the healing arts."

"A physician?"

"No, a warrior, but he was trained in youth by his father, who was a famed physician. Sayeed never followed his father's craft, but he remembered his teachings on the care of wounds."

"And he rode east?"

A dip of the head. "I have said."

"In search of whom? How came you here? Were you at Hattin?"

"Hattin? Ah, you mean Hittin …" The Saracen's brow wrinkled then, but he plainly resisted the impulse to ask what was in his mind and simply answered the question. "No, I was not. We were on our way to Tiberias, in obedience to the Sultan's summons, when ill fortune befell us."

Sinclair reached down and handed the water bag to the Saracen again. "Tell me about it, since we have nothing better to do, and then we will find your food and water. What happened to you?"

The dark-faced man sat thinking for a few moments, then began to speak.

HIS NAME WAS IBN AL-FAROUCH, he said, and he had been in the southwest, riding with a reconnaissance force near the town of Ibelin on the coast when a courier arrived to summon them to Tiberias, eighty miles away. They had set out immediately on receiving the command, and along the way had met a wounded man who had, mere hours before, escaped from a nearby village that was being attacked by bandits. The bandits, the fugitive told them, had numbered fewer than twenty, but the villagers, lacking their men of fighting age, had been unable to resist them. The name of the village, which meant nothing to Sinclair, had caught the attention of al-Farouch immediately, because he had an aged uncle, fond brother to his mother, who lived there. Angered at the thought of his uncle, who had always been kind to him and to his family, being molested and perhaps even killed by godless brigands, he had sent his men on their way, but had ridden with an escort of ten hand-picked companions to administer justice to the raiders.

Unfortunately, he said after a lengthy pause, in his anger and indignation he had underestimated his opponents, not merely their strength but their number, taking the word of the fugitive at face value. He and his party had ridden into a cleverly constructed ambush in a steep-walled wadi, and he had lost seven of his men, shot down from concealment, before he could even begin to collect himself. Only Sayeed, Arouf, himself and one other had managed to fight their way free, three of them, and two of their mounts, wounded. The fourth man had died of his wounds soon after their escape, as had his horse, and Sayeed had cut the throat of Arouf's horse some time after that, when the deep slash in its belly had finally split and spread, spilling the beast's entrails to tangle in its hooves. Arouf, pressing a cloth to his bleeding groin wound, had then mounted behind Sayeed, and the three had kept riding until they found this place, where they had stopped for the night. Sayeed, the only one unhurt among them, had stanched the bleeding in Arouf's groin first, sprinkling it with some powder that stopped the flow of blood, after which he had strapped the wound up tightly. He had then tended to al-Farouch's leg, the smaller bone of which had been snapped by a crossbow bolt. He cleaned the wound, set the bone as well as he was able, and then bandaged and splinted the limb, which he expected to heal completely.

They had spent the night here together, all three of them, and when the next day dawned they discussed what must be done. Their companions would be far ahead of them by now, and might even have stopped to wait for them, or turned back to search for them, but all three men knew that the odds against their being found without assistance left little hope. And so al-Farouch decided that Sayeed would ride out in search of the others. Arouf would have none of that, swearing he was sound enough to ride, now that the bleeding from his groin had stopped. He would ride out with Sayeed, overriding his brother's wishes for the first time in all the years they had known each other. He would take the northern route while Sayeed searched farther to the east. Al-Farouch, whose splinted leg made it impossible for him to mount a horse, would remain where he was, with a supply of food and water sufficient to sustain him for seven to eight days, by which time one or both of the others would have returned with help. The two then rode off, leaving al-Farouch's round shield hanging from his upended spear to serve as a sign on their way back.

"And now you know as much as I do, *ferenghi*," al-Farouch concluded, using the Arabic term for a Frank and lapsing back into silence.

Sinclair sat silent, mulling over what he had been told. If Sayeed had survived the storm and found his fellows, they would return here and that would be the end for him. He could still depart on the horse, he knew; one way or another he could contrive to mount it again, even without a mounting block, now that he knew its placid nature. He thought of looking out again to check that the horse was still nearby, but instead he leaned forward and spoke to the Saracen.

"How is it that you speak our tongue?"

"One of your tongues," the other answered drily. "When you spoke at first, in that first tongue you used, it fell upon my ears like the gibbering of *djinns*. What was that noise?"

Sinclair grinned for the first time in days. "That was Gaelic, the language of my people in Scotland, where I was born."

"You are not, then, a Frank?"

"No, I am what they call a Scot, but my family came there from France a hundred years ago. When the call went out for warriors to come here, I joined the army."

"Are you a knight, then? I see no badges of rank on you."

"I cast them off with my armor when I found myself afoot in the desert. There are too many ways to die out here without being foolish enough to seek one, weighed down with useless steel and heavy clothing."

"Ah, I see. Plainly you have been here long enough to learn a smattering of Allah's wisdom, praise His name … But you came here to kill Saracens, no?"

"No, not exactly. I came because my duty as a knight summoned me here, to Outremer. Killing or being killed is merely part of the knight's code."

"You are of the Temple, then?"

Something, some unidentifiable element of menace in the simple question, made Sinclair change the affirmative that sprang to his lips, but he managed to dissemble without either lying or, he thought, betraying himself. "I am a knight," he drawled. "From Scotland, many days from France by sea. Not all the knights in Outremer are of the Temple or the Hospital."

"No, but the Temple *djinns* are the most dangerous of them all."

Sinclair let that statement lie as it fell. "You did not answer my question, about how you came to speak the language of the Franks."

"I learned it as a boy, in Ibelin, where I grew up. There was a Frankish lord who built a fortress there, after the capture of Jerusalem, long before I was born. He took the name of the town as his own. I worked there when I was a boy, in the stables, and I ran and played with his son, who was my age. I learned to speak their tongue, as the boy learned mine."

Sinclair was frowning. "Ibelin … Mean you Sir Balian of Ibelin? I know him. I rode with him from Nazareth to …" He broke off, aware that he might be saying more than he ought, but al-Farouch was already nodding his head.

"It would be he. His name in our tongue is Balian ibn Barzan, and he is a powerful man among the *ferenghi* nowadays—a knight, but not of the Temple."

"Are you still friends, then?"

The Saracen shrugged. "Who can be friends, as Muslim and Christian, in a holy war of jihad? He and I have not met in years, not since we were boys. We might pass each other in the souk and not know it."

Sinclair slapped his good hand on his thigh and straightened his back, turning to squint out into the brightness behind him. "We should eat something. All men share that need, even in a jihad, no? When did you last eat?"

Al-Farouch thought, his lips pursed. "I cannot remember, but it was a long time ago."

Sinclair stood up. "I left my horse—your horse—saddled in the sun, and he must be suffering. If I bring him in here, close to you, will you help me to unsaddle him? It's difficult to loosen a tight girth with one hand."

"I will, if you can bring him close enough that I can reach him."

A short time later, the horse seen to and its saddlebags removed, Sinclair dropped the saddle to the floor of the little shelter and sat on it while he rummaged in the bag that held the food, withdrawing a large piece of dried meat and the sharp little knife. He threw the meat first and then the knife to the surprised Muslim, who caught it easily, hilt first. "Here, you have two hands and can cut better than I can. Cut us to eat from that, while I see to the rest."

The Muslim set to slicing the hard meat without comment, while Sinclair extracted dried figs, dates, and bread from the saddlebag for both of them.

They ate in a courteous, strangely companionable silence, each immersed in his own thoughts. Sinclair reflected upon the unlikelihood of the circumstances that had brought him to this point, placidly sharing a meal with an enemy who, under any other conditions, he would have attempted to kill on sight. He wondered if his silent companion might be thinking the same thing, but then his thoughts returned to the veiled threat he had suspected in the Saracen's question about the Templars, and he began to take solemn stock of it.

Sinclair had no means of knowing whether his cautious response had been any more necessary than his decision to conceal his knowledge of Arabic, but he felt comfortable with the way he had deflected al-Farouch's curiosity. He was indeed a Temple Knight, and he suspected that the Saracen would have accorded him little in the way of approval for that, but there was much more to Sir

Alexander Sinclair than mere membership in the Order of the Temple, and he had good reason to be reticent about who he was.

Sinclair was a highly placed member of the clandestine Brotherhood of Sion, the secret society within the Temple that had founded and created the Order for its own ends, decades earlier at the turn of the century, and which still supervised and guided the Order's policies. So secret was the brotherhood that not even its existence, let alone its activities, was suspected by the rank and file of the Order, and although many of the most senior officers of the Temple belonged to the brotherhood, many others of equivalent military rank lived out their lives and died without ever being aware of the brotherhood's existence. Prime among the latter was Gerard de Ridefort, the current Master of the Temple, who, although prized and honored for his courage, military skills, and high-principled audacity, had been deemed unqualified, thanks to his pride and hotheaded arrogance, to enter the brotherhood.

Membership in the Brotherhood of Sion was not lightly bestowed. Its members were few and bound by oath and loyalty to utter silence and secrecy, and they seldom met in plenary session. Whenever they did convene, it was under the guise of traditional celebrations called Gatherings, and those were always held in secure and private properties owned by senior brethren of the Governing Council. There the brotherhood would assemble, surrounded by their families and friends, most of them kinfolk, and while the celebrations and rejoicing went on above, in the public spaces of the hosting family, the brotherhood would gather secretly in the lower reaches of whatever castle had been chosen as the venue, to celebrate their own clandestine business of initiations, instruction, and promotion, their activities unsuspected by the other celebrants at the Gathering.

Individual members of the organization were not distinguishable in any way save one, and even that knowledge was secretly guarded, close held among themselves, although it was a distinction that no one who was not an initiate could ever see. Every man of them was selected from one of a federation of aristocratic clans known among themselves as the Friendly Families, all of which lived in the region of southern France known as the Languedoc, so called because the region had its own ancient language. The name literally meant "the tongue of Oc," or "the place where Oc is spoken." The association of the federated families dated back more than a millennium, to the first century of the Christian era, when the founders of each of the clans settled together in southern Gaul after their long overland flight from the Roman destruction of Jerusalem in the year 79.

Their collective Jewish roots were the greatest secret of the brotherhood, for their families had assimilated seamlessly into local society soon after their arrival, and they had now been Christian for a thousand years, blissfully ignorant of their Semitic origins. Only the initiates of the ancient Brotherhood of the Order of Rebirth in Sion knew the truth, passed down in secret throughout the generations of that same thousand years, and they alone undertook to shoulder the great responsibility entailed in that knowledge, their singular entitlement safeguarded and reinforced by the inflexible edict that only one male member from every generation of each of the Families could be eligible for initiation.

Sir Alexander Sinclair, chosen from among seven brothers in a family that had produced no daughters, had been admitted to the brotherhood on his twentieth birthday. None of his siblings, all of whom were now of age and two of them knights of the Temple while a third rode with the Order of the Hospitallers, ever suspected that their brother Alec held a secret station above and beyond any of theirs. And because the duties imposed upon him by the brotherhood had made it all but impossible for him to interact normally with his brothers in their workaday world of filial and familial obligations, Christian dedication, and feudal loyalties, they chose to believe that their brother Alec was an ingrate, guilty of turning his back on his family responsibilities. Alec had had no other option than to shrug and appear to accept their condemnation.

And so he had disappeared into the secretive world of the brotherhood, where the Governing Council, having assessed and quantified his every trait and capability, began to educate him in a specific way, for its own purposes. Alexander Sinclair, Knight of the Temple, was a spy for the brotherhood.

"You are deep in thought, *ferenghi*." Al-Farouch's French was fluent, despite the guttural overtones of his Arabic diction. Sinclair smiled wryly and scratched at his scalp.

"I was thinking about my situation here, thinking I ought to climb back up onto your horse and make good my escape before your friends arrive to rescue you."

"If they arrive. Nothing is certain but what is written, and it might be Allah's will, blessings upon His name, that I should remain here and die."

Sinclair thought about that for a while, then nodded slowly. "I find myself believing that Allah might be reluctant to discard a weapon as strong as I suspect you might be for him ... I was also thinking that I do not enjoy the thought of simply riding off and leaving you here alone to live or die, strange as that might sound to you."

The Saracen's eyes narrowed to slits. "More than strange. It smacks of madness. Why should you care what happens to me here, when every moment that you remain places you in deeper peril of being taken, *if* my men arrive?"

A bleak smile flickered on Sinclair's lips. "Call it a family weakness, bred in my bones: that no man of honor should ever leave another to die when he might either save him or help him."

"Honor. It is ..." The Saracen paused, searching for a word. "It is a *concept*, no? A reality without substance. One that is given much ... external recognition ... but is truly understood by very few."

"Even among the faithful of Allah?"

"Even so, alas, as I am sure it is among your own kind."

"Aye, yon's the truth ..." Sinclair had lapsed back into Scots, but even so he could see that the man across from him had understood his tone.

"What is your name, *ferenghi*? You know mine already."

"Lachlan Moray." The lie sprang naturally and unbidden to Sinclair's lips.

"Lachlan … That almost sounds like an Arabic name. Lach-lan Murr-ay."

"It might, to your ears, but it is Scots."

"And you have but little beard. I thought all Frankish knights had beards."

Sinclair scratched ruefully at his stubbled chin. "It is true. I would never be mistaken for a Templar were I in the midst of them. But if I stay out here much longer the beard will grow and I will regret that. I have an affliction, even in the eyes of my comrades, in that my face has little hair and my skin is … do you know the word 'delicate'?"

The Saracen shook his head, and Sinclair shrugged. "Well, as my beard grows, the skin grows scaly and itches painfully, and so, to maintain my sanity and keep from scratching myself bloody, I choose to keep my face clean shaven, when I can. Few of my fellow Franks can understand that." He said nothing of the fact that being clean shaven enabled him to wear a false beard of whatever shape and texture he required from time to time in the course of his work.

"Tell me of Hittin … Hattin, as you call it."

The request was straightforward, but couched as it was in a mild command, it caught Sinclair unawares so that he sat blinking, unable to think of a response.

The Saracen sat straighter, flexing his shoulders. "You asked me when you first arrived if I had been at Hattin, and the tone in which you asked caught my attention. I was not there, as you now know, but Hattin is close to the place you call Tiberias, and the Sultan, may Allah smile upon him, summoned us to gather there. Was there a battle there? Is that why you are here alone?"

Sinclair silently cursed his own carelessness, but there was no point in lying now. He sighed. "Aye, there was a battle."

"I see. And it was … decisive?"

"Aye, I fear it was. We were defeated. Your side was victorious."

"Allah be praised. What happened?"

"What happened? You ask me that? Have you ever been in a major battle, involving thousands of men?"

"I have, several times."

"Have you ever held supreme command in such a battle?"

The Saracen frowned. "No, I commanded my own men, but I am no general."

"Nor am I. So you know as well as I do that a warrior in a battle has little awareness of what is happening in the overall sense of the fighting. He only learns of victory or defeat from what he sees at the end of it. In the midst of it, he strives to protect himself and his men—to stay alive.

"This battle at Hattin was enormous. We had the strongest army ever gathered solely in the kingdom—more than thirty thousand strong. Knights, Turcopole allies and infantry. Your Sultan, Saladin, commanded at least twice our number, probably more, and we were beaten. I saw only glimpses of the main battle, from afar. I was wounded and unhorsed early, breaking my arm, and then was left behind in the fighting. I had a friend with me and we escaped together that night. We decided to make our way back to La Safouri, but we were overtaken by the storm."

"Where is your friend now?" the Saracen asked.

"Gone. Somewhere in the sands. He dragged me behind him for two or three nights—I was raving mad from my injuries—and then he went looking for water, leaving me asleep in a cave he had found. When I woke up the storm had arrived. I have not seen him since. He could be anywhere. I pray he is alive, but I fear he may be dead."

"So what will you do now? Where will you go if you ride away from here?"

"I have no idea. There might be no place for me *to* go." Sinclair grunted, part laughter, part disgust. "Perhaps that's why I am loath even to make the attempt."

Al-Farouch held up a peremptory hand, his head cocked suddenly as though listening. Sinclair strained to hear what it was that had attracted his attention, but he heard only the stillness of the desert, and eventually the Saracen lowered his hand, shaking his head.

"I thought I heard horses approaching." He looked at Sinclair, one eyebrow rising high on his brow. "I suggest, however, that if you are contemplating an escape from here you should leave now."

Sinclair turned his head slightly to gaze out into the gathering dusk, mildly surprised that the day had vanished so quickly. "I have been thinking about that," he said, before turning back to al-Farouch. "And I find that I have a conflict to resolve in my own mind. We spoke of honor briefly, a short time ago, and honor, in my life, involves responsibilities that we Franks call duty."

Al-Farouch nodded, his face impassive. "We, too, have duties, some of them more onerous than others."

"Very well then. Since you understand the concept, as you called it earlier, perhaps you can help me to resolve my dilemma. This day is almost done, so were I to leave now, I would be riding out into the darkness with nowhere to go and no knowledge of how to get there, for the sole purpose of avoiding capture by your warriors. I might achieve that anyway, simply from their failure to come here at all. Then, on the other hand, I might ride straight towards them in the darkness if they do come, for I have no means of knowing the direction they'll come from.

"My dilemma is this: if I ride off blindly into the desert now to avoid capture, with no knowledge of where I am going, will I be acting honorably, because it is my duty to win free, or will I be guilty of dereliction of duty by acting foolishly and endangering my own life needlessly? Do you see what I mean, Master Saracen? Is my duty better served by riding off in the darkness now, perhaps to die, or by remaining here and taking my chances?"

Neither man spoke for a moment, and then Sinclair resumed. "Besides, as I've told you before, I like not the idea of leaving you here alone … And so I have decided to stay here until the morning comes. Then, providing there is no sign of your men, I will make you comfortable and ride far enough away to avoid capture, and there I will wait. If your rescuers do not appear, I will return and eat with you, for nothing will have changed, and I will still not know where to go."

Al-Farouch ran the tip of his middle finger down the length of his nose and pressed it against his pursed lips. "Why do you say you do not know where to go? Were your losses at Hattin so grave?"

Sinclair rose to his feet and went to lean against the edge of rocky wall that formed their small shelter, staring out into the approaching night. When he spoke, he did so without turning his head. "Night comes quickly here, in the desert. In Scotland, where I grew up, the evening light at this time of the year can linger for hours after the sun goes down. There is no word for it in French that I know of, but we call that time of lingering betwixt day and night the gloaming ... It is the *loss* at Hattin, more than our losses, that concerns me—the defeat itself, rather than the casualties, although God knows they were appalling. Your Sultan, from all I know of him, is not a man to ignore an opportunity sent from God, and to his eyes that is how his victory at Hattin will appear. Tiberias will have surrendered to him by this time, I suspect, with the army crushed, and I already know his men have taken La Safouri, and probably Nazareth, too. Were I he, backed by a victorious army and knowing that the Frankish forces are in disorder if not completely destroyed, I would march on Jerusalem at once." He straightened up and turned back towards the other man. "And that, I fear, leaves me with few places to run ... When did you pray last?"

Al-Farouch blinked. "Some time ago, at the appointed hour. You were here. You simply did not notice."

"Should you not have faced the east?"

The Saracen smiled. "Allah requires our prayers, but being merciful, He does not insist that we torture ourselves when we are disabled. I will pray properly when I am able, but until then I will pray as I can."

"Well then, when did you last defecate?"

The Saracen's eyes went wide, but then he shrugged. "The morning my friends left, but I have eaten little since then, so I have had no pressing need."

"But you've eaten now. Can you walk on that leg at all, if I support you?"

"I believe I can."

"Good, and did your friends dig a latrine?"

"They did, close by but far enough removed to be inoffensive. It is ten paces to the right of the entrance."

"If I can help you there, are you capable of seeing to your own needs?"

"Yes, I am."

"Good. Now, if I help you to stand up and walk, will you attempt to kill me?"

The merest hint of a smile showed in the Saracen's eyes. "Not before you bring me back in here, despite my oath to destroy all infidels at any opportunity."

Sinclair grunted, then moved forward, his good arm outstretched. "So be it, then, let's see if we can raise you to your feet. Be careful of my other arm, for it is as badly broken as your leg, but not so well bandaged. Once you are up, we'll go outside and I will leave you to do what you must. Call out when you are done and I'll come and help you back."

By the time they had completed their business at the latrine, full dark had fallen, and they sat together in the darkness of the small corner that was their shelter. They talked of small, unimportant matters for a time, but the night was utterly still and they were both tired, so they soon fell asleep, head to foot in the narrow space, and Sinclair's last thought was that he would have to be awake and away by dawn.

SINCLAIR CAME AWAKE when a callused hand clamped itself across his mouth and chin, but his protesting reaction was stilled instantly as he heard a deep, guttural growl and felt the edge of a cold knife blade at his throat. He lay motionless, waiting to die. Dawn had yet to break, but there was movement all around him, and he knew he should have anticipated this development.

"Who is this *ferenghi* dog? Should I slit his throat?" The voice came from directly above him, and he felt the pressure on the blade at his throat increase, preparing to slash. But even as he began to tense for the blow, the voice of al-Farouch stayed the other's hand, ringing out with an authority that was absolute.

"No! Do him no harm, Sabit. He has shared bread and salt with me and I am in his debt."

The man called Sabit grunted and sat back on his haunches, removing his hand from Sinclair's face but continuing to hold the knife to his throat, although it was the flat of the blade that pushed now against his skin. "How can you be in debt to a *ferenghi*, Amir?" His voice was rich with disgust. "He is an infidel, and therefore you need not be bound by our holy laws in dealing with him. The very idea is laughable."

"And you would see fit to laugh at me for being compassionate, Sabit?" The hard tone of al-Farouch's swift retort was sufficient to make Sabit remove the knife from Sinclair's neck.

"No, not so, Amir. I was but—"

"You were but challenging my judgment, I believe."

"Never, Amir." Sabit knelt upright, swinging to face his superior. "I merely thought—"

"That is strange, Sabit. Thought is something I have never known in you before. I require no thought from you, merely obedience and loyalty. Are we in accord on that?"

"As you say, Amir." Sinclair did not have to see the man to know he was crestfallen.

"Excellent. Now offer thanks to Allah for His blessings and my good humor, then take the *ferenghi* outside and hold him where he cannot overhear us talking. He professes not to understand our speech, but I think we might have much to discuss here and it makes sense to be cautious."

"Allahu Akbar. My obedience is yours, as always."

As the man called Sabit lurched to his feet, al-Farouch changed languages, from Arabic to his rolling, heavily accented French.

"You should have ridden off last night, Lach-Lann, as we discussed, for now you are a prisoner. My lieutenant Sabit is a good man, but a man of firm, sometimes misguided ideals. He was set to cut your throat."

"I could tell." Sinclair fought to keep his voice calm. "I thank you for my life." He hesitated. "I heard him call you Amir. Did you not say your name is Ibn?"

"It is their name for me," the other man said. "I am emir to them, you understand? We live far from other speakers of our tongue. The Bedouin say 'Emir,' but where we live, we say it differently, 'Amir.' Now go with Sabit. He will look after you while I confer with my officers, for my men are here in strength. They will bring me up to date on all that has happened within the past week. In the meantime, Sabit will take you apart from us and hold you safe until I decide what must be done with you. Go with him, and give thanks to Allah that I was able to stay his hand before he could harm you. You will be safe in his hands now."

"I thank you again. Clearly you are a man of more authority than I had suspected. I will go with your man."

"Go now then. Sabit will assist you. Help him up, Sabit."

The last sentence was in Arabic, and as Sabit moved to obey, Sinclair was able to discern his face and shape in the strengthening light. He was a huge man, with the twin clefts of a deep scowl between bushy eyebrows, and a fiercely hooked and bony nose. He wore a spiked helmet with a folded white kufiya draped loosely over it, its ends thrown over opposite shoulders so that the folds covered the lower half of his face. His right eye was covered with a black patch, from which a livid scar stretched down, plainly visible even in the wan light, to disappear beneath the layers of cloth that obscured his mouth and chin, and the fingers of his left hand caressed the hilt of the long, curving sword that hung by his side. He extended his other hand, glowering fiercely, and Sinclair used it to pull himself up to his feet, where he stood swaying for a few moments before stepping towards the mouth of the fold in the cliff. The Saracen fell into step behind him, one warning hand on his shoulder.

A silence fell as Sinclair stepped out from the shade into the open, and he looked about him curiously. More than a hundred men, most of them still mounted, were staring at him in the dawn's light. Not a man of them spoke or moved as Sabit prodded Sinclair forward with a gentle finger, but every eye in the throng followed the Frank as he proceeded some thirty paces along the base of the cliff until his escort's hand closed over his shoulder again.

The big man pointed at the ground, waving downward flat-palmed with his other hand in an unmistakable gesture. Sinclair sat down without further prompting, leaning his back against the rock face, and watched as two of al-Farouch's men, their hands linked to form a chair, carried him out from the niche that had sheltered him. They stopped, facing their comrades, who roared out their greetings to their chief in a manner that left no doubt of the affection and approval they held for him. Sinclair was impressed but not really surprised by their welcome, based on his own impressions about al-Farouch's character and temperament. He was surprised, however, when the mass of mounted men parted to reveal a matched pair of white horses harnessed to a vehicle of a kind that he recognized but had never before seen. It was a battle chariot, a light, two-wheeled conveyance that was little more than a basket-sided platform mounted on high, slender wheels, but he saw at a glance that it had been equipped with a seat that would permit its rider to sit in comfort and control the vehicle despite his broken leg. A richly dressed warrior led the horses forward, and al-Farouch's attendants raised him up carefully to where he could reach out and haul himself into the seat. He raised his hand and waved to his men, drawing a renewed burst of cheering.

Moments later he issued a quiet command and the assembly broke up. Most of the men dismounted and formed into casual groups, while others, evidently officers of one description or another, followed al-Farouch's chariot as he led them away from the gathering to where they could talk without being overheard. Sinclair abandoned any thought of attempting to listen after that, for even had they been shouting at each other, hearing what they said would have been impossible from where he sat. Instead, he settled himself to wait in as much comfort as he could, aware of the formidable and watchful Sabit looming above him, and of the sun's gathering strength on his face. Careful to show no emotion, he covered his face with the folds of the kufiya the big man had tossed to him moments earlier, crossed his arms on his chest, and bent his head as though to sleep.

He was startled when Sabit prodded him with his foot, for he had not expected to fall asleep, but when he looked up wide eyed he saw the other reaching for him again with his right hand. He took it and hauled himself up to his feet, then adjusted the sling on his arm and followed the big man. Al-Farouch sat waiting for him in his chariot, and he was aware as he went that he was being scrutinized by every man there.

Al-Farouch nodded solemnly to him, then stroked the point of his beard between thumb and forefinger. He spoke in French.

"Well, Lach-Lann, it appears that you were right to be concerned about where you might run to, and I am impressed with the accuracy of your predictions. Tiberias surrendered to the Sultan as soon as they heard of our victory at Hattin. He was merciful, as always, and permitted the defenders to depart unharmed. Suffiriyya and Nazareth also fell to us, as you foretold, and the Sultan, may Allah continue to shed His light upon him, has besieged Jerusalem and is expected to win back the city and drive its defenders into the sea before we can arrive there. Palestine, your Latin Kingdom, is ours again, free of the Frankish yoke, and the other territories that you call Antioch, Edessa, and Tripoli will soon be equally blessed. Our lands will be united under Allah from northern Syria to Egypt."

Sinclair stood wooden faced as this was all recited to him, then nodded his head.

"What of the battle, my lord? Know you the extent of our casualties?"

"I do." There was no trace of raillery or gloating in al-Farouch's demeanor. "The Turcomer infantry attached to your knights was destroyed, without survivors. Of your original twelve hundred knights, more than a thousand died. The Crow of Kerak, the foul beast called de Chatillon, is dead, personally cut down by Saladin in fulfillment of his oath to do so." Al-Farouch paused, and a new expression, something unidentifiable, sharpened his gaze. Sinclair braced himself for whatever might come next, but it was not at all what he expected to hear.

"Also dead, I am told, at the express command of the Sultan, are more than one hundred Temple Knights, taken in the battle and executed later."

"They executed prisoners? I do not believe it. Saladin's name would never recover from such an atrocity."

Al-Farouch's right eyebrow twitched. "Saladin's *name*? You mean his reputation among the Franks? The Sultan's name is revered by the followers of Allah, by the warriors of Islam. It matters nothing, to any of the Faithful, what the infidels might have to say about his name or his reputation. This is the man who has sworn the holiest of oaths to sweep Islam clean of the pollution of the Franks, and he ordered the execution of the Temple Knights because he believes them to be the most dangerous men on earth. He has issued a decree that henceforth no Templar will ever be allowed to go free and fight against us again."

Sinclair could not think of anything adequate to say in response to that, and nodded. "What will you do with me now? Am I to die, too?"

Al-Farouch barked a laugh. "Die? No, you are not to die. I owe you a life. But you will be my prisoner, until such time as you are ransomed. Do not be alarmed," he added quickly, seeing Sinclair stiffen. "You will not be treated harshly, so be it that you cause no trouble. We will teach you to speak our tongue while you are among us, and expose you to the words of Allah and His Holy Prophet Muhammad, blessed be his name. We may even teach you to bathe and to dress like a civilized man, but that will depend on how long you remain among us. In the meantime, I have given Sabit charge over you. You will find him swift to deal out punishment and retribution, but he really is not a harsh taskmaster unless provoked. Your Frankishness would normally provoke him grievously, but I have warned him against permitting himself that enjoyment. Go with him now, but before you go, learn your first lesson in Arabic. 'Sala'am Aleikhem.' It means hello, greetings, welcome, and it also means farewell and goodbye. The response to it is to repeat the same words. And so I say to you, until we see each other again, Sala'am Aleikhem."

"Sala'am Aleikhem," Sinclair replied, wondering whether he ever would see his home again, for these people believed his name was Lachlan Moray and no one would ransom Sir Lachlan Moray, a Scottish knight with no affiliation to any major group. There was no Templar knight with such a name, and there was no one out there, even among the brotherhood, who might be capable of divining the truth of what had happened.

Sabit stepped forward and clamped a hand on his shoulder, and Alec Sinclair moved obediently in response, taking his first real steps into captivity as he made his way, under guard, to the horse— al-Farouch's horse—that had been reserved for him in the center of the Saracen formation.

THE COUNTY
OF POITOU
1189–90

ONE

Even before Ector shook him by the shoulder, Henry St. Clair knew he had been dreaming, caught in that wavering limbo between sleep and wakefulness that he had been visiting regularly since his wife died the year before. The noises in his dream had been disquieting and vaguely frightening—distant, but thunderous and threatening—and yet he had been incapable of doing anything about them, unable to move decisively or to raise his voice in question or protest. And then hands were grasping at his shoulders, pinioning his arms, and he awoke with a muffled cry to find Ector standing over him, weirdly menacing in the flickering light of the candle by the bedside.

"My lord! My lord Henry, wake up."

Henry stiffened, then relaxed, recognizing both his steward and his own familiar bedchamber as the last elements of his nightmare dwindled and vanished. He scrubbed at his eyes and pushed himself up onto one elbow, peering owlishly at his visitor.

"Ector? What is it? What hour is it?"

"Long after midnight, my lord, but you have visitors. You must dress yourself, quickly."

"Visitors? In the middle of the night?" He flung away his coverings, then paused, half in and half out of bed, squinting up at his steward. "Is it those thrice-damned priests again? For if it is they can all go to Hell, where I will supplicate the Devil to dig deeper pits among the coals for them. Their sanctimonious arrogance is—"

"No, my lord Henry, not the priests. It is the King. He bids you join him, as quickly as you may."

"The King." Henry's toneless voice betrayed his bewilderment.

"The King of *France*? Capet? Philip Augustus is here in Poitou?"

"No, my lord, I meant the Duke. The English King, Richard. Your liege."

"Richard of Aquitaine." St. Clair's voice flattened. "You dare to name him King, here in my house? His father would have us *both* gutted for even thinking that, let alone saying it aloud."

Ector hung his head, abashed at his gaffe. "Forgive me, my lord. My thoughts impaired my tongue."

Henry held up his hand. "Enough! He will be King of England soon enough, but Henry is not dead yet. And in the meantime, the son is here at my door." He jerked his hand in warning as Ector opened his mouth to speak again. "No! Be quiet and let me think. And while I do that, pray you for Heaven to protect us all from an ill wind, for no fair breeze blows any man to another's door at this time of night, let alone Richard of Aquitaine. Why did you not say sooner it was he?"

Still clad in the tunic and leggings he had worn the previous day, Sir Henry rose from the bed as quickly as his aging body would permit and crossed to the bowl on his nightstand, where he splashed water onto his face and scrubbed at his eyes and cheeks. Ector offered to bring heated water, but Henry simply grunted and reached for a towel, bidding him fetch a fresh surcoat and his cloak instead. By the time Ector had retrieved them from his armoire, Henry had adjusted what he was already wearing and slipped his feet into a pair of sturdy, fleece-lined boots.

"How many men has he brought with him? Is this a war party?"

"No, my lord. He is practically alone. One noble companion and half a score of guards at most. I had the impression they have ridden a long way and still have farther to go."

Henry shrugged into the first of the two garments Ector held out to him, a sleeveless white ankle-length surcoat without blazon. He wrapped the two sides around his waist and cinched them there with a leather belt. "How is his mien, his mood? Does he seem angry?"

Ector raised his eyebrows. "No, my lord. He seems ... excited, full of enthusiasm."

"I'm sure he is." Henry picked up Ector's candle and held it high as he bent forward to peer into a mirror of polished metal. He dipped his other hand into the bowl and splashed water on his hair and beard, rubbing it in with his fingertips and then combing and grooming himself with spread fingers. "But for what is he enthusiastic now? I wonder. His passions ever change from week to week. I wonder where he's bound, that he should pass by our very door. Did he say anything of that?"

"No, my lord. Not to me."

"No, of course. He would not. Well, I shall have to go and ask him."

St. Clair bared his teeth and nodded to his reflection in the mirror, then turned back to Ector, taking his knight's mantle from the steward's hands and sweeping it around above his head in a broad, circular motion, so that its voluminous folds flared out and settled perfectly across his shoulders, with the St. Clair crest prominently displayed on its left breast. He snapped shut the catch that secured the heavy cloak across his chest, then nodded again and strode towards the door to make his way down the broad, shallow staircase of stone that led to the main entrance hall, where a profusion of bright lights and bustling servants focused his attention on the large antechamber into which Ector had ushered his visitors.

"You set food and drink for him, I hope, before you came for me?"

"Of course, my lord, and replenished the fire as soon as he arrived."

"You have prepared chambers for them?"

"They are being made ready now, fires lit and the bedding aired and warmed. His retainers are already quartered in the stables and haylofts."

"Good man." St. Clair halted outside the doors to the anteroom, then spread his arms to settle his cloak more comfortably, and drew a deep breath. "Well then, let's find out what our lord and master wants now."

"HENRY, YOU SLUGGARD! By God's holy legs, you took your time in coming to greet us!"

Richard Plantagenet had risen to his feet as Sir Henry entered, dropping the meat he had been eating and wiping his greasy hands on the sides of his much-stained leather jerkin. But despite the apparent harshness of his shouted rebuke, there was no doubting the obvious pleasure with which he stepped towards the older man, his arms spread wide to welcome him in a great embrace. St. Clair barely had time to register a second man, also rising from the table, before he was swept up in a bear hug and swung off his feet, incapable of doing anything other than clinging to his dignity as well as he might. The big man holding him swung him around only once, however, before releasing him and holding him at arm's length, locking his eyes with the piercing blue of his own.

"You are looking wonderful, my old friend, as well as I had hoped to find you, and that is the best tidings these eyes of mine have looked upon in weeks. How long has it been, seven years? Eight?"

"Five, my liege," Henry murmured, smiling, aware that Richard Plantagenet would know to the day precisely how long it had been since last they met. "But do not interrupt your meal on my behalf, for you have evidently traveled far and must be hungry." A quick glance to the right had shown him a pair of wet, mud-spattered riding cloaks thrown over the back of a high chair and two long swords lying across its arms. April had been a long and dirty month of hard rain and blustering gales, and May, mere days away now, seemed set to be even bleaker and more unseasonably hostile.

"You're right, old friend, and I am ravenous." Richard spun away and returned to the table, where he picked up his discarded joint of fowl again and waved it towards his companion before sinking his teeth into the meat and ripping off a mouthful, which he chewed a few times and then thrust into his cheek, permitting himself to speak around it. "You'll know de Sablé, I suppose?"

The knight called de Sablé was still standing and he nodded courteously to St. Clair, who shook his head politely and stepped forward, offering his hand.

"No, I fear I do not know the gentleman, but he is most welcome here, as are you, my liege." He sized the man up briefly as their hands came together, looking up a few inches to meet de Sablé's bright eyes. The other bowed his head in return, smiling slightly, the pressure of his grasp tentative at first, then growing firmer in response to St. Clair's warmth.

"Robert de Sablé, Sir Henry," he said. "Knight of Anjou, and vassal to Duke Richard, like yourself. Forgive us for the lateness of the hour."

"Nonsense," Richard growled, then belched softly. "Forgive us? What is to be forgiven, that we remind him of his duty? Henry is my vassal, as you said, bound like yourself to keep the hours I keep, and if I am out and about all night, my vassals must resign themselves to accommodating me, even be it but once in five years. Is that not so, Henry?"

"It is, my liege."

"My liege, my lord, my lord, my liege. You used to call me Dickon, and beat me if I failed to please your every whim."

"True, my liege." St. Clair permitted himself a tiny smile. "But that was many years ago, when you were but a boy and needed shaping, as all boys do from time to time. Now you are Count of Poitou and Anjou, Duke of Normandy and of Aquitaine, and Lord of Brittany, Maine, and Gascony. I imagine few would dare call you Dickon to your face today."

"Hah!" Richard's eyes gleamed with delight. "Dare call me Dickon? Few would dare even to say what you said there. I'm glad to see your balls have not gone soft." He turned to de Sablé. "This is the man who taught me all I know of weaponry and warfare, Robert—taught me the elements of using sword and lance and axe and crossbow long before William Marshall of England came into my life, taught me to strive every day for perfection, to lift and throw, to build muscles. Marshall gets the credit for my youthful training, but I had learned most of what I know from this man here while I was yet a stripling lad. I've told you this before, I know, but now he stands before you in the flesh: the man who made me who I am."

May God forfend! The thought sprang unbidden to Sir Henry's mind, for although the compliments were flattering, there was much about who Richard Plantagenet *was* that scandalized every moral fiber in the elderly knight's being. He had taught the boy to joust and fight, that was certainly true; he had dinned weapons craft and military discipline into him from the age of eight until he was fourteen. And he had done it with a stern, single-minded tenacity born not of love, or even of admiration, but of duty, because in those days Henry was Master-at-Arms to the boy's mother, Eleanor, Duchess of Aquitaine. Eleanor who had been the Queen of France before she divorced her husband and married King Henry II of England to become Queen there, retaining her Duchy of Aquitaine, the largest and most powerful fiefdom in France. She had once been called the strongest woman in Christendom, but her strength had somehow failed her sons, of whom Richard was the third born and said to be his mother's favorite. Even in his boyhood, notwithstanding that he was soon known as a swordsman and fighter without equal among his peers, there were aspects of the young man's character that both chilled and repelled Henry St. Clair. And now, after long years of not having set eyes on his liege lord, he found he had no slightest wish to be regarded, even in error, as the man who had made Richard Plantagenet into who he was.

"Sit, man, sit you down. This is your own house and I am but a guest in it. Sit you and join us and tell us what you have been up to, hiding yourself away here for all these years."

Ector stepped forward and pulled a seat out from the table for his master, and Sir Henry sat, arranging the folds of his cloak carefully so that they did not impede his movements.

"Here, have some capon," Richard growled, pushing the serving platter towards his host before Henry could say anything. "Nothing wrong with your kitchen staff, I'll give them that. My meat never tastes this good. Spices or something ..." Richard savaged his meat again, his short red beard glistening with grease. De Sablé ate more fastidiously, nibbling at his fowl rather than rending it, and St. Clair took the opportunity to examine him more closely. The Angevin knight appeared to be in his late thirties, perhaps five years older than his liege, and his face was nobly formed, with clear brown eyes above a long, straight nose and a jaw that was clearly square beneath his spade-shaped dark brown beard. It was a stern face, yet not devoid, Henry guessed, of either humor or compassion, and he wondered briefly who the fellow was and why he should be here alone, in the company of Richard Plantagenet, one of the most powerful and mercurial men in all Christendom. Henry pulled a wooden trencher towards him, then served himself a wing from one of the cold capons. It held little meat, but he was not hungry. His mind was racing with the possibilities and portents of this unexpected visit. He picked up the meat and then laid it down again untasted.

"I was saddened to hear but recently that your father is still at odds with you over the succession. I had hoped that question might have been resolved long before now."

"Aye, as did we all. And it was, in truth, until the old boar changed his mind again. He is a stubborn old pig, for one who thinks of himself as a lion. I will have the better of him yet, though. God's throat, I will. Wait you but a while and see with all the world. He'll make me heir to England ere he dies, and he will not last long now, pray God."

Even although he knew there had been little love between the father and son, and he had heard reports of how the old King was visibly and rapidly declining, Henry St. Clair was nonetheless affronted to hear the son speak of his father's impending death so callously. Before he could think of anything to say, however, Richard continued.

"Still, the old boar did well for himself during his life, I'll grant him that ... and for me, as well, now that I think of it. Built me an empire, did he not? I've detested him all my life and even hated him at times, and yet I can weep for him, too, upon occasion. He may be a miserable tyrant but by God, he has been a man, and a king, to reckon with. I swear I know not how he and my mother lived together for so long without killing each other."

"Perhaps because he has kept her in jail for the past sixteen years."

Richard's head jerked back and he looked at his old tutor in shock, and then his face broke into a grin and he loosed a great guffaw.

"By God, you have the right of it. That probably had much to do with their mutual survival."

"How is your mother now?"

"Wondrous well, from what my people in England tell me. But one of these fine days she will regain her freedom, and then she will probably become more dangerous and unpredictable than ever! Eleanor will never finish pursuing her own designs."

St. Clair dipped his head in acknowledgment. "I cannot speak to that, my lord, for we live quietly here and are seldom made aware of what is happening beyond our gates. We seldom receive company nowadays, and since my wife, Amanda, died, more than a year ago, I have sought little to do with the world beyond my walls."

Richard's response was instantaneous, emphatic and not at all what St. Clair had wished to hear: "Then you need to get out more and move about in the world. Which is why I am here this night." Having uttered these ominous words the Duke fell silent, kneading a ball of bread between thumb and finger, his face pensive as he stared towards the roaring fire in the great hearth. When he spoke next, his words surprised the older man. "I had not heard of your lady wife's death, and I know how much she meant to you … That must have hit you hard, my friend, and it most certainly explains your ignorance of affairs in the world beyond your gates, as you say, so we will talk no more of that."

He stood up and removed his leather jerkin, and tossed it behind him to land on the chair that held their weather-stained cloaks. Sir Henry raised a beckoning finger to Ector and pointed to the garments, and his steward moved immediately to collect them.

"Your chambers should be ready soon, my liege, and you'll sleep warm and comfortably. In the meantime, we will have your mantles dried and cleaned, ready for you when you arise."

Richard grunted and watched idly as Ector left the anteroom, his arms laden with the two heavy cloaks and the Duke's jerkin. Then, when the doors closed behind the steward, he took his chair from the table and dragged it close to the roaring fire, where he subsided into it again, his feet stretched out towards the flames. His golden-bearded chin rested upon his chest, lower lip jutting in thought, and his fingers brushing absently at his personal crest, with its single left-facing rampant lion richly embroidered in gold wire against a blood-red shield-shaped background on the left breast of his tunic. The silence stretched, and when it became clear that the Duke had nothing more to say for the time being, St. Clair cleared his throat gently and spoke over the crackling of the fire, attempting to ignore the fluttering apprehension in his breast.

"You began to speak of why you came here tonight, my liege, something to do with my need to go out and about more. Am I permitted to enquire more closely about what you meant?"

Richard's eyes flared open, betraying that he had been on the point of nodding into sleep. He made a harrumphing noise in his throat and sat up straighter, turning in his seat to look over to where St. Clair sat opposite de Sablé at the table. "Aye, you are. I have need of you, my friend. I need you with me, by my side."

Henry fought to quell a surge of dismay upon hearing that. He allowed his face to express a lack of understanding as he asked, "Here, my liege, in Anjou?"

"No, damnation! In Outremer—the Holy Land." He glared at St. Clair for a moment, then clearly remembered what the older man had said about his detachment from worldly affairs. "I have been in close communication with the new Pope, Clement, these past few months. It seems we have had a plethora of popes in this past year, would you not agree? Urban the Third, dead in December of the year before last, then another Gregory, the Eighth, for two short months until last March, and now the third Clement, anxious to proceed with this new war after barely a year in office ... I suppose you heard about my father's commitment to winning back the Kingdom of Jerusalem and the Holy Cross for Gregory, last January?"

St. Clair shook his head, wide eyed. "No, my lord, I think not. Or if I did, the tidings did not penetrate my grief. My wife died mere weeks after Pope Urban's death."

Richard looked hard at the older man, then jerked his head in a terse nod. "Aye, well, Henry swore an oath to Pope Gregory in Gisors, about a month before we heard of Gregory's death, hard on the heels of Urban's passing. In truth, he made the pledge in Gregory's absence, to Archbishop Josias of Tyre, the only Christian see left occupied in all of Outremer. Anyway, the old man committed us all to the war, myself and Philip in particular, even though I was not there—but that should not surprise you, as well as you know him and me. The old lion saw my mere absence as no impediment to his paternal dedication of my life to the papal cause."

Although St. Clair was feigning interest in this information, he felt that his persistent ignorance was irritating Richard, who cleared his throat noisily and returned to what he had been saying. "Well, it is all arranged, it seems. The French levies are to wear red crosses on white surcoats, the English white on red, and the Flemish green—presumably on white. All highly colorful and rich with meaning, I suppose. We are all agreed to set out next year, but of course my father has no intention of going with us. This is all a ploy to set me safely out of the way while he goes about his own designs of putting my useless brother John on England's throne. He'll plead infirmity, sickness, and old age when it comes time to rally to the standards, you wait and see.

"But this third Pope Clement is not a stupid man, and he has made that more than plain to me. He can see clearly what's afoot here—thanks to the snouting and burrowing of his bishops here and in England—and he knows I will not meekly step aside for my useless, half-wit brother. And so he has expressed his sympathy for my concerns, because he has need of me—wants me to take up arms on behalf of Mother Church, in Jerusalem, as leader of his new Frankish army of deliverance that will win back the Frankish Kingdom from the infidels.

"That desire, were it the sole wish that Il Papa had, would leave me unimpressed, since I have intended to lead the army anyway, ever since I first heard of it. But the German Emperor, Barbarossa, jumped into Gregory's plans headlong before the old Pope died, swearing to raise an army of Teutons more than two hundred thousand strong. And that, of course, has all of Rome, Clement and all his cardinals, a-chittering in terror, because the last thing they need, or want, is to have the Holy Roman Church beholden in any way to German Barbarossa and his Holy Roman Empire, to say nothing of his unholy Roman armies. They could lose the papacy and all the world, were they to sit back and do nothing. And so, I represent the only hope they have of salvaging *their* Empire of Men's Minds."

The Duke plucked at his lower lip and gazed at Henry through narrowed, unfocused eyes before continuing. "Clement is wooing me, seducing me into leading a Frankish host that will counterbalance Barbarossa's presence in Outremer and keep the scales of power balanced in favor of the papacy. Our force will be no more than half the size of the German levies, for Barbarossa has almost three times the manpower available to him that we have, but Barbarossa is almost as old as my father, and I intend to use that age difference to my advantage. Our Franks will outfight and outperform his stolid German Goths and his Teutonic knights. And in return for providing that superiority, the Pope has offered me a guarantee—but nothing yet in writing, mind you—of the succession to England upon my father's death."

St. Clair wrinkled his nose. "I see. And do you trust this pope, my lord?"

"*Trust* him? Trust a *pope*? Do you think me mad, Henry?" Richard was grinning now. "What I trust, my friend, is my own ability to know, and to do, what is best for me and for my people. And so I have agreed to his request. I will command the army if he will aid me in the raising of it.

"Philip will be involved in the expedition, of course—but he already is, since the original agreement at Gisors. Since then, of course, in August, he alienated my father forever by chopping down the old man's favorite elm tree there, the so-called Gisors Elm, beneath which the King had signed so many treaties, including the one of which I speak. We came close to open war over that incident, and I was forced to side with Philip again, in order to protect my own holdings in France, where my liege loyalties are to him.

"Imagine what an upheaval that caused—the threat of a new war among ourselves in Christendom when the major threat to the papacy lies in Outremer! There was panic in the Vatican, and a flurry of papal ambassadors appealing to all of us individually. Philip allowed himself to be persuaded back into the fold and has restated his commitment to the Holy War. With him, to the prosecution of it and hence to our advantage, he will bring the most powerful vassals in his kingdom: Philip the Count of Flanders and Henry of Champagne. For his sins, poor Henry is nephew to both Philip and myself—did you know that? My mother is his grandmother by her first marriage in France. And, for a certainty, Count Stephen of Sancerre will be there. But *I* will hold command. The new Pope Clement is sworn to that, albeit I am not yet King and Philip has been crowned for ten years now. He is an organizer, our Philip, an administrator without equal, but it is I who am the warrior. If my father lives long enough to see the army raised, he will make noises about wanting to lead it, but that will be a nonsense, as I have said, presented for the show of it.

"Anyway, once the army is ready, we will set sail immediately for Palestine, and by the time we come home victorious, England will be mine beyond dispute, with the support and blessings of the Pope and all his court."

Richard stood up and braced an arm against the mantel, staring into the coals. St. Clair remained seated, frowning, his eyes follow-ing Richard and then shifting to where de Sablé sat watching, his face an inscrutable mask. Now he cleared his throat and spoke out.

"A hundred thousand men, you said, my lord. Forgive me for asking, but … who will pay for that?" He hurried on before Richard could react. "I mean, I know you said your father was the one who made the commitment to the venture, at Gisors, and that is as it should be, but will he carry through with it now, since the events of August, knowing you will prosper thereby?"

"Aye, he will." Unfazed by the question, Richard spoke over his shoulder, not quite looking at St. Clair but speaking to him nonetheless. "He will, because he knows nothing and will *learn* nothing about my agreement with Clement. And before you ask me how I can be sure of that, the answer is that Clement needs my goodwill today far more than he will ever need my father's. And to make doubly sure of that, I have made it clear to the Pope that I will have my own spies watching closely. Should I ever hear the smallest whisper of suspicion that the Holy Father might have been in contact with my profane father, I will resign from the army, quit the Holy Land immediately with all my men, and leave him to work out his own destiny, and that of Holy Mother Church, with Barbarossa and his Germans."

He thrust himself back from the fire and dragged his chair back to the table, where he leaned against the back of it, his forearms folded across its top. "As for the funding of the venture, I have told you the Church is willing to contribute gold under the terms of my recent agreement with Clement. And there are other sources of supply. That, too, was taken care of at Gisors. We initiated a new tax at that time, both in France and in our Plantagenet territories in England and elsewhere. It is called the Saladin Tax—a good name, don't you think?" He plainly thought so; St. Clair could see that from the way the Duke almost smiled as he mentioned it. "I thought of it and named it. It will be most useful when I apply it fully in England. Each man in the realm, priests *not* excluded, will pay a three-year levy of one-tenth of all his income. Some people think it is too onerous, I am told, but that does not concern me. England is the richest jewel in the Plantagenet crown. It can well afford the price I demand of it in such a noble cause. And besides, I would sell London itself to raise this army, could I but find a buyer with sufficient wealth." He thrust his lower lip out in a pout. "And a noble cause it is, Henry, apart from all the politics involved."

Having delivered that opinion, the Duke appeared to have reminded himself of his official persona, and he stepped gravely from behind his chair and seated himself before continuing. "This

upstart infidel in Palestine, this Sultan dog who calls himself
Saladin, has raised his foul head far enough above the sand to beg to
be stamped on. He has taken Jerusalem and Acre back from us,
although he will not keep them long, and his treachery has resulted in
the defeat of the Christian armies in the Holy Land and the death of
hundreds of our finest knights, including those of the Temple and the
Hospital. Not to mention the loss of the True Cross discovered by the
blessed Empress Helena six hundred years ago. For all of those transgressions he deserves to be struck down, and it is all in hand. We will
be in Outremer by this time next year, and you will be by my side."

"I ... see ..." Henry had to fight hard to keep his voice and his
face from betraying any vestige of the consternation and panic that
was threatening to overwhelm him. He counted slowly to ten before
continuing in a very calm voice, "In what capacity, my liege?"

Richard frowned. He was clearly reaching the end of his limited
patience. "Capacity? You'll be my Master-at-Arms, of course. What
other capacity would you expect?"

"Master-at-Arms?" The unexpected declaration left St. Clair
floundering.

"Why not? You think yourself unfit?"

"No," Henry responded, stung by the tone in which the question
had been uttered. "Not unfit, but perhaps no longer *fitted*, if you take
my meaning. I am old now, my liege, too long removed from the
field. This time next year I will be fifty, and I have not swung a
sword in years. In truth, since my wife died I have not even sat
astride a horse. There must be younger men at your command, more
suited to this task you would have me attempt."

"Away with that *old man* nonsense! My father is fifty-nine and
he was in the saddle, fighting me tooth and nail in Normandy, mere
months ago. Besides, it's not your muscles I require, Henry, it's your
brains, your skills and experience, your knowledge of men and
warfare, and, above all else, your loyalty. I can trust you with
absolute certainty, and there are few men about me of whom I can
say that."

"But—"

"No buts, man. Have you not heard a word I've said? The ruck of folk, both here and in my soon-to-be new kingdom, think I should take William Marshall of England to my heart. Yes, Marshall is the finest soldier of our time, bar me myself. But William Marshall is my father's man. Has been all his life, body and soul. So he can never be mine. He has my father's thinking and his prejudices. He dislikes me and distrusts me and he always has, seeing in me his master's natural but begrudged heir and resenting me for it. I will not have him come that close to my designs, for I distrust him even more than he does me. Is that plain enough for you?"

"Yes, my liege, it is … yet I would beg the privilege to be allowed to think upon this for a time."

"Think about it for as long as you wish, Henry, but think not to ignore my wishes. I will have it thus, and you'll refuse me, as your true liege lord, at your peril." Richard fell silent then, uncaring of St. Clair's reaction to his words, and sat stiffly, his brow knitting as he glanced around him, half turning towards the door at his back.

"Where is your son, young André?" He turned back to face his host. "Still out tomcatting at this time of night? He had better be, or I'll not take kindly to his slighting me." He stopped, struck by the expression on Sir Henry's face. "What's wrong, Henry? Something's amiss, I see it in your eyes. Where *is* the lad?"

The door opened at that point and a servant entered, his head obsequiously downcast, and scurried towards the fireplace, clearly intending to add more fuel. Henry raised his hand and voice, stopping the fellow in his tracks and dismissing him instantly. As the man hurried away, closing the door noiselessly behind him, his master stood and removed his heavy mantle, folding it gently over the back of his chair before he himself moved to the fireplace. There he silently set about selecting logs and placing them carefully atop the fire, grateful for the chance to collect his thoughts. He had forgotten how disconcertingly intuitive Richard Plantagenet could be on occasion, and as he placed each log and thrust it down into the coals with his booted foot, he cursed himself for his lack of caution in this particular matter.

Richard, however, had no intention of allowing his host to escape the hook. "Well, Henry? I'm waiting. Where is young André?"

St. Clair straightened his back and sighed, then turned to face the Duke squarely. "I cannot answer that, my liege, for I truly do not know."

"What's that supposed to mean? You don't know where he is tonight, or you plain don't know where he is at all?"

"The latter, my liege. I have no knowledge of his whereabouts."

Richard pushed himself upright in his chair, making a great show of wide-eyed surprise. "No knowledge of his—?" He turned to direct an incredulous look at the silent knight de Sablé. "This is a man who has but one son, Robert, and I have seen him spend more time with the boy in a single day than my old lion spent with myself and all my brothers in his lifetime. And now he does not know his whereabouts?" He turned back then to St. Clair, all trace of raillery vanishing. "When did you see him last, then?"

St. Clair shrugged. "It has been more than two months since last he spent a night beneath this roof."

"Then whose roof does he sleep beneath tonight? And before you answer *that* question, know that I noticed how you avoided my last one. Has he a mistress?"

"No, my liege, to the best of my knowledge he has not."

"So when did you last have contact with him? Take care, Henry."

St. Clair inhaled deeply, knowing there was no way to avoid answering. "Two days ago, my liege. Contact, but purely indirect, through another. I sent him food and clothing."

"Food and clothing? Is he a fugitive?"

"Aye, my lord, he is."

"From whom, and for what cause?"

St. Clair could not bear to look the other man in the eyes any longer, and he turned away towards the fire. "He killed a priest."

"A priest? By God's holy arse, this calls for more wine. Pour some for us, and then sit down and tell us your tale, for it sounds as though it must be worth an ear. And wipe the misery from your mien, my friend. Bear in mind the name and status of your audience.

We have yet to meet the priest who dares to look at us defiantly, ever since my father dealt with the Englishman Becket. Quick now, man, pour, and then tell us what occurred."

Heartened in spite of his own pessimism by his liege's obvious contempt for priests in general and by the influence he knew Richard could bring to bear if he cared to, Henry went to the table and poured three brimming goblets of wine while de Sablé stood up and pulled his chair over to the fireplace by Richard's. He served both of his guests, then dragged his own chair over to join them before returning for his own cup, sipping from it slowly as he returned thoughtfully to his seat, deciding how he would present his story.

Richard's patience, notoriously scant at the best of times, wore out rapidly, and as usual it was he who broke the silence.

"So, he killed a priest. How and why?"

"By accident," St. Clair replied. "Although the intent was there, and the man deserved to die. He was raping a woman."

"Raping a woman ... the priest?"

"Aye, and there were four of them, all priests. André came upon them accidentally, but there was a fast-flowing river between them and him and so he could not close with them quickly enough to stop them. He shouted to let them know he had seen them, fired a crossbow bolt at them, and galloped to the only bridge, half a mile downstream. It was too far. By the time he got back to where they had been, they had killed the woman and three of them had vanished, leaving a fourth man dead. André's crossbow bolt, loosed at random, had found a mark, falling from the sky to pierce the skull of one of them."

"And this fellow was a priest?"

"He wore the square tonsure of a Benedictine, so he was either priest or monk. But his friends had taken his clothes and the woman's, so André could tell nothing of the fellow's ranking from his habit."

"If André could not come close to them, and they were all unclothed, how could he know they were all priests?"

"He had recognized another of the four from across the river, a fellow he had met and had words with once before. This was a priest by the name of de Blois, whose family's lands abut ours. The rest was deduction. For if two of the four were priests, involved in criminal activities, then it made sense that the other two should also be priests. But that argument is moot now, for we know who the others are."

"How so? Are they in custody?"

"No, my liege, they are not. André gave chase, but when he did not find them immediately he sought assistance. He came directly home and told me what had happened—this was our own land—and so I sent the captain of my household guard with a party of men to retrieve the bodies and bring them back here. But there were no bodies there when they arrived. They found blood at the scene, and they found marks to indicate that something heavy had been dragged away, but nothing else."

"You mean bodies were dragged away, I presume?"

"Yes, my lord. There is a great hole close to that point, a vertical chasm that the people hereabouts call the Devil's Pit. It falls straight down into the earth and appears to have no bottom, and local legend says it simply appeared there one night, back in the time of my grandsire's grandsire. My captain believed the bodies had been thrown down there and were beyond recovery."

"And had they?"

"One of them had. The woman. And with her body, the priest's head."

"The priest's head …" Richard was frowning. "What happened to the rest of him? And who was the woman?"

"No one knows who the woman was, my lord. No one has asked after her or come looking for her, and none of our local women are missing. All the women within a circle of twenty miles from here have been accounted for. It would appear safe to say she was not from these parts."

"It would be equally safe to say she might not have existed at all, save in the mind of her creator, Sir André St. Clair—" The Duke forestalled Sir Henry's protest with a chopping motion of one hand. "I am not saying I believe that to be true, Henry, but were you and I judges, seeking the truth, we would have no choice but to consider that. With no proof of this woman's death, and no faintest knowledge of her identity, there is no evidence, other than the word of your son, that she ever existed at all. Even were she a stranger, she must have come here to visit someone, and her disappearance would have given rise to questions. So we will come back to that matter. Now tell me about the priest's body, headless as it was."

"The body of the priest was presented as evidence that the poor fellow had been murdered by my son."

"Explain that."

Sir Henry St. Clair nodded his head in acquiescence. "From what I have been able to piece together, my liege, the three miscreants stole the bodies, cut off their dead companion's head, and threw it into the Devil's Pit along with the woman. They then took his body back with them because he had a deformed hand that identified him beyond doubt as one Father Gaspard de Leon, a visiting priest from Arles. They then told a tale of how, on their way to join their now-dead brother, they had witnessed him in the act of apprehending a sinner in the act of committing sodomy with a young boy—"

"Pardon me—," de Sablé began, but Richard waved him to silence.

"Go on, Henry. Were you about to say they accused young André of sodomy with a boy?"

"Aye, my lord. I was."

"Say on, then. Tell me."

"They said that they had seen the scandalized priest challenge the pederast and attempt to save the boy, but the sodomite had sent the boy scurrying away and then seized his sword and killed Father de Leon, cleaving his skull. He had then cut off the priest's head and taken it away with him, wrapped in de Leon's priestly garments, leaving a naked, unidentifiable body behind him. He had not seen them, they said, being separated from them by the swollen river.

"As soon as he had gone, they made their way to the bridge and back to the scene of the murder, then followed the tracks of the killer's horse down the hillside to the Devil's Pit, where they arrived in time to see him throw the severed head down into the abyss.

Fearful for their own lives, they hid and waited until the killer left, then made their way directly to the castle of their landlord, Baron Reynauld de la Fourrière, and testified under oath to him, and to their superior, Abbot Thomas, about what they had seen, and adding that one of them, the priest called de Blois, had recognized the murderer, a local knight called André St. Clair."

St. Clair looked from one to the other of his listeners, both of whom sat stone faced. When he saw that they had nothing to say, he continued. "I found out all about this the morning after, when a squad of Baron de la Fourrière's men came hammering on my door, demanding that I surrender my son to answer the charges of sodomy and murder brought against him. Fortunately, André had left before they came, and I sent a messenger to find him, warning him to stay away."

"Sodomy." Richard's voice was flat and hard. "They accused André of sodomy?"

"Aye, my lord. They did."

"And you did nothing? I find that hard to credit."

"What could I do? For that matter, what could *they* do? André was beyond their reach at that time, and I knew I needed to make sure he stayed there, for I saw no hope of his receiving justice in this matter in the verdict of the Church. I asked myself what man of goodwill, in his right mind, would publicly give consideration to the possibility that three distraught priests might have beheaded their companion and disposed of his head to protect themselves, or that the single man accused in this case, who made no denial of having killed the dead man, might be telling the truth when he condemned his three priestly accusers for the rape and the murder of an innocent girl?

"And so I have not set eyes on my son or spoken with him since."

"Not once? Why not?"

"Because I dare not, my liege. I am watched constantly and, with very few exceptions, I know not whom to trust. There is a price on my son's head, sufficiently high to tempt any man to turn him over to the Church and what it must see as justice."

Sir Robert de Sablé glanced at Richard. "May I speak, my liege?"

"Of course you may. Speak up."

"It unsettles me that the woman has not been either identified or claimed, or even reported missing. I find that to be not merely incredible but deeply troubling, for much of it makes nonsense of both sides of this sorry tale." He looked directly at St. Clair. "Have you discussed this with your son at all?"

St. Clair's headshake was brief. "No. When first he told me of it, her identity did not appear to have great import. The urgency for me at that moment lay in taking immediate steps to retrieve her body, and her assailant's. There should have been ample time thereafter to establish who she was. But then the bodies vanished, and that set everything at odds."

"But surely—"

"Surely we should have discussed it later, is that what you were about to say? We would have, without fail, but la Fourrière's people arrived soon after dawn the following morning and by then André was already gone."

"Hmm ..." De Sablé looked down at his hands and then back to his host. "I trust you will believe me when I say I have no wish to cast doubts upon what you have told us, Sir Henry, but much of this affair, as I see it, bears upon the total absence of this woman's body and the apparent fact that no one has stepped forward to enquire about a missing woman. That, in itself, speaks strongly on behalf of your son's accusers, as I am sure you are aware. So I must ask you this, because your son's accusers will present it as their case: is it possible, or is it even remotely probable, that there never was a woman there and that these priests are telling the truth? Might not your son, taken in a guilty and forbidden act, have panicked and done murder to protect himself? And then might he not have taken the step of beheading the priest to conceal the true nature of the man's fatal wounds? If that were the case, then, he might easily have lied about the supposed woman and lied to cover up his own guilt and save his own life."

Richard laughed aloud, interrupting his earnest vassal, and as de Sablé's eyes opened wide in astonished protest, the Duke rose swiftly to his feet and turned his back on both men, walking away only to swing around again and lean forward against the high back of his own chair.

"Then where's the *boy*, Robert, the boy who was being buggered? Think you a gaggle of mortified priests would not have turned this county of Poitou upside down to find the little brat—and all of Anjou and Aquitaine too, should that have been required—merely to prove their case beyond all doubt?" He grinned. "Besides, it's evident you know nothing at all about young André St. Clair. I do. I knighted him myself three years ago, and he was foremost among all my candidates that year, and most other years, to tell truth. I found him honest, upstanding, courageous to a fault, and utterly, completely masculine in every aspect of his character. I swear to you, Robert, I have never met—and nor could you—a more unlikely pederast. André lacks nothing in charm and seductive powers, but it is all of it reserved exclusively for women, and he has never suffered from any lack of those. So let there be an end of this nonsense. The priests are lying, and I feel sure God in His Heaven is amazingly unsurprised. And as for the missing head, were it to be produced in evidence, transfixed from crown to chin with a bolt that obviously fell on it, it might cast the priestly version into doubt, would you not agree?" He glanced from one to the other. "Surely both those points are self-evident?

"I would find it far more interesting to know how André knew *precisely* how to aim that shot he loosed? It was no accident, I swear, for though fate may play a part in where a cast shot falls, it takes skill and unerring confidence to cast it perfectly in the first place. I doubt I could have done what he did, so smoothly and unerringly. I will have to speak with him about it as soon as may be."

Neither man responded to that, although both were now convinced, through Richard's expostulations, of André St. Clair's innocence of homosexuality, and therefore of all the charges against him. For there could be no doubting the Duke's championship of the younger man, it being known, but seldom openly discussed, that Richard shunned the company of women and surrounded himself at all times with young and comely men and boys of his own persuasion. It was the single aspect of Richard's character that repelled the staid St. Clair most profoundly. He found himself marveling now that he could ever be grateful for it.

Now, however, the regal Duke was leaning towards him, frowning and pointing an admonitory finger. "So," Richard said, more softly than his frown had led Henry to expect, "we agree that this nonsense of the priests is tomfoolery, and murderous tomfoolery at that. But before I decide what I must now do, there is one more thing I require of you, for Robert is right. The matter of the woman troubles me, too. Bring in your son, Henry, and do it tonight. I have a need to talk with him, and no one will dare accost him here, with me present." He crossed to where the two long swords lay on the arms of the chair, tossing de Sablé's to him and hefting his own like a walking staff. "Now it is late, and Robert and I will need some sleep before we make such a momentous decision as is in my mind, so take us to where we can lay our heads, my friend, and then send for the boy. Have him here when we awake and we will talk with him after we three have broken fast."

TWO

S ir Henry found his son asleep the following morning on a bench in the great hall, and he stood over the young man for long minutes, taking note of the disrepair of his clothes, the ragged, unkempt look of his hair and short beard, the reek of his unwashed body, and the lined gauntness that marked his face after two months of solitary hiding. He did not know how long his son had been sleeping there, but it had been after two in the morning when he had sent Jonquard, his stable master, to fetch the lad, and it was not yet seven, so it was improbable that the two could have returned more than an hour ago. He heard noises coming from an anteroom, where servants were cleaning up the debris of the previous night, and he decided to leave the boy to sleep undisturbed for as long as he could, for he doubted that his guests would be stirring for at least another hour and perhaps longer. He went directly then to the kitchens, where he instructed the cook to prepare enough hot water for a full bath, and to have some of his scullions transport it upstairs to the master's chamber; they were to light the fire in the brazier there and then to prepare his bath and summon him when it was ready.

The cook offered no sign that he saw anything strange in any of that, although Sir Henry had not used the wooden bath in his chamber since his wife died, but had bathed in the kitchens, like everyone else in his household, as recently as two months earlier. He merely nodded and told his master it would be done immediately.

Henry then made his way to the main gate tower, where he stood for a while, observing the scene beyond his walls and searching for any sign that he and his were under surveillance. When a servant came looking for him, something over a half hour later, to tell him that his bath had been prepared, Henry went to wake André.

André sprang awake, wide eyed and tense, as soon as his father touched him, and then he spent several moments peering about him, as though wondering where he was. Henry put him at his ease at once.

"You could not have had much rest, I fear."

André blinked rapidly, clearing his eyes of sleep. "Enough to do me, Father. I had slept for almost seven hours before Jonquard came with your summons, so I am well rested. I lay down here simply because the house was quiet when I arrived, and I must have dozed. What's wrong? Why did you send for me?"

"Duke Richard is here. He came late last night, alone save for another knight, and I told him your story. He asked me many questions, but he believes your tale, although he requires more information than I could give him, before he can do anything. And so he ordered me to summon you." He smiled down at his son. "But you are hardly fit to meet a Duke and a future King, looking and … *smelling* as you do. There is a fresh hot bath prepared in my chamber. Go you and use it, then make yourself presentable. Dress in some of your own finery so that you look like a knight rather than an indigent beggar. You have time. There is no need for breakneck speed, for Richard has not yet risen, although he may at any moment. When he comes down he and I will break fast together, and he told me last night he will wish to see you immediately after that, so do *not* fall asleep in the bath, no matter how tempting it might be. I will send for you when it is time."

André's relief was plainly evident to Sir Henry, who felt much the same way, and a moment later the boy was gone, obedient to his father's wishes.

The Duke appeared not long after that, in company with de Sablé, and both men greeted their host cordially, Richard asking immediately if André had yet appeared. Henry confirmed that he had and would join them when summoned, and then he led them into the anteroom, where Ector, showing remarkably few signs of having been awake for half the previous night, awaited them with a solid breakfast that he cooked personally for them, over a brazier set in the main fireplace, now swept clean of ashes from the previous night's fire. As soon as they were ready, he served the three men fresh duck eggs whisked in a flat pan with goat's milk and butter until they were solid, then salted and folded over fresh mushrooms and onions and accompanied by light, fluffy fresh-baked rolls straight from the kitchen ovens. They ate him out of stock, and after Ector had supervised the removal of the remnants of their meal and left the room, Richard turned to Sir Henry.

"Bring in young André and let's hear what he has to say for himself. But before you do, let me warn you that, if my suspicions prove correct, you might hear things for which you are unprepared. If that should be the case, I want you to say nothing, is that clear?"

St. Clair nodded, not even curious about what Richard thought he might be unprepared for. In his estimation, nothing could surpass his relief at seeing his son's name cleared. "It is, my liege."

"WELCOME, SIR ANDRÉ ST. CLAIR. You look older ... more *mature* than when we last met. But then you are ... two years older, at least. As are we all. Stand easy."

The young knight relaxed from the upright military stiffness he had maintained since marching in the door and coming to a halt before the table to salute his liege lord formally and ceremoniously, fist clenched upon his breast. He spread his feet more comfortably and placed his arms behind his back, gripping one wrist with his other hand, but continued nevertheless to stare respectfully at a spot somewhere slightly above the Duke's head.

"Your father has been telling us about your recent misadventures, and I admit I am surprised to see you looking as wholesome as you do, after two months of living in hiding. You look remarkably well."

He looks miraculously *well*, Sir Henry thought, hardly able to believe the change in his son's appearance. *You should have seen him but an hour ago.*

André had made good use of his father's stout wooden bath and had obviously used Henry's short grooming shears and metal mirror to trim his hair and beard in the morning light from the window. Now he stood before them as a knight, complete in a suit of supple mail over which he wore a mantle the twin of his father's own, the blazon of St. Clair embroidered finely on the left breast. He carried no weapons, however, and his mailed hood hung down at his back, leaving his head uncovered, for as an accused felon, he had no right to bear arms, especially in the presence of his Duke.

"Remarkably well," Richard repeated, musingly. "And remarkably guiltless, for an arraigned priest-killer."

André St. Clair did not even blink, and Richard, who had pushed his chair back from the table, waved a hand towards his companion. "This is Sir Robert de Sablé, who rides with me for Paris, to meet with King Philip. He is a man of great wisdom and sagacity, for all his apparent youthfulness, and he is familiar with your situation, explained to us by your father ... although I know not whether he be convinced of your innocence in this matter. You may greet him."

The young knight swiveled his head towards de Sablé and inclined it respectfully, and de Sablé returned the nod, his face expressionless.

Richard crossed his long legs and locked his hands below the upper knee, then bent forward and spoke quietly to André.

"This is not a formal court, Sir André, but an inquiry into the details of your story, as one of my vassals. And I must tell you here and now that, irrespective of my own beliefs, my main concern is this matter of the vanishing woman. With her dead body to back up your tale, your allegations against the priests would be unshakable. But lacking her completely as you do, without even a name or a description, you cannot provide even a smidgen of proof that she ever existed. We have no complaints of a missing woman anywhere, no knowledge of who she was or where she came from, and no possibility, it appears, of that knowledge miraculously appearing. Look me in the eye."

André did as bidden, and the two gazed at each other for long moments before Richard said, "It was the sodomy report that convinced me yours is more probably the true account of what occurred. But this other matter, your lack of evidence to demonstrate the truth of what you allege, could prove insurmountable. That, in itself, is likely to hang you … unless, by some miracle, you could conjure the woman's name."

"Eloise de Chamberg, my liege."

"Eloise de Chamberg … And whence came she, this spectral Eloise?"

"From Lusigny, my liege. It's nigh on thirty miles south of Poitiers."

"I know where it is, man. I own the place. But why have you said nothing to anyone about knowing who she was?"

St. Clair shrugged. "I could not, my lord. I have spoken scarce a word to anyone in months. Jonquard, who knew my hiding place and showed it to me that first day, never came near it afterwards for fear of being followed. He would ride by every few days and leave provisions for me in a clump of bushes under a nearby oak, and I would collect them after he had gone. It was only last night, on my way here, that I learned from him the full extent of what has been going on. That may sound strange to you, knowing how much time has passed, but it is true."

Richard sprang to his feet and began to pace the room with the irrepressible energy that Sir Henry, watching him closely, recognized from the Duke's early boyhood. Even then, Richard Plantagenet had been incapable of sitting still in one spot for more than a few minutes, and as he paced he ground his palms together, pressing them firmly one into the other and twisting them constantly so that, when he was most intellectually engaged, the sound of his weapons-hardened calluses rubbing against each other was clearly audible.

"Strange it may be," he growled eventually, "but no more strange than this: how come you, a knight of Poitou, to know a woman called Eloise de Chamberg from Lusigny?"

André accompanied his answer with the slightest shrug of his shoulders. "By accident, my liege. I met her by sheerest chance when I attended a tourney in Poitiers two years ago."

"And fell in love, eh? But why so secretive?"

For the first time, a trace of color showed on the young knight's face. "Because I had no choice, my liege. At first I seldom saw her, for my duties kept me far from Poitiers, and so I never spoke of her to anyone."

The Duke stopped, almost in mid-stride, and looked André straight in the eye. "And later?"

The flush spread farther, suffusing André's temples. "And later it became impossible to speak of her."

"I see, and I can hazard why. She is from Lusigny, and yet you met her in Poitiers and visited her there later. Why was that?"

"She lived in Poitiers then, with her parents. But fifteen months ago ... she was wed, by her father's wishes."

"Aha! For most men that would spell *finis*."

André nodded. "True, my liege, it would. But hers was a loveless marriage from the first, with a man almost three times her age who lived in Lusigny. It was her father's wish, not hers, and she was an obedient daughter."

"But plainly not an obedient spouse. You continued seeing her."

"I did, my liege, although we met far less often then."

"And how came she to be here in Poitou at the time of her ... misfortune? Need I remind you that, married or not, the lady is now dead and beyond the reach of clacking tongues, whereas you are very much alive and stand in need of her? Speak out, then."

A swift, uneasy glance at his father preceded the younger St. Clair's response, but then he raised his chin and looked directly at the Duke. "I received word from her, nigh on three months ago, that her husband would soon be traveling southeastward from Lusigny to spend a month visiting an aged, ailing brother in Clermont, and she had a plan, set in place months before, that would permit the two of us to meet. And so I arranged for an escort to conduct her on a prearranged visit to a distant cousin of hers, a recently bereaved widow who lives close by here, on the outskirts of our lands."

He glanced again at his father, whose face betrayed nothing of his thoughts. "It was complex in some ways, yet in others exceed-ingly simple, for no one knew her here, and her cousin knew nothing of me, or of the relationship between us." Again he gave the tiniest of shrugs, almost imperceptible. "It was straightforward and it worked well. The widowed cousin made her farewells to Eloise on the morning of the day she was killed, believing her safely on her way home to Lusigny, escorted by her husband's men-at-arms. But the men were in my pay, hired through a friend in Poitiers, and they brought her to the spot where she and I were to meet for the last time, for we had decided that to continue this charade was purest folly, tolerable to neither one of us. They settled her comfortably there to wait for me, and then they departed as ordered, to await my later summons ... I can only presume that when they heard no more from me, they eventually returned to Poitiers. They had been well paid, and in advance, and they knew our meeting was a tryst, so they would have—must have—assumed the lady had decided to remain here with me."

He paused, frowning in recollection. "Be that as it may, the priests found her before I arrived, and you know the rest, my liege, save for this: when Eloise failed to return home to Lusigny, no one could have begun to imagine where to look for her, because she had told her own household attendants that she was traveling north and *west*, towards Angers, to visit yet another cousin, whose husband had sent an escort to accompany her. It is hardly surprising, there-fore, that no one has come seeking her here."

"Hmm ..." Richard crossed the floor and stood behind his chair, grasping the knobs on its high back. "Explain, if you will, why you did not tell your father you knew this woman? It would have saved everyone a great amount of grief and frustration."

André's face had flushed bright red before Richard finished speaking, and he nodded, miserably. "I know now how foolish and misguided that was, but I only saw it today. It had not occurred to me before. I was distraught when I reached home that day and at the time it seemed the right thing to do ... to protect her name and reputation."

"And where were you the following morning, when the Baron's men came to arrest you?"

André St. Clair's eyebrows rose as if in disbelief that anyone could ask him such a thing. "I was at the Devil's Pit searching for her body. I had not slept all night and could not believe that two bodies could vanish without trace. I found the tracks my father's man had reported, and followed them to edge of the pit. Then I attempted to climb down into the hole, but it proved impossible. Within twenty paces down from the only point of access on the rim, I reached a spot where I could descend no farther without falling to my own death, and when I attempted to turn back I almost despaired of climbing out again. It took me more than an hour to make my way back up and even then I would not have succeeded without help at the end from Jonquard, whom my father had sent to find me and to warn me to stay far from home. He found me and pulled me out."

Duke Richard moved around his chair and sat down again, silent after that, staring at the younger knight, then turned to Sir Robert de Sablé.

"Robert? What think you?"

De Sablé inhaled deeply, and Henry, noticing the flattening of his nostrils, the frowning brows, and the implacable set of the man's mouth, braced himself for the condemnation he felt sure must follow. But de Sablé turned his eyes instead to where the Duke sat watching him. Unfazed by Richard's gaze, he shook his head slightly and raised one hand in a plea for patience and time to make his decision, while André, who had most to lose or gain from what would be said next, stood still, looking at no one.

Having watched the young knight as he was telling his tale, de Sablé now believed the man implicitly, and he was making a great effort to contain his own sense of outrage. No one would ever accuse Robert de Sablé of being naïve, and he had been fully aware all his life of the rampant corruption among the clergy at all levels of the Church's hierarchy. But his knowledge and his critical acumen had been sharpened through a more radical circumstance than any that influenced the vast majority of his fellow men. Robert de Sablé was a member of the secret Brotherhood of Sion. He had been admitted into the Order on his eighteenth birthday, and since then he had learned much, and studied more, about the Order's teachings, and the accuracy of its lore and its archival sources regarding the errors and misguided policies of the Catholic Church over the preceding thousand years. The corruption within the Church was worldly and cynical, certainly, and it cried out for correction. But murder and rape such as were involved here was beyond his experience and insulted his credulity. He drew himself upright.

"My lord Duke," he said, his frustration evident in his tone, "I know not what to say, other than that I am convinced we have heard the truth spoken here. But admitting that, I must admit, too, my own relief that the burden of responsibility is yours and not mine. You are Duke of Aquitaine, and this matter rests squarely within your jurisdiction, but I fear I can offer nothing of guidance in how you must proceed henceforth."

Richard rose to his feet again and resumed his pacing, his palms grinding together relentlessly, his eyes shining with a zeal that Henry recognized with both pleasure and misgiving.

In the course of the years he had spent shaping, training, and grooming the boy, he had learned to read Richard Plantagenet like a book, and now he found himself observing the Duke dispassionately, guessing, before Richard even opened his mouth, at what he would say. When swift, unprecedented judgments and decisions were required, Richard had proved, time and again with overwhelming consistency, that no man in Christendom, even his own formidable father, could match him in ruthless and precise decisiveness. Richard was brilliant, cynical, mercurial, overwhelmingly ambitious, relentlessly manipulative, and every inch the warrior Duke, and his proposal, whatever form it might take, would, Henry knew, be simple, clean, straightforward, and drastic. He clasped his hands together in his lap and crossed his ankles, knowing from the Duke's expression that a decision would quickly be forthcoming. Even so, the swiftness of Richard's response surprised him, demonstrating clearly to the older man that, once again, his former protégé had made up his mind beforehand and that his consultation of de Sablé had been no more than a formal courtesy.

"So be it," Richard said. "I concur. It is my task and my responsibility alone, as Duke of Aquitaine, to make the decision on what is to be done in this matter. When we ride out of here today, Robert, we will go together to visit this vindictive fool of a baron, de la Fourrière, and if he escapes my wrath with his barony intact I will be more astonished than he. I have more than enough pressing problems to occupy my time without having to step aside from all of them to kick the arrogant arses of my petty vassals. And speaking of arrogance, before we even set out, I'll send a captain and four men to arrest the unsaintly Abbot of Sainte Mère ... what was his name? Thomas?" This was flung at Henry, who merely nodded. "Well, he will lose his every doubt, just like his doubting namesake the Apostle, when he finds himself being frog-marched in chains to confront me."

De Sablé spread his hands. "And then, my liege?"

"And then they will both find themselves dealing with me in fourfold jeopardy, judging them as Count of Poitou, in which domain they hold their power, and then as Count of Anjou, as Duke of Aquitaine, and atop all of those as the future King of England, sired by a father who long since demonstrated his impatience with troublesome barons and meddlesome priests. By my decree, they will agree immediately to quash and annul this ridiculous charge of murder—and the laughable but despicable implication of pederasty against Sir André." He laced his fingers together. "The contumacious and murderous priests involved will be arrested, tried, and hanged. And should either one of their erstwhile patrons, Baron or Abbott, prove reluctant to proceed with that immediately, I will deal with them and their murderous brood as my father, the old lion, dealt with Becket. So help me God!" The Duke's voice was chillingly absolute in its sincerity.

"You may stand down, Sir André," he continued, not bothering to look at the young knight. "You are absolved and this matter is concluded, save for the final details."

Even before Richard turned to look at him, Henry's mind had skipped ahead to the *quid pro quo* that must come next. Richard Plantagenet did nothing without a *quid pro quo* being involved, and this one had been self-evident from the outset.

"My liege," he murmured, the rising inflection of his voice turning the appellation into a question.

"Aye, Henry, as you say, your liege." The King's mouth broke into a sardonic little grin. "I came here looking for *you*, but I will now require both of you to entrain with me in the coming venture in Outremer, for only thus will all threats against your son's life be annulled. André cannot safely remain in France once I be gone. Surely you see that, and you, too, André?" Both men nodded, and Richard smiled. "Then let us be resolved on it. We go to war together, for as powerful as I may be when I am here, I tend to create powerful foes, and these churchly knaves would find a way to arraign you again and kill you quietly as soon as they believed my back was turned.

"So! Henry, you will be my Master-at-Arms. And you, Sir André, will join the Temple."

"The Temple, my liege?" André eyes widened. "How may that be? I am no monk, nor fitted to be one."

Richard barked a short, humorless laugh. "Perhaps not now— you have made that amply clear—but such things can be arranged, and you may warm to the thought. But monk or no, you are nonetheless a knight, raised to that estate by my own hand, and you are a St. Clair, of the bloodline that produced one of the nine Founders of the Temple Order. And God surely knows the Order has need of you and will welcome you to ride beneath its black-and-white standard."

He glanced then from son to father. "Hear me now, and hear what I say. Two years ago—no, 'twas even less than that by half a year— two hundred and thirty knights of the Temple were lost in a single day at a place called Hattin—that was the battle I told you of last night, Henry. But more than a hundred of those were executed as *prisoners*, after the fighting, on Saladin's own orders. Think upon that, my friends. This fellow calls himself Sultan, the exalted ruler, but that atrocity alone demands the dog's death. Two hundred and thirty Temple Knights lost in a single day, and nigh on half of them murdered out of hand when the fighting was all over. And then, hard on the heels of that, he slaughtered hundreds more after he took

Jerusalem the following month. And his stated reason for that butchery? That the Temple Knights are the most dangerous men on earth." His eyes moved from father to son. "Well, they may have been the most dangerous men on earth *before* Hattin, but he has now ensured that they will be even more perilous to him and his in time to come."

He ground his palms together again. "But irrespective of its origins, the reality of this slaughter has left us facing a truth with which we have to contend, my friends: The Templars have been worse than decimated, for they have lost *five* men in ten, not merely one. They may be the most powerful and celebrated warriors on earth, the standing army in the defense of Christianity in Outremer, but not even they can endure losses on such a scale as has been seen these past two years. It has been accepted since the days of Julius Caesar that no military force can continue to function effectively once its strength has been reduced by more than one third of its complement."

He stopped again, giving those words time to sink home to his listeners before he continued. "There have never been more than one thousand Templars at any single time in the entire area of the Holy Lands. That is not something that is widely known, for most people today think the Temple is ubiquitous and indomitable. But their recent losses have amounted to more than five hundred, leaving a mere fragment of their former force in place. So the Order is hungry for qualified recruits." He looked directly at André. "They seek young knights, debt free, without worldly responsibilities, and sound of mind and body. Think you that description might apply to you, my young friend?"

André shrugged, looking uncomfortable. "It might, my liege, were it not for the shadow hanging above my head."

"That shadow has been banished. Forget it ever existed."

"I wish I could, my liege. But even were *I* to succeed in forgetting it, it will still be kept alive and reported on by others, perhaps even in Outremer, and the Temple is notably rigid and unyielding in its scrutiny of recruits. I have heard it said, if you will forgive me for being thus blunt, that not even kings or dukes have the power to impose their will upon the Order."

Henry St. Clair stiffened on hearing his son's words, fully expecting that they would infuriate Richard, but to his astonishment, the Duke merely smiled.

"True, that is absolutely true, so my influence would normally be little use to you in gaining entry. But look again, if you will, at my friend Sir Robert de Sablé here, and believe me when I tell you that there is more to him than meets the eye. In certain things, Robert has influence that I could never gain. He is, for one thing, one of the finest mariners in all of Christendom, albeit he holds that to have but little import in his life nowadays." He raised an inquisitive eyebrow at de Sablé, and the knight nodded in return, apparently submitting to some unspoken request. Richard grinned broadly and turned back to the others, drawing the long-bladed dagger from his belt and flipping it into the air, end over end, to catch it easily as it came down. Twice more he did it, and the others watched him, wondering what was to come next.

"I can tell you both a certain secret known to very few at this time. Sir Robert, like you, André, is not a member of the Temple." He spun suddenly and threw the dagger towards one of the wooden pillars that supported the high roof above them, and it crossed the space as a whirling blur, to hammer itself home point-first into the densely grained timber. In the silence that followed, Richard ambled over and worked the blade free, examining the point critically before he sheathed the weapon again.

"But Sir Robert has been *invited*, by the Governing Council of the Templars, to *join* the Order, and not merely as a serving knight but as the newly designated Master of the Temple, to replace the man Gerard de Ridefort, the current Master who has recently been reported missing yet again, believed captured in battle and very probably dead."

He grinned again with satisfaction in seeing the jaws of both St. Clairs sag open and their heads swivel slowly to gaze at de Sablé. When he considered they had had sufficient time to gape and be impressed, Richard continued. "Let me repeat that: Sir Robert has

been invited by the Governing Council of the Order of the Temple
to join its ranks. Never has such an invitation been issued before
now. It is unprecedented because the Temple has always been
jealous—and zealous—about those to whom it permits entry to its
ranks. But it has an even deeper meaning here, and now especially
for you, Sir André, because it makes it possible—and even likely,
given that Sir Robert professes himself convinced of your innocence—that you could be admitted to the Order, as a novice without
formal vows, prior to our leaving France. Thus both of you could
travel together in my train until we reach the Holy Land, each of you
preparing for the task that lies ahead, so that when we arrive you,
André, would enter the Order of the Temple as a serving knight and
you, Henry, would assume your own duties on my behalf."

Henry St. Clair bowed his head deeply.

"Excellent," the Duke said. "Now, let us be about our business.
First this pious, sanctimonious Abbot Thomas. He may not have
much fear of God in him, but by God's holy throat he will discover
such a fear of me this day as will make him howl with penitence.
André, go and find Godwin, the captain of my guard. He is an
Englishman, enormous, but he speaks our tongue. You won't
mistake him. Bid him take four men and ride to the Abbey of Sainte
Mère, to arrest the Abbot Thomas and to bring him to me in chains
at the castle of la Fourrière. *In chains*, mind you, and afoot. He is to
make the Abbot *walk*! I want this holy lout to suffer pains and fears
the like of which the sanctimonious hypocrite has never imagined
before this day. And send one of your own men with them, to show
them the way from here to there. Go. No, wait." He clicked his
fingers. "While you are there, tell Pierre, Godwin's corporal, to
prepare our horses and bring them to the entrance within the half
hour. You have all that?"

André nodded, murmured "My liege," and left the room. Sir
Henry watched him go, admiring his son's upright posture and still
mildly surprised at the ease of his own acquiescence to what had
been wrought here. He had known almost from the outset of
Richard's visit exactly what must result for himself from the

Plantagenet's wishes, and resentment and bitter frustration had been bubbling within him, tightly suppressed, since first he heard Richard's demands the night before. But now, as if by magic, all traces of resentment had left him, replaced by a grudging sense of admiration for this man who controlled all of their lives.

Despite his thoroughgoing awareness that Richard Plantagenet was being even more manipulative than usual, Henry had reasons of his own, besides the obvious, for accepting the Duke's will now, for there was no question in his mind that without Richard's ducal and regal support, his son André could have no life to speak of here in France. To avoid eventual arraignment and execution—or even assassination—after Richard's departure—and with him, Henry's—his son's sole option would have been to join the assembling armies anonymously and without escutcheon, as a free lance. Now, however, thanks to Richard's self-interest—for Henry did not believe for an instant that the Duke he knew so well was moved by any altruistic love of justice—both he and his son had been accorded an acceptable alternative. That his own involvement in the Holy Land campaign was a *sine qua non* of the entire proposal was an element no longer worthy of consideration to the veteran knight, for its validity worked now to the advantage of both of them, liege lord and vassal. In accepting Richard's proposal, Sir Henry had made a virtue out of necessity, seizing the opportunity to keep his son alive and share his future. Now, all things considered, no more than a small, niggling sense of foreboding remained in him, unable to be dislodged, and Henry knew he would have to accept that and live with it, because its cause was deeply rooted in the dark side of the complicated and unpredictable man.

He became aware that Richard was watching him closely, and he drew himself up to his full height, self-consciously sucking in his belly.

"We are going to have to toughen you up, Henry. You've gone soft."

"I told you that, my liege. Since my—"

"'Twill not take long. We'll have you fit again within the month." He grinned. "It may be the death of you, but if it be so, you will die in better health than you have now."

Sir Henry smiled. "It will not kill me, my liege. I shall probably enjoy it, once I begin."

"Well, young André will have no such problem. I'll have Robert here put him to work at once, to learn the basic, general disciplines of the Order, those elements that are generally known and accessible, at least." He cocked an eyebrow at de Sablé. "What think you, Robert? Will he have what is required for a Templar?"

"He has it already, my liege. All that will be required, from what I can see, will be a few … adjustments."

"Aye, to praying morning, noon, mid-afternoon, and evening, and three or four times more during the night. A damnably strange way of life for a warrior knight."

De Sablé smiled gently, negating the importance of what Richard had said with a flick of one hand. "That is the Rule of the Order, my liege. All members, without regard to rank, must abide by it."

"Aye, and that is why I could never join. I wonder God's Holy Warriors have any knees left to them with which to hold themselves upright and fight."

De Sablé's smile widened. "They appear to manage wondrous well, my liege, by your own admission mere moments ago. Besides, I have been told on good authority that the strictest measures of the Rule are set aside in time of war, and the application of the laws governing prayer is eased in favor of fitness and fighting readiness." He turned to the elder St. Clair. "What think you, Sir Henry? Will your son settle to harness?"

"With great good will, Sir Robert, for he has a hero of his own already serving with the Temple Knights in Outremer, and I am sure he will work with great zeal to join him there, so be it the man is still alive."

De Sablé quirked an eyebrow. "A hero? Who might that be?"

"A cousin, from the English branch of our family, although his family's holdings are now in Scotland, to the north, these past thirty years. He is Sir Alexander St. Clair, although, having lived among those benighted islanders since his birth, he calls himself by name according to their uncouth tongue."

De Sablé frowned. "How so? I do not follow you. You said his name is St. Clair."

"Aye, but he pronounces it *Sink*-lur, not Sann Clerr as we do."

"Sing-klur? That does sound strange … And why is he a hero to Sir André?"

The older man shrugged and smiled. "Because that is the kind of man he is. Why else? Alec—his own name for himself—is … heroic, a fighter of great repute and a veteran of the Temple. He spent two years with us, living in our household, soon after his admission to the Order, when André was but an unformed boy." Henry hesitated, seeing the expression on de Sablé's face. "What is it, Sir Robert? Have you heard of Alec St. Clair?"

De Sablé's slight frown cleared immediately. "I know not. But it seems to me I recollect … something. It is a very unusual-sounding name."

"Yes, for a very unusual man."

"And why was he two years here after his admission to the Temple?"

"You must ask him, Sir Robert, if ever you meet him, because I never did know more than that he was about the business of the Temple in some fashion. And that, of course, is secretive, to those who do not belong."

The outer doors swung open and Sir André entered, announcing that the Duke's instructions had been delivered and were being carried out. Richard moved impatiently towards the doors at once, summoning Sir Henry to join him and shouting back over his shoulder to de Sablé, as he strode from the room, that he would await him by the front doors within the quarter hour.

As soon as the other two had gone, de Sablé and the younger St. Clair stood looking at each other, the younger man clearly ill at ease in being alone with his new superior. De Sablé gazed at him for a few moments, and then nodded his head graciously.

"Your father has been telling me about your friendship with your cousin Sir Alexander Sinclair."

André St. Clair dipped his head, smiling slightly. "I could not call it a friendship, my lord. We liked each other, but I was a gangling boy at the time and Alec was a full ten years older, already a Temple Knight. We have not set eyes on one another in eight years, perhaps longer. But if Sir Alec is alive and still in Outremer, I will be honored to meet him again, and perhaps even fight beside him."

"So you anticipate fulfillment, traveling to the East?"

The question, innocuous as it sounded, had multiple meanings and implications, St. Clair knew, and he hesitated.

"Come here."

André moved closer almost with reluctance, wondering at the command, following as it had upon the unanswered question, and when the elder man stretched out his hand, he would have knelt had not the knight said, "No, take it."

No longer hesitant, André St. Clair took the proffered hand in his, and when he felt the unmistakable shape and pressure of its grasp, he answered it in kind, silently confirming their membership in the brotherhood. De Sablé released his grip.

"I had a feeling, but I should have had it sooner," he said, musingly. "I suspected your father might be of the brethren, but he did not respond to my grasp."

"No, Sir Robert, my father does not belong. But Sir Alec does."

"How did you learn that?"

"After my own initiation, of course. I had my suspicions soon after that, stirred by what I was learning, and remembering things that had puzzled me about him and his behavior when I was a boy. I asked my mentor and he confirmed it."

"So then, even as an initiate of our ancient Order, you had no thought of joining the Temple Knights?"

St. Clair's grin was open now. "None, sir, as I suspect you yourself had none. My loyalty was, and remains, to the brotherhood, and as I said earlier, I am—or I was—no monk."

"Well, you will be soon, although under the vows of the brotherhood rather than those of the Church. You know, of course, what I mean by that?" André murmured that he did. "I have no doubt the brotherhood will task you with some duties while you are in the

Holy Land. We must both make contact with the Council soon, informing them that we have met, along with the how and why."

André nodded in response, thinking briefly of Sir Robert's reference to vows. Upon being Raised to initiate status within the Brotherhood of the Order of Sion, each of them had been required to swear two vows that were closely related to, but essentially different from, the clerical vows of poverty and obedience. In the Order's breviary, the brothers swore to own nothing personally—which entailed personal poverty—but to hold all things in common with their brethren, and their oath of obedience was sworn in fealty to the Grand Master of their ancient Order, not to the Pope, and certainly not to the Master of the Temple. The third canonical vow, the oath of chastity, went unspoken within the Order of Sion because individual chastity was integral to the brethren's way of life. Within the Order of the Temple, the vow was insisted upon, and it posed no difficulty to those of the brotherhood who belonged to both orders. As he had so many times in the past, André shook his head in wonder at how little awareness outsiders had of such things, and that led him back to Richard Plantagenet, so that he looked at de Sablé and decided to be blunt.

"May I ask you something in the spirit of our brotherhood, Sir Robert?"

"Of course. Ask freely."

"The Duke seems mightily pleased with your appointment as Master Elect of the Temple, but for the life of me I cannot understand why that should be so. The moment you join the Temple, he will lose his influence over you, since no man can serve two masters and the Order is subservient to no temporal authority. It is unlike Duke Richard to be happy over losing a strong vassal. Can you shed light upon that for me?"

De Sablé laughed outright. "I can, and simply. His pleasure stems from the fact that my appointment, if it comes, lies in the future."

"Forgive me, but I don't understand. You said '*if* it comes.' Why should it not?"

"Oh, it will, but *when* it comes depends on whether or not the current Master, Gerard de Ridefort, be alive or dead. We suspect he may be dead, but we have no certain knowledge, for conditions in Outremer today are chaotic. The information that trickles back here to us is not always accurate, and in some instances not even true. So if de Ridefort yet lives, then I will wait until my services are required. And in the meantime, Duke Richard is well pleased because he has a use for me. I am to be his Fleet Master on the voyage to the Holy Land. He is assembling, ostensibly with his father's blessing, to this point at least, a great argosy, the greatest the world may ever have seen, to transport his armies, livestock, provisions, and siege engines by water, rather than overland.

"Think about it, lad. I am of the brotherhood, and until recently my Council-assigned task has been to tend to the trading ventures of a house established by certain families friendly to each other." The wording was noncommittal, but André St. Clair knew exactly what de Sablé was saying. "So, in order to fulfill my fraternal duties, I have spent decades learning everything I could of shipping and of cargoes, including the navigational and mathematical skills of commanding argosies at sea. Richard needs my services in that, and I, on behalf of the brotherhood, require his, in order to ensure that I reach Outremer alive and quickly. Surrounded by an enormous fleet, the odds in favor are greatly increased, and the Temple's risk of being and remaining Master-less is set largely at naught."

St. Clair nodded. "My thanks to you for that. It makes things much clearer. Now, what will you require of me from this time on, Sir Robert? Whatever you may have in mind, I can begin immediately. My father will see to the establishment of a crew to run these lands while we are gone. How long will we have, think you?"

"A month at least would be my guess, but it might be less, or even greatly more. Richard is keen to reach England, to set about the marshaling of his armies and his fleet, but for that he will remain dependent, as he always is, upon the goodwill and cooperation of his father the King. That is not a prospect that fills our liege lord with joy, although I believe that Henry will be at pains to appear tractable on this occasion, since he wants Richard safely out of England and bound for Outremer.

"But then, too, there is this ongoing matter of Philip's injured pride over the Vexin, and the imaginary indignities suffered by Alaïs. That, too, must be dealt with and settled to the satisfaction of both sides before any of this business can go further forward."

The silence that followed those words was brief, but fraught with meaning for both men. Alaïs Capet, the sister of King Philip Augustus, had been betrothed to Richard Plantagenet since childhood, shipped to England into the care of King Henry and Eleanor at the age of eight. But at the age of fifteen she had been seduced by her fiancé's father, who was old enough to be her grandfather even then, and she had remained his mistress ever since. It had been a short-lived scandal nevertheless, for by then Queen Eleanor had already been locked up in the prison where she would remain for more than a decade and a half, and no one, least of all Alaïs's cuckolded husband-to-be, really cared what became of the French princess.

The real grit in the dynastic ointment of the alliance between England and France, far more scandalous than the liaison between a lecherous old king and a silly, precocious girl, had sprung from the flagrant love affair between Alaïs's brother Philip and her betrothed husband, Richard. That the two men had been bedmates for years was something that was widely known but rarely discussed. The two of them had bickered for years, frequently in public, like an ill-matched husband and wife, with Philip Augustus playing the shrewish, jealous wife and neither man giving a thought to the situation between King Henry and Alaïs. Now, with Philip actively preparing to quit France to travel to the Holy Land with his army, the entire matter of Alaïs's dowry had arisen again between the two men, and this time it would not be easily deferred.

Alaïs's dowry, the cause of friction between the two royal houses now for more than a decade, was the rich and powerful French province called the Vexin, given as a marriage incentive and a token of the goodwill of the House of Capet to the Crown of England when the child Alaïs had traveled to that country to live with the family of her affianced groom. Originally intended to marry Henry's elder son, Prince Henry, her commitment had been changed in favor of Henry's younger brother, Richard, after the young Henry's early death. But irrespective of the reality that no marriage had yet taken place after nigh on twenty years, the strategic reality underlying the resentment and ill will over the disputed territory was that the boundaries of the Vexin lay less than a day's hard march from the French capital of Paris, and that had resulted in its being grasped and jealously held by King Henry, and latterly by Richard, ever since Alaïs first arrived in England.

Philip had wanted the Vexin returned to France, maintaining, with some justification, that since no marriage had been consummated, the dowry now stood forfeit and was the rightful property of France. Henry and Richard, who had used the intervening years to build a solid base of operations within the Vexin, on the very fringes of the French Kingdom, naturally and vehemently disagreed, but they had lost much of their argument in the conference at the French town of Gisors in January of 1188, when Philip had managed, with the assistance of the Pope, to have the Vexin placed in escrow, under his name, until such time as Richard honored his bargain and married the Princess Alaïs.

The silence passed without comment from André, and de Sablé continued as though it had not occurred. "That could take days, or it could take weeks, depending on how well the two of them can settle their differences and make amicable arrangements to share the leadership of the campaign."

"Will they be joint commanders?"

"Probably, in some form. But Richard is the soldier, Philip the negotiator who much prefers to administer rather than to fight. On the surface that should work well for the survival of the alliance, but between us, as brothers, neither man will settle for less than the primary leadership. For the time being, at least, Philip is the only king involved in this venture, and having that acknowledged by everyone acts an insulation to his pride. But as soon as Richard becomes King of England, that will change, and in reality—something you know as well as I—Richard will die before he gives up the military glory of being supreme commander of the expedition. Sooner or later, sparks will fly on the wind over that, and they will probably start fires where no fires are expected. But that will singe neither you nor me.

"Be ready to leave for England within the month, then, but before the coming week is out, get you to Tours or to Poitiers, seek out the brotherhood and report what has occurred here. From then on you will be instructed as required. I may or may not return this way from Paris, depending upon Richard's urgencies, but you will be summoned, no matter which way we go back to England, so be prepared. And now I must go, for he is waiting for me and you know how little he likes to be kept waiting, so I will bid you adieu, and we will meet again soon."

The two men embraced briefly, brethren now, and de Sablé went to join his Duke, leaving Sir André St. Clair with much to think about.

THREE

May went by, and then June, without another word reaching the St. Clair estate from Richard, but Sir Henry barely noticed the time passing. He was too intent upon regaining the conditioning that he had lost since his wife's death, aware that even before she died, he had surrendered to a life of comfort and sloth, smugly and silently claiming the privilege of an older man who had served his lord's—and before that his lady's—purposes well. Now, having learned all too belatedly that his self-indulgence had been both premature and ill advised, he felt the full weight of his age as he struggled to regain some of his former strength and the associated skills that had been his stock-in-trade.

He had begun by learning to ride again, suffering the pains of the damned as his body rebelled against the disciplines his muscles had forgotten. The riding itself was unforgotten, of course, but his stamina had atrophied and his old bones and sinews protested against the indignity of being battered and bruised as he fought grimly to recapture the ability to spend long hours and days in the saddle without respite.

He rode for five hours on the first day of his renewed odyssey, and when at length he returned to the castle and climbed clumsily down from the saddle, almost falling as his feet struck the ground, his aching muscles were screaming at him for rest. But he ignored them. Instead, he forced himself to walk into the training yard and take up his sword, after which, alone and face to face with a foot-thick, upright balk of solid oak that had been hacked and dented for decades by the weapons of trainee recruits, he launched himself into the ancient, elementary exercises designed to teach a novice the basic techniques of swordplay. He swung his sword against the post for more than an hour, religiously following the basic drills until he could no longer summon the strength to raise his arms, and then he staggered to his chamber, up the familiar stairway that he thought would never end, and fell face down on the bed like a dead man, before the sun even came close to setting.

He woke up late, in broad daylight, and barely had the strength to raise himself to his feet. Every muscle in his body felt rigid, cramped and corded like old, gnarled wood, and his buttocks and inner thighs were bruised as though they had been beaten with steel rods. He lurched towards the well in the courtyard, recovering his powers of movement very slowly, and doused himself in icy water, cursing savagely at the shock of it, but not as loudly as he would have liked, for fear of scandalizing the servants. He toweled himself dry with a piece of sacking, surprised to find himself feeling a grudging sympathy for all the young novices he had ground through the same punishing routine for so many years without a thought for their pain and misery.

When he was dry and feeling slightly fresher, he reeled towards the kitchens on legs that were achingly inflexible and still unsteady, unaware that no one, including the faithful Ector, had yet dared to speak to him. Then, when he had eaten, he made his way to the stables and called for his horse, only to discover that he was absolutely incapable of mounting it because his stiff old legs would not stretch far enough to permit it. He called irascibly for a leg up from a sturdy groom, and then had to suffer the additional indignity of requiring his feet to be placed in the stirrups, since his legs were not limber enough to permit him to find them unaided. By the time he clattered out of the cobbled yard and through the gates, the entire staff of the castle was holding its breath, waiting for him to explode as he had in bygone days, but when he disappeared without incident they heaved a collective sigh of relief and went about their daily affairs.

It took two full weeks for his body to begin adjusting to the demands he was thrusting upon it after such a long period of idleness, and there were several of those days when he believed he could no longer subject himself to such unending pain and punishment, but Henry St. Clair had never shirked his duty. He had, in truth, spent a lifetime training other people mercilessly, drilling discipline and obedience and acceptance into callow students, and he now used himself no less harshly than he had used them. He had no other choice, for he recognized his own weakness and would have died of shame had young Richard Plantagenet come back and seen him before Henry himself was ready to be seen.

But then came a day when the pain of hauling himself into the saddle seemed less severe, and when the bite of his swung sword in the late afternoon felt *cleaner*, somehow, the arc of its swing more crisp and decisive. After that, working each day harder than the day before, he improved rapidly in every area: bodily strength, stamina, agility, and horsemanship. His face and hands grew dark from riding daily in all weathers, and although his muscles appeared to him to be no bulkier or more solid, he could nonetheless feel them increasing in strength with every day that came. He could swing his sword now against the post for hours on end, smashing out slivers and splinters of the heavy oak, with only minor intervals of rest between attacks, and he exulted in the joy that simple ability brought him, for it was undeniable proof that he was hardening himself. Even his armor appeared to have grown lighter nowadays, he noticed, and he was barely aware of its bulk and rode fully armed and armored at all times.

Early that June, he shared his table with a French knight who had been passing by and claimed his hospitality for a night. His guest informed him at dinner that warfare had broken out again between the kings Philip and Henry, and that Duke Richard, snubbed yet again by his father in the matter of the accession to England's throne, had sided openly with Philip against King Henry, joining the French king in besieging his own father in Le Mans, the town where Henry had been born, and the place he was said to love more than any other. The knight, whose name was du Plessey, told Sir Henry that he had left Le Mans under siege two days earlier, carrying dispatches south, by way of Tours and Poitiers to Angoulême on Philip's personal behalf.

In spite of persistent questioning by his host, however, he was unable to provide any information about either André St. Clair or Sir Robert de Sablé, with whom André had been traveling constantly since Richard's visit in April, so Henry was unable to ascertain whether his son had been with Richard's forces at Le Mans.

Then, mere weeks later, on the sixth of July, a beautiful summer afternoon, André arrived home alone, in prime condition and glad to be back in his own territories, even though it would be for but a few days on this occasion. He, too, was on his way to Angoulême, it transpired, to deliver official documents from Sir Robert de Sablé in Orléans to the preceptor of the Temple commandery there.

André's arrival threw Sir Henry's entire household into a frenzy of celebration, for the young man was dearly loved by everyone and it had been months since anyone had seen him. Henry had accepted and accommodated the general excitement with good humor, sharing his son generously on the first day and night of his unexpected homecoming and making no attempt to engage him on anything more important than the standard generalities being bandied about by everyone else at dinner that night. It was not until the rest of the household had retired and even Ector had been sent to bed that father and son were able to sit and talk together over a jug of Henry's beloved pale yellow wine, purchased unfailingly each year from his favorite vineyards in the neighboring province of Burgundy, less than a hundred miles to the east.

Much of the idle talk throughout that day had been about Sir Henry's recent training regimen, with everyone eager to deliver his or her own report to André on the startling improvements in his father's appearance and overall health, and now, when André sought to bring the subject up again, Henry waved his comments aside.

"We have talked enough about me and what I have been doing. I am far more interested in you and your activities. What have you been doing? I have been presuming that you were with Richard's army, since he seems to want to keep Sir Robert de Sablé close to him, and from the single letter you sent me last month, I gather that wherever Sir Robert goes nowadays, you go, too."

André tipped his head, twisting his mouthy wryly. "Not always, Father, but I admit Sir Robert has taken a keen interest in my welfare and has been extending himself on my behalf ever since the day he chose to believe my story." He smiled more openly then, his voice growing less formal. "If the Temple Knights refuse to have me, it will not be Sir Robert's fault. He has decided that I am suitably qualified to be a Templar, and I am tempted to agree with him now, having taken time to think upon what is involved. Would it displease or disappoint you, sir, were I to become a full-fledged member of the Order?"

"A Templar monk?" Henry was surprised by the question. It had never occurred to him that his son might take up the burden of monk-hood. He sat frowning for some time, twisting an end of his mustache. "I really have no answer for that, André. Would it displease me? I see no reason why it should, on first thoughts. And yet already there are second and third thoughts spinning in my mind. Would it disappoint me? Hmm ... Two years ago, when your mother was alive, it might have, for she always dreamed of having grand-children, but now that she has left us, God rest her soul, the urgency of that regret is gone, too. You are my only son, and the last of our particular line, which means that if you die without sons, there will be an end of us." A tiny smile flickered briefly at one corner of his mouth. "Some might think that no great loss, I am sure. We have cousins enough, but none that are really close, and the one of those you most admire is already a Temple Knight and therefore a monk himself. So, should you decide to join the Order outright, you would be in good and noble company." He thought again for a few moments, then concluded, "No, André, I should be neither displeased nor disappointed, so be it that was what you really wished to do. And providing that I were able to spend time with you in Outremer before you took final vows, I would have no complaints."

"You know it would mean that I would have to give this castle and all my possessions to the Order upon your death?"

"I understand that, but what does it matter? There will be no one else with any rights to the place once I am dead and you become a monk. Better, perhaps, to donate it to the Order, where it may serve some useful purpose, than to leave it to be squabbled over after your own death by grasping relatives. No, I am convinced—if that is your wish, your chosen course, then so be it." He clapped his hands together once. "Now, tell me about the world out there. What is happening beyond my gates that I should know about? The last thing I heard was that Richard and Philip were besieging King Henry in Le Mans. Is that debacle still going on?"

"No, not at all. It is over, long since. The city fell after only a few weeks, in late June. Richard turned the populace out and burned the place down ten days ago. King Henry escaped just before the city's surrender and fled south, towards Chinon, and Richard followed hard on his heels as soon as he had issued the burning order. I was in Tours last night, at the Temple's commandery there, and in the course of the evening I heard several tales of what has happened since then, but I can attest to the truth of none of them. There are so many reports, from so many sources, that it would be foolish to attempt to distinguish truth from falsehood among them."

"Tell me some, at least, of what you heard."

André shook his head in disgust. "Some say the old man is fallen gravely ill, on his deathbed, his spirit finally crushed by the wanton destruction of his native city. And I heard that he was robbed by his own people after the sickness struck him—the followers and fawning hangers-on who ever flock about him—and he now has nothing left."

Sir Henry's brow creased into a quick frown. "That is iniquitous. But you say Richard pursued him. I presume he would have caught up with him once the old man fell sick, if not before. Did he then do nothing to stop this theft you describe?"

"I doubt he was aware of it, Father. Richard had other matters on his mind, and I gather he was ruthless in prosecuting them."

"Other matters … such as what?"

"It surprises me that you would even have to ask. The Vexin, first and foremost. Facing death, Henry did what he would never do in life. He named Richard heir to England, officially. That was three days ago, on the third of July, according to what I heard last night. At the same time and by the same report, he decreed that his wife, Eleanor, be freed from her prison in the tower at Winchester in England, where he has kept her these last sixteen years. And he formally relinquished any claim he might have held to the Vexin, agreeing to hand over the Princess Alaïs to Philip Augustus and Richard, so that Richard can marry her and settle the matter of the Vexin dowry—and with it, the entire issue of the English/French agreement to the Holy War—once and for all."

Sir Henry sat silent for long moments before he murmured, "The old man must be sick indeed, to have given up so much ... and Richard must have pressed him hard."

"Aye, Father, and he pressed even harder than that. Henry was forced to surrender castles and estates that he has owned all his life, and to cede territories to Richard that were never in dispute. They say that Richard left him nothing at the end, not even dignity. I also heard that, after he had conceded everything Richard demanded of him, the King prayed aloud that he might be allowed to live until he could achieve a fitting revenge on his ungrateful son, but died immediately thereafter, denied even that satisfaction by a God whom he flouted too many times. I can't swear to the truth of that, though. His death, I mean. Others present disputed that. Bear in mind I am only reporting second hand." André's tone assumed a note of bitterness. "Yet I heard, too, that Richard began weeping and praying for his father's soul a few hours before the old man died, starting the moment he had wrung everything he wanted from him."

"Who would have told you such a thing?" The frown on Sir Henry's face had deepened to a scowl of disgust. "Who would dare speak such words? Whoever he may have been, he was no friend of Richard Plantagenet." André made no attempt to reply, and his father went on. "You said you were in the Temple commandery in Tours, did you not? And it was there you heard such things talked about openly, among strangers? I find that hard to credit. Among the knights themselves, in their own quarters, yes, I could accept that they might discuss such things in privacy. But you are no Templar, and thus to have heard such tales, you must have been among the public crowds."

"No, Father, not quite." André shrugged his shoulders very gently, managing to deprecate his own importance with that gesture. "I was privileged to be in the company of a pair of Temple Knights whom I have come to know well these past few months. They work closely at all times with de Sablé, acting as couriers between him, Duke Richard, and the King of France on behalf of the Order. It was as their guest that I was able to overhear so much."

"Aye, but even so, André, unless drastic changes have recently been made, personal friendships have no standing in such things, not when it comes to oaths and secrecy. You are not of the Order. You do not belong, and you must therefore be treated—and mistrusted—accordingly. But I mislike the entire smell of this, the disloyalty involved in even speaking of such things."

André's brow wrinkled. "Disloyalty? How may that be, Father? We are discussing the Knights of the Temple. Their sole loyalty is to the Pope himself. No temporal ruler, be he emperor, king, or duke, has any claim upon their loyalty."

"I am aware of that, André, as aware as I am of the fact that you are not yet one of them … unless there is something you have not told me about your present situation? Are you informing me that you have already been raised to the ranks of the elect?"

His father's tone, raised in mock interrogation, was skeptical, and André was far from being surprised, but he had long since learned to accept that there were things about himself and his life that he could never reveal to his father, things they could never discuss. He waved one hand and shook his head before standing up and walking to the great iron brazier in the hearth, where he set his wine cup on the mantel before squatting down to throw fresh fuel from the piled logs on one side of the fireplace onto the dying fire, thereby gaining himself some time to shake off and conceal the guilt that always affected him at such times, even after years of living with the knowledge that his secret had nothing to do with his filial love and respect for his father. But his silence did not go unnoticed, for his father now asked, somewhat peremptorily, "What are you dreaming about down there?"

André rose to his feet fluidly. "The Templars," he said casually, lying without effort, as always, when it came to safeguarding the secrets of the brotherhood. "I was watching the flames licking the wood, and thinking that we won't see much wood in Outremer. Not firewood, anyway. The people there burn camel dung, I'm told. That reminds me of a tale I once heard about a Templar sergeant whose primary duty, for several years, was to have his men gather up all the dung they could find in the streets of Jerusalem, for fuel."

"That sounds like a worthwhile way to serve one's God ..."

André ignored his father's sarcasm. "Apparently Hugh de Payens thought so, for he was the man who assigned the duty."

"Hugh de Payens? Was he not—?"

"The first Master of the Temple, the Founder of the Order. Aye, Father, that was he."

"Hmm." Henry contemplated his son. "You think you really will join them, André, vows and all?"

A fleeting grin from his son reassured Sir Henry greatly.

"Oh, I think not, sir," André drawled. "It's an idea that flits through my mind from time to time, nothing more. I will fight as one of their force in Outremer, that is a promise given, but I doubt I will take the formal, binding vows."

"Then why are you so involved with them, with this de Sablé fellow?"

"I'm not." André's eyes had widened as his father asked the question. "Not involved with the knights, I mean. With de Sablé, yes, but he is not a Templar, not yet. We are both working for Richard. Working hard, too."

"Doing what?"

André's face quirked into a smile. "Well, Sir Robert is organizing what may become the largest fleet of ships ever launched, whereas I am training men to use the new crossbow, the arbalest."

"What's new about a crossbow? This ... what did you call it?"

"An arbalest, sir. It's the latest, most up-to-date development of the weapon. As you know, I've loved the crossbow ever since I was strong enough to load one, and of course Richard himself has, too. Well, he and I started talking after he and Sir Robert came here that day, and he wanted to know about the shot I made—how I gauged it, aimed it, that sort of thing—when I killed the priest, that de Blois slug. One word led to another and the upshot of it was that he charged me with the task of putting training in place for new levies of cross-bowmen immediately. Not to train arbalesters, you understand, but to train other men as teachers, and to place particular emphasis on train-ing with the new arbalest. He is very keen on it, and I can see why."

"Have you spent much time with him since you left home?"

"With Richard?" André shook his head. "No, barely any time at all. A half hour here and there, and perhaps three hours the day he set me to the training task, for he wanted to be sure I understood what he required of me. Apart from that, I have seen him only five times since then, all of them from a distance as he rode by."

"Good. That may be fortunate. Trust me, as your father, André. Be careful of Richard. Should you start spending more time close to him, you will find there are aspects of his character that will proba-bly offend you. I'll say no more than that, for you are old, smart, and ugly enough now to see such things for yourself and draw your own conclusions, but if you do find yourself growing disgusted at any time, in God's name keep your displeasure shielded from his eyes. Richard mislikes being disapproved of, almost as much as being crossed. He resented it as a boy and I doubt he has grown out of that." Henry watched his son's face darken with curiosity, but waved an extended finger in dismissal of the topic. "Tell me, then, why the enthusiasm for this new arbalest device? What is so different about it, compared with any other crossbow?"

André's eyes lit up with enthusiasm. "Power," he said. "Sheer, unbelievable power. And accuracy. It's named after the old Roman weapon, the ballista. Do you know what the ballista was?"

His father's head came up as though he had been stung. "Do I know—? God's teeth, boy, do you really think me that ignorant? I was a Master-at-Arms before you were even born! It was an artillery piece, modeled after the Greek *catapulta*, the original cross-bow. *Ballistae* were large, two-armed throwing devices, made of wood and powered by torsion ropes wound by ratchets, and they could hurl a stone or sometimes a heavy spear for half a mile and more, predictably and accurately."

His son was nodding eagerly, still bright eyed. "Aye, made of wood, as you said. Well, the arbalest has a bow made of sprung, layered steel. It is far stronger than any wooden bow ever made, and unlike the ballista, it is portable. It is cumbersome, but it can be carried and operated by a single man, and a skilled operator, trained in its use, can fire two bolts, with enormous power and accuracy, in a single minute, and kill armored men more than five hundred paces away. I have one of them upstairs. Would you like to see it?"

"I would."

"Well then, in the morning, if you can haul your ancient bones from your bed, perhaps I will grace you with a demonstration. I think you'll be amazed."

Henry smiled. "I'll be amazed if you manage to raise your tired carcass from slumber before I've dressed and broken fast. We shall see who feels more ancient come sunrise tomorrow."

André laughed. "Aye, we'll see. Sleep well, Father."

He left his father with a smile, enjoying this echo of their raillery of old, but as he made his way towards his cot, he felt the painful distance that was now between them, a distance born of knowledge and secrecy.

Sir Henry thought of the Templar Knights as being the elect, and although they might arguably be so, to a minor and very limited extent, André knew that his father was wrong, and that he could never imagine that his son was already one of the true elect: an initiated brother in an ancient and secret order whose existence Sir Henry, as an outsider, could never be permitted to suspect.

Accepting that awareness, years earlier, had been a difficult task for André, eased only by the recognition that it had been shared by every individual initiate of the ancient brotherhood into which he had been inducted, or Raised as his brethren called the initiation, at the age of eighteen, even before being knighted by Duke Richard.

The brotherhood conducted its affairs beneath a shroud of inviolable secrecy, with a simply stated purpose: to safeguard and study the incalculably valuable secret that was its sole reason for being. From the moment of his Raising to a full-status brother, André had grown increasingly fascinated with the reality of that secret, so that now, endlessly enthralled by what it all entailed, he found himself thinking of varying aspects of it at different times, every day of his life, no matter what he was doing or where he might be.

For more than a millennium, ever since the end of the first century of Christianity, its presence unsuspected and undreamed of by anyone outside its own ranks, the organization, the brotherhood, had been known to successive generations of initiate brothers as the Order of Rebirth in Sion, and throughout that time its members had been studying the great body of lore that lay at the root of its being. The secret they guarded so zealously and jealously was one so old and so alien to their everyday world that it defied belief, perhaps even more so now than ever before, after eleven hundred years. It had certainly defied André's belief when he first learned of it, and he now believed implicitly that it had affected every one of his initiate brethren, older and younger, living and dead, in the same way since time immemorial, for alien it was. Its substance was inconceivable, and awareness of its mere existence induced nausea, profound terror, and the appalling possibility of eternal damnation, with the irretrievable loss of one's immortal soul and forfeiture of any possible hope of achieving salvation on either side of death. And so the initiates questioned it vigorously and disputed its credibility with everything—every whit of logic, intellect, and instinctual horror and distaste at their disposal—beginning as soon as the trauma of their introduction to it had begun to wear off. And every individual initiate who fought against it came to appreciate, eventually, that every single one of his brethren, over the past thousand years, had shared the same odyssey and come to harbor at the end of it, at ease with the immensity of what he had learned to be the absolute truth. And one by one the entire brotherhood, to a man, became content to dedicate the remainder of their lives to proving that truth, by proving the truth underlying the lore of the Order.

That unity of purpose had survived unbroken, André knew, until approximately sixty years earlier, in 1127, when the Order had renamed itself by dropping the word *Rebirth* from its title, calling itself simply the Order of Sion. Only the brothers themselves knew of the change, and they smiled with pride when they thought of it, for after a millennium, the *Rebirth* had been achieved when a small group of nine knights from the Languedoc area, all of them members of the brotherhood, led by a man called Hugh de Payens, had excavated under the foundations of the Temple Mount in Jerusalem, and, after searching diligently and in secret for eight years, had unearthed exactly what the Order's lore had told them would be in that precise place.

Thinking about what he knew, and what his father would never know, André lay his head down that night feeling more like a stranger in his father's home than he had ever felt before.

THE NEXT MORNING, father and son were out in the training yard between the castle and its outer walls, waiting for sunrise, neither one enthusiastic about being there or about acknowledging the other's presence. Sir Henry stood back with the heavy arbalest in his arms while André stooped close to the front wall of the yard in the dim light of the newborn day, a quiver of heavy crossbow bolts dangling from his shoulder, and carefully examined the old and battered balk of oak used for sword practice.

"This will serve, for now," he said, striding back to join his father. "I'll shoot from over yonder on the other side. The light will soon be strong enough for us." He then led the way to the far side of the yard, less than fifty paces from the thick practice post, where he took the heavy weapon from Sir Henry and proceeded to arm it. Henry could see that his son was an expert in its use, for he pressed it front down against the ground and placed his foot firmly in the stirrup at the end, then leaned forward, bracing the butt end against his belly while he used both hands to wind the pair of swivel ratchets that dragged the bowstring of thickly woven leather back, against the pull of the steel bow, until it tipped and was held in place by the notched end of the trigger that protruded through the body of the weapon, at the end of the channeled groove that would hold the feathered bolt. It was hard work, and his father admired the way André performed the task with the ease and skill of a master.

"That's the worst part," André said, straightening his back and wiping a trickle of sweat from his eyebrow with the back of one hand. "Now we simply load the bolt and watch what it does."

"Is this the same device you said will throw a missile five hundred paces?"

"Aye, it is. Why do you ask?"

"Because it is less than fifty paces from here to the post you're aiming at. What do you hope to achieve there, in order to impress me?"

"Just watch. Pass me one of those bolts."

Henry pulled one from the quiver on the ground and straightened up slowly, one eyebrow raised as he held the missile out towards his son, who took it and placed it in the launching position.

"Aye," André said. "Heavier than you expected, was it not? And so it should be. That thing is solid steel. Now, watch." He raised the arbalest to his shoulder, sighted quickly with one eye closed, and squeezed the lever that operated the trigger. There was a loud, sharp *snap*, and Henry saw the end of the weapon leap high into the air. He grinned, meeting his son's eye.

"Unfortunate, that. The violence of that snap back must have destroyed your aim, no?"

"No, Father." André's headshake was definite. "Too much power involved for that. The bolt was clear and gone long before the nose began to rise. Look." He pointed to the post, but peer as he might, Henry could see no sign of the bolt.

"You missed the post," he said.

"No, sir, I did not. Look more closely."

Henry moved forward, peering towards the distant pole, his pace increasing as he approached it, and then he hesitated and stopped, unable to believe what he was seeing. The steel bolt, fifteen inches long and as thick as one of his fingers, was almost completely buried in the post, splitting the weathered wood vertically above and below its point of impact. Only the flighted end of the bolt remained visible, protruding a mere three inches. He reached out to touch it with his fingertips, then turned to his son.

"This post is solid oak."

André nodded, smiling. "I know, Father. Solid, aged, and seasoned, and battered now beyond its capacity to withstand much more abuse. I helped select it and set it in place there, you may recall, about twelve years ago. Now ask me again about the five-hundred-pace distance involved in a long shot."

"No need," Sir Henry answered, shaking his head slowly. "How many of these does Richard own?"

"Nowhere near sufficient to his purposes. That's the rub. He has very few real arbalests—this kind, I mean, with the steel bow. There are none at all outside Richard's own domains of England and Aquitaine. Bear in mind that no one has used these weapons in fifty years, so even the art of making them is lost to most armorers. The man who made this one I use is a smith with skills that surpass belief. He makes them very well, but he appears to be the only one who can, and he cannot make large numbers of them, nor can he make them quickly. He appears to be the only one, at this point, who knows the secret of springing the metal bows. He is training others now, apprentices, but that takes time." He paused for a moment, thinking. "Plain crossbows, with bows of wood and laminated horn and sinew, are easier to come by, but even they are scarce and precious nowadays, each one worth its weight in silver, perhaps even gold. And of course Richard's English yeomen have their yew longbows, and their bowyers continue to work as they always have."

Henry nodded, accepting his son's word without demur. The second Pope Innocent, using the power of his office, had banned all projectile weapons—bows and crossbows alike—fifty years earlier, and the proscription, despite its papal origins, had been unusually successful, honored and observed beyond credence by almost everyone throughout Christendom. The results of that success, inevitable and, as it was now turning out, unfortunate, had been that bowyers and fletchers everywhere outside of England and Aquitaine, deprived of purchasers for their products, had turned their skills towards other crafts, and projectile weapons had fallen into disuse. They were seldom seen nowadays, and those that did survive were ancient, worn-out things, barely capable of bringing down a hare or a deer.

The official explanation for the papal ban had been that God Himself found these weapons offensive and un-Christian, and their use against Christian warriors from that time on had been forbidden under pain of excommunication and eternal fire. But the truth underlying it—and the pragmatic reason for both the original proposal and its subsequent acceptance by the knightly class—was that the escalating power and strength of the weapons had made it possible for an untrained, landless, ragamuffin man-at-arms, or even a serf, to shoot down and kill a fully armored, highly trained knight from a distance far enough removed to offer the killer immunity.

Among the ruling heads of Christendom at the time of the proscription, only the young Henry Plantagenet, then Count of Anjou but later to become King Henry II of England, had possessed both the perspicacity and the self-sufficient defiance to ignore the papal decree from the outset, keeping the weapons in use—albeit ostensibly for hunting and training purposes—within his own territories. He recognized that these weapons were the strongest and most lethal killing machines ever developed for use by individual men in dealing death impersonally, and hence terrifyingly, from great distances and he therefore refused to deny himself the advantages they offered to him as a warrior and commander of armies. And later, adhering to his example almost inevitably, his third-born son, Richard, Count of Anjou and Poitou, and eventually Duke of his mother's province of Aquitaine, had adopted his father's enthusiasm with an even greater approval of his own.

It was the unexplained anomaly of that behavior—since Richard seldom aped or approved of anything his father did—that made Sir Henry now ask his son, "Why then, if he has so few of them, is he making you responsible for training men to teach other men to use them? That seems to be a waste."

"Not at all, sir. We are producing more of them all the time. Not with bewildering speed, but even so, we will need trained men to use them. But it is the *idea* of the weapon, its potential for spreading awe and fear, that excites Richard. His will be the only men in all the Frankish forces who have these weapons, and that will give him an advantage over all his allies."

"Wait! Think about what you are saying, lad. Do you honestly believe the German Redbeard will not have these weapons?"

"Barbarossa?" André shrugged. "He might ... He probably will, now that I think of it, for he's the only man in Christendom who cares as little for the Pope's decree as Richard does. But that merely proves Richard's correctness. Can you imagine the advantage the German would have, in lording it over all of us, had Richard no such weapons?"

"Hmm." The evident lack of interest in Sir Henry's grunt indicated that his thoughts were already far away from that, involved with other things. "So then, aside from that, if Barbarossa is so easily dismissed, are you telling me that Richard is merely interested in a perceived advantage over his own allies here?"

André blinked. "Pardon me, sir, but where is 'here'? I think I may have misunderstood your question."

"Here is *here*," his father snapped, "in Christendom. My question is: what, if anything, does Richard have in mind about using these weapons in Outremer?"

"Well ..." André was plainly mystified. "He will use them, most certainly—"

Henry cut him off, his voice strained, biting back a sudden, angry impatience. "I hope he will, *most* certainly, as you say, since the ban against them states clearly that they are forbidden solely from use against Christians. But the enemy we go to face in Outremer is most certainly not Christian, and I have been told, by several sources, that they themselves used these very weapons—bows, at any rate—to harry and destroy the last Frankish and Christian armies we deployed against them. I pray God that your Duke has a mind to that. And if that is not the case—although I admit I cannot imagine that it would be so—I will make it my concern to ensure that he is made aware of it."

ANDRÉ LEFT TO REJOIN Sir Robert de Sablé a few days later, promising to return at the end of the month, and the next three weeks passed quickly. On the morning of the last day of the month, helmed and shielded and wearing a full hauberk of steel chain mail coat and leggings, Sir Henry made the rounds of his lands, exulting in the sheer pleasure of being who and what he was and in the semblance of youth he had regained over the previous few months of hard, determined work. He no longer had to steel himself against the pains of training, on or off the drill field, and on this particular day he carried a tilting lance in his right hand and a plain, undecorated shield on his left arm. His sword hung at his waist, the belt that supported it cinched loosely over a plain black knee-length surcoat that was covered in turn by his military mantle, with the crest of St. Clair on the back and above his left breast.

He had ridden around the full perimeter of his lands that morning, a circuit of more than fifteen miles, and he was filled with exultation as he spurred his warhorse up the slope of the last hill that would bring him within sight of his home and the high road that bordered the eastern reaches of his estate from north to south, for he had been eight hours in the saddle by then and he felt as though eight more would cause him no concern. He felt better and more carefree than he had in years, and he was looking forward with pleasure to André's arrival that same day, after the intervening weeks spent in Angoulême, about some business set him by the knight de Sablé.

His horse surged easily up and over the crest of the hill, and Henry pulled it to a halt at the start of the downward slope on the other side, sitting easily in the saddle as he examined the scene spread out ahead of him. Half a mile away, to his left, on a rocky knoll surrounded by massive beeches that concealed an encircling river, sat his family's stronghold, its tall, square, hundred-year-old donjon jutting up from the bare rock crest, surrounded and protected by high, thick crenellated walls that could accommodate all his tenants behind their solid bulk in times of danger, and a drawbridge across the deep river gorge that could be raised to secure the donjon itself in time of attack—although the presence of the huge beech trees proclaimed that no serious attack had taken place here since they were planted, nigh on a century earlier. From the castle gates, a hard, wide, beaten roadway struck directly for a mile to the high road that bounded his lands on the east. He turned in the saddle to look back towards the south, hoping to see André approaching from that direction, but the road was empty. Turning back, he glanced idly towards the point where the road from the north crested a distant ridge, then stood upright in his stirrups as he saw movement—increasing movement—where he had expected none.

Three mounted men, two of them recognizable as knights by their shields and plumed helms, had already crossed the ridge and were riding down the hill towards him. Behind them the third man, less richly dressed and clearly a military sub-commander, rode at the head of a strong phalanx of marching men, in ranks of six, that was only now coming into view, its files stretching back and out of sight beyond the ridge. Henry knew they could not have seen him yet, high on the side of his hill, and so he sat there and watched their approach. The tenth and last rank of the phalanx of men-at-arms crested the rise, their pike blades reflecting the light, and immediately behind them the high box of a passenger carriage came into view, rising towards the summit of the road. It was followed by another and then a third, each carriage flanked by a pair of mounted knights flaunting the colors of their individual houses like peacocks. Three more vehicles followed the carriages, heavy, flat-bottomed wagons drawn by teams of mules and piled high with cargo, securely covered and strapped down, and a second formation of infantry, the same size as the first and preceded by another pair of knights and a sub-commander, brought up the rear. By the time the last men marched into view the leaders were nigh on a half mile down the hill.

Henry was intrigued, but not alarmed by the approaching party, for despite its strength it was clearly not a warlike group. The great road they were traveling had been built hundreds of years earlier by the Romans. It ran straight south and west towards Marseille, and, much like a river of stone, collected tributaries leading from all the cities of the northern half of France, from Brittany and Normandy, Artois, and Paris itself, the home of King Philip Augustus. These travelers were obviously wealthy and important, judging by the number of vehicles and the strength of their escort, and he found himself wondering who would need six score men-at-arms, with officers and no fewer than ten fully armed knights. A senior prelate with his staff, perhaps a cardinal or an archbishop, was his first thought, or perhaps the wife of a powerful baron or a duke, with her household.

He spurred his horse gently and angled it down the hillside to where he could come within hailing distance of the cavalcade, then reined in on the edge of a coppice, casually concealed within twenty paces of the road and surprised that no one had drawn attention to his approach. He was on his own land and in full chivalric armor, so he had no fear in presenting himself, but he had misgivings about not having been seen, for that meant the men leading the advance party were riding carelessly, and coming into their view too suddenly might provoke them into overreacting, out of guilt and surprise.

Moments later, the first of the two leading knights came into view, resplendent in black and yellow trappings, and Henry's back straightened in astonishment before his face broke into a smile. He had not seen this man in years, but he had trained him as a youth and had promoted him to be his own adjutant, fifteen years earlier.

"Sir Francis!" he called out at the top of his voice. "What would you do now were I a squad of archers instead of but one watching old man?"

The effect of his shout was salutary, for the marching men behind the two knights crashed to a halt instantly and then, at a snapped command from their mounted officer, the first four ranks spread out across the roadway. Twelve of the men knelt as they aimed their swiftly loaded crossbows towards the sound of Henry's voice, and twelve more behind them aimed over their heads. The leading knight, whose name Henry had shouted, must have been half asleep, for he pulled sharply on the reins and brought his horse rearing up on its hind legs, then spun it completely around, and by the time the animal's front hooves returned to earth he had his bared blade in his hand. His companion had spun away, too, and now sat his horse with his spear couched, its butt firmly gripped beneath his armpit.

"Who goes there? Show yourself!"

"Happily, Francis, if you will tell your men not to slaughter me on sight."

The knight called Francis frowned, but he raised his sword and waved down his men, bidding them hold, then called again to Henry to come out. Henry nudged his horse forward slowly and enjoyed the amazement that dawned in Francis de Neuville's face as he recognized the man approaching him.

"Sir Henry? Sir Henry St. Clair? Is that you?"

"Of course it is. Did you think you me a specter, in broad daylight?"

Both men slipped down from their saddles and embraced in the middle of the road. "By all the saints in Heaven, well met, Sir Henry. How long has it been, ten years? What are you doing here, so far from anywhere?"

"Twelve years, Francis, and I am riding my boundaries. This is my home. My castle is close by, over the hill there." He waved towards it, then indicated the motionless procession stretching back up the hill. "What are you doing nowadays, escorting churchmen?"

"Churchmen?" Sir Francis looked perplexed again. "Why would you think that? There are no churchmen here." He glanced at the other knight who had been riding with him. "William, you've heard me talk about Sir Henry St. Clair who was Master-at-Arms to Aquitaine when I was a boy? Well, this is the man." As Henry and Sir William exchanged nods, Sir Francis continued, "So you live nearby? I thought somehow you were in the north, towards Burgundy."

They were interrupted by a clatter of hooves as a trio of men came spurring down the hill to find out the cause of the delay. One of them, a black-browed giant of a man mounted on an enormous horse, scowled ferociously at Henry before turning his displeasure on Francis de Neuville, demanding in a surly, ungracious voice to know why the entire column had been brought to a standstill.

De Neuville looked at his questioner and managed to give Henry the impression that he had responded with a very Gallic shrug, although he was fully armored. "I stopped to speak to an old friend," he said. "And I have not yet finished greeting him. Move them on, if you wish. We will draw aside and I will catch up with you when I am ready."

"You should have done that without waiting to be told."

De Neuville's right eyebrow quirked as he raised his eyes to look at the mounted questioner. "And how would you know that, Mandeville? I doubt if you have ever had a friend to stop for in your entire life." He stepped to his horse and took its reins in his hand, then beckoned with his head to Henry. "Come, Henry, we can talk over there as they pass by."

Neither man spoke until the column had begun to move again, the scowling knight riding ahead in de Neuville's place while his companions returned to their positions. The marching column of soldiers trudged on, ignoring the two knights by the roadside, their eyes fixed in accustomed misery on the ground stretching endlessly ahead of them.

"Who was that fellow?" Henry spoke first, his eyes on the retreating form of the big knight.

"Mandeville. Sir Humphrey Mandeville. A jackass. He's Norman English and a lout, like most of his ilk. Ignorant and lacking in the basics of civility. Born over there, of course. He hasn't been here three months, but believes himself superior to all of us."

"Is he *your* superior?"

Sir Francis barked a laugh. "Not in *any* respect, although I'm sure he dreams of it. But what of you, buried here in obscurity? How long have you been here? You look fine."

"I am now. Thriving, Francis. Who's in the carriages?"

Sir Francis smiled, deprived of any need to answer, for the lead carriage had been drawing level with them as they spoke and now the leather curtains were pulled aside and an imperious voice called out over the noises of hooves and iron-tired wheels.

"Henry? Henry *St. Clair*, is that *you*?"

"Great God in Heaven!" The words were out before he could check them, but they went unnoticed, since the apparition in the carriage was already leaning from the window, shouting to the driver to stop, so that once again the cavalcade came to a halt.

"Well, sir? Have you no greeting for me? Have you gone mute?"

"My lady ... Forgive me, my lady. I was distraught. The sight of you blinded me ... I had no idea ... I thought you were in England."

"Hah! In jail, you mean. Well, I was, for years. But now I am here, at home. Come now, salute me properly and ride with me. You and you, out. Find places in the other carriages. De Neuville, take Henry's horse. You, sir, come and pay me your respects, as true knight to his liege, then tell me what you have been doing all these years since last we met."

As her two obedient women spilled hastily from the open door, clutching helplessly at their disarrayed clothes, Sir Henry St. Clair walked forward open mouthed, still grappling with the suddenness of coming face to face again with the woman who had once been the most powerful force in Christendom, Eleanor, Duchess of Aquitaine, former Queen of France and later of England. He climbed into the carriage obediently and sat silent, gazing at the woman across from him and caught up, as he had always been, in admiration of her forthrightness and the uncompromising, direct force she brought to every conversation.

"There now," she said when he was seated. "That is much better, and you may close your mouth and collect yourself, Henry, for we have much to talk about and I require you to be alert and as intelligent as I recall you used to be ... speaking of which, you look remarkably fine for an old man. You were much like my Henry in those days. And you look much the same today. Clean living, I dare say, for I doubt your leopard could have changed his spots. As a young man, I remember, you were remarkably toothsome, if stiff and unyielding and greatly old-fashioned in your notions of fidelity. How is Amanda, by the way?"

St. Clair finally found his tongue. "She died, my lady, nigh on two years ago."

"Ah, I can see it in your face. You miss her yet."

"I do, my lady. Intolerably at times, but less now than before."

"I know. Henry is barely in his grave and yet I find that I am mourning him too, and painfully, despite having hated him so long. The old boar kept me locked up in a tower for sixteen years, can you believe that?" She snorted, something approaching a laugh. "Oh, they call it a castle, and it's rich enough to be called luxurious, but a prison is a prison." She hesitated, then grinned. "But then, to tell the truth, I gave him little option. I am really going to miss him. Without him, I shall have little to rail about in future."

"So he is truly dead then, my lady? We have heard rumors, all of them conflicting, so we did not know what to believe."

"Oh, he's dead. You may take my word on that. He died in Chinon, on the sixth day of July, and some say he was tortured to death by Richard. That is absolutely untrue, and you may trust me on that, too. Richard is no angel, and he was ever at odds with Henry, but my son as regicide and patricide? That is simply impossible. Believe me, as his mother."

"I do, my lady."

"I did not doubt you would. God's throat, Henry, it's good to see your honest face. You're frowning. Why? Speak out. You always did before, uncaring what I might think."

Emboldened, St. Clair shook his head. "Thinking about my people, my lady, no more. I have been out riding since before dawn, so they will be concerned when I do not return. It came to me that I should send word to them, tell them where I am. May I ask how far we are going?"

"Not far, but you have the right of things, as usual. Use the window. Call for de Neuville."

St. Clair wasted no time, pulling back the leather curtains and leaning out. De Neuville was riding behind the carriage and trotted forward when Henry caught his eye. Eleanor, who had been watching, leaned forward.

"Francis, how much farther will we ride?"

"Less than ten miles, my lady. The advance party should be there by now, setting up your tents."

"Send back word to Henry's people, telling them he is detained but will return soon. You may use my name." When Sir Francis had saluted and wheeled away, Eleanor settled herself on her seat. "There, are you at peace now?"

"I am, my lady ... and grateful. But had I known you were coming this way, you could have stayed on my lands."

She smiled, slowly. "And bankrupted your estate? Be thankful you knew nothing, my old friend. I have more than two hundred in my train. It would have caused you nothing but grief ... although frankly, had I remembered where you live, I would have used you shamelessly. Queens and royal people do that all the time." She paused, gazing at him with eyes that were no less spectacular than he remembered them from almost three decades earlier. "Well, I have told you how fine you look, so now it is your turn. How do *I* seem to you, approaching my dotage? Be careful."

Henry found it surprisingly easy to smile at this woman who, at her glittering court in Aquitaine decades earlier, had fostered the troubadours who now swarmed everywhere throughout the land, singing their songs of courtly love and spreading her personal beliefs in the duties of noble men and the supremacy of women in teaching them those duties. "Before I set eyes upon you this day, my lady, I would not have thought it possible that you could be more lovely than you were when first I met you ... But you are."

She stared at him hard, then sniffed. "You disappoint me, Henry. I am an old woman and that is grossest flattery. The Henry St. Clair I knew before would never stoop to flattery."

"Nor would he now, my lady. I speak the simple truth."

"Then you never did before. I never had an inkling that you thought me lovely."

His smile broadened. "Well, your husband, Henry, if you but recall, was notably jealous. Had he suspected that I saw in you anything other than my lady liege, he would have served me my own stones, sewed in their sack."

"Hah!" Eleanor's laugh was startling, full bodied and rich with earthy delight. "He would have had to vie with your Amanda. One ball apiece, they would have had."

"Aye, they would …" His own laugh subsided. "But that was long ago, when the world was young …"

"How old are you now, Henry?"

"I will be fifty within the year, my lady."

"Why, man, you're but a child. I am sixty and seven, and my Henry was fifty-six when he died." She paused. "Richard is to be King of England. Did you know that?"

"Aye, my lady, I know. I saw him recently. He stopped at my door on his way to Paris, bare two months ago."

"Did he, by God's holy blood?" Eleanor's face had hardened. "And why would he do that?"

Henry half shrugged, his face void of expression. "He had need of me, he said. I am to sail with him to Outremer, as Master-at-Arms."

"Master-at—" She checked herself. "Well, he is clearly not witless, for all his other faults. Misguided, certainly, but not witless." Her eyes transfixed him, no whit less hypnotic than they had been decades earlier, when she could beguile even a pope. "And like a fool, you intend to go. I can see it in your face. You are going with him. Why, in the name of everything that's sane? The Holy Land is a place fit only for *young* men, Henry—virile, muscular idiots full of the wildness and passion of their youth and their endless lust for guts and glory … idiots and lost souls. There is no life there for women, and even less for elders without crown or miter. Believe me, I was there and saw it for myself. Why, a' God's name, would you even think of such folly at your age?"

He raised one hand, then let it fall to his lap. "I have no choice, my lady. It is my duty, called upon by your son."

"Balls, Henry. God's entrails, man, you have spent a lifetime giving naught but the finest service to our house—to me and to Henry and to Richard himself. Enough, man. You have earned your right to die at home, in your bed. You could have declined with honor. Not even Richard would be so—" She stopped suddenly, her great eyes narrowing to slits. "No, there's more to it than that. My son manipulated you somehow. Coerced you. That is his way ... But what was his lever? What hold did he find over you, to bring you to this? Tell me."

It was a command, peremptory and not to be evaded. Henry sighed and looked away from her to where the slowly passing countryside was visible between the curtain halves, seeing the dust lie thick and heavy on the cow parsley that lined the road. "I have a son, my lady."

"I know. I remember him as a child. His name is ... André, is it not?"

He looked back into her eyes, impressed again by her seemingly limitless capacity to remember such details. "Aye, my lady, André."

"A man now ... and a weapon against you. Is that not so? Tell me."

He told her the entire tale, up to and including Richard's intervention and solution, and throughout the hour that took she sat silent, her eyes never leaving his as she absorbed every nuance and inflection of his voice. When he finally fell silent, she nodded and pursed her lips, thinner than he remembered them, and the gesture drew attention to the hollowed cheeks beneath the high cheekbones that had always defined her startling and still-present beauty. He waited, and watched her eyes grow softer.

"And that, of course, explains why you look so *rudely* healthy. You have been driving yourself these past two months to recapture your lost youth. Well, you have not suffered ill from it, old friend. So, what happened to these damnable priests? Did Richard hang them?"

"The priests were tried before the Archbishop of Tours and their guilt clearly established beyond doubt, although, lacking the authority and single-mindedness of your son in prosecuting them, that might not have come to pass so easily. They were then disowned by the Holy Church and bound over to the secular law of the Duchy of Aquitaine for execution."

"And in the meantime you and your son were bound to Richard by unbreakable ties of gratitude and fealty ..."

Henry St. Clair noticed the irony in her tone, but he paid it no attention. "Aye, my lady. By gratitude more than even fealty, if such a thing be possible."

"Hmm …" Eleanor shifted in her seat and then reached out and pulled aside the curtain on her left, and spoke as she gazed out at the long, slanting shadows thrown by the trees on the sloping hillside above them. "It is growing late, my friend. We should be stopping soon, but it may be too late by then for you to ride back home alone. You must dine with us and return in the morning. In the meantime, come what may, I have a thought for you to dwell upon, Henry, and it is this: there has never been a tie, of any kind, that is unbreakable, given sufficient will, and power."

She turned her eyes back on him again. "Absolve yourself of any guilt you feel, even be it born of gratitude. I will talk to Richard about this. I will not tolerate this idea of forcing you to sail to Outremer. It is a nonsense. Besides, you know my son almost as well as I do. He was yours to mold for years. He is a creature of great passions and enthusiasms, ungovernable and unpredictable to all save me, it seems."

Sir Henry spread his hands apologetically. "My gratitude for your concern, my lady, but if it please you, I have no wish to be excused from this duty. I would far rather travel with my son to Outremer than bide alone here and fret for him. He is all I have left of family in this world, and life without him holds little attraction for me now that I am growing old. I might be a fool, as you suggest, but I would rather be an old fool near my son than be a lonely old hermit awaiting death here without him."

Eleanor gazed at him for long moments, then nodded her head slowly. "So be it, my lord St. Clair. I will say no more on it. We are both of us too old and gray to quarrel over the manner of our deaths. The Reaper will find us wherever we may be …" She nibbled her upper lip between her teeth in a mannerism he had long forgotten, and then she added, "You know why Richard was so intent upon enrolling you, don't you?"

When St. Clair shook his head in honest ignorance, she sniffed. "Well then you should. And take note, if it please you, that I said he *was* intent on it—knowing my son as I do, it would not astonish me at all to learn that he has either forgotten all about involving you or has changed his mind since then. A move's afoot in England to have him take the Marshal of England, William Marshall, into his train as Master-at-Arms, but Richard will have none of it, and I would be surprised were it otherwise. Marshall was Henry's man, dyed in the wool, as fierce and lifelong-loyal as a hunting hound. In Richard's eyes, Marshall will always represent Henry himself. And, truth be said, I cannot find it in my heart to fault my son for that."

She paused. "Besides, Marshall is all for England, first, foremost, and above all else. Richard, on the other hand, has more to govern. England is but a by-blow of his empire, and a backward one at that. God's throat, he can barely speak the language that they growl over there."

She stopped again, mulling her next words. "I suppose you know about Alaïs?" She read the answer in his face and grunted. "Aye, of course you do. You would need to be both blind and deaf not to know of it. It was inevitable, given what was involved, but yet I find myself feeling sympathy for the poor creature, goose though she be, for none of what happened to her lay in her control. She has been used and abused her whole life long and she never had sufficient backbone to brace herself for any of it. Myself, I would have killed someone, years ago, had any man tried to do the half to me of what was done to her. But Alaïs is not me, and now she is home in France again, disgraced, and unlikely to find another husband soon ... What is it?"

"What is what, my lady?"

"Whatever is in your mind. You have a witless, gaping look about you, so spit out your thoughts and we will talk about them."

Henry gestured mildly with one hand. "Merely surprise, my lady. I hear or see no bitterness or hatred in you when you speak of her."

A brittle smile quirked one corner of Eleanor's mouth. "Nor should you, for I harbor none against her. Did you not hear me when I said she has been used and abused her whole life? I have bitterness aplenty in me, Henry, make no mistake in that, but none of it is wasted on Alaïs."

"But ... she stole your husband."

"Stole? *Stole* Henry Plantagenet?" Her smile spread wider but grew no warmer. "Bethink yourself, my lord St. Clair, and remember the man of whom we speak. There never was a woman born who could steal Henry Plantagenet or bend him to her will for longer than it took for him to mount her, and I include myself in that. Henry was a taker in all things carnal. He saw, he desired, he took. Oh, I was his match for many years, but as soon as my looks began to change and I began to age, he looked elsewhere. And the old goat was lusty till the day he died.

"No, Alaïs Capet did not steal my husband. Far from it. She was but one of a long line of vessels for his convenience, used and discarded when the next in line stepped forth to catch his eye. But Henry kept Alaïs closer than all the rest, because of the Vexin. Had he discarded her, it would have cost him the Vexin or, at very least, a long and brutal war to keep it. And in the end, he lost it anyway, before he died. But Alaïs was no thief. And besides, by the time Henry first set hands on her, he had already put me away. I had been locked up for years by then, because he said he couldn't trust me to run free without fomenting plots against him with my sons. He was right, too. I can see that now. But hate Alaïs? Might as well hate the north wind for bringing down the snow as blame that child for what befell her.

"But her misfortune forced Richard's hand to what he did, once he was named as Henry's heir. He could hardly take Alaïs as his queen when all the world knows she spent most of her betrothal period sleeping with his father. The Church in England was scandalized and made no bones about it. They howled anathema at the very idea of such a marriage, and forbade Richard to proceed with it, under pain of excommunication. And so Richard's hand was forced. He sent her home to her brother, Philip, as was only to be expected."

"To be expected, perhaps, my lady, but hardly to be welcomed by her family. King Philip must have been beside himself when he learned of it."

"Nonsense. The only thing Philip might have been beside was his bedmate of whatever day it was when the tidings reached him. Philip cares nothing for Alaïs, Henry. He never did, from the day she was born. Women have no place at all in his affections. All he cared about was regaining the Vexin, and now that he has it safe, he will use his wronged sister as a weapon against Richard for whatever advantage he can gain. That is the total of his regard for her—she is a tool for negotiations."

"That is … inconceivable." His voice had fallen on the last word, hushed with disbelief, but Eleanor negated his awe with a tightly controlled flick of one finger.

"Nonsense, far from it. It might be unnatural, but then, Philip Capet can hardly be called a template for Nature's perfection."

"Aye, I suppose that is true. But what of you, my lady? Have you been to Paris?"

"God's throat, no! I have been in Rouen, about my own affairs, and now I am traveling home, for the first time in far too many years. I shall stay there for a while, I think, at least until Richard has been crowned in England."

"Forgive me, my lady, but will you not go to England to witness your son's coronation?"

She gave him a wintry little smile. "Absolutely not. Richard is more than capable of having himself crowned, and the last thing I need is to be there to witness it. That will all proceed perfectly well and naturally, and in the meantime I will take myself southward, across the Pyrenees to Navarre." She saw the incomprehension in his eyes and added, "To *Navarre*, Henry … the kingdom in northern Iberia. There to find a queen for England."

"A *queen*, my lady?"

She laughed outright. "Aye, a queen. My son is to be King of England and he needs a queen. *England* needs a queen. And I have found one in Navarre. In truth, Richard himself found her, three years ago. He met her at her father's court and wrote to me about her then. Her name is Berengaria, daughter of King Sancho, and now that Richard is no longer betrothed, I intend to generate a marriage. Sancho should prove to be a staunch ally in this coming war, accustomed as he is to fighting off the Moors who threaten him down there in his Iberian wilderness, and I feel confident he can be persuaded to dower his daughter amply for her role as queen consort. And be assured, Richard and England will make good use of whatever he provides for their Holy War."

"Berengaria. That is a beautiful name. But *King* Sancho? I have heard, it seems to me, of a *Prince* Sancho …"

Eleanor's eyes sought his, narrowing intently, but she detected no awareness of her son's rumored misconduct with the young Prince of Navarre. "The Prince is Berengaria's brother. When his father dies, he will become the seventh king of that name. For now, he is a nonentity, but I have great hopes for his sister. I have not met her yet, but by all accounts, including my son's own, she is a gentle, biddable creature … perhaps not greatly beautiful as we envision beauty, but regal nonetheless. So, if I can arrange the match, I will bring her to Richard before he leaves for Outremer."

The carriage slowed and came to a swaying halt as she spoke, and a babble of voices sprang up outside, with orders and instructions being shouted on all sides. Eleanor listened for a moment, then began to gather up the few belongings scattered on either side of her as St. Clair pulled aside the curtains and peered out into the gathering dusk.

"We have arrived, obviously."

The words had barely left her mouth when de Neuville rode up and bent forward in his saddle. "A few moments more, my lady, and you will be able to alight. Everything appears to be prepared, and by the smell of things, the cooks have done well. Rest you there for a few more moments, if you will, until your carriage can pull forward safely to your tent. A hundred paces, even less, and you will be there." He glanced at St. Clair. "Sir Henry, I have your mount secure. My groom will care for it tonight with my own." He saluted Eleanor and swung his horse away, and the Duchess smiled at St. Clair.

"Well, old friend, our visit is at an end—the most enjoyable part of it, at least—for when that door opens next, I must go back to being Eleanor of Aquitaine, with all the nonsense that attends upon being a Duchess restored to her holdings." She reached across spontaneously and gripped him by the wrist. "It has been *so* wonderful to see you,

Henry, and to spend this time with you. Men of your stamp are few and far between in my life nowadays. May God, if He is up there at all, bless you and your son in your future adventures, and may He forgive me for these next words. Put not your faith in princes. I know not who first said that, but he had the truth upon him when he did. Be careful of my son. I love him despite all he is in many ways, but I warn you as an old and trusted friend: do all you can for him but be you not too trusting, for he is governed by factors you cannot control, and guided by lights you would never wish to see or understand." She drew her head back, her eyes narrowing, her fingers still gripping his wrist tightly. "I tell you that out of love, Henry—a woman's love for an admirable man overcoming a mother's love for a wayward son— but if you ever say a word of it to anyone, I shall deny I said it and wreak official retribution on you in return. You hear me?"

"I do, my lady, and I shall heed your warning, unspoken though it was."

The carriage began to move again, lurching off the road and into the crowded meadow where the tents had been set up. Eleanor began to gather her skirts about her with one hand, bracing herself against the motion of the vehicle with the other by clinging to a braided silken cord handle on the wall by the door, until they came to a halt again.

"God's throat, I wish you well, my friend. Now, when the brouhaha begins, get you away from here and find Brodo, my steward. Tell him I sent you and he is to feed you well and find you some place suitable to sleep. I may not have the time to speak to you again and I know you will have no wish to waste your time among the fawning, squawking fowl that flock about me every- where I go. Eat well, sleep well, then ride home early and continue your preparations to do your duty by my son. And so farewell."

The carriage door swung open, and Sir Henry went out first into the clustering crowd, turning to hand the Duchess down safely. He bent over her hand and pressed it to his lips, and she smiled, then tapped him on the crown with one finger of her other hand before stepping past him to be engulfed by the multitude of her admirers.

FOUR

Henry St. Clair discovered, very rapidly, just how great a sacrifice he had made for his temperamental liege, Richard Plantagenet. Within days of his encounter with Duchess Eleanor, he found himself being inundated with new responsibilities, tasks, and activities springing from his appointment as Master-at-Arms, and soon he barely had time to notice how quickly the days and weeks were passing. It all culminated a month later, when he received a summons to join Richard in England immediately, and from that moment onward, he could not call his life his own.

"How soon is immediately?" Henry had barely glanced at the writing on the scroll that he had opened mere moments earlier, but that glance had taken in the peremptory instruction.

The Hospitaller knight who had delivered the summons shrugged his wide shoulders and lowered his eyes to the scroll Henry was holding, but he said nothing and his face remained expressionless. Sir Henry looked back down at the scroll.

"I see. It's all in here, eh? Well, you had better sit down while I read it. Have you eaten today? No, probably not ..." Henry turned to where Ector stood by the door, watching and awaiting instructions. "Bring food and drink for Sir ..." He turned back to the other man. "Do you have a name, Master Hospitaller, or are you merely a grim and spectral presence? Speak up, sir."

"My name is Gautier, Sir Henry. Gautier de Montdidier."

"Montdidier, you say? Then we should know each other." Henry moved to sit in a chair by the fireplace, waving to the other man to sit across from him. "An ancestor of yours and one of mine were among the founding members of the Temple. Did you know that?"

"I did."

"Then why do you wear the black mantle of the Hospital rather than the white of the Temple?"

Montdidier's lip curled in a smile, and he dipped his head slightly to one side. "Mayhap I prefer it that way, but in truth I have followed the Rule of Blessed Benedict since I was a stripling boy. I was orphaned at birth and raised in a monastery in England, so when I came of age to be a knight—my father had been one, killed in battle before I was born—it was but natural that I should join the Knights of the Hospital."

"Aye, I suppose it would have been ... Ector, food and drink for Sir Gautier de Montdidier, and see to it that his men are fed, too. How many did you bring with you, sir, and where are they now?"

"Six men, Sir Henry, and they are all in your courtyard, awaiting word from me on where they should go next."

"Aye, well, they may stay here for the night, but that will depend upon just how 'immediately' I am to leave, so permit me to read this missive of yours, and I will be able to give you a response."

In truth, Sir Henry had been ready for weeks, having put all his arrangements in place to ensure that his estates and lands would be cared for in his absence, presided over by a man Henry had known and trusted for years, the eldest brother of his dead wife. But the instructions in Richard's letter were succinct and to the point. Henry was required to make his way to England as soon as might be, in the company of Sir Gautier de Montdidier, there to take up his duties as Master-at-Arms *to Aquitaine*.

The distinction did not escape him, and it was an interesting one. There had been no mention of Aquitaine in his first meeting with Richard. The position he had been ordered to take up then had been Master-at-Arms to Richard, no more and no less. It was a small point, of no real consequence since Richard, as Duke, *was* Aquitaine, but Henry found its presence there in Richard's letter amusing. He surmised that the political situation in England had changed since Richard's return, and probably radically. But he was far from unhappy with the new development. He would feel much more comfortable as Master-at-Arms to Aquitaine, a position he had held and enjoyed for years in the service of the Duchess, than he would as Master-at-Arms to an army of Englishmen, with their guttural morass of a language.

There was no mention of André in the letter, but Henry had expected none. André had seldom been at home since first meeting the knight de Sablé, and he seemed to be enthusiastically caught up in preparations required for his upcoming admission to the ranks of the Temple Knights. Henry knew he would meet his son again in England before they set sail, and he was content with that, knowing the young man to be safe and well. He released the end of the scroll, allowing it to spring back into its cylindrical shape, then held it between the fingertips of both hands as he looked over to de Montdidier.

"Why you, Sir Gautier? Why did Richard send *you* to bring me to England, with but six men? Did he think me incapable of traveling alone?"

"I doubt that, Sir Henry. I believe it was the King's wish that you and I spend some time together, so that we could converse on the journey."

"Converse about what? I have no wish to demean or to insult you, Master Montdidier, but I doubt that you and I have anything in common. The difference in our ages alone would make sure of that."

"Perhaps because he thinks you might learn something from what I have to say. I am newly come from Outremer and I was wounded in the debacle of Hattin. I know that the King has assigned to you the task of finding some new means of confronting and defeating Saladin's armies. He believes I may be able to assist you with that."

Henry looked at the Hospitaller now with far more respect. "You may indeed. And God in His Heaven knows I require all the assistance He can send me. But how came you to survive Hattin that day? I have been told that Saladin murdered every captured member of the military orders, both Templars and Hospitallers, after the fight."

"He did. I watched them die and expected to die myself, for I was badly wounded. But I lived through the day, lying among the dead without being discovered, and I managed to crawl away into hiding after darkness fell. I had an arrow in my groin and was too badly wounded to have any hope of escaping, so I stripped off my surcoat, having no wish to be recognized as a Hospitaller, and managed to don a plain brown surcoat that I stripped from a dead man. I then surrendered myself the following morning. They took me captive, tended to my wound, treated me humanely, and eventually offered me for ransom with four other knights, none of whom were of the military orders. I was fortunate."

The doors opened and Ector entered, followed by two servants carrying food and wine on trays. They laid the contents of their trays on one of the tables and then left without having looked at either knight. St. Clair looked at the food, and then at Montdidier.

"Well, Master Montdidier, the King was right. I do wish to speak with you, at length. You are the first person I have met who was actually there that day at Hattin." He stood up and waved towards the table. "Eat, and when you have finished Ector will show you to a sleeping chamber, where you may rest for a few hours. I will dismiss your men to my barracks building as I leave, and I will see you later, but I have things I must do now. We will leave at dawn the day after tomorrow. In the meantime, my home is yours." He dipped his head in a salute and went out, closing the doors behind him and leaving the Hospitaller to his food and drink. A moment later, he was back.

"How did you come here, Sir Gautier? By what route?"

The other swallowed a mouthful of food. "From the west. Landed at La Rochelle, then followed the road northeastward through Niort, to Poitiers, and then northwestwards to here."

St. Clair nodded. "That's the best route. Far shorter than traveling northwest to Nantes and Saint-Nazaire. How long did it take you?"

"From La Rochelle to here? Five days ... today's the sixth. We traveled twenty miles each day, sunrise to sunset."

"Hmm. Well, we will need more time than that, returning. I'm taking four men with me, and a cart for my belongings, which means we will have to travel at the speed of the cart. We'll be fortunate to make fifteen miles a day."

"So, seven days."

"Aye, but no more than that. How long, think you, will we have to wait for a ship?"

"No time at all. We already have one awaiting us—the ship that brought me over here. It will remain there in La Rochelle for fourteen more days, then sail without us if we have not yet arrived. We would be presumed dead by then."

"I see. Then we had best make haste, and do what we can to remain alive." St. Clair nodded, as if agreeing with his own comment, then left again.

THE WIND HAD DIED SUDDENLY about half an hour earlier, and now Henry St. Clair stood on the stern platform of the ship bearing him and his party from La Rochelle to England, leaning out over the starboard rail and peering down into the waters below. He stood with his legs spread, his knees flexing against the erratic, unpredictable movements of the ship's deck, and his right elbow hooked around a rope that stretched up like an iron bar into the mass of rigging above his head. He was untroubled by the pitching, rolling motion of the deck beneath his feet, leaning forward in fascination, craning his neck as he watched the heaving water surging beneath him. At one moment it would seem close enough for him to reach down and touch the surface, and then within the space of a heartbeat it would swoop away and down, baring the entire side of the ship until the stern rose clear of the water. It would hang there for long moments, before the vessel tipped forward and plunged down the following slope of the wave, smashing prow first into the trough at the bottom and sending vast sheets of water sweeping backward over the deck to saturate everything before it drained away.

In the waist of the ship, he knew, the crew were working like madmen, trying to throw the trapped seawater out of the cargo hold faster than it came in, but conditions now were nowhere near as dangerous as they had been even an hour earlier. Then, with a gale howling over and around them, whipping spray and spume from the surface into an impenetrable fog, it would not have been possible for him to stand where he stood now. The waves, while still enormous, were smooth, their sides marked with patches of foam that rose and fell placidly as the swelling waters passed beneath them.

"It's dying down. For a time back there, I thought we would be lost."

Montdidier came to stand beside him, balanced against the motion of the ship as he stretched out one hand to grasp a taut rope. Behind him, Henry noted, visibility had improved considerably, but the low, leaden skies out there still masked the horizon, the line of sea and sky lost in dismal, hazy distance.

"Aye, it appears to be over, and it was bad while it lasted. I confess that for a while there *I* thought we were all going to die, too." He looked around the deck area and smiled a tight little smile. "But I had to come up to the platform here to safeguard my stomach. The noise and the stench of vomit down below were overwhelming. Now it appears that you and I are the only two of our party who are not retching and groaning, *hoping* to die." He released his hold on the rope and sat down with his back resting against the ship's side. "Come and sit here beside me. It's wet and unpleasant, but so is all the world at this point. Our last conversation was interrupted by the storm, and just as it was growing interesting."

Montdidier released his handhold and lowered himself carefully to sit shoulder to shoulder with St. Clair as the older man placed his hands flat on the deck and, with a deep grunt, hitched himself into a more comfortable position.

"Ahh," he muttered, "that is ... much better. These old bones of mine lack padding nowadays. The discomfort, however, is a small price to pay for being able to sit in the open air without being sick like everyone else. Are we still on course, think you? I saw no sign of land."

"No, nor did I, so I spoke to the captain. He told me we have been blown westward, into the Atlantic, but that we will head straight north under oars, now that the wind has died, and will soon find land again. After that, we will sail northwest again until we round the cape of Brittany, and then it will be north by east until we reach Cherbourg. From there we may see the coast of England, north of us. I asked how long that would take, but all I got in response was a shrug. It depends on winds and weather, he said, so it could take anywhere from seven days to thrice that long. In the meantime, we will stop in at Brest for fresh provisions, then make our way to Cherbourg, and from there it is a single day's sail to England."

"In other words, we must resign ourselves to whatever happens and be patient." St. Clair shivered, and pulled his wet cloak around him. "Well, we may be fortunate, I think, that we have so much to talk about, you and I." Another shiver shook his frame, and suddenly he was shaking as though palsied, aware that if he did not rid himself of his soaked clothing he would run the risk of falling sick. The younger men around him might be able to make light of chilled physical hardships, but he himself was much too old to tolerate such abuse. He pulled himself to his feet with some difficulty, feeling the stiffness that was already invading his bones, and bracing himself with one hand on Montdidier's shoulder.

"This is madness," he said. "I have clean, dry clothing in my sleeping space below and I intend to strip off these sodden rags and dress myself in something fresh and warm. You should do the same. Here, take my hand."

The Hospitaller took Henry's hand and rose easily to his feet. "I agree. I feel as though I have been wet and cold all my life, even though I know it has only been since last night." He paused. "But if you and I should come to know each other better in the time ahead, remind me regularly, if you will, that I have no desire ever to spend another night in the hold of a pitch-dark ship in the middle of a howling storm at sea. So let us go and dry ourselves as well as we may, and I will meet you here again within the half hour."

It was closer to an hour later when St. Clair finally emerged onto the deck to find the Hospitaller waiting for him. But he was dry and warm for the first time in many hours, and the sights that greeted him made him feel better than he had in days. The heavy cloud cover had broken up while he was below and the sun was shining now through a widening gap, and he noticed that the crew had manned the oars and were making headway against the visibly smaller waves. He also noted gratefully that the deck beneath his feet was beginning to dry.

No one paid the two knights any attention as they crossed in front of the burly crewman who manned the tiller and stood staring straight ahead towards the prow. They seated themselves near him, side by side on two large bundles of what looked like netting, and far enough removed from the helmsman that they could speak without being overheard. For a short time after that, they talked of generalities, but Henry was anxious to talk more of specifics and soon went to the heart of things.

"The last thing you said to me yesterday, just before the storm broke and we had to scramble for shelter, was that the kings who will lead us to the Holy Land need to absorb some facts that will stick in their craws. I have been wondering ever since. What did you mean?"

Montdidier's face grew somber. "I meant exactly what I said. The army being assembled now, both in Britain and in France, is no army at all. It is a collection of fragments—splintered factions and coteries—each of them with leaders and commanders who have agendas and ambitions of their own and an eye to their own advantage ahead of everyone else's. But all of them, kings, princes, dukes, counts, and anything else that's there, *all* of them need to be convinced somehow, and forced if necessary, into accepting the realities of where they will be going and what awaits them there. I have spoken with most of them and told them what I believe, what I know and have witnessed with my own eyes, but among all of them, only Richard Plantagenet deigned to heed what I said. The others had no wish to hear. They have their own beliefs, their own deluded convictions."

When the Hospitaller said no more, St. Clair prompted, "And those convictions are ... what? I think I could guess, but tell me anyway. What do they believe?"

"Stupidities." Montdidier dropped his hand to his belt and drew out a dagger with a long, narrow blade. He shifted his grip from hilt to blade and began to scrape the underside of his fingernails with the point.

"And? What are these stupidities?"

Montdidier was glowering, but then he straightened his back abruptly, sucked in a great breath and expelled it loudly, ridding himself of his frowning anger as quickly and as easily as another man might shed a cloak. "Why am I being angry at you, can you explain that to me? You are not involved in this at all … Not yet, at least. But you will be, believe me." He slipped the knife back into its sheath and crossed his arms on his chest. "They all believe that this new war, like all the other conflicts they have known, will be won by mounted knights."

"And you would have them believe otherwise."

"Of course I would, because I want them to destroy the Muslim armies and survive. They *must* be made to see how wrong they are— to change not only their minds but their methods and their fighting tactics. If they do not, they will all die quickly and uselessly, because everything has changed now. All the so-called wars they talk about, wars won by mounted knights, have been waged here in Christendom, and they have all been piddling little affairs, petty, parochial squabbles between greedy barons and whatever enemies they chose to confront at any time."

He turned to look St. Clair directly in the eye. "There has never *been* a war like the war going on today in Palestine, against the Muslim, against Saladin. Believe me in that, Sir Henry. That war is being fought in a different world, far from everything we know in Christendom, and the rules of warfare that we learned and know have all been changed. You have never been in Outremer, have you?"

"No, I have not. My duty to Duchess Eleanor kept me here at home when I might have gone, and I never had another opportunity to go, until now."

"Aye, that is what I thought … Well, believe me when I tell you that Outremer is completely unlike the world you know. You called it the Holy Land a while ago, but God Himself knows there's nothing holy about the place. It is a world the like of which these people who see themselves today as leaders will never understand and cannot begin to imagine. They are all too young to remember the lessons of the first and second expeditions we sent out, and too ignorant to concern themselves with the realities of the land and the climate in which they are destined to fight. Most of it is desert, as hostile and brutal as the people who live in it, and unimaginably dangerous to newcomers. It is a damnable place, filled with terrors and cataclysms, where sandstorms can spring up without warning and bury entire villages—entire *armies*, at times—storms so violent that the blowing sand will strip exposed flesh from a living man's bones.

"But even worse than any of those things, it is a place filled with zealots—fierce, unforgiving warriors who live and breathe the creed of their own god and his Prophet, Muhammad, and who are glad and willing to die in his service. These Muslim warriors—Saracens, Mussulmen, Arabs, Bedouin, call them what you will—can outfight our best, Henry, much as we might wish to deny it. And they are sufficient in numbers to outface a Frankish army three thousand strong, fielding ten men for every one of ours, and to destroy it, leaving but one man in every score alive."

There was a long silence as St. Clair thought about what the Hospitaller had said, and after a time, he held up one hand in supplication. "I do not disbelieve you, for I have heard similar reports from others. But despite all of that, and all the logic and scrutiny brought to it, these numbers that you cite defy belief. Nineteen men killed out of every twenty? How could *any* army, no matter how well trained or zealous, achieve such slaughter?"

"Missiles." The word was so gruffly uttered that St. Clair was not sure what the other man had said.

"I think I misheard you. Did you say *missiles*?"

Montdidier looked at him again, clear eyed and cogent. "Aye, that's what I said. Missiles ... arrows, if you're looking for precision."

"Ah, arrows. Arrows shot from bows."

Montdidier's face tightened with anger. "Aye, that's right. *Arrows*—projectiles shot from bows. They slaughtered us with arrows. They rained arrows upon us, like hailstones, constantly and from all sides at once. And then, at night, they shot our horses, knowing an armored knight is helpless when forced to fight on foot, in sand. Arrows, Master St. Clair. They used them to demoralize us, to unnerve and frighten us and ultimately to destroy us, forcing us to make desperate moves that we would not otherwise have undertaken. And we were helpless against them."

"I know, and I am not mocking you. I have heard something of this before. I was merely thinking yet again on the folly of the papal ban on bows in Christendom. It cost us dearly at Hattin. But yet … surely, once an arrow has been loosed, it is lost? It cannot be used again. And yet you are describing a *prodigious* number of arrows. There must be *some* exaggeration there."

"Aye, so it must seem to anyone who was not there. You are not the first to think that and question me. But I saw it with my own eyes." He rose to his feet in one fluid motion and moved to the side of the ship, where he laid both hands on the rail and stood gazing out at the water until St. Clair thought he must have said all he wished to and would say no more. The waves had continued to dwindle in size since the wind had died so that the ship was now moving far more smoothly, almost gently, and the sky overhead had become almost cloudless, the late-afternoon sun well down the slope towards the western horizon that was now clearly visible beyond Montdidier. But Montdidier turned again to face St. Clair, leaning back against the ship's side, his elbows resting on the rail behind him.

"Have you ever seen a camel, Sir Henry?"

Henry nodded. "Aye, both kinds—one hump and two—and several times. There is a fellow who brings a collection of strange and wild animals to Poitiers each year, to the Midsummer festival. People come in throngs and pay well to marvel at his beasts."

"So you understand that the camel is a beast of burden, very large, immensely strong and capable of carrying great weights for extended lengths of time, while an arrow is practically weightless.

Even a quiver filled with arrows—a score or more—weighs next to nothing compared to a sword or an axe. So let me ask you this: how many arrows, carefully packed and bound in bundles, do you think a fully laden camel might be able to carry?"

St. Clair puffed out a breath. "I have no idea, but from the way you ask I can surmise that the number would probably be greater than any I might suggest."

"Much greater. The sole limitation that would apply to such a load is the physical bulk of the bundles of arrows. Now imagine a number of those, all neatly tied up, with five and twenty arrows in each bundle. Each bundle would be approximately the thickness of a double fist." He illustrated what he meant by placing his clenched fists together, thumb to thumb. "Now imagine crates made out of lath and wire—cages, each as wide as an arrow's length, and sufficiently long and deep to hold ten bundles side by side, stacked four layers deep. Each crate, a light but strong cage, would hold one thousand arrows, and it would be no great feat of engineering to bind six such crates together on each side of a camel. That represents twelve *thousand* arrows, carried by just one beast."

St. Clair shrugged, smiling and spreading his palms. "An interesting premise, I will grant you that," he said quietly. "Given, of course, that one could even *find* twelve thousand arrows."

"Find them? Sir Henry, the army that defeated us at Hattin was made up almost entirely of bowmen—*mounted* bowmen, on horses much smaller than ours, wiry and spare, faster and much more agile. Each bowman carried his own arrows into the campaign, three or four quivers full at least. But Saladin had already thought beyond such things and seen what he must do. Months before he assembled his army, summoning them from Egypt and from Syria, from Asia Minor and all the other fiefs that he commands, he sent out the word for arrows to be made in numbers that had never been seen before, and for all of them to be shipped to the places where the different contingents of his armies would assemble."

"And he loaded them all onto a camel, is that what you were going to say?"

"No, Sir Henry, it is not. That would amount to only twelve thousand arrows. By the time he moved against us, coming to lay siege to Tiberias, Saladin had seventy—*seventy*—camels laden with extra arrows in his baggage train. I know not how many arrows they had in total, but when the slaughter at Hattin was over, the Muslims were boasting among themselves that they had transformed the infidel pigs from knights and soldiers into hedgehogs. I have never seen anything to equal the storm of arrows that were shot at us that day."

"Seventy camel loads … How do you know that?"

"I was their prisoner, and I speak their language. I heard them talking about it afterwards, and about the difficulties they had had in collecting the spent arrows after the battle."

St. Clair now felt distinctly ill at ease. "Wait now, because I am not sure I understand what you have said here. Are you telling me that the Christian army at Hattin was destroyed from a distance, without ever engaging the enemy? If so, it goes against everything else I have heard about the battle. What about the feats of the individual knights, and the charge of the Templars?"

"What charge?" Montdidier scoffed. "The Templars made no heroic charge at Hattin. Trying to close with the enemy was like trying to capture smoke. They outnumbered us hugely, and rode in circles around us, and every time we tried to charge them and engage them, their formations would disintegrate and scatter as we drew near. They would move away to a safe distance, permitting us to ride through and then closing in behind us, cutting us off from our own forces and exposing our flanks to their bowmen. The Temple Knights held the rearguard. They recognized what was happening, after several attempts to engage, and to their credit, they fell back to reinforce the King's encampment on the knoll above the battle. But the King's people had pitched their tents between the King's main force and the Templars, so that the knights were forced to ride around and between them, being shot from behind as they jostled one another, trying to find a way through the lines of tents and the thousands of guy ropes that confounded their horses.

"No solid portion of our army even came close to a hand-to-hand encounter with the enemy that day. Some individuals did, but they were few against hordes and they were swiftly slaughtered. Our infantry, almost twelve thousand strong, were allowed to march right through the Muslim ranks. It was the same technique—they simply moved aside and let our men pass through without a fight, and then they were followed and picked off piecemeal from both sides as they made their way down towards the lake. None of them survived.

"And that, for all intents and purposes, is the story of Hattin: we sat helpless on our horses and were shot down. We were outmaneuvered, outmanned, and out-planned, and our leadership was impotent in the face of the enemy's superior ability. It was not a glorious occasion for Christendom." He turned his face away, then hawked and spat, disgust and outrage radiating from him almost visibly. "*Leadership*, I called it. Hah! May God forgive me, but I have seen more leadership among a pack of rats than I saw that day at Hattin. Arrogance, stupidity, ignorance, and vaunting pride I saw aplenty, but leadership, ability, or inspiring behavior? God help us all next time, if we are foolish enough to go at all."

"Are you implying that we might see the same thing happen again, next time?"

Montdidier looked at him with raised eyebrows. "Do you doubt it? What has changed, between then and now? The arrogant old warhorses like de Ridefort are gone, but we've replaced them with even lesser fools. I swear to you, Master St. Clair, if we ride into battle in the same fashion in this coming war, arrogant in our notions of superiority, Saladin will meet us with exactly the same tactics and achieve precisely the same effect. That is why the kings must be made to see that change is needed."

St. Clair opened his mouth to speak, but closed it again, and the Hospital Knight waited.

"Is—?" Henry coughed to clear his throat. "There is a question I must ask, purely for my own peace of mind. Are there ... Is there any possibility that the defeat at Hattin was merely an accident of war? Might it have turned out differently had the armies met in another place, on another day?"

The other's headshake was terse and definite. "I doubt it. There might have been some minor differences in the way the fight was fought, but the outcome would have been the same. On the day after the battle, July the fifth, when the Saracen physicians were tending to my wounds, Tiberias, which had been under siege, surrendered—unsurprising, you might say, since the citizens had watched the slaughter from their walls the previous day—but five days later, on the tenth day of the month, Acre fell. And then, one after the other in rapid succession, Saladin's army captured Nablus, Jaffa, Toron, Sidon, Beirut, and Ascalon. All heavily fortified towns. After that, apart from a few scattered castles that still held out in remote spots, only the port of Tyre and the city of Jerusalem remained in Christian hands. And then Jerusalem went down to Saladin in September. None of those events occurred by accident."

"Aye …" St. Clair rose to his feet and rubbed his eyes with the heels of his hands. Sir Gautier simply waited, giving him time to think, and at last St. Clair said, "I am no king. I will, however, stand in your support of your views from this time on." He then crossed the deck to the starboard rail, where he stood with his back to Montdidier, staring quietly out at the distant horizon.

The Hospitaller hovered where he was for a moment, looking at St. Clair's back and the set of his shoulders, then walked away.

"GOD'S WOUNDS, Henry, tell me straight! If I wanted veiled hints and mysteries I'd call in a priest. You are my Master-at-Arms, so what I require from you is straight talk, with no muttered nonsense. You've seen this morning how we intend to transport our army to Outremer, but to this point you have said nothing, not a single word, about how we are to conduct ourselves when we finally arrive there and confront Saladin and his Mussulmen. How are we to approach this task, to come at them anew without suffering the same fate as Guy de Lusignan and the army of the Kingdom of Jerusalem? Damnation, man, I need guidance in this, before I speak to the others. Philip of France will scream outrage if he even begins to suspect that I have not yet found an answer to that."

Richard was right, of course. As Duke of Aquitaine, King of England, and co-leader of the new expedition to win back the Holy Land, Richard expected and needed some straightforward, unequivocal advice from his recently appointed Master-at-Arms. More accurately, he needed to know exactly what original and innovative tactics St. Clair was developing in order to offer his armies some hope of victory against Saladin's hordes. Henry had been riding around with his Duke for three days now, waiting for an opportunity to present his findings and proposals without the threat of being interrupted. Richard was increasingly preoccupied with the preliminary logistical arrangements for the sea voyage to Outremer. The great fleet would not begin to assemble for at least another two months, but the Fleet Master, Robert de Sablé, had already been planning with his quartermasters and subordinates for months, and shipping and supplies were being assembled in more than a score of major ports. That morning, Henry and Richard had ridden together, inspecting troops and reviewing plans. The time had passed quickly, and their work had been productive, with Richard seizing the opportunity to propose several pragmatic suggestions to de Sablé regarding the allocation of space aboard ships for horses, saddlery, and weapons, including their massive siege engines, broken down to be shipped piecemeal.

"Well, sir? Have you an answer for me?"

Seeing his opportunity arise at last, St. Clair spoke up quickly. "Aye, my liege, I have an answer. But I will need at least a full hour of your time to explain my thinking in this matter, and after that you yourself will probably wish to spend a day or two examining the idea."

They had just left the southern English coastal town of Plymouth, one of the main assembly ports for the King's Fleet, and were riding through a spacious meadow dominated by solitary trees, mature oak, elm, and beech, with a wide and pleasant stream meandering among them. Richard looked about him and tugged at his horse's reins, making the animal veer right, towards the point where the stream came closest to them.

"Come, then, if it is going to need a full day of thought from me, we will take the time now to sit alone over there on the bank of the stream and talk about it." He looked over his shoulder to where his constant bodyguard and companion, the taciturn but fiercely loyal Angevin knight called Baldwin of Bethune, rode in his accustomed place, four horse lengths behind his Duke. "Baldwin, do we have food and drink?"

"Aye, lord."

"Good, then we will stop here and eat by the stream, when you are ready."

Richard Plantagenet ate in the same manner as he did most things—with total concentration and impatient speed. Watching the Duke consume the fowl grasped in his hand, ripping at it with eager teeth and consuming tiny bones and all, his beard and chin slick with grease, Henry wanted to warn him to slow down and take time to savor the meat, but he knew better than to say anything. A need to eat had come between Richard and what he wanted to do next—it was a nuisance that had to be attended to, and enjoyment had no part in it. When Richard finally finished, throwing the remnants of the carcass into the stream and scrubbing the grease and fat from his fingers with a handful of grass torn from the ground beside him, Henry calmly set aside his own meal, unfinished, and prepared to deal with whatever the Duke might throw at him. He did not have to wait long.

"Montdidier tells me you and he spent much time conversing, and he says you grasped the import of his views more quickly than anyone else he has met, other than myself, of course. So, what have you to tell me?"

"No more than what you will have already determined, my lord: we need to make radical changes to the way we do things on this coming campaign, and we need to begin immediately. Truth be told, we should have started months ago, when the Hospitaller first arrived and began speaking the truth about what happened at Hattin. But at that time, apparently, few among your own people or your allies believed him. I admit I found it hard myself, at first, to believe that his has been the sole voice of warning and discontent to return from Outremer."

"Ah, but here's the difference. Montdidier is a man of principle, unafraid to speak the truth. Doesn't care what others think of him. That makes him rare. As for those who came back with different stories, I have no doubt at all that some of them did so to escape punishment for their own craven behavior, while others probably wished to make their deeds and their survival appear to be more heroic than they were. And the priests, of course, have their own explanations for everything. They seek to keep us all transfixed with guilt so that we will return as quickly as may be to redeem ourselves and expiate our sins. They tell us of our faults and sins, but they are priests, so they can tell us nothing of how to fight and win a war. But none of that matters, now, for we have the truth from a man we may trust." He paused for a moment. "So, what would you have me do? What changes have you in mind for our line of battle?"

"Stability, and consolidation." As he always did when they were alone and talking strategy, St. Clair spoke to Richard without honorifics, although he himself was unaware of doing so.

Richard blinked. "Explain that."

"Gladly. The army destroyed at Hattin was too mobile by far, and fatally vulnerable to the tactics Saladin used against them. I have become persuaded that what discipline there was among the Franks was splintered—too many factions among the army and all of them working against one another. King Guy's knights were jealous of the Templars, and despite their common cause, there was little love lost between the Templars and the Hospitallers. Then King Guy himself, because of his own weakness, was afraid of being browbeaten in public by de Ridefort and de Chatillon as he had been before, on several occasions. The Count of Tripoli, Raymond, along with his followers, presented the voice of reason, but they were disregarded by everyone because of Raymond's former truce with Saladin. And everyone was reaching out for personal glory, riding in disorganized sorties to engage the enemy and playing right into the hands of Saladin, who did everything to encourage them, then avoided their charges and wiped them out from a distance. Did Montdidier tell you about the extra arrows?"

"Seventy camel loads, aye he did. I am not sure I believe that. Too much margin for exaggeration."

St. Clair raised a hand in demurral. "Believe it, and learn from it. I have been thinking of little else since first I heard of it, and I am now convinced that the Hospitaller is right. It is an astonishing insight into an enemy we have yet to meet—a measure of how forward-thinking and original this Sultan is. He planned it months, perhaps years, in advance and had his people make those arrows a-purpose. That tells me he has great confidence in himself and in his people, and it tells me, too, that he has little regard for us, Franks of any description, as warriors. He took those steps and made those arrows purely because he saw how predictable the Franks would be when they finally came to battle, and then he used that predictability to destroy them."

"So we must become *un*predictable."

St. Clair dipped his head to one side. "No, not unpredictable, that would be suicidal. Merely *less* predictable. We will have to make Saladin and his emirs—that's what he calls his generals, I believe— we have to make them see, and believe, that we will no longer be enticed into chasing wildly after his formations. They will have to come to us this time around, and when they do they will find us ready for them."

Richard nodded again, still speaking quietly, his tone almost musing. "That appears to make sense. But in truth, Henry, how ready can we be, against such numbers? Mind you, there will be more of us this time than Guy and his unfortunate crew were able to field at Hattin. They barely had thirty thousand, and once we meet up with Barbarossa, our combined army will number three hundred thousand. But there may also be more of the infidel ranged against us, for Saladin's territories are vast. Only time will tell us that. But should they repeat their performance with hailstorms of arrows— and I cannot imagine why they would fail to do it—our men will have no defense against them. We will be shot down in droves."

"Perhaps, but only if we permit the enemy to come close enough to reach us."

Richard's head came up and his eyes narrowed. "Very well then, tell me. How do we keep them safely at a distance?"

"By out-shooting them. Your English longbows and your Angevin arbalests. Both will easily outreach the bows used by the Saracens. Their bows are puny by comparison. We will teach them to dread our arbalests."

"And so they should. They should dread them. But we have nowhere near enough of them—not even ordinary crossbows, let alone arbalests. And mine are the only ones in all of Christendom, so we can expect no help there from any of our allies."

St. Clair merely nodded, unimpressed. "We need no help. I have already taken it upon myself to presuppose your agreement and to requisition new supplies from your armorers, both here and at home."

"Have you, by God's holy, nodding head?" Far from showing displeasure, Richard quirked an eyebrow in amusement at St. Clair's effrontery. "When did you so, and how many did you ask for?"

"As many as can be made before we set sail. I asked for an initial five hundred, and more if time permits. And I did it a week ago, sending word home to Poitiers by a fast ship, since that is the only place the arbalest can be made today. Of course, not all of those will be the steel-bow type—I understand they are extremely difficult to make—so I have called for the next strongest kind, the heavy, layered bows of wood and horn. I also sent word to the secondary manufactory, in Tours, requesting five hundred lesser crossbows, of wood and sinew. And I required your English bowyers to increase their production, although I have since been told that they are already working at capacity."

Richard inhaled deeply. "So be it," he said. "You did well. Now, how do we train our men in their use before we have the weapons in our possession? That will not be simple, Henry, for none of the recruits we choose will have any familiarity with the weapons."

"True, but you have already set my son, André, to training trainers, and we can use the men he has already trained to teach the newcomers. How many arbalesters have you under command in Aquitaine?"

"In Aquitaine? Not many. I have more in Anjou, and others in Poitou ..." Richard pursed his lips, calculating. "Aquitainians, perhaps five hundred remaining, perhaps six. I brought two hundred of them here with me to England—twenty ten-man squads.

"And what of lesser weapons, other crossbows?"

"The same, I would think, if you are still speaking of Aquitaine. Perhaps a hundred or two more ... say, close to a thousand. But again, I have more in Anjou and in Poitou. And before you ask, I have a thousand English longbows in my train and will add at least a thousand more before we quit England."

Richard now settled his shoulders against the tree at his back and sat staring into the distance, reviewing the numbers he had quoted. Overall, they made up a very small percentage of the hundred-thousand-strong army he was raising against Saladin with the French king and their other, lesser allies, but he realized that it was due to him alone, and he reluctantly added credit to his father, too, that they had even that many. His spies had brought word that Frederic Barbarossa, the Holy Roman Emperor, was rumored to be raising an army of two and a half hundred thousand from his German territories as his contribution to the Pope's new war, but Richard had had his spies at work and he now thought it unlikely that the German emperor's battalions would contain many bowmen of any kind.

Richard's gaze focused again and he looked back at St. Clair. "Have you given any thought at all to how we should deploy these new forces you have dreamed up?"

"Aye, I have. The strategy is easily enough explained, but I have not yet worked out the precise tactical details. Now that I have your concurrence on the need to proceed, I will spend more time on that."

"And this is what you meant by stability and consolidation?"

"Aye, it is. As I said, the small moves are still unclear—they have not yet crystallized in my mind—but I know that we must use the new weaponry in tactical blocks, mobile but capable of standing in place and repulsing an attack in strength, and we must use them in support of our chivalry."

"And what of our infantry?"

"Again, to be used in blocks, in the manner of the ancients, where each man relied upon the support and strength of his neighbor."

Richard nodded with slow deliberation. "The ancients ... You mean the ancient Roman legions?"

"Aye, exactly. Solid, unyielding, hard hitting, self-reliant, tightly disciplined, and virtually indestructible."

"I see. That is quite a list of attributes."

"Aye, but it's achievable. And necessary, if we are to go against the legions Saladin will throw at us. We can do it, but we have no time to waste."

"What about these hailstorms of arrows?"

St. Clair shrugged. "If needs must, we will reinvent the Roman tortoise and cover our soldiers with shells of solid steel shields."

Richard contemplated the older man for long moments, then nodded. "Very well, do it. Is there anything more in your mind?"

"Aye, there is. The Saracen captured all the Frankish fortifications and cities in Outremer, and that means we will have to take them back by siege. I had thought to inform you of the need for siege engines for that, but we discussed that this morning and it seems well in hand."

"Aye. What we really need is training and trainers, both for infantry and bowmen. So here is what we will do. You will spend this night with me—all night, if necessary—and we will work on the principles and the logistics of these new ideas of yours until I am familiar with all that we will need. After that, I will attend to the rest of it myself and ensure that the right men are chosen and charged as a cadre to put those principles into practice. You, in the meantime, will return home as soon as may be and start training a new, greatly expanded corps of men to use these crossbow weapons—all of them. Use volunteers at first, since they are most likely to learn quickly, but raise others as you need them, from whatever source you deem suitable. I will give you carte blanche on that. I suspect that our French allies, and perhaps even several of the others, will wish to send some of their men to you for training, now that we can openly use these weapons against the Muslim. But what they should do first is send their best smiths to our armories in Anjou and Aquitaine, to learn the making of an arbalest." He checked himself, noticing the expression on St. Clair's face. "What is it, man?"

Sir Henry looked puzzled. "Your pardon, but do you mean me to go home before your coronation, or after it?"

"Are you mad, Henry? Before it, of course. This new need is far too important to put off for an entire month, especially over religious mummery. I want to see you gone within the week. I'll tell you all about the coronation when next we meet, you and I. Now, let us be up and away, for we have several miles to go and I want to start work on these plans tonight." He twisted his body to look at Baldwin of Bethune, who was sitting some distance aside from them, waiting to be summoned. "Baldwin, we are leaving now. Gather up what needs to be gathered and follow us, quickly as you can."

As Baldwin rose smoothly to his feet, Richard did the same, then reached down his hand to Sir Henry and pulled him up. "You have done well, Henry ... justified my faith in you. Don't ever stop thinking the way you do. Now, mount up."

FIVE

Sir Henry St. Clair sat spear-straight on his horse, looking down from a reviewing stand at the top of a high, sloping ramp. In front of him, stretching away on both sides, lay an enormous drilling field, its edges lost in distance. At his back, beyond the width of its protective moat, the high walls of the Castle of Baudelaire towered above him, cloaking him in a late-afternoon shadow that stretched far ahead of where he sat. The entire area to his right was given over to horses and horsemen, groups of knights and formations of mounted men-at-arms riding hither and yon, all of them deeply involved in their exercises. Henry was content to leave them to themselves. He was far more interested in what was happening in the left half of the field, where seemingly endless rows of crossbowmen, the closest of them almost directly below his reviewing stand, shot in aimed volleys at ranked targets far ahead of them. Farther away, beyond the concentrations of crossbowmen, he knew Richard's English yeomen were working with their deadly longbows, but they were so far distant that St. Clair could barely see them and could only guess at their activities. Like the horsemen that afternoon, they claimed but little of his attention, for his focus was concentrated upon the crossbowmen, the sole reason for his unexpected return to Aquitaine in mid-August of the previous year. It was now the middle of June in the year of Our Lord 1190, and ten months had passed him by like a headlong, badly fractured dream.

The task facing him on his return to Poitiers had been formidable, and he had barely known where to begin. But in the first week after his arrival, he had sent out teams of recruiters from Poitiers to visit every one of Richard's vassals in Aquitaine, Poitou, and Anjou and to stage demonstrations of their weapons' potency. These recruiters performed in Tours, Angers, Nantes, Nevers, Bourges, Angoulême, and Limoges, along with another hundred villages and hamlets scattered between and among those, and they announced after every demonstration that Duke Richard was looking for volunteers to fill the ranks of his new, elite artillery corps. More than a thousand men came forward to Poitiers within the first month of that campaign, and Henry set his trained Angevin arbalesters to work immediately, teaching the newcomers. By that time, too, the first new weapons had begun to arrive from the manufactories in Poitiers and Tours, the former supplying arbalests and the latter more simple, light, and versatile crossbows, and once the production had begun, the capacity rose steadily.

Now, after ten months of hard, grinding work, Henry had twelve hundred new crossbowmen fully trained—three hundred of them on arbalests—and more than two thousand new men under arms in various stages of training. More than four hundred of the latter group had been sent to him by the King of France, Philip Augustus, who requested with great civility that Sir Henry consent to train, on Philip's behalf, a cadre of men who could, in turn, return to teach more of their own in France.

All things considered, Henry felt the efforts he had expended had been more than worthwhile. Word had reached him that morning of Richard's arrival in France the previous week, and the same missive had warned him that the Duke, now crowned King of England, could be expected to arrive in Baudelaire sometime in the afternoon of that same day. That knowledge had prompted Henry to arrange this mass gathering of his new troops.

It was this magnificent training field, Sir Henry knew, that had prompted the Duke to impose his entire army, a mere two weeks earlier, upon the hospitality and duty of the castle's owner, Edouard de Balieul, Count of the surrounding lands of Baudelaire. St. Clair, who had delivered the tidings to Balieul, along with the King's army at the same time, was wryly convinced that the Count must feel that he had little to be thankful for. But there was no place comparable to Baudelaire within a hundred miles and it was perfectly suited to Richard's needs, lush with sweet drinking water for his troops and ample grazing for all the cattle and horses that the army required. Situated on the banks of the river Loire, close to the small town of Pouilly in Burgundy that supplied Sir Henry annually with his beloved golden wine, it also lay within forty miles—a three-day march—of Vézelay, the mustering point for all the various contingents assembling for the voyage to the Holy Land.

Satisfied that everything was as it ought to be, Sir Henry nudged his horse forward, starting it down the ramp to field level, then angling it left, to where a small, densely spaced group of grim-faced men were practicing with the heaviest arbalests, concentrating fiercely on the efforts required to arm the cumbersome weapons. They each held the body of the device firmly upright, one foot through the stirrup on the front end while they worked to turn the two-handed winch at the rear that pulled the heavy bowstring, against the enormous pressure of the steel bow, to its full lock. St. Clair sat watching them until the frowning instructor drilling them looked up, saw him sitting there, and slowly made his way to stand beside him.

"Master-at-Arms," he said, his voice low, deep, and far different from the abusive howl he used to chivy and upbraid his students. "I hope you are pleased with all you have seen today."

Sir Henry nodded back. "Well enough, Roger. What about you? Are your French students making progress?"

"That all depends on how you would define progress—" He raised a hand to hold Sir Henry's attention, then raised his voice to its usual hectoring pitch. "You there, Bermond! Put your back into it, man. There's no time to waste with those things. Too slow and you'll be dead before you can pick it up again. You're supposed to fire two shots each minute, not one shot every two!" The man he had shouted at now began working twice as hard, his arms churning at the winch handles. Sir Roger de Bohen turned back to his interrupted conversation. "That's part of what I have to deal with. They think they're being demeaned because they're French, and they're always muttering that our Angevins have an unfair advantage in having used these things for years, even though these particular fellows are just as raw and new to their weapons as the Frenchmen are."

St. Clair smiled. "Come, Roger, that is not quite the whole truth. The Angevins have grown up seeing the weapons used all around them. They have at least a degree of familiarity with them. The French, on the other hand, have never laid eyes on a crossbow, much less the biggest crossbow of them all."

Roger de Bohen and Henry St. Clair had known and respected each other for two decades, and spoke as friends. "You're splitting hairs, Henry, and you're wrong," de Bohen said now, keeping his voice low to avoid being overheard. "These Frenchmen are feeling put upon because, even starting from scratch with no advantage on either side, they are nowhere *close* to being as good as the Angevins are, and at this rate it will take months to whip them into any kind of battle readiness."

"But they will learn, will they not?"

"Aye, they'll learn … Of course they will." De Bohen shrugged and swung away, speaking back over his shoulder as he returned to his charges. "The question is, will they learn quickly enough?"

St. Clair watched him as the other returned to his task, and then he kneed his horse and pulled its head around until he was heading directly towards the far left side of the field, where the block formations of Richard's English archers were firing massed volleys of arrows that fell on their target area like sheets of windblown rain. But even as he rode towards the English ranks, his mind was still with the crossbowmen behind him, and with the potential they offered of being able to lay down a heavy, defensive screen of missiles against the kind of attack that had destroyed the Christians at Hattin.

The English longbows could lay down amazing volleys from great distances, shooting in high arcs over hundreds of paces, but what St. Clair needed from his crossbowmen was an intermediate killing power to augment the longbows: shorter, but no less lethal, volleys fired straight out and kept on low trajectories. He had been working for months now on training solid, coordinated formations of short- and intermediate-range crossbows that would work in conjunction with smaller but much harder-hitting teams of arbalesters. These troops would be capable of generating sufficiently lethal interference to discourage any sustained attack by the vaunted Saracen light archers, and would therefore increase the odds in favor of the Christian infantry and knights in any confrontation. That, at least, was his theory, and Henry was well aware that he had pinned his reputation to its success.

The sound of distant cheering, far off to his left, attracted St. Clair's attention, and as he turned to look for the cause, he heard one of the nearby English yeomen shouting the King's name, so he nudged his horse forward to where he could watch Richard approach, and he wondered, as he had many times in recent months, at the sheer confidence and regal ability that radiated from the so-called *English* monarch who, despite having spent much of his boyhood in the country, had always disdained it, barely spoke the language of the people he now ruled, yet had captivated all the fighting men of that warlike land, inspiring spontaneous cheers whenever he rode by.

Today, as was his habit when mixing with his own soldiers, the King rode almost alone, refusing a formal escort and accompanied this time only by two knights, one on each side, and two squires riding behind them. One squire carried the royal sword, with its hilt of gold and its scabbard glinting with precious stones, while the other bore the King's flat steel pot-helmet with the narrow golden coronet worked around its burnished rim. Richard was bare headed, his mailed cowl pushed off his head to hang down his back, leaving his long, red-golden hair to blow free in the breeze of his passage. He wore a magnificent cloak of crimson silk worked with gold thread, its sides thrown back over his shoulders on this occasion to reveal the white surcoat with the red cross of the Holy Warrior and not the standard of Saint George that he normally wore on the breast of his tunic—three elongated golden lions passant on a field of brilliant scarlet. Beneath the surcoat, he was armored in a full suit of gleam-ing mail, and his battle shield covered his left arm, its single black lion rampant facing left against a bright red field.

To his men, and to the world at large, Richard Plantagenet was every inch the warrior king, but Henry barely noticed him after the first, analytical look in which he gauged the monarch's temper and judged it to be pleasant. Thereafter, his eyes remained fastened on the knight who rode at the King's right shoulder, his own son, Sir André St. Clair. He had expected that André would be returning, as he was now working permanently as an interlocutor of some kind between the Fleet Master de Sablé and the King. It had been many months since Henry had last seen him, and his first thought, even from as far distant as they were from each other, was that the lad looked older—older and more mature, which was as it should be, and happily carefree, which was even better. He noted, too, that his son yet wore his own knightly mantle, bearing the device of St. Clair, which meant that whatever else had been occupying his time, André had not yet joined the ranks of the Temple Knights. For just a moment, St. Clair was overwhelmed with pride in his son, with anticipation of the simple pleasure of sitting with him, hearing his voice, listening to his opinions. He felt a lump swell up in his throat and swallowed it down gratefully. Then, schooling his face to show nothing, he spurred his horse forward.

Richard saw him coming and greeted him with a shout from a long way off. Although Henry could not make out the King's words, he inferred from the broadness of Richard's wave towards André that he was showing Henry his thoughtfulness in having brought his son along. Henry waved back, reined in his horse, and dismounted, acknowledging that he had been recognized and waiting until the King's party reached him. When they did, he stepped forward and brought his clenched fist to his left breast in salute to his liege lord, but Richard was already staring off, over Henry's head, his ever-shifting attention captured by something beyond the line of Henry's vision. Henry stood waiting to be addressed, and for long moments nothing happened, but then Richard looked down and smiled at him.

"Henry St. Clair, old friend. Forgive my inattention and bad manners in seeming to ignore you, but I thought I saw someone I did not expect to see here." His eyes flicked away again, then returned to Henry. "But that is neither here nor there. We have been in the saddle all day and stand in need of relaxation ... that and stimulation." He straightened his shield arm and worked with his other hand at freeing the clasp that held his cloak in place. "Tomkin! Take this, quickly." As one of the young squires moved quickly to take the monarch's shield and cloak from him, Richard continued speaking. "You look hale and hearty, Henry, and I hear tales from all directions that you have been doing sterling work here. There!" He finally rid himself of cloak and shield and stood up in his stirrups, pushing his elbows back and flexing his back muscles. "I recall I promised to tell about the coronation next time we two met ... and no doubt you will be panting to hear all."

He looked about him at the expressions on the faces of the others in his small group and then laughed. "Well, my friend, if that is the case you can put your tongue back into your mouth. You were the fortunate one, to be far gone on that occasion. It was tedious, Henry, tedious. Was it not so, Sir André? Apart from the single instant when I felt that crown come down solidly upon my head, to be sure. That one moment made the entire thing memorable and worthwhile. But the remainder of the event was boring beyond belief, all muttered Latin amid solemn dirges sung in a sea of smelly, swirling incense." His eyes moved away again, narrowing with interest.

"Damn me, it *is* Brian." He glanced back at Henry, obviously impatient to be gone. "I must have words with my English captain, Brian of York, over yonder, my friend, so I pray you, bide you here with your son while I do so, or come with me if you so wish. This should not take long." He jabbed his horse with his spurs, and Sir Henry turned his head to look at his son, who was watching him expectantly, flanked by the other knight who had come with him and the King. Henry judged the stranger to be almost his son's age, perhaps a year or two older. He nodded courteously to the stranger and spoke to his son.

"Well, what think you? Shall we join the King?"

Sir André smiled and shrugged. For a moment, Henry thought he detected a tinge of something unexpected, almost a bitterness, in his son's eyes, but when he looked more closely there was nothing there to be seen, and he thrust the thought aside.

"If he is going to fight afoot with the English soldiery," André was saying, "as I suspect he is, we ought not to miss the spectacle, for I am told he does it rather well." He bent forward in the saddle, reaching out towards Sir Henry, who grasped his hand warmly. "Good day to you, Father. Permit me to introduce Sir Bernard de Tremelay, who has accompanied us from Orléans."

Sir Henry again nodded cordially to the newcomer. "De Tremelay, you say, from Orléans? Was there not a Master of the Temple once who had the same name and came from Orléans?"

"Sir Bernard de Tremelay." The stranger nodded, smiling. "Your memory is excellent, Sir Henry. That was more than thirty years ago, and he was Master for barely a year. He was elder brother to my grandfather. I heard much about him in my youth, for he was highly regarded, but I never met the man. Shall we join the King?"

The three men prodded their mounts towards the place where the King and his two squires had dismounted in front of the small knot of kneeling English yeomen whom Henry had been watching earlier. By the time they arrived Richard was already rousing the kneeling men to their feet, laughing and slapping at the cumbersome padding the men wore.

" … on your feet," he was saying. "A fighting man need kneel to no other. A bending knee may indicate a pledge of fealty from time to time, but a bent knee that stays bent means subjugation, and I'll have none of that in men who are my friends. Brian!" he called to the instructor, the only man among the English yeomen who was not swaddled in padding. "Pick me your three finest among this crew. No, wait. That would be … injudicious. I'll pick my own three, and take my chances. You will supervise the fight." He scanned the twelve astonished men in front of him, then raised a hand. "Now listen, all of you. I pick three of you, and we fight. Three single

bouts, to a fall or a solid hit. Brian will judge." He favored all of
them with his dazzling grin, all flashing eyes and gleaming teeth.
"But be warned, any man fool enough to hold back to spare my
royal kingship and dignity will find himself digging latrines for the
next two weeks. Is that clear? It had better be. I want to beat all three
of you honestly and fairly because I am the better fighter. And if you
can beat me, best me, knock me on my arse in the mire, then you
had better do it, for I will not thank you for insulting me by holding
back. And besides, I have a golden bezant for any man who knocks
me down—three of them, if need be." He looked from man to man
again, meeting each one's eye, then chose his opponents with three
flicks of an index finger. "You, you, and you, let's fight. Someone
among the rest of you lend me a quarterstaff, and we'll set about it."

Word spread quickly, for the King's behavior around his soldiers
was well known, and even before he and his opponent faced each
other for the first of the three bouts, a crowd had formed, encircling
the fighters tightly so that the remaining nine yeomen of Brian of
York's group had to busy themselves forming a protective cordon,
keeping the press back sufficiently far to afford the fighters room to
move freely. But the nine of them were not sufficient to control the
surging crowd. Those at the back of the throng jostled for a better
view, pushing the people in front of them forward, and Sir Henry
himself soon had to requisition additional "volunteers" to hold back
the crowd.

The first bout began innocuously, both men circling to the left,
easily balanced on the balls of their feet, their quarterstaffs held at
the ready and their eyes intent upon each other. They were watching
for the slightest hint of a coming attack, judging and interpreting
every nuance of shifting balance, every flickering shade of expression. The yeoman, a tall, wide-shouldered young fellow called Will,
whom St. Clair would have sworn to be less than twenty years old,
had the enormous arms and wrists of a longbow archer, and he
appeared to be unimpressed by the fact that he was face to face with
his King in single combat. He was poised and cool and showed not
the least sign of being intimidated as he moved easily in concert

with Richard, gliding smoothly, knees lightly bent in readiness to spring.

Henry was not surprised that it was Richard who made the first move, lunging forward to his right, the staff in his hand suddenly transformed into a whirling blur of violent motion punctuated by hard-hitting, clattering blows that would have broken bones had they landed on anything other than his opponent's weapon. They would certainly have forced most men to fall back and give ground, but the young yeoman stood firm and met the attack strongly, parrying and absorbing the flurry of blows easily and seemingly without effort, so that Richard soon stopped in mid-swing and sprang away, ending the clash and landing lightly poised on his toes. The younger man went after him immediately, giving him no time to rest, and for a space of whirling, rattling blows and stifled grunts it was Richard who went on the defensive, even yielding ground to the inexorable strength of young Will's advance before he managed to regain the advantage by feinting ingeniously and almost disarming his opponent with a backhanded chop that forced the archer to spin nimbly away to his right. That spin, a miraculous recovery against an unforeseen blow, should have resulted in the end of the contest, for it exposed the archer's back fatally to the huge blow that followed as the King swung around in a full pirouette, continuing the arc of his backhanded chop into a massive, sweeping downswing. But the young archer's evasive move was so sure and swift that it carried him beyond Richard's reach, and instead of striking him squarely between the shoulders, the tip of the King's staff merely grazed the center of the heavy padding at Will's back and glanced off, continuing downward to strike the ground hard and giving the young man an opportunity to recover and regain his poise.

After that, neither man seemed willing to take any risks, and for a while the action swayed back and forth as first one and then the other sought to take the initiative, but that state of affairs could not last long—not with Richard Plantagenet being watched and judged by his own men. He feinted right and then sprang to his left, slashing backhanded again in the hope of catching his opponent off guard. The archer was there to meet him and smashed the quarter-staff right out of the King's hands, drawing a grunt of surprise, quickly followed by a howl of approval, from the watching crowd.

Disarmed and shaken as he was, Richard nonetheless gave his opponent no time to improve upon his advantage, but flung himself forward into a head-tucked, rolling tumble towards his fallen weapon, barely missing Will's legs in his charging dive. The yeoman was forced to step aside as the King passed directly beneath his arms and snatched up the fallen quarterstaff in lunging to his feet. Sir Henry had to stifle a grunt and bite down on an admiring smile, for this action was pure Richard Plantagenet—the kind of spontaneous, unpredictable, and brilliant feat that made the man so beloved of his soldiers of all ranks; a move so unexpected and yet so sure and sudden that the King, re-armed, was back on the attack before anyone, including his opponent, could recover from their surprise. He cut young Will down with a heavy, powerful blow to his padded thigh that crushed the man's protective padding and paralyzed his leg, sending him toppling sideways to his knees, hands flat on the ground, head hanging, with no other choice but to yield when the butt of Richard's quarterstaff pressed down against the back of his neck.

The watching soldiery went wild with approval when Richard grinned and gallantly assisted his battered and vanquished adversary to his feet, making a great show of being out of breath and pushed almost to the limits of his strength. And yet, as he handed young Will from the fighting arena, he was already beckoning to the second man to step forth and face him.

This bout was far shorter and less exciting than the first, perhaps because Richard was flushed with victory and enthusiasm, or perhaps because the second yeoman was dismayed by what he had already seen. Whatever the reason, the second man crashed down solidly, flat on his back with both wits and breath driven out of him mere moments after the onset, having failed to anticipate or counter any one of a trio of blows that struck him within a brace of heart-beats and left him senseless.

The third man stepped forward slowly and judiciously, holding himself erect save only for very slightly bent knees that gave his posture the merest suggestion of a crouch. He held his quarterstaff across his chest with both hands and gazed at Richard through deep-set, almost slitted eyes. Richard, standing hipshot across from him, stared back calmly, his own quarterstaff gripped gently upright in one hand, its length resting against his shoulder. Sir Henry already knew the third man's name was Hawkeye—he had heard it shouted by his friends—and looking now at the man's expression he could understand whence the name had come. There was something of the raptor about this Hawkeye, with his low hairline coming to a point in the middle of his forehead, a great, narrow hook of a nose, and wide black pupils beneath straight, archless brows.

There was no questing for position between these two; they stood square to each other and breathed deeply, neither making any attempt to begin the joust, content for the time being to take each other's measure, and as the moments passed a stillness fell over the watching crowd. Henry's horse snuffled and stamped, rebelling against the bite of a fly, and he reined it in ruthlessly, willing it to be quiet and stand still. The two adversaries had not moved until then, but as though the horse's stamping foot had been a signal, both men exploded into action, leaping towards each other across the space that separated them. From that moment on the air was filled with the hard, staccato rattle of wood against wood as they belabored each other hard and fast, each seeking to penetrate the impenetrable curtain of the other man's defenses. And then, between one blow and the next, the man called Hawkeye leapt backward, away from the fight, landing in a crouch and flinging himself forward again immediately, catching his opponent in the very act of beginning to lunge after him. The concussion as their bodies met was almost palpable to Henry, but Hawkeye had the advantage of both momentum and surprise, and Richard went staggering backward, off balance. One heel landed awkwardly on the uneven surface, striking a half-buried stone, and unable to right himself, the King fell heavily, flat on his back and shoulders, his arms flying wide and the heavy quarterstaff tearing loose from his grasp.

It was Hawkeye's victory, and not a single person watching doubted it, and yet, in the instant of that recognition, Hawkeye hesitated. It was barely for a moment, the merest flickering of an eye, but Henry saw it clearly and so did every other man there. For the briefest instant, the man called Hawkeye remembered the identity of the adversary he was about to defeat, and then he collected himself and leapt in for the kill. But he was already too late. In the instant that had elapsed by then, Richard, impossibly well conditioned to the doing of impossible things, had brought his knees up to his chest, rolling far back onto his shoulders and from there, with no break in his fluid movements, he had flipped forward again, kicking his powerful legs up, out, and down in a springing lunge while at the same time thrusting himself up straight-armed like a tumbling acrobat and powering his entire body back to a standing position. It was a prodigious feat of physical prowess, but he did not complete it, because before he could regain the point of balance, his rising body met Hawkeye's coming forward, arms upraised for the killing stroke. And instantaneously accepting the reversal, Richard gripped the armor at Hawkeye's neck with both hands, raised one foot, lodged it above the other man's groin, and threw himself backward and down again, pulling the yeoman with him and then launching him onward with a powerful thrust from his bent leg, propelling him high over his head to land heavily and roll face down, unmoving.

There was neither sound nor movement among the group surrounding the circle. The only noises came from Richard himself as he came to his feet, then pulled himself up to his full height, swaying and looking down at Hawkeye's inert body. Finally he waved a hand towards his downed opponent.

"Well, by God's throat, have you all been stricken mute? Is he alive, or have I killed him?"

His words broke the spell that had held everyone, and in a moment people swarmed around the man on the ground. "He's breathing," someone shouted. "He's alive! Here, be careful. Stand back and let him breathe." And with that the noisy enthusiasm of the soldiers quickly returned to normal as they discussed the pros and contras and technical details of what they had seen.

High on his horse above all of them, Sir Henry St. Clair saw the unconscious man's fingers twitch and then clench into a fist, and then he watched Richard stride forward and pick up not only the quarterstaff he himself had been using but the one belonging to Hawkeye as well, before he returned to stand looking down at the other man, his expression unreadable.

When the man called Hawkeye opened his eyes, he found himself at the center of a ring of well-wishers, with Richard of England himself kneeling at his side. The King smiled at him and spoke, but Hawkeye's wits had not yet returned to him and he understood nothing of what the monarch said. Later, when he thought back on it, he knew that Richard had rewarded him with three gold bezants—more wealth than Hawkeye had ever held in his hand or would ever see again—but he remembered nothing of what had transpired. He knew only what his friends told him about the incident, and he took satisfaction in knowing that he had given the Plantagenet a good fight and had actually knocked him off his feet, flat on his back, in a bona fide fall. That was what had earned him one of the bezants. The other two had been added purely for the quality of the fight he had provided, according to his friends. And even so, Richard had gone further, in an act of unheard-of magnanimity, and presented the other two fighters with a silver mark apiece, in token of his gratitude for their loyalty and fellowship, he said.

Sir Henry St. Clair was familiar with the entire ritual from many years earlier, and the vagaries of whatever might happen on any individual occasion had long since lost any power to impress him. He invariably experienced, however, an unwilling, even grudging admiration for the sheer effrontery of Richard's performances in ingratiating himself with his gullible followers. His blatant self-aggrandizement at such times never failed to take Henry's breath away, and the veteran knight shook his head every time at the willful blindness of people in allowing themselves to be so shamelessly and openly manipulated.

But even as that thought came to his mind, he looked beyond the unfocused aura of the King's presence and found himself being truly astonished by the expression on the face of his son, for there, where he would have expected to see tolerant amusement and even admiration for Richard's flagrant mummery, Henry saw instead a faint frown. It was barely there at all, recognizable only to a man who had spent a lifetime fondly watching the face of his only son. What was the expression? Was it disdain, suspicion, disapproval, outright dislike? Henry decided that all of these applied.

He became aware then that he himself was frowning and must have looked troubled to anyone watching him, and so he quickly cleared his face of all expression. He casually swung his horse away, resisting the urge to look at his son again but determined to find out, at the first opportunity, what had so changed André's opinion of his champion and savior, the Plantagenet King who had, at last report, been his hero.

THE CHAMBER ALLOCATED to Sir Henry St. Clair was comfortably appointed, as was only fitting for the quarters of the army's Master-at-Arms. It was reasonably snug and secure from drafts, its floor made of carefully matched flagstones and strewn with fresh rushes save in the area surrounding the fireplace. Its high, bare walls were hung with heavy tapestries, and its furnishings were well and solidly constructed, the heavy oaken bed raised well clear of the floor. When Sir Henry swung open the door from outside and held it for André to enter ahead of him, he found his steward, Ector, already there, supervising the replenishing of the blazing fire in the brazier by one servant while keeping an admonitory eye on the laying of a table with food and drink by two others. As soon as he saw his master enter, Ector clapped his hands sharply, signaling his minions to finish their tasks immediately and remove themselves. When the door had closed behind them, he bowed to Sir Henry.

"Will there be anything else, my lord?"

Sir Henry shook his head, waving the steward away. "Go to bed, Ector. I'll have no more need of you this night."

He watched the steward leave, then turned to where his son, having already removed his surcoat and sword belt and laid them across one end of the newly set table, was ignoring the food but sniffing appreciatively at the long-necked silver ewer containing his father's favorite wine. Half smiling at André's earnest preoccupation, Henry shrugged out of his own mantle and removed the belt that held his long sword, and hung them over a peg set high in the wall beside the door before he moved to sit in one of the two chairs flanking the fire.

"So tell me, then," he asked without preamble, "what kind of falling out have you had with our liege lord, Richard? And do not even think about pretending you don't know what I'm talking about."

This was the first time the two men had been alone together since Richard's joust with the yeomen hours earlier, so the words, and the criticism they implied, caused André St. Clair to pause in the act of pouring the wine into two of the pewter goblets Ector's men had left on the table. He turned to look warily at his father, one eyebrow quirking upward, then straightened up slowly, lowering the ewer's bulbous base and replacing it carefully on the table. Then, in a movement clearly designed to give him time to think, he flexed his shoulders backward with a slow, exaggerated rolling motion and brought his elbows in close to his sides, raising his forearms in unison until his bent knuckles came together beneath his chin.

Sir Henry watched all of this intently, admiring the discipline that kept his son's face so innocently empty of expression even while he must be wondering what had prompted the question and how much his father knew or had guessed. Henry was content to wait until his son should choose to respond, and sure enough, after scrutinizing his father for a count of ten, André dipped his head slightly sideways in what might have been the beginnings of a nod and returned to pouring the wine. He replaced the stopper in the ewer, set the flask down, then carried both cups to where his father sat by the fireside watching him. He handed one over wordlessly, then took the other fireside chair and looked down into the blazing heart of the brazier between them.

"Having been to England now, with all its chills and shivers, I find it strange that one should need a fire at night here in the summertime in the middle of France."

"Aye, but the here you are referring to is not the middle of France. It is the middle of an old stone castle in west Burgundy, dark and damp and drafty and far removed from sunlight, winter or summer. It is *always* cold in here. And you are avoiding my question."

"No, Father, I am not." André looked up at his father. "I simply have not found the words yet to reply to it correctly."

"How so? Can it be that difficult? We two are the only ones here, so you run no risk of being denounced for sedition or disloyalty, no matter what you say. You are at odds, in some way, with the King, that much I know simply from watching you. But Richard was pleasant with you when we met today, so whatever occurred between the two of you must have been minor. Otherwise you would probably be in prison in disgrace."

"Aye, or even executed … True, Father. But bear in mind that you yourself warned me to keep my disapproval masked should I ever encounter anything to incur it." He shrugged. "So I did. I encountered something … distasteful. Something I had not sought, nor thought to find."

"Distasteful. No stronger than that?"

"No, not unless I dwell upon it, and I try not to do that, because when I do, my distaste increases to dislike."

"Hmm. Tell me, then, about this distasteful episode."

André's expression hardened. "It was no episode, Father. It was far more than that. I have found distastefulness to be a constant in the man. A trait … a flaw I cannot bring myself to countenance."

Staring at his son now, and seeing the cold, stern disapproval on his face, Sir Henry felt stirrings of chill gooseflesh raising the hairs on the back of his neck as he imagined the tenebrous, threat-filled specter of Richard's notorious homosexuality looming behind André's head and gesturing obscenely.

"Do you hate Jews, Father?"

"What?" So abruptly different was the question from what he had expected that its incongruity threw Henry off balance. "Do I—? No,

I do not hate Jews." But then he hesitated, before blurting, "What concern is that of yours? Why would you ask me such a thing?"

"Forgive me. Most people do hate them, I find. They call them Christ killers." He frowned, and when he spoke again his voice was quieter. "Richard ... Richard does not like Jews."

Somewhere deep inside him, Henry felt relief unfolding like a blossom. "I see. And that is what you find distasteful?" He nodded gravely, not expecting a response from André. "Well, it's hardly an unusual opinion, is it? But having said that, and taking your exalted opinion of the man into consideration, I suppose it is understandable that you might be disappointed, particularly if he makes no secret of his dislike. But Jew hating is something of a social pastime every- where, not merely here in Anjou and Aquitaine but all throughout Christendom, sanctioned and often even fomented by the Church itself." He paused, musing, then continued. "So I have to ask you this: do you find the pastime unequivocally distasteful everywhere you encounter it, or only in Richard's behavior?"

"He is the King, Father. His behavior sets an example everywhere, for all his people. And in England, many of those people are Jews."

"Ho, now!" His father held up his hand, "Rein yourself in, there. Many would argue strongly against that. You will find people aplenty ready to tell you loudly that Jews are Jews, no more and no less, irre- spective of where they are. They live within the confines of their own strange religion and lead their secretive lives to their own ends, shun- ning the company of non-Jews but thriving through usurious commerce with Christian folk and neither owing nor offering alle- giance to anyone or anything Christian. By those precepts, the Jews of England will remain forever Jews and will never be English, as their counterparts here will never be Angevin or Aquitainian or even French."

André had been staring at his father, narrow eyed, while Sir Henry spoke, and now he nodded. "You could, you might argue that ... but would you, Father? Do you believe it?"

Sir Henry flicked the question aside with a one-handed gesture. "That is neither here nor there, although in fact I do not believe it and have not for years. What we are dealing with here is you and your beliefs, since those appear to clash with your King's. So let us deal with that."

André looked away from his father's gaze as he raised his cup and drank off almost half its contents. "Deal with that, you say. But I seem to be incapable of dealing with it sanely, at least for the time being."

It was Henry's turn now to turn aside and stare into the flames, collecting his thoughts before presenting them to his son's judgment, but presently he rubbed the back of one finger gently against the end of his nose. "Have I ever told you about Karel?"

"Karel the Dalmatian, the Magyar. Your boyhood tutor." André smiled. "Aye, you have, many times, but I have not heard you mention his name in years, not since I was a tadpole. I remember you saying often that there was far more to Karel than he ever chose to let people see."

"Most people looked at him and saw the Outlander: the strange-looking fellow with bushy hair and narrow eyes and the thick-tongued way of speaking. They never thought to try to look beyond that front that he maintained. And that was all it was: a pretense, a mask held up in front of the real Karel to protect him from the attentions of those he considered fools."

André tilted his head sideways, an expression of gentle amusement playing about his eyes. "I gather, then, he thought most people fools?"

"He did. And by his lights, he was correct, for Karel equated foolishness with frivolity, and most people prefer being frivolous to being serious all the time.

"He was a lawyer, you know, long before he ever thought to turn soldier. His family was wealthy and powerful in their own land, and some bishop there took note of the boy, recognizing his abilities even in childhood, and sent him off to Rome to be educated at the papal court. He had a mind for legal matters, it transpired, and he quickly made a name for himself, winning advancement to great heights, by his own admission years afterwards, at a very early age—" He broke off, hesitating, but still smiling that same whimsical smile. "I suspect now, although it *is* mere suspicion, unsupported by any evidence, that he may have been a priest or even a bishop by the time he was done, and I would not be surprised to learn he ranked even higher than both. But in any event, something went very badly wrong. Something he learned or experienced in Rome repulsed him, and his disgust was terminal. He walked away, left Rome and all it had meant to him, and cloaked himself in absolute obscurity, in the last place anyone would ever think to look for a cleric and a lawyer ... or a bishop, for that matter. He took up arms as a mercenary.

"That was in 1133, in Germany. He entered into a contract to fight for a German nobleman, Conrad of Hohenstaufen, the man who later became King Conrad III. Karel served with Conrad's armies for twelve years, then left for reasons of which I know nothing. He had entered Conrad's service as a fugitive lawyer, and he emerged twelve years later as a highly regarded military officer, and that is when he came into my life. My father had met him years earlier, somewhere in Germany, and they had become friends—God alone knows how or why. Anyway, when he left his position with the German King, he came looking for my father and took a contract with him, as a mercenary, tasked to train the St. Clair men-at-arms in modern weapons craft. He did it very well, too, and when his contract expired, he stayed on in my father's employ, charged with the primary task of educating me, albeit as a soldier, not as a cleric or a student. And for the next ten years, in his own unique and inimitable way, that is precisely what he did."

André was leaning forward in his seat, listening closely. "He educated you, you mean, or he taught you to fight?"

His father shrugged with one shoulder. "Both, and at the same time, for there is no difference. Karel created no divisions in what he did. He saw no differences between learning how to fight and learning how to write. The tools we use for each might appear to be different, he used to say, but all of them are controlled by our minds, and it is our application of what our mind tells us that makes each of us different, makes one man better than the mass of his fellows, makes one in each group stand out head and shoulders above all others, no matter what the pursuit that they are following may be."

André was wide eyed. "Your Karel sounds to me to have been a wondrous character."

"I doubt I could have had a finer mentor or a better instructor. And you would have liked him, had you ever met him. But he died before you were born."

"You have never told me any of this before." There was a plaintive note to André's voice.

"When you were a boy, you had tutors of your own and Karel was already dead. Why should I have wished to bore you with tales of a dead man? I fed you snippets of his wisdom from time to time, little things that I thought might amuse you." Sir Henry paused again, his gaze unfocused, then went on. "You have to understand that no one ever questioned Karel's teachings, or asked me what I was learning in my classes. No one cared, I see now, because my father could neither read nor write, but he could see me training in the arms yard every day and could tell at a glance that I was thriving and acquitting myself well. That was enough for him. My mother, on the other hand, was already sick of the palsy that would kill her by the time I was fourteen, so she had neither the strength nor the will to check into my learning. And there was no one else to care. But fortunately, I was never happier than when I was seated at Karel's feet, learning of wonders. And as I grew older, he spoke to me more and more openly about what he believed, and about how he saw a man's responsibilities—any man's responsibilities—as laid out for him by God. He understood and talked about many aspects of God and godliness—righteousness and piety, things that the ruck of men, including most of the priests I knew, could never have imagined, let alone learned. And he had very strict beliefs and stern opinions concerning God and men and their relationship each to the other."

"How did he die?"

"Of a pestilence, one that seemed to be everywhere that year. His death left a great hole in my life that would not be filled until I met and wed your mother. But I remember clearly that, on the very last occasion when I saw him well, we spoke of this very matter of Jews and how they are so hated everywhere."

"Truly, Father?" André sounded slightly skeptical. "That was a very long time ago, and your memory might be playing tricks with you. I know mine does with me from time to time."

His father eyed him sideways, one eyebrow rising in amusement. "Think you so? Well, it might be as you say, were I as old as you appear to think I am. But in this instance I know there is nothing faulty about my memory, because that last conversation became a very special one for me. I recalled it time and again, remembering every word of it because it was the last time we had ever spoken.

"Karel had never been able to come to terms with that widespread hatred of Jews, because it seemed to him to be at odds with everything he had come to believe as a boy. He had asked me why I thought the Jews were always blamed for everything that befell the Savior." Henry smiled softly to himself. "And before I could come up with a single reason, he went on to point out that if we agree and believe that Jesus was born into our world to give up his life in expiation for our earthly sins, then we also ought to believe, logically, that everything that happened surrounding those events was part of the divine plan, and that, God being by His very nature omniscient, every eventuality of that planning had been foreseen and accounted for. Why then, he asked me again that last afternoon, were the Jews alone vilified for behaving as they did? Their God and ours were one and the same. Had He forsaken them to nurture us? Or were we to believe the Jews the only sinners among mankind, guilty by themselves, beyond all doubt, of creating the need for the Savior's sacrifice? If that were so, was it only afterwards that all the other races, including the arrogant Romans, were turned into sinners, contaminated by the behavior of the Jews?"

Sir Henry shook his head now, as if bemused. "I must have been twelve years old, and I remember that even at that young age I was able to see through the stupidity underlying those questions. I remember mentally digging in my heels, too, and telling Karel what I thought, and then being astonished when he agreed with me.

"'Of course it is nonsense,' he said, and he gave my head a push, the way he did when he was pleased with me. 'It is an insult to any person with the ability to think logically from one step to another. If the Jews had ever been the only sinners in the world, there would never have been any reason for Christianity to exist. The Jews believed they were already the chosen people, so all that would have been needed was for a Jewish Messiah to come down to earth and do whatever Jewish law demanded need be done. But that is not what happened. The message spread from Israel to all the countries of the world, which then became the Christian world. No one argues with that, do they? So tell me, young Henry St. Clair, what do you think is the real reason underlying all the nonsense about the Jews?'"

"Did you have an answer for him?"

Sir Henry raised an eyebrow. "Would you have offered one, had you been as old as you are today?"

André smiled and dipped his head, appearing to acknowledge his father's point, although what he was actually thinking was that he could, indeed, have answered the question at great length and to Karel's complete satisfaction. Instead, he merely nodded and asked, "So what did he say then?"

"I have never forgotten what he said. He said it was the priests— Karel was fond of blaming most things on the priests and on the Church in general—who promulgated the anti-Jewish filth to suit their own wishes at some time or another in the earliest days of the Church, some dire occasion when they needed to find a scapegoat to take people's attention away from whatever they themselves were up to. Karel believed that firmly. The Jews had proved to be an easy target, he said, and the Church took note and marked it, so the guilt by association was never let go."

A silence elapsed before André casually asked, "How do you feel about that, Father—the scapegoat explanation? Do you subscribe to the idea?"

Sir Henry had slipped down gradually in his seat since their conversation began and was stretched almost full length, his legs crossed at the ankles in front of the fire, his chin sunk on his breast-bone. Now he sniffed and pulled himself up again before reaching for his cup on the floor.

"I think I always have subscribed to it." He sipped his wine and grimaced. "Blech! My wine's hot ... too close to the fire." He stood up and reached for André's cup. "Give me that. The ewer should still be cold. One more before bed, eh?"

When he returned with replenished cups, André had thrown fresh logs on the fire and was watching the flames curl up around them. He accepted his fresh drink without looking up, and Henry sat back down and continued speaking as if there had been no interruption.

"I don't doubt that the Jews have been made into scapegoats, but I can't tell you why or when it happened. I *can* tell you, on the other hand, that it was not always that way. The Jews of Judea were always a contentious people, fighting among themselves long before Jesus came into the world, and they were always harshly, arrogantly intolerant of anyone who did not share their faith or revere their grim, implacable God. It is a matter of record that the Romans detested them for all the trouble and upheavals they caused. The Roman province of Judea was a tiny place, after all, in terms of the overall empire, but it fomented disruptions, civil, religious, and military, far beyond what should have been the scope of its capacities, and when its contumacious people finally rebelled to the extent of declaring war upon the Romans, the imperial authorities deemed the situation in Judea to be intolerable and destroyed the entire nest of them.

"They sent in the legions, who tore down the city of Jerusalem itself and stamped out resistance, as only the Romans could, wherever they found any signs of it. They laid siege to the mountain fortresses the Jewish insurgents held and destroyed them all, one by one, taking as much time, as many years, as that required. And since the religion of the people lay at the center of all their discontent, they destroyed the focus of that religion: they tore down the temple and put its priests to the sword. They were inexorable and utterly merciless because that was the Roman way. They killed or enslaved as many of the populace as they could capture, and generally made the province of Judea uninhabitable, so that the Jews could never trouble Rome again. But—" He sat up straighter, digging the tip of a little finger into one ear, then examining it critically before wiping his finger on his leg.

"But all of that was retribution for the sin of rebellion against Rome. It was punishment justly earned in Roman eyes. It contained nothing of the kind of mindless hatred that Christians show towards the Jews today."

He sipped at his wine and rolled it around his tongue, savoring it for a while before adding, "The Jews gave us their One God, André. People tend to forget that. The God we worship came to us directly from the hands of the Jews. We should be grateful to them for that, for giving us our God. But no, we choose to shun them, when we are not abusing and persecuting them.

"Karel told me once that he had known several families of Jews throughout his travels, and he believed that they were ordinary people just like Christians, save that they believed differently about how their God expected them to behave. After all, Jesus was a Jew. No getting around that, Karel used to say. So where did the breakdown occur? When did the breakaway happen? When did it become perfectly acceptable for Jesus to have been a Jew all his life and for all eternity, for His Father to have been the God of Israel, and for Christian people to dream and speak of returning to Sion—which is Jerusalem—and to speak glowingly and lovingly of biblical Israel, yet hate all Jews? Where, he would ask—and he would ask anyone and everyone who showed the slightest interest in what he had to say—*where* was the logic in that?"

He glanced at his son, as though in the hope of hearing an answer, but when it was clear that none was forthcoming he went on, raising both hands almost apologetically and spreading his fingers wide to indicate that these thoughts were Karel's and not necessarily his own.

"Well, *his* own answer to that unanswerable question was that the logic was priestly—'sacerdotal' was the word he used—and because

of that, it was invisible and incomprehensible to ordinary men, since
it lay in the repository of most of the other logic of priests everywhere: deep in the lightless tunnels of their rectums." Sir Henry
laughed aloud. "I used to love it when he said things like that. I was
always afraid that some band of scandalized bishops might come
leaping out of hiding and condemn the two of us for heinous and
unforgivable behavior.

"He used to say—and he was *insistent*—that priests were seldom
clever and even less often intelligent, but that most of them were
cunning and all of them self-serving. The majority of priests, he
held, those mediocrities who were destined never to be bishops or
prelates or princes of the Church, owed their positions to being born
as younger sons to parents who could not support them, which
meant that, as young men, they had all faced the same limited
choice: become a knight, or take the Church's cloth. For all of them,
and probably for a wide range of reasons, the thought of a military
life with all its brutal hardships had been abhorrent, and so they had
opted for the easier way, a life lacking in general hardship
and supported by the contributions of others. They entered the
priesthood."

Henry sat up, gulped the wine remaining in his cup, then rose to
his feet and crossed smoothly to the table, where he set the goblet
down.

"And that, my son, is all that I can tell you about my peculiar
beliefs regarding the treatment of Jews," he said, turning his head to
glance over to where André sat watching him. "Has anything I have
said been of assistance to you in your dilemma over Richard's
behavior?"

"I have no dilemma, Father. I have a revulsion."

Something that might have been a tic of annoyance flickered
between Sir Henry's brows. "That's a strong word," he said.

"And I don't use it lightly," André replied. "This is not simply
anti-Jewish sentiment on Richard's part, Father. I am talking about
mindless and inhuman cruelty, inflicted for the sheer pleasure of
doing so and observing the results."

That caught Sir Henry by surprise. He looked keenly at his son, trying to read his face, but seeing nothing he could identify, he slowly made his way back to the fire. "Very well, then, tell me what you mean by that, because it is a very strong indictment. 'Inhuman cruelty inflicted for the sheer pleasure of doing so and observing the results.' I would expect to hear something utterly infamous in the way of charges to back such a statement up."

"Well then, would you accept a report of the King's guards being sent out into the streets to arrest any Jews they find and bring them back for the entertainment of the King's guests at dinner? That in itself might not qualify as infamous, unless you consider that the entertainment consists of their being pinioned by men-at-arms and held erect while their teeth are pulled out with pliers ... *all* their teeth."

The silence that followed seemed vast. André sat tensely, leaning forward in his chair and waiting for his father to respond.

"You saw this? You were there?"

"No, sir, I was not. It would appear that I have a happy knack of being absent on such occasions. But it has happened more than once, and I have been told of it each time by people who were present and whose word I trust."

"What people?"

André shrugged. "The knight you met today, for one, Bernard de Tremelay."

"You trust him, you say?"

"Implicitly, Father. I have known him now for eight months and he is become my closest friend, almost from the moment we first met."

Sir Henry looked steadily at his son, one eyebrow rising slightly. "I find that strange ... you tend not to make friends that quickly."

"I know. But we liked each other from the outset, probably because of how we met, if truth be told. We were the only two young men in one particularly large and grave gathering of humorless gray-beards, and I fear we found companionship in quiet laughter. He was the one who gave me the most detailed description of the abuse of one unfortunate Jew … the first one to suffer that way, I believe. I was away from London at the time, but Bernard told me all about it, in great and lurid detail, when I returned. He was sickened, and he sickened me, too, with the telling of it."

"And you say Richard condones such things?"

André barked a sound that could have been the truncated start of a laugh. "Condones them? Better say foments them. Father, this is Richard's notion of a wondrous way to keep his friends amused." He looked away for a moment and then looked back to where his father stood thunderstruck. "As I understand it, the first occasion was almost accidental, one of those things that simply comes about unplanned. One of the Golden Clan made a comment to the effect that he was having trouble with a Jew to whom he owed money—"

"The Golden Clan? What does that mean?"

André frowned and shook his head. "Forgive me, Father, it is not something I would expect you to know about and certainly nothing you would ever approve of. The term is a pejorative, recently coined in England, a name used to indicate certain of King Richard's cronies. The unnatural ones who have no use for women. They were originally called the Gilded Geldings, until someone pointed out that they were anything but gelded."

"Quite. So what did this fellow say about the Jew?"

"Something about the fellow having his teeth in him. Whatever he said, it was evidently enough to spur Richard to shout, 'Then let's have the whoreson's teeth out!' and he sent his guards to arrest the Jew at his counting house and bring him back to the King's Hall at Westminster. They pulled his teeth publicly that night, at dinner, apparently with such notable success that the entertainment has been repeated at random several more times, whenever the King or any of his guests feels bored. He simply sends his men out to find a Jew. Their Jewishness alone is condemnation enough to justify their so-called punishment."

"God in Heaven!" Sir Henry's jaw dropped and he groped for the back of his chair, then lowered himself back into his seat "That is …" His voice failed him; his mouth moved, but no words emerged until he stopped trying, swallowed, and shook his head slowly. "That is infamous. And no one has complained? What about the bishops?" He slashed his hand in dismissal as soon as he spoke. "No, that would be a waste of time and effort. They would do nothing, except perhaps to bray encouragement. But surely some of the nobles must have complained of such outrages."

"Complained?" André St. Clair sounded as though he might either laugh or weep. "To whom should they complain, Father? To the King, about his own conduct? Would you dare that?" He held up a hand, palm outward, to silence a response. "Yes, you probably would, but what would you achieve? At best you would draw down his rage for offending him and his sensibilities. And at worst, what? Who knows? This is Richard *Plantagenet* ... Besides, if you spoke out everyone would think you mad, to champion a Jew in any way. No one would have any sympathy for you, no matter what Richard did to you. You would stand alone, and you'd stand condemned."

"As would you, were you to speak out." Sir Henry's voice was measured, filled with regret. "So, what are you to do now, my son? It seems clear you have no wish to continue as you are at present."

André, however, demurred. "No, Father, that is not so, and that is what makes this choice so difficult for me. It may seem clear to you, as you say, that I have no wish to continue as I am, but it is far from clear to me. I have had many duties and responsibilities thrust upon me in past months, and few of them have stemmed from Richard. The truth is that much of my loyalty is now willingly committed to Robert de Sablé, and he, in turn, is bound to Richard and knows nothing about what we are speaking of tonight. The most frightening thing of all, perhaps, is that, in spite of all I know, I still see much in Richard to admire. The man is a phenomenon, both in his strengths and in his weaknesses. He is a mass of indivisible contradictions. Cruel and inhumanly unjust as he can be in this matter of the Jews, he possesses at the same time all the military virtues and the strengths that I admire and to which I aspire. And his people— *all* his people—appear to love him, from afar at least, in principle, be they in Normandy, England, Brittany, Aquitaine, Anjou, or at home in our own Poitou. All his allies in the gathering army look up to him and are proud to be numbered among his host, even Philip Augustus and the Count of Flanders. So I am still unable to decide what I must do, but I will not be quitting the army. Perhaps all I can hope to do is avoid attending any of the King's dinners." He rose and laid his drinking cup on the table.

"It is late. The fire is almost out again, and although I myself am not tired I have kept you too long from your bed. I'll go and take the night air for a while and leave you to sleep. You have to be on parade at dawn and I do not, so I can be more dilatory in rising than you can … but I have much to think upon before I sleep this night." André smiled lopsidedly, then embraced his father warmly. "Thank you, Father, for listening. Sleep well."

Henry undressed slowly and climbed into bed, blowing out the last candle. He did not expect to find rest easily that night, after listening to his son, but he fell asleep almost instantly.

SIX

ndré St. Clair had much on his mind when he left his father
that night, and without any conscious awareness of seeking
height, he soon found himself answering the challenge of
the guardsman on the battlements at the top of the highest tower of
the keep of Castle Baudelaire. He met the challenge, identified
himself, then went to lean against the side of one of the embrasures,
gazing out into the enveloping blackness. Were he to lean forward,
he knew, the dying campfires of Richard's army would be visible
below, a river of embers stretching away on both sides, edging the
winding path of the river Loire. In front of him, however, in the
distant west, there was nothing visible at all, which meant that either
the night was moonless or the cloud cover was absolute, and he
glanced up, unsurprised to see the heavy blankness of a starless sky.
He sighed and turned his back on the emptiness, lodging his
buttocks against the sill of the embrasure and crossing his arms on
his chest, then allowed his thoughts to drift.

The following morning he would set out with Richard and all his
army for the Burgundian town of Vézelay, where, according to tradi-
tion, the bones of Saint Mary Magdalene had been enshrined twelve
hundred years earlier. It lay a three-day march to the west from
Baudelaire and had been the officially approved assembly point for
the armies of western Christendom ever since the sainted Abbott
Bernard of the Cistercian monastery of Clairvaux had dispatched the
Soldiers of Christ from there on the first campaign to recapture the
Holy Land from the Muslim Seljuk Turks, ninety-five years earlier
in 1095. Now, this month of June in the year 1190, all the puissant
forces of Frankish Christendom would gather there, to be blessed

and freshly rededicated to their purpose by Holy Mother Church, after which the entire assembly would travel southward to Lyon on the river Rhone. From Lyon, the French King and his followers would make their way across the Alps of Savoie to Torino and thence south to Genoa, where Philip had hired the entire Genoese fleet to transport his army eastward. Richard's forces would march directly south from Lyon through his own ducal territories, following the Rhone to Marseille, where his English fleet would be awaiting them under the command of his admiral, Sir Robert de Sablé. The embarkation would work smoothly, André knew, for it had the benefit of long and careful planning with an eye to every conceivable contingency.

Despite the impression he had given to his father earlier, he really had little difficulty, moral or otherwise, with the thought of accompanying Richard to war in person. The André St. Clair who had emerged from hiding a year earlier, under threat of death from the trio of venal priests, might have balked at doing so, but he was a different person from the man who sat now at the top of Castle Baudelaire, considering his options. That younger man, more naïve and perhaps more self-absorbed than André St. Clair was today, might have been sufficiently foolish and intolerant to endanger himself by showing his disapproval of the King's behavior, but much had changed in the intervening year to blunt the point of young André's impetuosity.

His initial encounter with Robert de Sablé, triggering fraternal recognition between them, had quickly brought about a complete renewal of André's commitment to the Order of Sion after a lengthy period in which isolation and responsibility for running the family estate had caused a drifting from the brotherhood. De Sablé had brought an end to all that. André was now constantly moving between one place and another, ostensibly on business related to de Sablé's task of readying the fleet but in reality serving as a courier between de Sablé and the other members of the Governing Council of the Order, whose members were scattered widely across the provinces of what had once been Roman Gaul. For a thousand years,

beginning in the Pyrenees and the Languedoc, then extending
outward into Aquitaine, Poitou, and Burgundy and as far west and
north as Brittany, Normandy, and Picardy, the ancient confederation
of clans who called themselves the Friendly Families had spread
throughout the land, taking their influence and the ancient, secret
brotherhood of their Order with them. Now, working with a few other
members of the brotherhood as a full-time liaison between the
outlying members of the Governing Council—which was how he
had come to meet his friend and brother Bernard de Tremelay—
André no longer had any doubt about his future admission to the
ranks of the Temple. That was already a *fait accompli*, guaranteed by
the goodwill of the Council of the Order of Rebirth, that small group
of powerful men who had, since its beginnings, dictated the fortunes
and directions of the Order of the Temple, even while the vast majority of Templars were completely ignorant of their existence.

The origins of the Templars, a mere seventy-two years earlier, in
1118, were already legendary. Every boy old enough to thrill to tales
of adventure and great exploits knew how the veteran warrior Hugh
de Payens had gathered about him a tiny band of knights, nine of
them including himself, and dedicated them to defend and champion
Christian pilgrims in the Holy Land against the swarming hordes of
Arab bandits who for years had lain in wait for them at every turn in
the roads. Calling themselves the Poor Fellow Soldiers of Jesus
Christ, de Payens and his men had undertaken monastic oaths of
poverty, chastity, and obedience and had quartered themselves in
some abandoned stables on the Temple Mount within the city of
Jerusalem and from there, in the face of incalculable and seemingly
impossible odds, they had won spectacular successes against the
marauding bandits, making the roads of the Kingdom of Jerusalem
relatively safe to travel for the first time since the capture of
Jerusalem in 1099.

Thereafter, within less than a score of years from the date of their
founding, championed by Bernard of Clairvaux, who had written a
rule for their new order, their successes and their heroic prowess had
become so renowned that their recruitment numbers had swollen

almost beyond counting. They had become widely recognized and revered throughout Christendom, first as the Knights of the Temple Mount of Jerusalem, then as the Knights Templar, and eventually quite simply as the Order of the Temple, although their official name remained the Poor Fellow Soldiers of Christ and the Temple of Solomon. There were other military orders in the world today, most notably the Knights of the Hospital and the Emperor Barbarossa's recently formed Teutonic Knights, but the Temple Knights had been the first of their kind, the first monk knights, and their glory would never fade.

That was the legend. The truth was as sparse as legendary truths must always be. The reality, a secret known only to the initiates of the Order of Sion, was that de Payens and his eight original companions had all been Brothers of the Order of Sion, and they had been sent deliberately to Jerusalem to unearth a treasure. As described in the lore of the ancient Order, this treasure had been laid down there eleven hundred years earlier, at the time of the destruction of Jerusalem and its people by the Roman General Titus, son of the Emperor Vespasian. Estimates of the slaughter carried out there varied, but few doubted that upward of six hundred thousand Jews had died, and many sources, most of them Roman records, claimed twice that many had perished. Whichever was correct, the Jews had ceased to function as a race in their own homeland since that time.

Notwithstanding that, according to the lore that had directed de Payens and his companions in their search, a large number of the Jewish priestly caste—inheritors of the original Jerusalem Assembly, the communal church supervised during their lifetimes by Jesus and his brother James the Just—had foreseen the tragedy and escaped the destruction and the bloodbath that followed, first burying the bulk of what they could not carry with them, the written records of their community, beyond the reach of even the rapacious Romans.

Safely out of the doomed city, these people, sometimes called Essenes, had then made their way overland, traveling in large but loose-knit groups for mutual safety. South and west they walked, to the Nile Delta, Cairo and Alexandria, and then westward for years across the immensity of Africa, always keeping within sight of the great Central Sea on their right, until they reached the Narrows and managed to cross out of Africa and into Iberia. From Iberia, long before it became Spain, they made their way northward on foot again, crossing the Pyrenees eventually and arriving in Gaul, where they settled in the region now known as the Languedoc.

Highly aware of who they were and what they represented, they were determined to return one day to their homeland, to claim their inheritance and unearth the treasure they had buried there. Rome had decreed their deaths, and thus their safety and their very survival depended upon their ability to conceal their true identity from others. And so they worked at doing precisely that, blending and mixing seamlessly into the primitive and unstable society that was Roman Gaul, less than a hundred years after Julius Caesar's conquest of the region. They were not to know that more than a millennium would pass before their return, but they planned carefully and methodically nonetheless.

Originally more than thirty families strong, from the start of their new lives in Gaul they called themselves the Friendly Families. They established a communal integrity that fitted easily within the tribal units of the Gallic world and would persist while centuries elapsed and each of the original families expanded to become a wide-branching clan. Their assimilation was so successful that within four generations only a select few of them—and absolutely no outsiders—knew that their families had ever been Jewish.

They adopted the new religion of Christianity with everyone else when it arose, but among themselves they formed a secret brotherhood they called the Order of Rebirth in Sion, the *Rebirth* anticipating their own renewed embrace of their ancient religion and their traditional way of life once safely returned to their home in Jerusalem. The elders of the Families decided that they themselves, the patriarchs, would be the only members of their clans to safeguard the knowledge of their Jewishness, practicing their rites and ceremonies secretly, away from the eyes and knowledge even of their own loved ones, purely as a matter of protection.

As the years passed, without incident or alarum, and the longed-for return was still deferred, they decided upon recruitment to ensure the safety of their sacred knowledge. One male member, and only one, of each ensuing generation of each of the original families would be considered eligible for promotion to membership in their brotherhood, and his suitability would be judged by the membership at large, with the criteria for admission clearly defined. The male offspring of any woman who wed outside the Families were ineligible for membership, and since none but the Brotherhood of the Order knew anything about it, no one ever suffered by that.

Apart from the requirement of direct male descent from Friendly Families blood, honor and integrity, intelligence and righteousness, single-minded purpose, and the ability to maintain close-mouthed secrecy at all times and under all conditions were the *sine qua non* elements of eligibility. Within a very short time, as the original Families grew larger, there was never any shortage of eligible candidates, so that in the event that no single member of a given generation of one family was thought fit for membership, then none would be chosen and the eligibility would pass to the next generation, with no slur of any kind against the family.

The system was set into place with great care and great planning, and from the outset it worked magnificently. Because of the need to ensure the very highest standards of behavior and performance in each candidate, the scrutinizing and evaluation process was slow, painstaking, and continuous. No one could be admitted before reaching the age of eighteen years, but entry was often awarded long after that age, since each son born into a generation had to be given his opportunity to be evaluated. No candidate ever understood anything about what was happening to him during the early stages leading to his initiation; he understood only that he was being prepared for something momentous, that it was secret, serious, and solemn, and that the people preparing him, his mentors and sponsors in the work, were the people in his life for whom he held the highest regard. Only after his initiation, when he was Raised to full membership of the Brotherhood of the Order, would his early training begin to make any sense to him, and only then would he realize that he, perhaps the only living member of the brotherhood in his entire family, was the only one who knew the brotherhood existed. That was often the most difficult element of initiation for a new member to understand: that he was cut off forever, in a very basic and fundamental sense, from the remainder of his family, knowing a truth about himself and about their origins that he was forbidden to share; forever unable to discuss with them, or even to acknowledge, an area of his life that would continue to grow greater and more important to him while they remained unaware of its existence and oblivious to its significance.

André St. Clair had been troubled by that only infrequently for several years now, but this evening it had come home to him to sting like a serpent's venom, enhanced by the irony of his father's ignorance of what they were really discussing. Sir Henry St. Clair, the noble Angevin, was intensely proud of his heritage and his family's ancient and honorable lineage, and he meant every word of what he said when he claimed to have no prejudice against Jews, and his son had not the slightest doubt of that. But notwithstanding Sir Henry's integrity and his genuine goodwill, André also knew that his father would be insulted and outraged were anyone to attempt to make him believe that Jewish blood ran in his veins and that his ancestors had been Judean priests. Furthermore, it would be inconceivable to him, utterly incomprehensible, that his own son should adhere to those beliefs and in accordance with them should dedicate his life to ensuring that the ancient teachings they involved would come to pass in today's world. That reality would be forever alien to the old man, and André had no choice but to grit his teeth and come to terms with it, for there was nothing he could do to change a whit of it.

The disgusting business of the tooth pulling was real enough, but it was a relatively minor piece of knavery, and André had used it deliberately to shock his father into seeing how serious were his concerns. But the real villainy, André knew, lay in the less ostensibly brutal but far more widespread and lethal persecutions of the Jews throughout the length and breadth of England in the previous half year. It had begun on the day of Richard's coronation, the third of September in the previous year, 1189, at his notably, some said scandalously, masculine coronation dinner. The Bachelors' Feast, it had been called, and no woman of any rank, including the King's mother, had been invited. Towards the end of the proceedings, when everyone was far gone in drink, a delegation of Jewish merchants had come to offer gifts and good wishes to the new monarch. But they had been stopped at the entrance to the King's Hall, their gifts confiscated, and then they were stripped and beaten before being thrown out into the streets, where they were pursued by a mob who followed them right into the Jewish quarter of London and there set about burning the houses of the Jews who lived there.

No one made any attempt to stop the mob until the fire began to spread to the neighboring Christian district. On the day that followed, Richard publicly ignored the atrocity, other than ordering the death by hanging of several men who had been instrumental in the burning of Christian-owned properties. The Archbishop of Canterbury, who was present at the time, said no single word in defense of the hapless Jews, content merely to comment that if they chose not to be followers of Christ, then they must be prepared to be treated as followers of the Devil.

With such examples of mercy and forbearance for guidance from their King and their Archbishop, it surprised few observers that the citizenry of England's great cities indulged in orgies of anti-Jewishness in the months that followed, their hunger for the blood of the "Christ killers" bolstering their hysterical determination to wrest back the Holy City from the godless Saracens. André had been on the way to visit the King's Quartermasters of the city of York when the last great outrage occurred there in the days leading up to Easter, a mere month before his return to Anjou. It was all over by noon on the day he arrived at York, but everyone was still talking about it.

He learned that a vengeful mob had collected and then chased a crowd of nearly five hundred terrified Jews—men, women, and children—into the fortified Tower of York, which they then surrounded, screaming for the Jews to come out and face their "punishment." In the expectation of certain torture and appalling slaughter, the Jewish elders decided to be merciful to themselves. All five hundred committed suicide.

André knew in his heart that similar atrocities had occurred in his own homeland from time to time, but the scope, the regularity, and the bloodthirstiness of the uprisings in England had soured him forever against that country, and the tacit approval of its newly crowned King had effectively killed any enthusiasm and willing support he might have shown for joining in Richard's military adventures. Only his greater duty, his fraternal obligations to the Order of Sion, prevented him from divorcing himself completely from the company and service of the English King, and even so, knowing the importance of what he had to do on the Order's behalf, the younger St. Clair was finding that overcoming his repugnance and maintaining a veneer of enthusiasm was far from easy.

His thoughts were interrupted by the sounds of movement close by, and he turned to look across at the guard on duty on the other side of the tower platform, who had been joined in his corner by another man. Their voices reached him as no more than a murmur, but as he looked, André saw the newcomer start to move in his direction, silhouetted against the glare of the sentry's fire basket. He straightened up and rose to his feet just in time to recognize his friend and companion from Orléans, Bernard of Tremelay, who greeted him with raised eyebrows.

"St. Clair? I thought you would have been fast asleep by now, after all the riding we have done these past few days."

"Then clearly you think me weaker than you are. Why aren't you abed by now?"

"I was, but I could not sleep. Too many matters on my mind, I suppose. Tomorrow will come quickly enough, but I thought to defer it a while by staying awake. So, what were you thinking about up here all alone?"

André waved in farewell to the watching guard, then followed de Tremelay down the narrow steps to the causeway beneath the battlements, holding his response until he was beneath the line of the guard's sight.

"That membership in our brotherhood sometimes comes at great cost."

They had begun descending the next flight, but de Tremelay stopped and turned to look up at André behind him. "Your father again?" André nodded. "Well, it's true, Brother. It does. But when you find yourself fretting over that, remember this: just when you think that cost has grown unbearable, it can grow worse. And it will, without fail. Trust me, despair is the only road left open to us." And then he barked a great, guffawing laugh and swung back to his descent.

"Bernard, in honesty, has anyone ever told you what a turd you truly are?"

"Aye, a few." This time de Tremelay did not pause and the words drifted back over his shoulder. "But when you're a turd, people walk around you, rather than risk treading on you. Trust me on that, too." He laughed again as they reached the bottom of the stairs, then grasped a handful of André's surcoat and pulled him gently but firmly back into the shadows at the side of the stairs, where they could be neither seen nor heard.

"Bear this in mind from now on, lad," he said in a low voice that held no trace of humor, "and don't ever forget. In a few days, when we reach Vézelay, you will be accepted into the outer ranks of the Order of the Temple formally, as a postulant. After that, if you keep your nose clean and look to your assignments, you will become a novice, and eventually, all things being equal, you'll end up a full-blown knight of the Temple, privy to all its secrets and its so-called sacred lore. You believe it's difficult now, keeping secrets from your noble father? Well, that difficulty will seem like nothing within a matter of mere days.

"Wait until you enter the temple and are shut off among people whose every thought is alien to all that you know and believe. Wait until you find yourself floundering among the pig-headed ignorance and unquestioning stupidity you'll find within the ranks you are about to join, where the knights all firmly believe they are God's chosen and the world's elite—and many of their sergeants think the same way—and you will not be able to breathe a single word about the truth you know: that their sacred and secretive Order was invented by the brotherhood to which *you* belong, to safeguard *that* Order's sacred secrets.

"Your entire existence in their ranks will be a lie, and you will have the salt of that rubbed into your awareness every time they wake you in the middle of the night to pray in a ritual that holds no truth for you. You will know better, but you will have no other option than to comply and to observe their false rites, and you will never be able to say a word in protest or complaint. Now that, I suggest to you, might cause you some real difficulty. And that, unlike the minor business with your father, represents the real cost of belonging to our brotherhood.

"Fortunately, of course, your isolation will not last forever. As soon as you have passed all the tests and met all the qualifications for achieving full membership, the strictures surrounding you will be relaxed and members of our own brotherhood within the Temple ranks will see to it that you are assigned to duties in which you can be used to best advantage."

He grinned again, squeezing St. Clair's shoulders in his hands. "But I promise you, albeit I have never been inside a Temple gathering, your next few months are destined to be sheer misery."

"Aye," André sighed. "I have been warned about all that already. But I want to thank you for the obvious delight you have taken in reminding me of what lies ahead."

"It does lie ahead of you, André, but by the time we reach Outremer, it should be over and you'll be back in the world of living men. Now get you to bed and sleep well, then rise and greet tomorrow's day bright eyed. They say it's going to rain, so it will be a long, wet pilgrimage to Vézelay, and we'll endure great misery before we find comfort again."

THE MORNING SUN ROSE DAZZLINGLY above the snowy peaks of the Alps in the eastern distance, illuminating the great banner of the

Order of the Temple that stood proudly alone, reflecting the blinding rays back from the crest of a hill that overlooked the fields
surrounding the town of Vézelay. The banner did not flap in the light
breeze, as did some others in the throng below the hill; it hung rigid,
weighted along its bottom, from a bar at the top of an enormously
high pole, allowing its equal-armed, eight-pointed red cross to stand
out stark, challenging, and unmistakable against the pure white of its
field, proclaiming the Order's pre-eminence. Beneath it stood its
formal guard of ten armored, white-clad knights, and around them,
covering the entire hilltop and neatly laid out in regular, rectangular
patterns, lay the campsite of the Order's personnel: knights and
sergeants of the Temple, the majority of them new and untested,
recruited only recently to fill the Order's depleted ranks after the
tragic losses sustained in Outremer.

More than a thousand fighting men were drawn up in formation
there, on the downward slope of the hill in front of their foremost
line of tents, and fewer than one hundred of those had ever been
involved in a real battle. The knights among them, fewer than six to
every score, wore plain white surcoats, emblazoned not with the
black cross of the Temple but with the brilliant red, long-bodied
cross of their mission to regain the Holy Land. The remaining men,
the Sergeants of the Order, wore the same red crosses over surcoats
of plain brown, save for a scattering of senior sergeants who wore
distinctive black surcoats signifying their rank.

Below and in front of the Templars, the remainder of the armies of
Christendom seethed and eddied like fields of grain in a high wind,
save that no field of grain, even when rich with wildflowers, could
ever show such a profusion of colors. They completely filled up the
fields that stretched away towards the little town of Vézelay, which
was hidden in the distance by a forest of tents and pavilions. To the
right of the watching Templars, the ranks of Richard Plantagenet's
followers stood banked, block after solid block of them, horse and
foot, interspersed with formations of the King's crossbowmen and
archers, who were easily distinguishable by their drab colors and their
lack of formal armor. Within that host, the individual colors of the

various divisions could be discerned in places among the surrounding welter: the wine-red standards of Burgundy stood firmly alongside the dark, rich blue of Aquitaine, and the greens and gold of Anjou and Maine were visible behind those, as was the black and crimson of Poitou, along with the blue-and-white stripes, pale greens, and yellows and reds of Brittany and Normandy and, of course, the golden lions of St. George's England on their crimson field, flapping above all the others on a gigantic silken banner and supported by no less a churchman than Archbishop Baldwin of Canterbury, who had personally levied three thousand Welshmen, mainly archers, to join Richard's host.

Opposite this panoply, ranged on the Templars' left, were the forces of Philip Augustus and his allies. As befitted the dignity of a French King, Philip's own royal standard, the golden fleurs-de-lis on a sky-blue field of the House of Capet, appeared to be at least as large as that of his English ally, and behind it were clustered the colors of his own major allies and vassals, comprising the flower of the nobility of Christendom. The brilliant colors of Stephen, Count of Sancerre, were prominent there, as Richard had foretold they would be, more than a year earlier. So were those of Count Philip of Flanders, and Henry the Count of Champagne, nephew to both kings, accompanied by an entire cavalcade of lesser French nobility. The German Louis, Margrave of Thuringia, had lent his stature to the French King's use, as had a huge number of knights from Denmark, Hungary, and Flanders. And there were bishops everywhere among the throng on both sides, many of them clustered in prayer in a vast gathering between the two armies, but many, many more among the armies themselves, armored over and beneath their vestments and accoutered for war, hungry for the blood of any Saracen foolish enough to come within their reach.

André St. Clair sat gazing down at the spectacle from a knoll at the front edge of the Templar formation, several horse lengths ahead of the leading rank, with his immediate superior, Brother Justin, the Master of Novices, on his left side. Justin was a scowling, grim-faced veteran who stank like rancid goat cheese. St. Clair was two horse lengths away from him, but the acrid smell of the older man threatened to take his breath away every time he inhaled. Brother Justin was flanked on his own left in turn by their expeditionary force's taciturn commander, Etienne de Troyes, whose austerity and utter lack of tolerance for public spectacles like this were legendary. De Troyes was what his brethren in the Order of Sion called a Temple Boar—*un sanglier Templier*. He did not belong to the Order of Rebirth and had, in consequence, no knowledge or suspicion of the Order's existence.

One of the most highly ranked Templars in all the Frankish territories of what had been Gaul, de Troyes, like so many others of his ilk, was utterly intolerant of everyone and everything that was not a part of his world, and within that narrowly circumscribed world there was but one entity of any significance: the Order of the Temple. Anything that interfered with his intense dedication to the Temple and its priorities was not to be tolerated. On this occasion, however, much as he disliked the restraint, Sir Etienne could not disdainfully dismiss the goings-on below and absent himself. He was the Master of the Temple in Poitou, which made him the senior officer of the Order present in Vézelay that day, and he had thus a responsibility to observe all that happened. The Temple neither owed nor accorded fealty or allegiance to any temporal king or lord. Its loyalty and fealty lay wholly with the Pope in Rome, and its representatives were here this day as the Pope's personal emissaries, although they would fight with both of the Kings below against the common Saracen enemy.

Brother Justin had designated St. Clair a courier that morning, against the need for someone to carry dispatches to, or gather information from, anyone in the armies below. The designation was extraordinary, everyone knew that, since St. Clair was a mere postulant to the Order, admitted a mere two days earlier, but Justin was taking blatant advantage, and to no one's surprise, of André's filial relationship with the Master-at-Arms below. At their backs, bound by the discipline of the Order's training, the Templar ranks were utterly silent, the only sounds they made emanating from the restless movement of horses that had been standing still for too long. By contrast, the noise from the army massed ahead of them was chaotic, a low rumbling of a hundred thousand voices overscored by louder, sometimes strident shouts of command, unintelligible from this distance, and the constant braying of trumpets and horns. André's horse stamped and whinnied, sidling closer to Brother Justin's mount and fighting against the rein when André, almost revolted by the man's stench, tried to bring it back.

"Where is your father? I can't see him."

Ignoring the frowning presence of their field commander on his left side, Brother Justin had spoken brusquely from the corner of his mouth, without moving his head, and in response, unaware of what might be permitted him in this situation, André leaned forward in his saddle and turned his head very slightly to his right, to peer down the slope to where the standard of St. George waved over a churning mass of brightly clad bodies, human and equine, that made nonsense of any attempt to discern order.

"He's there somewhere, Brother Justin. He will be in the thick of it, among the throng. Has to be. He organized this whole thing on King Richard's side—protocol, procedure, order of precedence, everything—so he must be in there somewhere."

As St. Clair spoke, Etienne de Troyes uttered a disgusted curse. His patience with the distant proceedings was exhausted. Sawing savagely on the bit, he swung his horse around and sank his spurs into its flanks, spurring it up the hill, his entire body radiating the intensity of his displeasure. Brother Justin watched him go from the corner of his eye before he breathed out and spoke again, in what passed for his normal voice.

"The Marshal is plainly not pleased with what's going on down there. Nor should we be, I think. We can see everything there is to see, except those things we want to see—and that includes action—but do we understand any of what's going on? The only thing I can recognize with any certainty is that huge, unholy cluster of bejeweled bishops in the middle yonder, between the two armies, waiting to play their part in this mummery. If even half of those prating, pathetic whoresons are allowed to pray at us, we'll all die of old age before we ever get off this hill."

St. Clair was astonished to hear such words from the mouth of the Master of Novices, but he had the good sense to betray no reaction. Despite that, however, he felt a need to say something, and so he cleared his throat. "Little fear of that, Brother Justin. Richard Plantagenet is in charge down there. He has no more affection for high priests than his father had. Those bishops will all pray, but they will pray together when the time for prayer arrives."

The Master of Novices grunted but made no other response, evidently having remembered that he was speaking to the merest nonentity. But then he added, unexpectedly, "Aye, they will, like as not. The Archbishop of Lyon will lead them—and the Abbot of Vézelay will assist."

They were interrupted by the clattering of hooves as one of the senior knights, whose name André did not yet know, rode forward and reined in on Brother Justin's left, speaking to him as though St. Clair did not exist.

"What's happening down there? De Troyes is angrier than a wet cat."

"I know he is, but nothing's happening. He simply can't stand the waste of time. It would make a saint angry. There's a hundred thousand men down there, and they're all due to leave this day, but they are up to their armpits in bishops, panting to pray again."

The other knight hawked and spat. "These past three days have been a bishop's dream—one endless, sweaty Mass with panoply and chanted prayers and roiling clouds of incense. But enough's enough. Now it is time to pack up all the tents, load all the wagons, marshal the armies, and strike out on the road."

He turned his head, his eyes taking in St. Clair but dismissing him instantly as of no import, and nodded to the Master of Novices. "You mark my words. We'll either be off this hill and on the road by noon today, or Richard Plantagenet will stand excommunicate." His voice sank to a cynical growl. "And with Holy Mother Church relying on him to lead this entire campaign, exterminate Saladin and his Saracens, and win the Holy City back for Rome, excommunication would appear to be unlikely."

"De Chateauroux!" The voice cracked from the heights behind them like the sound of shattering rock, and the knight beside Brother Justin straightened up with a jerk. "Shit! Keep an eye out. See if you can detect any movement between the camps. Anything at all! Here, Brother Marshal!" De Chateauroux shouted an acknowledgment and pulled his mount into a dramatic, rearing turn, setting his spurs to it before its front hooves reached the ground, plainly having no wish to draw the displeasure of de Troyes.

From the corner of his eye, André saw Brother Justin turn to watch the other man leave, then swing back towards him. "You stay here," he snarled, "and if you see anything change down there, any movement of any kind by a large group, send for me at once."

André heard him clatter off in pursuit of de Chateauroux, but made no effort to watch him. He already felt conspicuous sitting where he was, a mere postulant, not even a novice, yet clearly being accorded preferential treatment. He had noticed no signs of resentment from any of his fellows, but he was shrewd enough to anticipate that it might be there somewhere, hidden beneath a veil of seeming indifference, and he had no wish to make matters worse by appearing to gawk or to preen.

A short time later, during which nothing of any moment had happened below, Brother Justin came back.

"You, St. Clair. Marshal de Troyes wants to go down there, in his official capacity as Marshal, to spur the sluggards along. You are to ride down and find your father the Master-at-Arms and inform him that the Marshal of the Temple wishes to confer privately with the two monarchs. Do you think you can manage that?" When André did not react to the sarcasm, he went on, "You see that boulder over there?"

"Aye, Brother Justin." The boulder was too enormous not to see, a singular, inexplicable stone of gigantic size, dwarfing the mounted knights who sat in its shadow.

"You will ride down there and find your father, but you will go escorted, as a formal courier from the Marshal, riding under a baucent pennant." He turned in his saddle, stuck two fingers in his mouth, and whistled loudly, attracting the startled attention of a young knight behind him who clutched a long lance bearing the triangular baucent banner of his squadron. "Come over here, you," he shouted, and waited, arm outstretched, until the young standard-bearer obediently came to join him. Different from the great banner, the lesser baucent was the battle standard of the Temple—a plain, black, equal-armed cross on a white field—and the right to carry it was a great honor that was hotly contested among the rank-and-file brothers of each squadron formation. Brother Justin nodded an abrupt acknowledgment of the man's courtesy, then waved a thumb towards St. Clair without removing his gaze from the standard-bearer.

"I need you for extra duty, Brother. You will ride down to the valley below, escorting this courier who, although he is but a postulant, has well-hidden virtues. You will stay with him until he concludes his business with the Master-at-Arms of King Richard's army, then return here with him. I will inform your squadron commander of where you are and what you are about." He turned now to André. "As for you, as soon as you have completed your task and know where the Kings choose to meet with the Marshal, you will climb to the top of the boulder down there and signal us with this baucent. For the English camp, hold the pennant in your right hand, for the French, the left hand. If they choose to meet between the armies, close by the bishops, raise it above your head with both arms. I'll have the sharpest eyes here on watch for you and you'll stand out with your virgin's shroud." He was referring to the still-new, brilliantly white postulant's robe that St. Clair was wearing. André nodded wordlessly. "You send the signal yourself, you understand? The standard-bearer's red cross might well be lost to sight among all the other crosses down there." He looked again at the standard-bearer. "You understand that? You are to give him your baucent and let him use it to send the signal. That's important. Is it clear?"

"Aye, sir. I am to give him the baucent for the signal. But will I take it back again?"

Brother Justin pulled back his head as though he had been slapped. "Aye, of course you will. It is a baucent, in God's name, not a walking staff." He hesitated, then sniffed loudly and spoke again to André. "As soon as you send us the signal, the Marshal and his party will make their way down to the appointed place while you make your way back up here and report to me. Clear? Then go, and waste no time. Marshal de Troyes will be awaiting your word and fretting."

St. Clair nodded and followed his escort as the standard-bearer hitched his shield higher, tightened the reins in his left hand, raised his lance in salute to the standard, and spurred his horse forward and down the hill.

IT WAS TWO HOURS LATER by the time St. Clair returned, and the first thing he noticed when he reached the crest of the hill was that they had broken camp in his absence; all the tents were dismantled and stowed for travel. He saluted the Master of Novices, who dismissed him immediately with a contemptuous flick of one hand. Nothing loath, André moved gratefully to join the fifteen hopefuls with whom he would share his life for the foreseeable future, both as postulant and novice brother. There were no prospective sergeant brothers among them; all were of the knightly class and were already either knighted or advanced in their training, ranking at least as squires. Their formal induction as novices, they had been told, would take place in the cathedral in Lyon, and until they reached there they would continue to wear the shapeless garment known as the virgin's shroud. But until they were formally accepted as novices they would continue to act, and to be treated, as servants of the Order. This was in keeping with the way of the Temple, and none of the postulants was dissatisfied with their lot. Lyon lay but a five-day march southeast of Vézelay, and thus within the week they would be launched as knights of the Temple.

They ranged in age from a gangly, knock-kneed stripling of about sixteen to a serious-looking, dark-skinned man of about André's own age, with whom St. Clair had shared his entry ceremony two days earlier, but with whom he had not spoken since. Now, as André approached silently to sit alongside him, the fellow spoke quietly out of the corner of his mouth, taking care not to move his head or attract any attention to himself.

"What was all that about? A postulant riding with a baucent escort? Who are you?"

"Name's St. Clair. André."

"Ah! I know who you are now. They sent you on an errand to your father."

André frowned, wondering what had prompted the tone of that comment. It had sounded like bitterness, perhaps cynicism. He answered evenly nonetheless. "They did. Do you disapprove of that?"

"It's no affair of mine. I was simply curious. Don't be offended by my lack of manners. I'm a Frank."

St. Clair risked a quick sideways glance at the man, more than half convinced he had heard a smile in the fellow's voice, but there was nothing to be seen. "Who are *you*?"

"They call me Eusebius, after the holy man. My mother was devout. I'm from Aix. Provence."

"Ah! That explains the outlandish speech. Well met, then. I'm from Poitou."

He saw the slightest inclination of the other man's head, and then they both fell silent and sat rigid as a sergeant rode by, frowning as his eyes passed from man to man. When he had gone, Eusebius cocked an eyebrow and glanced down to where a leather bag was cinched to André's belt. "What's in the bag?" he asked quietly. "You didn't have it when you rode down the hill."

"Observant." André smiled to himself, intrigued. The stranger was astute, articulate, intelligent, and might even be likable. "Dried figs, compliments of Tristan Malbec, King Richard's sutler." Tristan Wry Nose, as he was known, was senior quarter- master of Richard's armies, but long before that he had been senior steward and quartermaster to Eleanor of Aquitaine for years, until she was imprisoned in England, and then he had become Richard's.

The man called Eusebius smiled too. "It sounds as though you know the sutler passing well."

"Well enough to ask no quarter of him. I have known him since before I learned to walk, and as a friend of my mother and father, he has been feeding me sweetmeats and dainties since before that. He warned me not to eat these all at once, because it might be years before I see another one. I'll give you one later, if you like."

Eusebius stared straight ahead, but nodded. "My thanks for that. I will enjoy it. I have not eaten a fig in years. So what is happening down there now? And where is the Marshal?"

The man fell silent again as the sergeant, who had finished his inspection, swung around and began to make his way back towards them, glancing from man to man and clearly hoping to find someone who would give him a reason to play the tyrant. Neophytes as they were, however, none of them was sufficiently naïve to give him the slightest opportunity to be displeased, and when he was less than halfway along the formation someone called him and interrupted his scrutiny of the ranks. From the way he rode off rapidly in answer to the summons, it was clear to all of them that he was just as glad to be quit of them as they were of him. But still, apart from a very minor stirring in the ranks, none of the postulants moved, and only St. Clair spoke, still soft voiced and for Eusebius's ears alone.

"Everything's over down there now," he said, as though he had been speaking all along, "thanks to our humorless Marshal de Troyes. From the moment of his first greeting to the Kings, it took less than an hour to organize the closing service, short and solemn, with only one brief *Te Deum* sung before the final blessing. And then the trumpets started blowing the assembly. Now, even though we be too far back in the ranks here to see it, the armies are moving out—and we are yet more than an hour shy of noon. I think that is remarkable."

"Hmm." Eusebius glanced at St. Clair and then returned his gaze to where it ought to be. "What I find remarkable is that I have no least idea of what you are talking about. What is remarkable about the fact that the armies are moving?"

"Because for the last two days it has been looking more and more unlikely that they ever would. The Kings, Philip and Richard, were at odds, unable to agree to anything. Two days of incessant parley had produced nothing in the way of concord. But according to my father, much was achieved last night, on the surface at least. The Kings called a privy council that went on until near midnight, under heavy guard, with Richard swearing that the army would strike out for Lyon today, no matter what, and that no one would sleep until the entire agenda drawn up by the bishops had been dealt with. And so it was."

The blast of a bugle brought them to attention, and junior sergeants began to move up and down the lines, straightening the formations and preparing everyone to evacuate the hilltop. For a while there was no more talk, with everyone's attention concentrated upon the task of an orderly withdrawal. It was not until their squadron was riding down along the hillside, still far above the immense spectacle of the armies eddying in the valley below them, that the two men were able to resume their conversation, and again it was Eusebius who initiated the discussion, having looked around to ensure no officers were watching them or listening.

"So, this meeting last night. What did it achieve?"

"Agreement," André responded, keeping his voice low, although the noise of the column's movement, with the clatter of hooves, the clanking rattle of armor and weapons, and the creaking of saddle leather, would have made eavesdropping impossible. "A formal treaty of friendship and mutual amity and trust, all signed and sealed and witnessed by an army of priests. A solemn cessation of hostilities. England, including all of Anjou, Poitou, and Aquitaine, along with the remaining territories belonging to the House of Plantagenet, to be at peace with France and its allies henceforth, abjuring all conflict while England and France remain jointly engaged in the service of the Lord God. In the event that either monarch be killed before the war is ended, the other will assume command of his armies and redouble their efforts on behalf of Christ and Holy Church. Should either monarch break that pledge, he will stand excommunicate and the united bishops of both realms will attest to the justice of the punishment."

"You there! You, with your lips moving! I hope you are praying, insect, but even if you are, do it in silence. I see your lips move one more time and you'll be drawing extra latrine duties for the coming month. You hear me?"

"Aye, Brother Sergeant." André kept his face blank. Neither man had seen the sergeant approach, but now that he had singled out André, the two became models of dutiful decorum. For the next four hours, until they reached the point where they would stop for the night, they behaved themselves, making no attempt to communicate. Between them, for all that, a comradeship was born and grew stronger throughout the remainder of that day.

After dinner that night—a chaotic event, it being the first time the field kitchens had made shift to feed a thousand men at once— the two men sat by a fire for the hour before curfew. It had been a long, tiring day, so they soon found themselves alone, the rest of their companions gone to sleep, and they returned to the topic they had been discussing earlier that day.

"So Philip and Richard both agreed to that arrangement you described?" Eusebius was impressed and made no secret of it, shaking his head in mock disbelief. "I would not have believed that had I heard it yesterday. I have been told those two have been squabbling like jealous, ill-tempered fishwives ever since they arrived here, yowling and circling each other like two long-clawed cats in heat—" He broke off, looking warily at St. Clair. "Does that offend you, to hear such things?"

André merely looked at him, straight faced. "Why should it offend me? Because I count myself a friend of Richard, or because you suspect me of unnatural tastes?"

Eusebius stared back at him, unsure of how to respond and unable to decipher the look on his face, and André allowed him to hover on the edge of apprehension for several heartbeats longer before he said, "In truth, I found the long-clawed-cats-in-heat image was an apt one. Very good. Now hear me, my friend. If we are to be friends, and it seems to me we could be, then we have to start trusting each other. I swear to you that no matter what you say to me, I will not run off and report you to the Master of Novices. Not for speaking what is in your mind. Are we as one on that?" He watched until Eusebius nodded. "Good, then carry on with what you were saying. You had them fighting like cats in heat."

Eusebius sat blinking for several more moments, then nodded his head. "Excellent. So be it … Fighting bitterly is what I was saying, with that unmatchable venom of former lovers. The queenly side of Philip's nature has been on hugely admired display, I'm told. Probably because his royal nose is out of joint." He paused, and then grinned with relish. "Mind you, you can hardly blame him if you think about it at all. He has been the only king in all this land for ten years, and now his former lover has a king's rank, too. That, plus a bigger army, a deeper treasury, a more appealing personality, and a stronger, well-earned reputation as a warrior, to boot. Not to mention that he owns a bigger fleet, even stronger than the Genoan navy that Philip has had to hire at great expense to ship his own army. And none of that is made any easier for him to bear by the fact that Richard is too cock-a-hoop and too flamboyant ever to consider sparing Philip's dignity by toning down his own performances." He shook his head again. "That must have been a stodgy bowl of oats for Philip Capet to choke down all at once. It must have really stuck in his throat. And yet you say he has swallowed all of it, his pride as well as his bitter gall, and come to terms? What about the matter of Alaïs?"

St. Clair spread his hands and made a moue. "Settled, apparently. Richard has promised to wed her."

"God's nose!" Eusebius straightened up in shock, but managed to keep his voice down to an impassioned level that maintained their privacy. "After all the shouting and the dancing that has gone on all these years, he's going to marry her? Well, by God's kneecaps I find that difficult to credit, but I will take your word for it … although I would wager he will never touch her anyway, wife or no."

"Why would you say that? He has a son, you know."

"He's reputed to have one, you mean. No one that I have ever heard of has seen the brat, and you'd think if it were true he'd take the little bugger everywhere with him, just to let the soldiers know he's as potent in bed as he is in battle."

St. Clair could only dip his head to that, unable to respond yea or nay, and soon afterwards the trumpet sounded curfew and the two men made their way to their tents.

The next two days were nothing but marching, eating, sleeping, and starting all over again. At the end of one long march through heavy, rain-soaked woodlands, St. Clair was gratefully clutching at a large pannikin of hot venison stew from one of the commissary stations and making his way towards the fire his new comrades had built against the dampness of the evening air, when he heard his name being shouted. It was his friend de Tremelay, with a loaf of bread beneath his arm and a skin of wine dangling from his shoulder. The two ate together, sharing what they had, and André's new companions were courteous enough to seek their cots soon after they had eaten, leaving them alone so that they could talk for the short time that remained before curfew. They had exchanged their daily trivia, speaking in generalities, and after a momentary silence, de Tremelay asked, "So, how are you finding the hardships of belonging to the Temple?"

"Barely noticeable to this point, for which I humbly offer thanks. Most of the nonsense attached to harassing newcomers seems to be set aside while we're on the march. No time for playing silly games. And I've found one fellow I like, another postulant. Good sense of humor and an intellect. His name is Eusebius."

"That's a bonus, at least. Be thankful for it. Will the fleet be there when we arrive, think you?"

St. Clair had been thinking about Lyon, where they were scheduled to arrive two days later, and it took him a moment to realize what de Tremelay was talking about. "You mean in Marseille? Why would it not be?"

De Tremelay flicked a piece of wood he had been holding, sending it tumbling end over end into the fire. "I can think of several reasons.

Were they crows, they could fly from England to Marseille in two days. But they are ships, so they have to take the long way around, all the way down along the west coast, through the Bay of Biscay, with the roughest seas in all of Christendom, down past Portugal and east from there, around Moorish Iberia, then north again along the eastern coast. One bad storm could sink half of them and scatter the others like leaves on a pond. Or they might run afoul of the Moors' galleys, along the Iberian coastline or even in the narrows of northern Africa. The Moorish fleet can't match our ships for strength, but their galleys are fast and lethal and they could cause severe damage to our plans."

"No, I think not." André shook his head. "This is June already and the worst of the spring gales is long blown out. The Bay of Biscay should be calm by this time. At least, that is what de Sablé told me. Besides, he will be in command of the fleet himself and it's a fighting fleet. His ships—the ten biggest, best, and fastest vessels ever built in England—are warships, pure and simple, newly built and designed for exactly the kind of sailing he'll be called upon to do in coming to Marseille from London. I don't doubt they will be there waiting for us."

"Well, I'm sure you are perfectly correct in that." De Tremelay's voice was little more than a rumble, and it dripped now with sarcasm. "And they'll see us comfortably laden, too, no doubt. We'll each have a comfortable little hole somewhere within the ship, where we can crouch in utter misery among our dying, stinking equals and puke our entrails up all the way from Marseille to wherever we land in Outremer. Where will we land, do you know?"

"If we can land safely, it will be at Tyre, on the coast of Outremer. That's the only port left open to us—Saladin and his hordes control all the others. But first we have to make the voyage, from Marseille between Corsica and Sardinia to Sicily, and then from Sicily to Cyprus, and thence to Tyre."

"Is that a long trip?"

"No. We'll be at the mercy of wind and tides the whole time, but according to Robert, all going well, we should be no more than a month at sea."

"Sweet Jesus, that's a long time to be sick. Have you ever been seasick?"

St. Clair shook his head. "I never have, although I understand it is not pleasant. Have you?"

"Aye, several times. It is the strangest thing, for when you're falling sick at first, with your insides falling into themselves and curdling with every swoop and swing, you think you are going to die and you're afraid. But later, when you're in the midst of it and *really* sick, you realize that Hell could be no worse than what you're going through—"

"And your greatest fear becomes the fear that you might *not* die!" St. Clair finished the sentence for him.

De Tremelay scoffed and looked St. Clair straight in the eye. "They say women can't remember the pains of childbirth after they are done. Believe me, my friend, that is not the way with seasickness. I will never, ever forget what that is like and I have no wish ever to experience it again, although I know I will on this voyage. That should be enough to guarantee me a place in Paradise, think you not? To plunge voluntarily through Hell in order to redeem the Holy Land … I'm going to bed. We'll be in Lyon the day after tomorrow. Did your father happen to mention how long we will remain there?"

"Yes. He said if we stop at all, it will be overnight, no more. We're not supposed to stop there, but he is convinced that it will only be practical that we should, and that the timing of our arrival and departure will have to be arranged in advance, as we draw nearer the town. The army will split there, probably the morning after we arrive, and Philip's force will head east while we strike south along the Rhone to Avignon and Aix, and then to Marseille. By the time we reach Lyon, we postulants should number a score, perhaps more. I know there's another party of knights on the way to join us from the commandery at Pommiers, a few miles northeast of Lyon, and they're supposed to bring at least six more postulants. Our induction in Lyon will be a private Temple ritual, with no effect upon anything to do with the army. I assume it will be carried out while we are in the city, during one of the prayers of the night office."

"You are probably right, but it will be a secret, so how would I know? Enjoy it, anyway. Once you've taken the plunge, you'll see precious little of me and our other brethren for a while. The Temple will keep you too busy to have time to dwell upon our needs, at least until you take your initial vows." He stood up to leave, then hesitated.

"What?"

"You said something I didn't understand, when you were talking about reaching Lyon. Something about the planning required to arrive there on time … What did that mean?"

St. Clair grinned and stretched like a cat, then leaned towards the fire again, one elbow braced on a knee. "Think about it, Bernard. Tomorrow, instead of riding blindly and feeling sorry for yourself, look about you as we march and think about it. Have you ever seen anything like this? You have been working for and with de Sablé, organizing Richard's fleet, but this is even bigger. Massively bigger. You can't tell from a casual glance, because it's not as visible as a fleet with all its masts—here you can only see what's close around you—but we are surrounded by, and part of, more than a hundred *thousand* men, plus all their horses, wagons, equipment, and accoutrements. Seriously, think hard: what is the largest group you have ever traveled with, prior to this?"

De Tremelay's brow creased in thought. "A hundred men," he said eventually. "I rode down into Navarre with my liege lord when I was younger, about eight years ago, and there were a hundred and nine of us, not counting camp followers."

"And how many of those were there, think you?"

He shrugged. "Grooms, servants, cooks, smiths … Who knows? Twenty, perhaps? Perhaps a few more than that."

"So your party of a hundred was closer to seven score, one hundred and forty. Do you remember whether you had any difficulty finding camping places on that journey?"

"Aye, we did, every day. I remember well, because I had to scout for them and I hated it. I had to ride out every day, all day, miles in front of the main party, looking for good camping spots. Sometimes I'd have to ride all day to find one."

St. Clair stood up and looked about him at the sleeping camp. "This camp of ours is huge, isn't it? More than a thousand Templars—far more, as you say, if you count the servants and handlers. Must be close to three hundred more, counting them.

"And we are but one camp. There must be at least another hundred camps like ours out there—two hundred, if each of them be only half our size. Do you really wonder why planning every aspect of our route of march is important? When we began to march yesterday, we did not all march straight ahead. Most of us marched diagonally to one side or the other, until we formed a moving front two miles wide. Tomorrow, we will do the same again, spreading our front farther until we are four miles in width."

"Why will we do that?"

"Because if we do not do that, my friend, our hooves and wheels and marching feet will destroy all the land we march through on our two-mile front. There is no road in all this land strong enough or wide enough to bear our weight, and the fields might take years to recover from our passing as it is. When we encounter forests, and we already have, our passage through them will leave them blasted. One hundred thousand men, and then their horses and wagons. It is a miracle that we can move at all on such a scale, but when we reach Lyon, it will probably take at least a full day to march the columns into place from all sides, and then they'll have to camp in the fields surrounding the city. It is a frightening undertaking. The mere thought of it has tired me out, so now it is my turn to bid you a good night." He stood up just as the curfew sounded throughout the camp, and nodded in farewell to his friend. "Sleep well, and try not to wonder where we are going to find enough supplies to feed us on the way."

"Damn you, St. Clair, I will be awake all night now."

André grinned as he turned away. "Well, if you are, keep good watch."

SEVEN

A ndré St. Clair did not doubt for a moment that his life had changed radically with the formal conclusion of the induction ceremony in Lyon, for after it no single element of his daily life remained as it had been before. The rigid schedule of the Order's regimen, based upon the ancient Rule of Saint Benedict, with variations and extensions added by Saint Bernard for the Rule of the Temple, stipulated an unvarying rotation of formal prayers and scriptural readings that occupied most of the monks' time both day and night, and that was merely the most obvious of the changes affecting him and his fellow novices. But there were no intervals in the work periods between these prayer sessions in which a novice might snatch a moment for himself. It was as though the entire Rule by which they now lived had been designed to deprive the arrivals, collectively, of any memories or comforts that they might have retained from earlier, more familial times.

André watched the ceremony unfold with a feeling akin to amused incredulity, for he recognized elements of the proceedings that echoed, and sometimes came close to aping, passages and fragments of the ritual he had undergone years earlier on his Raising to the Order of Sion. But although this occasion resonated with pomp and solemnity, he experienced none of the sense of revelation that had overwhelmed him throughout the other. It was, he thought, as though the ceremony had been cobbled together by a group of men groping self-consciously for ways to impart a sense of occasion to an otherwise sterile event. There were prayers and incantations aplenty, intoned by Templar priests and dignitaries among clouds of incense, and there were formalized, secretive rituals carried out in near-darkness, lit only by one or two candles, but it was glaringly obvious to St. Clair that there was no substance to the reality and no meat in the broth of the concoction. The induction ceremony was a spectacle designed to awe and intimidate those who participated in it, and most particularly the inductees. By the time they had undergone all the variations of the ritual involved, they were benumbed with visions of the greatness of the commitment they had made, and convinced that they were doomed to live thenceforth in perpetual meditative silence and would never again have time for frivolous personal pursuits.

In the few furtive moments when they did manage to scratch out whispered conversations among themselves, the former postulants tried to pretend that things were not as awful as they seemed, and that every monk within the Order suffered the same hardships, but they could see that was not true. The novitiate was a period of deliberately engineered trial and tribulation, intended to cull each intake of recruits remorselessly, to winnow out those who were unfit for the monastic life that lay ahead of them.

Well warned of that in advance, André was resolved not to be discouraged, determined to bite down on his dissatisfaction and struggle through, single-mindedly, to the end of this purgatorial process. He told himself that he was prepared for anything the Order's martinets might throw at him, and he set himself to obeying every command and instruction instantly and meticulously, no matter how demeaning or dehumanizing the tasks set him might seem. And in what little spare time he had, greatly assisted by his ability to read, he learned huge sections of the Temple Rule, hundreds of paragraphs with numbers and subsections, by rote. Even so, he grew incredulous each time it occurred to him—and it did so daily—that the rules under which they were all struggling had been greatly relaxed in order to accommodate the rigors of life on the march.

It had taken them five days to win free of Lyon when all was said and done. The bridge over the Rhone there had collapsed on the first of those days, buckling under the weight of men and wagons crossing it, killing more than a hundred men. Richard had been forced to spend the next three days collecting boats and skiffs from miles away, up and down the river, to ferry the remainder of his troops across to the south bank. Thereafter, fortunate if they could travel twelve miles in a single day, the sixty thousand men of Richard's corps had made their way steadily south for eight more days, marching on a three-mile-wide front until they reached the town of Avignon and swung down towards Aix, another day's march distant. And as they progressed, to everyone's astonishment, they continued to attract recruits.

On that eighth night, however, to the wide-eyed astonishment of those of his peers who witnessed the event, André St. Clair was summarily arrested and taken into custody by a squad of sergeant brothers acting under the orders of the Master of Novices. With no explanation, or even an opportunity to collect any of his meager possessions, he was confronted, his wrists and arms were shackled at his back, and he was marched away.

He spent the next few hours under close guard, locked in a mobile jail, one of the four that traveled with large bodies of Templar soldiers. It was a windowless, wagon-mounted, solidly built box of heavy wood, ventilated only by an iron-barred slit. No one informed him why he had been taken, or of what he stood accused, and he felt hopelessness and dismay like balls of lead in the pit of his stomach because, after less than two weeks as a Temple novice, he knew that he had no voice and no identity, no authority with which to challenge this injustice.

Then, in the middle watches of the night, after vigil and long before matins, when the darkness was still absolute, he was taken before a tribunal of senior knights assembled by torchlight in the Marshal's tent. There he was arraigned by Brother Justin, the Master of Novices. He read out St. Clair's full name—just his name—from a scroll of parchment that bore several ornate and official-looking waxen seals before raising his head and looking André up and down in silence. André stood erect, his head held high, sick with tension. He could smell the unwashed odor of Justin's notorious sanctity from where he stood, four paces from the man, who stood slouched and scowling, his bottom lip sagging pendulously and his potbelly bulging against the stained fabric of his surcoat.

"You stand accused of perfidy, André St. Clair, accused of crimes so grievous as to annul all claims you might have held to entitlement for membership in this great Order." He lowered his head, perusing the scroll again before he proceeded. "And yet … there would appear to be some doubt … some *minor* doubt … concerning the details of the charges." He lowered the scroll abruptly, releasing it to close upon itself before he began to twist it into a tighter roll. "You are to be taken under guard to Aix, to the Temple House of the Commandery there, to answer the charges against you, in the faint hope of demonstrating that they are false and that you have been maligned and remain, in truth, faithful to the depositions you have made in joining this Order. May God assist you. Take him away."

No one else among the tribunal had said a single word, but as St. Clair turned away he saw a face he recognized at the rear of the tent, behind the gathering: one of the postulants with whom he had been inducted. Assigned even at this ungodly hour to some kind of menial duty on the Marshal's behalf, the fellow now hurried away, head bowed, but André was convinced the fellow had missed nothing of what was said. He was surprised that the foul-tempered Brother Justin had not noticed him and had him ejected at the outset. But just then one of his own guards took him by the elbow and led him outside, swinging him to the right outside the flaps of the Marshal's tent, to where he saw the bulk of the mobile jail again, outlined in the flickering torchlight and hitched this time behind a heavyset horse.

His guards hustled him forward, and then he was lifted and pushed, almost thrown, and he fell on his knees in a corner of the jail box as the heavy door slammed at his back and the wagon lurched into motion. He was weak and trembling, his legs suddenly bereft of strength, and he had to fight hard against the urge to vomit. In misery more abject than any he had ever imagined, he felt his heartbeat surge towards panic as he grappled with the impossibility of the only explanation of all this that would come to him: somehow, against all probability, the false testimony of the three dead renegade priests must have resurfaced, so that he stood accused again of murder.

He sought to calm himself by practicing the new discipline he had been forced to acquire as a Temple novice, reciting the *Paternoster* of his daily prayers. He shut out everything from his mind except the repetitive drone of the words until his mind was numb, keeping count by numbering the knots on his prayer cord until he had repeated the prayer the requisite number of one hundred and forty-eight times for the day. Day had not yet broken by the time he finished, the cell was too narrow to permit him to lie down, and the rocking motion of the wagon was such that he could not possibly sleep. And so he lodged himself upright again and began anew to count his prayer knots against the next day's required tally.

He had recited one thousand and twenty-six *Paternosters*, ten fewer than a full week's quota, before the wagon swayed to a halt, and in the time that had elapsed he had discovered, much to his surprise, a stoic inner calm that felt secure. He had also calculated that one hundred and fifty of the prayers, repeated deliberately and clearly, would fill up roughly one hour of time. He had to close his eyes tightly against the blinding brilliance of the light when the door to his cell swung open, and he was content to allow his guards to move him about and guide him downward slowly until he was standing on the ground again. He felt the sun's heat on his face and arms, and then they pushed him forward into the coolness of shade, and he opened his eyes cautiously.

He had been aware of their arrival in a city, one he had presumed to be Aix, for he had heard and felt the rumble of cobblestones beneath the wheels of the cart some time before, and the sound of raised voices echoing from close-crowding buildings had been unmistakable. Now he could see that he was in some kind of enclosed yard, with buildings on all four sides, one of them pierced by opposing doors through which the wagon had entered. The two guards who had escorted him from the Templar camp were moving about now, occupied in minor tasks and paying no attention to him for the moment. Directly in front of him was a wide doorway, framed in pale yellow sandstone and fronted by a broad flight of shallow steps of the same stone. Set into the arch above the doorway, a shield bearing the arms of the Temple had been carved in deep relief, and two white-clad guards, wearing the red flared-arm cross of the Temple on their left breasts, stood beneath it, flanking the great oaken doors. One of them gazed at St. Clair incuriously while his companion watched the men who had accompanied him.

Even had he not known their destination, St. Clair would have recognized the details he could see. He knew this must be the new Temple House of the Aix commandery, for he had heard it being described admiringly several years earlier, by someone who had watched it being built and had been crowing about the rich color of the stone, quarried on his own land nearby.

He closed his eyes, lulled by the warmth of the afternoon, and felt himself swaying, but before he could even straighten up, he felt his escorts' hands on his arms again and he was propelled gently towards the doorway, where the guards leaned in to pull open the heavy doors. It was dark and cool inside, and his guards led him forward for some twenty paces before they stopped again, this time in front of a broad table, flanked by two more of the Temple House guards, behind which a wide passageway ran right and left.

His escorts snapped to attention and saluted a knight who had stepped from behind the table, his face expressionless. The knight listened while the senior escort explained who they were and why they were there, and then he took the warrant the man offered, thanked the two men courteously, nodding to each of them in turn, then dispatched one of his own men to escort them to the refectory in search of food. As they left, he turned slowly and gazed at St. Clair for long moments, until the sound of departing footfalls had dwindled into silence. Then he spoke to the single remaining guard.

"Find Brother Preceptor and tell him the prisoner has arrived."

The man snapped a brisk salute and spun on his heel to march away, and the knight's gaze came back to where St. Clair stood straight backed, staring at him defiantly.

"Follow me."

He walked away, along the wide passageway on St. Clair's right, moving with the authoritative gait of a man who had never doubted his own power. André blinked, tempted for the briefest of moments to stand firm and be as defiant as he felt, but then he remembered that he did not know what kind of trouble he was in and realized that defiance might not be in his own best interests. The man ahead of him was pulling away rapidly and had not even glanced around to see if he was following, and so André grunted and set out after him. He stepped out briskly, surprised to find himself enjoying the simple movement.

Twenty paces farther along, another passage crossed the one they were using, and just beyond that junction their passageway ended in a pair of doors that filled it entirely, height and width. The knight threw open one of the doors and stepped sideways, holding it for St. Clair, who hesitated at the unexpected courtesy, glanced at the man, then walked right through and came to an abrupt halt. A second set of heavy doors now barred his way, exactly like the first and separated from them by the distance of three paces.

"Sound barrier," the man said, and stepped past André to swing open the second set of doors. André blinked and walked past him again, then halted just inside the doors, looking about him. The only need for a sound barrier that he could imagine was to shelter the ears of the sensitive innocent from the screams of the tortured guilty, and the thought instantly banished the stoic calm he had achieved with his *Paternosters*.

The large chamber they had entered appeared to be windowless, and yet light was spilling into it from somewhere. He tilted his head back and looked up, but still he could see no windows. High walls on both sides of him were paneled with wood and draped with richly woven tapestries. Ahead of him, on each side of a stone wall containing a massive fireplace, stood more ceiling-high doors, and he realized that daylight was streaming through from behind them, too.

An enormous iron basket in the hearth contained a roaring log fire that threw heat out to where St. Clair was standing, just inside the door, and three vast stuffed couches fronted the fire in an open box formation, with the pelt of a great beast that St. Clair knew, from paintings he had seen, to be a tiger spread on the floor between them and the fire. Throughout the room oversized iron sconces, some of them with several arms apiece, held what appeared to be hundreds of fine, clear-burning candles. On his left, against one wall, a long, heavy table held an array of cups and tall, decorative ewers, together with what appeared to be an abundant supply of foodstuffs covered with cloth. The very sight made his mouth water, and he reflected, bitterly, that this bounty was unlikely to benefit him in any way. He was the prisoner here, mired in ignorance of what he had done, but under no illusions about the seriousness with which his transgression was being viewed.

St. Clair distinctly heard the doors close quietly at his back and turned to see the unknown knight in the act of unhooking a ring of keys from the belt at his waist. Without a word, the fellow stepped forward, gently turned St. Clair around, and unlocked the manacles that bound him, removing them and tossing them carelessly against the wall by the fire, where they clattered to the floor. Unbound, St. Clair tensed and prepared himself for whatever might come next. If the chance came to defend himself, he would not hesitate.

"Subterfuge, Sir André, subterfuge … Elaborate by necessity. This will all be explained to you, once the others arrive. In the meantime, I'll wager you might enjoy a cup of wine."

Without waiting for a response, and clearly not expecting one, he stepped to the table and picked up two heavy, long-necked ewers, turning back to cock one eyebrow at St. Clair, who had been eyeing the scuffed and battered condition of the sheathed broadsword that hung from the belt at the Templar's waist. He hoisted one of the containers slightly higher than the other.

"We have a choice, thanks to the Bishop of Aix. One of these contains the deep blood-red nectar of Burgundy, the other, pure amber magic from the Rhine. Which would you prefer? I'm Belfleur, by the way. Plain Jean Belfleur, of Carcassonne. Red or gold?"

"*What?* What is this about? Why am I here? What—?"

"As I said, all will be explained. Have the red." Belfleur busied himself pouring, and handed St. Clair a brimming cup. "But we must wait until the others join us."

"What others?"

"Patience, my friend, contain your curiosity, I pray you." He waved towards the three couches fronting the fire. "Come, have a seat. I will not ask you about your journey here, for it could not have been pleasant, but I will tell you that when our business here is concluded, you will have access to a hot bath, to wash away the stink of your imprisonment, both literally and symbolically, and to fresh clothing, fitting for your rank. Your own weapons and armor will be returned to you."

St. Clair could do no more than nod reluctantly, acknowledging his recognition of the other's goodwill and feeling oddly abashed at his own feelings of resentment. But he moved obediently to one of the couches and sat down slowly, relaxing gradually and gently over the next quarter hour as the full-bodied red wine spread its own goodwill inside him. Neither man spoke again, but the silence between them held no trace of strain. Both were content, for different reasons, to await developments.

The effect of the wine, the heat of the fire, and the long night without sleep all combined to seduce André, who had no awareness of nodding off until he heard the doors swing open at his back and leapt to his feet, dropping the empty cup he still held as he swung around to face the imposing group of men who now strode into the chamber and spread out in a loose crescent, facing him. There were nine of them, of varying ages, some of them wearing armor and one, a Templar, standing half a head taller than any of the others. Red haired and ruddy faced, with bright, pale blue eyes, there was something about this man that reminded St. Clair instantly of Richard Plantagenet. This man was every inch a soldier and warrior, and he exuded the same kind of reckless self-confidence. He was the first to speak, tilting his head a little to one side as he looked directly into André's eyes.

"Sir André St. Clair. Welcome to our House. I am Benedict of Roussillon, Count of Grenoble and Preceptor of the Temple Commandery of Aix." He extended his hand, and André stepped forward to bend over it, but before he could begin to bow he felt the unmistakable pressure of Roussillon's grip on his own hand pulling him up, and he returned it, his eyes widening in astonishment. The preceptor of the Temple of Aix was a Brother of the Order of Sion.

But the Count was already turning to indicate the others in his group, the first of them another Templar. "Here you have Henri Turcot, the Castellan of Grenoble and my staunchest ally, as well as deputy preceptor of the commandery there. Henri has just arrived, having ridden all night from Villeneuve-les-Avignon. And with him came this young man, Henry, Count of Champagne, a brother of our ancient Order, but far removed from his home."

The young Count smiled and inclined his head towards St. Clair, who responded by bowing deeply. Henry of Champagne was known to him by repute, nephew to both Philip Augustus of France and Richard of England through Eleanor of Aquitaine's first marriage to King Philip's father.

As Count Benedict went on to introduce the others in his company, some of whom were far advanced in age, St. Clair found himself becoming more and more awe-smitten as the awareness grew in him that the people he was meeting so casually here were the most powerful and influential men in the territories ruled by the two monarchs leading this third great expedition to the Holy Land, and that they were all members of the Governing Council of the Order of Sion. Their names were familiar to him because they were already legendary within the Order, honored and revered by all the brotherhood, but it was becoming more and more disturbingly evident to him that they had all assembled here in this place to meet with *him*.

Recognizing St. Clair's confusion, one dignified member of this cadre, whose name was Germain of Toulouse and who appeared to be the eldest among them, called the others to order and reminded them that their guest had not yet been informed of what was taking place here, and within moments they had all removed their outer garments and made themselves comfortable wherever they could find a seat. When they were settled, Benedict of Roussillon stood up again and, speaking clearly and courteously, described the circumstances of this strange situation for St. Clair's benefit.

St. Clair had been brought here, he explained, because the Council of the Order had assigned him a momentous task, a task for which he was uniquely suited, for a number of reasons, all of which would be explained to him in due course. Because of its importance, however, it was also a task that demanded utter secrecy, over and above the standards of secrecy already demanded by the brotherhood. No one, de Roussillon emphasized, other than the nine elders present here plus one more—the man to whom St. Clair would report during the performance of his task—could be permitted to have any inkling of what St. Clair would really be doing in Outremer after his arrival there. De Roussillon reiterated that, driving the point home not merely to St. Clair, it seemed, but to the entire assembly: no one must ever have any suspicion that André St. Clair had any other purpose in being in Outremer beyond his duties as a knight of the Temple. So important, and so sensitive, was this assignment that it had been deemed crucial for St. Clair to be brought here for instructions.

Having set the proper tone of gravity for what was to follow, Sir Benedict then added that the chambers within which they now sat had been secured against any possibility of disturbance or infiltration. All discussions relating to the matter in hand would be held behind closed and guarded doors, and St. Clair would be given a thorough explanation of the background underlying his mission, along with explicit and unambiguous instructions on how to proceed, once he had committed himself to achieving the objectives set him.

When he had finished explaining that, Sir Benedict asked André if he had understood everything he had been told, and when St. Clair responded that he had, de Roussillon immediately declared a half-hour adjournment for food, since many of the people assembled had not yet eaten that day. After this, he explained, all meals would be served formally and, as was usual, in the refectory of the Temple House with the other Temple brethren, and would be eaten in silence, to the accompaniment of scriptural readings from the daily office. On this sole occasion, eating together in private would permit the various brethren to exchange information from their various home locations. The meeting broke up at that point and everyone moved to the tables, where the food was uncovered and proved, although all of it was cold, to be something of a banquet.

André St. Clair enjoyed himself thoroughly, making polite conversation with everyone who spoke to him, and acutely aware that he might never again be able to eat, drink, and relax in such an august and distinguished company. The allotted time passed quickly, and at the end of it the gathering was reconvened and the serious business of André St. Clair's instruction began.

The white-bearded Germain of Toulouse began the proceedings, speaking from his place at the center of the semicircle of chairs that faced the single chair where André sat alone.

"Sir André St. Clair, welcome to this formal session of instruction, initiated with the concurrence of the plenary Governing Council of our Order. We are aware of the circumstances under which you were brought here, and would be unsurprised to find you angry and frustrated. Unfortunately, it was necessary to have you removed from your situation under the threat of official displeasure and investigation, and to have those events witnessed and reported. You are a member of the novitiate of the Temple, and had you been summoned in any other fashion, the very fact of your being summoned might have generated precisely the kind of attention we wish to avoid. When our business here is completed you will be returned as a free knight, your honor vindicated and your reputation unblemished ... Have I said something amusing?"

André had flicked a hand, indicating that he wished to interrupt, and now he smiled in embarrassment over the elder's question. "Forgive me, Brother, for my temerity, I had no wish to smile, but the thought of returning to Brother Justin, the Master of Novices, with my reputation unblemished has a certain … resonance that engaged my attention. The smile was merely unwilling disbelief … mixed, perhaps, with a small amount of terror."

"Ah, Brother Justin. Of course." Germain of Toulouse smiled. "He is redoubtable, is he not? But you need have no fears of the Master of Novices. His fraternal loyalty is beyond question."

"Fraternal? He is one of *us*?" The question was jerked out in astonishment.

"Of course he is one of us, and of incalculable value, considering the post he holds and the influence he wields within the Temple ranks. He will have no idea of what you are about, under his care, but he will do everything in his power to assist you upon request, and if you ever need to be away for any length of time, it is Brother Justin who will make it possible for you to do what you must do."

St. Clair was flabbergasted, reviewing a mental image of the irascible Master of Novices, with his evil-smelling body, his stained and ragged clothing, and his pendulous lower lip that protruded almost as much as his swollen, tunic-straining belly, but the elder was speaking again and he quickly pushed all other thoughts from his mind, concentrating on the old man's words.

"You have a cousin in Outremer, already with the Temple, is that not so?"

"Yes, sir, I have. A cousin of my father's, from Scotland. Sir Alexander Sinclair."

"And you have met this man?"

"I have, albeit briefly. He lived with us for a while when I was a boy."

"And the two of you were friends."

It was not a question, but André thought for a few moments before he responded. "No, sir, I cannot say that is accurate. We liked each other, I believe. I certainly liked him. But I was a mere lad, less than twelve years old, and he was already a trained and dedicated knight, sworn to the Temple. He was kind to me, and gracious, in that he spoke to me freely and with courtesy, and always showed me great consideration. Never once do I recall him speaking down to me or belittling me for anything I said to him. I admired him greatly, but I would be flattering myself to say that we were friends."

"I see. And so, were you ever to see him again, would he remember you, think you?"

André shrugged his wide shoulders. "I do not know, Brother Germain. I would like to think he would know me, but I cannot be sure, after such a long time."

"Would you know him?"

"Again, I think I would, and I would love to be able to swear I would, but I might not. He might have changed beyond recognition."

"Aye, he might ..." The older man's words were almost sighed, and he sat silent for the space of several heartbeats before he nodded, as though to himself, and continued. "The truth is, he may be dead." He inhaled sharply and looked directly at St. Clair, his voice gaining strength and clarity. "We simply do not know, nor does anyone we have been able to contact in Outremer. Sir Alexander Sinclair fought at Hattin and has not been seen since. No one saw him die, and no one saw his body on the field thereafter. Nor was he numbered among the knights slain on Saladin's command after the battle. He might well be alive somewhere, a prisoner of some Arab sheikh or emir, being held in slavery or perhaps for ransom, albeit it has been more than two years now, closer to three. Your first task on reaching Outremer will be to find him. Find Sir Alexander Sinclair. Either that or establish his death beyond dispute."

St. Clair had been watching the faces of the other brethren as Germain of Toulouse made this announcement, and what he saw in them prompted him to make a comment that he would not normally have considered uttering in such company.

"You make him sound very important, Master Germain."

"And so he is. Your cousin, Sir André, is one of our most valuable agents in all of Outremer. His reputation among his peers is legendary, his military prowess equally so, but he has other qualities, undreamed of by his fellow knights. Gifted with an ear for languages, he was tutored by a trio of erudite Shi'ite philosophers from Aleppo, Damascus, and Cairo, who, for reasons of their own, taught him not only to speak Arabic fluently and without an accent but also to write it effortlessly and beautifully. They also taught him about Islam and the differences between the Shi'ite and Sunni sects, placing great emphasis, as was only natural, upon the disadvantages suffered by their own, the minority Shi'a sect, and its persecution at the hands of Sunni caliphs. Do you know much of that?"

"Not really," St. Clair said. "I know that the religion of Islam has two kinds of followers, Sunni and Shi'a, and there is little love between the two. I know too that the Sunni are more numerous, greatly outnumbering the others." He hesitated, then added, "I have also been told that their differences stem from the death of the Prophet, Muhammad, created by the quarrel over who should be his successor. The Sunni caliphs assumed the mantle of his leadership, but the Shi'ites believe the Prophet himself named his son-in-law to follow him and the caliphs disregarded his wishes and seized the leadership from the righteous claimant."

The old man nodded, visibly impressed. "You know more than most of your fellow travelers, for the ruck of them believe simply that all Saracens are the Devil's henchmen, existing only to be put to the sword. More than that, as Christians, they have no interest in either knowing or learning. The purpose of the armies, they believe, is straightforward and to the point: they are going to Outremer to wipe the enemy from God's Holy Land, and in the doing of that, should they capture lands and territories that will enrich their kings and leaders, then those leaders will give thanks—humbly, one supposes—to God. There is but one enemy, to the Frankish warrior, and he is the Muslim Infidel. The fact that he may be Sunni Muslim or Shi'a Muslim goes ignored."

Germain looked around the assembly, catching each man's eye before he continued. "Of course, among the Christian leadership, that difference, that schism, is viewed as proof of the falsity of the religion of Islam. That it should have such a profound split at the very base of its existence, they say, demonstrates clearly that its foundations are fatally flawed, and that, of course, is a vindication of the purity and wholeness of Christianity, in that there are no comparable differences of belief or basic philosophy in its ranks."

The old man's mouth quirked in a grin and he cocked his head slightly to include his friends in the audience. "The difference between the Eastern, Orthodox rites of Byzantium and the Roman rites of our homelands are, of course, not differences at all, according to these theologians. They are merely nuances of interpretation. And of course, those same theologians do not even suspect our Order's existence, so how could they suspect a difference in our philosophy or beliefs? We must educate them one day, my friends, for their own good."

Most of the men listening to him were smiling at his little joke as he turned back to St. Clair. "But I was talking about your cousin and how important he is to our affairs in Outremer. By the end of his time with his tutors, your cousin had been transformed into a man who could effortlessly pass as a Muslim among Muslims. He traveled to Outremer and spent three more years living and working as a civilian trader attached to a Cairo-based trading house, traveling widely out of that city and uncovering and providing us with information.

"From there he moved to the Latin Kingdom of Jerusalem, abandoning his trader persona and taking up the duties of a Temple Knight within the Jerusalem garrison, circulating throughout the kingdom, ostensibly as a high-level courier but truly functioning as liaison between the brotherhood and certain active but equally secretive sects within the widespread but small Shi'a community—activities which he knew would not endear him at all to the Sultan Saladin and his Sunni supporters, among whom his current companions must number.

"It is one of the greatest ironies of our existence that, despite the overwhelming importance of Jerusalem and Palestine to everything it stands for, our Order is, and for the time being must remain, very poorly represented there. Were we discovered, was our existence even suspected, the Church would root us out and destroy us as heretics. And so that need for secrecy makes it nearly impossible for us to function in Outremer. We have been thrust into a situation there where we have had to make use of every advantage available to us, and that has included befriending the Shi'a community, which in Jerusalem is almost as small and endangered as our own. The Saracen Sultan, Saladin, is Sunni, as are all his hosts. We therefore have actively sought out friendship and alliances among the Shi'a community, proceeding on the ancient theory that the enemy of my enemy is my friend. Your cousin Alexander was our main liaison in those activities, and most particularly in our dealings with an association that operates within the Shi'a community much as our own Order does within ours. They call themselves the Hashshashin, the Assassins. I see you have heard of them."

St. Clair's eyes had widened on hearing the name and he nodded, mute.

"Well, do not let what you have heard harden you against them. As usual in such things, where little is known and much is feared, what is broadcast is seldom even close to the truth. The Sunni have used their numerical superiority and their ill will, both political and religious, to blacken the name and reputation of the Assassins. But that is unimportant here. What is important is that the Assassins represent no threat to us. On the contrary, they and we are natural allies and have mutual interests, not the least among those being a fascination with the geometry and the arcane lore of the Ancients. Like us, the Assassins are a closed, secret society, and theirs is the repository of a vast wealth of knowledge that we hope one day to share in equality. We had suspected that was so for decades, but Alex Sinclair established it beyond dispute … I can see you have a question. Ask it."

"But …" St. Clair frowned, shaking his head very slightly in his impatience, "how could he have established that beyond dispute, without—?"

"Without betraying our own Order's existence? We had been aware for some time that, in order to gain the trust and confidence of the Assassins, we might have to show our own trust by exposing our own existence to them. Sir Alexander had the authority, at his own discretion, to proceed on that basis. When the time was right, he chose to do so, and his judgment has been amply rewarded."

"And what if he had misjudged? What if he had trusted the wrong people with his information, what then?"

Germain shrugged. "What then? All that anyone would have is the word of one man, unsupported by evidence. What harm could ensue from that? No, there were checks and counterchecks in place. Nothing irreparable could have occurred."

"And what now, then, should he be dead? Are you telling me you do not know how to proceed from there?"

"On the contrary, we know that your cousin left a complete and up-to-date report for us before setting out for Hattin. We even know where he left it. But the messengers, and there were three of them, who were entrusted to collect and forward that report to us, were all killed in the aftermath of Hattin. To the best of our knowledge, the report must still be where Sir Alexander left it. Should you be unable to find him when you reach Outremer, you will have that location in your possession so that at the very least you may find the report and send it to us."

"And if I do find my cousin?"

"Then you will deliver the Council's dispatches to him and work with him thereafter, assisting him in his endeavors."

"I see." St. Clair nodded slowly, his gaze moving from one to the other of the assembled group, although he continued to address Germain of Toulouse. "May I ask another question, one which you might find presumptuous?"

"Of course. We are putting your life doubly at risk, so ask us anything you wish to know."

"Why is this more important now, today, than it was a month ago? I was arrested and brought here in haste. I could have been more subtly contacted weeks and months earlier, without risk or difficulty. I have been working with members of the Council for at least that long, on Sir Robert de Sablé's behalf."

Germain hesitated, then nodded. "Correct. And you *would* have been brought in a month ago, save that several developments occurred about that time and had to be verified and then considered at great length for their ... *political* import. It would have been pointless to involve you before we were sure of what our path must be. Now we are sure, and our decisions have been made. But I am not the man to tell you about what they involve. Master Bernard, will you continue from here?"

Germain of Toulouse moved away and sat down, making way for another speaker, only slightly younger than he was. André St. Clair felt his heartbeat speed up slightly as the newcomer smiled at him before beginning to speak. André knew, from the information he had received from Robert de Sablé, that this was Master Bernard of Montségur, one of the trio of Joint Masters who supervised the affairs of the Order of Sion within the three ancient territories in which it functioned. The first and oldest of these three "regions" was the Languedoc, covering the entire region north of the Pyrenees, including the provinces of Aquitaine and Poitou and the walled towns of Montségur and Carcassonne; the other two were known as Poitou and Champagne, and together they covered the remaining area of what had once been Roman Gaul, with the Champagne region covering the northern third and Poitou the entire central area. Each of the three Masters—their ranks elected and held for life— was responsible for the Order's affairs within his own region and acted as coordinator of the Regional Council. Of the three Joint Masters, de Sablé had told André, Bernard of Montségur was the most influential. He was also the one who conducted the Order's direct liaison with the Order of the Temple and the network of Brothers of Sion who functioned within the Temple on behalf of its much older avatar.

"As my brother Germain says," Bernard began, "much has changed in recent months, and, as always, we are late once again in learning of those changes. My brethren here all know what I am speaking about, but we have judged it important that you, too, Sir André, should be aware of what is involved. A ship arrived in Marseille from Sicily a month ago, and it carried information that might, in itself, have been encouraging, had it not been connected with another, more troublesome development. Does the name Conrad of Montferrat mean anything to you?"

St. Clair shook his head. "No, Master. Nothing at all."

"Hmm. Well, are you aware of Barbarossa's expedition?"

"To the Holy Land. Yes, I am. Everyone is. He is riding at the head of an army of two hundred thousand men, traveling overland from Germany. His host alone will outnumber the combined armies of King Richard and King Philip."

"Correct. And do you know what this man calls himself?"

"Barbarossa?" St. Clair nodded. "Frederic of Hohenstaufen, Holy Roman Emperor, named Barbarossa for his red beard. Is that what you meant?"

"Yes, it is. But as Holy Roman Emperor, he rules an entity that is neither holy nor Roman. Nor is it an empire. It is a polyglot mass, a sprawling federation of barbaric and decidedly unholy German tribes. And it is far more Greek than it ever could be Roman." Bernard saw the confusion on St. Clair's face and added, "I speak now of religion, Sir André, not race. Barbarossa cleaves to the Eastern rites of the Orthodox Church, as it calls itself, and the See of Jerusalem has always been maintained by the Eastern Church, headed by a Patriarch Archbishop."

"Aye, Master, I knew that. Warmund of Picquigny was Patriarch there when first we took Jerusalem. It was he who, along with the second King Baldwin, gave Hugh de Payens his charter to proceed with setting up his knights. Yet I detect something in your tone that hints at friction there, and to the best of my knowledge there never was any such friction."

"Correct again. There was none. Not then, and certainly not on the surface. The Church's presence in Jerusalem then was dominated by the Eastern rite, but the military power there was all Frankish, which meant it was Roman. The war that brought them there was called Pope Urban's War, after all. But now things have changed, as I said. After he recaptured Jerusalem, Saladin permitted the Orthodox Christians to return to the city last year, with no other penalty than a light tax, and he allowed them once again to take over the administration of the holy places. That means that all the sacred Christian sites in Jerusalem are now back in the hands of the

Patriarch, and the imminent arrival of Barbarossa and his hordes has thrown everything into hazard, because once they arrive and Saladin has been defeated and thrown out again, the predominant weight and power there will be that of the Eastern rite, and Rome's power will be eclipsed."

He stopped, watching narrow eyed as St. Clair thought about that, but before the knight could comment he continued. "Why should we care about that? Eastern or Roman rite, they are both Christian and therefore misguided in the eyes of our Order, correct?" St. Clair nodded, and Bernard brought his hands together in a single loud clap. "No, Sir André. Wrong. The moment Barbarossa seizes power in Jerusalem—and think not for a moment that he will fail to do so—one of his first concerns will be to establish preeminence for his own Teutonic knights. They will take over all the duties and responsibilities of the existing Orders there—the Templars and Hospitallers. They may leave some of the Hospitallers in place, the serving Benedictine brothers who minister to the sick and wounded, but they will remove the military brothers, and they will most definitely expel the Templars. They have no choice if they are to establish preeminence for their own Teutonic Order—the Temple has to go. And since the Temple constitutes the veil disguising and enabling our presence in the Holy Land, that means that we, the Order of Sion, will be ousted, too, our works, indeed our entire mission, abandoned unfinished. Do you begin to see why your cousin is so important to us now?"

St. Clair was frowning openly now, plainly uncomprehending. "No, Master."

Master Bernard nodded. "Your lack of understanding stems purely from the enormous dimensions of the next logical step. If Sir Alexander Sinclair has been sufficiently successful in forging alliances with his Shi'a counterparts, he may be able to establish a solid presence for our ancient Order there, even after the Temple has been dispossessed."

"Forgive me." St. Clair held up one hand in entreaty. "I am still struggling with what you said about the Temple being ousted from

Outremer. I find it difficult—no, more than difficult, I am finding it impossible—to imagine anything like that. It would take an open act of war by Barbarossa to achieve such a thing." St. Clair looked around the assembly, seeking support but seeing only solemn faces. "The Temple will not meekly surrender its power in Outremer and simply sail away … will it?"

"No, it will not. That is what we ourselves would have said until mere weeks ago. But then the ship that I mentioned earlier arrived in Marseille, with tidings that altered everything we knew. The man who brought the information to us was familiar with what he described, and he bore written testimony from others to reinforce his claims. And here is what we now know to be true." He nibbled at his clean-shaven upper lip as he sought the proper words for what he would say next.

"From all that we have been able to gather from reports, we have become convinced that Guy de Lusignan, the King of Jerusalem, is a fool and a weakling. Guy was driven into the folly of the fight at Hattin by conflicting advice, all of it bad, from the Master of the Temple, Gerard de Ridefort, and his arrogant and disgusting cohort Reynald de Chatillon. Had Guy been anything less than a poltroon, he might have ignored both of them and made his own decisions, but he did not. And his folly did not end at Hattin. He was captured there by Saladin, who treated him well and later released him, upon Guy's promise to fight no more but to return home to France.

"No sooner was he free, however, than he broke his promise, on the unsurprising grounds that an oath issued under duress to an infidel cannot be binding. He then proclaimed himself King in his own right. But he was already late and feckless yet again, because a new player had arrived in Outremer. Do you know anything about Tyre?"

St. Clair shrugged. "It is a city. I know no more than that."

"A coastal city and a great port. It was once an island, until Alexander the Great captured it by building a causeway to it from the mainland. That causeway is still there, forming an isthmus and straddled now by a great defensive wall that makes the city almost impregnable from the landward side. Saladin besieged Tyre hugely within days of winning the fight at Hattin, and so hopeless were the defenders that they were already negotiating terms of surrender when a ship sailed into the harbor there. Aboard that ship was an adventurer called Conrad of Montferrat. He and his companions were headed for Jerusalem and knew nothing about the war, nor about Saladin or Hattin. They had sought to land at Acre the previous day but had been warned off, with word that the Saracens had captured the city four days earlier, and so they had sailed for Tyre.

"As soon as he learned what was going on, Conrad took charge. He immediately cut off the surrender negotiations and prepared the city for a long defense. Saladin, who saw that he was now facing a long, sustained siege rather than an easy capitulation, promptly left Tyre and marched off southward with his armies to capture Jerusalem and Ascalon. He knew that Tyre was isolated and posed him no immediate threat, whereas Jerusalem was a prize ripe for the picking.

"Conrad, now the acknowledged commander of Tyre, became the *de facto* leader of the Franks, but Guy himself arrived in Tyre, having broken his oath to Saladin, and demanded to be acknowledged as King. Conrad shut the gates against him. The kingship issue was unresolved, he said, and should await resolution when the armies of the Frankish kings arrived in Outremer.

"The following spring, Guy led a tiny army, supported by a few ships, in an attack on Acre, further down the coast."

The old Master paused and shook his head, looking at no one in particular. "That was sheer stupidity, a gesture fully worthy of Guy of Lusignan, whom no one, even in his finest moments, ever accused of being either sensible or wise. The Acre garrison alone, I am told, was more than twice the size of his entire army, and Saladin, who was resting but a short march to the south, could have stirred at any moment and annihilated the upstart King and his followers as one might swat a fly. But Guy had no other option available to him. If he failed to attack Acre, making a last defiant and insane attempt to engage the enemy and win, he faced extinction.

And so he did the only thing he could do, stupid though it might appear to be. Perhaps he had hopes of a miracle. He certainly had need of one. And by the living God of Moses, he found one."

"As the sole conflict being waged directly against the Muslims in Outremer, Guy's silly little siege attracted attention. A fleet of Danish and Frisian ships arrived later in the year, followed quickly by another from Flanders and northern France, and then Louis, the Margrave of Thuringia, arrived from Germany, leading another contingent. They all went directly to Tyre to Conrad, but it seems that Conrad, for no reason anyone can name, somehow made himself intolerable to all of them, so that eventually they all marched and sailed south to join Guy outside Acre, where Saladin had finally moved to attack the tiny Frankish army. It was then that our informant left to bring home the tidings of what had occurred, and the last word he heard before leaving Outremer was that Conrad had finally condescended to join the other Franks and lend Guy his support against Saladin."

As Master Bernard's words faded away, André had a vision of the scene before the towering stone walls of Acre and the tents and banners of the besieging Franks, but he had no time to dwell on it before another voice demanded his attention.

"So there you have the situation now in force—at least as far as we may perceive it." The young Count of Champagne had risen to his feet. "The situation appeared to be tolerable when all we had to concern ourselves over was the advancing threat of Barbarossa, still half a thousand miles distant. But the addition of this new element has altered everything."

St. Clair was aware of feeling stupid, as though he had missed something self-evident, and on the spur of the moment he decided to confess his ignorance. "Pardon me, my lord Count—"

"Your lord nothing, address me as a brother. We are all brethren here."

"Aye, forgive me. But I am missing something. What is the relationship between Guy's siege of Acre and the threat of Barbarossa?"

Henry grinned, a wide, attractive flashing of white teeth, dipping his head to one side at the same time. "I am glad you asked that. I knew you ought to ask it, but I was beginning to wonder if you might not. Good man. On the surface, there is nothing at all connecting the two, until you think about it, Brother. We here have had time to do that. You have not.

"The siege of Acre itself is not important to us, but the people involved in its execution are, and most particularly the newcomers: Louis, the Margrave of Thuringia, and Conrad of Montferrat himself. Both are high born, German, and proud in the arrogant ways of their kind. Both, by birth and feudal loyalty, are sworn vassals to Barbarossa. Conrad is a cousin. Their mere presence in Outremer ahead of his arrival paves the way for his conquest and for our dispossession." He raised a hand quickly to forestall any questions St. Clair might have.

"You must bear in mind that the Templars in Outremer hold the line of battle on our behalf, but they are no longer the Army of Jerusalem, as they have been for eight decades. Now they are merely warriors fighting for a victory and a homeland, like everyone else in the field. And no matter what the people here at home might think of them and their supposed invincibility, the Templars have competition now that did not exist in earlier times: Barbarossa's Teutons. He created them and shaped them. Here in the West we know little about them, but what we do know is troublesome. We have no yardstick with which to take their true measure at this time, but we know that he modeled his Teutons specifically upon the Knights of the Temple and the Hospital and we know that among their own kind their reputation is unsullied. But their motivations, obscure to us but dictated by Barbarossa, are, we fear, greatly different from those upon which they were originally modeled. The loyalty of both Templars and Hospitallers is to the Pope and the Roman Church, and the Teutons are loyal to Barbarossa and the Orthodox Church. And nothing, Brother, *nothing* on God's earth is more dangerous than military campaigns based upon religious differences."

Count Henry crossed his arms over his chest and cocked one eyebrow at André, almost but not quite smiling. "You said that it would take an open act of war by Barbarossa to dispossess the Temple, but you said it in a tone that made it clear you think that could not be. My suggestion now is that you might wish to review that opinion and consider clearly what is at stake here, when all is said and done. Do you really believe such a war to be impossible, while openly recognizing the current war between Christianity and Islam, and the ongoing internecine war between the Sunni and Shi'a branches of Islam itself? You believe it to be impossible that Roman and Orthodox Christians might clash in the same way and for more or less the same reasons—mere form and ceremony—that Sunni and Shi'a do? How can you think in such an illogical manner? Remember, we are discussing a potential struggle for ultimate hegemony, Brother André, with the prize being the minds and souls of all the world's Christian folk—plus, of course, all that they possess in worldly goods—and the winner's strength will surely rest upon the steward-ship and possession of Jerusalem and the Holy Land."

The Count eyed St. Clair again with the same amused expression he had used earlier. "Are you convinced of that now? Or must I seek other words to bring you to understanding?"

"No, Brother, I understand. How could I fail to, after that? But it is nonetheless disheartening to hear."

"Aye, it is, but the fact that you should say exactly that makes it heartening that you are one of us. So, now that you have a basic, albeit hazy, understanding of what is involved, here is what will happen next. You will spend the next three days listening to all of it again, related from other perspectives and made relevant by others among our brethren here, so that by the time you leave, even should you be disinclined to believe me at this moment, you will be completely aware of what you are about and what you must do when you arrive in Outremer. From the moment you leave here after that, you will deal with one man alone, in everything related to this task that we have set you. You already know that man. He is Robert de Sablé and he will be your liaison with this Council. He himself will have two deputies, neither of whom will know your name unless something happens to de Sablé, at which point the first of them will open written instructions and learn your identity.

"In the meantime, you will return to your own detachment bearing documents that exonerate you completely of all charges and explain, officially, that you were taken in a case of mistaken identity. You will then leave for Outremer as scheduled, and your primary task will begin the moment you set foot in Outremer. By that time you will be a fully fledged knight of the Temple, your acceptance formalized on the journey, most probably in Sicily, where Richard is scheduled to stop for reprovisioning. But you will have another duty, too, and its importance will be paramount to you. As soon as you embark for Outremer, even before you leave Marseille, you will begin to learn to speak and read Arabic. That has been arranged, and we already know you have a quick ear and a gift for learning languages." He paused and looked around at his companions. "Does anyone wish to add something, or may we set Brother André's schedule for the next few days before we adjourn again?"

No one had anything to add, and so André St. Clair received his instructions and fell into a world of intense tutelage the like of which he had never imagined.

THE ISLANDS OF SICILY AND CYPRUS
1190–91

ONE

The shipboard voyage from Marseille to Sicily was miserable for everyone, and André had sailed among his peers as a Temple novice, the lowest of the least, assigned to the very bowels of an ancient, rancid-smelling vessel, to live in penitence, filth, and squalor for every moment of their confinement, save only for a single period of one hour each day when they were allowed to go up onto the deck for fresh air and exercise.

Below decks, in theory, he and his fellow novices were supposed to spend their time in prayer, listening to readings from the scriptures and from the Temple Rule, and in reciting and learning the articles and sections of the Rule itself by rote. In reality, however, all of the brothers who were to do the readings fell seasick, unable to sit still and read, head down, in the stinking, fetid, heaving hell of the lower deck. And so most of the men aboard spent the entire voyage groaning, vomiting, retching, and squirming in agony.

Although André St. Clair was spared the worst of this, by the time they dropped anchor off Messina, he had not spoken sensibly to a living soul for weeks. And when he was finally permitted to go ashore, to the Temple Commandery in Messina, he went with no idea where he might find his father. He did know, however, that Sir Robert de Sablé, the Grand Master of the King's Fleet, was the liaison assigned to him by the Council members at Aix en Provence, the man who would direct him in all that he did on the Order of Sion's behalf in Outremer; he knew, too, that de Sablé would know where to find Sir Henry. Accordingly, with permission from Brother Justin, he made his way directly to the Master of the King's Fleet.

And so it was that he came to dine that night in the refectory of the great building that had been commandeered for the administrative staff of the army and the fleet, with his father, and with the King himself.

The King was restless—too long at sea, he said, and too long cloistered since then with kings, princes, and churchmen. Sir Henry smiled at hearing this, but said nothing, and Richard half turned towards him.

"Grin if you like, Henry, but I can see in your eye that you know exactly what I'm talking about. It was bad enough at sea, but ever since we landed I've been choking for air, surrounded by puling priests and bleating bishops. I swear by the smile of Christ, too much incense can block a man's lungs, leave him gasping, unable to breathe. God's balls, but I thought I might go mad out there at sea, had we been cooped aboard ship for another day. People puking and heaving everywhere, and the smell of it threatening to taint every bite of food we had. But now, thanks to the sweet and gentle Jesus, the praying and the prating seems to be behind us for a spell.

"I feel the need to bestride a horse and let God's fresh air blow the salt out of my hair and lungs, and to forget about the tomfooleries of affairs of state for a while ... Oh, I know they're necessary and laudable for a hundred reasons, and they give the clerks and clerics all a reason to keep breathing, but they are intolerably tedious, Henry. Will you not grant me that? So! My horses were off-loaded days ago and my stable master tells me they are now recovered from the voyage and ready to be ridden, so I am taking a hunting party out at dawn, to bring back fresh, untainted meat, free of the smell of puke, for all of us. You two will join us, eh?" Both men merely nodded, not even glancing at each other. There was no point in attempting to demur or disagree once Richard Plantagenet had made up his mind on something like that.

The hunt went well, and the entire party—ten men, excluding servants—had acquitted itself well when Richard called a halt late in mid-morning and led them back towards Messina. They were less than halfway back, however, when they encountered signs of impending trouble. A messenger came galloping, his horse blowing and badly winded, to tell Richard that Philip of France had returned to Messina and was calling for an immediate parlay. That left the English King nonplussed, for Philip Augustus had sailed off for Outremer two days before in a fit of pique, angry at, and probably jealous of, the way in which the Sicilian crowds had flocked to welcome Richard's flamboyant arrival two days after his own advent had gone unremarked. But Philip, who was notoriously prone to seasickness, had sailed into a violent storm mere hours after his departure, and it had taken his damaged ship almost two days to limp back into Messina, where he was now tapping his foot impatiently and awaiting Richard's return.

Richard cursed under his breath, then turned to Sir Henry, who was riding at his knee. "Damn the man! Am I never to be free of his tantrums? I thought he was safely gone and out of my concerns for a while, and now he's back, puling and whining that no one shows him the respect he demands. The damned fool simply does not know that you cannot demand respect, that you have to earn it. Blast him to Hades."

Henry sat silent, well aware that Richard was merely giving vent to his frustration and needed no input from him, and the irascible King continued, warming to his theme and unaware, beneath everything, that Henry was even there. "God's holy arse! As if I didn't have enough on my platter, dealing with Tancred, the upstart idiot King of Sicily. Now there's an ample cause to make a monarch curse his lot. Tancred the King! Tancred the Tosspot, Tancred the Pisspot, Tancred the Thief! God damn his thieving soul, I'll have his guts dried and strung to my new arbalest."

He looked again at Sir Henry. "I cannot rest until I deal with the upstart fool and show him what he deserves. He stole the kingdom from my sister, threw her royal arse into one of his jails, and now refuses to return her dowry, to which he has no slightest right. I swear to God, I have been thinking upon ways to gut him, and now I can't, until I have consoled my wayward cousin Capet. Philip Augustus indeed ... I've seen crows that are more august than this foppish Frenchman."

Sir Henry wisely refused to meet his son's eye when he became aware of André staring at him. Tancred had seized the throne two years earlier, upon the death of King William the Good, husband to Richard's younger sister, Joanna Plantagenet. On mounting his new throne, and never imagining for a moment that Richard would come to Sicily under any circumstances, Tancred had imprisoned Joanna and impounded her substantial dowry. He had hastily released her several days before, immediately upon her brother's unexpected arrival, but he had ostentatiously failed to release her dowry, and Richard had been preparing for days now to redress that situation. Within hours of disembarking, he had dispatched squadrons of elite forces, some of them English, others Aquitainians, to secure several prime locations, defensive and aggressive, surrounding Messina itself. Simultaneously, in a lightning-fast and unexpected move the previous day, he had seized and garrisoned a strong monastery at La Bagnara, on the far side of the Straits of Messina, installing his sister Joanna safely there under guard. He already had nine-tenths of a *fait accompli* in his hands, and the last thing he needed now was an additional degree of difficulty like the one presented by the petulant reappearance of Philip of France.

As the walls of Messina began looming in the distance, the hunting party encountered a contingent of Richard's English yeomen who were arguing loudly and obviously highly upset. Tensions within the city, it appeared, had broken out that morning into open hostilities between the English soldiery and the local Sicilian merchants. The Sicilians traditionally disliked foreigners of any description and made no secret of their distaste. They had taken to disparaging the English soldiers as "long-tails," implying, with no subtlety at all, that they each concealed the Devil's tail beneath their clothing. But early that morning one English man-at-arms had argued with a baker over the price and weight of a loaf of bread, and the surrounding crowd had risen up against him, stomping the fellow to death in a demonstration of hatred that quickly escalated into a street riot in which more than a score of English soldiers had been slaughtered, their bodies thrown into public privies as an additional insult.

Richard waved Sir Henry to his side and spurred his horse towards the city, but long before they reached Messina they began to encounter increasing numbers of their own Angevin troops. The English, they said—those who had not been killed in the morning's rioting—had been driven from the city, and the great gates had been locked to keep them out. The Griffones, the English soldiery's own insulting name for the local Sicilians, were now lining the tops of the city walls, jeering and howling abuse at the English yeomen, whom Richard and his party could now see milling in the space before the walls.

It was plain to André, as they approached the scene, that the hundred or so English yeomen in this particular group were spoiling for revenge and waiting only for a leader to rally them to the attack, and naturally enough, they flocked around Richard when he rode over to them, expecting him to be that leader. But Richard had other concerns that ran more deeply than the emotional currents affecting his men. He stood up in his stirrups and called them to attention, then waited until they all fell silent. When he was sure he had their undivided attention, he drew his sword and sat back into his saddle, holding the magnificent weapon high.

"You all know this sword," he told them, keeping his voice low enough that they had to strain to hear him. "Think you I would sully it by accepting insults from these louts and leaving its blade to grow dull from lack of use? We will teach these Griffones to mind their manners, lads, rest assured of that, but we must do it my way ... the way I am constrained to do it. Easy enough for you brave bulls to cry out and go rushing in to fight bare handed, but I have to think and act like a king, and see it from the viewpoint of a king. So here's what we must do."

He swept his eyes around the crowd that stared up at him, meeting the eyes of every man there, however briefly. No one moved or made a sound, and he stood up in his stirrups again and raised his voice more strongly this time.

"There are dead Englishmen in the streets of Messina this day. Is that true?"

A massive roar from a hundred throats verified that it was, and he chopped it into silence with a downsweep of his blade. "Then, by God's almighty beard, they shall be avenged, every man of them. Their deaths will not go by unpunished. Messina and its rabid citizens will pay dearly on behalf of every Englishman done to death in its streets this day, or I am not Richard of England! I will have justice. *We* will have justice! This I swear to you."

For long moments there was a chaos of noisy approval, and not once did Richard glance at any member of his hunting party as he waited patiently for the tumult to die down. Instead, he concentrated on judging the precise moment when the noise began to fade, and raised his arm high, commanding attention as the silence fell again.

"In the meantime, I ask for your trust, and your understanding. I stand here as King of England, but you men *are* England, and you are here for a sworn purpose. God's Holy Land awaits your coming, groaning beneath the feet of the infidel hordes. So think, then, upon this. It is our sacred duty to our God to come with every man intact to fight the Saracen, and every man we lose, 'twixt here and there, is one less sword to raise on God's behalf. We could storm Messina here today, but the gates are locked and the walls are manned against us, and we have nothing here to use against them, no ladders, nothing. They, on the other hand, would meet us with torrents of arrows, spears, stones, and boiling oil. We would lose too many men, and I cannot permit that.

"But I swear to you now, by the bowels of Christ, tomorrow is a different matter. Tonight will be for talking, but if they will not see sense and make apology for what they have done, then come morning, we will be here again, but this time properly prepared, and Messina and its people will weep for today's folly. Then we will drink Griffonish blood."

Again he waited for the shouting to die down before continuing. "But you must know, in truth," he told them, "I have no wish to shed another drop of English blood here in Sicily if it can be avoided."

The last grumbling voice died away as that sank home, and Richard spoke into a profound silence. "Every single man left lying dead on the island of Sicily," he pointed out to his quiet listeners, "is one man lost uselessly to our great and holy endeavor. So here is what I want you to do now. I want you all, every man of you, to go back to your camp and wait to hear from me. I will send word to you at dawn of what is happening. And as you go, tell everyone you meet what I have said, and turn them back with you. Above all else, trust me and believe in what I say. Now go, and God be with you."

Richard then sat and watched the disgruntled yeomen withdraw reluctantly in the direction of their encampments. Only when the last of them had vanished from sight did he turn back to face the walls of Messina, the evidence of his fury stamped upon his face, but to André, it was also clear that he was determined to keep his passions under rein. Richard's eyes now swept the scene in front of him, taking in the broad, open space leading to the enormous gates and then scanning the densely packed rows of abandoned stalls on each side before rising to look up at the press of figures lining the tops of the walls. Finally he spoke.

"I am going forward to the gates, to talk with the captain of the guard—assuming that there is one. Even a rabble such as this must have someone in command of a main portal. Henry, you and André will come with me, as will Baldwin, but we will not approach directly in the open. That would be tempting the Fates, inviting attack by some fool with no brains. Come, we will leave our horses over there beneath that big brown canopy where they will be safe from bowshot, and make our way from there under the protection of the market stalls—or such protection as they offer. Four of us will be adequate. An envoy and his escort. Any more than that might be provocative, and this is no time for needless provocation. The rest of you will stay here with the horses and await our return."

They dismounted beneath the large canopy and then struck out towards the gates, moving cautiously as they wound their way among the tables, carts, and booths of the marketplace, aware that they became increasingly vulnerable to attack from above as they approached the walls. But no one molested them or hindered them, and soon they arrived in front of the gates and moved close to the portals, where they were concealed from above by the high, outthrust arch over the lintel.

It became apparent within moments, however, that there was nothing Richard or anyone else could do there. The high, featureless barrier of the oaken gates remained locked against his summons, and no one responded to his challenges to open them and talk with him. The King was literally talking to a wall, and ran a very real risk of appearing foolish and ineffectual. His face close to the wood of the doors, he inhaled deeply through his nose, then nodded tersely and accepted the inevitable.

"So be it. We can do nothing here, so we will go back. Henry and André, take the lead. I'll follow, and Baldwin will guard our backs."

"Aye, my lord." André glanced at the King before starting to turn away, and his eyes rested for a moment on Baldwin of Bethune, Richard's constant bodyguard and companion. True to his nature, the giant, taciturn knight from Anjou had said no single word that day in André's hearing, and he said nothing now, merely drawing his sword from its sheath. André drew his own, seeing his father from the corner of his eye in the act of doing the same, and then he stepped out into plain view of those above the gates and began to lead the way back, through the market stalls, to where they had left their horses and the others of their party.

It was only as they re-entered the maze of market stalls that André felt the first awareness of danger. They had passed the same way in approaching the gates, but now something had changed. He grasped his sword more firmly and walked with extra caution, his eyes moving ceaselessly, scanning the alternating patterns of light and shadow among the stalls and canopies surrounding them. His father, sword in hand, was moving parallel to him on his right, perhaps two paces distant and half a pace behind, and Richard was almost directly at André's back, perhaps a pace farther away. Behind Richard, André knew without looking, Baldwin would be walking backward, his eyes scanning the heights behind them for threats. André's misgivings increased; something was wrong here.

He started to speak, to offer a warning of some kind, and had begun to turn his shoulder when a flicker of movement on his left captured his attention. He twisted immediately to look at it, tightening his grip on the hilt of his sword, but there was nothing there to see. There was only an empty stall, like all the others, save that it had a rear wall of black cloth. But as his eyes adjusted to the blackness, he saw another movement in the shadows and reacted instinctively as he recognized what he was looking at: a man, dressed completely in black, on the point of loosing a bolt from a crossbow. He shouted and flung up his sword to the side as fast as he could, intending to warn Richard and push him back, but he knew he was too late. And then he heard a ringing clang and felt an enormous concussion strike him head on. He had a flaring, light-filled vision, a momentary impression, of being hurled aside and in upon himself, and after that he knew nothing.

Afterwards, long after the event itself, when the furor and the excitement had abated and he was finally able to think about it, André St. Clair tried to string together the series of events that had led to his being where he was that morning, precisely placed to save the King's life in the warren of litter-strewn aisles that separated the market stalls crammed into the space fronting the high, blank walls of the city of Messina. He knew that had he been one foot to either side of where he stood at the crucial moment, he would not have been able to do what he did, and Richard of England would have died there on the offal-strewn ground of the deserted marketplace.

IT TOOK SOME TIME for André St. Clair to regain awareness and when he did, he found himself in a world of agony, his right hand and arm aflame with dementing pain. André's upflung sword had intersected the trajectory of the lethal crossbow bolt precisely, and the steel missile had struck the exact center of his blade, about a hand's breadth beneath the cross-guard, and driven the length of it violently backward to smash into the King's chest and shoulder and send him toppling to the ground. In the course of that violent, spinning movement, Richard's own sword, reflexively outflung, struck the back of André's head hard, stunning him.

André's sword had been destroyed by the impact, its clean length twisted and warped beyond repair, and the hard-shot steel projectile, loosed from no more than a hundred feet, had driven a hole clean through the tempered, half-inch-thick blade. The King, struck by the full force of the bolt-driven blade, had been knocked senseless for a time, and the links of his light mail tunic, the only armor he had worn to the hunt, had been driven into the flesh of his chest, leaving a pattern of bruising. Unfortunately, it appeared that Sir André St. Clair's right hand, fingers, and wrist had been broken, perhaps beyond repair, by the wrenching impact.

Within moments of the attack, Richard and his small group were surrounded by the remainder of their hunting party, and soon after that the scene of the attack was thronged with English soldiery. By the time Baldwin returned carrying the unconscious would-be assassin over his shoulder, Richard and André had been loaded onto stretchers and were being transported by wagon to the King's own tented enclosure, where the King's physicians busied themselves immediately in seeing to the comfort of Richard and his stout defender.

Baldwin's interrogation of his prisoner had been brief, simplified by the fact that the fellow was no hero and had no tolerance for pain, especially when that was coolly and systematically applied by someone like the big knight from Anjou. The would-be regicide had confessed immediately, spitting out every detail of what had occurred. The man turned out to be a sergeant of some description, in the employ of King Tancred. He had somehow learned that Tancred and Richard were sharply at odds with each other and had consequently decided, without forethought, to remove Richard as a threat to his own King's welfare.

The physicians eventually decided that nothing had been broken in St. Clair's hand or arm after all. But they agreed that everything had been outraged and that it might be weeks, perhaps even months, before Sir André would be able to use his arm again. Every bone and tendon in his hand, wrist, and elbow, and even his shoulder, had been hugely wrenched and strained, not sufficiently so to tear the joints apart, but nearly enough so to provoke grave frowns and shaken heads among the King's august physicians. The bruising, they agreed, would be spectacular—the entire limb had already begun to turn black—and none of them was willing to speculate on how long its effects would last, but they were absolutely in accord that the only effective healing agent they could offer would be time, in whatever quantities might be required, so they encased the knight's arm in a rigid framework of splints, bracing the joints in such a way that they could not be moved before the physicians themselves deemed it appropriate to attempt to move them. And then, because he was in great pain, and because the King himself was greatly in the young knight's debt, they dosed him heavily with opiates for three whole days.

WHEN ANDRÉ ST. CLAIR finally opened his eyes again and felt sane and normal, his father was sitting by his bedside, staring at him with unfocused eyes. André tried to sit up, but discovered that he could not move a muscle, and his effort produced only a grunt, which served to bring Sir Henry's attention back to the moment at hand. The Master-at-Arms straightened up in his chair and then bent forward, frowning in concern.

"André? Are you back?" He blinked in doubt. "Are you awake?"

André forced himself to relax, not even attempting to move his head. He had closed his eyes when he grunted and now he lay still, mastering his breathing and wondering whether his voice would be as unresponsive to his mind as his body had been. But at length, when he felt ready, he worked his tongue to stir some saliva in his dry mouth and swallowed it, then spoke.

"Father? What are you doing here?" He blinked his eyes and looked about him, realizing that he was not in the Temple Commandery. "Where am I?"

"You are in King Richard's personal quarters, in his sick bay."

"How long have I been here?"

Sir Henry sucked in a great breath and then nodded, as though satisfied with something, although he made no attempt to answer his son's question. "Good," he said instead. "You are well. We knew you would be, but the King's medical staff cared only for your comfort, so they have kept you drugged. But they took the splints off yesterday. Now you are merely bandaged."

André counted silently to five, absorbing that. "And how long have I been here?"

"Four days since you were ... wounded. Three of them spent unconscious, lashed to a special framework built for you under the direction of Lucien of Amboise, the King's chief physician. An amazing device. Kept you completely off the ground, suspended in the air, on pulleys. I never saw anything like it."

"Was I raving?" André was suddenly smitten with fear of what he might have said in his sickness, thoughts of the Order of Sion and its secrets whirling through his head, but his father's eyebrows rose in astonishment.

"Raving? Not at all. You were like a dead man most of the time ... most of the time when I was here at least, and I have spent much of the past few days here, with King Richard's permission."

"Am I still drugged?"

"No. Master Lucien estimated that you would awaken naturally ..." Sir Henry looked about him in mild surprise, "about now. He said mid-morning, and that is what it is. How do you feel?"

"I can't move."

"No, you can't, because you are still tied down to prevent you from moving carelessly. Apart from *that*, how do you feel?"

"Better than I did before. I remember vomiting ... It hurt abominably. And I remember not being able to think clearly ... seeing strange visions and hearing strange noises. I feel better now, and I'm relieved to know that I am not paralyzed. I thought I was, when I first awoke. Otherwise I feel well. Can you undo these ropes?"

"No ropes, they are leather straps. But I think you had better keep them on until Master Lucien decides they can be removed." Sir Henry fell silent for a moment, and then in a voice filled with wonder he asked, "How did you do that?"

"Hmm? Do what?"

"What you did in the marketplace. How could you be that swift, to bring your blade up like that, to exactly where it needed to be?"

André turned his head slightly on the pillow until he could look directly at his father, expecting to find the older man smiling at him, teasing him, but Sir Henry's face betrayed no humor and it was now André's turn to frown.

"You mean blocking the shot? I could not. I didn't *do* that, Father, not intentionally. It was an accident … happenstance. I moved, trying to shout a warning and wave Richard down, but I was too slow … far, far too slow. How is the King?"

Sir Henry cocked his head, wrinkling his eyes as he deliberated with himself over what his son had said, and then he murmured, "His Grace is in perfect health, and all the world believes he owes that health to the brilliance of your defense of his royal body in the face of attack."

André shook his head slightly, rolling it gently from side to side on the pillow. "Not so. He owes it to Fortuna, the Roman goddess of chance, for it was sheer good fortune that I was there and moved when I did. I didn't see the bolt coming. It was loosed from within thirty paces, too fast to see, and I barely saw the man who fired it … What happened to him, was he caught and killed?"

"Caught, but not killed. He was an idiot and he acted alone, thinking he would be rewarded for it by Tancred. Baldwin captured him and Richard pardoned him, gave him five silver pieces, ostensibly in gratitude for his poor aim, and let him go. Richard came out of the affair well in everyone's eyes, Sicilians as well as our own, by forgiving the fellow and making light of his attempt. But look you …"

André waited, and when his father said no more he prompted him. "Look you what, Father? What were you going to say?"

Sir Henry shrugged. "I—I was going to say something that seemed to make no sense, but I think it needs to be said anyway. You are convinced—" He hesitated, then plunged ahead. "Yes, you are convinced that your saving the King's life was an accident. I can see that. But I disagree. You could not have done what you did had you not been prepared to do it, poised to do something. You did what you did because you were ready to do it, to react to whatever came. I believe that just as strongly as you believe your own explanation, but what is even more important is that *Richard* believes it, and so does everyone else. If you get up from the bed now and declare that the entire thing was an accident and your actions were completely without merit, you will do yourself a great disservice, my son."

"How? It seems to me to be the honorable thing to do … to speak the truth."

"Honorable, perhaps, but foolish in this instance. Think about where we are and what lies ahead of you." Those words struck home, although not in any way Sir Henry could have understood. "Look at the people who surround you, André, in this endeavor of ours. Do you see much there of honor? Of nobility and integrity? I think not. Not in the way you and I were taught to think of those attributes." He shook his head in frustration. "Look, I speak here as your father who loves you, and I have nothing but your good in mind, even if I seem to be saying things. André, none of us can afford to neglect or to give up any advantage offered to us. Each of us is a single soul among an army too vast to count, marching against another army that some say outnumbers us as the grains of sand in the desert outnumber the stones …

"You have an opportunity to improve yourself here, perhaps an opportunity to outlive your fellows and survive this coming war with honor—although that is, as ever, in the hands of God. You saved the King's life! It matters not that you believe it to have been an accident. That you were there at all was an accident. That Richard was standing where he was at that precise moment was an accident. And it was an accident that the Sicilian bowman recognized the man walking through the marketplace as the King of England. But the fact remains that when the fellow's missile reached for the lion heart of England's King, it struck and pierced your sword blade, punching a hole clear through the metal of your blade. Had your blade not been there in place, that bolt would have sundered Richard's heart and ripped on through his spine. That. Is. The truth! And that truth can work to your advantage. Known as the King's Rescuer, you will walk apart from other men. The word of your speed and skill will run ahead of you and warn lesser men to treat you with respect. But only if you keep your counsel to yourself about what you say you believe happened. No one will give a rotten fig for a common knight who had a momentary flash of good fortune then threw it away."

"Aye, Father, I hear you ..." André's tone was sufficient to interrupt his father's warnings, and Sir Henry fell silent, eyeing his son and waiting for him to speak. André lay thinking about what in fact lay ahead of him in Outremer, and how his task there might be simplified were men to think of him in the way his father had described.

"Very well, then, so be it. You have convinced me and I am persuaded. I will speak no more of accidents." He paused, then grinned. "So what will happen now? Paragon or not, I am yet the meanest creature in the world: a novice brother in the Order of the Temple."

His father smiled. "Aye, mayhap, but that will not last for long. Your hardships will be easier to bear after this, I believe."

Flat on his back, André raised a sardonic eyebrow. "Think you so? I fancy Brother Justin, the Master of Novices, might be unimpressed by my new-won fame ... Will we stay here long in Sicily, think you?"

"Well, yesterday I would have wagered that we would not stay here long. Richard has thoroughly cowed Tancred and his rabble now, and I'm sure the thought of a long sojourn in Messina, with Philip crying and whining at every imagined slight, holds no allure for him. But all of that changed this morning, with the arrival of enormous tidings. Barbarossa is dead, his army scattered. The entire world has been cast off balance. I doubt now that we will leave here before spring."

For several moments André could not speak. Frederic Barbarossa, who had held the title of Holy Roman Emperor for more than three decades, was a leviathan among men, aged in years now but hardly less fit and battle ready than he had been when he first claimed his empire, thirty-five years earlier. At the age of sixty-odd, he had retained sufficient power and influence to recruit an army more than two hundred thousand strong and to lead it in person, overland by way of Constantinople, to Outremer. He was a legend by any standard, truly a name with which to conjure.

"Barbarossa is dead? How? What happened? Are you saying Saladin defeated him?"

His father shook his head. "No, not at all. Barbarossa never reached the Holy Land. He drowned, apparently, somewhere near Byzantium, crossing a mountain river, they say. Fell off his horse, fully armored, into icy water. The armor held him down and he was dead by the time they pulled him out. He was an old man, you know. They are saying it was the shock that killed him ... the icy water ..."

"Sweet Jesus!"

Sir Henry's voice was firmer now. "We had word this morning, on a ship out of Cyprus. The vessel was crammed with Barbarossa's people—high-ranking ones, barons and counts, lords and knights, all of them making their way homeward. Apparently the army began to break apart the moment the old man died. No one strong enough or politically acceptable enough to the others to rally the forces and keep them together. Within a week of the event—his death—his army had all but disappeared. More than two hundred thousand of them, there were, and they scattered to the winds, blown into nothingness."

"What about his son, the Swabian fellow, Frederick? What happened to him? He would not simply have abandoned his father's body and fled. There must be more to the tale than you are telling me."

Sir Henry shrugged. "No one seems to know anything with certainty. No one even knows if any of the army marched on towards Outremer, but no one seems willing to believe they did."

"Hmph. No one on that ship is willing to say otherwise. If Frederick of Swabia or any of the other leaders march on to Palestine, the ones aboard this ship, and all the others like them who ran for home, are going to look like cowards, don't you think?"

Neither man spoke for a space then, each of them thinking through the significance of these tidings, until André said, "This alters everything."

"How so, everything?"

"Well, not everything ... But it certainly alters the political urgencies that have been causing Richard and Philip and the Pope so much concern. With Barbarossa dead, the Eastern Orthodox threat to papal rule in Jerusalem is greatly eased, which will translate directly into breathing space for us and for our armies."

"I don't follow you. It won't change anything in Outremer. Conrad of Montferrat will still be at King Guy's throat, trying to take his place."

"Aye, but his zeal will be considerably diminished when he hears of the death of his imperial cousin. As long as he retained the threat of Barbarossa's power to back his movements, he strutted finely. Lacking it, I think he might be more amenable to compromise than he has been. I think it certain, however, that once the word arrives in Palestine that Barbarossa is dead and his army scattered, Guy and his followers will be encouraged enough to maintain their positions and wait for Richard's arrival, however long that takes. And therefore I can see no flaw in your thinking. We will probably stay here for the winter and sail again come spring. That will breed an entirely new set of complications, but there is nothing you or I or anyone we know can do to alter any of that, so we may as well accept it."

Sir Henry rose. "I had best be gone. I have taken too much time lately for my own concerns. And the King will probably want to talk with me, once he has absorbed these tidings. If he does decide we are to stay here until the spring, I'll have to set about building winter quarters for the whole damned army. Sweet Jesus, that is going to be a painful exercise, in this godforsaken place ... You stay abed and set your mind to wellness. Farewell, I will see you again tomorrow."

IT TOOK TEN FULL DAYS for the injuries to André's hand and wrist to heal sufficiently for him to clench his fist, and even then his fingers were still too tender and the bones of his hand too sore to permit him to exert any real strength in the clench. His forearm, elbow, and shoulder were completely restored by that time, their color almost returned to normal, but his hand was still a fearsome sight, a mass of multicolored bruises.

On the fifteenth day after sustaining his injuries, he finally swung his feet off the bed, set them squarely on the floor, then pushed himself upright with the assistance of a stout stick in his left hand. He stood for a moment, weaving gently until he mastered his balance again, then took a deep breath and stepped away from the bed. That, at least, was what he attempted, but his feet did not move and he fell straight forward like a log, and had to be helped back onto his cot.

Three days later André was walking easily, but it was to be another week before his hand grew strong enough for him to hold a sword again with any kind of authority, and only then was he judged fit to be discharged from Lucien's care and to return to the company of his fellow novices, whose training had been proceeding throughout his absence. On the morning of the day he was discharged, Richard himself thrust open the door to the room where André sat breaking his fast with two other knights, and leaned in.

"Here," he called to André, "you will need this." He brought up his arm in an underhand sweep, tossing a long, sheathed sword to where André was rising to his feet. André caught the weapon and held it at arm's length, seeing that it was wrapped in a thick but supple sword belt. He turned back towards the door, but Richard had already gone, leaving the door to swing shut at his back. André looked from one of his breakfast companions to the other and saw that both were gazing at him owlishly from beneath raised eyebrows. He shrugged and grinned, a little shamefacedly.

"I lost my other one," he said, and then he unwrapped the belt from around the sheathed weapon and drew out the blade. It was magnificent, a King's gift, and he brought it to his eyes to admire the rippling light that played along the fold patterns of the glorious blade. It was neither elaborate nor ostentatious in its finery but simply superb in every detail, and even the heavy leather of its sheath was worked and subtly embossed, its interior of sheepskin shaved until it was no more than the suggestion of a nap. He remembered the sword he had owned before, a useful, unpretentious weapon that had given him honorable service for years, and he knew that this one was worth a hundred times as much as that had been. This was a sword fit for a king, given him by a King. He had not the slightest compunction in accepting it, for he knew that he would put it to good use in the times that lay ahead.

Returned to duty, he soon lost himself in the urgency of making up the ground he had lost to the other novices, and his injured hand hardened rapidly under the daily discipline of battle training. His days were filled once again, but far more so than ever before, with the monastic rituals and daily prayers of the Temple Rule, and when he was not praying, he was completely preoccupied with training, sharpening his fighting skills and rebuilding the strength of his sword arm. The days, weeks, and months passed by without his really being aware of their going and, more importantly, without any real awareness on his part of the world beyond the walls of the Temple Commandery. He knew of Christmas and the Feast of the Epiphany at the time of their occurrences, but solely because of the liturgical impact they had upon the daily discipline of the novices. And then he lost awareness of time again until the beginning of Lent, in early March of 1191, when the normal activities of the novices were suspended in order to accommodate a three-day period of increased prayer and fasting, called a retreat. During this time the novices were expected to do nothing more than pray and meditate in penitential silence, standing or kneeling at all times, save for the few hours when they were permitted to sleep.

On the morning they were dismissed from their retreat, directly after matins and long before the first false dawn began to lighten the sky, André was summoned by Brother Justin.

With an absolutely clear conscience, aware that he had done nothing wrong, André presented himself immediately before the Master of Novices, suspecting and hoping that this might have something to do with the Order of Sion. Brother Justin appeared as ill tempered and intolerant as ever, but he said nothing disparaging, merely nodding to André and informing him without preamble that he had been instructed to send him at once to Sir Robert de Sablé, whose quarters were inside the city of Messina.

André, struck by a sudden thought, looked down at the filthy surcoat he had been wearing for months. "Should I go as I am, Brother, dressed like this?"

Justin frowned. "Aye, you should, of course you should. How else would you go? Sir Robert knows you're a Temple novice and you have nothing to hide. Were you to go out differently, and be recognized, it could lead to the kind of questions we don't want people asking. But take a horse from the stables. De Sablé may have other work for you. Here." He held out his hand, bearing a small scroll that he had been holding all along. "Give this to the stable master and he'll give you a decent mount. And if anyone asks you where you are going or what you are about, tell them you are on an errand from me to your father. That's what is in the scroll. Now be off with you, and whatever Sir Robert may require of you, be careful."

IT WAS CLOSE TO NOON that morning when Sir Henry St. Clair was finally able to return to his quarters, duty free for the time being, and he was surprised and pleased to find his son in his day room waiting for him, perched on the wooden bench that ran along the wall where Tomas, Sir Henry's loyal assistant, sat permanently on guard against those who would waste the time of the Master-at-Arms. It had been several weeks since father and son had last spoken to each other, but Sir Henry wasted no time in leading André into his private chamber and closing the door firmly behind him.

"What's wrong, Father? You look concerned."

"I am. Why are you here? I am happy to see you, of course, but I know you must be here for some specific reason, some reason grave enough to justify your being granted leave to come a-visiting at this stage of your training."

André's eyebrows shot up. "How would you know about that? The details of our training are supposed to be secret."

"Aye, like so many other things. Sit down." As André moved to obey, taking one of the two chairs by the single large work table in the room, Sir Henry continued, "I have many friends, my son, as befits an aging man, and some of them are Knights of the Temple.

As it happened, I shared a pot of ale with one after dinner a few days ago and we talked of many things, one of which was the training of this latest batch of Temple novices. He knew, of course, that you are one of those and he was merely attempting to console me for not being able to see you." He eyed his son closely. "So come on, spit it out. Why are you here?"

"Jews, Father." André spoke the word bluntly, deliberately, watching to see what effect it might have on his father, but whatever reaction he might have anticipated, he received nothing. Sir Henry merely blinked, then sat down across the table.

"What about them?"

"That is why I am here."

"You make no sense, son."

"No, Father, I fear I do, to my own ears at least. Do you recall the last time that we spoke of Jews and of the King's regard for them?" He did not wait for his father's response. "I have come here directly from Sir Robert de Sablé, and at his urging. He sent for me this morning and had me released from my duties for the day, purely so that he could pass along to you, through me, his grave concern for your safety."

When André paused, Sir Henry spoke out. "Well, while I am duly grateful for Sir Robert's concern for my safety and well-being, I believe that what I do and how I behave has nothing at all to do with him and should be beneath his attention. Be so good as to pass that information along to him, with my gratitude, of course."

"No, Father, with respect, I will do no such thing. You are being obtuse. Sir Robert has no interest in chiding you for misbehavior. He fears for your welfare, because he sincerely believes it to be in the interests of the armies and the venture upon which we are engaged. He could have sent a warning to you by other means, but he chose to communicate through me for a variety of reasons, the very least of which is that he and I are friends. But the issues that concern him in this are far greater than any personal friendship."

Sir Henry frowned slightly. "Issues such as what?"

"Policy, ambitions, politics, and schemes. William Marshall, Marshal of England, and Humphrey, Baron of Sheffield."

Sir Henry leaned an elbow on the table's edge, tapping his pursed lips with two fingers. "Explain."

"Do I need to, Father? It took no great understanding when it was explained to me this morning. Richard is King of England, but he is also Duke of Aquitaine and of Normandy and Count of Anjou, Poitou, Brittany, and a host of other territories, none of which are English and all of which have offered up their men to this mission to free Outremer. You are, by title, the King's Master-at-Arms, but in reality you are Master-at-Arms to your liege lord Richard, Duke of Aquitaine, and as such you represent in your very person the identities and the hopes of every soldier in the armies of Richard and Philip who is not English. If you fall from favor and are dismissed, then William Marshall will assume your place and this entire army will fall under English control. That must not be permitted to happen."

Sir Henry nodded slowly, agreeing but conceding nothing. "I can understand how that might be of concern, but what of Humphrey of Sheffield?"

"I am surprised that you would even ask. I know the fellow, Father. He is a gross, slovenly pig, without honor and unworthy of his knighthood, let alone a barony. It has come to Sir Robert's attention, from a source he claims is unquestionably truthful and well informed, that you have crossed paths with this swine … and have, in fact, come nigh to crossing blades with him."

Sir Henry shook his head abruptly. "Not so. I do not like the man, but I have had no active quarrel with him."

"Can you be sure of that, Father? Would he agree? The information that Sir Robert received was that you had come to Humphrey's attention, unpleasantly, over the matter of a certain Jew called Simeon, here in Messina. Simeon was a well-known figure in this city, apparently, a merchant but not a money lender, but he disappeared from sight, with his entire family, at an inopportune moment and has not been seen since."

"An inopportune moment for whom?"

"For Sheffield. Who else would care? Humphrey is a rabid, dedicated Jew hater. It is one of the things, and probably the single most significant thing, that enables him to maintain the friendship, if such it is, that he shares with Richard. It is Humphrey's responsibility, it seems—although it is something not openly acknowledged—to provide Jews for Richard's dinner entertainment spectacles. According to Sir Robert's informant, this Simeon had been earmarked for one such spectacle, after an altercation with one of Humphrey's associates over a debt. But he vanished, as I said, along with his family. Your name came up in connection with the disappearance, something about a warning in advance of a nocturnal visit from Baron Sheffield's men-at-arms. Humphrey believed the report and took it to the King. Fortunately for all of us, the King was ... preoccupied and did not have time to listen to the report. In the meantime, Sir Robert, having heard of the matter from his own spies, took it upon himself to intervene, providing an unsolicited explanation for your conduct that was a direct contradiction of the tale Baron Humphrey had received. The Baron, who is deeply in Sir Robert's debt and had no reason to suspect the Master of the Fleet would even know you, believed what he was told, and so nothing more will come of it. But Sir Robert wishes you to know what happened, and while he would not presume to tell you how to behave, he begs that you will at least be more circumspect in future."

Sir Henry sat silent for long moments, digesting what André had said, and then he inhaled deeply and nodded, lowering his chin to his chest and pinching his lips between two finger ends. Finally the Master-at-Arms looked up. "So be it. I acknowledge it. I acted rashly, although it did not seem so at the time. In future I will be more ... careful. But was it truly only fear for my political position that made your friend act as he did?"

"Can you doubt it, Father? Think about what is entailed."

"I have, and he is correct. And seen from that viewpoint, my responsibilities are larger and more complex than I had believed. I shall be more careful from now on."

"No, Father. If it pleases you, I would like you to stay away from any involvement with Jews in future. Everything surrounding them is fraught with danger amounting to insanity."

"Aye, but only because our King chooses to make it so."

"Our King and his bishops. The Church condones it."

"My son, the Church *fosters* it. But should ordinary men of good-will then hide their heads and condone it, too, giving tacit consent to atrocities that would disgust the gentle Jesus in whom we are taught to believe?" He shook his head, once and with finality. "Do not ask me to do that, André. It sits well with neither my nature nor my honor, so we will speak no more of it. You have delivered your message, and I have heeded it." He hesitated, then added, "You said your friend told you the King was preoccupied and did not hear Sheffield's report, but did he say why? When did this happen?"

"I don't know, Father. I did not think to ask. I was too worried about the ramifications of what he was saying. But looking back on it now, on the urgency Sir Robert betrayed, I have the distinct impression that it had all happened very recently."

"Hmm. Within the past few days. It had to be then." He checked himself, cocking his head at his son. "Have you heard about the sodomy confessions? No, I can see you haven't. There's probably much good to be gained from living the cloistered life." He thought for a moment, then went on. "Less than three weeks ago Richard decided, for reasons known only to himself and God, to confess to being a homosexual deviant. He cloistered himself with an entire convocation of bishops in a private chapel here in Messina, belonging to a local dignitary, and there, amid clouds of incense, he made a full and purportedly public confession of his addiction to sodomy, begging forgiveness of God and the Holy Church and supplicating the strength to resist temptation and mend his lustful, impious, and unnatural ways henceforth. Amen."

"My God! This is not a jest, is it? He actually did that?"

"He did. I thought at first that might have been why he was preoccupied and unable to deal with Sheffield's report, but then I realized that the Simeon affair came after that. So de Sablé must have been describing the events of the past few days when he spoke of Richard's preoccupation. Which means Eleanor's arrival, four days ago."

"Eleanor's arrival? The Duchess Eleanor, the King's mother? Is she here in Sicily?"

"She is. Arrived the day before yesterday, and the place has been buzzing like a hive ever since. You and your fellow novices must be the only people in Sicily not to know."

"But why? What is she doing here? I thought she had returned to England."

"No, nor will she. She is back living in Aquitaine, in Rouen and sometimes in Chinon, which she always loved. She merely came here to deliver a gift to Richard."

"A gift." André's voice was flat, his face blank as he sought to make sense of what he had just heard. "What kind of gift would bring her all the way here to Sicily to deliver it herself?"

"The gift she was going to find for him when last I saw her. A wife."

The words dropped like bricks into a still pond, and for a long time neither man spoke.

"A ... wife ..." André's voice was much lower now, deliberately hushed, and his father's response matched his out of sheer caution, even though the heavy doors at his back were solidly shut.

"Aye, from Navarre, south of the Pyrenees. The Princess Berengaria. Eleanor went to her father's court and sued for the match in person, successfully. King Sancho will be a strong ally for Richard. Years of experience fighting the Moors down there in Spain."

"Aye, but ... This King, Sancho you said? Has he no knowledge of ... of what Richard is? What hope they to achieve by this, and how is Richard reacting?"

"He appears to be reacting very well, to most people's surprise. Fortuitous timing, I suspect, considering how fresh he is from being absolved and forgiven for all the abominations of his former ways. With that all comfortably behind him, I am quite sure he sees himself reborn and newly disposed towards cohabitation and fatherhood. But in truth, an uncharitable soul might wonder whether our monarch could have heard, say a month or so previously, that his mother was on her way to visit him with bride in tow, and decided to prepare himself accordingly."

"Yes, perhaps he did. Nothing would surprise me in that. But in God's name, Father, the mere idea! You know Richard even better than I do. So are we now to give credence, all of us, thanks solely to the verbal blessings and forgiveness of a chapel full of bishops, to the public pretense of Richard Plantagenet *married*, and a *paterfamilias*?"

"Unimportant whether you or I believe or not, André. It will be done, be assured. England will have a Queen and perhaps in the course of time a Prince Royal, and Richard will be seen to be a man. There is no contesting the fact that an heir for England is Richard's first priority, overarching all other responsibilities. If he fails to come up with a son, the throne will go to his useless brother John. And even I, who have spent less than a single month in England and have no wish to return—even I know that to be a prospect no one wishes to consider."

"Ye gods!" André was shaking his head. "This is the King who would not even have a woman at his coronation dinner! And now he is to surround himself voluntarily with women. Eleanor, Joanna, and this, what's her name, Berengoria? Mother, sister, and wife. They will drive him insane."

"Her name is Berengaria, and it is my understanding that she is a quiet thing, demure and … complacent."

"Complacent? I hope she is, for by all the gods, she will need to be."

"Besides, Eleanor is leaving for home again in a few days—actually for Rome first, then Rouen. Richard made sure of that with no loss of time. And Joanna can be malleable enough, with proper treatment. She will cause no trouble, lacking her mother's presence. Besides, she'll be company for the poor bride once the husband rides off to war."

"So when is the wedding to be?"

"Not during Lent, that much we can rely on. But after that, who knows? The bridal party is all here, although I doubt that Philip

Augustus will attend, and there is a profusion of sanctified bishops ready and salivating at the thought of pontificating when Richard Plantagenet is brought back into the fold of sexual orthodoxy. God help us all."

"Will you attend?"

"Of course I will. I shall have no choice, as Master-at-Arms. But you should be a Templar knight by then, so you will not be expected to be there."

André gave a little grin. "Perhaps not, but we will have to wait and see. How is Philip taking all this, really? Do you know? He must be out of countenance, his lover to be wed and his sister spurned at the same time, despite a bishopric full of holy oaths to the contrary."

"Aye, as you might expect, he is not happy. But Philip has been a king all his life, and thus he is a pragmatist. He will learn to live with the realities involved."

"Aye, no doubt ... and with the unrealities as well." He twisted his face into a grimace. "So be it, then. There's nothing any of us can do, as you say. But I do have your promise to be more careful in your dealings with the Jew baiters?" He returned his father's nod and stood up. "Excellent, then. I shall return to Sir Robert and tell him about this, and then I should return to the commandery. Fare thee well, Father. I hope to see you again soon." He stepped forward to embrace his father, but Sir Henry grasped him by the upper arms, staring into his eyes.

"When will your novitiate be complete? When will you join the Order?"

André smiled. "I really don't know, Father. They don't tell you things like that. They won't even unbend sufficiently to tell you if you *will* join the Order. But I can promise you that, like the King's wedding, it won't be before Easter, because it can't happen during Lent. In the meantime, I fret sometimes about the vows ..." His grin widened as he watched Sir Henry's eyes, and before the older knight could frame the question springing to his lips, André added, "The poverty and obedience are simple enough. Those are part of the life I have chosen, but the chastity worries me, because I did not choose that …" He was being facetious, but his humor became tinged with chagrin when he saw that his father had taken him literally. He grimaced and took his father's hand again, holding it in both of his. "That was a jest, Father. A poor one, I see now, but I was trying to make you smile.

"And now I must go. Until next time, stay well. And remember, no more foolish risks over Jews. Risks I cannot forbid you, but foolishness is governable, is it not? Adieu."

TWO

On the tenth day of April 1191, which happened to fall that year on the Thursday of Holy Week, Sir Henry St. Clair, enjoying the lift of a ship's deck beneath his feet, was prepared to believe he might yet make a sailor out of himself. The sky was clear, cerulean blue, the sea beneath the hull was smooth and calm, and a gentle wind, just strong enough to fill the sails above and behind him, seemed to herd King Richard's gigantic fleet in front of it like a flock of sheep. Perhaps half a mile away across open water from where he stood at the prow of King Richard's personal warship, a line of sixty-four ships spread out to each side, seeming to fill the sea from horizon to horizon, and yet he knew that they were but a tiny portion of the King's fleet. The vessel on which he himself stood, a long, sleek galley flying the royal standard of England and powered by both sail and oars, was one of a sub-fleet of ten identical warships that was King Richard's maritime pride and joy. All ten had been built to exacting specifications designed jointly by Richard himself and Sir Robert de Sablé, Master of the Fleet.

Engineered from the outset as fighting ships, each of the ten galleys had been built to be self-sufficient. Each carried thirteen anchors, in anticipation of sudden, severe, and perhaps even frequent need to cut and run, and in addition each carried three spare rudders, a spare sail, and a crew of fifteen men, commanded by a captain or master. Each one also carried thirty oars and three complete sets of ropes and rigging, and provided accommodation for a hundred heavily armed men and their equipment. They were long, slender craft, each of them fronted with a pointed spur on the

307

prow for ramming the enemy, and they were propelled by two rows of oars. They had been built to ride low in the water, yet to have enough strength and resilience to handle high seas without difficulty. Fast, versatile, and predatory, their primary purpose was the defense of the remainder of the huge fleet.

Caught in a vicious storm the previous month, on the first leg of their long voyage from Dartmouth to Lisbon, the ten vessels had been scattered and one of them had been lost. Now five of the remaining nine, including the King's own ship, formed the eighth and rearmost rank of the fleet of two hundred and nineteen fully laden ships, transporting Richard's entire army to Outremer. The other four were ranging freely, chivying the lines of ships ahead. The sixty-four vessels directly ahead of the rear line formed the seventh rank, and six more lines stretched out ahead of that, beyond Henry's vision, each line narrower and containing fewer vessels until the first of them, the vanguard, held only three massive and impressive ships called dromons, slow and at times ungainly, but sturdy and always dependable—*seaworthy* was a word Sir Henry had heard applied to them with great respect by Robert de Sablé.

Henry had been told that could one have soared above it like a bird, their formation would have appeared as a gigantic triangle upon the surface of the Mediterranean. It was possibly the largest accumulation of warships ever assembled since the time of the Trojan Wars.

Behind him, Sir Henry could hear the King's voice raised in raillery, and he found it easy to imagine the strained, uncertain smiles on the faces of Robert de Sablé and the other officers of the fleet clustered around the monarch on the rear deck. He counted himself fortunate not to be part of the gathering. Although things appeared to be going well this day, no one, every man in that group knew, could afford to place a wager on how long the relative calm would last. Richard had been like a raging bear for nigh on two weeks now, ever since the thirtieth of March, when Philip Augustus had thrown a tantrum, ostensibly outraged at the possibility of accidentally finding himself face to face with the woman Berengaria, "the bovine Navarrean slut," as he called her, who had "compromised and dispossessed his little sister, Alaïs." That Berengaria had never met or known his sister and had had nothing remotely to do with Alaïs's years-long fall from grace was immaterial to Philip, who was simply indulging himself, giving free rein to his petulance and jealousy. But at the height of his dudgeon, his passions fueled by his own fulminations, he had confounded everyone by issuing orders to summon his Venetian fleet, which was waiting offshore, and then to marshal and embark the full complement of his French and allied forces. He had then set sail for the Holy Land without a word to anyone outside his own circle, and without consulting his English colleague and co-leader.

Richard, taken by surprise like everyone else, had had no other choice than to react as the situation demanded, abandoning whatever plans he had been working on and issuing orders of his own to marshal his troops and proceed with their embarkation as quickly as possible. The alternative, doing nothing and thus leaving Philip to do as he wished, entering Outremer as the savior of Jerusalem at his own pace and under his own conditions, was simply unthinkable. Now that the German King-Emperor Barbarossa was dead, there could be but one savior of Jerusalem: Richard Plantagenet.

And so the English King's mobilization had proceeded from disorder to chaos, unexpectedly begun and poorly organized there-after despite all Robert de Sablé's experience and expertise in such things. For days nothing had appeared to go smoothly and no one appeared to function with laudable distinction: ships had been loaded and manned and then unloaded again because of uneven ballast or improper provisioning—a lack of properly laden and stowed water, or the omission of sufficient food and stores to keep crew, soldiers, and livestock fed for as long as was required. The harbor of Messina and all the tiny coves and inlets up and down the coast for miles in both directions had been reduced to conditions of utter chaos for days on end, with proliferating traffic difficulties that gave way to other, fresher problems as they themselves were resolved.

Eventually, however, order had been returned to the fleet, and on this Holy Thursday morning they had finally set sail, the entire panoply of the fleet afloat presenting a spectacle of splendor to the awestruck Sicilians who lined the cliff tops to watch them sail away. God and His saints had smiled on the English host throughout the day of departure, and now, having taken up their individual positions in relation to the whole fleet, the two hundred and nineteen ships of Richard's force had been sailing south and east for the better part of an entire day, under the sailing orders compiled and distributed throughout the fleet by Sir Robert de Sablé. The following day would be Good Friday, and Sir Robert had estimated that they should drop anchor off Crete in time to celebrate the rejoicing Mass of Easter Sunday.

In the meantime, the Princess Berengaria was safely installed in one of the three huge dromons of the first rank, accompanied by her chaperone and future sister-in-law Joanna, the former Queen of Sicily, and sharing the security of the great vessel with the major part of the bullion in Richard's war chest, watched over by a strong contingent of the King's personal guard. Richard, knowing his betrothed and his sister to be comfortably and securely lodged, consequently felt entitled to enjoy a degree of freedom again with his own friends and chosen companions, a good three miles behind and securely out of sight of the ladies. Small wonder, Sir Henry thought cynically, that the King was in a jocular mood.

"Sir Henry! How did you acquire the privilege of being able to spend your time alone up here, admiring the beauties of our fleet?"

Henry recognized the voice and twisted around to where he could smile at Sir Robert de Sablé without removing his elbows from the point of the ship's rails. The Master of the Fleet had quit the King's group, who were still talking loudly at the stern, and had made his way forward to the bow of the ship.

"Sir Robert, good day to you. I earned this privilege, as you call it, on the parade grounds of Messina, moving large numbers of heavily armored, sweaty, unwashed bodies around rapidly in mass drilling units, until they were fit for nothing but to fall into their cots and sleep like the dead, to the great relief of those officers responsible for their behavior and well-being. Now that we are at sea I can no longer do that, and so I am permitted to rest and recuperate, rebuilding my depleted strength in preparation for use again when we disembark."

"And is that what you were thinking about when I came by?"

St. Clair smiled again and shook his head. "No, in truth I was thinking that I could almost be content as a sailor, were the life always like this."

"Aye, no doubt, Sir Henry, no doubt of that. And were that the case we would have no trouble finding crewmen. But the sad truth— the one seamen and merchants try in vain to keep concealed—is that for every day we have like this, we may have twenty of the other ilk, when the entire world seems tilted up on end, awash in swirling brine and spewing vomit, and buffeted by chilling, roaring winds like those that scattered us like dead leaves on the way to Lisbon last Ascension Day."

Sir Henry nodded and turned back to look at where the sun was beginning its descent towards the western horizon. "You must thank God, then, for days like this."

"Aye, and I do, every time I see one. But I never allow myself to become complacent. I never trust the weather, Sir Henry. Never. Not even when I can see the blue and cloudless sky all around me. It can change within minutes, from smiles to screams, faster than a willful woman's temper."

St. Clair raised an eyebrow. "Surely you don't feel that way today? Today is perfect."

"Aye, it is, and that is why I distrust it. It is yet early in April, Sir Henry. We are barely clear of winter, and summer remains months away. Believe me, if this weather holds throughout the night, I shall be grateful. If it remains with us for two entire days, I will be even more grateful—and deeply astonished. And now, if you will forgive me, I have to see to my duties."

Resuming the mantle of Master of the King's Fleet, de Sablé nodded courteously and moved away, signaling with a crooked finger to Sir Geoffrey Besanceau, the Master of the King's Ship, and then walking with him to where the helmsman stood at the stern, leaning forward against the pull of the tiller. Sir Henry watched them go, arguably the two most important men in the entire fleet, and saw no irony in feeling a stir of gratitude that as Master-at-Arms, his responsibilities were far less onerous than theirs. He swung back to look to his front again, where the wide line of vessels appeared unchanged. King Richard, he noted idly, had fallen silent, and now the only noticeable sound was the steady swishing of the oars that propelled the galley.

Someone on one of the vessels far ahead shouted, and the sound carried clearly across the water although the words were unintelligible. St. Clair wondered briefly if that was because he was too far away to hear clearly or because the words were in a language he did not know. He assumed that it would have been the latter, for that formed the backbone of one of his greatest plaints as Master-at-Arms. He was constantly harping, not merely to Richard but to all the allied kings and leaders and any intermediate commander who would listen, upon the increasing urgency governing the need for clear-cut, crisp, and concise communications.

The Arabs—Henry always thought of them first as Arabs and only afterwards as Saracens, the currently fashionable name for them—had two great advantages, he would point out at every opportunity. First, they were as numerous as the grains of desert sands, drawing their warriors from a vast area that stretched all the way from Arabia, Syria, and the immensity of Babylon and Persia down through Palestine and westward across the Delta of the Nile to embrace Egypt and its neighboring territories across the north of Africa. Reports of Saladin's fielding a hundred thousand men and more were commonplace. And they were apparently inexhaustible, capable of generating new multitudes of warriors as soon as earlier hosts, having done their duty as they saw it, began to drift away homeward to visit their families and tend to their affairs before returning another day.

The second and greatest advantage that the Arabs enjoyed over the Franks, however, was that they all spoke the same language, and St. Clair found himself marveling constantly at that. No matter whence they came in the Islamic lands, they all spoke, and most of them read, Arabic. There were regional differences, of course, but only in the spoken tongue, and none of those variations prevented fluent communication. The written language, of course, was immutable throughout the Saracen empire. St. Clair despaired at times of ever bringing the importance of that single, staggering fact to the attention of the Frankish leadership. In their eyes, the Saracens were infidels and therefore savages, forever beneath their notice, other than for the need to fight and destroy them. But who cared that they all spoke a single language? How important could that be? They spoke gibberish to civilized, Christian ears.

Henry St. Clair had been moved to fury on many occasions by this arrogant and ignorant indifference. It seemed unimportant to these fools, he often thought in the privacy of his own mind, that their own men often could not speak to each other. And that inability was not merely a matter of gross differences, like Frenchmen being unable to speak with Germans, Englishmen, Danes, or Italians. It was far worse and far more serious than that: a Frenchman from Paris simply could not understand a sailor from Marseille, and few from Marseilles could speak Oc, the language of the Languedoc. It was the same in England and in every other country in Christendom—people from different regions of the same country could seldom understand one another.

Henry grunted in disgust and pushed the thought from his mind. It was an old and pointless train of thought, promising nothing but frustration and ill will. But he allowed his thoughts to return to his long-lost friend Torquil, a Danish mercenary. Although neither of them had ever understood the other's language, they had enjoyed many adventures together before Torquil eventually fell to a random crossbow bolt in a squalid little scuffle in the foothills of the Alps. Torquil had been a great eater and a renowned scavenger who could find food, it was said, in an empty coffin, and his greatest coup had been the "capture" of a "stray" shoat outside of the besieged city of Le Havre, in one of the several wars between King Henry of England and his rebellious sons. The shoat had still been suckling when Torquil took it, the sow's milk still trickling from the corner of its mouth, and to this day the smell of roasting pig brought back visions of that night and the succulence of that meat, the first that Henry and his friends had eaten in more than a month. Thinking of that now, and remembering the occasion, he felt the first stirrings of hunger and went looking for his pack, where he had stowed his personal rations: a thick, heavily spiced sausage, several sticks of goat cheese, a jar of olives pickled in brine, and a loaf of still-fresh bread. He ate alone at the galley's prow and watched the sun set, noting how the temperature dropped swiftly as soon as the light was gone. A short time later, in the gathering dark, he drank some water and lowered himself to the deck, where he rolled himself in a blanket against the vessel's side, out of the chill of the April evening and out of the way of anyone else who might come up there.

He fell asleep to the gentle rocking of the waves, and when he awoke, still in darkness, he knew instantly that something was different, but it took him several moments to identify what the difference was. First came the silence, deeper and more profound than it had been when he fell asleep, and even as he absorbed that, it was broken by low voices and movement as other men began to stir and rouse themselves; and then the silence unfolded further, becoming the stillness of an absolute lack of motion. Someone had set a burning lantern into a metal bracket on the ship's bow above his head since he had fallen asleep, and the flame within it burned perfectly, a golden leaf of purest fire surrounded by a lambent halo containing not even a flicker of variation. As he lay looking up at it, with a growing sense of wonder, he realized that the comforting motion of the deck beneath him, the rocking that had lulled him to sleep, had vanished, too. Somewhere behind him, on the rowing deck, there came a loud clatter, followed by a string of oaths and cursing and other, less recognizable sounds that increased in volume and variety as he listened. And finally, scrubbing at his eyes with the heel of his hand, he sat up and looked about him, his breast filled with nameless apprehension.

His first instinct was to check the sky for signs of bad weather, but there was nothing threatening to see up there. The entire firmament seemed cloudless, washed in pale rose and violet, and the few stars that remained visible were fading rapidly in the dawn light. He recognized that the light source was behind him, and pulled himself to his feet, facing the east just as the first blazing edge of the sun tipped the farthest rim of the horizon. It was a scene of flawless, staggering beauty, and he remembered that this was Good Friday, the day on which the Blessed Savior had been crucified for the salvation of mankind. All the auspices, it seemed to him at that moment, boded well for the human race that morning. He turned slightly to his left, towards the body of the ship, to see if anyone else had noticed the beauty of the dawn, and was mildly surprised to see that the rail was lined two-deep with men, all of them gazing silently outward. After a moment of smiling and having none of them return his smile, he realized that they were not looking at him or at the rising sun at all, but were gazing fixedly ahead of the ship, southward. Mystified, he followed their gaze and felt his mouth sag open in wonder that he could have looked this way before and failed to see what was now so glaringly obvious.

The surface of the sea was like glass, unbroken by the slightest ripple or hint of movement, and stamped upon its surface everywhere were perfect replicas of the ships that floated motionless above them. Nothing stirred anywhere; not even a passing seabird disturbed the utter perfection of the image. And then someone coughed somewhere at the stern of the ship and the sound marked the end of the reverent silence that had held them all. Men began to talk then, and to move about, and the first tentative stirrings quickly took on purpose and intent.

Sir Henry folded up his blanket and thrust it into his pack, then lodged the pack securely beneath the ship's rail before making his way back to the stern, where Master Besanceau was conferring with several of his officers. As he neared the rear platform, the ship's drummer drew himself up to attention and began to beat out a regular, high-pitched rhythm on his tightly stretched drumhead. It was clearly a summons of some kind, and St. Clair surmised that it would be answered by the commanders of the other four galleys of the rear line.

"Have you ever seen the like, Master-at-Arms?"

The speaker, who had come up behind him unnoticed, was a man called Montagnard, one of St. Clair's own officers, in charge of the hundred men billeted on the galley. He was a strange and taciturn man, Sir Henry thought, who would go for days on end without saying an unnecessary word, and then would suddenly break his silence, speaking fluidly and betraying a varied and convoluted background. Clearly this was one such day.

"The weather, you mean? No, I never have. It is almost uncanny. What is happening, do you know?"

"We are becalmed."

"Aye, I can see that. But is this a common thing? How long does it last?"

"It's not uncommon. I've experienced it once before, in the Bay of Biscay, when we were trying to beat into La Rochelle and suddenly the wind died and did not blow again for two days. It is a frightening experience, almost a religious one, for there is no rhyme or reason to it. No one ever knows what causes it or how long it will last. It is strange, though, is it not?" He nodded towards where the two Masters were conferring deeply. "It even upsets them, and it takes much to do that. You know what they say about it, don't you?"

"No, what do they say?"

"God is holding His breath." Montagnard turned to face Sir Henry now. "And what happens when you hold your breath? You have to release it again, sooner rather than later. Even if you are God. And depending upon the length of time you have been holding it, the gust, when you release it, may be strong."

"You mean it's going to storm?"

"Not necessarily, but it might. In the meantime, we are among the few people in the fleet who can move at all. We have our oars. Most of the others must simply sit and wait for the wind to come back. That should please the priests, at any rate."

"Why should they be happy?"

"Look about you, Master-at-Arms. It's Good Friday and a beautiful day without a breath of wind ... perfect conditions for reminding men how vulnerable and at risk they are in the face of God's omnipotence. You watch, every vessel in this fleet will be a sounding vessel for the Blessed Jesus this day. You will hear hymns being sung from every direction before the sun sets, you mark my words."

Henry smiled and was about to reply when he noticed movement on the water, and he stepped to the rail to watch as rowboats approached from each of the other four galleys. Moments later the first of them drew alongside, and its passenger, a galley commander, clambered aboard and joined the group around Sir Robert, followed soon after by his three colleagues. They did not remain aboard for very long, and within the half hour, all four of the rear-line galleys had begun moving forward, like sheepdogs, towards the becalmed vessels ahead of them, spreading advice and encouragement to their less fortunate companions as they rowed among them. Only Richard's own galley, which was also, and less than incidentally, the galley of the Fleet Master, remained behind, forming a rearguard of one vessel. When the word was passed to ship oars and be at ease, St. Clair quickly realized that de Sablé preferred to be there and alone, where he could anticipate anything the sea might throw at him, rather than in the midst of the fleet where he could be at a severe disadvantage in the event of a sudden reversal of fortune.

Montagnard had moved away and was nowhere in sight when Sir Henry looked around for him, and as the Master-at-Arms turned back towards the stern, he was just in time to see de Sablé's broad back as the Fleet Master disappeared into his cabin, leaving the deck strangely quiet. Silent crewmen were lounging everywhere, some of them staring off into nowhere, others sitting or lying against the sides of the ship with their eyes closed. Sir Henry smiled faintly and nodded to himself. He could see it was a time to wait and be patient, for nothing any of them could do would affect the span of time for which God chose to hold His breath.

That Good Friday became the longest day Sir Henry had ever known, for in the tiny shipboard world of his confinement there was absolutely nothing that he could do to take his mind off his enforced idleness. He dozed a little, but quickly grew tired even of that, and such was his boredom that he actually welcomed the diversion when the three bishops aboard the ship emerged onto the stern deck with their acolytes about an hour after noon and began to conduct the services for Good Friday. It became evident immediately that not everyone on board could attend the ceremonies at the same time, but some of the officers quickly worked out a plan whereby men were able to come on deck, in groups of twenty at a time, and spend a quarter of an hour praying, taking Communion, and breathing God's fresh air before returning to the densely packed cribs that were their sole accommodation. Some time later, in verification of Montagnard's prediction, voices began to rise in prayer and song from all directions, some of them emanating from identifiable ships, while others were mere vibrations in the air, ethereal and shimmering with distance. And then, at the third hour after noon, a silence fell, as deep as the silence that had surrounded them all day. Jesus was dead and the world would remain in spiritual darkness until the dawn of the third day, when his Resurrection would proclaim the universal salvation.

Sir Henry St. Clair noticed a small gust of wind tickling the hair at the nape of his neck. He had been dozing again, leaning against the rail in the foremost point of the deck, and the sensation, the first stirring of air he had felt in the entire day, snapped him awake instantly, so that he straightened to his full height, wondering what had happened. And then he heard voices being raised at his back and the hammering of running feet as someone rushed up to elbow him aside and take his place. The man leaned forward tensely, peering straight ahead at the horizon, and then he growled, "Oh, shit!" and spun away, running back towards the stern, shouting for the shipmaster, Besanceau. Henry watched him go, and noted the way in which everyone else was watching him, too, and then he turned back to see what it was that the fellow had seen to cause him to react as he had.

He could see nothing, other than what looked like a slight thickening above the line of the horizon, as though someone had smudged a stick of charcoal unevenly across the line separating sea and sky, blurring it in places. He narrowed his eyes and peered more carefully, and he had the impression, for a moment, that the smudged line was purple. He could no longer feel any stirring in the air, and the stillness was as profound as ever. But then, high atop the mast of one of the ships ahead, a flag snapped into motion and flapped several times before subsiding again to hang as limp as it had been before. Sir Henry felt his heart begin to beat more strongly and his gut stirred with formless apprehension. Something was in the offing, he knew, and the shouting that was now rising in volume at his back reinforced what he was feeling.

The purple line on the horizon thickened even as he watched and was soon discernible as an advancing line of clouds. Another gust of wind sprang up but died away quickly, only to be followed minutes later by another that blew harder and lasted longer. Henry watched in silence as three crewmen lowered the sail completely and folded it with great care before lashing it tightly to the spar that held it, then lashed the spar in turn, binding it solidly to the ship's mast. Moments later, his gut tensed again as he saw the stroke drummer take up his position in the waist of the ship and the oarsmen set themselves, seven to a side, ready to start pulling on his signal. The signal came, and the men bent to their work, pulling steadily as they fought against the ship's inertia and eased it into motion with agonizing slowness. Its speed increased rapidly, and the rowers seemed to have less difficulty in their task.

A movement on the stern deck caught Henry's eye, and he glanced over there to see Richard himself, resplendent in full mail and scarlet surcoat, standing spread-legged beside and slightly behind Sir Robert de Sablé's right shoulder, his massive arms crossed over his chest. On de Sablé's left, his face twisted into a ferocious scowl, Sir Geoffrey Besanceau stood tossing a dagger into the air, end over end, catching it and flipping it again each time the hilt smacked back into his open palm. He never glanced at the dagger, every ounce of his attention dedicated to peering ahead into the gathering murk.

A door opened from the soldiers' quarters and men began to emerge onto the narrow deck, evidently attracted by the sounds of activity after such a day of quiet. The tiny deck space rapidly became congested and the congestion threatened to interfere with the orderly running of the ship, and so the men were ordered back to their quarters. As the last of them left the deck, clearly disgruntled, Henry approached the King, who greeted him cordially enough but seemed disinclined to idle conversation. Henry knew his man well enough to be guided by that, and so he merely stood there, silent, until Robert de Sablé noticed him there.

"Henry," he said, and quirked one side of his mouth in a humorless grin. "You remember what we spoke of yesterday, about not trusting the weather?"

"Aye, I do, very well. Is that line over there what I think it is?"

"Aye, it is, if you think it marks trouble brewing. It's a storm front, coming rapidly."

"How rapidly?"

Again the quirk at one side of the other's mouth. "A half hour at the most ... at worst, half that."

"What can we do?"

"Nothing, my friend. We have already done all we can do. We sent out word throughout the fleet this afternoon to be prepared for anything: a gale, a tempest, a simple storm. When this thing approaching us arrives, each shipmaster will be responsible for his own craft and crew, and if he has done as bidden, each will be as well prepared as the next. It may be a simple squall, or a line of squalls, but it looks too large for that, and anyway, from here, there is no way of telling. All we can do is wait and take what comes. No man owns expertise when the wind blows hard and the sea starts churning itself to froth and spume. We can but try to hold our bows towards the cresting swells, and then we pray. You should start praying now, my friend, and since you are a landman, you should find a safe spot by the scuppers in the prow and tie yourself firmly into place. Ship oars!" The last two words were loud and urgent, a shouted order, and the oarsmen quickly raised their oars to the vertical, raining water down upon themselves as the ship's motion changed suddenly.

"Aha," said de Sablé, almost to himself, "and so we begin." The deck had tilted steeply without warning, sending the prow high into the air, and de Sablé reached for a hand hold and waved with his free hand to the ship's master at the same time as the vessel dipped again. The oars went back into the water, and de Sablé spoke again to St. Clair, this time without looking at him. "Go you, now, Henry, quickly, and do what I told you—tie yourself strongly down and hold on tight. My lord King, you should do the same."

"What, tie myself down? No, I'll tie a rope about my middle and anchor it to a rail, but I shall stay here with you." Richard looked at Sir Henry. "But you, Henry, you must do as Robert bids you. You no longer have the strength you had in youth and I need you in Outremer. Get you to safety. I have no wish to see you washed away. Go."

Sir Henry made his way back to where he had stowed his pack and bound himself into place beside it, securing it to himself with a short length of rope and then binding himself firmly to the ship's rail, close to one of the holes in the vessel's side that allowed the trapped water of inboard waves to stream back into the sea. He barely had time to finish the last knot before the storm broke over them, and from that moment on he lived in a screaming, wind-and-water-filled hell, unaware of time, or day or night or anything else that made human life sane or desirable. He was aware of changing colors in the cloud rack from time to time, and on one occasion he found himself being painfully battered by pebble-sized hailstones that piled up in sheltered places on the deck like shoals of splintered ice. Then it was rain that stung his face, whipped horizontally by the howling wind, and some time after that he became aware that the temperature had plummeted, his soaked clothing chilled to the consistency of rough board. He thought he may have passed out about that time, and had no notion of how much time might have passed, but eventually he came awake again to find himself being thrown from side to side, his head banging painfully against the side of the ship at every roll. His clothing was still icy cold, but now there was sufficient light for him to see that the folds of his surcoat were thick with fresh snow. Then came a looming lurch of fear as he sensed something swinging at him, and he lost awareness of everything again.

He awoke some time later and the storm was still howling about him, and after that he drifted in and out of consciousness, mildly aware, somewhere in his mind, that the storm seemed to be dying down. He woke up again when he felt someone grasp him by the face and pinch his cheeks together, shaking his head gently. He opened his eyes and saw one of the crew members kneeling above him, peering at him closely.

"Ah, he's alive," the fellow muttered. "That cut on his head, all bleached and open like that, I wasn't sure there ... Right, come on, then, old man, let's cut those ropes and see if we can get you back up on your feet."

IT WAS EASTER SUNDAY, late in the afternoon, and if there were any priests celebrating Mass or offering thanks for their deliverance from the storm, they were doing it privately and in silence, in whatever quarters they had been able to appropriate for themselves in the aftermath of the destruction. Sir Henry St. Clair knew he was still alive, but he knew little else of any import, and he had not yet decided whether to be grateful for his survival or to regret the lost opportunity to die in the tempest and be rid of the aches, pains, and griefs that beset him now.

He sat braced on a coil of rope, staring at the junction where the sides of the ship came together at the bows. He had at least two cracked or broken ribs, the pain of which made it impossible for him to stand and lean forward against the rails, and so he was forced to sit there, unable to see over the wooden sides in front of him. His back was propped against two other, smaller rope coils balanced on the first, and he forced himself to ignore both the pain of his ribs and the inconvenience of not being able to see anything, and to concentrate instead upon the small amount of information he had managed to glean to this point. The man who had found him half dead in the scuppers had known who he was, and had summoned another man to help carry him back to the rear of the ship, where someone else had tended to his injuries—Henry had no idea who that had been, but they had strapped up his ribs and bound a cloth tightly over the gash in his right temple before sending him back, supported between two crewmen, to sit where he had spent much of the previous few days, in the foremost point of the ship's bows and out of the way of most of the vessel's crew.

Twenty-one men had been lost. That much Henry knew beyond doubt, having overheard a report on casualties being delivered to someone he assumed to be Besanceau on the stern deck while his injuries were being treated. He had assumed that the missing men were his own, landsmen like him and unused to being afloat, whereas the ship's crew might reasonably be expected to survive a storm at sea. And besides, he recalled now that the galley held a complement of fifteen crew members only. But if that were true and all the missing men were his, then that meant they had lost one-fifth of their shipboard complement without their ever having had an opportunity to strike a single blow against the enemy. That thought depressed him, and he turned himself, very slightly and with great difficulty, to look back over his shoulder to where another man leaned against the side of the prow, gazing outward.

"Hey," Henry grunted, drawing the man's attention. "What can you see out there?"

The fellow scanned him from head to foot, then looked back over the side. "Nothing," he growled. "An empty ocean. Not a ship in sight anywhere, except one wreck, close enough to see, turned upside down and dragging its mast. Must have air trapped inside, keeping it afloat …" He turned back, his head bent, and looked at Henry from beneath heavy black brows. "How do you feel? Better than you look, I hope. You're trussed like a stuffed swan. Who are you, anyway?"

Henry eased himself back around to face forward again, hoping to find some comfort. "Name's St. Clair," he gasped, catching his breath and almost wheezing with the effort of moving. "They tell me I've broken some ribs, and I … aah! … I believe them. Come up here where I can see you, will you?"

The other man crossed to where he could lean an elbow on the rail and look down at Henry, nodding in sympathy. "Broken ribs are not likable. Broke two of my own last year, in Cyprus. Slipped on a greasy plank, carrying a sack, and fell against a pole on the ground. Took me months to get better. I'm called Bluethumb. I'm one of the rowers." He held up an almost purple thumb, and Henry could not tell if the discoloration was a birthmark or the result of an old injury, but before he could ask, Bluethumb said, "St. Clair, eh? The Master-at-Arms? That St. Clair?"

"Aye, that one. Can you help me up to where I can see, just for a moment? I can't move on my own—too tightly trussed, as you said."

"Let's see, then." The man called Bluethumb bent his knees and squatted, taking Henry beneath the shoulders, then lifted him smoothly with a strong thrust of his thighs. Henry sucked in his breath sharply, but felt surprisingly little pain, and then lost all awareness of anything else as he stared at the emptiness of the waters all around them. The only thing to be seen in any direction was the wreck Bluethumb had described.

"My thanks," he said eventually. "You may sit me down again."

When he was back in his makeshift seat, propped up by the ropes, he allowed himself, for a brief moment, to wonder what might have happened to his son, but there was little to be gained in doing that, and so he sucked in a deep breath, then expelled it forcibly before speaking again to Bluethumb. "What about the King, is he well?"

One eyebrow rose as though the man were surprised to hear the question asked. "Of course he's well. Why would he not be? He could walk on water, that one. Tied himself to the stern rail and fought the tiller with the helmsman throughout the storm. No wonder his people look at him the way they do. The man's like a god."

"Aye," Henry said with a nod. "He can be magnificent at times, far more so than ordinary men … So what will we do now, do you know?"

Bluethumb grinned and held the discolored digit up again. "I told you, I'm a rower. They don't ask me for advice. They tell me where to go, and when, and how fast. And I'd better get back."

He straightened up to leave but Henry stopped him with a wave of his hand. "If you would, should you see Sir Robert de Sablé back there, please give him my respects and tell him where I am and that I should like to speak with him when he can find a moment."

The rower cocked his head. "Me? Walk up and talk to de Sablé, just like that? He'd have me thrown overboard."

"No, he would not. Mention my name as you approach—Sir Henry St. Clair—and tell him I asked you, sent you to him. Here, let me—" He began to fumble for his scrip, but the oarsman snapped a hand at him.

"I don't want your money, Master-at-Arms. I'll tell him what you said, and fare ye well." He left without another word.

Sir Henry flexed his back muscles cautiously and tried to find some comfort against the piles of hard rope. He had not yet permitted himself to think about the significance of the emptiness out there beyond the ship's walls, but now he began attempting to visualize the cataclysmic power of the storm they had survived, and to wonder how many ships might have sunk completely, simply vanishing beneath the waves and taking their crews and passengers with them. He discovered very quickly that he had no stomach for such wonderings, and no means whereby he could control his imagination's sickening leaps and lurches, and so he was happy when de Sablé's voice distracted him.

"Well, Master St. Clair. Are you badly injured? I saw you being attended to on the stern deck but had no time right then even to cross the deck and find out what was wrong with you."

"There's nothing wrong with me, Sir Robert. Nothing serious, I mean. A bang on the head and a few cracked ribs ... I am pleased to see you looking so well. And I heard the King served as helmsman in the storm."

"Throughout it." Sir Robert brought his hands together, squeezing them in the way Richard himself frequently did. He was grinning broadly now and shaking his head in admiration. "He rode out the tempest with the aplomb of a veteran seafarer who has seen everything that Neptune has to throw at him. It truly was remarkable.

I would not have believed it had I not been there to witness it in person. The King tied himself to a thwart and manned the tiller with the helmsman for hours on end. Certainly, had he not done so, we might have been in even sorer straits than we were. I thought we were all dead men when the soldiers' quarters started to break up beneath the pounding of the waves— Did you know about that?"

"Yes, I heard it being reported. Twenty-one men lost."

"Aye, they were washed overboard when the superstructure holding them began to give way and tilted outboard. We yawed, torn off center by the sagging weight of the falling structure, and came as close as ever we could to turning broadside to the waves. It was only Richard's ferocious strength, combined with the helmsman's skill, that saved us. I had been thrown into the scuppers by a wave and I lay there and watched him fight to bring the bows back into line." He looked about him to be sure that no one else was listening, and when he was sure they were not being overheard, he added, "You and I, Henry, should both fall to our knees this day and give thanks for our King, and forgiveness for all the flaws we so often find in him."

"Amen," Sir Henry said, nodding.

De Sablé had moved to the bow rail, where Henry could look up at him without having to twist his body. He glanced away, towards the horizon, then uttered a snort, part grunt, part bitter laugh.

"That weather ... My friend, that was something undreamed of, something from our nightmares. I have never encountered anything like that. That was a storm to keep the most adventurous and intrepid mariners safe at home, on land, forever."

Henry could hear commands being shouted at his back, followed by the clatter of running feet and the creaking of stiff ropes above and behind his head, the rhythmic grunts of men pulling in unison on both sides of the deck and the squeal of ropes running through blocks.

"We're preparing to increase speed," de Sablé explained, "hoisting the sail so we can go in search of others."

"What others?" Henry asked, recalling the empty seas around them. "How many men and ships did we lose, do you know?"

"We lost them all, Henry." De Sablé waved expansively towards the horizon. "They are all gone, scattered on the wind like ashes. It's going to take days to gather them all together again."

Henry's eyes widened. "To gather them—? You mean we'll find them again? They are not all destroyed?"

Now it was de Sablé's face that registered surprise. "Destroyed? Great God, no, they are not destroyed. We may have lost a few of them, to collisions and calamities, but that is only to be expected when you have so many ships at such close quarters in stormy conditions. There's one drifting close by that you can see, dismasted and capsized, but the others have merely been scattered and blown before the wind and tides. They are ships, Henry, built by men who know and love and hate the sea in equal measures. They are designed to weather storms and outlast them, even storms as large and violent as that one was. They'll find the closest land to wherever they may be, and then they will begin to reassemble."

Henry was mildly flummoxed, trying to visualize the scene that, if de Sablé was correct, had to be unfolding beyond the horizon. "Where is the nearest land?"

"From where we are right now?" Sir Robert shrugged. "At this point, your guess would be as valid as mine. But I will be able to answer you easily as soon as we have discovered where we are right now. We have been blown off course. That much is certain. But how far, and in what direction, is what we must now attempt to discover."

He held up an open palm to forestall Henry's next question. "We are in the Ionian Sea, and we were sailing east by south from Sicily towards Crete when the storm struck. That was two days ago. We know that the coast of Africa lies on our starboard side at this moment, because we are headed eastward, directly towards the rising sun, but we do not know how far away it is. But by the same reckoning, we know that the coast of Greece and its islands lies ahead of us, so we will continue south and east on our present course until we sight land. With good fortune, that will be Crete, but then again, it might be any of a chain of islands, all of which will serve us equally well, since from any one of them we can be in Crete within days." He hesitated, and then gave a tentative half smile. "Of course, we might have been blown backward altogether and the next land we sight could be Sicily again. Only time will tell. In the meantime, we have our sharpest-eyed crewman up on the cross spar, squinting in all directions. He'll sight land soon, and the moment that he does, our fortunes will improve."

Sir Henry nodded. "Thank you for that. I often think there can be nothing worse than lacking information on which to base a decision. And speaking of information, may I ask if you know which ship my son was on? I have been thinking he must be dead, and to hear you say otherwise is an enormous relief."

"I can tell you it was one of the four Templar vessels, and all four of them were placed in the second line, directly behind the King's three dromons. Where they may be now is anyone's guess. And now I must return to my post. Are you comfortable? Is there anything I can provide for you?"

Sir Henry shook his head and thanked the Fleet Master graciously, then eased himself gently back against the ropes and closed his eyes, feeling the coolness of a gentle breeze ruffling his hair and lulling him to sleep, while around him the sounds of shipboard activity regained their normal levels. The last clear thought that crossed his mind before he dozed off was the notion that the King would not be pleased if anything untoward had happened to any of his three great dromons, for among them they carried his greatest treasures: his war chest, his sister, and his future Queen.

THE MASTHEAD LOOKOUT spotted the first stray within hours of their setting out, hull down on the horizon to the south of them, and de Sablé issued orders immediately to intercept it. It was a heavy-bellied cargo carrier and it wallowed about like an old sow, but ungainly as it might have been, it had survived the storm in good order and it changed its own heading as soon as it became aware of the galley bearing down on it. Within an hour of that, they found another ship, and then another, until they had gathered more than a score of followers by the end of the day. Some of the vessels had fared much better than others, and there were a few that were in dangerous condition, but de Sablé kept them together throughout the night and there were no further alarums.

The following day, because their presence and bulk had become substantial, they attracted many more survivors, and their numbers swelled to three score and more. Three days after that, they sighted land directly ahead on their easterly course, and they arrived in Crete that afternoon. They numbered more than a hundred vessels by that time, including seven of the eight remaining galleys, and as they approached their anchorage at the foot of Mount Ida, the masthead lookouts were reporting more ships approaching from all around with every minute that passed. But no one, anywhere, could provide any information on the whereabouts of the three dromons.

Richard expressed grave concern, and Sir Henry had no doubt that it was genuine, but he found himself wondering cynically whether the monarch might be more concerned about the loss of his treasure chests than he was about his wife and sister, and he was still wondering about that when Richard dispatched all eight of his recovered galleys that same evening, four to search the Greek coastal islands to the northwest and the north, while the other four swept on east, towards Cyprus.

Sir Henry was relieved to be able to leave the ship and go ashore in Crete, for the simple reason that he could then lie down and stretch himself out in a well-strung cot, to the great benefit of his aching chest muscles. He lay abed for three days after that, giving his body time to recuperate, once again at the insistence of Richard's physician, until word came to him from Richard that they would be leaving the next morning for the island of Rhodes, where a large number of their missing vessels had made landfall. Knowing his time abed had done him good, he felt sufficiently recovered to rise and move about, and he walked as far as the harbor, a distance of close to half a mile, before he felt the first twinge of pain.

They sailed to Rhodes without incident the following day, and found the remainder of their former fleet already there, waiting for them. The reunion was occasion for modest celebration, once they had ascertained that no more than seven vessels of the original two hundred and nineteen—disregarding of course the missing dromons—had been irretrievably lost. Henry St. Clair stood once again at the prow of the King's galley as they approached the ancient harbor on the northernmost tip of the island, famed throughout the world for its great lighthouse, and as the ship entered the shelter of the bay, his eyes moved restlessly among the hundred or so vessels awaiting them there, seeking the four recently built warships that belonged to the Order of the Temple, but in the absence of distinguishing insignia, he was unable to tell them apart from the remainder of the tatterdemalion collection. André would be somewhere among the forest of masts, he knew, but he had no idea how he might arrange to meet with him. He felt confident that they would remain in Rhodes for at least a week and perhaps two, for the entire fleet had to be provisioned yet again and many of the vessels had suffered serious damage that would have to be repaired before they could go anywhere. And so he concentrated upon his own responsibilities for the time being, focusing upon establishing a daily regimen of drill programs that would address the chronic problem of keeping very large numbers of men from idleness and temptation by keeping them gainfully engaged.

The sole remaining difficulty, and it was always a large one, involved finding and securing a training ground, or perhaps multiple training grounds, large enough to accommodate their numbers and close enough to both the army's central campgrounds and the harbor to make regular movement to and from both locations relatively simple. He sent out word for his training officers to assemble and then, after reviewing the priorities facing all of them, sent them off in pairs to scour the surrounding countryside for suitable sites.

When at last three expanses had been identified for drilling grounds, the sounds of marching feet were audible everywhere as the thousands of foot soldiers from the fleet made their way there in ordered units. The horsemen were allocated different sites and times to report, as many of the horses were still being unloaded from the newly arrived ships. And thus, transition was achieved, continuity was asserted, and novelty quickly became routine.

Ten days later, while Richard and some of his English barons were inspecting cavalry at one of the three horse camps Henry had set up, a messenger came galloping with word for the King that two of the galleys he had sent to find the Princess Berengaria had been sighted returning from the east, under sail and oars, and were expected to enter the harbor within the hour. Richard abandoned the inspection immediately, and he insisted that Henry accompany him, to be present should an instantaneous decision be required.

It was closer to two hours than one by the time the two galleys approached the harbor piers, but the commander leapt down from the bows as soon as his ship came close enough, and made his way directly to where the King and his entourage stood waiting. The Princess Berengaria and Queen Joanna were safe, he reported, but their ships, perhaps because they were the largest in the fleet, had taken the brunt of the storm winds and been blown far and away to the south of everyone else, ending up, by the time the storm finally blew itself out, off the island of Cyprus. All three of the dromons had remained together until the end, but as they neared the port of Limassol on the south coast of Cyprus, one of them had run aground on the reefs known as the rocks of Aphrodite and had foundered, with much loss of life.

Two of the great ships remained intact, their precious cargo safe, but the galley commander's urgency was all reserved for the fate of the third. The ruler of Cyprus, he reported, was a man called Isaac Comnenus, a Byzantine who titled himself Emperor but had behaved more like a bandit chief in this instance. Richard cut him off with a wave of his arm.

"Hold, there. What mean you by that—a bandit chief? Speak plainly to me now, for this is important. Forget all the fine words and flourishes and tell me as a man what happened and what this Comnenus fellow did."

The commander cleared his throat, and it required two false starts before he found his tongue and sufficient confidence to speak out plainly. "He has behaved shabbily, my lord King. His people looted and despoiled the dead men who were washed up on their shores after the shipwreck, and once the waves died down and it was discovered that the wreck could be reached from the shore, the survivors were taken ashore and penned up as prisoners, given little in the way of aid or care. And then they discovered that there were chests of gold aboard, and the people there went wild. Before they could bring much of it ashore, however, the Emperor Comnenus and his men arrived and confiscated everything ..." His voice faded away and he stood frowning.

"What, man? There's more, is there not? What of my ladies aboard the other ships?"

"They are well, my lord, but—"

"He has not harmed them?"

"No, my lord. But at first he would not let them go ashore. Threatened them with prison should they land on his shores. He changed his mind later, once he thought there might be gold aboard those ships, too, but by then the two ladies had decided they were safer aboard their ships than they would be elsewhere. Emperor though this fellow calls himself, he has no army worthy of the name, and no ships at all. But, sire, there is more ..."

"More?" Richard's face darkened by the moment. "What you have told me is enough already. I shall have things to say to this Comnenus when we meet, for he sounds like no Christian monarch to me, let alone an emperor. What more could there be?"

"Your vice-chancellor, my lord."

"Nevington. What about him? Is he dead?"

"Aye, my lord. He drowned in the wreck of the ship and was one of the people washed ashore."

Richard was frowning slightly, but then his brow smoothed out. "The seal! Is it safe?" Lord Nevington, as vice-chancellor of England, always wore the Great Seal on a ribbon about his neck, for it was his responsibility to keep it with him at all times, so that in the event the King needed to sign and seal an official document of any kind, the seal would be close by and ready for his use.

"Those who found it stripped it from him, not knowing what it was, but Comnenus seized it and now wears it around his neck."

"God's balls, man, tell me you jest with me!" Richard's voice had risen to a roar of fury. "Are you saying this … this filth-crusted, hunchbacked imbecile now holds the Great Seal of England, in addition to the gold I brought to pay my men?"

The mariner merely nodded, wide eyed.

"Then by the living Christ I will have the whoreson's scrotum cured and made into a bag to hold my seal from this time on!" He swung around to St. Clair. "Henry, set things in motion now, today. Send out orders to break camp at once and put one of your officers to find Robert de Sablé and send him to me in my quarters. I want the fleet loaded by tomorrow night, every man and horse and every item of stowage ready for the tide the following day. We are going to Cyprus to teach this crotch-sniffing, flea-infested *Emperor* that when he chose to thieve from us, he picked the wrong victim in Richard Plantagenet. And you—" The King pointed and the galley commander straightened his shoulders, bracing himself. "You have done well, to come back here so quickly and so well informed. Now I have further need of you. Do not permit your men to come ashore tonight, for I need you to leave again tomorrow, before the rest of us. Return to Cyprus immediately, you and your companion there, leading the four Temple ships that I will have assigned to your care. The Templars will protect my sister and my betrothed until such time as we arrive. And you may promise your crew, from me in person, that they will be given time ashore, and money to spend there, in recompense for the extra duties I am putting upon them." He looked over to the small group of nobles who had accompanied him and beckoned to a splendid, golden-haired young knight who might easily have been described as beautiful. "D'Yquiem, if you will, present my respects to the Marshal of the Temple and ask him if he would be kind enough to seek me in my quarters within the hour."

The young knight saluted smartly and spun away to his task, and Richard nodded abruptly, dismissing everyone else with a back-handed wave before striding off in the direction of the building he had taken as his personal quarters.

THREE

Jean Pierre Tournedos had been born into a mercantile family that owned a modest fleet of trading ships, and at the age of twenty-six was invited to join the Order of the Temple as an associate brother and to dedicate his knowledge and his exceptional skills, at an appropriate price, to the design and construction of a prototype ship that would permit the rapidly expanding Order to move away from its reliance on land bases. Working with a small group of colleagues, Tournedos designed a large vessel with the capacity to ship both men and cargo, including livestock. But what made the ship unique was that it was designed to house a highly disciplined crew of fighting monks, accustomed to living in penitential austerity, in close quarters that normal mariners would not have tolerated. Manned by such a highly disciplined and religiously obedient crew, the vessel was also capable of serving as a ship of war should the need arise, with triple banks of oars, fighting platforms, and a metal-clad ramming prow. It also incorporated specific modifications that permitted it to function as a monastic vessel at times, although that concept, of a monastic ship, was as revolutionary in its time as the notion of military monks had been ninety years earlier.

Since adherence to the Rule was all-important in the daily life of the brethren, additional space had been created within the hull, directly below the rowing deck, for the brethren of the Order to assemble for common prayers and services. It was a cramped and crabbed space, entirely lacking in comfort, and only along the narrow central aisle could a man stand upright without stooping, but the men who would use this space had no regard for physical

comfort and would gladly offer up their discomfort to God, in penitence. The central aisle offered the sole access to the space. The
brethren would enter by the aisle, then crawl or climb to their
assigned places in the spaces that flanked it, where they would sleep
at nights, and at other times sit, and sometimes kneel, for the prayers
and readings of the daily Rule. That commitment was extraordinary
at a time when every inch of shipboard space was precious, but it
had been deemed necessary for the spiritual and physical welfare of
the monks who would be crewing the vessel.

In the years since then, three sister ships had been built, and five
more were now in preparation, to the same design, forming what the
Templars now called the Mediterranean squadron, based in the port
of Brindisi, on the outermost heel of the Italian mainland. One of the
earliest preceptories built by the Order in Italy, Brindisi had in
recent years begun to assume significant importance to the emerging nautical interests within the Temple Order, situated as it was
within easy sailing distance of a cluster of shipbuilding yards that
had been there, some said, since Roman times. The vessels they
produced were expensive and highly prized.

Tournedos, now the squadron's commodore, had sailed south and
west from Brindisi to Messina, to join the great fleet assembled by
Richard of England for the expedition to the Holy Land, and in
Messina he welcomed aboard his own vessel the senior members of
the Order's latest reinforcing expedition to Outremer, including
some of the highest-ranking Templars in all of Christendom, all of
whom were eager to inspect the ships of which they had heard so
much. And at the same time, they took aboard the newest crop of
reinforcements, including the least of the Temple's least—the latest
contingent of low-level recruits and novices.

Now Tournedos stood on the stern deck of his ship, looking
about him at the surrounding scene. They had anchored that
morning, after entering Limassol on a rising tide, and the island of
Cyprus towered above him, its rugged hills appearing to offer no
hint of warmth or refuge. Gazing at the scene and at the port,
Tournedos, who had somehow managed to visit the island only

twice before in all his years of sailing, decided yet again that the island of Cyprus, beautiful as it might be, held no allure at all for him. He turned his eyes away and looked to his right, where, perhaps a quarter of a land mile distant but no closer to the shore, two massive ships, the dromons he had been sent to find and protect, dwarfed his own. Between him and the dromons, moving rapidly under oars towards the closer of the two ships, a remarkable young man, of whose existence Tournedos had been unaware until the previous day, stood in the stern of his ship's boat, gazing straight ahead to where an access ramp was being lowered from one of the great ships to await his arrival. Tournedos scratched absently at his bearded cheek with the tip of one finger, then turned again to look at the outlying anchorage behind him, where three more newcomers were now arriving. He scanned them once again, for perhaps the sixth time since being warned of their approach, looking for symbols by which to identify them. They were Christian ships, easily distinguishable from the low, rakish galleys used by Muslim pirates, and they had approached from the east, perhaps from Outremer itself, which would explain his inability to identify them. He sniffed, knowing he would find out who they were within the hour or soon thereafter, and turned away again to squint at the high, densely packed buildings surrounding the harborfront of Limassol.

According to what Tournedos had been told, the so-called Emperor of this place, Isaac Comnenus, had misplayed a minor opportunity for advantage into a looming disaster for himself and his countrymen. With an option plainly open to him to win favor and acclaim when the survivors of the great storm were blown into his harbor seeking assistance, Comnenus had chosen instead to abuse, affront, and insult the future Queen of England and her companion, the former Queen of Sicily, thereby giving intolerable offense to the implacable man who was husband-to-be to the first and brother to the second. Richard of England, the man becoming increasingly known as the Lionheart, had been much closer to hand than the hapless and badly informed Isaac had ever imagined, and now Isaac must pay for his folly and greed. Richard's fleet, bearing his entire army, would arrive in Limassol the following day, and when it did, and the army disembarked, life would become extremely interesting for everyone in the region, and most particularly for the self-styled Emperor of Cyprus.

ANDRÉ ST. CLAIR STOOD nervously, poised on his toes and ready to leap as soon as the man in the prow of his boat gave the word. Close by him, though the space between it and him varied constantly in distance, height, and angle, a sloping platform dangled dangerously, supported by hanging chains and strapped underfoot with wooden cleats to make it easier to climb up its steep incline. André swallowed hard and flexed his fingers, his eyes flickering briefly again towards the helmsman handling the tiller expertly and easily in the stern.

"Wait for it," the big man growled, maintaining his pressure on the tiller while keeping his eye on the end of the hanging platform. "It's not going anywhere without you. Wait you ... Wait ... There ... *Now!*"

André jumped, his feet landing solidly on the ramp while his left hand clamped in a firm grip on the chain that served as a hand rail. He released his breath explosively but without changing the expression on his face, then looked back at the boat master, nodding his thanks. As he looked away again, raising his eyes, the ship above him, the largest André had ever seen, leaned sideways on a swell, looming over him, and he felt his gorge threaten to rise. He swallowed it down determinedly and threw himself into the task of pulling himself up the steep surface, making sure that his boots were firmly anchored against the wooden cross-straps before he took each step, for the wooden ramp was wet and slippery and he had no wish to slide down into the sea wearing a full suit of mail. Halfway up the great, swelling side of the dromon, where the ramp folded back upon itself for the second, almost level segment of the climb, he found a flat, hinged platform between the flights and stopped to make sure that he would be presentable when he emerged onto the vessel's deck. Richard had not quite warned him about that, not in so many words, but he had mentioned the mid-climb platform and observed that it seemed to be a natural place to pause and make sure one's appearance was ... appropriate ... before proceeding to the deck. Ladies were temperamental creatures and much influenced by appearances, had seemed to be his message, and André had been attuned to it.

While he worked at straightening his clothing, a niggling voice somewhere far at the back of his mind murmured about the sin of personal vanity and the scandalous impropriety of any Temple brother having any dealings with women of any description. He knew that when the time came to take his final vows, he would be required to abjure all contact with women. For the time being, however, he was content to bear in mind that he was not yet a Temple Knight; that he was still answerable to, and bound to obey, the wishes of his liege, Duke Richard; and that there would be time enough in future for penitence and self-denial. He therefore twisted his shoulders and adjusted his mantle until it hung comfortably, and as he did so, he, too, eyed the three new vessels that had entered the anchorage. He knew none of them, but did not expect to. His knowledge of ships and shipping extended to whatever deck lay beneath his feet at any time, and there it ended. André St. Clair was not and would never be a seaman. He knew that every seasoned eye on every ship in the anchorage would be trained on the newcomers, and they would be either welcomed in or driven off. Either way, it was of no immediate concern to him.

His mantle finally settled comfortably about his shoulders, he set about the climb again, rising swiftly to the gate at the top of the ramp, where he was awaited by a brightly dressed group of five dignitaries, three of whom were more richly attired than the others, and all of whom regarded him as though they had found a rat crawling around the edges of their deck. One of the three best dressed would, André knew, be Sir Richard de Bruce, the Norman-English officer in command of the three dromons as a group. The other two, he suspected, would be the individual captains of the two remaining vessels, and the two less brightly caparisoned officers would be senior lieutenants. A swift scan of the deck showed him that there were no women in sight. He stepped forward immediately, through the gate that one of the common seamen was holding open for him. He made a choice instinctually, choosing the tallest and haughtiest-looking of the group, and drew himself to attention, saluting as he did so.

"Sir Richard de Bruce? I bring you greetings from King Richard and written personal greetings for his betrothed, the Princess Berengaria, and for his beloved sister Joanna, Queen of Sicily. My name is André St. Clair, and I am a knight of Poitou, liege to Richard as both Duke of Aquitaine and Count of Poitou."

The introductions and amenities dealt with as briefly as possible, de Bruce, the type of self-important martinet who set St. Clair's teeth on edge, informed André in clipped, formal words that the ladies had retired to their quarters for their midday meal, and that he would inform them of Sir André's arrival. In the meantime, he directed one of the senior lieutenants, pointing with the hand that held his letter from the King, to conduct Sir André to a sheltered spot on the rear deck outside the superstructure, where he could sit on a pawl and collect himself in privacy while he awaited his summons to attend upon the ladies. Mindful of Richard's admonition, André said nothing more, merely nodding formally and turning his back on de Bruce and his group to follow the ship's smirking lieutenant to the spot indicated, where he stood looking out towards the three newly arrived ships, purging his anger at the insult of his reception by reviewing the conversation he had had the previous day with Richard Plantagenet.

Richard had summoned André to the stem deck of his galley—a place where they apparently might not be overheard. There he had sat in his shirtsleeves, working busily. He needed someone, he explained, for a task that he could not trust to any man who might think to cross him.

"And then I remembered you," he said, "praying in the solitude of your penurious cell aboard one of the Temple ships." His face split in a grin and his voice rose. "I know your sword arm is well enough by now, but are your knees yet functioning, after being bent in prayer on a wooden floor for so long?"

He did not wait for—and clearly did not expect—an answer, but proceeded directly to say that he would be sending André with the Temple squadron to Limassol in Cyprus. Richard and the others would follow with the tide, a day or more later.

"Limassol is where my dromons ended up, with all their cargo: my wife-to-be, my sister, and my war chest—all the moneys I have raised to fight this war. All of them there, at the mercy of this demented Emperor."

"Emperor, my liege?"

"Aye, some petty fool of a ruler in Cyprus, a Byzantine who stole the throne, is threatening the safety of my women and has laid his thieving hands upon the Great Seal of England, wearing it around his neck like a gewgaw. I am sailing to root him out and kick his smelly arse out of Cyprus and into the sea. I need speed, and the Marshal of the Temple, Etienne de Troyes, agreed to let me borrow his four fast ships—of course, only after I'd mentioned the danger to our war chest, and how the loss of it would severely curtail our campaign in the Holy Land. For their part, the Templars, bound by their duty, will guard the ladies—guard them to the death—and they will keep their holy distance, terrified of contamination.

"André, I must be wary at all times of those with whom I deal. The potential for treachery and double dealings, for secretive and surreptitious alliances and plots among all this upheaval is enormous. Philip alone, I know, would be willing to pay anything to anyone, if they would undertake to destroy the possibility of this marriage my mother has contracted between England and Navarre. And he is but one of the enemies I have among our friends. Even the Marshal of the Temple must be suspect in my eyes in this affair, because his sworn loyalty is to the Pope, and the Pope would dearly love to lay his hands upon some means to keep England without an heir, and consequently at the mercy of France and Philip Capet and his staunch ally, Holy Mother Church. Rome has not yet forgiven me for my father's sin in killing Thomas Becket. And Philip will never forgive me for rejecting him … him first, and then his sorry sister."

He sighed. "I can take no other man's word for what has happened or for what is going on, because the stakes involved are so enormous that I will always wonder if what I am being told is truth, or whether someone has been suborned in order to set me on an errant course. You will do no such thing. It does not lie within your nature." He picked up two folded and sealed packages that lay on the far corner of his table and tossed them, one after the other, to André. "These are for Joanna and the Princess Berengaria. Joanna's is the one marked with the pen stroke by the seal. I want you to take these to their dromon immediately and deliver each one personally to the lady for whom it is written. Trust no one with that task. Do it yourself. Request an audience with both ladies in my name, then remain with them and wait for their responses, for I have asked each of them different questions and made it clear that I will be relying heavily upon the accuracy of their answers.

"I do not know the Princess well, but my sister Joanna was never anyone's fool, even as a bosomless chit of a girl. Indeed she is more her mother's child than any other of our brood. If there is something rotting around her, Joanna will have nosed it out and dealt with it by now. She will have information and opinions that will be invaluable to me. You read and write, too. I remembered that with much pleasure. It triples and quintuples your value in this. Listen closely to all Joanna has to say, and then make notes of all you judge to be important."

André would also bear a letter to Sir Richard de Bruce, whom Richard described as "a good seaman and an able commander, but distant, unfriendly, and disdainful." De Bruce would be instructed to give André a complete report and assessment of the situation in Cyprus, and to provide him with money, which Richard believed André might need for the purpose of bribery in order to gather information.

"When I arrive in Limassol, I want you there, waiting for me. You and I will then withdraw together and you will inform me of everything you have learned. Everything, André. Is that clear? Do you understand exactly what I require?"

André nodded.

"And now, by God's Holy guts, I have to meet with bishops, who will wish to pray, no doubt, for the safety of my future bride." He paused, and then a grin of pure devilishness transformed his face. "I will confess to you, but never to them, that I thought, last night, about my betrothed's safety. Were she to be ravished and returned to me fruitfully pregnant, it might save me a deal of unpleasantness, would you not agree?" He blinked then, owlishly, his smile fading but not disappearing. "No, apparently you would not. Very well, Sir André, get you gone, and keep your mouth shut, your ears open, and your wits about you." André had saluted and left then, striving manfully to conceal the shock he had felt at Richard's cynical remarks about his future bride's safety, and telling himself that the King had meant not a word of it.

When André was summoned at last, he was taken to a doorway in the stern of the great ship, where a guard knocked and then stepped aside. André moved into his place as the door opened inwards and an armored guard peered out at him and then moved aside in turn, beckoning him to enter. The doorway was low, and André had to stoop to pass within it, squeezing past the guard, who sucked in his paunch and tried to make himself as small as he could while the visitor passed him. Once inside, André was astonished to realize that the chamber he had entered was tiny and that the low ceiling barely afforded him the space to stand upright. It was dark in there, too, the only natural illumination being a grid pattern of bright beams of sunlight that painted the floor in checkered squares from an overhead hatch, making the dark shadows even darker by comparison. The few smoky lamps he could see mounted on brackets fastened to the ship's beams did little to dispel the gloom. He sensed rather than saw human shapes, female shapes, on both sides of him and counted three in a dark corner to his right and two on his left. Two ladies sat at a small table that held the remnants of a simple meal. He could see from their attitude that both of them were looking at him, so he bowed deeply and addressed himself to both of them.

"I pray you will forgive me, ladies, for I know not which of you is which and the light in here is very poor. My name is André St. Clair, knight of Poitou, and I bring you greetings and written words from my liege lord King Richard, who sent me here in haste to promise you that he is coming, with the remainder of his fleet, and will be here tomorrow to speak with you in person."

"Ooh, la! Richard has found himself a clever one." The speaker was the woman on his right, and something in the tone of her voice, a measure of maturity that he would not have expected in the young Princess, led him to wager with himself that this was Joanna Plantagenet. He stared hard into the gloomy corner where she sat and decided to take a risk of appearing stupid, rather than to stand there mumchance like an awkward boy. He smiled, showing his teeth, and raised an eyebrow. "Clever, my lady? May I ask what prompts you to think that?"

"Why, the cunning way you evaded the trap of having to guess at which of us was which, for that was a guessing game you could not have won without offending one or both of us. St. Clair, you say? Are you related to Sir Henry, who was Master-at-Arms to my mother?"

"I am, my lady. He is my father."

"Then I know you, knew you, when you were a child. Step closer."

André did so, relieved to know that he had guessed correctly, and as he did so, Joanna raised the flimsy, dark-colored veil that had obscured her features, and her face came into sight, almost shining in the gloom surrounding it. He remembered her, too, from his childhood, for she had been several years older than he was, and from the time he was a toddler until he was old enough to run away from them and hide, she and her friends had used him mercilessly in their games whenever they could. He had never thought of her in those days as being comely, but now he realized that she must have been, and he had simply been too young to notice. Her face, he saw now, was striking, and he recalled vaguely that men had once called her beautiful, before she wed, but the word that had sprung into his mind upon first seeing her face unveiled was *strength*.

She wore a white wimple that concealed her hair and outlined her face, and the veil over that, now thrown back behind her head, was secured by an ornate comb. Framed by the edges of the wimple, her forehead was broad and high and unlined—she was barely thirty, he knew, several years younger than her brother Richard—and her brows and lashes were pale golden, framing eyes that were deep blue above high, tight-sculpted cheekbones, a straight, strong nose, and a wide and mobile mouth. But there were tiny crow's-feet at the corners of her eyes and at the sides of her mouth, and he remembered hearing that she had been a well-wed Queen, although her elderly husband had been unable to breed a son upon her. She was now a widow of several years' standing.

All of this passed through his mind as she beckoned him to lean closer, and he realized that she was scanning his face as closely as he had hers. But then she nodded very slightly and the skin across her cheeks and below her eyes seemed to go smooth, as though she had somehow tightened it deliberately. "I remember you. You were a very pretty little boy and you have grown into a very pretty man."

There was something in her voice, an inflection of some kind, that struck André as odd, but he disregarded it as she continued speaking. "You have not yet met my sister-to-be, have you? Berengaria, this is Sir André St. Clair, one of Richard's ... friends." Again he caught that strange tone, a note approaching disdain, but this time, as he turned with a smile to face Berengaria, the implications of it washed over him, so that he felt himself flushing with mortification all the way from the back of his neck. He froze, the smile dying on his lips, and then straightened angrily, stung beyond prudence.

"Madam, you wrong me," he snapped, outraged that anyone would think to classify him as one of the effete group of dandies that clustered around the King. "Your brother is my liege lord and I, his loyal vassal. He honors me with his trust, upon occasion, and I find no dishonor in the fact that he regards me as a friend. But I am *not* one of his … *friends*." The emphasis he placed on that last word left no possibility for error in interpreting what he meant, and he saw Joanna Plantagenet draw back sharply as though in reaction to a sudden threat. Only then, too late, did he recognize the rashness as well as the harshness of his reaction to her comment and realize that he might have misinterpreted *her* meaning, but the damage had been done. He braced himself for her rebuke, but for several moments she said nothing at all, merely looking at him closely, a tiny frown between her brows.

Joanna drew herself upright in her chair. "Forgive me, Sir André."

Surprised by the mildness and forbearance in her reaction, André bent forward from the waist, placing one open hand upon his breast. "It is already forgotten, my lady."

Once again the former Queen gazed thoughtfully at him, her wimpled head tilted slightly to one side, and then she nodded. "So be it, then. Berengaria, let us begin afresh. I present to you Sir André St. Clair, a knight of Aquitaine in my brother's service and clearly a man to be highly trusted and regarded … Sir André, this is the Princess Berengaria of Navarre, the future wife of your liege lord, my brother, Duke Richard. I name him Duke to you because it is in my mind that his rank as King of England may mean little to you in person …" She allowed that sentence to fade away, and André bowed again, this time to the Princess, but he yet found it easy to smile back at Joanna.

"I swear to you, my lady, that were your brother King of Aquitaine, rather than Duke, it might sound like a higher rank, but it could neither influence nor increase the duty or loyalty that I acknowledge and dedicate to him as Duke today." He turned again to the Princess and bent his leg to kneel before her on his right knee. "My lady Princess, I must now ask your pardon for what I have just said. Your future husband's title as King of England may mean little to me as a knight of Aquitaine and Poitou, but I will happily swear personal allegiance to you and to your honor when you become both Queen of England and Duchess of Aquitaine."

Now it was the turn of Princess Berengaria to raise her veil and bare her face to his inspection, and as she did so he became aware of and then tried to ignore the ripe and shapely fullness of her breasts as they lifted in response to the raising of her arms. He could almost feel Joanna's eyes boring into him, gauging his reaction to what he was seeing, and he concentrated intensely upon keeping his eyes on the Princess's hands as she arranged the folds of her veil about her head. At the same time, however, his mind was full of the thought that to waste such lavishly endowed beauty upon a man like Richard Plantagenet must be both a crime and a sin, for the very fullness of such a lushly feminine body would repulse the King, who surrounded himself at all times with tightly muscled, tautly beautiful young men. And what perplexed and preoccupied him instantly thereafter was the possibility that Berengaria herself might suspect and simply accept what lay ahead of her, as Queen to a man who had no liking or desire for women.

The Princess, who was smiling at him now, inclined her head good-naturedly. Before she spoke a word to him, however, she turned to the guard who remained standing with his back against the cabin door, pretending to be unaware of anything that was going on around him.

"Leave us, if you will. Wait outside." She looked over to where the other three women sat huddled in the opposite corner. "You, too, may retire, ladies. We shall call you should we have need of anything." The guard drew himself up and saluted, then ushered the ladies-in-waiting out ahead of him, leaving the royal ladies alone in the darkness of the cabin with André, who remained kneeling at the feet of the Princess. When the door had closed solidly behind the departing guard, the Princess turned her smile back on André. "Master St. Clair, you are most welcome here, as a friend and confidant of my betrothed, Richard, and there is no need for you to suffer there upon your knees. Stand up, sir. Did you not say, upon entering, that you bear written words from the King?"

Her voice sounded vaguely foreign, slightly alien in its cadences and vowel sounds but not offensively so, and it crossed his mind that he had never journeyed beyond the Pyrenees to her father's kingdom of Navarre. Her people there, he knew, had lived under a constant condition of warfare for hundreds of years with the Muslim Moors to the south of them, and that condition of constant readiness for conflict was one of the things that had made the prospect of alliance with King Sancho VI of Navarre seem so attractive to Richard's mother in brokering this marriage.

"I did, my lady. Pardon me, I have them here, in my scrip." He rose to his feet and fumbled in the pouch at his waist, producing the two small cylinders and squinting at them in the poor light before handing the appropriately addressed tube to each of the women, who immediately set about opening them. Berengaria, smiling absently, waved to indicate the room behind André. "Be at ease, Sir André, while we read these. There is a comfortable chair behind you that I often use … This will not take long."

André bowed his head obediently and moved to the chair the Princess had indicated, and as he turned to sit in it, he saw Joanna lower her eyes quickly to her letter. He would have smiled back at her, but she gave no further sign of knowing he was there, and so he turned his attention to the Princess Berengaria, glad that his eyes had now fully adjusted to the darkness of the room and that he was able to see her clearly, and even more glad that he now had this opportunity to look closely at her while she read Richard's letter, which appeared to be long and substantial.

What could Richard Plantagenet possibly have to say, even in writing, that might engage the goodwill and curiosity of someone like you? he wondered, gazing at the way a tiny lock of black hair had worked its way from the confines of her wimple and now curled delightfully on the skin of her left cheekbone, and almost as though she felt his eyes on it, Berengaria raised her left hand absently, without taking her eyes from the page she was reading, and tucked the errant curl back out of sight beneath the white linen.

Black hair, he thought then, seeing how stark her eyebrows were against the dusky pallor of her face. Black hair and eyes so dark that they, too, looked inky black. At the moment, however, as she read, those eyes were downcast, and all he could see of them was the sweeping fullness of long, curling lashes that seemed to lie directly against the flawlessness of her cheeks.

Richard's Queen, André St. Clair concluded then, was beautiful in a way that he had never encountered before in his amatory wanderings throughout his home territories. She was vibrant, he decided, and alive with the promise of great joys, and the unfamiliar duskiness of her skin gave her an air of strangeness that suggested other lands and warmer climes. He had known many women with dark hair and dark eyes, so it was not merely her coloring that made her different; in fact in all his life, now that he thought about it, he realized that he had only ever met four women who could properly be called blond, with flaxen hair and bright blue eyes; four, out of ... He stopped there, unpleasantly surprised to discover that he could not supply that number, even for his own use. Four out of how many? How many women had he known to any degree of intimacy? Or even known well enough to feel attracted towards? Very few, he knew, and he set out to count them, working backward from Eloise de Chamberg, who had died in the woods of his father's estate the day that indirectly caused André's accession to the ranks of the Temple. Several he remembered well and easily, including all four of the flaxen-haired women, none of whom, he was surprised yet again to discover, he recalled with much pleasure. But then, when Berengaria stirred again and lowered the letter, he abandoned those thoughts and focused upon her.

She did not so much as glance in his direction. Her lips, full, red, were softly pursed, he saw now, the corners of her eyes gently wrinkled as she stared off into some unseen, private distance. Gently, absently, she scratched softly with one fingertip at the fabric of her bodice, beneath the sudden swell of her breasts, unwittingly drawing his attention back to her abundant femininity. Did she, could she, know that her future husband was a man-lover? And if she did, could she hoodwink herself into thinking she might change him?

André really had no experience in such things, and he made no moral judgments on the matter. Some such men he could quite easily accept as friends and comrades, ignoring their proclivities without discomfort, while others of their ilk—and there appeared to be more of this kind than of the first—he much preferred to avoid completely, finding them to be less tolerant of others than they expected others to be of them. By and large, however, he was content to live his own life and leave them to theirs. But from his own observations he had learned, inarguably, that such men tended to flock together, thriving upon mutual attraction, and they had little time, and less use, for women. He had also seen enough of them sufficiently advanced in age to prove that theirs was not a condition one outgrew. It was not a phase to be passed through and then forgotten. André was convinced that this condition—he knew no other word to describe it—was a permanent thing, an immutable state of being, and he suspected that the love of a mere woman, irrespective of her ardor or fidelity, would be powerless to change it. He had no doubt that Richard would perform his duty and provide an heir from Berengaria, but neither had he any doubt that, once that task was done, the King would leave the woman to the rearing of the child, while he went off to frolic with his friends. That was the lot of many women, he knew.

He felt himself frowning, perplexed by Berengaria's apparent lack of concern over something so self-evidently destructive. Could she really be blissfully unaware of all of this? She was but newly arrived here, from a sheltered home, judging by all he had heard, although that thought caused an uncomfortable stirring at the back of his mind, a faint memory of mutterings from several years before, linking Richard romantically with her brother Sancho. He thrust that thought aside and began again.

She was newly arrived here, and had not yet been sufficiently exposed to strangers to cause any pollution of her thoughts concerning her future marriage. No one would dare risk giving such offense, not against Richard Plantagenet, and not by furtive whisperings. Who other than Joanna, acting selflessly as friend, future sister, and adviser, could have told her?

Besides, this wife was a queen, born and bred with duty ever present in her mind, and the duty of a queen was to bear sons, just as the duty of a king was to sire them. Richard had undertaken publicly to set aside his lustful, unnatural tastes and breed an heir for England, and André, thanks to the high regard in which he held Richard as hero, had no difficulty, when he thought about it in that light, in believing that he would.

Joanna, having now finished reading, addressed André. "My brother says I am to trust you completely and to confide in you without reservation ..." She looked across the table at Berengaria. "Did he say the same to you, Berry?"

The Princess nodded, and Joanna turned slowly back to André, tilting her head a little to one side and regarding him with wide eyes. "I wonder, can you have any knowledge of how great a tribute he pays you in that? I have never, ever known my brother Richard to say that of any other man. You must be a very signal and singular young man, Sir André St. Clair ... But we have much to discuss, so let us be about it. Richard has asked me several questions about what has happened here since we arrived, and he wants you to hear my answers. I can only presume he has asked the same of Berengaria."

"He has," the Princess agreed.

"Well, then, would you prefer to speak with each of us alone, or may we do this thing together, all three of us?"

"Together would probably be best, my lady, unless you object. We are comfortably placed, unlikely to be disturbed or overheard." He pointed to the open hatch over their heads. "Providing, be it said, that we keep our voices low. That opens on the deck above, and I suggest that we proceed as though there were a large-eared spy perched up there, with one hand cupped over each ear. My lady Joanna, would you like to speak first?"

They sat and talked in low voices, the three of them, while the pattern of sunlight crawled across the floor of the cabin, and when it eventually faded towards nothingness, André summoned help from the deck and they paused in their discussions until candles and new lamps had been brought in and lit. St. Clair had much to think about when he left them and returned to his own ship, where he immediately set about making notes on what they had discussed. By the time he sought his cot that night he was almost exhausted, and he fell asleep thinking of both women, seeing their different beauties separately in his mind's eye and regretting, perhaps for the first time, that his status as a Templar would soon divorce him from any opportunity to spend such a guiltless, pleasant interlude in the company of women.

RICHARD'S GALLEY DID NOT ARRIVE until late the next morning, and when it did appear it was accompanied by two more of his galleys, but there was no sign of any following fleet on the horizon behind it. André boarded the boat that Tournedos had provided for his use and made his way to the King's ship as soon as it dropped anchor, but even before he reached it he could see that he had been preempted by a larger boat from one of the three unknown ships he had seen arriving the previous day, and he murmured to his helmsman to keep distance between them and the strangers. The foreign craft was a medium-sized barge, painted in red and deep green and crewed by a team of eight oarsmen. It had a stern platform capable of seating ten men, for André counted all of them, all knights and all fully armored and bearing their own heraldic identities, none of which he recognized.

His curiosity was now fully engaged, for it seemed to him, as he watched the unknown knights clamber aboard the King's galley, that they had an air of hard use about them: their shields, the few he could see, looked peculiarly old and worn, almost shabby, as though from long use, and their chain mail had a scrubbed look, too, almost a burnished finish, that intrigued him. The devices of their personal insignia seemed faded, too, the colors leached and dowdy. He watched as the armored knights crowded the galley's deck, seeming to absorb every available inch of space, and he signaled to his own helmsman to pull even farther away and wait.

Time passed slowly after that, but moments after the last of the boarding party had clambered aboard, the barge that had carried them eased back from the galley's side to make way for a much smaller boat that emerged from the other side of the ship and made its way slowly forward to await yet another passenger, this one departing. André sat up straighter as he saw the man approach the ship's side, and recognized the stern, frowning, eternally humorless face of one of his best-known and least liked compatriots, Etienne de Troyes, the Master of the Temple in Poitou and the highest-ranking member of the Temple Order in the current expedition. De Troyes stepped down into his boat without looking around, then seated himself in the stern and pulled the hood of his mantle over his head as his single oarsman pulled strongly away from the galley.

It was almost an hour later by the time the group of ten visitors returned to their barge, and Richard himself accompanied them and stood looking down at them until they were under way. André knew the King had seen him, but he sat waiting until Richard glanced in his direction and beckoned him in before turning away.

The last of the storm had long since subsided, but the water was still choppy and the waves sufficiently unpredictable for André to misjudge his timing in leaping from his boat to the netting on the galley's side. The boat's side dipped just as he jumped, and he fell short, clawing at the hanging nets and narrowly avoiding falling into the sea. He climbed aboard the royal ship with his legs soaked from the knees down, and with seawater squishing between his toes he left a puddled trail of footprints on the decking as he walked towards the stern, where Richard now sat dictating to one of the clerics. Behind them, a gaggle of officers, onlookers, and hangers-on hovered, eyeing St. Clair as he approached and making no secret of their disdain for his wet appearance. André kept his face expressionless and ignored all of them, the King's presence forcing him to resist the urge to drop his hand to the hilt of his sword.

Richard looked up as St. Clair approached and raised a quizzical eyebrow as he saw the wet trail, but he said nothing about it, merely nodding and holding up a finger in a mute request for a few moments more in which to complete his business with the cleric. In a low voice that André would have had to strain to hear, had he been curious, the monk read back to the King what he had written, and after listening to all of it Richard nodded and dismissed the man.

"André. You have the information I require?"

"Aye, my lord."

"Excellent." He raised his voice for the benefit of the crowd at his back. "Leave us, all of you, for you already have enough to talk about and some of you have much to do. But be sure that if I see you between now and when I finish with Sir André here, it had better be from a distance where the thought of being overheard or listened to would never occur to me. Off with you. Wait!" He held up a hand to stay them as they began to move. "Percy, you have your instructions and I require you to pass them along to your own people now, so that when the squadron following us arrives, everything will be in readiness for it. No one to go ashore until I give the word, but once you have that, I want the landings to go smoothly. Neuville, yours is the task of setting up my tent and guarding it. Disembark your guardsmen from the dromons immediately, and make sure that they are well supported by companies of archers and crossbows, then set us up on yon high eminence, there on the right, overlooking the beaches and the town's main gate. The so-called Emperor of this sad place may yet be there, within the gates, so make you sure he can cause us no nuisance.

"And you, my lord of Richmond. Take you my royal barge across the bay in one hour's time, but not a minute sooner or later, and see to it that King Guy is safely, and not too quickly, ta'en aboard and ferried ashore an exact hour after that, so that by the time you set his foot on land, our royal enclosure is prepared and securely guarded. Neuville, that should give you three hours from this moment. And now away, all of you, and leave me to my dealings with Sir André."

As his entourage scattered, muttering among themselves and not a few of them casting glances towards André that ranged from simple curiosity through suspicion to outright hostility, the King beckoned André forward and waved him to the single chair beside his own at the table.

"Come, sit and talk to me. The bulk of the fleet will be delayed, for another day or two at least—too many damaged chicks and raddled old hens among the flock. But a squadron of our fastest vessels, loaded with some of my best troops, will be here by night-fall." He looked around at the port ahead of them. "So, seeing no burning buildings in the town, I take it that my guards are still aboard the dromons and my ladies are both well and in good health?"

"They are, my lord, and looking forward to being reunited with you."

"And what of this creature Comnenus, has he threatened them or molested them in any way?"

"No, not directly. The lady Joanna keeps her wits about her at all times and is a fine judge of men and their motives. It was she who interpreted this Isaac's early actions and decided, once he began approaching her with conciliatory gestures and invitations to go ashore, that it would be safer and more prudent to maintain a distance between him and everything aboard the two remaining dromons."

"Good for Joanna. But one can only presume that de Bruce would have reached the same conclusion on his own, had she not been there." He hesitated, watching André's face. "Do you not think so?"

"No, my lord, with respect, I think not. I spoke at length with the commodore this morning and he gave me the distinct impression that he does not approve of the direction taken by the Queen. He believes that, had he been at liberty to accept Comnenus's initial invitation to parley, much could have been achieved without hostil-ity. He regards your sister's stance as being an interference in his affairs and an affront to his authority."

"Hmm. And do you believe he is right, that he could have settled matters amicably with Comnenus?"

"No, my lord. Comnenus had already spurned our requests for assistance when our ships arrived and sought leave to use his harbor. He had by then despoiled our dead and seized our treasure from the wreckage on the rocks. It was only after that, once he had guessed that the surviving ships held more treasure, that he became concilia-tory. He had no ships capable of attacking our dromons, and no army sufficiently organized to mount a land-based attack. So he had no other option than to try to win our ships by guile. Your sister was right to do as she did. Had she not done so, no one can really say what might have happened, but there is a real possibility that we might now be involved in a situation with royal hostages and a lost war chest held in ransom."

"Aye, I've little doubt that's true." The words emerged as a deep growl. "Tell me about this Comnenus. All that I have heard is hearsay and reports at distance. I presume you have garnered more immediate information?"

"Aye, my lord, as much as I could find." St. Clair sat back in his chair and steepled his fingers beneath his chin, settling his thoughts into sequence and only faintly aware of the coldness of his feet in their heavy, wet boots. "He is a strange man. I found that out immediately—a tyrant of course, and crazed, some say. He is largely detested—not merely disliked—by his own people, whom he treats savagely. He is Byzantine, and we knew that, but it seems an uncle of his truly was Emperor in Constantinople. That's what Isaac swears, anyway. He arrived here some six years ago, from Constantinople, and contrived almost immediately—no one seems to know exactly how—to wrest control of the entire island from the Empire. It was that feat, apparently, along with his supposed imperial family connections, that inspired him to name himself Emperor.

"As I said, everyone seems to hate him, and yet he maintains his hold on power with an iron grip and a mailed fist. His own people talk of his grasping greed and his treachery, and his cruelty is supposedly hard to believe. I had it from de Bruce this morning, and he had heard it earlier from a number of people in the town of Limassol, that many of the island's most prosperous and wealthy families have fled beyond the seas since he seized power six years ago. And those who remain do so only because they cannot escape. They are tied to their holdings here and they live in a state of despair because of Isaac's greedy demands and depredations of their property."

"The man sounds like a monster," Richard growled, sublimely unaware that he might have been listening to a recitation of his own methods of raising taxes to furnish his war in Outremer. St. Clair, however, noticed no irony.

"That is nothing," he added. "Apparently he treats his own officers and underlings so viciously, flogging and fining them at every turn, that they hate him almost to a man."

"Then why don't they kill him? That makes no sense at all. Does the fool know nothing about leadership? What kind of madness would drive a man—a leader of any description—to abuse the very people he needs most to keep him in power? The fellow clearly is crazed, sitting atop his island empire. Like this nonsense with the dromons. Did he think for a single moment that no one would come looking for such lost treasures? Did he think, for even the blinking of an eye, that those who came searching would be weak and witless? The man is an idiot."

"Perhaps, perhaps not," St. Clair replied. "The tale is told—and widely believed—that when he was much younger and apparently a strong and extremely able warrior, he went to war in Armenia among the Byzantine armies of the empire, and was captured and sold into slavery. According to this story, which persists even though Isaac himself seldom speaks of it, he spent many years thereafter in foreign lands, always shackled in heavy chains like a savage animal because he was so strong and rebellious. He came out of the experience with a rabid, deep, and abiding hatred for Westerners like us— he calls us Latins—because we kept him chained up for all those years." He paused, then added, "That might explain his initial inhospitable reaction to the discovery of two strange Latin ships anchored off his shores, seeking assistance."

"Aye, when you say it like that, I am tempted to think it might … but it makes me no less anxious than before to smear the wretch into a paste, the way I would a crawling spider. What else do you have? What about the early developments in all of this?"

André shrugged. "All accidental and not at all unusual, from what I could discover. The storm blew itself out eventually here on Cyprus and the three dromons had been driven by high winds the entire way. De Bruce believes that was due to the sheer bulk of the vessels. The vastness of their sides and stern surfaces acted as sails, catching greater amounts of wind than any other ships could harness, and consequently driving their big hulls farther and faster than any of their fellows. Be that as it may, they caught sight of the island at dawn of the third day of the storm, when the wind and the seas had just passed their peak but were still immensely powerful. The dromons were already too close to the shore by then and the one nearest to the land was driven onto the shoals and shallows that the islanders call the Rocks of Aphrodite. Once there, solidly aground, it was battered to pieces by waves and wind, and there was nothing either of the other ships could do to assist.

"The fury of the breakers among the rocks was such that very few aboard the ship survived to reach the shore. Over the next few days, the local fisher folk and islanders came down onto the shore, as is their wont, to salvage what they could. But the fisher folk found gold in the wreckage there, and the word soon reached Comnenus.

"We have been told that he did not know much at first, only that gold coins had washed up on the beaches and among the rocks, but that was enough to bring him sniffing. He saw your Great Seal around a fisherman's neck and confiscated it, unknowing what it was. And then, later on, one of his fellows dived down and reported finding chests and boxes filled with gold in the wreckage on the sea floor.

"Hours after that, it appears, word came to him that two more ships, giant things blown in from the westward, had arrived off Limassol and were seeking permission to land. 'Westward' meant 'Latin' to Isaac, and he sent back word at once to deny the foreign ships entry. At the same time, he imprisoned everyone who had survived the shipwreck. It was only later, once he had questioned some of the local observers and had a chance to think things over, that he began to see that the two great ships reported by his Cypriots as having sailed away were likely to be the ships off Limassol, and they were therefore likely to contain more of the same treasure.

"His first reaction was to go rushing off to Limassol in order to impound the two ships—one of his own captains told us that. But he did not dare leave the scene of the wreck until he was sure that every fragment of the treasure had been found. He trusted no one and expected neither loyalty nor honor from any of his people, since he never showed any of either thing to them. And so he waited, ranting in his impatience, until every coin had been recovered, and many people took note of his anxiety.

"Several days later, he returned to Limassol, only to find that he was powerless to move against the two dromons. He had been told that these were enormous ships, but because he had never seen a ship much bigger than a fishing boat—the dromon on the rocks had been smashed to kindling before he reached there—he had had no way of knowing what 'enormous' really meant, until he set eyes on them. He knew at once that he had nothing with which to threaten these beasts."

Richard was listening closely, frowning, and André continued. "It was at that point, once he had examined all his options, that he became conciliatory, offering friendship, aid, and hospitality to his unexpected visitors. To give him credit, he had at least sent word earlier to de Bruce that he was not in Limassol but had been detained inland, attending to affairs in Nicosia, and that might have worked had he not been undone by his own people, who told us everything they knew. De Bruce knew precisely, to the moment, when Comnenus had come back from visiting the wreck, and he knew, too, exactly what had been retrieved from the wreckage and what had been done with the survivors and with the bodies of the dead."

"Wait. You say Comnenus's own people told de Bruce all this? Why then would de Bruce disagree with what Joanna chose to do? He must have known she was right."

"No, my lord, he knew she was a woman, with little understanding of the realities of war and politics—"

"God's guts, man! Joanna was a reigning queen for years. And in Sicily! She knows more about politics and the way they work than de Bruce will ever learn."

St. Clair nodded. "Aye, that is probably true. But de Bruce, to give him justice, believed he would have been dealing with Comnenus from strength. Cyprus has no naval strength to speak of, and whatever it has in the way of an army is in sad disrepair, an untrained rabble with no pride and no spirit. There are no knights in all the island, incredible as that may sound. The Emperor has driven them all away to other lands, fearful that they might plot to overthrow him. In short, de Bruce believed he could easily assert his superiority."

"Not from on board a ship, he could not. He would have had to land first."

"Aye, sir, and he could have. He had a full company of your own guards aboard—two-thirds of a company at least. Two hundred disciplined men. He believes he could have captured all Cyprus with those, because Isaac's own people would have abandoned him."

Richard looked dubious, tilting his head. "Perhaps ... but perhaps not. In any case, it is not relevant. Joanna put her foot down. What then?"

"That is the most of it, my lord. There is more, but it is all incidental and will come out in answers to your questions as you pose them. For the time being, at least, that is all I have."

The King scratched his beard in thought, then nodded, decisively. "So be it. You have done well, provided what I need. Now I can make a decision, which I could not have done an hour ago. Within the hour, should I so wish, I can launch my forces against this base-born fool of an Emperor with good reason and sound conviction. My thanks for this. Go you now and find something to eat and we will talk again later, once I have had time to think about all you have told me. No, wait. The Princess Berengaria ... how did you find her? Her mood, I mean. Was she ...?"

"The Princess was well, my lord, and in good health and spirits. She will be awaiting your arrival today with great anticipation."

"Aye, indeed ... Was she ... What did you think of her? Is she not delightful to behold?"

"To behold ... Yes, my lord, she is. Delightful. She will make a beauteous bride and a regal Queen."

"She will ... She will, to be sure. Once more, my gratitude is yours, Master St. Clair. Farewell for now."

FOUR

André St. Clair fully expected the King to launch an attack against Isaac Comnenus immediately, but Richard did nothing of the kind, showing good sense and forbearance instead. He sent off a letter to Comnenus early that very afternoon, compiled with the assistance of a crew of bishops, that was astonishingly mild, given the provocation he had received. If Isaac would release the survivors of the wrecked dromon, with all their goods, and return Richard's missing treasures, including the Great Seal of England, which was useless to anyone else, then Richard would take no further steps against Cyprus or its Emperor but would set sail again for Palestine with all his forces and not come back.

And while the letter was being delivered, King Guy of Jerusalem was brought ashore without incident and installed in Richard's royal pavilion, a mile east of the city gates on a heavily guarded hill. The remaining ships and men of Richard's advance squadron came into view on the horizon, sure to arrive before nightfall as predicted. But even before the fleet had dropped anchor in the various spots assigned to them, Comnenus's response to Richard's letter arrived, and as the envoy bearing it rowed out towards Richard's galley, Isaac Comnenus himself appeared on the beach before the town. He paraded himself in front of a ragamuffin gathering of soldiery, who erected portable barricades before the gates in what André St. Clair, watching from the deck of his own ship and unaware of the King's letter, took to be a display of defiance and challenge.

And that was exactly what it was.

Isaac's response to the King's conciliatory letter was so abrupt and outrageously high-handed that those of Richard's advisers who read it could only shake their heads and mutter about the fellow's obvious insanity. He would not release his captives, Isaac said, nor would he return a single piece of gold. The Latin interlopers, he said, had injured his reputation by invading his territories and treating him as unworthy of their respect, and they had therefore earned his anger and the forfeiture he had imposed upon them. They must now accept the humiliation and the losses they had so justly earned. He expected to hear no more of them, he stated, other than reports of their departure in the immediate future, and he reminded them to be grateful that he had responded at all, since no Emperor would normally deign to have dealings with a mere King.

Several people told André later that Richard stood wide eyed with shock as his chancellor read this response aloud, and then he laughed a savage, barking laugh and ordered an immediate landing of three hundred men-at-arms, screened from attack by two hundred archers and crossbowmen, on the beach where Comnenus was parading.

They landed within the hour, and although Isaac's defenders came forward bravely enough to meet them, they had never before encountered anything as chilling or effective as the massed volleys of bolts and arrows that Richard's people poured down onto their heads from ships anchored close to the shore. The defenders, including Isaac himself, scattered quickly, running back into and through the town behind them, leaving the field to Richard's troops.

Throughout that evening and the remainder of the night, Richard gave priority to the unloading of his warhorses. Some of these had spent upward of a month at sea, and none was in any condition to be ridden, let alone ridden into battle, but long before dawn that morning the word circulated that Richard was in need of volunteers—two score of them—to ride with him before daybreak along the coast to Kolossi, five miles away, where Isaac and his men had supposedly ended up the previous evening.

As soon as he heard that being shouted to one of the guards on the prow from a night guard on the pier, André, who had been up on deck most of the night, restless and unable to sleep, went looking for his ship commander, claiming his right as one of Richard's vassals to respond to the call for volunteers. But Tournedos, barely risen from his bunk to face the day, shook his head, disclaiming any ability, as a naval commander, to grant such a request from a knight. He sent him instead to ask permission from the senior Templar officer on board.

André had never spoken to the man in question, a renowned and popular knight called Don Antonio del' Aquila, but he had seen him many times since boarding the ship. He found him now on the long stern deck, leaning against the rail near the sergeant brother guarding the helm, and talking in hushed tones with another dark-faced knight. They were clearly preoccupied, but the knight listened to St. Clair's request, albeit impatiently, frowning at being interrupted, and never taking his eyes off the man to whom he had been speaking. But then he curtly refused his permission, dismissing André with the tone of his voice.

Astonished at the finality of the man's response, André challenged the Templar's right to refuse him. He stubbornly insisted that he had not yet taken the oath of obedience to the Order and could not, therefore, be bound to accept or obey any order that was not a direct command.

Del' Aquila, who was known affectionately within the Templar community simply as Aquila, had been about to resume his interrupted conversation, reaching out to grasp his companion familiarly by the shoulder, but now he stopped and straightened slightly, raising an apologetic finger to the other man before turning back to face his challenger. The flickering light from a lamp on the bulkhead cast shadows on his face, and André expected to see anger stamped there. Instead, Aquila stood watching him calmly for long moments, showing no discernible emotions. He was a youngish man, in his fighting prime, and André estimated him to be thirty-two or thirty-three. He had a thick reddish-brown beard, although it looked black in the shadowy predawn light, and he kept it close-cropped beneath the mailed hood of his hauberk. His white surcoat bore the long-shanked red cross of the Temple Knights of Outremer front and rear, but in the frontal upper left quadrant of that cross, between his left breast and his shoulder, he also wore the equal-armed black cross with the flared ends, the cross-patté, that had been the original emblem of the Order before its investiture with the bold red cross signifying the Blood of Christ. Very few men wore both insignia, and all of those were knights who had distinguished themselves, and thereby the Order, in battle.

Aquila stood staring at St. Clair, eyes narrowed, teeth nibbling gently at his upper lip, and then he inhaled deeply and turned away towards the other man. "Forgive me, Signor Loranzo, but I must attend to … this. If you would wait for me in my quarters, I shall return as soon as I may."

The other man bowed deeply and moved away, and Aquila crooked his index finger at André. "Come. Walk with me."

As André fell into step beside him, the other man asked, "Why do you want to ride with Richard?"

"The Duke is my liege lor—"

"I know that, Master St. Clair, but why do you wish to ride with him?"

André blinked, mildly surprised that the other man should know his name, but he replied, "It is my duty, as his vassal."

"No, your duty as his vassal is to obey his every command. He has issued no commands in this. His call was for volunteers. Now let me ask you again: why do you wish to ride with him?"

"To—" André checked himself, aware that he was looking for a lie to justify his wishes, then smiled in spite of himself and conceded defeat.

"To feel a horse between my legs again."

"After so long at sea, you mean." Aquila had not been looking at him and had not seen him smile.

"Aye."

"Do you think you are alone in that?"

"No, not—"

"Quite." They had turned and crossed in front of the disarmed tiller and were now pacing slowly along the right edge of the stern deck, aware of the watching eyes and the listening ears of the guard at the helm behind them, but now, at the farthest point from where the guard stood watching them, Aquila stopped, turning inward so that he and St. Clair were almost nose to nose, and as he did so he grasped André by the wrist and frowned, as though snarling angrily at him, and lowered his voice dramatically. "Do not move. Do not look away from my face. Listen to what I am saying to you. Listen, as we are being listened to! Let us suppose I granted you permission to ride off with your lord. You would ride for perhaps five miles, on a beast that might prove fit to handle such a distance after a month at sea. And you might encounter this Cypriot Emperor and his crew of fools, after which you might fight them. But you might equally end up on a less than fit horse, on questionable terrain, fighting against men whose skills, though ludicrous, have the potential to be lethal on occasion. Suppose that one of those inept warriors were fortunate enough to strike you down and kill you by accident." He paused, allowing his words to hang between them, while his eyes never flinched from André's.

"So there you are," he continued, his voice little more than an intense whisper. "Sir André St. Clair, dead on an unknown scrap of land in the middle of nowhere, having achieved nothing, and all that you have gone through in this past year is set at naught, a waste of time and effort. And not merely your own time and effort but the efforts of all those people who have worked with you throughout that time in order to prepare you for the task that has been set for you in Outremer." He stopped, watching confusion and then understanding bloom in André's eyes, then cocked one eyebrow and nodded, confirming what he saw there.

"We had already decided," he said, in a louder voice, "those of us in command here, long before this call King Richard has made for volunteers, that the affairs of the Temple must, as always, take precedence over those of a mere king. Our task, our dedicated duty, is to reach the Holy Land alive and to replenish the strength and the fighting blood that our sacred Order has lost in the battles of the past few years. Our reserves there have been severely depleted, our continuing existence endangered, so we cannot afford to lose, or even to risk, the life or welfare of one single man before we come face to face with Saladin and his swarming hordes. The fate of Christianity itself, in Christ's own land, might depend upon each single man of us, or even upon a single one of us … And who can say who that one man might be?

"So, we remain aboard our ships, or within our own community should we land. We hold ourselves intact, and we avoid becoming caught up in such petty, prideful, unimportant squabbles as may kill good men to no useful purpose. Do you understand me?"

The only thing that André had truly understood until that point was that once again, and unexpectedly, he had encountered a fellow member of the Order of Sion who was aware of his secret purpose in visiting Outremer. He had also understood Aquila's message beyond a doubt, and now he had not the slightest trouble in seeing the strength of the reasoning underlying the man's refusal of his request, and the acknowledgment of that made him feel both foolish and selfish. The prattle about the fate of Christianity itself depending upon the Temple was no more than that—prattle designed for the ears of anyone who might be overhearing them. The true message André had received was that he was constantly being watched and guarded, even against himself, by his concerned brethren in Sion. He inhaled deeply, then raised his head and nodded.

"I do, Brother Aquila. I understand … completely. And I regret having brought myself to your attention on such a trivial matter. Forgive me."

"No need, for no harm was done. But you remain on board from now on unless King Richard summons you directly."

André found a smile and inclined his head. "I can improve even upon that for you, Senor del' Aquila, for I have had this conversation with myself, in other circumstances. I will attend upon King Richard only if he summons me as my liege lord, the Duke of Aquitaine. Otherwise I shall remain here and take no foolish risks. I owe no fealty to the realm of England."

Even as the two of them spoke, Richard and his party were

already setting out to ride west towards the town of Kolossi, and hearing them go, for it was yet too dark to see them, André felt no slightest pang of regret at remaining behind. Aquila's admonition had reminded him of the priorities that governed his life now, and he spent the rest of the morning tending to his weapons, and most particularly to his crossbow, cleaning it of the salt and corrosion that had accumulated on it over the previous months at sea, then cleaning and polishing his supply of bolts and making sure that his supply of bowstrings was in prime condition, dry and well protected against dampness.

After the midday meal, lured by the sights and sounds of the butts where other crossbowmen had set up shooting posts and targets, he went ashore with two other knights and spent an hour at practice until Richard and his party arrived back from their sortie, laden with plunder. The story of their successful raid spread quickly and was greatly enjoyed. The men had found Isaac's encampment undefended, all of its occupants asleep and not a one of them having considered that the enemy might follow them that night. Richard had attacked immediately, and the ensuing engagement had been a rout from the start, the enemy leaping out of their beds in panic and fleeing for the hills, making no effort to don their discarded clothing or weapons or to fight or defend themselves. Isaac had disappeared and was presumed to have fled among the mob, reportedly heading inland, through the Troodos mountain range to the north, towards Nicosia, seventy miles away, and Richard was in high good humor. The day was Sunday, the twelfth of May, the feast day of Saint Pancras in the year 1191, and it was to prove momentous in several ways other than the defeat of the hapless Isaac, the first of those being the sighting of the remainder of the fleet on the horizon, well ahead of schedule.

André had already listened to several versions of the morning's events by the time he heard about the incoming fleet, and he was on his way back to his boat on the beach when he heard a familiar voice shouting his name and saw the King himself cantering up behind him. Richard's color was high and he was very obviously pleased with himself. He swung down from his saddle and flung one arm around André's shoulders, pulling him strongly and effortlessly down and inward across his chest in the semblance of a wrestling grip. "I missed your face this morning," he began, before removing his arm. "Thought you would be with me when I called for volunteers, but then I saw that yours was not the only Templar visage missing from the throng. None of you came with me. Why was that? Does the Temple have a message that it wishes me to be aware of?"

André grinned ruefully, flexing his right shoulder, which, months after his injury, could yet be tender at times. "Yes and no, my lord. I tried to join you but was reminded, as was everyone else who sought permission, that my first duty to this expedition is the rebuilding of our Order's presence in Outremer. It was pointed out to me that an inglorious and pointless death at the hands of a buffoon in a small Cyprus field would do little to benefit the Temple, whereas my presence in the Holy Land might achieve great things on God's behalf."

"Hah!" Richard's bark of laughter confirmed that not even the Temple's policies could overcome his goodwill this day. "Whereas my own inglorious and pointless death in the same venture would have no impact at all upon the Temple! God's balls, these people are arrogant beyond credence." He hesitated, the merest fraction of a pause. "But you remain my vassal, do you not? You did not swear any vows while I was away?" He saw André's head shake in denial, and his grin grew wider. "Then that is marvelous, because this day, before the fleet makes harbor and before God can lay claim upon your loyalties, I require you to achieve great things on *my* behalf, my lad." His grin still in place, he glanced about him almost furtively, like a small boy contemplating mischief, then plucked at André's sleeve, pulling him sideways to where they could stand together in the sheltered angle of two wooden, open-sided sheds. "There is something I require you to do for me, you alone and right this very minute, while the decision is yet ringing in my mind."

"Of course, my lord. What is it?"

The King looked him in the eye, appeared to hesitate, and then plunged on, his words tumbling over each other in his haste to get them out. "I need you to commandeer a boat."

"Already done, my lord. I have one here, close by."

"Good. Then take it and get you out to the dromons in the bay. Present yourself there to my betrothed and inform her that she and I will be wed today, this evening, before the dinner hour. I will send an escort for her and my sister when the time is right. In the meantime, she is to dress and make herself ready. She will have several hours in which to prepare—two hours, at least, and perhaps three. I have already spoken with Father Nicolas, my chaplain, on the way back from Kolossi. He will conduct the marriage rites, as is his privilege, and he is even now making the necessary preparations for the remainder of the ceremonies. We will use the Chapel of Saint George the Dragon Slayer in the castle of Limassol, which is already ours, and the assembled bishops of our various domains—we have the Bishop of Evreux here, and another from Bayonne, as well as a few archbishops—will name and anoint her formally as Queen of England and place the crown upon her brows as soon as we are man and wife. Tell her all that. And warn Joanna to make sure that everything is as it ought to be. Bid her bring her own women and Berengaria's, too, to insulate the Queen from such a hedging-about of grim, unsmiling churchmen … And be sure to inform de Sablé's man, Coutreau, of how many women will be going ashore, for he will need to provide suitable transport for them—a barge, to keep them stable, and with a canopy to keep their hair and headwear free of risk from the wind and their clothing safely dry in the crossing. It would do me little good to have them row through wind and rain to appear there as a bedraggled brood, amidst all the ranks of peacockery that will assemble once the word of this is spread." He stopped abruptly, then grasped André's shoulder again, and the pinch of his digging fingers penetrated even the chain-mail shirt beneath André's surcoat. "Do you understand all I have told you?"

"Aye, my lord." André quickly rattled through the instructions he had been given, enumerating them succinctly for the King's benefit, yet thinking all the time that this had come into being very quickly and without warning, and he wondered why that should be so. Lent was long over, and the natural post-Lenten nuptial period of Easter, with all its overtones of rebirth, renewal, and fecundity, had passed without comment, thanks to the Easter storm and the scattering of the fleet. The betrothal might now have been extended indefinitely, without incurring as much as a raised eyebrow, since the urgency of the impending campaign in Outremer now eclipsed everything else and was growing larger with every day that passed. So why, André wondered, was there such an urgency in Richard to perform this wedding now, within the space of a single day? There had been no mention of it the day before, after André's visit to the Princess. Might it be such a sudden imperative, he wondered now, because the King, riding the high wave of victory over this island's tyrant, needed to make the leap in full flight, before his courage failed him completely? He searched for signs of panic or desperation in Richard's demeanor and discovered that he could see evidence of both, and in profusion, although both were muted and strongly held in check.

Richard, unaware of André's scrutiny, was talking again. "Good. Tell my lady it will be splendid. There is a monastery here in Limassol, a Benedictine fraternity, and I am told they sing wondrously well, so we will have music and light—solid banks of the finest white candles—and copious, billowing clouds of fragrant incense. Tell her that, lest she believe she is being cheated of a Queen's nuptials. Make sure she knows otherwise … Music and light and incense to set all the senses reeling … and a nuptial feast to follow, to be sure, oxen and sheep and swine already turning on the spit, and fish and fowl being prepared as we speak—" The King broke off, his face suddenly filled with doubt, and looked back over his shoulder. "At least, I trust they are … I spoke to—" He turned back quickly to André. "So be it. Go and do as I bid you. I have other things to see to and other folk to instruct. Quickly now. There's little time to be lost and none at all for wasting."

Before André could complete his salute, Richard was gone, swinging himself up into the saddle and pulling his mount sharply around, setting spurs to it and surging towards and through the crowds on the beach, scattering them with no regard for their safety as he bore down on them. André went in search of his boat.

This time his arrival at the dromon's side was unexpected, and after his boat captain had hailed the deck, André had to bide his time in silence until someone eventually threw him down a rope ladder, his advent evidently having been deemed insufficiently important to warrant the effort of lowering the heavy access ramp. He had had to stand uneasily in the bobbing boat as his two oarsmen manipulated the small vessel with great skill until one of them managed to hook an oar between two of the hanging ladder's rungs and angle it in to where André could catch it. He grasped the rope sides of the ladder in both hands, then leaned back against the sagging pull of it, looking up the swelling side of the enormous vessel and wondering how he would manage to climb up there in a full suit of mail.

"My thanks," he called back to the senior oarsman. "If I don't drown, I should not be long."

He was dry, at least, when he reached the level of the deck, and consoled himself that only his own men, beneath him, could have seen his undignified scramble to pull himself up the ship's side, but he was angry at having been put in a position where he needed to run the risk of falling into the sea, unobserved by anyone above. A seaman on the deck opened the gate in the ship's side to admit him, and two deck officers turned casually, and insolently, André thought, to inspect him as he strode forward. One of them, the senior of the two, judging by the braid on his tunic, opened his mouth to say something, but André shot up an arm in front of him so that the heel of his hand almost smacked against the fellow's nose.

"Stand at attention when you speak to a King's messenger, you ill-mannered lout," he snarled. "I represent Richard of England here, in person, and bear tidings from him to his betrothed and to his sister Joanna, Queen of Sicily. Would Richard himself be required to suffer your insolence and lack of regard on his arrival? Would he be forced to drag himself aboard your ship by hand?" He ignored the increasing pallor of the hapless officer's skin and pressed himself relentlessly forward into the fellow's face. "Rest assured that I shall inform him of the possibility when I return to him this afternoon. And don't you ever again lose sight of the fact that this is not, and will never be, your ship. It is a King's ship. King Richard's ship." He snapped his head sideways and jabbed a finger towards the second, younger officer. "You! Nitwit! Shut your drooling mouth and turn Sir Richard de Bruce out here this instant. Now!" He roared the last word, cutting short the man's attempt to respond, and the fellow spun on his heel and scampered through a door in the stern wall. André stood staring after him, making no effort to relax his rigid features.

"Sir ... Master Sai—"

"Be silent! You had your opportunity to speak as I approached the ship, and you chose to remain aloof and deliver silent insults instead of assistance or courtesy. Now you will learn how it feels to wear wet rags and heave upon an oar as a common seaman, so do what you can to prepare yourself."

As the officer stood gaping in dismay the door behind him opened and Commodore de Bruce emerged, his glance moving curiously from one of them to the other so that André knew the junior officer had already told him what was happening.

"Master St. Clair," he said, the beginnings of a frown puckering his brow, "I had not expected to see you again."

"Clearly. And neither had your pet ape here. I want this man stripped of his rank and duties now, for laziness and disrespect, crass insolence to a King's messenger, and *lèse majesté*, insult to the King himself." He raised a hand quickly, palm outward, to forestall de Bruce's protest. "Do as I say, Master de Bruce. Do not attempt to sway me or to excuse the man's conduct, I warn you. He is unfit to be an officer of any kind, even a ship's officer, and were he mine to command I would have him flogged and forced to serve in the ranks. So see to it that my wishes in this are carried out. I shall expect to see it done by the time I leave here, which should be within the hour, and I intend to make full report of what has happened to King Richard in person."

"I have no such authority aboard this ship, sir. The ship's commander—"

"Are you not commodore of these dromons, then?"

"Yes, I am, but—"

"No buts, Master de Bruce. Either you command or you do not. Which shall I tell King Richard?"

De Bruce's shoulders slumped slightly. "Very well, then, I shall instruct the captain … But, Sir André, this man is senior lieutenant of this ship."

"Was he, by God? How then are the mighty fallen. Now, if you will, send word to the ladies Berengaria and Joanna that I attend them here with urgent tidings from the King."

De Bruce drew himself erect and bobbed his head. "Of course. At once." He turned an icy glance upon the condemned officer. "You, sir, will wait in my quarters."

As both men left, leaving only the junior officer on deck, extremely subdued and crestfallen, André turned his back and stared out over the distant bow of the ship, aware that the seaman who had held the gate for him was standing rigidly at attention, his eyes on André and his face absolutely without expression. *I wonder what you thought of that,* he asked himself, beginning to wonder if he might have been too hard on the lieutenant, making a point merely to emphasize and simultaneously purge his own anger. The thought barely lasted a moment, however, for he knew he had been right— he recalled the manner in which the fellow had sneered at his appearance the previous day, the first time André had come aboard the ship. There had been no real offense given or taken on that occasion, but the man's attitude of disdainful intolerance had been noticeable and, André now realized, memorable. He put the fellow from his mind just as the door opened at his back and de Bruce re-emerged to tell him that the ladies would receive him at once.

ANDRÉ ST. CLAIR HAD WONDERED from the outset at the suddenness of the King's determined resolve to be wed at once, and he had thought even then, listening to Richard talk of singing monks and massed candles and assembled bishops and archbishops, that the abruptness of it all was likely to be causing enormous inconvenience to everyone involved, from cooks to housekeepers and quarter-masters, nearly all of whom must have been caught as flat-footed as he himself had been by the monarch's impetuous and imperious decision. He was completely unprepared, however, for the storm of furious and impassioned disbelief and protest that his tidings precipi-tated among the women on the dromon. It broke over his head out of a clear blue sky and left him reeling, mouth agape, and beginning to perceive, yet unable to comprehend, the enormity of the crime he had been cajoled into perpetrating upon, and in the eyes of, Richard's women. It mattered not that he was merely the messenger, guiltless of complicity or wrongdoing; someone had to bear the brunt of their collective outrage, and he was the closest and most qualified recipient for their ferocious indignation.

Afterwards he would realize, with gratitude, that the worst of it was brief lived, solely because the women had no time to waste on him once the gravity of their situation began to make itself felt. They were plunged into a frenzy of preparations, and he was quickly forgotten. St. Clair found himself standing in a whirlwind of panic-inspired noise, amid a seething blizzard of women's clothing that seemed to fill the air entirely, and moments after that he had been ejected from the cabin.

Although vaguely dazed, he had acquired the knowledge that he needed most: there would be nine women in the attending group to be collected by de Sablé's barge. The Princess would bring her aged dueña, who had been her nurse from infancy, and two younger ladies of Navarre; Joanna would be accompanied by her own senior companion and servant, Maria, and by three Sicilian women, two of them widowed and the other single, who had been her ladies-in-waiting when she was Queen in her own right.

He made his way towards the exit gate in the side of the ship, noticing only as he arrived there that the access ramp had been swung out and lowered into place, and the sight of it reminded him of the other matter he had set in motion. The same seaman was standing by the gate in the ship's side, and André told him to alert his boat's crew that he would be there soon. He then turned back to where the junior lieutenant stood watching him warily, poised on the balls of his feet.

"Call Sir Richard for me."

"Yes, Sir André." The response was as clipped as any one expected on a parade ground, and the lieutenant spun smartly away to deliver the summons. Sir Richard de Bruce emerged from his quarters moments later and came, stiff faced, straight to André, who nodded brusquely.

"The other fellow, what have you done with him?"

"I have confined him to his cabin, Sir André."

"Not good enough. Strip him to his tunic, put him in chains, and hold him under guard, publicly, over there in that corner, to await the King's verdict. It will do your self-satisfied fool no harm to see the world for a time through the eyes of those less fortunate than he is. He needs to be reminded that, as an undistinguished officer aboard one of the King's ships, he ranks only slightly higher than the ruffians he commands and can ill afford to give offense to anyone, let alone anyone who might be in a position at some time to seek revenge on him. What is his name, by the way?"

"De Blois, Sir André."

St. Clair's eyebrows shot up, but then he smiled. "D'you say so? One of his kinsmen did his best to kill me a little while ago. He failed, of course, but I found him decidedly unpleasant to be around, and now I find it interesting that this fellow is another de Blois. Family traits, Sir Richard ... Family traits."

André left the commodore staring after him and went directly to the gate, which the seaman held open for him. His boat was waiting at the bottom of the ramp, and this time he jumped aboard easily and settled himself in the stern as the rowers swung away from the great ship. And there André learned another lesson about the strangenesses of the maritime fraternity. He asked his boat master, the helmsman, if he had any idea where they might begin to look for the Count of Coutreau, the Deputy Master of the Fleet, and the fellow looked all around the assembled ships, then pointed unhesitatingly to one of the newcomers.

"Over there, sir," he growled, "aboard yon Englishman."

"How can you know that?" André was truly astonished, and the big helmsman grinned and tapped the side of his nose.

"The standard, sir, the high flag yonder at the masthead, higher than all the others, with the three green triangles on the white field and the twin tails. That's the standard of the fleet commander. Goes with him from ship to ship, so the rest of the fleet knows where he is at any time. Green triangles is the deputy, and means the Master himself isn't here. His standard's triangles are blue. Same flag, otherwise."

André was duly impressed. "You tell me so," he said, "but is it always thus?"

"Always, sir. Without fail. Where the Fleet Master goes, his standard goes, and mounts to the top of the mast. It's only good sense, sir, when ye think on it. In time of trouble, or in war, when people look for guidance or command, they look to the masts for the flagship, the one that flies the Master's standard. That's where the Master is, and that's where command is held."

"By Heaven, that is inspired! Who thought of that?"

The helmsman dipped his head, tapping the side of his nose again. "Someone smarter than me, sir ... and a few years older. I don't think there's ever been a time at sea when that wasn't the way of things. Like I said, it's only good sense, isn't it, when you think on it?"

"Aye, you're right, it is." André's face broke into a slow grin. "The same kind of good sense that keeps men away from women when there's marriage in the offing ... Take me to the Fleet Master now, directly."

SEVERAL HIGH-RANKING MEMBERS of the Order of the Temple attended the royal nuptials that evening, to witness the marriage and the new Queen's coronation, and by all reports it was a grand occasion, with massed banks of candles turning the air golden in the chapel while incense billowed. The monks of no fewer than five monasteries combined with those from Christendom to generate chanted prayers the equal of which had never been heard in Cyprus. The large number of bishops in attendance, all of them decked in their finest jeweled robes and attended by their retinues of sumptuously dressed acolytes, turned the scene into a glittering riot of colors and fabrics, and yet the bride and her women, despite the lack of notice they had received, succeeded nonetheless, and in spite of all this churchly splendor, in dazzling the eyes of every layman present, and no doubt those of many a churchman, too.

André and his companions did not even hear the singing of the massed monks. Like almost everyone else in the port of Limassol who was not involved in the actual marriage festivities that day and night, their time was entirely taken up by the arrival of the fleet. They had all had duties apportioned to them hours before the first ships made harbor, and their afternoon and evening fled by in brutal, backbreaking work that lasted well into the darkest hours of the night. They worked alongside others, in gangs or groups, although the Templars formed their own work parties and held themselves apart from everyone else, and each group was assigned to a specific task by the officials responsible for the orderly disposition of the incoming ships and their cargoes.

By the time the initial levies of dockside workers fell into sleep that night, whether they were locally conscripted laborers or arbitrarily assigned soldiers and seamen, they were all worn out and senseless from lack of rest, and tempers had been sorely frayed and blood spilt in more than one dockside tussle. And still the work of disembarkation continued, the various tasks taken over by fresh crews and gangs.

St. Clair rose as usual for morning prayers, but he had had little sleep in the previous thirty-six hours, and so he felt no guilt about finding himself an obscure corner afterwards and curling up to sleep again unseen while his fellows went about their assigned daily chores. He awoke refreshed about an hour before noon to discover that the day had been declared a day of rest and celebration to mark

the King's marriage, and then, attracted by loud voices and the deli-
cious aroma of roasting meat nearby, he made his way to the ship's side
and saw several score of men gathered around a cluster of cooking fires
on the beach close by his ship. A cask of beer had been mounted on a
trestle on the sand, and the sight of it sitting there in the bright sunlight
dried his mouth, so that he felt the lust for the cool taste of it against
the back of his tongue. He went to his quarters, almost empty at this
time of day, took off his mailed hauberk and dressed himself in plain
tunic and leggings for the first time in weeks. Then, glad as a boy to be
without armor, he strode ashore and made his way directly towards the
fires and the celebration going on there. He helped himself to a flagon
of beer, and then someone cut him a slab of meat from one of three
carcasses roasting on spits, and he wedged it between two thick slices
of fresh bread and went looking for a place to sit and eat it in comfort.
He found a log large enough for two people to sit on by one of the fires
and settled down to eat and to listen.

The talk around him was all of the previous night's wedding
feast, and the arrival of the force from Outremer, with its three ships
bearing King Guy and his entourage of highly placed dignitaries and
a hundred and sixty knights. André had little interest in the wedding
talk, knowing he would soon learn more than he needed to know
about it, but the topic of the visitors from Outremer interested him
greatly, for he had seen some of the knights the previous day and
had been impressed by their dour and hard-worn appearance. He
could not begin to imagine why King Guy, the rightful King of
Jerusalem, should leave the country in a time of war, accompanied
by so many battle-ready knights, unless he had been ousted in some
manner that defied understanding, but he learned more about that
situation in the first half hour after his arrival at the cooking fires
than he could have learned in a week in any other place, because the
men around the fires, by sheer good fortune from his viewpoint,
were members of Richard's own guard. As such, they were
inevitably privy to more trustworthy information than were many of
the King's more high-born followers, because the guards were
present around the King's person on all public, formal, and even

semi-private occasions and thus were normally taken for granted, ignored and all but forgotten by the people they were there to watch.

The first thing that sank through to him from all that he was hearing was that Philip of France, on landing at Acre, had chosen to support Conrad of Montferrat over Guy de Lusignan in the matter of their conflicting claims to the crown of the Kingdom of Jerusalem. That really surprised André, for it had been made clear to him by his own brotherhood, months earlier, that Conrad was both cousin and vassal to Barbarossa, the so-called Holy Roman Emperor, and that both of them were adherents of the Eastern Orthodox branch of Christianity. Each had publicly avowed his dedication, years earlier, to reinforcing the Orthodox Church within the Kingdom and the city of Jerusalem, twin affirmations that had been noted with alarm and then condemned by the Roman papacy and had resulted in the frenzied papal support that had fomented the current Frankish campaign to recapture the Holy City. But Philip himself was one of the two leaders of that campaign. Barbarossa was dead now and his army no longer a threat to Rome's ambitions, but if Philip of France was now siding openly with Conrad of Montferrat in opposing the legitimate claim of Guy de Lusignan to the Kingdom of Jerusalem, then the French King was thumbing his nose, deliberately, at the Pope ... which meant, by direct association, that he was including Richard, his nominal partner and coequal, in that defiance. That, André knew, was a major error on Philip's part, for it would force Richard to make a choice, and a commitment, that was likely to benefit no one.

André had little personal sympathy for King Guy's plight, because de Lusignan was no man's idea of a heroic leader, especially when his record was compared with that of Richard. Guy had demonstrated time and again, with depressing repetitiveness, that his inconsistency was limitless and that he was incapable of holding, for any length of time, a position or an opinion that was purely his own and uninfluenced by anyone else's thinking. Despite that, however, and even though his own deplorable behavior had done nothing to strengthen his situation, Guy's claim to his crown was legitimate, albeit decidedly flimsy.

The undisputed claimant to the crown of the Kingdom of Jerusalem, or the Latin Kingdom as most men were now calling it, had been Guy's wife, Sibylla, the sister and sole surviving heir of King Baldwin IV, the Leper King. No one had disputed Sybilla's succession to the throne after the death of her brother's only male heir, a sickly nephew who had not survived childhood, but everyone had been outraged by her choice of a consort. She had chosen her current lover, Guy de Lusignan, to rule with her, and coerced the aged Patriarch of Jerusalem into crowning the fellow not merely as a Prince Consort to the Queen but as the legitimate King in his own right. Her barons, the entire nobility of her realm, were scandalized, for they regarded Guy as an interloper, an adventurer, and a shameless opportunist.

He had arrived in the kingdom sometime earlier, an unknown from France, supposedly well born but with a background that was murky and shaded by rumors, and had succeeded somehow, in spite of that, in ingratiating himself sufficiently with the local barons to persuade them to appoint him as regent in the young heir's minority. His regency had been less than spectacular, and on the sole occasion when he had to make a show of force against the Saracens, at a place called Tubania, he had all but run away from the confrontation. That buffoonery had cost him his regency, although the young heir had died soon afterwards, rendering the annulment moot, but it had also cost Guy all his credibility in the eyes of the barons of the kingdom.

André swallowed a last mouthful of food and wiped the grease from his lips with the back of one hand before drinking deeply and then turning to look at his nearest neighbor, a slight, clean-shaven man with a hooked nose and a hollowed-out face that seemed lacking in lips and teeth. The fellow also had almost excessively broad shoulders, and he had sat down quietly beside André only moments earlier and was now diligently attacking a thick slice of juicy pork. He paid no attention to anyone at first, but when André greeted him he looked across at him and grunted, then stuffed the meat in his mouth into one cheek. André had noticed that he had brought nothing with him to drink.

"Good pig," the fellow said. "Did you have some?" He spoke narrowly, barely opening his mouth, so that his accent—André had no idea which region it sprang from—sounded tight and nasal, but his words were understandable at least, and André was pleased, for the odds of having found, at first try, someone with whom he could converse straightforwardly among this enormous force were greatly less than even. He swallowed a belch and nodded.

"No, I think what I ate was goat, but it was good. When was the day of rest declared? I missed hearing about it until I woke up and caught the smell of roasting meat, about an hour ago."

His neighbor sniffed. "Last night at midnight," he said.

"What about the people unloading the ships?"

"What about them? Somebody has to unload the ships. I worked all afternoon, yest'day, then had to go on watch last night. I saw you out there, too, with one of the Templar crews, didn't I? You one of them?"

André grunted. "Aye, a novice, lowest of the low. Not a Templar yet, but not a common nobody either, so I can't win at anything, anywhere." He hoisted his empty flagon. "I'm going to get more beer. Can I bring you one?"

The man looked about him as though surprised to discover that he had none, and then made to get up. "I'll come with you."

"No, then we'll lose our seats. Stay here and finish your meat."

By the time he returned, his new companion had finished eating and was staring morosely into the fire in front of him. André handed him a flagon of beer and sat back down beside him.

"Interesting that King Guy should turn up here, all the way from where you'd expect him to be, when we're supposed to be on the way to help him. Don't you think?"

"Interesting?" The guardsman shrugged. "No. I mean ... I suppose it is if you care. But who cares? Besides, we're not going over there to help him. We're going over to kick the Saracens out of God's country, aren't we? To take it back for the Church ..." He shook his head. "Can't see much in favor of our helping him, when I think about it ... *if* I thought about it ... He's not much of a king at all, if you ask me. I mean, our boy, Richard, now *there's* a king. Looks like one, dresses like one, and behaves like one. That's what a king's supposed to be ... a fighter. A scrapper, d'you know what I mean? Someone who knows what's his and'll take your head off if you so much as look sideways at it. That's a king. These other characters ... Well, I mean, look at Philip ... Or don't. I'd rather not. Do you look at him and see a king right off? I think not. Oh, we all know he *is* one ... and he talks like one and wears the fine clothes, but he's too prissy. He's too ... I don't know what he is, what the word is, but he's too *something* for my liking. Something that he needs to be but isn't. Certes, he'll have you murdered in your bed or stabbed in a dark alley if you cross 'im, but he'll never stand up and damn you to your face before he rips your head off with his bare hands, like Richard will ... And this King Guy's the same way, from what I've heard."

"What have you heard? What's your name, by the way?"

"Nickon ... Nich'las, really, but Nickon's what I get. What's yours?" André told him and he nodded. "Aye, well, André, from what I've been told, this Guy, this Jerusalem King, looks as though he should be good in a fight, but he doesn't often get to fight, if you know what I mean. Not too many people confident of his leadership ... He's the one caught all the blame for the big battle at Hattin, where your lot and the Hospitallers got slaughtered and we all got kicked out of Jerusalem. They say he lost it all single-handedly, 'cause he didn't know his arse from his elbow and couldn't make up his mind whether to stop and fight or run and hide ... Anyway, one of the nobs he brought with him was talking to the King—our King—day before yest'day, and I was on duty, right there within reach of 'em. Anyway this fellow, some big baron from Jerusalem, he was saying that Guy was the one who set up the siege of Acre, two years ago, and he's been holding Saladin's crew tied up there ever since."

He cocked his head, looking sideways at André. "He was captured and held prisoner by old Saladin himself, did you know that?" André shook his head, pursing his lips, and Nickon nodded solemnly. "Well, he was, for more than a year ... Mind you, being a prisoner and a king probably isn't the same thing as being a prisoner and a plain old sweaty guardsman, because Saladin let him go after that, on condition that Guy promised not to fight against him again. So Guy promised, and he got out, and then he started raising an army right away ... Well, a promise to a godless heathen's no promise at all, is it? 'Specially if it's made under ... you know ..."

"Duress."

"Right. Anyway, it took him a while, but he finally raised an army and sct sicge to Acre ..." Nickon tilted his head, eyeing André from an angle. "You've 'eard about Acre, haven't you? You know what it is?"

"Yes ... and no. I remember hearing something vaguely, but it was a long time ago and I didn't pay much attention. I had no notion at the time that I'd ever be going there. Tell me about it. What's so important about Acre?"

"Well, it's a port, isn't it? One of the places that Saladin overran and swallowed up right after Hattin. The only place he didn't get, right at that time, was Tyre, another port, farther to the north, and he would've had that as well if it hadn't been for Conrad of Montferrat. I'd never heard of him before yest'day, but I've heard a lot about the whoreson since then, I'll tell you. He's a German, some kind of baron or high lord, one of Barbarossa's people, and he turned up in the Holy Land by accident—" He checked himself. "Well, not by accident, not really, but nobody there knew he was coming, and he sailed right into the harbor at Tyre with a fleet of ships full of knights and soldiers on the very day the people in charge was getting ready to surrender the city. Put an end to that, Conrad did, and right quickly, and the upshot was that Saladin withdrew ... Nobody really knows why he withdrew, but he did, straight away. Turned around and marched away down south and captured Acre instead ... And his army's still holding it, even though they've been under siege for two years now, and King Guy's the fellow who started the siege."

André wrinkled his brow. "Wait, now ... I understand all that, but what has it to do with Conrad and Guy being enemies?"

"Nothing, my old lad ... and everything. I can see why you're still a novice. Conrad and Guy are two cats fighting over the same mouse ... The mouse is the Kingdom of Jerusalem, and there's nothing happens in the Holy Land that isn't touched by it. Conrad sailed into Tyre by accident and rescued it. Now he's Marquis of Tyre. Guy sailed into Jerusalem and tupped its Queen—though she wasn't the Queen then, not yet—and now he's the King of Jerusalem. Conrad is envious. The kingdom's bigger than a pissy little port and he wants it for himself. And according to what this nob was saying to the King yest'day, he might get it, one of these days ... See, he's arguing—and there seems to be a lot of people over there who support him—he's saying that Guy was only king there because his wife, this Sibylla, was the rightful queen. Sibylla died last year ... she's gone. Ergo, according to Conrad and those who'd like to see him on the throne, Guy no longer has a claim to the crown."

"But Guy was crowned legally, was he not?"

The guardsman turned and looked at André from beneath raised eyebrows, lifting his arms in appeal. "I don't know. Somebody forgot to invite me to the coronation."

"Aye, well, he was, by the old Patriarch Archbishop of Jerusalem."

Nickon slowly pushed his lips out into a pout that was all the more impressive because he had no lips to speak of, his mouth little more than a horizontal slash. Nonetheless he managed to convey great skepticism, perhaps because of that, and as André began to ask him why, he lifted one hand and shook his head slowly from side to side.

"Ask yourself one question, lad ... Do you really believe Montferrat and his cronies care for a moment about what some doddering bishop might have done five years ago? There is a *kingdom* at stake here, lad. The actions of one bishop, patriarch or not, won't stand up for a single heartbeat against the urgency of that ..." He paused, and then his face broke into a wrinkled grin. "And I can tell you that with certainty, because I heard the Jerusalem baron fellow say the same thing, word for word, to King Richard yest'day, after the King said what you did, about King Guy's coronation …

"See, they don't care about what's legal. All they care about is setting Conrad on the throne and throwing Guy out into the desert. Ever since Conrad first landed in Tyre and heard about what happened at Hattin, he's been working at undermining Guy and taking his place. He's never stopped, not for a moment … When Guy won free from Saladin and went to Tyre, the first thing he did was ask for the keys of the city from Conrad, because he was the King and this was all that remained of his kingdom. Of course, he didn't get them. Conrad accused him of uselessness and cowardice right then and there and told Guy that with the disgraceful defeat at Hattin, he had forfeited the right to call himself King. And then, shortly after that, he turned around and claimed the kingdom for himself and kicked Guy out of the city. He wasn't shy about claiming the crown like that. He'd already gone from nobody to Marquis of Tyre, so the step to kingship couldn't have looked like much of a challenge.

"After that, instead of going away—because the fact was he had nowhere to go—Guy simply stayed outside of Tyre and worked at raising an army beyond the walls, and Conrad did nothing to discourage him … in fact he sent him men because he had more people inside the city than he could feed. Guy eventually gathered about seven hundred men, most of them Templars and many of them from inside Tyre, including the Master of the Temple, de Rid-some-thing-or-other."

"Gerard de Ridefort."

"Yes, him … and that made all the difference, because once Guy had the support of the Templars behind him, others kept drifting in to join him, and soon he had several thousand under arms, all of them eager for a fight, and in the month of August he marched them south and set siege to Acre. A little while after that, fearing to lose the advantage to Guy, Conrad led some of his own people to join the siege. He and Guy managed to cooperate for a while, and to his credit, Guy held his end up really well in the one big clash they had with Saladin's forces outside of the city. But the army soon split up into factions—Guy's people against Conrad's—and that's the way it remained for more than a year ..."

"And? There's more. I can hear it in your voice."

"Aye, there is ... And then King Philip showed up with his half of the army ... He met with both several times, weighed one up against the other, and chose Conrad. That's why King Guy is here. He decided he couldn't wait for Richard to come to him, because Philip's been telling everyone that Richard is more interested in dallying with his friends than in reaching the Holy Land. So Guy left Philip and Conrad in front of Acre and he sailed here with the pick of his best knights, hoping to convince Richard of the need to hurry to Acre and bring Philip to heel."

"And will he, think you?"

"Will he convince the King, you mean?" Nickon twisted his face. "King Richard's advisers might tell you he will ... Personally, I think he already has, because Richard listened very carefully to all he had to say, and when he had finished talking he gifted him with new clothes and armor ... Guy's old clothes were threadbare and his chain mail rusted and falling apart. He also gave him fifteen hundred pounds in silver marks and various other treasures to replace what he had lost ... Now, I've been in attendance on the King for many years, and I've never known him to do a thing like that for someone he doesn't like, or doesn't intend to help."

"Hmm. And based upon that familiarity and experience, what d'you think he'll do now?"

He never did receive an answer, for even as he asked it, one of Nickon's friends came striding urgently towards their fire with word that brought both men to their feet. Isaac Comnenus, he told them, had sent envoys to Richard, suing for peace and a settlement of their differences, and Richard, precipitate as ever, had already agreed to a truce and committed to meet the Emperor outside the gates of Limassol at mid-afternoon. The King would ride out in full panoply, and Nickon and his fellows were recalled to duty immediately, to escort him, dressed in full parade armor. Within moments, Nickon had vanished in the direction of the city gates, and André was alone again, mulling over what they had discussed and trying to decide what to do next. He knew that he did not want to miss the confrontation between his King and Isaac Comnenus, so he went back on board his ship, collected his crossbow against the possibility of finding time to practice later in the day, and set off on foot, his crossbow and quiver dangling from his shoulder, towards the appointed meeting place on a slightly elevated plateau on the flatlands slightly to the west of the city gates.

FIVE

A ndré St. Clair arrived at the chosen venue in time to find himself a good vantage point atop a large, solitary boulder, close enough to the activities to watch both parties approach and to see and hear everything that happened.

Isaac arrived first, in what he must have supposed was full and impressive splendor, riding on a magnificent stallion that made André raise his eyebrows in admiration. But when Richard arrived astride an equally splendid mount, he was so sumptuously bedecked in gold weaponry and jewelry, with magnificently worked garments and priceless accoutrements, that the Cypriot Emperor was stricken dumb by his grandeur and so abashed that he positively groveled in front of the English King.

The proceedings went swiftly. Isaac begged, with great humility, to be forgiven his transgressions. Humbly he offered all the castles in Cyprus for the billeting of Richard's soldiers and promised to contribute knights, mounted archers, and infantry to the Frankish campaign. He offered fifteen thousand pounds of gold in retribution for the moneys he had stolen from the wrecked dromon and offered to surrender his only daughter as hostage to his future good behavior. Richard, still disposed to be magnanimous, for whatever reasons, accepted Isaac's capitulation graciously and then, summoning the captain of his own guard, ordered the immediate return of the magnificent pavilion that he had captured from the Emperor's abandoned camp at Kolossi. The two rulers sealed their truce with the kiss of peace, and Richard returned to his castle in Limassol, while Isaac remained to watch over the erection of his grand pavilion on the spot where they had signed their truce. André left him there and set out for the archery butts, thinking that, for a man whose reputation in such matters was that of an impetuous hothead, Richard had handled the Cypriot Emperor extremely well.

He was intercepted by one of Richard's knights before he could reach the butts, and the young dandy ordered him brusquely to attend upon the King immediately, then wheeled away, leaving André to make his own way to the castle. Stung by the younger man's loutish ill manners, André whistled loudly at his back, and when the fellow turned around, he called him to order, tore a strip from him for his high-handed and offensive attitude, and then demanded to know where the King expected to be met. The answer was, as André had known it would be, that he was to come to the King's quarters, but by the time he heard the answer, he had reached the haughty young knight and was within grasping distance of his ankle. He took a firm grip on the ankle and jerked the knight's foot from the stirrup, then thrust the open palm of his other hand beneath the exposed boot's sole and thrust upward, hard and straight. The knight, caught completely unawares, flew out of the saddle and crashed loudly to the ground, where he lay gasping, unable to catch his wind. Before he could even begin to recover, St. Clair was looming over him, his booted heel pressing gently but firmly into the fallen man's throat, and the point of his bare dagger dangling to trace gently over the man's nose.

"Now, sir," André murmured, his words quiet but clearly audible. "It is painfully clear that someone needs to talk to you about good manners, comportment, and a proper show of modesty and forbearance. You are a young and foolish knight, who looks at a man like me, dressed as I am in simple tunic and leggings, and sees nothing admirable, nothing noteworthy, nothing to indicate that I might be worth cultivating, or even slightly worthy of respect." The point of the dagger rapped gently but smartly against the bridge of his nose. "That, sir, is because you are a fool with much to learn, and evidently little in your head with which to absorb any of it." André inserted the point of his blade into a nostril and tugged gently upward, raising the fallen man's entire body by the nose. "Listen closely, now, Sir Ignorance, to what I tell you. I, too, am a knight, of longer duration, more experience, and probably higher status than you. That makes you even more of a fool, for not being able to see that without requiring to have it pointed out to you. My name is André St. Clair. Remember it. And I am an Angevin from Poitou, vassal and liege to King Richard, who knighted me in person, five years ago. So, if my lord should ever summon me again, and send you to find me, you make sure you approach me with proper respect, lest I turn you into a hunchback by the simple means of kicking your ill-mannered arse up into the space between your shoulders. Do you understand me, my pretty?" He pulled the knife point harder against the nostril. "Do you?"

It was clear that the fellow wanted to nod eagerly, but could not have done so without cutting his own nose, and so André held him there for a few more moments before stepping away to allow him to struggle to his feet.

"Are you aware that I have not asked for your name?" he asked. "That is because I have no interest in knowing it. But it also leaves you with the knowledge that I will not speak about this afterwards. Be satisfied with that, and do not even think about evening the score on this. Do I make myself clear? For if you do, so help me God, I will cause you great grief. Now go back to the King and tell him I have to dress, but will be in his quarters within the hour. Go!"

"WHAT DID YOU DO to young Dorville?"

More than an hour had passed since his arrival in the King's quarters, and from the occasional veiled reference that Richard had made but not pursued, André had suspected this question might be coming in one form or another, and so he was able to keep his face innocent and empty of expression. "Dorville, my lord? I know no one called Dorville. Should I?"

"You know damn well who I'm talking about. The knight I sent to summon you."

"Ah, that fellow. I merely gave him a small lesson in humility, my lord. It should not go to waste."

"Humility. Dorville. How did you do that? And don't even think to lie to me. I want the truth."

"I simply pointed out to him that I believed I deserved more respect than he was showing me, my lord."

"And where exactly was he while you were pointing this out to him?"

"He was on his back, sir, at my feet. His Adam's apple was beneath my heel."

"What did you enjoy most about doing that to him?"

"The expression on his face when he realized where he was, my lord."

"Hmm. And what did you like least about him?"

"His smell, sir. It was too ... sweet, too womanly."

"I shall have him change it. I will enjoy doing that, too. You realize he is not one of us?"

André frowned. "Not one of us? I don't understand."

"No reason why you should, but he is one of Philip's men, born and bred in the Vexin, during my father's occupation of it. I believe he detested my father, the old lion, even more than I did. Anyway, he was left here with us, when Philip flounced away, to act as messenger and liaison between France and us should the need arise. He is supercilious, tends to be overly ... critical. Seems to believe that everything we do and everything we have is not quite to the standards that he would impose, given the opportunity. But then he is very young. I find him occasionally hard to stomach, but he is pleasant to behold. Now, I need you to take the ladies hunting in the morning."

André stood motionless, caught off balance by what he had heard and rendered incapable of responding, but then he found his voice and his mind started working again and he shook his head. "No, my lord, forgive me but I may not do that ... I am forbidden, as a novice of the Order, to consort with women. It is expressly forbidden, one of the strictest requirements of the Order. Failure to observe that would disqualify me for acceptance."

"Aye, it might. But would that really trouble you? I have work enough to keep you employed on my behalf forever, if you but say the word."

"No, my lord, that cannot be ... although I realize that even saying such a thing is unforgivable. But I cannot, in honor, withdraw from my situation now. I am already committed, not yet under oath but clearly understood to be within an inch of committing fully. Besides, I cannot understand your objections now. It was your idea that I should join the Order."

"Aye, it was. But that was before I'd had the choice to think things through—and those damned priests were yet alive. Everything has changed since then, and now I need you."

André began to shake his head, but Richard held up an imperious hand. "Enough, say no more now. I was but jesting, although not completely so. Perhaps half jesting. And perhaps testing ... Take some time and think this matter through thoroughly. You yet have time before anyone expects you to take formal vows, and that means you have time to change your mind for good and sufficient reason. In the meantime, I still need you to take the women hunting in the morning. I can arrange a special dispensation for you, through the Master of the Temple in Poitou, the man de Troyes, and I will. You have no choice in this, André. It is not a request, it is a command. I can't take much more of this, being surrounded constantly by women ... it will make me mad. Joanna has decided that she wishes to go hunting and I know my sister. She will not stop harping on it now until she has her way, but I want her to go hunting, and to take my lady wife Berengaria with her. She hunts well, I'm told—rides like a man and kills like a fox, as does Joanna. You will enjoy them, I believe, once you overcome your monkish reluctance, but that is the way it has to be ...

"I offered to send my guards with the two of them, but Joanna would hear none of it. She wants someone she can converse with, someone with sufficient brains, as she put it, to walk and talk at the same time without tripping over his foreskin. The main thing is, she wants no guards at all. She simply wants to hunt—no pomp, no panoply, and no visible presence. She will dress as a huntsman, as she always does, and no one seeing her from more than ten paces' distance will ever suspect she is a woman. Berengaria will do the same, apparently. She has her own hunting armor, Joanna tells me. Joanna says, and I agree, that they have no need of any massive escort. But at the same time, Berengaria is my wife, the Queen of England, so I cannot allow her to go off into the countryside unattended, at the utter mercy of the gods. There must be someone with her, someone trustworthy and responsible, in case they encounter an emergency or have an accident." He shrugged. "So you became my natural choice as custodian of my bride."

André spread his hands in protest. "But why me, my lord? There must be—"

"Joanna asked for you by name, André, so there's an end of it. You obviously impressed her greatly."

"Impossible, sir. I was with her and the lady Berengaria for less than an hour."

The King smiled slightly, his eyes crinkling. "That, my young friend, is far more than enough time for women to weave plots and make plans. I shall inform my sister that you will await her at the stables at dawn. You will be there, will you not?"

"Of course I will, my lord, if you insist."

"Excellent, I do insist. And you will dine with us tonight. It is time you met King Guy, anyway, and came to know some of his knights. You will enjoy them. They are our kind of people, André, honorable, straightforward, unafraid to speak their minds. Besides, your father will be at table tonight. I sent him to Famagusta a few days ago, at the head of an armed sweep, and he returned this afternoon. He'll be looking to see you, as you will be him, so you will enjoy the evening. I'll see you at table."

RICHARD MAY HAVE SEEN André at table that evening, André had no way of knowing, but the two of them certainly did not speak. There was too much noise to converse without shouting anyway, and too many new people to meet. André liked almost all of the Latin knights that he met, and he asked if any of them had knowledge or recent tidings of his kinsman Sir Alexander Sinclair of the Templars. Three of them remembered Alex more or less clearly, although none of those could recollect having seen him after the Battle of Hattin. André swallowed his disappointment and continued asking questions, not about Alex Sinclair now but about anything he could think of having to do with Saladin and the Saracens and their ways of waging war. He ate well, this being the King's table, but he drank sparingly because he did not want to miss a word of what was going on around him. He found himself fascinated by these men and with what they had to say in response to his questions, because they were all veterans of the desert wars and every man of them had fought the enemy face to face.

He went looking for his father later, at that stage of the evening when the amount drunk began to dictate the volume and intensity of the arguments, debates, and outright quarrels that were taking place everywhere, but Sir Henry was nowhere to be found, and André guessed that he had simply slipped away to his own quarters, satisfied that both his presence and his absence would go unremarked at this time of the night. Despite his profession of Master-at-Arms, Sir Henry had always been decidedly fastidious and generally avoided exposing himself to occasions like these, where there was always a danger of being felled by an unexpected blow from some overheated drunkard.

Now, sober and looking around him detachedly, André decided that his father was a clever man and his example was worth following. Besides, he reminded himself, he had to be up early, to take the two Queens hunting, although he thought he would rather have stuck thorns in his eyes than be committed to that. He knew, without thinking about it, that the activity would bring him grief from his fellows, no matter how loud or public the dispensation from Etienne de Troyes might be. Women, he was learning quickly, were anathema to the Temple. Even the brief association he had had with Queen Joanna and Queen Berengaria, mere conversation and initiated at the King's personal insistence, had been noted and unfavorably viewed. Tomorrow's outing would not go unnoticed either, he knew, but he had no choice. He walked away from all the revelry just as two knights were beginning to circle each other with drawn blades in a hastily cleared space on the floor.

It was a fine night, and by the time he walked out through the city's gates towards the harbor, he had left the sounds from the dining hall far behind him. But then there were other loud voices being raised ahead of him, and he heard the clash of steel on steel again, more urgent than the sounds he had left behind in the hall. The knights in the hall had been fighting for sport, in an arranged bout, else they could not have drawn steel in the King's presence. These men ahead of him had no such restraints, and in all probability they neither knew nor cared where the King might be. He could tell from the noise of the curses being thrown around that blood would be spilled quickly and perhaps copiously. He knew, too, that the fighters would be men-at-arms and that if he went closer to them he would be bound, as an officer and a knight, to intervene. And at this time of night, to confront unknown, angry, and drunken foot soldiers and try to face them down would be madness. No one but a total fool would expose himself to such a risk; an unknown, unaccompanied officer alone in the dark could be an irresistible target to an angry, disenchanted ruffian.

He stopped and stood listening, peering into the darkness ahead of him. He was close enough to hear what was happening but too far away to see or be seen. He hesitated a moment longer, then made up his mind and walked away from the sounds of the brawl, and mere moments later he realized that he was walking towards the small plateau where Richard and Isaac Comnenus had met earlier that day. As he recognized the place, the towering shape of Isaac's imperial pavilion came into view, ringed about and illuminated by the flickering torches of Richard's guard, who had been assigned to ensure the comfort and security of their former foe.

Knowing he would surely be challenged if he continued on his present route, he turned again to head back towards the beach, the noise of the brawl now faint, off to his left and moving away from him. A full moon emerged then from behind a cloud, and its light flooded the entire plain, making it almost as clear as day, so that he could see the forest of masts in the harbor ahead of him, outlined against the sky. Something stirred at the edge of his vision, in the direction of Isaac's pavilion, and he glanced that way but saw nothing. Intrigued then, because he knew something there had attracted his attention, he stopped and stood watching for a while, one upraised foot propped on a knee-high boulder, bent knee serving as a brace for his elbow, to see if whatever it had been would move again. It did not, and as he stood there, hunched forward and motionless, one of Richard's guardsmen came marching on his rounds. The man passed solemnly on his way without even a slight pause to check for irregularity, and soon disappeared from view behind a fold in the terrain.

And then, in the instant before André straightened up to resume his walk, a figure darted out from the shadows of a pile of rocks and began to move quickly but furtively straight towards André. Whoever the man was, he was almost scuttling, crouched over and flitting from one patch of shadow to the next and turning to peer back over his shoulder every few steps. André did not move. He remained bent over, watching the running man and wondering what he was witnessing, aware that if he straightened up and the runner saw him, he would have to give chase and might lose the fellow. But who could he be, and what was he doing?

Clearly, he had come from Isaac Comnenus's pavilion, and equally clearly, he was doing everything in his power to avoid being seen by the King's Guard. The running man must be one of Isaac's Cypriots, André reasoned, for no one in Richard's army would have dared to risk offending the King by doing something foolish to the Cypriot Emperor. But then again, what if one of Richard's own men, perceiving Isaac to be a greater threat than he really was, *had* thought to dispose of him? It was not such an outlandish thought. The selfsame thing had happened to Richard in the marketplace in Sicily. Isaac Comnenus, André now realized, might already be lying dead in his pavilion, murdered by the man who was now running directly towards him, completely unaware that he was there.

The moon had gone behind a cloud again and the night now appeared to be darker than it had been before. André straightened up and moved quickly forward to intercept the man, and as he did so he heard a startled intake of breath, followed by the quick slither of steel from a scabbard and then the whistling hiss of a hard-swung sword blade. He had no time to draw his own weapon and only his own reflexes saved his life. He dropped down, tucking himself into a forward roll, diving beneath the slashing blade and bowling his adversary over, sweeping the legs from beneath him. He spun on his shoulders as he felt the other man go flying and thrust himself up and onto his feet, drawing his dagger as he rose.

The other man had landed well and had not lost his grip on his weapon, and he was already surging back to his feet again, one arm straight-braced against the ground and the other, his sword arm, extended for balance. André made to lunge forward, meaning to kick away the bracing arm and knock the fellow down again, but the other man was catlike, fast and strong, and he brought his weapon in and down again in a scything blow that would have cut through anything it met. Fortunately, André had seen the danger and changed direction, springing backward instead of forward, and the tip of the blade swept by his right knee, missing it by a hand's breadth. He threw himself forward again, flipping the dagger to his left hand and leaping as soon as his left heel touched the ground, lunging straight armed at the other man's neck, then sweeping his right leg forward and around to kick the swordsman's legs away. He almost succeeded, but the other man was already springing back and away. André's foot caught him on the ankle and sent him staggering, and by the time he regained his balance, André had his own sword in his hand.

The sounds of their blades clashing brought the guards running from the pavilion, and the sight of them coming spurred the runner to greater efforts. He loosed a flurry of blows that André was hard pressed to withstand, and then he stepped in and slammed a shoulder into André's chest, sending him staggering, so that he fell on his back, the sword jarred from his hand. Casting a swift glance towards the running guards to make sure they were still far enough away, the other man reversed his grip upon his sword, holding it two-handed above his head and pointing downward like a spear, preparing to stab it down into André's breast, chain mail and all. But as he reached the height of his extension and hesitated as he aimed the blow, the iron hilt of André's dagger, thrown from the ground with all St. Clair's strength, struck him in the throat, crushing his Adam's apple and dropping him like a pole-axed ox.

Moments later, three running guards arrived and crouched, weapons drawn, around the two supine men, and when André tried to rise, one of them stepped forward and held a sword point to his neck. André subsided and raised his hands.

"I have no weapons. My name is St. Clair. Sir André St. Clair of Poitou, vassal to King Richard. You have a sergeant among you called Nickon. He knows me. Is he on duty with you tonight?"

"Aye," one of the men growled, glaring truculently. "What of it?"

"Take me to him. But first, let me look at this fellow." He rose slowly to his feet and the guards came closer, keeping their weapons ready. André leaned over the fallen runner, reaching to search for a pulse beneath the jawbone. He found one, and it seemed strong and steady, but then the moon came out again and he saw the face of the man who had tried to kill him and might possibly have killed Isaac Comnenus. More puzzled than ever, André rose to his feet and waved the guards' threatening sword wearily away.

"Come," he said. "I need to talk with Nickon, at once. One of you may hold a weapon on me if you feel a need to ensure I won't try to escape, but I want the other two to keep close watch on this fellow. I suspect him of murdering the Cyprus Emperor, the one you are supposed to be guarding. I watched him pass through your patrols as though you were not there, and he came from the pavilion. So until we know what he was doing there, keep him here, on the ground and under guard. And if he tries to leave, tie him down. Now, one of you take me to Nickon."

They found Nickon surrounded by his fellow guards, in hot debate, and André was mildly suprised to note that Nickon, whom he had taken to be just another guardsman, evidently ranked higher and had more authority than his fellows, all of whom clearly looked to him for guidance in whatever was at stake here. St. Clair interrupted their wrangling and tugged Nickon aside, then launched into what he suspected his prisoner might have done. But the angry incredulity on the guardsman's face quickly leached the certainty from his suspicions and he stopped speaking, almost in mid-word.

"Isaac's not dead," the guardsman said. "He's gone, with all his people, on horseback, headed for the mountains at full gallop. Ran over two of my guards on the way out and killed one of them, one of my very best. My lads were looking to their front, never expecting to be struck down from behind ... especially not by the people they were guarding. I don't know what's going on, but that whoreson Cypriot will choke to death on his own bile if I ever set eyes on him again."

André pointed back over his shoulder with his thumb. "I have a prisoner back there, a French knight. I caught him running from your guards, from this pavilion. Two of your men are holding him now and I want you to keep him close and take him directly to the King. I know who he is, but that will do us no good if he escapes. He would vanish into the mountains just as quickly and as easily as Isaac has and we might never catch him again. Whatever is going on here, this man holds a key to it, so Richard will want to question him. In the meantime, have you searched the pavilion? Are you sure Isaac is gone?"

Nickon grunted, a sound of sheer disgust. "Aye, I'm sure. We haven't had time to do a thorough search, for the whoresons only ran a few minutes before you showed up here, but I sent men inside to check as soon as that happened. There's no bodies in there, no blood, but I don't know what else is there or what they might have left behind. All I know is, they've gone, and from the speed at which they left, they won't be coming back. You say this knight you captured is French?"

"Aye, one of Philip's men, left here as liaison with Richard."

"Then we had best drag his arse in to Richard as quickly as we can and leave it to the torturers to find out what he was doing." Nickon turned to one of his subordinates and started snapping orders to assemble his men, leaving only four behind to protect the magnificently ornate pavilion, which Richard would be glad to reclaim, against looters.

Richard was furious. He listened in perplexity as André recounted how he had seen and then intercepted the French knight, and his eyebrows rose high when André described how Dorville had tried to kill him. Only then did the King have the Frenchman brought before him under guard, and André sensed, as he watched and listened from a position in a rear corner of the audience chamber, that the King was reluctant to believe ill of the fellow. As his questioning of the French knight progressed, however, it was plain that the monarch's patience, notoriously short lived at the best of times, was being notably tested by the French knight's truculence and disdain.

Eventually Richard lost all patience. "God's balls, do you take me for a fool, sir?" he roared, after one sneering answer to a straightforward question. "D'you think to laugh at me? Well, by the joyousness of Jesus you'll find that I mislike being laughed at by prancing fops." He snapped his fingers at the guard captain in attendance. "Take this man belowground and find out the answers to the questions I have been asking him. See if red-hot iron will loosen his tongue more quickly than civil questions can."

Dorville did not last long before he changed his attitude. One encounter with a heated poker laid against his shoulder was all it took to dispel his hauteur, and the mere threat of facial disfigurement with the same poker loosened his tongue completely. To his credit it could be said, as Richard himself pointed out to André later, that he believed he had been successful in his activities and that his efforts could not be undone, and so, sensibly enough, he saw no tangible benefits in suffering disfigurement or mutilation after the fact. Accordingly, once he had gathered himself together and succeeded in pulling the tattered shreds of his dignity about him, he was completely open about what he had done, even evincing pride in his accomplishment.

He had gone to Isaac under cover of darkness, he now confessed, and told him that Richard had played him false and intended to return that night while the Emperor's followers were sleeping and arrest them all before clapping Isaac into chains. In doing so, he had played deliberately upon Isaac's well-known terror of being chained up, knowing that the Emperor would hear only the word *chains* and would lose sight of everything else in his scramble to escape.

Dorville claimed to have acted purely upon his own initiative. His sole intent was to assist his master, King Philip Augustus, to achieve his own designs in Outremer with Conrad of Montferrat. By involving Richard in an ongoing and time-consuming fight here on Cyprus and thereby postponing the departure of the English fleet, Dorville had thought to provide additional time to advance Philip's purposes. He had acted without accomplices, he said, and he was emphatic about King Philip's having no knowledge of what he had planned.

Richard listened to all of this with one hand propping up his chin, his elbow resting on the arm of his chair, and when Dorville finished speaking he remained there, thinking about what the French knight had told him. Finally he straightened up and looked at the prisoner from beneath lowered brows, his chin now on his breast.

"So," he growled at last, his voice pitched ominously low, "you have repaid my hospitality with double dealings on behalf of your own master ... and you have thrown me into a war I did not seek. So be it, then. You will spend this war in the chains you used to frighten Comnenus. A double set of chains, I think, as a reward for your courtesy and a symbol of my gratitude." He lifted his chin, narrowing his eyes as he watched Dorville's reaction. "You believe I am making sport of you, do you not, with this talk of gratitude? I am not. Were I not grateful, you would be on your way to your execution right now. As it is, I have decided to be lenient and permit you to live a while longer." His face broke into a tiny smile. "You have given me a perfect reason to impound the Jew's stallion. He's far too unsightly to own such a magnificent creature, and I have been lusting after it since first I saw it."

"My lord?" One of the men standing close to Richard spoke up, and his voice was high and querulous.

Richard glanced at him. "What is it, Malbecque?"

"My lord, Isaac Comnenus is not a Jew. He is Byzantine."

Richard's face began to redden angrily. "Not a *Jew*? Isaac is not a Jew? Are you mad, my lord Malbecque? Of course he is a Jew. Have you ever met an Isaac who was not? Shame on you for even suggesting such a thing. Of course he is a Jew. I knew that the first time I set eyes upon him. He has Jew written all over him, from the hooked nose to the curly, wiry hair. But that is neither here nor there. He was a usurper when he came here, seizing the throne, and now I am taking it from him. The land is fertile and will feed our armies well. And the taxes Isaac formerly collected will go to assist our great endeavor, while the island itself will be a perfect launching base for our incursions into Outremer.

"There is the source of my gratitude and mercy, Master Dorville, for you have dropped all these riches into my hands when I could not lawfully have achieved them by any other means. So dwell upon that in your imprisonment. Think upon all you have provided for me and my armies, enabling us to thwart and confound your master more completely than before." He snapped his fingers. "Take him away and keep him far from my sight. And remember, manacles and leg irons, two sets of each. Go."

As the prisoner and his escort marched out, Richard called for a council of war with all his advisers and dispatched Sir Henry, as Master-at-Arms, to send runners to summon them to attend upon him immediately. He then turned to talk with some of the other notables around him, and André took the opportunity to slip away quietly. Richard appeared to be deep in conversation with one of the senior English barons, and André brought himself to attention, bowed deeply towards the monarch, and spun on his heel to march out. He took less than three steps before stopping abruptly as Richard called his name.

"My lord?"

Richard came right up to him and laid one hand on his shoulder, then leaned forward to whisper confidentially, "I heard that it is likely to rain heavily tomorrow morning. One of my huntsmen says so and I have seldom known him to be wrong in such things. You had best take a wagon and tents with you."

"My lord?" André could hardly believe what he had heard. "Are you saying I should proceed with the hunting expedition, after this, when we are in a state of war?"

"Of course I am. What else would you have me do? I doubt we will be fighting pitched battles tomorrow morning in the woods where you'll be hunting. Isaac has no army, let me remind you, and my guess is that he'll run for Nicosia, although he might go due east and hope to find some of his ships in Famagusta. I'll dispatch a squadron of galleys there in the morning and they'll be waiting for him if he arrives. Either way, he will pose no risk to you or to your charges … Which reminds me that I hold his daughter here, as hostage, at Isaac's own insistence. I shall have to think about what to do with her …" He thought about it for the space of four of five heartbeats, than dismissed it with an impatient flick.

"No matter. In the meantime, be sure you take tents with you and a wagon to carry them, along with anything else you might need, including extra men, servants, in the event you have to spend more time out there than anticipated. If it does rain heavily, and the women become soaked, they could make your life more than simply miserable. Dry them off, keep them warm, make them comfortable, feed them well …" The pause that came then seemed ominously long, but then he added, "And keep them out there for as long as you can."

André's stomach lurched, for he could smell trouble coming towards him as the King continued. "You will earn my gratitude for every additional hour you can win me. Oh, and I have discussed it with the Deputy Master, de Troyes. He understands my situation here, and since you are not yet sworn a brother of the Order, he has acceded to my wishes in this matter, so you may go in good conscience. Here comes your father again, so I will release you now. He and I have much to discuss before the others arrive, and this could end up being a long session. Think yourself well out of it. Fare thee well." He clapped André on the shoulder and sent him on his way, and father and son exchanged smiles and greetings in passing.

Moments later, André was alone again and growing ever more despondent as he attempted to analyze the welter of misgivings that was plaguing him, the first and most troubling of them stemming directly from the conflicting loyalties of his obligations to the King and to the Order of Sion. He had no difficulty at all concerning the Order of the Temple, for membership in that organization was merely a protective coat he would wear to make it easier for him to do what he must do on behalf of the Order of Sion. But he yet felt guilty over Richard, his liege lord, who could be permitted to suspect nothing, ever, about André's true loyalties.

And then, he reflected, there was the matter of the King's women, which, he had begun to think in recent days, filled him up inside with hollow, reverberating emptiness and stirrings of temptation and anticipation. He felt no real guilt over that, but somehow he believed that he *ought* to, because he found both women attractive, in their different ways, and something inside him was warning him sibilantly about violations of trust.

And yet whose trust would he be violating if, in fact, he went any farther in pursuit of the urgings, to this point mainly formless and unfocused, that had recently been swimming lazily at the deepest reaches of his mind? Were he to indulge his attraction to the Princess, now Queen, Berengaria, whose trust would he betray? Surely not Richard's. He doubted that King Richard would care much, if at all. And would his admiration be a betrayal of trust to Berengaria, rebuffed and barely tolerated by an unnatural husband, and sneered at by the rest of the world? He had heard before he met her that she was less than beautiful, and he was prepared to admit, upon recollection, that when first he saw her he had thought that judgment accurate. But then, with astonishing speed, he had become aware of certain things about her—her smile, and the smoothness of her skin, and the absolute absence of flaws in her face—and he could not recall when she had changed within his mind to being beautiful, although it had all taken place in a matter of hours, not even days.

The same held true for Queen Joanna. He could find no betrayal of trust in the thought of holding her willingly within the circle of his arm, clothed or unclothed. This woman was a widow and a Queen, perhaps a little past her prime at thirty, he would have said days earlier, from what he understood of women, but certainly not yet old, and accountable to no man for her actions.

He suddenly realized he had become aroused by what he was allowing himself to think, and he straightened his back and squared his shoulders, shaking his head from side to side as though to repel his thoughts the way a dog will shake water from its coat. He was to be a Templar knight, and no matter how little import he might place on that distinction, there were considerations to be taken into account that he could not ignore. His honor was involved. If he were to become a Templar, then he would be required to take the vows. Two of these were variants of vows he had already taken when he joined the Order of Sion: the vow of total obedience to his Master and superiors, and the vow to hold no worldly goods in person, but to share all in common with his brethren in the Order. Only the third vow would be completely new to him, but that, a vow of chastity, was the one that caused him most concern. Left to his own choices, he would never have considered taking such a vow. But if he were forced to take the vow, then he would live by it, and that thought rendered his idle speculation over the King's ladies unthinkable. Then, striving determinedly to empty his mind of all such thoughts, he struck out towards the harbor and his billet aboard ship.

SIX

The morning dawned gray and heavy with solid clouds that filled the sky from horizon to horizon, but the two Queens were at the stables by the appointed hour, escorted only by a single huntsman apiece, and as Richard had promised, both were dressed appropriately for the day ahead and practically indistinguishable from the men surrounding them. They behaved as the men did, too, at that hour of the morning, moving in silence and without expression, guarding themselves against intrusion until they had fully banished the fuzziness of sleep and adjusted to the coming of the new day.

André watched them sourly as they moved about, each checking her own saddle gear and neither one making eye contact with him, and in spite of himself he found himself grudgingly admiring their absorption in their tasks and the competence with which they checked buckles and bindings, saddlery and stirrup leathers. Even Berengaria's unmistakably feminine lushness was invisible this morning, banished with all the normal trappings of femininity and flirtation, the frills and flounces, veils and draped gowns that they wore when they were being mere women. This morning both were unmistakably aristocrats, their fathers' daughters, imperious and self-confident, born to the hunt and entirely comfortable in heavily shod, knee-high boots, leather breeches and tunics, and plain, dull riding cloaks of thick, waxed wool that covered them completely. Each carried a quiver of arrows, with a short, heavy hunting bow slung crosswise over her cloaked shoulders, and was accompanied by a huntsman whose job it was to carry her spears and extra weapons, but neither woman appeared to be paying a whit of attention to the silent attendants.

The four-wheeled wagon that André had requisitioned the night before, on the King's instructions, stood in the roadway outside the stables, harnessed to a pair of sturdy workhorses. Covered by an arched canopy of finely tanned leather stretched tautly over hoops set into the wagon's sides, its bed was piled with tightly rolled tents made from leather and heavy, layered cloth, and with bulky bundles that André had not yet examined, although he presumed that many of them were the extra blankets he had ordered. There were several chests in the wagon, too, and although he knew nothing of what those might contain, he guessed they might hold personal posses- sions of the women, brought along in case of need. The wagon was manned by three of Joanna's household staff, the senior of them her steward of many years, a lugubrious Sicilian known only as Ianni, and André somehow felt that it would have been Ianni who thought to bring along the chests. A second, larger wagon, this one with a team of four horses, stood beside it and was manned by a crew of butchers under the supervision of a senior cook. This vehicle and its crew would deal with whatever the hunt produced, cleaning, skin- ning, and butchering the meat, and even cooking some of it should the need arise to feed the assembly.

The hunting party would ride initially only as far as the entrance to the stretch of forest that was fenced and reserved for Isaac's personal use, a distance of something less than three miles. Beyond that point they might either ride or walk, depending upon conditions and the prey available for hunting, which could range from small game like hares and roe deer to larger deer, wild boar, and even bear. André walked to where Sylvester, the master huntsman, stood alone making his final preparatory assessments, running his eyes over the entire party, one at a time and missing no single detail of the check- list that he carried engraved upon his memory after many years of supervising parties like this one.

"Ready?" André asked, and the huntsman nodded, feeling no need to speak. André nodded back. "So be it. Let's move them out. Will it rain heavily, think you?"

Sylvester started walking towards the wide stable doorway, and

André went with him, thinking that the man's reputation for being taciturn was well deserved, but when they reached the open doorway Sylvester braced one hand against the wall on one side and leaned forward, looking up at the lead-gray skies.

"Trouble with clouds like this," he said in a low voice, "is that you can't always tell what they're going to do. It's solid cover, so there's not much chance of the sun breaking through ... not before noon, at least. But it's high, too, so there's no danger of getting rained on within the hour, either. It will all depend on what the wind gods do. If they decide to blow the right way, we could hunt all afternoon in sunshine. If they blow the other way, we could all drown trying to reach home again." He glanced at André. "Your guess is as good as mine. But it's your hunt."

André grunted, glancing back over his shoulder to make sure no one had come up behind them to listen to what they were saying. "Well, there was never any option of not going. The King was adamant about wanting the ladies out from beneath his feet today, so let's get them started."

"Master St. Clair, do you intend to cancel our outing today?" The voice was Joanna's and it rang out clearly from the depths of the stables, cool and imperious. André turned smoothly, forcing himself to smile widely as he did so.

"No, my lady, I was merely checking the weather with Master Sylvester. We are all ready, and the weather is in God's hands as it should be, so mount up, if you please, and let's be about it." Moments later they clattered out onto the cobbled surface of the road leading to the city gates, the main party of Joanna, Berengaria, and their two huntsmen, accompanied by André and Sylvester. Behind them, and present more for the sake of protocol and appearances than for any need of protection, rode their military escort, a twelve-man squad of armored pikemen led by a sergeant and a standard-bearer carrying Richard's personal lion rampant banner. And following those, bringing up the rear, came the two wagons with their attendant crews of butchers and laborers. André's eyes darted about incessantly, searching for signs of military activity as they moved along from the stables towards the gates, but although he saw soldiers busying themselves here and there, he sensed none of the anticipation that would indicate large-scale preparations for war or even for battle, and he quickly decided that if any major developments were in the offing, they would not take place until later in the day. He stopped watching for alarums and turned his attention to the business in hand.

By mid-morning the hunt was well under way, and André had been impressed by the hunting prowess of both women. While stalking the woods mere minutes after starting the hunt and gliding slowly and silently through the misty, dew-wet stillness of a coppice of trees, Joanna had suddenly frozen, waving her companions to silence with a flick of her wrist. André, crouched behind her on her right, had turned his head gently to look at Sylvester, who had frozen in mid-step and was now looking at him, the expression on his face showing clearly that he had no idea what Joanna had sensed or found. But almost in that same instant, and in utter silence, a magnificent stag had surged to its feet from the low clump of bushes in which it had been browsing and stood listening, its head cocked towards the north, away from the hunters, and its body poised for flight. They were slightly behind and to one side of the animal, fewer than forty paces separating it from Joanna in the lead. André began to hear the beat of his own heart as he fought to keep still, and then he felt a tickle in his nostril, the earliest beginnings of an urge to sneeze.

Joanna, he now realized, had been advancing with an arrow nocked into the bow in her left hand, holding the shaft in place with her index finger, and now, with infinite slowness and patience, she began to raise the bow to the firing position. It seemed to take forever, and the stag stood where he was, looking away from her in three-quarters profile, his nose raised, sniffing at the air for anything resembling danger. André glanced at Sylvester again and noticed that the huntsman was frowning slightly and looking downward, towards Joanna's feet. He swiveled his own eyes to see what the other man was looking at and realized that Joanna, too, had stopped in mid-step. She had the bow up by now, but she was off balance, her right foot where her left should be, so that she could exert no pull on the bowstring. But even as he realized that she could not make the shot, Joanna achieved what he would have said at that moment was impossible: she straightened smoothly and stepped forward onto her left foot, pushing against the straining bow stave with her straight left arm and pulling the string smoothly back to touch her cheek. The stag flinched and began to leap away from the sound that it had heard, but the arrow was already flying true. It smacked solidly into the beast's chest behind the point of the shoulder and burst its heart, dropping the creature where it stood. André could not even gather himself to congratulate Joanna on what she had done. He simply stood there, staring at her, open mouthed, and she returned his look with one of her own, raising her eyebrows quizzically as though to say, "There, you see?"

An hour or so later, he witnessed another demonstration of the same kind of virtuosity, this time from Berengaria, when a large hare broke cover unexpectedly. They had not known it was there, for they had been tracking a boar at the time, but suddenly there was the hare, bounding on its powerful hind legs and leaping nimbly from side to side as it raced for safety across the far side of the clearing they had entered. The Princess had been the first to see it and she spun easily to follow it, bow already fully drawn as she led it and gauged the timing and direction of its leaps, and by the time he had realized what was happening, André had also accepted that she was too late. But she released smoothly and her arrow struck the hare in mid-bound, piercing it cleanly and sending it tumbling half a heartbeat before it would have been safely out of reach among the long grass at the edge of the trees.

Soon after that, close to noon, Sylvester suggested that they stop to eat. They had lost the boar trail on stony ground and they were glad to stop and eat from the baskets of bread, fruit, and cold meats that the cooks had prepared for them. The sky was still covered by high, dull cloud, and Sylvester asked the women if they wished to hunt on or if they had had enough and were ready to go home. There was no discussion. They would not be leaving here, Joanna said, until they had some good wild pig to take with them. She looked to Berengaria for confirmation, and the Princess nodded in assent, her attention focused on the cold roasted pheasant she was clutching in both hands. André watched and listened to all of this, content to say nothing, and greatly surprised at how much he was enjoying the outing.

It started to rain as they were preparing to resume the hunt, and at first it was light, a shower that everyone believed would soon pass over, but it did not, and as time went by, the downpour increased so that they were soon seriously inconvenienced. They were deep in the woods, in hilly terrain, and the roar of the downpour on the canopy above their heads was deafening, but the masses of leaves above merely intercepted the rain and deflected it so that instead of falling on the forest floor as normal raindrops, it tended to pool on the broad leaf surfaces and then spill from one leaf to another, gathering momentum and volume until it fell in solid streams, penetrating even the wax-scraped wiry wool of their foul-weather cloaks. André leaned close to Sylvester at one point and shouted into his ear.

"Were you the one who predicted heavy rain to Richard?"

The huntsman cupped his hand over his mouth to shout above the noise of the rain. "Aye, but I meant nothing like this. This is worse than I have seen in years. There's a cavern about half a mile ahead of us, up on top of the scree slope, in the face of a cliff. Found it a few weeks ago, first time I came hunting here. It's a struggle to get up there, but it's big and dry inside and we can light a fire, if there are no bears in there."

"A fire? Is there wood there?"

"Probably. Depends on who has been there recently. The locals have been using the place as a shelter for hundreds of years, and most of them stock the place with firewood before they leave. There was a pile there when I found the place." He shrugged. "Of course, some people will use up every scrap of wood that's there and won't replace a stick. Do you want to try it?"

"Lead on! It's big enough, think you?"

"Oh, it's big, much larger than it looks to be from outside, because the entranceway is really very small, barely three paces across, compared to the space inside, which is about ten times that wide. And it's deep, too, with high roofs. There are three big connected chambers, one behind the other like beads on a string. Front one's the biggest, open to the outside. The back one has some light in it during the day—a kind of glow that comes down like a fading sunbeam from somewhere up above—and the middle one's always dark."

André smiled at the huntsman. "Like a fading sunbeam … I like that. Let's hope there are no bears in there today."

They approached the cave mouth with great caution, having picked their way carefully up the treacherous scree slope, and when they were all in readiness, with arrows nocked and ready to draw, Sylvester threw a succession of rocks into the darkened cavern, pausing each time to listen for sounds that would indicate that the cave held tenants. Nothing emerged, and no sound disturbed the silent darkness beyond the cave mouth. Eventually Sylvester himself, carrying a heavy, spring-wound arbalest primed and ready at the level of his waist, stepped slowly into the entrance and paused there, framed in the opening and lit from behind, inviting any animal inside to charge at him. He remained there for a count of ten, and then he straightened slightly and disappeared into the darkness.

Minutes later, having made sure that no animals were lurking in the farthest recesses of the three linked caverns that stretched backward for at least sixty paces into the cliff, the two men stood together again, this time looking out into the driving rain. Behind them in the first cave, they could hear one of the other hunters chopping dry wood into kindling, while another of their number worked patiently with flint, steel, and finely chopped and shredded bark and grass to start a fire. The two women had gone into the farthest of the caves, the dimly lit one, and there Sylvester had shown them a cleft in the floor over an underground stream that offered a natural and pleasant latrine. He had then left them together to do whatever they needed to do.

"How far are we from the wagons, do you know?" André asked him.

Sylvester pointed off to their right, down the scree slope. "Half a mile, if you go that way, straight through the brush and across a steep gully with a stream at the bottom, but it will be heavy going in this rain." He flicked his hand towards the left, the way they had come. "If you go back that way, on the other hand, there's an easy path—we crossed it at one point, you may recall—that swings back around to where they'll be now. A mile and a half, perhaps two."

"An easy path? Easy enough for the wagons to follow if we sent for them to come here?"

"Aye, to the bottom of the slope, at least, but if you wanted anything after that, you'd have to hump it up the slope on your back."

"That's what men-at-arms are for, when they're not fighting. I think we should send for them."

Sylvester turned slowly and looked at him. "Now why would you want to do that?"

André met his look squarely. "Because this rain shows no sign of slackening and we have two ladies with us. They may not look like ladies, dressed as they are, and they have not been behaving like ladies through all this, because neither one of them has made a single complaint, but sooner rather than later the discomfort of this weather is going to penetrate their calm, which has been admirable until now. The rain may ease soon—it certainly ought to, because it can't continue this way forever—but in the event that it does not, then we ought to be prepared for whatever eventuality might arise. And one of those eventualities, I believe, is that the lady Joanna might not change her mind about remaining here until she kills a pig. If that happens, then we might end up spending the night here."

"The King would not be happy with that," Sylvester growled, but André shook his head.

"I don't know, my friend. I think you might be wrong there. You yourself put the notion into Richard's head yesterday when you told him it might rain heavily today, and that is why we brought a wagon filled with tents and blankets. It was the King's idea that we might be stranded by the weather, and he bade me be certain that I brought the necessities to keep the ladies dry, warm, and comfortable. He trusts us both implicitly in this. We have sufficient men to guard them, and we brought the cook along to feed everyone. So oblige me by sending your best man to find the wagons and their escort and to bring them here as soon as may be. I will inform the Queens of what is happening." He hesitated. "By the way, the third cave, at the back, with the latrine. Is there an updraft in there? Could you keep a fire burning in there without choking to death?"

Sylvester shrugged. "I don't know. I've never thought about that. I always use the fire pit in the front cave."

"Hmm. Well, we'll soon find out. There must be a chimney of some kind in the roof there. If light can get in, then air must be able to get out by the same route."

THE DOWNPOUR HAD NOT abated by the middle of the afternoon, but the temperature had plummeted so deeply that it felt more like a winter's day in England than anything one might ever expect to encounter in Cyprus. And then the wind came up, gradually at first, then strengthening to a gale and later still to a howling, lethal fury the like of which none of them had ever seen. In the forest below their cliff face, whole trees were uprooted and sent flying while others, older and more established, were shattered and sundered by the power of the winds, weak forks ripped apart and great limbs and branches torn away and transformed into flying weapons. Awe-stricken, but too wet and tired and miserable to really care about the reasons underlying the phenomenon, no one could explain it and no one tried. When they grew bored with watching the catastrophe, they concentrated all their energies upon drying themselves and their clothing, and staying warm.

The wagons had arrived and been unloaded long before the wind arose, every able-bodied man in the party turning to the task of carrying cargo up the treacherous slope of shifting shale and rocks beneath the cliff face and stowing it in the front cave, where a veritable bonfire now roared. When everything was safely moved, André sent them all out again, this time to find a sheltered spot in which to conceal the wagons and horses, and then to gather firewood to stave off the rapidly increasing cold. He had gone with them, as had Sylvester, leaving behind only a single elderly man from the cook's crew to tend to the ladies, should they require anything. That, too, had been before the storm winds really asserted themselves, and they had still been gathering piles of wood when one savage, icy gust of swirling wind plucked one of their number up bodily and threw him down the rocky slope to land unconscious, one arm broken and his head bleeding against a stone. That caused them to cut short their fuel gathering and settle for transporting what they had gathered up into the safety of the caverns as quickly as they could move.

There had been no question of continuing the hunt in such weather, or even of making the journey homeward to Limassol, for they had all seen with their own eyes the power of that wind. Instead, St. Clair had set all hands to preparing for a night in the cave. The twelve men-at-arms had been put to work at once, building an angled wall of stones and rubble across the narrow entrance to the cavern in order to deflect the force of the gusts that howled through the opening. The top of it was still half the height of a man short of the entrance's highest point, but it was high enough and strong enough to reduce the howling force of the wind to tolerable levels. Behind the wall, in a wide ring around the central fire pit—the floor of the main cavern was easily thirty paces long and almost the same in width—they had set up four leather tents as sleeping quarters, where they would be out of the wind gusts that still spilled into the cave from time to time. They could not drive pegs into the stone floor, but they were able to raise the tents solidly nonetheless by securing the guy ropes to heavy stones, and while all of that was happening, the cook and his crew were roasting a haunch of venison on a spit that they had placed over a second fire.

Sylvester had also ordered small fires lit in the central and rear caves, and the one in the rear chamber burned clean and well, as he had thought it would, whereas the one in the central chamber had to be extinguished immediately, before its smoke drove them all out into the storm. Having proved that the rear chamber could be kept warm and ventilated, he offered the two Queens the option of sleeping in the main cave with the rest of the party, in one of the four tents, or of sleeping by themselves in the rear chamber. He was unsurprised when they opted for the latter, for Ianni the steward had already been hard at work fashioning beds and seats by the fire from piles of tents and blankets, and generally converting the space for the women's use, even to the extent of lighting fat candles in standing sconces against the walls and having portable tripods set up as washstands, with ewers of heated water for their ablutions.

André bowed to the Queens and told them that he would have some hot food sent in to them when it was ready, but as he turned to leave, Berengaria called him back and thanked him, although for what, he could not have said. Her courtesy surprised him, for they had barely exchanged ten words all day, but he bowed slightly in acknowledgment and thanked her in return, and then was truly surprised when Joanna asked him to be seated for a moment, since she had several things to say to him and to ask about.

Someone had moved four knee-high boulders close to the fire that Sylvester had built close by the back wall of the chamber, where the smoke rose swiftly and cleanly upward, disappearing into the heights without causing any discomfort, and two of them had been converted to seats by the simple addition of a wad of padding to each. André thought the padding might be folded leather tents, but even as he looked at them, one of Ianni's men came by with a third pile of cushioning and set it atop another boulder, pressing it into shape. André nodded his thanks to the man and crossed to it, looking inquiringly at Queen Joanna, who stared back at him openly, then sat down across from him, crossing her booted, leather-clad legs and gripping her knee between interlaced fingers.

The effect of that simple movement hit André squarely beneath the rib cage, taking his breath away. He had been looking at both women all day and had, he thought, grown inured to the fact that they were women dressed as men, but they had been wearing heavy woolen cloaks all day, too, and all of them, himself included, had been concentrating on other things, and that had greatly dissipated the impact of their appearance. Now, however, they had laid aside their cloaks and the leather cuirasses they had worn for hunting, and both had found time to brush their hair, but they had not yet had any opportunity to change their clothing completely and they were now wearing only light, knee-length tunics, much like surcoats, over leather breeches that revealed, shockingly, the shapes of their legs and hips, so that by raising her armored knee and grasping it the way she had, Joanna Plantagenet had filled his mind and vision, instantly, with the awareness of her body. In looking away so quickly, he had undone himself further, because Queen Berengaria, similarly clad— although the word that came to him instantly was *unclad*—had been moving towards him, bending slightly forward so that the shape and fullness of her breasts were emphasized.

He closed his eyes instinctively, feeling the warm flush of redness creeping over his face, but when he opened them again, neither of the women appeared to have noticed anything amiss.

"I have been most impressed with you today, Master St. Clair," Joanna said clearly. "The task you were given is an imposition that could easily have been placed upon someone else. I know that, because I am the one who asked that you be given it, for my own selfish reasons. But you have discharged it admirably, with great patience and without a single frown or complaint, albeit it has turned out to be a far more hazardous and lengthy task than any of us could have guessed at. You have performed your duty and fulfilled your obligations wondrously, and my brother shall hear of it directly. My sister here thinks the same and will add her voice to mine. And for all you have done for us today, we now thank you."

"It was my duty, my lady, as you say, but it was also pleasurable. May I—may I ask why you asked for me?"

Joanna flicked a glance at Berengaria, then looked back at St. Clair, her head tipped slightly to one side and a tiny frown of annoyance, or it might have been perplexity, creasing the skin between her brows. "Because I thought you have a mind, sir, and might be capable of conversing sensibly, so why would you jeopardize that opinion by asking such a foolish question now?" When she saw the uncomprehending look that drew from him, her frown deepened. "I think—" She sat up straighter. "It cannot have escaped your attention, surely, Sir André, that the majority of your fellow knights can barely speak at all, once the topics of exercising, training, killing, and warfare have been exhausted. My brother tells me you can read and write with fluency. Is that correct?"

"It is, my lady."

"Then that alone sets you apart from all your so-called equals. I have been aware for years of an appalling truth, but I heard it expressed again by Bishop Charles of Beaulieu, less than a month ago, and it shocked me afresh: not one knight in any two hundred chosen at random can either read or write. And they do not even care! In fact they sneer at people who can, and for reasons that are obvious most of those are clerics, who must read and write in order to fulfill their obligations. And thus the gulf between knights and clerics is deepened with bullish stupidity. The fact that you are literate, Master St. Clair, marks you as being different from the ruck of your fellows and raises the possibility that you might be able to talk of things other than war and warfare—topics that a woman like me, or my royal sister here, might enjoy listening to and talking about. That is why I asked for you by name."

"I see." André nodded. "And I see, too, why my question annoyed you. Forgive me, my lady, I was not thinking clearly. Quite honestly, it had never occurred to me that anyone might find the ability to read and write to be an admirable trait. I have taken abuse over it for so long that I try to keep the ability secret nowadays." He paused. "You said you had some things to say to me and to ask about. I am at your disposal."

"Ah, if only you were …" Her face betrayed nothing of what she was thinking, and for a moment André grappled with the meaning of her comment, so that he missed what she said next, becoming aware of it only when he realized that her voice had been raised in interrogation and she was now staring at him, clearly awaiting an answer to a question. He pulled himself back to attention quickly.

"Pardon me, my lady, but I was distracted for a moment, and I missed what you said last."

"I was talking about whether or not Richard might be concerned by our failure to return to Limassol tonight. I asked you if you had thought to send a man back to tell them that we are well but will remain here until the storm abates."

"Ah. No, I sent no one." He picked a twig up off the floor and flicked it into the fire. "Your brother is clever enough to see that these conditions arc foul and intolerable, and to deduce that we will find some place to wait out the storm."

"Yes," Joanna agreed, nodding. "Bu—"

"Besides"—André, staring into the fire, was not even aware that she had begun to speak again—"any man out alone in weather like this, and in territory as wild as this, would run a grave risk of being killed or injured—blown over a cliff somewhere or killed by a falling tree. Had I sent someone out, and he had been hurt or injured, then nothing would have been achieved except the loss of a valuable man, and we would be faced with coming back again to look for him or find his body. No one in Limassol may know where we are now, but by the time they can organize a search party tomorrow, we will be well on our way home again and we'll meet them coming towards us."

Joanna nodded her head at that, accepting his logic, and after that they made more small talk for a while, until one of the cook's men cleared his throat from the entrance to the chamber and announced that the food was ready and would be served to them within moments. André rose quickly to his feet and left the women to prepare for their meal, then made his way back into the main cave to join Sylvester and the other huntsmen.

It had been a long and tiring day, and when their stomachs were full, no one appeared to want to move far from the fire, although a hardy few made their way outside to relieve themselves. Around the fireside the talk was desultory at best, and soon heads began to nod here and there and men began to make their way into the tents and out of the way of the occasional gusts of wind that still burst into the cave and whistled and buffeted around in the vaulted heights above their heads. Before long, the first long-drawn-out snores began to roll, and when André caught himself nodding in the fire's warmth he struggled to his feet and helped himself to a double armful of bedding, then made his way back to the chamber where the women were.

He coughed to let them know he was outside their quarters, then told them he would keep guard there, sleeping across their doorway, just to ensure that no one from the outer cave would be tempted to go wandering in the middle of the night. The possibility of that, he knew, was minuscule, but he made his bed on the floor from a double layer of folded leather tents, laid his unsheathed sword, his helmet, and his mailed gloves alongside it, and wrapped himself warmly in blankets over his leather hunting clothes before he lay down. Moments later he heard the sounds of someone throwing wood onto the women's fire, and then came a few brief whispers. Ianni emerged from the cave, carrying a candle, and stepped carefully over André, bidding him a whispered goodnight as he passed.

For some time after that, André lay listening to the sounds of the two Queens talking. He could not make out a word, although he did not really try, and he wondered what they were doing and what they looked like as they prepared for bed. But he soon fell asleep, despite his prurient imaginings.

HE CAME AWAKE in a surge of panic, surrounded by flickering yellow light and struggling to sit upright and to reach for his sword at the same time. He did not know where he was, only that someone's hand had covered his mouth and nose while he slept. Before he could struggle upright or cry out, however, the hand tightened, pinching his nostrils and pulling him backward, and a sharp voice hissed in his ear, telling him to be quiet. It was a woman's voice, and all at once he remembered where he was and his vision cleared, so that he saw the woman's face close to his own and promptly froze. Joanna's eyes were wide, as though with fright. He relaxed, and she immediately released him and moved back, placing her hand between her breasts and inhaling, a deep, quavering breath.

"My lady," he said, sitting up quickly now but keeping his voice low and turning his head to scan the passageway behind him. "What is it? What's amiss?"

She waved her hand at him and shook her head, and he became aware that she had knelt beside him to awaken him and was now sitting back on her heels, staring wide eyed at him, her hand still fluttering apprehensively over her breast. She was wearing proper feminine clothing, he noticed now, albeit night attire. Voluminous and concealing, it shrouded her body from his eyes, yet made him instantly aware that her body was there, soft and feminine and close enough for him to touch, were he to stretch out his hand. As he thought that, she stopped fluttering her fingers and held her hand still, the palm upraised towards him, and took another great breath.

"Lord, sir, you frightened me. I did not expect you to awaken so violently … or so noisily. For a moment I thought you would bring everyone running to see if we were being murdered in our sleep."

St. Clair hitched himself higher, finding a more comfortable seat, aware of the night chill where the blankets had fallen from his shoulders. He was wide awake now, but he rubbed finger and thumb in the corners of his eyes, clearing them of the last vestiges of sleep as Joanna began to speak again.

"There is nothing amiss, Sir André. I merely found myself unable to sleep. I did not wish to disturb my sister Berengaria, so I thought I might see if you would be good enough to talk with me for a time. I have remade the fire …"

Puzzled, but flattered, St. Clair unwrapped himself from his blankets and moved towards the fire, where, for the next few minutes, they both worked hard at overcoming the awkwardness they felt over what had taken place. Berengaria had not stirred, so it seemed that they had not made too much noise, but St. Clair got up anyway and went quietly out to the middle chamber, carrying one of the candles. He met no one and heard nothing other than the wind beyond the front entrance, and soon made his way back to where Joanna sat by the fire.

They talked quietly together for more than an hour, and St. Clair enjoyed it thoroughly, for Joanna began by asking for his opinion of

Guy de Lusignan, both as a ruler and as a man, and when he had obliged her, she responded by giving him her own opinion, and it was greatly different from anything he had ever heard anyone else say on the topic. As a woman, she said, she found herself attracted to the fellow, because he presented himself as a portrait of so many of the things women looked for in a man: tall and strongly built, yet proportionally pleasing, he was comparable to her own brother, if not quite so massively muscled. His teeth were excellent, she remarked, white and even, with no gaps, no obvious spaces, and no visible rot. He kept his dark hair and beard clean and neatly trimmed, too, she said, which was sufficiently uncommon to be noteworthy, and his skin was deeply tanned and pleasant to behold, the backs of his fingers, hands, and wrists covered in a noticeable scattering of fine dark curling hair that she and many of her sex found attractive and even alluring.

He had undergone severe hardship in the past few years, she told André, but even so his clothing, while faded and threadbare, had been well maintained and kept clean. Richard had, of course, provided him with new clothing, raiment befitting his regal status, but even so, the condition of the old garments spoke for itself. This was a man who was fastidious and painstaking over appearances. But all of that being said, she continued, her attraction to him, woman to man, had been purely superficial.

"Had he struck me as being more than surface-deep, had he really appealed to me, underneath, as a man, I would never have taken the time to examine him as closely as I did. But the more closely I observed him, the less I saw to like. He is weak. Having been raised with Richard as my brother and then spending years as wife to my dear husband William, I understand and recognize strength. I also recognize its absence, the lack of it, with great ease. Our noble King Guy is not reliable, at depth. Which is, of course, why he has earned the reputation that the German Montferrat, and now Philip Augustus, seek to use against him—" She broke off and inhaled a deep, sibilant breath. "But he is the rightful King, for the time being, and that is … inconvenient, to say the least, for my dear brother."

She had been gazing into the fire as she talked, but now she turned her head to look André directly in the eye. "Do you understand why I say that? Have you spoken with anyone of the politics surrounding this entire affair?"

"The religious politics, you mean? Yes I have. But I cannot convince myself that it is as important as everyone else seems to think."

"You—?" Joanna stared at him in amazement. "I cannot believe I heard you say that. You do not think it is important? Do you not, then, believe in God?"

St. Clair laughed, easily. "Of course I do, but what is at stake here, in this squabble between de Lusignan and de Montferrat, has nothing to do with God. It is a struggle between two groups of men—very large groups, be it said—all of whom purport to worship the same God. But one group calls itself the Eastern Orthodox Church and is ruled by a patriarch archbishop, while the other calls itself the Roman Catholic Church and is ruled by a pope. Each swears, calling upon the full authority of Heaven to attest to its righteousness, that it holds the one, correct, and inarguable means to achieve salvation. And both desire to govern the land where Jesus lived, because both believe it to be sacred, and both believe there is worldly treasure to be amassed by controlling it. Think you I am being cynical, my lady?"

She had been looking at him through narrowed eyes but now she laughed and shook her head in what looked like admiration. "No," she drawled, "not cynical, not really. But I think you are a very dangerous man."

"How so, my lady? I am but a simple knight."

"Aye, but a simple knight with his own ideas and his own way of looking at things most people never become aware of. That, sir knight, makes you highly dangerous, to people who would wish you to behave as they think fit. What do you think my brother should do in this instance?"

"I believe he is already committed, my lady. He has recognized Guy and given him sustenance and support. I cannot say he would have done so quite as willingly had Philip not thrown his support behind de Montferrat, but the die is cast now. Before that, I know the King was under ever-increasing pressure from Rome—he is surrounded by a plague of archbishops and bishops as you know— to safeguard its papal interests in Outremer, and most particularly in Jerusalem, should we ever win it back. But this turnabout by Philip, in support of Montferrat and the Orthodox camp, would seem to fly deliberately in the face of the Pope, and that mystifies me, for I would not have thought Philip brave enough or defiant enough to go directly counter to the Pope's wishes and authority."

Joanna merely nodded. "You may be right, or close to it. Perhaps he has reached an agreement of some kind with the Eastern Church in Constantinople. It would surprise me greatly were I to discover that there was less scheming among the followers of Orthodoxy than there is among the followers of Rome." She sat silent for a moment, then added, "What are you smiling at? Did I say something amusing?"

St. Clair's smile widened. "No, my lady, you said nothing amusing. What amuses me is that I have yet to hear a man say what you just said. They are all, by and large, far too afraid of the Church and its power ever to dare say such things. I agree with you completely, but hearing you express your opinion surprised me, that is all. I could not help but smile."

"Hmm. Spend more time around me, Sir André. I will soon have you wheezing on the floor, clutching your ribs in pain from laughing. One of the saddest things about being a woman is that you are not supposed to think, or even to be capable of thought. Even my brother Richard subscribes to that belief—one of the few masculine perceptions of women he shares wholeheartedly with every other man. But the Churches, both of them, Eastern and Western, are run by and for men, so what can a mere woman do, other than hold her own opinions and express them when she can?"

André nodded in agreement. "Aye, well, whatever has caused Philip to side with Conrad, it has drawn a strong dividing line between the factions, so that Richard now stands squarely in Guy's camp. Although I dare say he would declare that Guy stands in his ..."

Before Joanna could reply to that, they were interrupted by an explosive snort from the bed behind them, and both of them turned to see Berengaria, eyes tightly closed and her mouth making sleepy, sucking noises, turn over to face them and then subside back into sleep, her unbound hair obscuring much of her upper face and her bare neck clearly visible in the scoop beneath the edge of her blanket.

"Think you those lines will remain drawn once we arrive in Outremer?" Joanna was looking at him again, and St. Clair shrugged.

"I think, my lady, that much of that will depend on Saladin and on the situation that we find in force when we arrive there. If the Saracens come against us hard and fast, then they may achieve the effect of fusing our forces into one effective whole. But should Saladin even begin to suspect the kind of strife that besets us now—and the man did not become the Sultan of all Islam by being a blind, unseeing fool—he will hold back his armies and allow us to destroy ourselves. And we would do that, left to ourselves, Christian against Christian, Orthodox against Roman, through petty bickering and venal jealousies and greedy politicking. Pray he never does find out."

"I will, because I will be there myself, so you need have no doubt of that. I might even pray for you, too. Not that I am much of a prayer. I am too much like you, I suppose, for I have a mind of my own and I prefer to think for myself, and that displeases a surprisingly large number of people." She hesitated, then added, with a tiny smile, "For all I know, it might even displease God. In any case, I might pray for you."

St. Clair smiled faintly. "I would be grateful for that, my lady."

"Oh, do not say that, Sir André. For a while there, I was considering seducing you ... and for that you truly would have been grateful to me. But I decided instead that I like you, and so chose to leave you to your destiny, which may be sufficiently complicated to confound you already, without any contributions to your debauchery from me."

"I—" His mouth remained open and his eyes grew wide, and she smiled lazily at him, enjoying the play of emotions and reactions that he could neither control nor begin to understand. He became convinced for a few moments that he had misheard her, until his eyes on her face told him otherwise. She put a hand to her mouth to stifle a laugh, and when he appeared to have mastered himself and overcome the urge to say anything, for fear of sounding stupid, she spoke again, her voice quiet and gentle.

"Will you not ask me then what I meant about leaving you to your complicated destiny?"

He was frowning at her now, and shook his head in a gesture that was almost unnoticeable. "No, my lady, I think not."

"Are you aware, then, of having a destiny?"

"All men have destinies, my lady."

"No, Sir André, that is not so. Emphatically not so. All men— most men—may have fates awaiting them, but very, very few have destinies. Destinies change the paths of peoples and of empires, André. I believe you have such a destiny. And so, I believe, does my beloved brother, in his own twisted way."

"Forgive me, my lady, but I have no idea what you are talking about."

"I know that. That is why I find you so attractive."

Joanna's stare was so direct, so challenging, that St. Clair found himself unable to hold it, and he turned his eyes away from her, thinking furiously and unaware that his own gaze had returned to Berengaria.

"You find her beautiful, do you not?"

It took several seconds for the import of what Joanna had said to penetrate his awareness, for he had been looking at Berengaria's sleeping face, oblivious to what he was doing, but now he stiffened and straightened his shoulders.

"I think I misheard you, my lady."

"I am not your lady, André. I might lie with you and enjoy you, and you me, but I could never be your lady. But Berengaria could, and probably will be, albeit secretly and very quietly."

St. Clair could hear his heart pounding loudly in the pause that followed, and when Joanna spoke again it seemed to him he could hear a smile in her voice. "Would you like to bed a queen, Sir

André?" She paused again, briefly this time. "Come, sir, it is time to grit your teeth and banish blushes. You may bed both of us, would you but say the word. Then we would all three be pleased enough with our lot, and life could go on with never a wrinkle to mar its smoothness."

André did not even dare attempt to answer, for he was afraid, yet far from convinced, that the Queen of Sicily had lost her sanity, and the thunder of his own pulse was deafening in his ears. He sat motionless, making no attempt to look at her, and she bent forward and took him by the wrist, tugging at him.

"André, look at me. Look at me, and listen! Look at me!"

He turned his eyes with painful slowness to look at her and found her frowning at him.

"Sweet Jesus," she said, more to herself than to him. "You are even more innocent than I suspected. You are unfit to be permitted out alone and unguarded. André, listen to me, and if you have never heard anything before in your life to do with women, hear this." She squeezed his wrist with both hands now, this time hard enough to cause pain, and he flinched and looked directly at her.

"Are you listening to me? Good. Now hear this, from a woman with no wish to deceive you and a Queen with no need to lie. Berengaria is yours for the taking. I am, too, but there is naught in it for me but pleasure. For you and Berengaria, on the other hand, there is much more at stake. You are to beget a son on her, an heir for Richard."

As he made to leap to his feet, she leapt ahead of him and pushed him back down. "Listen, you stupid man! Do you think I would jest with you on such a matter? It is a fact. Richard has planned for this, and arranged it with great care, and there is nothing you or anyone else may do to alter it. He will, if need be, use the full power of his liege right to your fealty and order you directly to the task of doing it as duty, and if you refuse his wishes he will deal with you accordingly. Believe me, I know whereof I speak, and you know my brother well enough to know that he will not be crossed in anything he sets his mind to as he has in this. Richard has no fear of popes or bishops or prating priests, and there is no other monarch alive who could force his hand and make him change his mind."

She checked herself, seeing the look in his eyes, then flicked her hand sideways, as if to clear such thoughts away, and resumed in a more gentle voice. "But none of this is anywhere near as bleak as I have made it sound, believe me. Nor would it be unpleasant in any degree, especially with regard to my sister Berengaria." She spread her fingers wide and drew a deep breath. "Richard took Berengaria to his bed on their wedding night, witnessed by all who were required to be there to stand witness, but he made no attempt to couple with her. She is no virgin, nor was she expected to be one, but she is virgin to her husband, because Richard is a man's man and that means his Queen will be no man's woman, officially at least, for the remainder of her life."

"That is scandalous! She was brought to Sicily to wed him by his mother. How could Eleanor not know about her son and his vices?"

Joanna looked at him wide eyed. "Who said she does not? Did I?"

"No, but—"

"There are no 'buts,' Sir André. My mother is no man's fool and there is nothing she does not know about her sons ... nor her daughters, for that matter. She knew what she was doing."

"Then how could she do such a thing to this young woman?"

The naivety of his question brought a hard edge of impatience to Joanna's voice. "She could do it because this young woman is her father's daughter, bound to obey his wishes in this as in all other things. Her father is King of Navarre, and Eleanor's son is King of England and ruler of an empire that includes Gascony. My mother arranged the perfect alliance, matching Richard with Berengaria, one of those brilliant instances of logic and initiative in political reality that have made my mother renowned throughout her life for her political acumen.

"Richard has tribulations uncounted in Gascony and no time to deal with them. The entire region is a rats' nest of treasonous bandits. They call themselves landowners and noblemen, but they are no more than brigands who have no love for Aquitaine, and even less for my brother or for his House, whether it be called Plantagenet or Poitiers. And to the east of Gascony lies Toulouse, a foe to both

Gascony and Richard. That single fact, that enmity between Toulouse and Gascony, is the sole thing holding back open rebellion by both powers against Richard's lands and authority. But our farsighted mother has contrived to liquidate that threat."

She paused, collecting her thoughts, then resumed in a stronger voice. "The day he married Berengaria, Richard endowed her with title to all his lands and holdings in Gascony." She saw St. Clair stiffen slightly with shock. "Gascony's southern border is the northern border of those territories ruled by Berengaria's father, Sancho. He is a sound and solid man, a strong King with a powerful and experienced army, kept in the field for years campaigning against the Muslim Moors in Granada, to the south of him. And now that his daughter holds title over Gascony, Sancho will work to ensure that Gascony and Navarre stand united against Toulouse, thereby taming the Gascon bandits in his daughter's name and forming a firm cushion between Angevin Aquitaine and any threat from its eastern neighbors. You must admit, that is all logical. Will you not agree?"

St. Clair nodded. "Aye, it is, admirably so, but it does not—"

"Of course it does, Sir André. Royal duty and responsibility excuses anything necessary to the well-being of the kingdom. Berengaria has always accepted that. Besides, she is … complacent. That was the word my mother used in describing Berengaria's ability to absorb what Richard would do to her—or would *not* do to her might be more accurate. My mother has always known what few men ever know, that any woman, no matter how neglected or abused, can, if she has the will and the desire, find solace for herself almost anywhere.

"But even so, my brother is not wholly without conscience. He told the child what their life would be like, before they slept on their wedding night, and he told her that he would not object were she to satisfy her needs discreetly with some man who could be relied upon to keep his silence." Joanna paused dramatically. "And then he went even further. He told her that, should she get herself with child, he would accept the infant and claim it as his own. And then he selected you for the task."

"What? *Selected* me—? No! No, that is impossible. It's unthinkable. I refuse to believe it."

"Why, in the name of God? Why, André? You know my brother.
You know who and what he is. Why would you find this difficult to
believe? I knew it weeks ago, from the way he thrust you into prominence every time we turned around."

"But ... But—" André reeled back in his chair. "That is infamous, madam! To suggest that the King would ever consider having
anyone else, let alone *me*, sire a son for him! How could you even
hint at such a thing, you who know him better than I do, when all
the world knows him to be entirely capable of doing his own duty?
Need I remind you that your brother has already fathered a son?"

"Ah! The famous little Philip, of course!" Joanna pulled herself
up until her spine was straight, and looked into the flames, her face
unreadable. "The little bastard prince. The French King's bane ...
No, sir, you need not remind me of that fable. That child exists, but
he is no more the son of Richard Plantagenet than I am. He is an illusion, an artifact created for the common people to perceive. But I
would have thought that, even with your unworldly eyes, you would
see through such a simple subterfuge."

"Explain that, if you will."

"I will. You asked me but a moment ago how I, who know him
better than you, could even hint that my brother might be capable of
such a thing. Well, I can *hint* at it without hesitation because I *do*
know my brother far better than you ever could. He has decided
upon you, in this, because he has already done the same thing once
before, successfully, in the matter of the child from Cognac, young
Philip Plantagenet." She held up a hand, palm forward, to keep him
quiet. "I pray you, think about that for a moment, before you spit at
me for saying it. Think for just a moment."

She began picking off points on the fingers of one hand. "Think
about the obligations of kingship, André. The first and greatest of
them is to sire an heir, to carry on the line securely, thus guaranteeing
the safety of the realm and its people. The people *are* the realm, *any*
realm, and the king is dependent upon their goodwill. A king who

fails to get an heir is intolerable, which is why so many royal marriages are brief. The queen bears the brunt of failure when the progeny are girls. When there are no progeny at all, she is declared barren and put aside. The king himself is never at fault—except when he can be proved sexually deviant to the extent that he cannot sire a child. Now that, I suggest to you, must be a chilling thought for a man of my brother's nature and ambitions."

Joanna allowed those words to hang in the air between them for several moments before she went on. "Richard, as I'm sure you already know, needs to be seen as a paragon—fearless and invincible in battle, ready to laugh and drink or wrestle and fight with anyone at the nod of a head or the wink of an eye. And he presents a hearty, smiling face to all the world when he plays the convivial King of England. But this is a King of England who shuns the company of women, who surrounds himself with comely and effete young men, and who has been rutting with the King of France since they were boys together, so that in France their dalliance and their constant, jealous squabbling long since became a matter of tired jest, and the knowledge of it threatened to spill out into the ken of the common folk of Aquitaine, Anjou, and other parts. It was the priests who put an end to that, of course. Richard might care nothing for what the common folk might think, but the Church knew better. And so a ruse was designed, to gull the people, not merely the people of Richard's domains in France but the people of England, who would one day become Richard's subjects.

"The yeomen of England, as they call themselves, require their kings to be heroic in bed as well as on the battlefield, and being heroic in bed, in that basic, low-born sense, involves the seduction of women and the coupling of breeding pairs. The lower classes, particularly in England, I am told, have no understanding of the true male brotherhood that Richard dreams of and espouses, or of the ineffable love between noble fighting men that was enjoyed by the likes of Alexander and Caesar. And so to set idle tongues at rest, certain advisers, shall we call them, deliberately planned an adventure for Richard with a young woman in Cognac—a region far enough removed from his usual haunts to serve the desired purpose admirably—with the resultant, widely remarked birth of a fine boy."

"But he did it."

Joanna almost smiled. "Did he? No, my dear André, I fear I must disappoint you there. Someone—I have no idea who—once said that a leopard cannot change its spots. My brother's spots are equally unalterable. Why do you think this adventure was arranged so far away from home? Had Richard merely wished to bed a wench, he could have clicked his fingers, anywhere, and been surfeited with willing, panting women. But that was not the way it transpired. Certain people took great pains to find an eligible woman of good family, a young, impoverished widow, and made certain arrangements with her. The Duke would be seen with her in public, paying close and flattering attention to her for sufficient time to set tongues a-wagging. The gossips would grow busy, but the lady would be amply recompensed for any embarrassment she might suffer from that, and in the meantime, when the Duke was not around to disport himself with her in private, she would be notably entertained, albeit secretly, by a young knight of spotless blood and wondrously fine appearance and physique. When she became pregnant, as she surely would, the young knight would move on, content and more than amply paid for his services, and she would name Duke Richard as the father of her child. In return, Richard would reward her with gifts of buildings, lands, and money, and would happily acknowledge his paternity and name the child an heir to his estates. It worked out very well, for all concerned. The mother is now wealthy and independent, the smug matron of an acknowledged heir, and Richard has a living symbol of his virility, his sexuality, and his love of women, to parade before the crowds whenever he so wishes."

"But what about the real father? Has Richard no fears that he might step forth one day and state his case?"

Joanna smiled again. "Would you, were you that man? What would he gain, other than to lose all he may hold at the time, including his head? Besides, the poor man died at the battle of Hattin."

St. Clair sat deep in thought and gnawing gently on the inside of his lip. Eventually he looked up to face her. "I believe what you say, my lady. Your story has the ring of sound logic." He fell silent again, gnawing and thinking, then straightened abruptly. "But even so, were all this proved true, I cannot yet see why the Duke—the King—would make me part of his design in repeating such a thing."

"Come now, Sir André, you are too modest and it ill becomes you here. Think of it from my brother's point of view. You are perfectly suited to his needs in this: young, dashing, dedicated, honorable, and bound to him by the laws of fealty and duty, besides which your bloodline is pure and your antecedents are flawless. Richard would be more than happy to see a son of the ancient house of St. Clair assuming his patrimony and his name with an unsullied bloodline. God knows he has professed himself sick beyond detestation with his own."

St. Clair stared at her with wide, startled eyes. "What d'you mean by that?"

"Precisely what I said. Richard has said many times, and once in my own hearing, that his blood, the sacred, royal blood mixed from both our parents, has soured and befouled his entire life. What did he say, exactly? Let me think … Ah, yes, he said, 'The blood flowing in my veins is a mixture brewed, stewed, and then spewed out in Hell, the same noxious, evil filth that animates my brother John, may he rot alive. Better that it should die out with me, wherever and whenever it does, and that fresh blood, uncurdled, should go on to rule in England after my death.'"

She waited a long time for his response. Something, a small stone or a resinous knot of wood, exploded in the heart of the fire, sending fragments leaping in several directions, but St. Clair seemed unaware of it. Finally, as though fearing he might never speak again, she prompted him. "Well?" she asked. "What do you think of that?"

He inhaled sharply and turned to look at her. "I find it unbelievable, yet all too credible. And … I find it frightening, above all else. But—" He stopped, and squeezed both hands tightly over his temples, his eyes clenched shut, and then he lowered his hands again. "I find all of this difficult to comprehend, my lady, in simplest truth. Am I truly to believe … Are you really saying that, if I choose to approach the Queen, she will lie with me, and neither she nor the King will be angered?"

"I am saying more than that, my friend. If you father a son upon her, he will be legitimized at birth and crowned King of England in due time. That I can promise you."

St. Clair swallowed. "And if I … do this, this *thing*, as you suggest … will I then have access to you, too?"

The look she gave him then was open, wide eyed and serious, with no hint of amusement. "Of course you will. Did I not say so? It will fall to me to be your chaperone, the Queen's senior companion, elder sister by marriage, and lady-in-waiting, present in her royal company at all times. I am a widow and a dowager, expected to be physically dried up and spent. But I am thirty-four years old and in the full flow of my womanhood. I have no need for undying love, nor for any bright-eyed, lovelorn eagerly panting young man to flatter me by pretending to swoon at my feet, but I have great need of straightforward carnal pleasure. Keep me smiling that way and I will be your dearest friend, my friend, for who would ever dream that you would rut with the Queen of England while she shared her bedchamber with the Queen of Sicily? You will live like the Sultan himself, in your own seraglio, with two crowned queens as your willing odalisques."

"And … you say Berengaria knows of this?"

"She does. She has not quite decided to proceed, and she believes you know nothing yet, but she is … favorably inclined towards you already, and her eyes when she watches you are full of wondering."

The silence grew and stretched again as André St. Clair fought to keep his face unreadable and to quell the sickness that was roiling in him, a sickness caused not by the prospect of having two royal mistresses but by the callow, callous, and absolute disregard for his honor that was being shown by Richard Plantagenet and his sister. Aware that he must speak and act with extreme caution in the time ahead, he sat silent again while counting his own heartbeats, and when his count reached twenty he sat up straight and cleared his throat.

"Well, lady," he said. "I ... I must think on this. I had ... I had planned to do other, very different things with my life in the coming campaign. I am to join the Temple Knights ... or I was, until this moment. Now I know not what I must do about that, other than sleeping on it and deciding what must first be done. For how will we achieve this ... this condition you describe? It cannot begin to happen while I am yet a Temple novice. I will have to free myself—and fortunately I have not yet taken vows—and rededicate myself to your brother's service. After that, I presume, things can be made to flow more smoothly."

"Aye, that they can." Joanna's voice was barely louder than a breath as she leaned in towards him and pulled his face to her hungry mouth, covering his lips with hers. He shuddered and convulsed, suddenly quivering with a rampant lust he had been unaware of until that moment, and he had already begun moving over to her when someone coughed and snorted loudly in the middle cavern, startling them apart. André swung upright, drawing his sword and striding out into the other chamber, where he heard urine spattering against a wall as one of the men-at-arms, still more than half asleep, relieved himself. In the distance, beyond the outer chamber, the night was silent, the howling of the wind having finally abated.

He went back into the rear cave and bade the lady Joanna a good night, then moved back out to his own bed, raging at himself and wondering if he had been as big a fool as he imagined in not taking her there and then, when he had had the opportunity. But no sooner had he formulated the question in words than he realized that he had been shocked into doing the right thing, thereby safeguarding his own honor despite his worst intentions. Sick at heart, he lay down on his makeshift bed again and thought about the perfidy of princes, sure that he would be unable to sleep for the remainder of the night. Then, like a flash of light reflecting from a distant pool, a well-known face sprang to his mind, quickening his heartbeat, and all at once he smiled, amused in spite of everything by the way in which absurdity can often become reality. He knew where he must go next, and he smiled again. Moments later, he began to snore.

SEVEN

"Ah, there you are, St. Clair. Where in Hades have you been?" The voice came from the open door, and André rose to his feet, turning to face the apparition that was shambling towards him but not looking at him. Brother Justin, Master of Novices, was peering through screwed-up eyes at a parchment in his hand, but he had been blinded in stepping from the bright sunlight beyond the doorway into the dimness where André sat waiting for him, and now he flapped the parchment in frustration and peered about him myopically until he caught sight of André on the far side of the entrance hall.

Flanking St. Clair on each side, two clerks were supposedly hard at work transcribing documents, but both were listening avidly, heads cocked for nuances of tone and emphasis, for they knew that something was afoot. St. Clair had stormed in some time earlier and had demanded that two of their fellows go separately to find the Master of Novices and bring him back as quickly as might be. The two had attempted to demur, claiming to have no time for such goings-on, but St. Clair had reacted in fury to that, drawing his long sword and sending them scampering to obey him. Neither one had yet returned, but now Justin was here and clearly had known that the knight St. Clair would be waiting for him.

Justin's eyesight was evidently adjusting rapidly, for he addressed the clerks next, his voice dripping sarcasm. "Keep working, brethren," he said. "God's work is never done, and yours will bear no interruption. St. Clair, come with me."

André followed the irascible monk along a narrow passageway

435

that led to the stone-walled room that Justin had appropriated for his own use. As the older man threw open the doors and marched inside he pointed with a thumb to a high stool that stood beside a long work table beneath high, vaulted windows.

"Sit."

Justin moved to the far end of the table and picked up three small, tightly rolled missives, and he spoke as he broke the seals and scanned their contents briefly. "Your cousin has shown up in Acre, alive and apparently well, though some of his Templar brethren appear to dispute that opinion. Word reached us two days ago—a messenger from a trading ship on its way to Malta. I've had people hunting for you since the night before last, so I know you have not been in the castle, or aboard a ship in harbor or even in Limassol. That would be called desertion by some people I know, and at best it indicates a lack of responsibility. Where were you?"

"Being responsible. I was about the King's business."

Brother Justin put the three messages down carefully and drew himself up to his full height, looking squarely at André St. Clair for the first time. There was something new in St. Clair's voice and it had captured his ear immediately, and now Justin spoke slowly, his tone calm and measured.

"And since when has any king's business taken precedence over that of our Order?"

"Never before, Brother. And not now. That is why I am here."

Brother Justin pulled a nondescript piece of rag from his sleeve and used it to brush crumbs from the dingy, much-stained white robe stretched tautly over his belly and then, clearly requiring still more time to think, he wiped the corners of his mouth with it, drawing attention to his bulbous, mottled nose and pendulous lower lip before stuffing the rag back whence it had come and nodding his head ponderously.

"You still have not told me where you were, and as your Master of Novices I must insist on knowing."

"I was hunting, ten miles or so beyond the city, in Isaac Comnenus's hunting grounds. We were caught in the storm yesterday and had to spend the night in a cavern. Came back this morning, shortly after dawn."

Justin was looking at him strangely. "The King's business sent you hunting without him? That seems strange. I saw the King last night, here in this castle."

"I have no doubt you did. He was not with us. He set me to accompany and attend his wife and his sister, the ladies Berengaria and Joanna, both of whom are excellent hunters, better than many a man I know."

Brother Justin shivered suddenly and looked about him, rubbing one hand against his arm. "It is cold in here," he muttered. "I should have a fire. No matter how intense the heat of the day outside, these old stone walls keep it out there and keep these big rooms cool. I distinctly felt the temperature fall again there, moments ago ..." He raised his eyes to gaze up at the vaulted and groined ceiling. "I know you have many things you wish to tell me, Sir André, but first I must ask you for clarification on one small matter. Am I to believe you spent a night in a cave with Queen Berengaria and Queen Joanna? Alone with two women, but for some hunters?"

"Hardly alone, Brother Justin. There were twenty-six of us there, in addition to the two Queens."

"Twenty-six. And how many of those were women?"

"The only women there were the two Queens, and even they were dressed as men."

"I see. And does this ... expedition have anything to do with your seeking me out now?"

"Everything."

"Then clearly you have much to tell me. But before you do, and while I yet have a voice with which to speak, is there anything you wish to ask me?"

"Aye, Brother. Where has my cousin been for so long?"

"In prison, in the hands of the Saracens. He was at Hattin, but managed to escape alive, only to be taken soon afterwards."

"So why did we not know this sooner? We knew the names of most of those killed and captured, did we not?"

"Aye, but apparently your cousin changed his name—his whole identity, in fact. He knew that Saladin had executed every Templar and every Hospitaller captured at Hattin, so he concealed the fact that he was a Templar. The battle was long over when he was captured, and he had rid himself of everything that would identify him with the Temple. He even took the name and ranking of his closest friend, a Scot like himself who had been his boyhood companion, a fellow called Lachlan Moray, who was also a knight and died at Hattin, but was not of either military order."

"So Alex denied the Temple?"

"He did, for the greater good of our Order of Sion."

"How can you know that?"

"Because the word we received was sent to me, not to the Temple. It was not written by a Templar."

"I see … And I suppose therefore that I will be permitted to know nothing about this greater good that he perceived."

"I did not say that. In fact you will know everything about it, and about Sir Alexander's task and duties for the brotherhood. But first I want to hear the concerns that brought you here in search of me. You have never come directly to me before, so why would you do so now? I confess I am greatly curious."

St. Clair then told him everything, omitting absolutely nothing, so that for the ensuing hour and more Justin sat rapt, watching André's lips and missing not a nuance of the tale unfolding in front of him. When the younger man fell silent at last, neither of them made any attempt to speak for a long time. It was eventually Justin who broke the silence.

"Hmph," he grunted, then fell silent again for a short time before adding, "Well, then, why are you here? Why would you not simply go ahead and take what you have been offered? You have sworn no vows and undertaken no obligations to this point that might prevent you from doing so. Most men would do anything to gain what you are offered. You have not refused the honor, have you?"

André was frowning. "No, I have not. Not yet, but—"

"Then why tell me about it, in God's name? Why would you even hesitate in this?"

"You yourself used the word that stops me."

"I did?" Justin frowned now. "What word was that?"

"Honor, Brother. It is an ideal, and a reality that I value highly, particularly since it seems to be greatly out of use and favor nowadays."

"Aah ... Honor, I see. Yes, honor can be inconvenient."

St. Clair shook his head. "I disagree, Brother Justin. I believe that honor is never inconvenient, and the lack or absence of it in any situation repels me. I see nothing of honor, no slightest trace of it, in what I have described to you here."

"And so you will have none of it, is that what you are telling me?"

"Aye, sir. It is."

"You set a high standard for others to follow, then."

"No, I do not. The standards I may set are mine alone, for me to follow. I expect no others to accept my dictates. They are my own, as is my honor."

Justin pursed his lips and nodded. "Good man. So mote it be. I expected no less of you, and you have my full support. But tell me, why did you not go directly with this to de Sablé? He has your interests at heart and holds higher rank within the brotherhood than I do. He also wields more influence in matters like this."

St. Clair had started shaking his head as soon as Justin spoke de Sablé's name. "I dared not. Sir Robert is a good man and I know him well and I believe he trusts me, but he is close friends with Richard—has been for years. They are even related, cousins of some kind. I simply dared not take that kind of risk with this. It is too dangerous ... Not that I thought he might betray me to Richard. He would never do that, I know, but he might betray himself inadvertently, and bring about his own destruction by showing his disapproval in some way. His honor, too, is great, and strictly guarded, and that would make it difficult for him to conceal his distaste over Richard's treatment of the Queen. I could not forgive myself were he to be killed because of something I told him when there was no need to do so."

"Hmm. You are probably right. It is too dangerous. We may never know with certainty whether you were right or wrong, but we do have other options and I think you were correct in choosing as you have ... What's wrong?"

St. Clair had been frowning. "Nothing, save that you do not appear to be surprised by anything I have told you."

"Should I be? Do you mean I should be shocked and scandalized at venality and carnality, the lusts of these men and women? What would make you think that? I joined our brotherhood when I was eighteen, Brother André, as you did, and since then I have studied without rest to advance myself inside our Order and find the true Way to be with God. And most of what I have learned has been based upon the gulf created between God and men when our ancient Way was lost in the destruction of Jerusalem in Roman times, after the deaths of Jesus and his brother James. After that, as our ancient lore teaches us, humanity was left to wander in the wilderness, vainly attempting to find their way to God by following the errant footsteps of mere men, who were as mortal and as weak and foolish as those who followed them, no matter what great names and titles they bestowed upon themselves. Stripped of godliness, there remains in man's nature nothing but feeble, fragile, and self-seeking humanity. So no, I am not surprised. My task is to find some way to make use of what you have told me in order to benefit the aims of our brotherhood. Thus I am glad you came to me first, for the aid we must now seek lies within the Temple Order itself, and de Sablé is not yet one of them.

"We need to keep you here, from this time on, beyond Richard's reach, and that could be but a temporary respite at best, since he may yet come looking for you as your liege lord. We can hope all his attention may be absorbed in the coming days by this Isaac Comnenus nonsense, but the only truly effective way to keep you beyond his reach is to induct you formally into the Temple as a knight. To that end, I will call upon some of the brethren to assemble as soon as may be."

"You mean to induct me alone, without the other novices? How can that be done?"

"By speed and stealth, born of necessity. And not only can it be done, it can be done quickly. We have reason and motive. All we need now is a sufficiency of knights to conduct the ceremony."

St. Clair grimaced. "Reason and motive. Is merely saving me from the King's clutches, in the matter of an escapade of which we cannot speak, sufficient to provide both of those? How will you justify this to others?"

"Easily. First of all, the King has nothing to do with this. Be clear on that from the outset and bear it in mind from now on. I told you that your cousin appears to be alive and well, but that several of his fellow Templars might dispute that. Sir Alexander, not for the first time, is causing grief among his fellow Templars, challenging their standards at times and scorning them at others. He was ever a prickly man, your cousin, prickly and unyielding in his righteousness, but he was seldom wrong, a fact that, while it reflected well upon his name, did little to endear him to his less uncompromising peers. But now he has come back from captivity among the Saracens pouring out allegations of incompetence and corruption within the Templar hierarchy, along with other ideas that do little to endear him to his fellows, and when they challenged him on what he was saying—challenged him very bluntly, I understand—he vanished again, into the desert. The other Templars over there now say he has been suborned and seduced by Saladin and his ungodly beliefs, and they want him stripped of his rank and membership in the Order, and then banished, excommunicate."

"Sweet Jesus! Can they do that?"

"Aye, if they see a need for it. They are Christian monks—men of God and thus entitled to punish wrongdoing or dereliction of duty mercilessly. They can do it, never delude yourself on that."

"How long has he been free? Was he ransomed?"

"No. According to what I read, he was set free in an exchange of prisoners. But be all of that as it may, he has information that we of the brotherhood gravely need, information that he was sent out there to gather years ago, and it has been many years since any of the Council of the brotherhood have had direct dealings with him. Alexander Sinclair trusts no one at face value and never has. Now we have someone to send to him, from within the Temple, whom he will be inclined to trust instinctively. You and he were friends once, so he will trust you more easily than someone he has never met. Therefore you will be the one promoted and dispatched to bring him back into the Order, where he may be examined by his peers of the Temple. That will, at least, be the ostensible purpose underlying your induction and rapid dispatch to Acre—the requirements of the Temple and your duty to meet and execute those requirements, involving a special dispensation and a rapid induction and promotion predicated upon your family connections and your former friendship with Alexander Sinclair.

"Whether you can convince him to return and be judged, of course, remains to be seen. Your real objectives, however, when all is said and done, will have nothing to do with the Temple, *per se*. Your true task will be to reestablish communications between him and the Governing Council of the brotherhood, and to effect the recovery and transfer of the information Alexander holds for us."

"And that information consists of what?"

Justin grinned, a vulpine, leering twisting of his uncomely features. "If I could answer that, Master St. Clair, there would be no need to send you all the way to Acre in such a rush, would there?"

"Hmm. What about the vows—where will I take those?"

"Two of them you have taken already, with merely minor differences. You'll simply repeat them. I'll be the one to lead you through that part, so I will put the words in your mouth and you will merely respond. These are illiterates, for the most part. No one who is not of our brotherhood will notice that the wording of the first two vows is different."

"I have no concerns over those two. It's the third of them that concerns me."

Brother Justin raised both eyebrows. "The vow of chastity? But you have already made your choice on that matter, with your decision to spurn the two Queens. Soon now, in a mere matter of weeks, you will be in Acre—or outside it—and believe me when I say you will find little there among the daughters of the Faithful of Allah to threaten your chastity. Added to which, of course, will be the incentives to chastity provided by the Rule of the Temple itself ... No, you will take your vows in the course of the admission ceremony, and you may never even think of them again thereafter. De Troyes will officiate, as senior member of the Order here in Cyprus."

"De Troyes? He is not a member of the brotherhood."

"No, he is not, thank God. He is exactly what we require in this instance, in terms of probity and credibility. Not even Richard Plantagenet will dare challenge the acting Master of the Temple here in Cyprus. Le Sieur de Troyes is *un sanglier du Temple*, a Temple Boar, with no interest in life other than the Temple and its form and rituals. That is why he will officiate at your induction, because once I have explained the situation to him he will see, immediately, the need to ship you off in order that you may remove the very real danger to his beloved Temple that your cousin seems to represent."

"How can you be sure he will believe everything you tell him, without question? We have little to go on, save hearsay."

"Hearsay and imagination, Brother André, and you must never underestimate the power of imagination. Men like de Troyes have none of it. Their lives are barren and arid, tied to the daily trivia of humdrum existence. They live in a world without colors, so that when they meet someone like you or me, with the power to talk persuasively and to draw and describe sweeping pictures with our minds and voices, they are easily gulled. By the time I have finished talking with Etienne de Troyes, he will believe your cousin is a bigger threat to the Temple than Saladin himself, and he will begrudge the time it takes to initiate you in the Temple Knighthood, so great will be his need to see you on your way to Acre. Then, while the enthusiasm is still upon him, I will send him to King Richard with the tidings of your promotion and departure."

St. Clair inclined his head. "You obviously believe what you are saying, so it would be churlish of me to doubt you further. When will this all take place?"

"As soon as I can arrange it. Today is the fifteenth day of May. I will have to consult with some others of the brotherhood before I can commit to a specific time, but immediately thereafter, if I can gather sufficient bodies."

"So how long will that be?"

"Tomorrow. Almost certainly we will be able to proceed by tomorrow night."

André nodded. Inductions always took place at night. "Will I be able to visit my father before I leave?"

"No, because you cannot leave here now until you are a sworn Templar. But Sir Henry may visit you here, if he can find the time. If we induct you tomorrow night, you will be gone the following day, so you had best send word to him to visit you tomorrow. And mind you warn him to say nothing to the King." He paused, and then added, "Forget that. I will see to it myself. Is there anything else troubling you? You look … worried."

St. Clair shrugged. "The ceremony, I suppose. The Raising. I have no idea what to expect. Is it complex?" He looked decidedly relieved when he saw the veteran Master of Novices sit back on his stool and grin at him.

"It is a secret ceremony, Master St. Clair. You know that. But it is no Raising. Accept my word on that, if you will, and rest assured that there is nothing complex or meaningful about it." Justin stood up from his stool and crossed to a cupboard against the wall, where he opened a door and removed a flat-bottomed flask and two horn cups. He poured two generous measures of the golden liquid the flask contained, then stoppered the flask and closed the door on it again. He carried both cups to the table. "Honey mead," he said, handing one cup to André. "God created it for moments like these." They both sipped appreciatively and Justin sat down again.

"Remember where this ceremony sprang from, first of all. In the beginning were the nine Founding Brothers, and all of them were brethren of the Order, the sole Order in existence at that time—the

Order of Rebirth in Sion. Through their own efforts, the founders completed the task set them, the unearthing of the Order's treasures, and thereby achieved the rebirth for which it had been named. Thereafter, it became simply the Order of Sion, although its work, unlike its rebirth, is far from complete." He sipped again. "Of course, when they returned to Europe with what they had found, they succeeded in impressing, and in terrifying, everyone in the upper levels of the Church, so that, in their scramble to placate the brothers and to ensure that they maintained the secrecy surrounding what they had found, they heaped praises and plaudits on the men who called themselves the Poor Fellow Soldiers of Christ but were known to everyone else as the Knights of the Temple Mount. And soon recruits began flocking to the standard, demanding to join the order of the new knighthood, as Saint Bernard had called it.

"And thus was born the Order of the Temple. But none of the recruits now flocking to the Temple Mount were brethren of the Order of Sion, and the secrecy of the original nine brothers was well known, although since it was secret, none knew what it entailed. And so, purely in self-defense and for the protection of the brotherhood, Hugh de Payens and his eight friends dreamed up a new ritual that would satisfy the people clamoring for admission and for the trappings of secrecy and arcane rites. They decreed that all initiations would be held at night, in darkness, and they coined new ceremonies out of nothing, ceremonies that have since become entrenched and almost hallowed in observance. Ninety years of use has made them seem portentous, but they began as nonsense, and nonsense they remain." He hesitated. "Mind you, having said that, I have no wish to dismiss all my Templar brothers without respect. They may not be literate or well schooled in social manners, but many of them, including even the Temple Boars, devote their lives and their vocations to the pursuit of sanctity, albeit in the churchly, Christian sense. And that is greatly admirable, even in the eyes of those of us who see their error from our own ancient and privileged viewpoint. We can see them as misguided, but we cannot think of them as foolish, since their sincerity is undoubtable and their error one that has consumed the world.

"You, Brother, have been sufficiently fortunate to be Raised in the Order of Sion, and you have had to work and study diligently to achieve each step in your progression to your current status. You will find none of that work, or anything to resemble it, within the Temple. The rites you will experience are largely meaningless, and the only work a man need do to progress through the ranks is military—training and fighting. You are already adept in those areas, and so believe me, you need have no fear about the initiation rites. By the time you enter the Chapter Chamber for the ceremony, you have passed every test set you and your acceptance is assured. The ritual in the Chamber is merely a confirmation, for the benefit of the Temple congregation. There will be other rites you may attend from time to time, whenever opportunity arises, but those, too, will be secret and concealed within the Temple's secrecy, shared only by our brethren."

He raised his cup in salute, and André answered him, then both of them drained their cups of the sweet, fiery liquid, after which Justin belched loudly and rose to his feet.

"And now I have to start making arrangements. I will send one of the brothers to your father, inviting him to be here tomorrow at mid-afternoon and warning him to say nothing about it to anyone at all, including the King. Will he be bound by that, think you?"

"He will, Brother Justin, he will."

ANDRÉ ST. CLAIR was in the tilting yard of the castle the next afternoon and had been there for an hour, training hard, hacking and swinging his broadsword against an upright post until he began to believe that he might never be able to raise his arms again, when he was approached by a sergeant brother who told him that Brother Justin wanted to see him immediately.

He found the Master of Novices where he had left him the previous day, huddled over the long work table in his own room, and the moment he set eyes on him he knew something had gone wrong.

"What?" he began. "What is it? Has de Troyes vetoed your idea?"

The look that Justin threw at him then was part anger, part puzzlement. "What are you talking about? No, de Troyes has vetoed nothing. Everything there is in hand, to this point. But your father will not be coming to visit you."

"Why not? He said he would be here by mid-afternoon."

"Aye, he did, but that was before the madness erupted in the city."

"What madness? What is going on?"

"You did not know? No, clearly you did not. Well, it is nothing unusual. Your liege lord has merely remembered once again that he hates Jews, and so they are turning the entire city upside down, rooting them out wherever they are to be found."

"Rooting who out, Jews? There are no Jews in Limassol."

"There are Jews everywhere, Master St. Clair, if you wish to look closely enough, but this persecution of them is a crime in the eyes of God. Something triggered this latest madness sometime before noon, but I know not what it was. I know only that Richard was incensed to hear of it and ordered the arrest of every Jew in Cyprus. And since he believes Isaac Comnenus is a Jew, he has turned out his entire army and assembled them on the beaches between the city gates and the harbor, preparing to hunt him down. It truly is a madness. Anyway, as Master-at-Arms, your father is involved in the midst of it all, but he found time to send word here and to wish you well in the event you do not see him before you depart for Acre."

"How did he know I am going to Acre?"

"I had my man tell him, in explanation of why you wished to see him today."

"So why are you angry about that?"

"Angry? I am not angry. I am merely frustrated not to be able to find some of the people I wanted to have present at your ceremony tonight. We can proceed with it, so be prepared an hour after dark, but there will be five, perhaps six people missing whom I wanted to be there. Ah well, we will talk afterwards. And tomorrow you will leave for Acre on a fast galley, one of the Temple's best, bearing dispatches for the senior Temple officer there who is at this time, I believe, the Marshal himself, a knight of the Languedoc who shares your given name, André. He is André Lallières of Bordeaux. Do you know the name?"

"No, should I?"

"I thought you might. He is one of us, Raised on the same day I was, and his family is one of the originals. Be ready for tonight. You will be summoned by two knights."

"What must I wear?"

"Exactly what you are wearing now. Your virgin's shroud. They'll take it from you and you will be dressed formally after the induction. Now go and leave me to do what I have to do between now and then."

The rest of that day passed with a slowness that St. Clair could not believe, but pass it did, eventually, and he was waiting impatiently as soon as darkness fell over the city.

Eight hours later, at daybreak on the seventeenth of May, he stood on one of the wharves in the harbor, flanked by two knights whose finery was less new and striking than was his. He wore the full white surcoat and red cross, brilliantly new and unused, of a fully fledged Temple knight. It covered a suit of mail so new that it was as stiff as the equally new and heavy knee-high boots that encased his feet and legs. The mailed hood encasing his head felt strange and constrictive, but the helmet he wore over that felt solid and comfortable. His own sword, the gift from Richard, hung at his waist, and behind him stood his personal attendant, a sergeant brother assigned to him that morning for the duration, whose primary duty was to keep both Sir André and his personal armor, equipment, and weaponry in prime condition and ready for battle at any time. André stretched himself and flexed his shoulders beneath the unaccustomed tightness of his mailed hauberk. He had not worn a full mailed suit since joining the novitiate, and as he watched the approach of the boat that had been sent for him, he wondered how long it would take him to grow used to it again.

The boat bumped against the wharf close by his feet, and André turned to his two companions and bade them farewell as his attendant passed the two chests that held their possessions into the boat, then climbed in after them. Brother Justin, unusually splendid in a fresh white surcoat and burnished mail, wished him God speed, and the other knight, Etienne de Troyes himself, hung a rigid leather cylinder containing dispatches around André's neck, then drew himself erect in a formal salute and wished the new knight every success with his mission in the Holy Land. The little boat was pushed off from the wharf and began to steer towards the galley that would carry André St. Clair and his dispatches into Outremer.

EIGHT

*K*reeee ...

The distant, high-pitched scream drew André St. Clair's eyes upward to where the hawk hung impossibly high above him, visible only as a floating speck against the flawless blue of the morning sky. Motionless then, his neck tilted sharply backward, André watched it drift silently on whatever currents were sustaining it up there, lifting and wafting it on a cushion of air pressed gently but firmly against the spread of its wings. As he watched, holding his breath, the black shape altered and then swooped down and around in a great arc, until the wings began to beat again, bearing the creature easily upward to its previous height.

"How big do you think that thing is?"

The voice came from behind him, and André shook his head. "Difficult to tell," he answered. "There's nothing up there to judge it by, not even another bird. It could have wings as wide as your arms' span, seen from here, or it could be less than half that size and only half as far away as we think it is."

"D'you think someone might be controlling it?"

"I doubt it." St. Clair kept his eyes on the distant bird. "Most falconers will keep their birds hooded until they spot a quarry and release them only then, directly to the hunt. They are wild things and will return to the wild if they are given sufficient opportunity, no matter how well trained they may be. That's why the falconers are so jealous of them. They do not enjoy seeing their precious killers flying around loose for any great length of time."

"Speaking of time, it is nigh on noon and it looks as though we have been played for fools."

St. Clair broke his gaze from the hawk and stood up in his stirrups, stretching his arms high over his head and counting aloud
slowly to twenty. He then bent his elbows and held his arms horizontally, keeping his head steady as he twisted slowly from one side
to the other several times, pulling each elbow as far back in its turn
as possible, grunting gently with the exertion. That done, he rolled
his head with greatly exaggerated extension, three times to the right
and three more to the left, and only then did he gather up his reins
and respond to the other man's comment.

It was the thirtieth day of May in the year 1191, and he had been
in Acre now for ten whole days, during which he had sent out
inquiries about the whereabouts of his cousin, Sir Alexander
Sinclair, explaining who he himself was and offering a substantial
reward to anyone who could arrange a meeting between the two of
them. He had had no qualms about doing so, and no fears that
anyone might challenge his right to conduct himself as he saw fit.
The letter he carried from Etienne de Troyes had explained
succinctly to the Temple officers in command at the siege of Acre
that St. Clair was in Outremer on a special mission for the Temple
and must be accorded full cooperation and any assistance he
requested. Now he half grinned and spoke over his shoulder.

"We have not been played for fools, Harry. I may have, but you
have not. You are here at my invitation, to keep me company, and
there is nothing foolish in that. Unless, of course, you feel foolish
for accepting the invitation. Our host may have simply been delayed
by something unexpected. That happens to us all, from time to
time." He was grinning as he swung his horse around to where he
could see the man at his back, but Sir Harry Douglas was in no
mood to return the grin. He sat frowning, disapproving of everything
involved in this excursion, which he believed unauthorized, into
needless danger.

Long before dawn that morning, telling no one about their
departure or about where they were going, they had left their
fellow knights encamped at the oasis they called Jappir, a mere
hour's ride from the siege lines around Acre. They had ridden

inland from there and were now deep inside hostile territory, more than three leagues from where they had set out, and facing a land- scape that Harry could never have imagined before he set eyes upon it that morning. They were surrounded by an ocean of rocks, a vast plain of smoothly rounded boulders of all shapes and sizes, some of them as large as houses, some as large as castles, and others, the pebbles of the scene, merely as large as hay wains or peasants' huts. Any one of these could conceal an entire group of men, and Harry and André had not eyes enough between them to keep sufficient watch. It was all Harry could do to resist the temp- tation to keep his horse moving constantly so that he could scan the horizon without pause.

Harry kneed his horse forward and rode slowly around the cluster of massive stones that crowned the tiny hilltop, the highest point for miles. There appeared to be no more than six of them in the grouping, but they occupied the exact center of the small hilltop and were piled together as though gathered and set in place by a giant. They were also high enough to be visible from miles away, the tallest of them towering far over Harry's head, a tapering, sand- sculpted monolith more than twice as high as he was on his horse's back.

"Laugh if you want to, St. Clair," he said quietly, his eyes probing the horizon, "but I don't like one wee bit of this. I think you're mad to be here, and I am even madder to have come with you. I enjoy your company and you can be a droll whoreson at times, but this, this is insanity. There could be legions of fleabags out there right now, watching us from behind every stone in sight, even taking aim at us, and we would never even see them before we died. Let's move on, in God's name. That way, even shut in on all sides, we can at least entertain the illusion that we might be able to run between the rocks and save ourselves."

André St. Clair shook his head gently. "I have no doubt you may be right, my friend. And God in His Heaven knows that your abili- ties to maintain the sanctity and integrity of your own fragile and cowardly skin are legendary. But I believe, nonetheless, that it would be an error to leave so soon. The man we are here to meet might, as I said, have perfectly valid reasons for being late."

"You call this late? He has slipped by several hours beyond late."

"One hour, Harry, one hour at most. No more than that. We arrived early."

"Well, I'm glad at least you didn't name him Sinclair."

André looked at him quickly. "What is that supposed to mean?"

"This fellow, he could be anyone. Might even be a Muslim bandit, hoping to take you for ransom. We have no proof that he's the man you seek."

"No, we have not. Nor have we proof that he is not. So we will wait. And with the grace of God, we shall see." He tugged at his reins and nudged his horse towards the edge of the hilltop, and Harry moved forward to join him, gazing out at the eerie sameness of the countless stones in this strange stretch of desert. St. Clair arched his back again, raising his bent elbows to shoulder height, then pressing them backward. "Master Douglas," he said, "I intend to climb down from this saddle now, to stretch my legs and wait in comfort for a spell. You should do the same. But in the meantime, think of something different to talk about ... something pleasant and positive."

Douglas said nothing, but both knights swung down from their mounts and busied themselves in loosening their saddle girths to give their horses a brief respite.

"Did no one ever warn you people never to relax your guard?"

The voice came from directly behind them, so close that the speaker had had no need to shout, and both men spun around so quickly, fumbling for their weapons, that anyone watching might have laughed at their consternation. Harry Douglas was quicker to react than St. Clair. His sword cleared its sheath as he completed his pivot, and he had it half raised to attack before the significance of what he was seeing struck home to him. André had been less well balanced when he heard the stranger's words, and he had to shuffle his feet quickly before he could begin to turn around, but his hand had barely closed about his sword hilt when he identified what he was seeing and straightened up immediately. He did not relinquish his grip on the hilt—the folly of such naïve behavior had been drilled into his skull years earlier—but he felt the tension bleed from him as quickly as it had sprung up as he swept his gaze from side to side, searching for others. There were none. The man facing them was alone.

"Who are you?" Harry asked the question before St. Clair could formulate it.

The stranger merely looked back at him. "Who should I be? Whom did you expect to find here, so far into the desert and at such a time of day? I am Alexander Sinclair."

It was all he needed to say, and André felt his heart leap in his chest with relief, not because he had doubted who this was but because he had doubted his own ability to recognize his cousin after so many years. He might, he felt now, have recognized the face, changed though it was, but the voice, deep and resonantly alien in its Scots intonation, was unmistakable and unchanged. Before he could say a word, however, the stranger looked from Harry to him.

"You are young André, I can tell. I remember your eyes, and the wee crook in your nose. Had you no' mentioned that in the message you sent me, I would never have answered you. I have but little truck wi' people nowadays."

André smiled, feeling euphoric, for he had heard little good of this man since arriving in Outremer, and he had begun to suspect that his cousin might, indeed, have turned away from everything he once knew. Now, however, within moments of setting eyes upon him again, he knew deep down in his heart that Alec Sinclair was no whit less than, or different from, the man he had always been. He was tall and lean, dark eyed, gaunt faced, and long legged, with broad, strong shoulders. His beard was iron gray and clipped short, and in conjunction with the edges of the close-fitting mailed hood he wore beneath his helmet, it emphasized the deeply graven lines of his face. He wore the full dress of a senior Templar knight, with the equal-armed black cross embroidered on his left breast, in the upper quadrant of the white surcoat bearing the long red cross on its front and rear. The chain mail of his hauberk and hood had the burnished look about them that André already knew to be the result of years spent in the desert dryness, being scrubbed and polished every day by blowing sand, and he carried a long-bladed sword, harnessed somehow to hang at his back, between his shoulders. In that single glance, he registered that Sinclair's leggings were different, too, ankle length rather than calf length, and flared from the knee down so that they could be worn over heavy, thick-soled riding boots.

"Then I am glad I sent the message as I did," he said in response, his wide smile still in place. "But it was nothing subtle. I merely thought you might remember the incident. Well met, Cousin. It's been too long a time, too many years. And say hello to my friend of friends here, one of your fellow countrymen, Harry Douglas. Harry, this is my cousin, Sir Alexander Sinclair." He extended his arm and Alec gripped it firmly, smiling with the astonishingly bright, warm eyes that André remembered well. But then André twisted his arm subtly and gripped his cousin's hand in both his own, and beyond a momentary flicker of surprise, Alec betrayed no reaction, but returned the required counter grip of brotherhood. He then turned to Harry and shook with him, too, initiating the grip himself this time and receiving no reaction.

"Well met, Sir Harry Douglas," he said. "Do you know what we are talking about, your friend here and I?" When Harry shook his head, Sinclair laughed, a single sound deep in his throat and swallowed before it could emerge completely. "That beak of his," he said. "With the bend in it. 'Twas I did that for him, one summer afternoon when he was yet too young to do anything other than bleed. I turned quickly, to see what he was doing, and there he was, right at my back. The butt of the spear beneath my arm caught him from the side as I came around, and it mashed his nose across his face. It was a marked improvement, for even as a boy he was too comely, but I was tormented by guilt over it for at least an hour." He paused dramatically. "Well, it felt like an hour. But in honesty it could have been less." He stopped, then looked from one to the other of them, and his face grew sober.

"You will have heard, no doubt, about how changed I am since I returned from my captivity among the Infidel?"

He had spoken to both of them, but he was looking at André, and André returned the look openly, nodding. "Aye, we have heard some drolleries, but as you see, they did not deter us from coming to find you."

"Aye, and had I known for certain it was you seeking me, I might not have brought you so far out into the desert for a meeting. But I have learned that very few men are worth trusting nowadays, and I was never the great truster of people in the first place. I thought, just from the way your message was worded, that you might be who you said you were, but I have heard nothing of you since last we met, more than twelve years ago. It was not inconceivable that you might have told the tale to someone, who then thought to use it as a lure to draw me out of hiding. And it was possible, too, that you were being used against me. But here you are in the flesh, a Knight of the Temple, and I can see you're still the lad I knew and liked. How is your lady mother? I have never stopped being grateful to her for the way she took me in that year."

"She died a few years ago, but she remembered you fondly. She would often talk of you, years after you had gone. But my father is well, and aged as he is, he is coming to Outremer with Richard, as his Master-at-Arms." Before Alec could react, he asked, "Why would anyone seek to draw you out of hiding, Alec? Why are you *in* hiding, for that matter?"

"Och, that's a long story and for another time and place. But it grieves me to hear about your mother. Is that why you have been at such pains to find me? Has it to do with … family affairs?"

"Yes."

"Friendly, I presume?"

"Oh yes, very much so. I have much to tell you. But before I tell you anything, you have to tell me how you did that, how you were able to creep up on us so quietly."

"Quietly? The two of you were making so much noise I could have ridden up behind you with an entire troop without your hearing me."

"For a few moments, perhaps, we were making noise, but where were you before that? Where did you come from?"

Alec Sinclair smiled. "I was in hiding, watching you and listening. Close by, as you suspect, but you'll pardon me if I don't tell you exactly where. I will tell you, however, that the opportunity it afforded me to hide and observe is why I chose this spot."

His cousin thought about that for a few moments, looking around him speculatively, and then he nodded. "Accepted. Were the secret mine, I would not reveal it, either."

"And speaking of secrets," Harry Douglas intervened, "I know that you two have things to discuss—confidential family matters that do not concern me—so I will leave you to talk. Now that you are here I am prepared to believe that there are no fleabags watching us and waiting to attack. I shall unsaddle our mounts and feed them some oats, and then I will walk about among the stones and try to find your horse, Sir Alexander, for I presume you did not walk all the way out here in full mail. Should I become lost, I will whistle loudly, so if you will keep one ear apiece cocked to the air, I'll be obliged. And so, in which direction should I seek your horse?"

Sinclair raised an arm and in a slow and elaborate mime pointed directly north, and Harry nodded in acknowledgment and began to walk away, leading the two horses, until Sinclair stopped him again.

"I know you have been out here in the kingdom for a while, but I doubt you have been *here* before. Be careful walking among those stones. Keep your eyes open and your wits about you, and don't stick your bare hands into open holes. This place is a paradise for vipers."

Harry nodded. "My thanks for that. I promise you, I will keep my hands where I can see them at all times."

"HE SEEMS LIKE A GOOD MAN," Alec Sinclair said as Harry vanished behind a boulder, leading the two horses. "But then, he is a Scot, so I should not be surprised. Mind you, he does not sound like one."

"He is a good man, in every sense," André replied quietly, "and he is his *own* man, which is far more important and appears to be an unusual attribute out here. The Temple brothers, knights and sergeants both, walk somewhat in awe of him, and that makes Harry uncomfortable, so most of the time he avoids people altogether. He always was a quiet man, from what I've heard, but now he is one of the most celebrated knights in all of Outremer, and that does little to increase his comfort."

Sir Alexander pointed to a pair of smallish stones, then reached back over his shoulder and drew the great sword from behind his back. "Can we not sit down while we talk? I have been standing for hours. You'll pardon me, I hope, for drawing steel, but I canna sit with this thing in place." He stepped to one side and carefully leaned the long-bladed weapon upright against a stone.

"That is an impressive weapon. I do not believe I have ever seen its like."

"Then you have never been in Scotland. Two-handed broadsword. They are common there."

"That blade must be more than five feet long."

"It's certainly long enough to keep the pests away when you swing it around your head."

André laughed and looked again at the impressive blade, gauging the width of it at a full hand's breadth where it met the double crossguard. "What were we talking about?"

"About your friend. You said he was uneasy. Why?"

André crossed his arms on his chest. "Well, he is a monk, and some of those make a religion out of discomfort. But were I to guess seriously at a realistic reason, I would say he feels guilty for missing the disaster at Hattin. He was at the springs of La Safouri with the rest of the army a few days before the battle, but he was sent off with dispatches to the garrison at Ascalon the night before de Chatillon and his cronies talked King Guy into abandoning the oasis and marching directly for Tiberias. So most of his friends ended up dead."

"And he feels guilty because he survived, you think? Then I shall have to talk to him. I was there that day, and believe me when I tell you that Harry has no need to berate himself for his good fortune in being somewhere else. So how came he to be in Acre?"

"Because he fought his way out of Ascalon, just before it fell, then spent the following months acquainting himself with the land of Palestine, sometimes on horseback, mostly afoot. The entire region was in chaos, for after Hattin, the Muslims were invincible and our side could barely field a force of cavalry. Every city in the Latin Kingdom went down, as you know, and it seems Harry was there at most of them, usually in the thickest of the fighting. He was wounded a few times but he came out alive every time, and men began to say he was indestructible. In a time when there were no senior officers anywhere, to plan or take command, men rallied to Harry, forcing him to be a leader despite his own unwillingness. And eventually, he led a tired and tattered little army back to Tyre."

"How long ago was that, do you know?"

"No, but Harry can tell you. It must have been half a year after Hattin, at least."

"Aye, at least. So he reached Tyre. They must have fetcd him when he arrived, after so long."

"They tried, I'm told, for the men who had been with him sang his praises everywhere they went, and God Himself knows the Franks had need of heroes in those days ... conquering heroes first, but failing those, defiant heroes. Especially in Tyre."

Alec Sinclair nodded. Tyre remained the only Christian-held city in all the Holy Land, the only place that had not fallen to the Saracens, and in the weeks and months after Hattin it had filled to overflowing with the remnants of the Christian army. Conrad de Montferrat, the German Baron who had snatched the city from Saladin's grasp a bare moment before it was lost forever, ruled it with iron discipline, even claiming sovereignty over the last of the Templars there, which in itself was a measure of how far the Temple's star had plunged after Hattin.

"There were fewer than a hundred Templars—knights and sergeants both—in the city when Harry arrived, and he brought only three more with him among his followers. But Gerard de Ridefort was already there."

"And not entirely pleased with the situation, I understand."

"Apparently so."

There was no need for either man to say any more on that matter. De Ridefort, notoriously choleric and intolerant at the best of times, had been reduced to seething impotence in Tyre, bitterly resenting his subordination to de Montferrat and the obligation that went with it to accept orders from the German and obey them meekly, upon pain of expulsion from the city with his knights. There had been no slightest doubt in the Master's mind that Conrad would expel him and his congregation out of hand at the first sign of insubordination or opposition, and he had told his Templars that. He also made no secret of how much it nauseated him that he, as the embodiment of the Temple Order, could do nothing to resist or to change that situation, for he had lost his entire command structure, not to mention four-fifths of his entire command, during and after the battle at Hattin. He was reduced to watching and biding his time, powerless, grim faced and tooth grinding in his acknowledgment of that.

De Montferrat was a newcomer to the Latin Kingdom, a German whose primary loyalty was to the Holy Roman Empire, which meant to Constantinople and its Orthodox Christianity. By extension of that, and there was no great leap of understanding required to appreciate the subtleties involved, de Montferrat's ideal military order was the Emperor Frederic Barbarossa's Order of Teutonic Knights, which meant that other Orders, namely the Hospitallers and Templars, were inferior and less than ideal. In Conrad's eyes, it was only right and proper that the Teutonic Knights should and would provide the future strength and protection of the Christian presence—*Orthodox* Christian being plainly understood—in the Latin Kingdom. And given sufficient time, he believed, the Latin Kingdom itself might well become the German or the Teutonic Kingdom. In the interim, he was determined that the graspingly ambitious and politically unacceptable *papal* Christianity, Roman Catholicism as it was now known, would be shut out from Jerusalem and forced to return to Rome, taking its knights and its Frankish adherents with it. And neither the Templars nor the Hospitallers, both inextricably linked to the Roman Catholic Church, would be permitted to operate in Outremer thereafter.

"Barbarossa's death must have come as a shock to Conrad," Sinclair mused, and his cousin nodded.

"Aye, and unwelcome."

"Completely. Think about that from his viewpoint, if you can imagine it. There he is, sitting strongly in the throne he built himself, awaiting the arrival of his cousin the Emperor with an army of five hundred thousand men, sufficient strength to enable him to thumb his nose at everyone from Saladin to Richard Plantagenet and Philip of France. He must have felt omnipotent, invincible ... And then in a clatter of hooves comes a worn-out rider with the word that his universe has fallen apart: his Emperor is dead, his mighty army scattered, and all his hopes and promises no more than smoke blowing in the wind." Alec shook his head in wonder. "I know not how I might adjust to such a reversal, such a *vast* reversal. But then, I am not Conrad de Montferrat. And yet, for any man to go from heights to depths so quickly ... And then, no sooner was he down than the next blow struck him: Saladin released de Lusignan. The confluence of timing is incredible."

"Aye, it is—literally incredible. I doubt that was coincidence, Alec, no matter what so many people say. Saladin is no man's fool. He released de Lusignan upon Guy's sworn word that he would not again take up arms against Islam. Everyone knows that, and they laugh at him because of it, thinking him a fool not to know that no Christian need be bound by an oath given under duress to an infidel. But think about that for a moment, if you will. Saladin has been fighting us for years and has had many dealings with our highest-ranking officers and potentates. Do you really believe he is stupid enough to be unaware of the sneering contempt in which every Frank holds him and his? Bear in mind, this is the man who has welded the entire world of Islam, from Syria to Egypt, into one entity, melding and commingling two caliphates and fielding what is probably the largest army ever assembled by any one man in history—greater than Xerxes or Darius, perhaps even greater than Alexander. Do you not think it makes more sense to believe that this Sultan, seeing the danger to his supremacy that existed within Tyre in the person of de Montferrat, might think it advantageous to release King Guy, knowing beyond doubt that Guy would break his given word immediately and march on Tyre, there to claim his kingship and his other rights from Conrad?"

Alec Sinclair smiled, gazing out into distance. "Aye, it makes perfect sense, and I have never thought otherwise. It worked out perfectly, too, did it not? Guy and Conrad were at each other's throats within days."

"But not for many days. The wind changed and the smoke from the fire he lit blew back into Saladin's face when Conrad threw Guy out of Tyre and Guy marched south to besiege Acre. He took the Templars with him, under de Ridefort, and that brings me to the end of Harry's story."

"The *end* of Harry's story?" Sinclair crossed one ankle over his knee and grasped it in both hands, leaning backward. "How can that be? Harry is still with us."

"True, but bear with me. De Ridefort, being the man he was, saw a large and immediate advantage to be gained in promoting Harry to high rank within the Temple. Harry was popular among the brethren and equally well known and liked among the army's other elements, so de Ridefort thought to raise him to one of the key positions left vacant after the losses at Hattin. He told Harry what he had decided, and Harry declined, graciously but firmly. He wanted no part of such distinction, he said, and when de Ridefort refused to accept that, Harry, just as stubbornly, refused to be browbeaten into changing his mind. He was a monk, he told de Ridefort, and he had joined the Temple to be simply that, a monk, adhering to the Temple Rule and seeking salvation in a life of prayer and duty."

"Harry won the argument, obviously."

"Aye, he did. De Ridefort was beside himself, but there was nothing he could do. Faced with the simplicity of Harry's stance, and with the full light of the public scrutiny he himself had initiated with never a thought that he might be rebuffed, he had no choice. So for perhaps the first time in his life as a Templar, he accepted what he could not change. But he let it be known in no uncertain terms that he considered Sir Harry Douglas to be in breach of his vow of obedience—"

"Which he was."

"—perhaps, that is debatable—but also derelict in his concern for the welfare of the Order and fundamentally unworthy of the high regard accorded him by so many misguided people."

"Harsh words, but that sounds like de Ridefort. He was a vindictive man."

"Vindictive? Perhaps. I never knew him, but I have probably heard more about him than about any other man since I came here. There were many negatives attached to him—implacable, humorless, intolerant, irascible, intractable—but I believe now that all of these were a natural outgrowth of his extreme conviction. He was a giant among men and an inspiration as a leader, passionate, given to extremes, and his greatest passion was his loyalty to his religion, even above his loyalty to the Temple. He never suffered fools gladly, and he never tolerated any threat to what he truly believed to be God's kingdom upon earth, but within those terms, Gerard de Ridefort's integrity was boundless."

Alexander Sinclair regarded his cousin calmly, his face empty of expression, then nodded slowly. "Aye ... Well, as you said, you never knew him." His tone was as bland as his facial expression, and André could only stand blinking at him, wondering if he had been rebuked, while Alec continued: "So how has the Master's death changed your friend? He must be different, now that he is free from disapproval?"

"No, Harry is the same. He lived in isolation for months, within the Templar fraternity, for there were many who had snubbed him at the outset, afraid to do otherwise lest they attract de Ridefort's displeasure, and then when de Ridefort was killed, that October, Harry discovered that he preferred to remain alone, content with his own company. He had seen who avoided him before, and had no wish to consort with them again simply because they were no longer afraid of de Ridefort. Then, somehow, when I arrived, he and I became friends, and we have been close friends ever since."

"How long ago did you arrive?"

"Ten days ago."

"Hmm. You know I heard about de Ridefort's death at the time. I was still a prisoner then, but the tidings of the Temple Master's death swept right across the Saracen world, and there were celebrations everywhere. I know he was executed, beheaded, but I never did discover how he was captured. He was long dead when I was released and I had other matters to concern me then."

"Well, it was exactly as you might have expected him to be captured: in the thick of things." André stood up and crossed to where Alec's sword stood propped against a stone. "May I?" When Alec nodded, he took the sword in hand, holding the long, gleaming blade out in front of him and eyeing it as he spoke. "There was a fight that day, a savage one, but not big enough to be called a battle because it sprang up suddenly, outside the walls of Acre—a spontaneous clash, rather than a strategic confrontation. And strangely enough, it was the only fight of its kind that I have heard of in which Guy commanded brilliantly and distinguished himself." He stepped to one side, swinging the long sword with him, slowly, hefting it for weight and balance. "Stranger still, Conrad was there that day, too, and the pair of them managed to cooperate effectively. It was October fourth, 1189, and I remember the date solely because it was the day Gerard de Ridefort died." St. Clair smiled ruefully, then returned the blade to where it had been propped against the stone. "Beautiful weapon," he said as he sat down again.

"Classically perfect de Ridefort behavior," he continued, "a straight frontal charge against a superior—no, an *overwhelming* concentration of enemy cavalry. It was the third recorded time in his career as Master of the Temple that the man suspended all common sense, in the blind belief that God would protect him and his righteousness, and committed his forces suicidally against impossible odds. And as on the two previous occasions, the enemy merely split their formations and flowed around his charge, yielding nothing in the way of ground or advantage, content to stand off and shoot down the charging monks as they rode by, and then to smother the remainder with the sheer mass of their numbers. And de Ridefort survived again. He always did. And he was taken prisoner. But this time the Saracens executed him out of hand."

"*Sic transit gloria mundi.*"

"Something like that. You didn't like him, did you?"

"De Ridefort?" Alec Sinclair pursed his mouth in distaste. "Didn't like him, didn't trust him, couldn't tolerate him. He cost me too many good friends over the years, with his pig-headed, self-righteous stubbornness and bigotry. You may call it inspiration, but I called it bullying and obstinate idiocy. The man was the perfect Temple Boar. Not a thought in his head that did not have to do with the Temple, its glory, its dictates, its dogma, its needs, and when it might require him next to bathe. That is a very narrow path to walk through life." He slapped both palms down on his thighs. "So you are here on Council business. When were you Raised, and where?"

"Like you, on my eighteenth birthday. And at a Gathering in Tours, in the house of one of the Council members."

"And when did you decide to join the Temple?"

André waggled one hand from side to side. "I never did ... not really. That decision was made for me, by King Richard."

"The man himself, the Lionheart? I am impressed."

"You need not be. He is my liege lord. And that, too, is a long story for another time. More important now, I have dispatches for you—a wealth of information and instructions, I believe. They are in my saddlebags, so I'll give them to you when Harry comes back."

"Do you have any idea what they concern?"

"Yes and no. They are from the Council. I was amply provided with dispatches when I arrived, some for the Commander of the Kingdom of Jerusalem, from his Temple superiors in France, but most of them for you. They all looked similar on the outside, so I had to be careful not to mingle them. Yours, however, were labeled in Arabic. I spent a long time receiving careful instruction in Arabic."

"You speak Arabic?" The astonishment in Sinclair's voice was worth all the time and trouble and effort André had expended, and he permitted himself a tiny smile.

"Barely. I understand it far better than I speak it, but I do speak a little … atrociously, I've been told. "

"And you learned it over there?"

"I did, from a number of distinguished teachers, mostly in Poitiers, some in Marseille."

Alec Sinclair immediately switched languages. "Tell me, then, about what you have learned."

"Many things, in a broad range of subjects. The Koran, of course, first above all, the words of Allah and His Prophet, without which nothing in the Arab world makes sense. Then much about the diversity and complexity of Islamic society, and of the various elements within it. I can also speak with authority, and from either viewpoint, on the differences between the Shi'a and Sunni sects."

"That is amazing." Sinclair had been grinning as he listened, but now he said in a low, serious voice, "Cousin, I swear that that is probably the worst Arabic I have ever heard spoken, even by a Templar *ferenghi*."

"So why were you sent to find me? You, I mean, and not someone else?"

"Because the members of the Council knew we are cousins and we know each other. And because no one had heard from you in a very long time and there was very real concern that you might be dead. My understanding is that you had been entrusted with some matter of grave importance to the brotherhood and had been engaged upon pursuing it for years, until the outbreak of the war and your disappearance. My task was to find you and to acquire the information you had collected, then return it to the Council."

"If that was all that they required of you, you had no need to learn Arabic. What do you know about this information I was collecting?"

"Nothing, really. Nothing at all."

Sinclair looked closely at him, then looked away. "Then there is something lacking here … something that neither one of us knows. How large are these dispatches you have brought for me? Are they heavy? Bulky?"

"They are heavy, considering that they are merely written missives. And they are in two large wallets, both of them full."

"Aha. And what were you to do with them in the event that I was dead?"

"Read them, and then try to complete your task."

"But then you would have had to start from the beginning, from the very outset. And I had been working at it for years. Even speaking Arabic, you would have been able to do nothing."

"Perhaps not, but I had—I have—a list of names, three names in all, of people with whom you are known to have associated in the past. I was to contact them and try to reconstruct your activities, hoping to find whatever reports you might have left behind ... in concealment."

"Hmm." The single sound was dismissive, perhaps contemptuous, but Sinclair had made up his mind. "Well then, we had best collect these wallets of yours and be on our separate ways. It sounds as though I have much to read, and I believe the quicker I set myself to the task, the better it will be. Can you whistle for your friend? I will ride back with you as far as I can, but I will leave you before we draw near to the camps at Acre, for I have no wish to be seen. When I have read everything and understand what is required of me, I will send them back to you, for you to read. It seems appropriate that, if you are to run the risk of being killed with me, you should understand what we are attempting to do. I presume something is required from both of us in any case, although there is little to be gained from speculating as to what. But I will also send you instructions on where to meet me next time. It will not be as difficult or far away next time, I promise. Now call for Harry."

FOR A MILE OR TWO the men spoke of generalities until they fell into a comfortable silence, and for some time there was nothing to be heard but the clopping of hooves and the creaking of saddle leather, and St. Clair found himself thinking about the absence of metallic bridle sounds. None of the knights wore metal bridles. That was one of the first things he had noticed on arriving here. Sound

traveled far in the desert air, and many a knight had died uselessly
in the early days of conquest here because of a jingling bridle. He
was brought back to awareness by the sound of his friend Douglas
clearing his throat before starting to speak again.

"May I ask you a question, Sir Alexander? A question I have no
right to ask?"

Alec looked drolly at Harry. "An impertinent question, you
mean. You may ask, but it sounds portentous and formal, so I may
choose not to answer it. Ask away."

"One of the first things you said to us today, about not knowing
whether to meet us or not, was … Well, you said a few things, in
fact, that have been troubling me ever since, but you began by
saying that few men are worth trusting nowadays, and that you
thought André's little tale about his nose might have been used as a
lure to draw you out of hiding."

"That is correct. So, what are you asking me?"

Harry threw up his hands in exasperation. "You are a monk, like
me, like André here. We are all three Templars, and that means that,
apart from our prowess against the enemy, we own little to cause
concern or envy among our fellows, who are all as poor as we are,
having taken the same vows. Were you saying that your fellow
Templars wish you ill? And if not them, then who? Wait, wait …"
He slowed himself down and began again. "What I am asking you,
Master Sinclair, is why an honored knight like you, a veteran of
years of service here, should be in so much fear of his own kind that
he feels the need to live alone and in hiding. That is my question."

"There is no short answer to that question, Harry," he said eventually. "Yes, there are some among my fellow Templars who, if they
do not wish me ill, certainly do not wish me well. But not everyone
in this army is a poverty-sworn monk with no ambitions, and I have,
whether or not you choose to believe it, excellent and defensible
reasons for living alone and in hiding. It is not such a great departure from our chosen way of life, if you stop and consider it, Harry.
I live alone, so I find I am free of temptations most of the time. I also
live very simply, feeding myself upon what I can catch, barter, or

infrequently grow, and I have ample time for prayer and contempla-
tion of the vale of tears we live in. I live, in fact, not so much like a
monk as an anchorite … or even an eremite." He fell silent then, and
let the younger knights mull over his words before continuing.

"Much of the trouble I have had in the recent past has sprung
from my being held by the Saracens. You may have heard mention
of that before, in fact I mentioned it myself, did I not?"

"Aye," André said with a nod.

"Well, simply put, that is the source of my troubles."

"Your captivity?" André said. "Forgive me, but I must be misun-
derstanding. How can the fact that you were a captive cause problems for you now? Did you convert to Islam?" He was half jesting,
but contrived to look perturbed, nonetheless, and Alec smiled.

"No, I did not … not quite. But I did something almost as repre-
hensible. I enjoyed portions of my captivity."

André glanced sideways at Harry, as if to make sure that he was
hearing the same thing. "You enjoyed it? Captivity?"

"*Portions* of it."

"Which portions would those have been?"

"The people, for one thing, the ordinary Saracen villagers,
women and children and old men. Whenever we Franks think of
them at all—and we seldom do because all our attention is taken up
by the men, the warriors—we think of them as nomads, wanderers
with no permanent homes. But not all of them are nomadic. The
village in which I was held was prosperous, after its fashion, and the
tribe had lived there since the days of the local emir's grandfather,
growing sufficient goats and crops in the normal way of things to
keep themselves alive and provide a small surplus for trading. But
their village was built over an underground water source and they
had many date palms, and that was the source of their wealth and
permanence. Once I grew accustomed to being there, unable to
escape, I found myself growing to like them. I understood and
spoke their language, although none of them knew that, but that
helped me greatly towards understanding who they were and how
they lived.

"I was a prisoner, and so naturally enough they put me to work, slave work for the most part, although it was little different from their own. Everybody in that village works in some fashion, for there is no room for unproductive bodies. They watched me closely at first, suspicious and hostile and probably afraid I might go mad and murder all of them some night while they slept and all their men were away at war. But as time passed and they observed that I worked well and was no threat to anyone, they began to show me small kindnesses—an extra bowl of broth, or an additional mouthful of bread or hummus. One of the old men, whom I had once voluntarily helped to carry a heavy load, carved me a wooden pillow of my own. And so when the time seemed right, I permitted myself to 'learn' their language, repeating selected words aloud and very cautiously, taking great pains to make them sound correct yet slightly alien.

"I felt quite guilty, I recall, for they were all delighted with my efforts, and particularly with the fact that I would even try to learn their tongue. But they were very supportive, and within the space of several months I was able to converse with them. I had to be careful, at first, not to betray myself by 'learning' too much, too quickly, but the discipline of that proved beneficial, and soon I could rattle on about most things, although I professed to know nothing at all of the Koran. I was a *ferenghi*, after all, a foreigner and a Christian. And then, eventually, I was released and returned here, to Acre. And that is when I first found trouble."

It was Harry's turn to ask a question. "How? Why? What did you do?"

"Nothing much. I have never been much of a talker, so I listened while others talked, and I disagreed with some of what I heard—with most of it, in fact—and I said so. And every word I said was repeated and twisted out of recognition and then thrown back to me as accusations. They said I had been traduced by the enemy, that I was a Saracen-lover, that I could no longer be trusted and should be placed in quarantine, isolated from decent Christians who might be influenced and suborned by my heretical beliefs."

"Heretical? Was that word used?"

Sinclair grunted in disgust. "Of course it was used. But the fool who used it did not even know what it means. He knew only that he had heard it used impressively by some angry priest who was bent on frightening someone. Can you read, Harry? Can you write?"

Harry made a face. "Aye, I can write my name, and I can read it, too. But not much else."

"Then you are better off than the next hundred of your fellows. André here can read and write, I know, because he could do both already when first I met him, and he was but ten years old. But André is unusual in that, for someone who is not a churchman. Most knights cannot read. Not one of them in any hundred may be literate." He paused for only a moment, and when he continued, his voice took on an oratorical cadence, deliberately assumed, so that as he continued to speak, it grew in volume and articulation until he was declaiming, his voice ringing out over his horse's pointed ears.

"Knights have no need to read, or to write. They have no time to waste on such things. They are educated only in warfare and fighting, and they will know nothing else for the duration of their lives. And yet being men, they are too stupid to recognize or accept the frightening vastness of their own ignorance, and so in hope of sounding wise and seeming clever, they quote and misquote their betters and, all too frequently and unfortunately, their benighted peers as well, filling the air with the belching emptiness of bellicose ignorance being misquoted by fools and ignoramuses. That is the grand total, the sum contribution to our existence, of most of the men who compose this army. And set above those, we are asked to believe, are their betters ... the makers of military opinion and shapers of belief. But sadly, they, too, are knights for the most part, no better informed or educated than their underlings." He stopped dramatically, then resumed in a much quieter, deadly serious voice.

"And then there come the clerics, last of all, but powerful beyond credence—the priests, the churchmen, the so-called men of God. More than all others combined, these, I believe, are the true malefactors of our time. Their ignorance is of another order. Malignant, oppressive, and tyrannical, they are consumed by their own self-importance and all too often just as tragically blind and bigoted as the most ignorant of their followers."

Harry Douglas was looking at Sinclair with rounded, awe-stricken eyes, his mouth slightly open as though he was about to speak but could not move his jaw, which was for several moments exactly true. But then he found his tongue and managed to say, "You told them that? You said that to the priests?"

The beginnings of a grin tugged at the corner of Alec's mouth. "No, I did no such thing. D'you think me daft? All I did was observe aloud that, having lived for years among the enemy, I had never seen any of them eat human flesh, fornicate unnaturally or with animals, or consort knowingly with devils in order to conjure magical defeats for Christian armies at their hands. I said that Saracens were, in many surprising and enlightening ways, remarkably similar to our own people at home, in loving their children and honoring their elders, attending to their civic duties, producing taxes for their governors, and voluntarily leaving their families behind and riding off to war when they were called upon. And having said so, I refused to change my opinions or my testimony." He shrugged. "That was sufficient to outrage them and to have me cast from the society of my supposedly civilized cohorts. And so I left, almost three months ago."

"Would you like to return now, with us?"

Another shrug. "No, I think not. I have been alone now for almost longer than I stayed in camp on my return, and I find I prefer it … Besides, I am not completely alone, not all the time. I have friends who visit me from time to time." He glanced around. "Look, we are out. That always amazes me, the speed of the change."

It was true, they had ridden abruptly out from the boulder field and were now in an open desert of sandy ground, thinly scattered with desiccated, long-dead shrubs among which the largest pebble visible was barely the size of a man's thumb. Ahead of them now, perhaps a mile away, the sand began to slope upward into dunes, but at this point there was nothing beneath them but bare earth and sandy clay, and at their backs a straight line, almost a solid wall, of boulders, seemingly man-made in their appearance of regularity and the straightness of the line of demarcation. St. Clair suddenly felt exposed and vulnerable, highly aware of the openness surrounding them, and involuntarily he sat up straighter in his saddle, dropping his hand to the hilt of his sword and stretching one leg forward to touch the shield that hung from his saddle bow. Beside him, at precisely the same moment, Harry Douglas did the same thing, and Alec Sinclair smiled to himself and peered ahead, to where the distant dunes appeared as a low-lying cloud on the horizon, then flicked at his reins and brought his mount surging to a canter.

Behind him, Harry spurred his horse to catch up, and as he drew alongside, followed by André, he shouted, "Why do you dislike bishops and priests so much? I mean, I have no great opinion of them myself, but you really appear to detest them."

Sinclair barely glanced at Harry as he shouted back, "You wrong me. I said nothing of bishops and priests. I said men of God. It's far more complex than priests and bishops."

Harry reined in without warning and sat frowning until the other two reined in their mounts and rode back to him. "What's the difference?" he asked when they arrived.

Sinclair made no attempt to pull his mount around again, so that all three of them sat in a mounted triangle, their horses' heads meeting in the middle.

"Have you ever seen an ants' nest, Harry?" Sinclair asked him. "A broken one? It is a scene of chaos, with thousands of ants scurrying everywhere, trying to salvage and rescue all the things they feel to be important."

"Aye. I know what you mean."

"People are like ants. They are social creatures, and there are certain things they need, and certain things they will go to any lengths to achieve. And of all those things, one of the greatest in importance is a sense of order and design. That is part of the nature of man—an urge to have order and design. It applies in everything we do. And nowhere is that more true than in the worship of God. God may be all-knowing and all-powerful, but His affairs in this world are run and organized by men, and it has always been so. In the beginning was God, and when the first man grew aware of Him, the first priest stepped forward to interpret the One to the other. It may or may not be that the outstretched hand of the priest was incidental, but from that time forth, all priests have subsisted on the largesse of the common people.

"In the security of our homes in France and in England, we tend to think of men of God solely in terms of the Pope and his archbishops, his bishops and his priests. Few of us ever stop to think that in the East, in Constantinople, there is another Church, also Christian but different from that in Rome, yet organized and run by priests like those of Rome. Roman Catholic and Orthodox Christian—the same God, in virtually all respects, but different in each realm, because the men of God who run the two Churches differ in their beliefs and in their interpretations of God's will and wishes. Thus we have Christian friends and supposed allies worshipping one God and killing each other for the differences in what they each believe is truth, according to the men of God to whom they look for guidance. God is merciful, we are taught, but men of God need not be. Their task is to convert the world to their particular beliefs."

He looked from one to the other of his listeners. "So much for Christianity and its supposed unity. But look, too, at Islam. Is it different? No, it is not, not in the sense I am talking about here, because it, too, is run by the men of God. They call themselves imams and mullahs and a range of other names, but they are priests and bishops in every way that we would recognize, in that they seek to control the minds and the lifelong behavior of their fellow men and they live off the goodwill and wealth of the common people. And even they, from the beginning, have fostered divergence in their struggling for power from the outset. No sooner was the Prophet Muhammad declared dead than his followers began to squabble over who would succeed him and control the power of Islam. And mark that word 'control.' It is remarkable how often you will find it cropping up, in dealings with the men of God.

"So today, within Islam, you have Shi'a and Sunni Muslims, each tearing at the other's throat at every opportunity, and each convinced, because their men of God insist it must be so, that Allah is great, as is Muhammad His Prophet, but these others, be they Sunni or Shi'ite, have debased God's wishes and become the enemy, to be damned and obliterated in God's holy name. Shi'a Muslim and Sunni Muslim, Roman Catholic and Orthodox Christian. Bigotry and jealousy and fearful bloodshed entrenched in all four, and four bowed necks beneath the heels of the men of God.

"Would you like to hear more of what I believe, or have I said enough to provoke you, perhaps, into thinking for yourselves?" He looked again from face to face. "Enough? Excellent. We three may or may not meet again, but if we ever do, I would ask you to avoid directing my thoughts again towards the sweet men of God. Shall we ride on? We are yet far from journey's end."

THE FOLLOWING DAY, having found Alec Sinclair and completed the first part of his quest, André talked his new friend Harry Douglas into taking him on a tour of the siege works, which were enormous, far and beyond anything St. Clair had imagined. His focus during his first week in Outremer had been on finding his errant cousin, so that he had really not taken time to look about him and observe the conditions in force here. But now, he was awestricken by the scope of the activities.

Acre had been under siege now for two years, and the assault had long since lost all of its initial excitement and momentum, settling down into grinding routine and the extended periods of boredom common to all static forms of warfare, with only brief and terrifying clashes occurring occasionally between the two opposing forces. And the extent of the siege works was so vast that André had great difficulty in comprehending the complexity of the strategies involved on both sides. Acre itself, now held by a stubborn garrison of mixed Saracen warriors, was one of the oldest ports in Palestine. Built up to prosperity by the Phoenicians hundreds of years earlier, it had developed into a polyglot and extremely wealthy community, attracting merchants and trading fleets from all over the world, and before its capture by Saladin in 1187, it had been renowned as one of the most notorious fleshpots anywhere.

Under the rule of Muslim law, all of that changed. The fleshpots had vanished overnight, the Christian churches were stripped of their crosses and bells, and the mosques of the city were refurbished and reopened, but the conquering Saracen army turned its attention immediately to strengthening the city's walls and defenses, and for four years now that work had been continuing.

Then, when the original Frankish army had arrived two years later, under the command of Guy de Lusignan, a new momentum had been established. The Christian fleet, composed mainly of Genoese and Pisan fighting ships that dwarfed the Arab dhows and galleys, immediately took command of the seas surrounding the city and established a naval blockade, and it was left to Guy and his small army to blockade the landward side of the city, an undertaking more easily described than achieved.

The city of Acre was vaguely triangular in layout and built on a hook-shaped promontory, its north–south axis tilted slightly to the northeast and southwest, so that the sea fronted it west and south, and it boasted both an inner and an outer harbor, the inner harbor defended by a massive chain that could be raised against incoming ships. On the landward side, the city was protected by a brace of high, parallel walls reinforced by barbicans and towers, the latter spaced closely enough to permit withering crossfire to be laid down against any attacker. These walls had been built by the Templars and the Hospitallers, whose presence in the city in the years before the battle at Hattin was ubiquitous. In the earliest days of the siege, the Frankish attackers came to appreciate how well those walls had been built and quickly learned the folly of attempting to engage the enemy by attacking them directly. Instead, they set up their siege engines and catapults and concentrated all their heaviest firepower on what was estimated to be the strongest but most vulnerable point in the walls, a right-angled corner in the northeastern salient controlled by a high tower known as the Accursed Tower. Settling in to the siege, however, they were acutely aware that their backs were vulnerable, their entire rear exposed to attack should the Sultan bring his armies to the relief of Acre.

It was at that point, Douglas explained to St. Clair, that the Trench was thought of, and for more than a year the Latins labored to build a wide, fortified ditch that stretched two miles inland from the sea and cut off the city from help from the landward side. Saladin's army began to arrive piecemeal soon after that, but they were unable to challenge the Latin besiegers who sat safely inside their Trench, attacking Acre from the one side and defending themselves against attack by Saladin from the other. But Saladin set up a blockade of his own, on the landward side of the Trench, establishing a heavily manned presence along a three-mile line that effectively curtailed most of the Frankish efforts to bring in supplies. Only occasionally could they land supplies from the sea, because their ditch had a very narrow intersection with the beach, and the Saracen forces concentrated there were constantly on the alert for attempts to smuggle material ashore. Food and supplies did manage to filter through, from time to time, but never enough, and never often enough. In recent months, however, according to Harry Douglas, more and more reinforcements had begun pouring in from every land in Christendom to swell the ranks of the besiegers, and the Christians knew that the city garrison was starving and would not be able to hold out much longer.

On the twentieth day of April 1191, Philip Augustus of France landed in Acre and assumed the overall command of the siege from his nephew, Prince Henry of Champagne. He quickly established his French command post in front of the Accursed Tower and added his own siege machines to the heavy concentration of catapults, trebuchets, and mangonels already in place there, fortifying his own artillery pieces with redoubts made of iron and stone.

That day, having climbed to the highest point of the defensive earthworks on the Trench, facing Acre, André and Harry stood watching the French catapults lobbing horse-sized boulders remorselessly at the walls of the Accursed Tower—so called, Harry said, because legend had it that the thirty pieces of silver used to pay Judas Iscariot had been minted there. But something else caught St. Clair's attention, a strange-looking device, a long cylinder of sorts, save that it had been cut in half and laid lengthwise on the ground, its far end snug against the wall of the tower that loomed over it.

"What's that thing, over there?" he asked, pointing at it.

Harry squinted, not quite knowing what he was referring to at first, but then he made a harrumphing sound. "Oh, that. That's what they call a cat."

"A cat. It's obviously a siege engine of some kind, but what does it do?"

"You don't know what a cat is? Have you never seen one before? They've been around since the days of the Caesars, in one form or another."

André shook his head. "I have heard of them, but I have never seen one. This is my first siege."

"Well, it works like the old tortoise formations the Romans used to use to defend themselves against falling volleys of arrows. This thing is an armored half cylinder, mounted on wheels. You can see them along the bottom if you look closely enough. The top surface is smooth metal, strong enough to repel anything thrown or dropped down onto it, including Greek fire, the gelatinous mix of pitch and naphtha that clung and burned with a fury unmatched by anything else in nature. Inside, beneath the roof, teams of sappers move it into place, right up against the walls, and then they dig down and in, undermining the walls."

"Does it work?"

Harry shrugged. "In theory, yes, and I've seen it work on several occasions in the past, but not here. These people have been digging away down there for months, since long before Philip arrived, and to this point they have been less than successful."

"Hmm." St. Clair turned away and looked to his right, to where the royal standard of France hung limply above Philip's pavilion. Nothing moved there, and there were no signs that the King might be in residence, although the standard's presence indicated that he was. "That reminds me," he said. "Guy de Lusignan arrived in Cyprus a few days before I left. He had a substantial number of knights and nobles with him, but he was most unhappy with Philip."

"I can imagine."

"Can you? Then tell me why. Some of his knights told me that Philip had chosen to back Conrad against him in this matter of the kingship of Jerusalem. I know the word of that upset Richard and his supporters, but I had my hands full at that time—I was being inducted into the Order—and I did not have time or opportunity to explore what was going on. What do you know about it?"

"Not much. I was here throughout the affair, but being an intimate of none of the main players, I know little about what was involved, other than the common barrack-room chatter and the opinions of a couple of knights whom I respect." Harry paused, considering something, and then resumed. "You know, I presume, that Guy's claim to the throne was through his marriage to Sibylla? Aye, well, when Sibylla died, Guy's kingship died with her. Oh, he's been hanging on to it since for all that he is worth … which, come to think of it, *is* all he is worth. But the plain truth is that Guy can no longer really call himself King, because the next heir in the legal line is Sibylla's sister Isabella, and she has been married for years to a husband whom she might already have named King, quite legally, had she been so inclined. Humphrey de Toron. Does the name mean anything?" St. Clair shook his head. "Well, he was stepson to Reynald de Chatillon."

"Aha! Now there's a name I recognize. The one Saladin beheaded? They called him the Templar Pirate?"

"That's him. Saladin decapitated him in person, for just and long overdue cause. The man was a disgrace to everything the Temple is supposed to stand for."

"So his stepson is to be King of Jerusalem?"

"God, no. Heaven forbid. The man is a bigger disgrace than Reynald ever was. He is a useless, cowardly poltroon already several times disgraced, and atop all that he is an outrageously public homosexual, which might be ignored in practically anyone else, but demands recognition in one who is married to a reigning queen."

"Oh …" André decided to say nothing of what had sprung into

his mind about another similarly married to a queen, and contented himself by asking, "And this man is married to Queen Isabella?"

"No, he *was* married to Queen Isabella, until very recently. Conrad of Montferrat took care of that. I know not how he achieved it, or how much it cost him—he must have had to dig *deep* into his purse—but he had the marriage annulled. Because it was a royal marriage, there must have been substantial and elaborate briberies involved—although one has to wonder where Conrad could have found a sufficiency of corrupt priests and bishops to achieve that kind of thing." He waited to see if André would respond to his sarcasm, but St. Clair showed no reaction. "Whatever it cost, it was achieved quickly and effectively. Humphrey's indiscretions and public misconduct were sufficiently notorious that it surprised no one when he was finally brought to account for them and his marriage was annulled. So Humphrey de Toron is no longer wed to the Queen of Jerusalem, and Conrad de Montferrat will be, as soon as it can be arranged."

"Ah! And I presume Guy must have learned of this before he left in search of Richard?"

Douglas dipped his head. "That's what drove him out. The word arrived soon after noon on the Friday, and Guy was gone from here, with all his followers, by dawn on Saturday. They struck for the coast and clearly they found a galley to transport them."

"They found three, and they wasted no time in seeking Cyprus. And so, what is happening now with this impending marriage, do you know?"

"How would I know that? I'm a monk, André, a Templar like you. Potentates and kings do not consult me when making their decisions."

"Well what do your cronies say? It is a juicy topic, made for speculation. Surely you must have heard something?"

"Nothing, save that it has not yet happened. The two lovers have been unable to coordinate their travels and their duties ... and it seems both of them must be present for the wedding to take place."

"No, that is not so. Not when the Church is involved. It could be done by proxy, were the officiating priests sufficiently powerful. And the Patriarch of Jerusalem, who would officiate in such a match, could make it so. Conrad is of the Eastern rite, I know. I presume the Queen, Isabella, would be, too." He inhaled sharply. "I am going to have to find out more on this matter, for it sounds more urgent than I would have thought a month ago." He looked about him again, then grasped his friend by the shoulder. "Thank you for this, Harry, for bringing me out here, but now I must return to camp. There are some people to whom I need to speak." He did not mention that one of those was the senior Templar commander in the line, nor did he add that his current credentials were sufficiently impressive to ensure the commander's cooperation, and anyway, Harry had already started walking back, content with the explanation he had been given.

A WEEK DRIFTED BY, during which André heard not a word from his cousin but was kept occupied by infrequent, minor skirmishes that kept him and his brethren patrolling various points along the walls of Acre. Then one morning, directly after matins, on his way to the camp refectory for a breakfast of water and chopped nuts and grain, someone clamped a hand on his right shoulder, and he spun around to find his cousin at his side. He opened his mouth to speak, but Sinclair cut him off with a gesture.

"You and I have to speak, now, and I have no wish to sit in the kind of company we are likely to find where you would go, so come with me and let's find a horse for you. I have food enough for both of us, and the quicker we are gone from here the more pleased I shall be."

André followed Alec wordlessly, aware that several of the men around them were casting unhappy looks at Sinclair, but even trying to avoid attention, walking with their eyes cast down, they were not able to escape unobtrusively. Someone raised his voice in a jeering catcall, announcing that there was a Saracen-lover among them, and within moments the two cousins were walking through a storm of verbal abuse. André reached reflexively for his sword hilt, but

STANDARD OF HONOR

Sinclair seized his elbow, telling him to keep walking, look at no one, and say nothing. And that worked for a spell, until a burly bullock of a fellow deliberately walked in front of them and barged straight into Alec, leading with his shoulder. André had tensed as he saw what the other intended, but before he could do anything to intervene, Alec stiff-armed him from the side, knocking him off balance for a moment, and took the brunt of the other man's shoulder charge upon his own shoulder, so well braced in anticipation that he barely rocked to the impact. He then sprang back and away, raising both hands in placation as though the collision had been his fault.

"Forgive me, Brother," he said, both hands still upraised.

The other man blinked in amazement and then his face clouded in fury. "Don't you 'Brother' me, you infidel turncoat," he snarled, then crouched and shuffled forward, arms spread like a wrestler. The last thing he expected at that moment was the speed he encountered. Alec Sinclair's hands shot forward and grasped the lout by the front of his surcoat, pulling him strongly forward and off balance to crash, nose first, into the flat steel brim of Sinclair's helmet as Alec thrust his head forward. He then released the man, leaving him to rear up in agony, both hands to his ruined face, while he stepped quickly backward for a second time, raising his knee to his chest and pivoting slightly to kick out viciously, and driving his booted heel into the other man's midriff, below the peak of his rib cage, making nonsense of the protective powers of the chain-mail hauberk the other wore.

André stood gaping at the swiftness of the punishment, but then he bethought himself and looked around defensively, only to see that everyone else appeared to be as shocked by the violence as he himself was. They were all Templars and all monks, and violence to a brother was unconscionable. Name calling was one thing, and apparently acceptable, but physical violence to a brother was a violation of the Temple Rule and endangered the immortal soul. And yet Sir Alexander Sinclair had been provoked and assaulted. Only when he was threatened with further assault had he reacted, and the fact that he had done so briefly, effectively, and with finality did not go unremarked.

No one offered to interfere this time as the two kinsmen walked away in the direction of the horse lines, and neither André nor Alec spoke a word to each other until they had retrieved Alec's horse and one for André and had ridden obliquely into the dunes southeast of the siege works, remaining close enough to their own lines to give them a reasonable certainty that they would be safe from Saracen patrols, yet removing them completely from the threat of interruption by their own.

"Why do they all dislike you so much?"

For a moment, St. Clair thought his cousin was not going to answer him, but Alec was merely looking around, checking the lay of the land. "This will suffice," he muttered, almost to himself, then set about laying out food and drink. He kicked a hole in the side of a sandbank, large enough to accommodate his hips and allow him to sit in comfort, his lower back supported by the rising bank, and as soon as André saw what he was about, he did the same. Alec then went to his saddlebags and took out a number of wrapped bundles before returning to lay a plain cloth out on the sand between their seats and piling it with surprisingly fresh-looking bread, some slices of cold meat that looked like goat or lamb, a twist of salt, a small jar of olives in spiced oil, and a flask of water.

"They dislike me because they are afraid," he said eventually. "Afraid of what I might have done, of what I might have learned, of what I might know, or even of what I might not know. They know no shortage of things to be afraid of."

"But they are monks, Alec, men of God." That earned him a swift, sidelong glance filled with skepticism, and he flushed quickly, remembering their earlier discussion. "Well, you know what I mean. They should know better than to doubt a brother simply on hearsay."

Alec looked at him in astonishment. "That is the first truly stupid thing I have heard you say since your arrival, Cousin. *They should know better* ... How could they know better? They have no way of learning otherwise and no one is willing to teach them differently.

These men are monks in name only, André. You know that. And they are far from being what I call men of God. And because of that, their observance of the monkish code is limited to attending prayers all day and night, and muttering endless *Paternosters* in between. Most of these men believe their entire salvation depends upon killing Muslims and saying one hundred and fifty *Paters* a day, yet none of them can count … How does a man who cannot count keep track of one hundred and fifty repetitions of a prayer? The truthful answer is that he does not, and so he simply never stops, preferring to say a few more prayers in sanctity than to run the risk of not saying enough and thereby sinning.

"These are simple, ignorant, unimaginative men, André. They believe what they are told to believe, they behave as they are told to behave, and they are all convinced, utterly and beyond hope of change, that no one among them is capable of engendering a single worthwhile thought. They believe that thoughts and opinions, along with planning and directives, emanate from above, from beyond their experience. And so they listen to what they are told, and they behave accordingly because none of them would ever dare to question anything that came down to them from on high. Thus, they have heard that I am intractable, that I hold opinions that run contrary to the Order's view of things, and since they know that means I ought to be punished, yet can see that I have not been punished, they are confused. And confusion breeds fear and panic."

"And so they abuse you, rather than remain silent and be thought to agree with you?"

"Something akin to that, yes."

"So tell me, then, about Muslims. What is it you believe that so upsets everyone?"

Alec Sinclair nodded, then busied himself with eating, chewing his food thoroughly and making no attempt to say anything further until he was replete and had washed down his meal with water from the flask. André, who finished at the same time, leaned back in his sand chair and folded his hands over his belly.

"That was good. Thank you. So, are you going to tell me?"

"Of course I am. I believe that Muslims are people, just like us, with all the same needs, desires, duties, and obligations, albeit they differ in interpretation."

"So you have said. But that belief hardly seems radical enough to cause the kind of concern I see on the faces of your brethren when they look at you."

Sinclair nodded again. "Carry it, then, to the next step."

"I don't understand what you are saying. Carry what to which next step?"

"The belief I have. Take it beyond a casual thinking about the ordinary people, and think of it from the viewpoint I am about to suggest. It will make things easier for you to understand.

"I have been out here for more than a decade now ... closer to two decades, in truth." He reached up and removed his helm, then loosened the bindings that held his mailed hood tightly in place. He pushed it back and off his head, and scratched vigorously at his shorn scalp. That done, he squirmed, twisting his buttocks in the sand until they were more comfortable, then leaned back and clasped his hands behind his neck. "There! That's much better. Now, back to history.

"I was of middle status in the brotherhood, just like you, which meant that I had learned enough of the Order's lore, in certain specific areas, to enable me to go forth and build upon what I knew. Like you, I had learned the tongue of the Saracens before setting out, taught to me by men of great learning, Arabs all, who had much in common with our senior and most learned Councillors of the brotherhood. I could have gone to Outremer alone, right then, but that would have meant operating alone thenceforth, with no support, thousands of miles from home. Much simpler, the Council thought, for me to join the Order of the Temple, where we already had a well-established network of the brotherhood working in secrecy. And so I joined the Temple and came out here, and since then, until I was captured after Hattin, I went about my primary work ... Does the name Masyaf mean anything to you?"

"No. Should it?"

"Probably not, but that was where I was sent first by the brother-hood, after my arrival here in Outremer. I was attached to an intake of Templars assigned to garrison duty in the fortress at Safita, the one the Templars call Castel Blanc. It's in Syria, north and east of Tyre. My instructions were to establish myself there, and then to contact Rashid al-Din Sinan, using an intermediary in the town of Masyaf."

"Sinan? I know that name. Isn't he—?"

"The Old Man of the Mountain. Aye, he is. The imam of the cult called the Assassins."

"God's eyebrows! Why would you be asked to contact him? To what end?"

"To several ends. There are certain matters in which the imam and our ancient Order share a common interest, not the least among those being what would appear to such as you and me as ancient and indecipherable mysteries. Rashid al-Din Sinan prides himself upon being something of a mystic and a clairvoyant, and he is an ascetic. He is also supposedly pious and demonstrably ruthless, and his reputation frightens even Saladin, who should twice have died at an Assassin's hands long since and remains alive today only through the best of good fortune and blind chance. How Sinan and the brother-hood first came into contact with each other I know not, but the relationship is now more than forty years old."

"And you were commanded to contact him …"

"Aye, I was. Jacques de Saint Germain, who had been the Council's main liaison with the imam for more than twenty years, had died some time earlier, and I was his replacement. Sinan knew I would be coming, so I had no difficulty in finding him, especially through the Temple."

"I don't follow."

"Then pin your ears back, lad, for there are clearly huge gaps in your knowledge. The Assassins are a terrifying group and they hold all of Outremer in a thrall of fear. But forty years ago, in seeking to expand their power and influence within a new territory, they over-reached themselves and killed King Raymond II of Tripoli. In retaliation, the Templars were turned loose against them, operating from their bases at Castel Rouge and Castel Blanc, and they wrought havoc among the local populace until Sinan was forced to sue for truce. And ever since then the Assassins have been paying a heavy annual tribute to the Temple in return for the liberty to conduct their own affairs."

"But they are Muslims ... how can the Temple treat thus with the enemy?"

"Because they are not the enemy. Your interpretation is wrong. They are Shi'a. Ismaeli Shi'ites descended from Persian roots. They are the deadly enemies of Saladin and his Sunni followers, but any enmity they may feel for us is merely incidental. Rashid himself, the Old Man, was born in Basra, in Iraq, but he came into Syria as *dai*, or Imam of the Cult, only a short time before the killing of Raymond of Tripoli. That may have been one of his early moves to assert his dominance, but if it was, it was a costly error. Soon after that, he entered into a relationship with the Temple. The two organizations have much in common, when you sit down and think about it. Both are closed societies with arcane rites that they conduct in secrecy, far from the sight and hearing of ordinary men. Both are ascetic, too, in every sense of the word. And both are dedicated to death, in a manner of speaking—dedicated to high and vaunting ideals and prepared to die gladly in battle to achieve and protect them. Neither one has much difficulty in appreciating the objectives of the other."

There was a silence then, and when André accepted that his cousin had no more to add, he prompted, "So this is why your brethren distrust you, this association with the Assassins?"

"No, by God's wounds! None of them even knows about that. That liaison was a personal relationship, a clandestine thing that I did not particularly enjoy. It ended when I was taken prisoner by Saladin's people. I have not spoken to the Old Man since—although now, as you will see when you read my orders, I will have to. In telling you of this, I was trying to give you some idea of how much I have learned of many things ... and how little I truly know. The simple truth is that I made a friend among the Muslims when I was their captive, a close friend and perhaps the best I ever had. He was my captor, the man who took me, although the reality was nowhere near as simple and straightforward as that sounds. His name is Ibn al-Farouch, an emir in Saladin's personal guard." He smiled as he saw the astonishment spread over his cousin's face. "It's a long tale, but I think you might find it worth the hearing, if you have the time."

André looked about him. "I seem to have no pressing engagements to detain me from listening."

Thus, for the next hour and longer, André sat rapt while Alec Sinclair told him first the story of the Battle of Hattin and the loss of his friend, Sir Lachlan Moray, and then of his encounter with the injured Saracen and his subsequent capture by the search party who came looking for their missing leader, al-Farouch. And thereafter he listened eagerly as Sinclair described his life among the Saracens and his eventual and reluctantly acquired admiration and respect for his enemy and their ways.

"They have so much more than we do," Alec concluded. "They have everything that we possess, but all of it, it seems to me, in greater measure, and they appear to appreciate it more than we do. Certes, they live in a harsh land, and most of them spend the major part of their lives living under tents instead of a solid roof. But even that permits them to remain largely clean. They pick up their tents and move to a fresh area whenever they so wish, whereas our peasants at home build a hovel in one squalid spot and there they stay for years, living in their own stink and sharing their abode with swine and cattle. And when the Prophet's followers do aspire to build fine buildings, they construct them, it appears, out of light and air, with only gracious, swirling, weightless lines of stone and marble to hold them together. Completely unlike our dark, dank, and windowless piles of heavy granite stone.

"And they are *clean*, André. Saracens are clean in a way that we in Christendom can never comprehend. The words of the Prophet Muhammad lay upon them, as a burden, an obligation to purify themselves weekly at least, and before all religious festivals. They see no sin in cleanliness, whereas we, in our world, avoid it as we would the plague. Cleanliness, in our world of Christendom, is looked upon as some form of sinful depravity, as some Devil's lure that will lead straight to fornication and the evils of the flesh. However, I am grown convinced since my return to freedom and the civilized company of my companion brothers that the rank, rancid stench of foul and filthy unlaved bodies and stinking, unwashed nether garments must militate strongly against any temptation to sin willfully with a bearer of such odors."

He lapsed into silence then, and André sat mute for a time, thinking over what he had heard and what it meant. He then surprised himself by spouting words he had not known were in him, waiting to be said.

"I agree with you completely," he said, earning himself a glance of mild surprise from his cousin. He shrugged. "I know it would earn me little in the way of praise were the truth known to our fellow Templars, but I am a bather myself, although I keep it secret nowadays. I grew into the habit of it while I was in southern Provence, studying with my Arabian tutors at a villa belonging to one of the senior Councillors of the Order of Sion. The tutors were Muslims, to a man, as I am sure yours were in your time, but since there is nothing Christian in the beliefs of our brotherhood, there was no ritual conflict to hamper them from pursuing their own ways and living their lives according to the Koran."

He smiled, recalling something from the distant past. "The senior of them, a learned man I soon came to revere for his wisdom, took exception to the smell of me when I first arrived to take up my studies, and by the time he had called in his servants to search for and find the wild, dung-covered goat that had somehow found entry to his chambers, I had begun to sense that I might be smelling a little ripe. He went on to point out, with great patience, that since I was of the brotherhood and only nominally and of necessity a Christian, I could afford to behave in a civilized manner while I was on premises owned by the brotherhood, which meant that I was free to bathe without fear of reprisals, and consequently blessed thereafter to be able to absolve my friends of the need to pinch their noses and suffer my rank odor."

Alec had been listening closely to this, one arm crossed over his breast and supporting his other elbow while he scratched the tip of his nose idly with the nail of his little finger. "This tutor. You say he was the eldest of the group? Might his name have been Sharif Al-Qalanisi? I know the chance is—"

"Yes! How could you—?"

"Because he was my teacher, too, in the same place, in Provence. The Villa Providence, home of Gilbert, the Master of St. Omer, great-nephew of Godfrey St. Omer, one of the nine Founders of the Temple. Al-Qalanisi must be nigh on seventy now, for he was over fifty when I knew him. How small, the world in which we walk, do you not agree? Pardon me for my enthusiasm, but you were describing an experience I once had, too, in minute detail. And did he then encourage you to bathe daily?"

"He did. And I did as he bade me, so that in the space of half a year, while learning Arabic, I had grown so accustomed to the pleasures of bathing that my return to Christian smelliness and filth was almost intolerable. I could not believe how everyone *reeked*. The stench of my companions took my breath away at times, and so I soon learned to avoid their company, and Sharif Al-Qalanisi, God bless him, had taught me a way to keep myself reasonably, or at least tolerably, clean. As you know, there are occasions when it is considered laudable and indeed obligatory for a Christian man to bathe—Easter springs to mind, as do the feast days of several major saints—so that all in all, a man may bathe as frequently as once every season, should he so desire. But that is only part of the struggle. Even if they washed their bodies, very few men will wash their clothing at the same time. It was that little truth, passed on to me by Sharif Al-Qalanisi, that enabled me to bathe as often as I was able to arrange it, so be it I kept a set of suitably rancid, sweat-stained clothing to wear around my fellow novices. But when I was alone, I would wear clothing that smelled as fresh and clean as hillside air on a cool morning." He nodded emphatically. "The only sin a sane man might connect with cleanliness is the hypocrisy and ignorance that leads the Christians to deny its worth. Tell me, therefore, what else do they have that you consider superior?"

"Superior to what we have? Are you sure you want to hear that?"

"No, consider what we have been discussing ... We are of the Brotherhood of Sion, an entity unto ourselves. I want to know what else the Saracens have that you consider superior to the *Christian* equivalent."

"Ah, I see. There is a difference. So, let me see. Well, I could start with honor—the true kind, that has all the solidity and worth and value that is seldom found among the ranks of Christendom today. The Saracens have that in profusion, whereas among the Frankish ranks today, from kings to pikemen, honor is merely a sound mouthed by knaves to gull fools. Then there is integrity, closely linked to honor in that the one cannot exist without the other. Next might come fidelity, to ideals, to commitments, to agreements, and to good—truly good—intent. The military virtues I will not include, for they are simplistic rituals played out by mindless fools for the most part—bravery, courage, constancy, mercy, and compassion, though it seems obscene even to include those latter two by name. But all of those may be adhered to or abandoned in the heat of battle by men of either side, with no one being any the wiser. No, I think I will make suffice of honor, integrity, and fidelity. The Saracens possess all of those three in greater mass than do the Christian Franks."

St. Clair nodded. "Tell me this, then, for it is puzzling me. You say that you only discovered these things, and reluctantly, while you were prisoner in the hands of the Saracens, yet you have been dealing with Islam and with the Muslim Sons of the Prophet ever since you arrived here. Why were you not aware of these things before? You must have had some inkling that it was so."

"No, not so. My liaison with Islam prior to my being captured had nothing to do with the Saracens. I was dealing with the Assassins, and they are Shi'ite, originally from Persia. And not merely that, but I was dealing personally with Rashid al-Din Sinan himself, the Old Man of the Mountain, and he is not an endearing man to be near. The Assassins are single-minded and humorless, like all zealots, merciless and incapable of compassion. They are very much like their counterparts here, the Templars. In all the years in which I dealt with the Old Man and his minions, I handled them with care and expected truth in our contracts and justiciary precision in our dealings. I never doubted their fidelity to their leader and the agreements he made with us, but I never thought of them at all in terms of honor or integrity as I understood those things. They might have had their own versions of each, within themselves, but there was nothing there of either one that I could recognize. It was only when I fell among the Saracens and came to know Ibn al-Farouch that the scales of blindness began to loosen and fall from my eyes."

"And so when you came back you defended them when you heard them maligned."

"Whenever I heard them unjustly maligned I did, yes."

"Hmm. No wonder, then, that people look askance at you. And you say you have had no dealings with the Assassins or their leader since you were captured four years ago?"

"None at all, no."

"Do they even know you are yet alive?"

"They do now, for I have made it known to them, this past week. That's why you have not heard from me. The dispatches you delivered made it clear that I need to renew my relationship with them, and so I set about that right away. But my prime contact had moved on two years earlier, and once I found out where he had gone—no easy task in itself—it took me three whole days of cajoling and explaining before he would even see me. He simply did not believe I was me. He was quite sure that I had died at Hattin, for they had acquired the names of all the Frankish knights who survived the fight and the ransoms that followed, and of course mine was not among them. I had to convince him that I had changed my name from Sir Alexander Sinclair of the Temple to plain Sir Lachlan Moray, knight of Scotland, when al-Farouch captured me, because Saladin was executing Templars and I saw little future in being known as one."

"Is the Old Man still alive?"

"Oh yes. Alive and well, and as malignant as he ever was. I am to meet with him the day after tomorrow. He has been at al Kahf, the

Eagle's Nest, his favorite, unreachable stronghold in the northern mountains, but he is already on his way back and will be here, within riding distance of us, by tomorrow night."

"What will you say to him? And is he still paying tribute to the Temple?"

Alec sat up straighter and stretched mightily. "I have no notion of what to say to him. He will tell me what he expects to hear. Rashid al-Din Sinan is not an easy man with whom to make idle conversation. Yes, he is still paying tribute to the Temple. But before I can tell you any more and still make sense—"

He half raised one hand, finger pointed, in a tacit order to be quiet and listen, and far off in the distance, rising clearly in the desert air, they heard what sounded like the noise of battle. Both men surged to their feet and set about shaking the sand from their clothing, looking around to where their horses waited quietly.

"Take the dispatches with you," Sinclair said. "They are in my saddlebags. Read them tonight, then meet me here tomorrow at the same time. I'll bring food again. But you will know what's involved by then and you will be able to understand what I intend to do when I explain it to you. Now let's see what all the shouting is about."

The din grew noticeably louder as they approached the rear lines, and eventually they came to a place where they could see that the entire army was up and shouting, facing towards the northeast while armed riders ran up and down in every direction, cheering and screaming, all semblance of discipline abandoned.

"What is happening out there?" André shouted. "Can you see anything?"

Alec Sinclair was standing high in his stirrups, shielding his eyes with one hand as he peered towards the distant horizon, and he stood motionless for a long time before he settled back into his saddle. "Richard of England," he said, turning to his cousin. "Finally he comes. I can see his great standard out in front of everything else." The English host is out there, filling the horizon with an admirable blur for as far as the eye can see. A very large, broad blur. They've been a long time a-coming and there were more than a few here who said they never would arrive, but they are here now. They must have landed up the coast, at Tyre, and marched from there, then made camp early yesterday and set out on the last leg to here long before dawn, for the sun's been up less than two hours. You told me they were more than a hundred thousand strong. Were you exaggerating?"

André bridled a little. "No, I was not. Why should I need to exaggerate? When you combine Philip's French and allied levies—Burgundy, Flanders, and Brittany—with Richard's English and Angevins, they total nigh on seven score thousand, according to my father. One hundred and forty thousand men, with weapons and munitions, horses and livestock, servants and camp followers in addition. The fleet required to carry them numbered more than two hundred and twenty large vessels and there was not an inch of space left available in any one of them."

"Excellent. Then we should soon see things start to happen more quickly around here, once they are settled in and have had time to flex their muscles. The raptors will be lusting for blood. Acre will not stand long against them now, and once it falls, the legend of Saladin's invincibility will be forever tarnished."

Alec looked away again, back towards the fevered activity in the Trench, then stooped and pulled the dispatch wallets from his saddlebags. "Here, make sure you take time to read these tonight, no matter what madness happens here to celebrate this arrival. This reading is more important than anything else you could conceivably be called upon to do. Chew on it and digest it. We will talk about it in greater depth tomorrow, before I have to leave to meet Rashid al-Din. For now, I am instructed to talk with your friend Sir Robert de Sablé, if he is with the main host there, and it were best I did that alone. If I find him, I will deliver greetings to him from you, but we do not wish to attract unwelcome attention by seeking him out together. So fare ye well, for now, and meet me here in this same place tomorrow, even if it is allocated to some incoming group in the meantime. It should not be. Everything has been laid out already in the flat area southwest of the Trench, but you know how it is with armies. Some bright lad might decide to erect a general's tent right on this spot between now and tomorrow at this time. We'll meet here anyway, because no one will know us or care who we are, and we will move on elsewhere if we must."

André waved and watched his cousin spur away towards the approaching blur, as he thought of it, then tucked his wallets into his saddlebags and turned his horse back towards the stables. He knew that planning had been under way for weeks and probably for months to accommodate the enormous influx of personnel and materiel that Richard's arrival would precipitate, and that a veritable city of street grids had been prepared in the area to the southwest of where he now sat his horse, with encampments for the various contingents of infantry, cavalry, sappers, engineers, and assorted others that made up the vast army. This afternoon, he decided, he would watch the great arrival unfold, keeping well out of everyone's way. In the evening he would read Alec's dispatches, and the morrow would look after itself.

As he kicked his horse into motion he was wondering what was going through the minds of the garrison commanders in Acre as they watched the approaching dust clouds of Richard's army blot out the sky.

NINE

The night had passed relatively peacefully, once the first chaotic arrivals and dispersals had been overcome, an event that lasted throughout the entire day and well into the hours of darkness. But the furor died down eventually, and the strident, heckling voices of the marshaling sergeants had dwindled and faded slowly as the last remaining units of the incoming forces were received and led away to where they would set up their encampments for the next few weeks at least.

André St. Clair had plugged his ears with fine white candle wax and spent more than four hours, two of them by candlelight, reading and then rereading the contents of the two wallets he had transported across the seas for his cousin. He now felt he understood most of what was required of Alec, and of himself, but what he had yet to learn could now come only from Alec, and he was impatient to return to their interrupted discussion. He contrived to miss matins that day, surmising accurately that the activities of the previous day and night might have resulted in a general lapse of enthusiasm for midnight prayers, and he made his way to the horse lines to select a mount more than an hour before the sky began to show the first hint of the coming day. He then made his way out into the desert, riding by the pale light of the last, lingering stars until he reached the rendezvous, where he dismounted and off-saddled his horse, then tethered the beast to a dragging iron tent peg so that it would not wander far, and slipped a nose bag containing a handful of oats over its head. That done, he left the animal to munch contentedly and fashioned himself another seat in the sand.

An hour later, the sun long since risen, it was evident that something had happened to detain Alec, and André resolved to wait another half hour before returning to his own tent. It was pointless even to think of going in search of his cousin, for he had no vaguest idea of where to begin looking, and he could not even guess at what kind of changes would have been wrought in the general camp layout by the overnight addition of a hundred thousand men. But he had no desire to remain here alone for much longer, for the sun was growing measurably stronger and he had not thought to bring any kind of shelter against it, reasoning that their business there would be concluded in short order and that the two of them would then return to do whatever needed to be done.

He smoothed a rectangular area of sand with one hand and stuck a poniard, hilt first, into the center of it to create a sundial. Then he sat back to watch the shadow creep slowly towards the line that he had traced as marking half an hour. When shadow and line crossed, he waited a few minutes longer, then rose up and sheathed his blade, moving to saddle his patient horse. He had thrown the saddle across its back and was tightening his girths when he heard an approaching noise and looked up to see Alec, his face solemn.

"Well, welcome to you, Sir Knight of the Mournful Face. You took your time arriving. Where have you been?" He was still working beneath the horse's withers, tightening the straps, but when he heard no answer to his gibe he straightened up and looked across to see no warmth in his cousin's face. "Alec? In God's name, man, what's wrong? You look as though you have lost all you value. What's happened? Is it de Sablé?"

Alec Sinclair managed to shake his head, but strangely, as though he were numb or impaired in some manner. Then he swung his leg over the cantle and slid loosely to the ground, collecting himself fluidly and with ease. But still his eyes were unfocused.

"De Sablé is well. I left him only a short time ago. Come and sit down." He moved past André on stiff legs and lowered himself to the depression in the sand where André had waited for him. André felt apprehension coiling strongly in his gut, and he patted the horse's flank and left it standing there as he went to sit on the sand beside his cousin.

"Alec, tell me what is troubling you. You went to look for de Sablé yesterday, so why did you have to meet him today?"

"Couldn't find him yesterday. He had too much marshaling to attend to. But I remembered what you had told me about his joining the Temple, and so I left word at the commandery that if Sir Robert were to appear, he should inform him that I had come seeking him. He sent for me this morning and I've been with him ever since." Alec sat up straight and drew a great breath, and André could see that his cousin was in some kind of torment, his eyes haunted with awareness. Before he could say anything, however, Alec bent forward quickly and seized a double handful of the fabric of André's surcoat, pulling him close and into an embrace.

"André— Your … your father is dead."

The words, emerging choked and close to indistinguishable, washed over and through André with no effect. He heard them, and a tiny portion of his mind may have absorbed their meaning, but their significance had absolutely no effect upon him. He was highly aware of the discomfort caused by the position into which Alec had pulled him, and he could feel the links of his cousin's mailed shoulder digging painfully into the skin of his face. He even felt slightly embarrassed about the intimacy of this unexpected embrace, thinking they might be compromised were anyone to see it, but the words he had heard held no meaning for him. His father was dead. He knew that must be important, but his face was pressed against his cousin's clothing, against his armor, and he realized that Alec Sinclair bore the same aroma as his father, the same beloved, unmistakable tang that marked Sir Henry St. Clair, and in that instant, in the space of half a heartbeat, the barriers fell and he heard what Alec had said.

Afterwards, much later, he would recall Alec gazing at him solemnly, his eyes wide and concerned as he told him how Sir Henry had been waylaid and struck down, with two of his junior officers, as they made their way back one night from a popular hostelry towards their quarters in Famagusta, where they were coordinating the details of a mixed strike force, horse and foot, that was to be led by Guy de Lusignan against Isaac Comnenus's forces the next day. Their assailants had not been identified, let alone captured, but there was ample evidence that the attack had been carried out by one of several well-organized guerrilla groups operating out of the foothills to the north of the city.

Sir Henry St. Clair had fully discharged all his responsibilities to the liege lord whom he had served so faithfully throughout his life. He and the two officers with him had received full military honors in their funerary rites, Alec Sinclair said, and the King himself was in attendance, accompanied by an entourage of some of the senior lords and barons of his holdings throughout Christendom, including Sir Robert de Sablé. The Archbishop of Auxienne had offered prayers for the souls of the slain heroes, and Richard of England himself had spoken highly of his Master-at-Arms and how he had learned much of what he knew about fighting under Sir Henry's tutelage.

All of these things, André knew in moments of lucidity over the course of the following few days, might be cause for pride and pleasure at some unknown date in the future, but for the time being, while he was feeling the cavernous emptiness that had filled him, it was all meaningless.

When they returned to camp, Alec Sinclair, fretful over his cousin's condition, set about seeking the best in medical aid that he could find, for André had fallen into a state of deep melancholia and refused to be shaken out of it. And as was not unusual among the Frankish populace of Outremer, many of whom had now lived there for generations, he chose to engage the services of a celebrated Muslim physician whose acquaintance he had made several years before, although he would tell no one where or how. The truth was that Saif ad-Din Yildirim, reputedly a first cousin to one of Saladin's most trusted associates, was in fact Shi'a and an associate of the Assassins.

Yildirim promptly set André St. Clair upon a regimen of liquid foods and powerful opiates, designed to keep him abed and asleep most of the time. There was no logical explanation, he said, for Sir

André's reaction to the death of his father, but he had seen similar cases among men of his own religion and was quite sure that the effects would soon pass, aided by sleep and rest. And sure enough, Alec discovered, so it was.

Yildirim suspended the administration of the opiates on the morning of the fourth day following the onset of André's strange symptoms, and André St. Clair awoke at his usual time before dawn the next day with no memory of having been ill. When Alec questioned him, he remembered receiving the tidings from Alec, and he was subdued and saddened, but he now behaved as any other young man would on losing a well-loved parent.

A little later that same day, André came seeking his cousin in the knight's new quarters close by the Templars' tent, the great, bannered pavilion that served the Templars in the field as a mobile commandery. Although Sir Alexander Sinclair would have refused to place himself so close to the heart of the Temple Command a mere week earlier, the reason for his profound change of heart was simple: Sir Robert de Sablé's personal pavilion now stood squarely beside the Templars' tent. Scarcely less elaborate than its imposing neighbor, de Sablé's pavilion had been erected several days earlier, after Sir Robert had formally resigned as King Richard's Fleet Master and accepted his new posting as Grand Master Elect of the Order of the Temple of Solomon. Alec had sought out de Sablé as soon as he heard that the veteran had arrived, and had offered his personal services immediately and without reservation, for the two of them had known each other for more than two decades and had been Raised to the Brotherhood of Sion in the same ceremony, on a warm August night near the ancient town of Carcassonne. De Sablé had embraced Sinclair enthusiastically, and instantly appointed him to his personal staff. And that, very markedly, had been the end of Alec's loss of popularity.

André found Alec working diligently when he arrived, frowning over a letter he was writing. He sat quietly until his cousin had completed what he was doing and sat back in his chair.

"I owe you a great deal, it seems, Cousin. I have been told that there is no better or more renowned physician in these parts than Saif ad-Din Yildirim."

Alec flicked his fingers in a gesture of dismissal. "Nonsense. You owe me nothing. You are all the kin I have out here, and selfishness insists I look after you, since you are a mere child. Yildirim is an old friend and was happy to oblige me in this. How are you feeling now? Any ill effects from the opiates he fed you?"

André smiled. "None. But I seem to remember dreams that I would enjoy examining more closely now." His face sobered. "Let me ask you this again, Alec, but one more time and for my own satisfaction, simply so I can be sure that my memory is serving me correctly. Am I correct in believing that my father was struck down at night, returning to his quarters from a hostelry where he had eaten with two friends?"

"Two associates, both his subordinates. All three of them were killed, the assailants unknown. We have to believe there were multiple assailants, since otherwise the odds would have militated against all three being killed. Your father's age might have worked against him in a long struggle, but the men with him were both serving officers, both experienced veterans, and both at the top of their profession of arms. Those two would not have gone down easily. Ergo, multiple assailants and most probably from ambush. But we have no way of knowing how many or who they were."

"And this was when, do you know? How long after I had left Cyprus?"

"Hmm. De Sablé said you would ask that. Three days after you left Limassol. Your father had been shipped to Famagusta that same day, the day you left, before daybreak, and had arrived there that same night. He had been in Famagusta for two days when the incident occurred."

"So I was still at sea … I understand the King himself was there to speak for my father at his funeral?"

"He was. He traveled to Famagusta for the funeral rites. He and several others, including an archbishop."

"Aye, well the King's presence would have pleased the old man.

I am grateful to you, Cousin, for this courtesy." He inhaled loudly and straightened his stance. "I really came here this afternoon because you and I have unfinished matters to discuss. We never did talk about the material you gave me, and I had spent the entire night absorbing it all. I have since spent another hour, today, reviewing what I remember, and I am now ready to discuss these matters further with you, if you so wish." He paused, but for no more than a moment. "I recall you were to meet with the imam, Rashid, the day the tidings of my father's death arrived. Was that meeting a success?"

"It did not take place. As soon as I found out what had happened to your father, I sent a message explaining that I had been rendered unable to attend upon Rashid al-Din at that time and requested that we might arrange another meeting. He was courteous enough to agree, although in fact he had little choice, but that is neither here nor there. The meeting yet lies ahead and nothing has been lost, other than a few days of time which is not pressing."

"I see. Then I regret that my personal woes had to interfere in your duties. Accept my apologies for the inconvenience I have caused you. It was not deliberate."

"What?" Alec's face broke into a grin as he stared at his earnest cousin. "Are you twitting me? You expect me to believe you know nothing at all of what has been going on here these past few days? André, I love you dearly, but you ask too much of me in this." He stopped, then hesitated again on the point of speaking, and then the grin faded from his lips. "You really don't know what has been going on, do you? André, my failure to meet with Rashid al-Din had nothing to do with you. Even had you been in perfect health, he and I would not have met … Do you remember the eclipse? No? Nothing at all? Well then, we had one, on the afternoon of the day following your … indisposition. In the middle of a heavy skirmish between a large contingent of their cavalry and an equal one of ours, God drew a curtain over the face of the sun. Three hours it lasted, from start to end, and it put the fear of Christ into our soldiers. We of the brotherhood knew what was happening, of course, because our savants know how to predict such events, and the Saracens were unsurprised by it, but our ordinary soldiers and sergeant brothers knew nothing, and they were panic stricken, convinced that God Himself was hiding His light from them.

"Since then, we have all been waiting on the edge of the abyss. Acre is tottering, Cuz, on the verge of falling. It has been common knowledge for more than a month now. There is only so much that flesh and blood can withstand, and then it all collapses, and the garrison of Acre has been subsisting on nothing at all for months now, defying all the odds. Anyone with a brain in his head knows the siege is over, in all but fact. And since the eclipse, for the past four days, Richard has been negotiating with Saladin's envoys, and no one expects the status quo to last for more than another day or so.

"You may think you have been sick for a spell, but you have barely been inconvenienced. Richard, on the other hand, has been deathly ill. The doctors call what ails him *leonardia* and have all kinds of high-sounding explanations for it, but the truth is they have not the slightest idea of what is wrong with him. His hair is falling out in clumps, his gums are rotting, and his teeth are loose enough to wobble with a fingertip. He is a mess. And yet, throughout his illness, he has been involved in discussions with Saladin, seeking a resolution to this war. They bargain back and forth and neither is really inclined to surrender anything to the other. But at least while they are negotiating, no one is dying. What point was there in speaking, in the interim, to Rashid al-Din? That would have been vanity piled upon vanity. Thus, we have both waited to see what will transpire in Acre."

"And what will happen, think you?"

"Once the city falls, you mark my words, the situation will return to prewar levels. The Hospitallers will re-man their hospital, the Templars will repossess the Templar Castle, and the King's administrative crew will resume their occupation of the royal basements."

"And what of Saladin? Don't ask me to believe he might offer himself as hostage for his people's behavior."

"I would not dream of it. Saladin will do as leaders always do— he will negotiate an honorable outcome for himself and his closest associates, and he will leave his minions to their fates … or those of them, at least, who cannot help themselves."

"You are being harsh, are you not? Nothing that I have heard of Saladin indicates that he would simply abandon the people of Acre, after their heroic defense of the city for so long."

Sinclair shrugged. "He may, he may not. Much of it will depend upon the demands that Richard makes. If he digs in his heels, then Saladin will have little option but to humor him. It does not make for heroic behavior, but it is not uncommon in war for the losers to die. Look what happened to us at Hattin."

"Hmm. I suppose you are right, and only time will tell us what the leaders have decided. Would this be a good time for us to talk further about what was in the dispatches you gave me to read?"

"Aye, it would, Cousin. There is no time like the present, for when you arrived, I was preparing for the next step in what needs to be done. How well do you feel, in truth?"

André almost smiled. "Well enough for anything you might throw at me. I felt a twinge of weakness earlier today, but now I feel as well as I have ever felt."

"So be it then." André stood up. "Come with me. We'll stop at the stables and from there—" He stopped and looked André up and down from boots to helm. "I think I will have everything you need. But first, horses, and some food from the field kitchens. You pick out two good, stout mounts and I'll collect the food."

"And drink. Don't forget to bring water."

"I'll pretend I did not hear that. Get the horses. I'll rejoin you in a few minutes."

"How long will we be gone? Shouldn't we leave word with someone?"

"Aye, with de Sablé. I told him where I was going. I'll send him word from the kitchens that I've taken you with me."

"I've been here before. This is the road Harry and I took when first we went to meet you, in the desert of stones."

"Correct, Cousin. It is the self-same route, and we are going to the self-same place. The outer edge of the stone field should be coming into view at any moment."

"Why would we go there, Alec?"

"Because I have good reason to go there, one that will make perfect sense to you, too, once I have explained it. Do you remember when you were here that first day, how intrigued you were by how I had been able to approach you unheard?"

"Aye, I remember it well. You said it was because we were making so much noise that we could not have heard you. You also said that you had been standing for hours."

"I did? Did I really? That was ..."

"Careless is what it was, for it set me to thinking. I would be prepared to wager that you have a hiding place nearby. You looked me up and down moments ago and told me that you had everything I would need, but we have not stopped moving since then and your saddlebags appear to be empty. The food and drink you brought is the only burden you carry. Therefore whatever else you have that I might need must be located where we are going. And there is always the additional consideration that, while the location there might suit you for any number of reasons, all of them would be greatly increased if you had a convenient hiding place nearby from which you could spy upon those who come to meet you."

Alec Sinclair grinned. "Well done, lad. We'll be there soon and you can see it for yourself."

They rode in silence after that until the high pinnacle of the monolith in the center of the clearing where they had first met came into view, and as they approached it, Alec pointed out how the natural elevation of the little rock-crowned hummock made it easy for any watcher to see clearly what anyone on the summit was doing. Before they came too close to the central clearing, however, Alec led them aside, following a trail so faint it was barely discernible among the boulders, and it led them out and around towards the back of the knoll. Alec stopped in the shadow of a particularly large clump of stones, then turned his horse towards it and moved forward to where it seemed his horse must walk straight into the side of the stone. But then he dismounted, and taking hold of his horse's woven leather bridle, he led the animal sharply around to his left and downward, following the abrupt edge of what appeared to be a large hole in the ground.

Following close behind him, André saw that it was indeed a hole, its sides smoothed by ages of use by people following a narrow but manageable path that wound downward in a tight spiral to vanish some distance below. He advanced carefully, following Alec, and soon found himself in a natural atrium, a wind- or water-worn hallway in the living rock, open to the skies. They were perhaps ten paces below the level of the ground above, and the blue sky over their heads was almost circular in section. Behind André, hidden in shadow, was the entrance to a cavern that turned out to be the first in a progression of caves culminating in a large, high, well-lit space with a dry, sandy floor. A fire pit in the center of the floor appeared to have been used for centuries, and the entire space was criss-crossed with beams of light that shone directly in as though from windows.

"Amazing, is it not?" Alec Sinclair dropped the bags he was carrying by the fire pit and led his horse over into a far corner of the large cavern, where he began to unsaddle him. "I felt exactly the same as you when I first saw it. It took my breath away and left me mute. It still shakes me when I think about it, but I've grown used to it nowadays and it takes someone like you, seeing it for the first time, to remind me how awe-inspiring it really is."

"How did you ever find it?"

"Never did. I had to be shown it, just like you. In my case, by Ibrahim, my main contact with the Old Man." He swung the saddle off his mount's back and carried it back to drop it by the fireplace. "Leave that," he said, waving his hand to take André's attention away from his own saddle. "Come and see this."

André followed him as he scrambled up a high incline and thrust his upper body through a hole in the roof. It was larger than it appeared to be, and there was ample room for the two of them to stand up there together, side by side.

"You have to be careful to stay quiet climbing up," Alec said, "but it is worth the effort, would you not agree?"

André could say nothing, able only to gape in wonder. He was standing with his head projecting through a hole in the ground, almost completely surrounded by the bases of the central cluster of boulders dominating the tiny knoll where he had waited with Harry Douglas for the arrival of Alec Sinclair, and he could see the entire scene perfectly, looking directly through the gaps at the bottom of the boulder cluster.

"You were here all the time. You could hear every word."

"Every syllable. I was impressed by the charitable way you made excuses for my tardiness."

André stooped and made his way back to where he had left his horse partially saddled. He completed the job of unsaddling, lugged his saddle and blanket to the fireplace, then crossed to a high wooden bin against the wall.

"What is in here?"

"Dried dung, some of it camel but mostly horse. We hoard it as fuel. It's the only kind we have ... camel dung and horse dung. There is a seam of anthracite—a hard, shiny, hot-burning coal— about ten miles from here, and when time permits, we haul fuel from there, too. But most of the time we burn dung."

"And in here?" André was standing now in front of two large wooden chests with ornate hasps, and as he spoke Alec was already in the act of bending to open one of them.

"Clothing, for a range of purposes. Which is our next priority. Strip out of your armor. It is time to take on the protective coloration of the landscape." He pulled open the top of one of the chests, exposing a welter of brightly colored garments. "You should make a fine-looking Muslim. Have you worn Saracen clothing before now?"

"Only twice before, at home and very briefly—you can imagine the notice it would have attracted. I have a basic understanding of what is required and how the various garments fit."

"Excellent, then let us make a start on it. Quickly now, strip down and I will help you don new finery. Ibrahim should be here very soon."

"Ibrahim is already here, Almania."

The words, spoken in Arabic, were uttered close to André's ear, and he spun around so quickly that he almost fell on the uneven floor. "How came—?" he gasped, dropping his hand to his dagger hilt. He did not finish the thought, for he saw the curling hairs on the back of the brown hand close to his jaw and felt the flat width of a blade pressing firmly upwards against the soft skin beneath his chin and he knew, beyond dispute, that the blade would have a very sharp edge. He tilted his head back, yielding to the pressure of the blade until the skin of his entire neck was tautly stretched, then remained motionless, his eyes focused on the face of the man who had come up so silently behind him and now stood eyeing him askance, smiling sardonically and daring him to move.

The fellow wore a tall, tapering helmet of shining steel, from which hung a facial mask of fine steel links, protecting his face without impairing his vision, and he stood with his own chin elevated almost as far as André's, his body braced slightly rearward against the tension of the outstretched arm that was forcing André up onto his toes. Beneath the hanging links of his visor, the skin of the stranger's face was a deep, dark brown, making the lines and shadows on his skin seem black, and his eyes were equally dark beneath bushy brows. His mustache and beard were so black that they appeared to have blue light in them, and although the mouth beneath them was closed now, André had seen the gleam of white teeth shining through as the fellow smiled. This man, André knew, was dangerous; tall, lean, and broad shouldered. He could see little of him below shoulder height, but he surmised that the man would be dressed from head to foot in flowing black.

"Ibrahim! I vow you are improving, in spite of yourself. I barely heard you come in this time." Alec's Arabic was flawless and betrayed no indication of surprise.

"You did not hear me at all, Almania." The dark eyes did not leave André's for an instant, even as the knife-wielder spoke to Alec.

"I was already here when you named me. Who is this *ferenghi*?"

"My cousin, André St. Clair." He looked at André and switched back to their tongue. "André, say hello to Ibrahim al-Khusai, my liaison with the forces of Rashid al-Din Sinan." Another swift switch and he was speaking to Ibrahim in Arabic again. "André is the one for whom I summoned the services of Saif ad-Din."

Alec had made no reference at all to the dagger being held beneath André's chin, and now André saw Ibrahim's eyes narrow to slits. "The one who lost his father?"

"The one."

Ibrahim blew a small snuffing noise through his nose and lowered his blade. He took a step backward and returned the dagger to its sheath. "That is an affliction no man should have to bear but, by the will of Allah, all men do. I lost my father less than two months ago, may Allah smile upon his memory, and the grief has barely left my bones." He turned to Alec. "But you did not hear me coming, Almania, be truthful."

André took the opportunity to scan the Assassin now from head to foot, seeing that he had been right in assuming the fellow would be completely robed in black, but over his long outer garment, Ibrahim wore a knee-length tunic of the finest open-link chain mail André had ever seen. Over that, he also wore a cuirass of shining steel to match his helmet, and a magnificent long-bladed scimitar hung from the belt at his waist.

He was still glaring defiantly at Alec, but Alec merely dipped his head slightly, dismissing the point as unimportant. "I was not listening, in truth, because I had no need to hear you coming, my friend. But truthfully, I *smelled* your presence the moment we entered the main cavern. I have told you before, you may recall, that cinnamon, in the amounts by which you consume it, is a highly recognizable aroma. You are inured to it and therefore unaware of how strongly you smell of it, but in your kind of work, it could get you killed."

Ibrahim had stopped listening, having obviously heard and been bored by this before, and was staring now at André, his eyes moving up and down the length of his body. Now he nodded to himself and held up his hand. "I will help this one to dress like a man." He turned his head back towards Alec. "Tell him to take off his clothes."

"Tell him yourself. He speaks your tongue."

Ibrahim straightened in surprise. "You speak Arabic?"

"Not well, but I do," André replied in the same tongue. "I learned it before I ever left our homeland to come here, because our brethren there, who are the allies of your imam, Rashid al-Din, considered it wise to have me learn your language early, taught by a number of your finest scholars who live among them today, sharing common knowledge with our brethren."

"So be it. Now, to our task. Disrobe, if you will."

André removed his armor and his clothing, and Ibrahim instructed him thoroughly thereafter in the wearing of Muslim clothes, showing him the manner of applying and properly adjusting each separate garment, so the overall effect was one of loose and unrestrictive comfort. He ended by showing the Templar how to don the flowing headdress called the kufiya, and how to fasten it into place, tugging the securing band firmly into position, and then examining his own handiwork with a critical eye before nodding in satisfaction. "Thus it should hang," he grunted. "You have the feel of it?"

"I have it now, but whether it will stay with me, I know not." He could not have said why he had decided to say nothing about knowing the clothing already, nor why he chose to continue feigning ignorance.

"I will attend you from now until we meet the people we must meet. By then, you should know how to wear your clothing. It is not difficult. Our children can do it." He glanced at Alec, who had been watching. "Come, Almania, we should be on the way already."

As they saddled their horses, André spoke to Alec again in French. "What is that name he called you? Almania?"

"It's the name of a tribe of Germans, the Alemanni. He thinks it means Englishman and he has called me it for years. I've tried to tell him different but he pays no heed, so now I simply accept it. And apparently there is no name for Scotland or for Scots in Arabic."

"Where are we going now?" he asked. Ibrahim was leading the way out of the caverns.

"We are running errands, delivering messages to certain interested parties and to one in particular. There is no real need for you to come along, save that I think it is time we showed your face to the people with whom we have to work. That may or may not include the Old Man himself, for that is where we are ultimately going, but whether or not he will consent to receive you is something we will not know until the moment arrives. So think of this as an orientation journey, to meet these people, see where they live, and take note of how they deal with us."

Ibrahim had ridden ahead and vanished among the boulders soon after they set out, but now they glimpsed him coming back towards them, and he drew rein about a hundred paces ahead, waiting for them to catch up to him. Alec continued, "You should find it interesting, because it will be like nothing else you will ever encounter out here. They would as happily slit our throats as look at us, but they do not dare, because they know we are under the protection of the imam, Rashid al-Din. They do not know why that should be so, but they accept that it is, and so since we are not Sunni, yet are People of the Book, they tolerate us, irrespective of how much or how little they understand of the reasons for our presence here. They know, too—and I have no idea how or how much they know of that, or where they came to learn of it—that even although we appear to be Templars, we are nonetheless different from the other Templars with whom they have dealings. Some things we are simply not meant to know or understand, and that is one of them."

He waved to Ibrahim as they began to draw level with him, but continued talking to André in French. "Thus, you will find most of them courteous, if not exactly friendly, but never, ever forget who these people are, André, and never think to trust them. They are the Hashshashin. The Assassins. Our brotherhoods may have arcane commonalities, but we, as brothers, have nothing in common with them. Beware of them at all times." He switched smoothly into Arabic again, for he had seen Ibrahim's shoulders straighten on hearing the name Hashshashin. "Forgive me, Ibrahim my friend, for my lack of courtesy in speaking our *ferenghi* tongue, but my cousin here still finds it easier to listen and learn in our own tongue than in yours. I was explaining to him the history of your brotherhood and its successes since the advent of Rashid al-Din to Syria, more than forty years ago, but it strikes me now that you are far more qualified than I to speak of your brotherhood's intentions and ambitions, and listening to you speak of such things in your own tongue would be a great benefit to him. Will you not honor us both by educating my cousin from your own point of view?"

Ibrahim, it transpired, was more than willing, despite his lingering air of disgruntlement. For the next two hours he talked without pause and surprised both his listeners by being articulate and well informed, with clearly defined opinions and beliefs amplified by analytical and even philosophical observations on what he and his Shi'a people had been able to achieve in their campaign against the Sunni caliphate, personified at this time by Saladin himself, who had called for the extermination of the Assassin brotherhood. In retaliation, he told them, Saladin had been marked for death three times, and on the first two had escaped by sheerest blind chance. But the third attempt, carried out by Ibrahim in person and according to the specific instructions of Rashid al-Din, had achieved what failure could not. On that occasion, the Sultan had awakened to find warm hotcakes and an Assassin's dagger lying on the pillow by his head. There could be no mistaking the message: Saladin's life was safe nowhere, not even in his own tent, under the care of his personal bodyguard, among the legions of his army.

Since that day, Saladin had taken to sleeping in a secure wooden pavilion that he had specially made and took with him everywhere, and he had never again called for action against Rashid al-Din and his followers.

Long before Ibrahim's commentary ran out, they left the boulders and their surrounding plains far behind them and struck up into the mountainous terrain of the northern region, arriving at a high mountain village as the shadows began to darken late in the afternoon. It was a large village and unusually prosperous, according to a grunted aside from Alec, who suspected that its wealth came solely from banditry. André was formally introduced to the headman and his council by Ibrahim, before sitting down to dine with them. The men talked openly enough throughout the meal and showed no overt signs of hostility to the strangers in their midst, but Alec would tell André afterwards that he had been highly aware of the differences between the men of this village and those who lived in the village ruled by his friend and former captor Ibn al-Farouch. There was no humor here, he noted, at any stage of the proceedings. Everything was deadly dull and serious, tinged with overtones of hardship and tragedy. No one laughed, and he did not remark a single smile around the fire pit or around the dining table.

The three visitors slept beneath the open sky, wrapped in blankets against the night chill, and they were up and away soon after daybreak, heading northward again. As he had promised, Ibrahim inspected André's appearance before they left, and made him presentable with a few sharp tugs and tucks, explaining all the while exactly what he was attempting to achieve. And by the time the next day dawned, their business with Rashid al-Din, the Old Man of the Mountain, was completed and André and Alec were homeward bound, uncaring of what any casual observer might think of the finer adjustments of their dress.

The previous night, just before darkness fell, André had seen, and had been seen by, Rashid al-Din himself, but he had not met the great man, if *great* was the appropriate word to describe him. He had accompanied Alec to the meeting place under a sunset sky of brilliant golds and burnished browns and orange, and had then drawn aside to wait outside when one of the guards had held up a hand to bar him from entering. This had been expected, and Alec had already explained that he might or might not be summoned to go inside after Alec had informed Rashid al-Din of who he was and why he was there. There was no way, Alec had said, to foretell how the imam might react, for in matters such as this Rashid al-Din took pleasure in being known as a man of whims and varying moods.

Either he would summon André to his presence, or he would not.

In the event, the imam did neither. André had been standing to one side of the door, removed by several paces from the orbit of the guards, when his attention was drawn by a minor disturbance of some kind in the doorway itself. It had turned cold as soon as the sun sank beneath the peak at their backs, for they were high in the mountains here, on the pinnacle fortress known as the Eagle's Nest, and he had just finished wrapping himself in his cloak against the chill of the night air. And then, hearing a surge of movement behind him, followed immediately by complete silence, he had turned around slowly to find himself being watched by a man he knew could be no other than Rashid al-Din.

Part of his certainty stemmed from his instant awareness of the tension gripping the guards as they eyed the man, their entire attitude conveying awe and apprehension so clearly that it seemed to him as though their very bodies were straining backward, away from the man who stood between them. And then he grew aware of the man himself and the air of stillness that hung over him like a shadow. Like most of the Assassin brotherhood, he was dressed completely in black, but this man's black seemed personal and it transcended darkness; he exuded blackness, and as André looked at him the thought formed in his mind, *and icy cold ... blackness and icy cold.*

He realized then that he did not know how to react or how to behave. He felt a nervous gathering of tension at the base of his neck and thought, for a wild moment, that perhaps he ought to bow, but he dismissed the notion as soon as it occurred to him and willed himself to remain erect and motionless. If he were not to be summoned, but were merely to be looked at and inspected like some inert lump, a faceless prisoner or a slave, then he would give no man the satisfaction of seeing him as submissive, and so he squared his shoulders and gazed stonily back into the cold, basilisk stare of the man watching him. The face was flat and close to featureless, almost completely concealed by a heavy, full beard of wiry iron-gray hair with wide, white streaks running from the outside edges of the nose to come together beneath the chin. Beneath twin, pointed tangles of coarse gray eyebrows, glassy, opaque eyes stared at him emptily, expressionless and unreadable. They reminded him of serpents' eyes, utterly lacking in humanity or warmth, and he held their gaze resolutely, refusing even to blink as he mentally detailed the impressions this man had already made on him without speaking a word or offering a hint of recognition.

Arrogance was there, above and before all else, clearly discernible in the way al-Din held his head and even in the way in which the trailing ends of his black turban hung down to frame his face, as though positioned by someone who sought to achieve precisely the effect that he had captured. Intolerance was there as well, in the curl of the lip and the dead dullness of the sagging bags beneath the expressionless, unyielding eyes. Pride was there, too, he knew, although he could detect no overt sign of it, and so were monstrous vanity—denied and disavowed, no doubt, but there beneath the facade of faceless humility nonetheless—and sneering disdain for any but himself. André St. Clair decided then and there that he did not like Rashid al-Din Sinan, the Assassins' Old Man of the Mountain, and that he had no wish to have any dealing with him on any pretext, even in obedience to the Council of the Order of Sion. And as that thought entered his mind, the other man slowly turned and stalked back inside the doors, the guards closing them reverentially and with evident relief at his back.

ALEC EMERGED FROM THE MEETING HOUSE about an hour later, frowning to himself as he tracked down André, who was warming himself by the fire the guards had built in the courtyard, and his first question, asked in French, was about Rashid al-Din. "He came outside to look at you when I told him who you are. Did you see him?"

"How could I fail to? He stood less than five paces from me, staring right at me."

"And what did you think?"

André looked around him. There were more than a score of

people in the courtyard now, and about half of them had gathered around the fire. "Do any of these people speak French?"

"Not that I know of. It is highly unlikely."

"No more unlikely, surely, than that we should speak Arabic?"

Alec's answering grin was tiny and brief, accompanied by a shake of the head. "Different thing, Cousin, believe me. You and I learned their language so that we could converse with them for our own purposes. These people have no such incentive. They are simple and unlettered, for the most part, seldom leaving these heights, and atop all that they are zealots. They despise us and everything we represent. They see us as godless infidels, damned eternally for our refusal to accept Allah and His Prophet. Why would they wish to sully themselves by speaking our foul infidel tongue? These men do not speak or understand French, upon my oath."

"Then I shall tell you what I thought of your Old Man of the Mountain. I thought he was one of your perfect men of God. He is a zealot, but he is also a fanatic on the scale of a Nero or a Tiberius, consumed by self-love and convinced that only through his personal intercession can men ever hope to achieve salvation, and therefore he will do all in his power to foment war for his own purposes and to his own ends. He is filled up with self-righteousness and intolerance and hatred. He preaches bigotry and slaughter in the name of God. He is insane with the need to make other men insane in fighting for their gods and his own ambitions. I loathed him at first sight, and the mere prospect of having to treat with him at any time, for any purpose, makes me want to vomit. Apart from that, I found him quite impressive, in a flat-faced, inhuman kind of way."

Alec quirked one eyebrow. "Well, he certainly seems to have made an impression on you. I wonder what thoughts you inspired in him."

André tried unsuccessfully to cover a quick grin. "I believe in first impressions, Cousin, and they seldom lead me astray. As for what he thought of me, I could not care less. What did you and he talk about?"

Alec was quiet for several moments, as if deliberating whether or not he wanted to challenge André's opinions, but then he shrugged and answered the question in a voice filled with disgust. "More than I wanted to talk about. First thing I found out was that I had stepped into a mess I didn't even know was there. I didn't do what any fool knows you have to do—I did not check my understanding against reality before jumping into the action, and placed myself at a disadvantage by not knowing everything I should have known. And, as it always will, that failure undid me when the last thing I needed was to be undone. Damnation! I'm still angry, but the truth is there's no one to blame but myself."

"Like what? I have no idea what you are talking about."

"Conrad and the Templars … De Montferrat and de Ridefort. I thought to distance them from each other, for my own purposes, one of them now being dead, but as soon as I brought the matter up, Sinan became incensed, and I knew I had missed something. Sure enough, he told me all about it, and I was taken completely by surprise. It mattered nothing that I was still a prisoner of war when all of it took place, because I am a dealer in information first and foremost and should know better than to make such errors."

"I still don't know what you are talking about."

"I know. I know you don't … But I don't want to discuss it right at this moment. I'm hungry and I can smell roasting goat. Let's find some food and a place where we can sit and eat it and talk privately, and then I'll tell you all about the debacle."

A short time later, fortified by roasted goat and freshly baked bread, washed down with cold water from a nearby stream, the two Franks settled themselves by the side of a dying fire and stirred it into life. No one paid them any attention at all, and eventually Alec Sinclair sat up straighter and brushed crumbs from the front of his robe before starting to speak.

"What I found out was that Conrad crossed Rashid badly, months ago before I was released from my captivity. Rashid is still so angry about it that he would not even allow Conrad's name to be mentioned, and I ended up looking like a fool. Apparently one of Sinan's ships, laden with treasures of various kind, was forced to seek sanctuary in Tyre from a violent winter storm early in this new year. I am told there are protocols governing such situations, and that the laws of sanctuary offered by harbors to visiting ships are quite as stringent as those offered to sinners by churches, but for a variety of reasons on this occasion the laws were suspended by Conrad. He had opted some time before, for reasons of his own, to shun the call to arms sent out by Richard of England to all the knights and men of Outremer. We all knew that, but somehow failed to pay it the attention it deserved, for Conrad is German, kin to Barbarossa, and newly named but not yet solidly established as the Count of Tyre.

"The Templars had left Tyre long before this happened, to lay siege to Acre with de Lusignan, and they had taken their war chest with them, which meant that Conrad had lost his largest and most ready source of funds. He was courting the good opinion of Philip of France at the time, too, and that was not an inexpensive endeavor. But he knew there was no love lost between the English and French Kings and he sought to turn that to his own advantage. The primary import of all that at the time, however, was that Conrad was almost bankrupt, and the Arab ship in his harbor was heavily laden with goods and cargo of great value. And so he impounded the vessel and killed its captain.

"Well, when Rashid al-Din learned of what had happened, he sent envoys to Conrad, explaining who he was—a Shi'a prince— and requesting the return of his ship and its cargo and crew on the old basis that the enemy of my enemy is my friend. Conrad refused, and the messengers were sent home with fleas in their ears. And needless to say, nothing was ever restored to Sinan.

"It was a loss of great magnitude to the Assassins and they would have gone to great lengths to make sure that no hint of their discomfiture would ever filter back to amuse Saladin. By the time I was released, the story of the captured ship had long since been overshadowed by other events. But I should have known about it nonetheless. I was lazy, and I did not dig deeply enough before committing myself to a course of action I would regret."

"But what could you have discovered, and how would you have known where to look?"

"I would have looked where I ought to have looked before doing anything else. I would have looked among our own Brethren of Sion here, the few who deal with such matters. And had I done that, I would have found out everything about the episode."

"So … Apart from the damage to your pride, if what I am hearing is correct, there had been no great setback to what you have been asked to do. Am I correct?"

"Oh yes. Conrad is a dead man. He merely does not know it yet. No one makes a mortal enemy of Rashid al-Din Sinan and survives to talk about it. Conrad is now under *fatwa*. His death has been decreed, his killers dispatched. All that remains to be finalized is the manner and the timing."

"Then your duty is fulfilled. You have achieved your objective without even having to do anything. That seldom happens in life today."

Sinclair cocked his head and regarded his cousin steadily. "Aye," he said. "I suppose that is true, save that we cannot dictate the timing of any of this, which could be a disadvantage." He paused. "We never did talk about that aspect of my orders, you and I. How did you feel when you discovered my instructions in the dispatches? Have you anything you wish to say? Anything you would rather not do?"

"Well," André's voice was musing. "I must admit I was dismayed that you should be asked, and by our own Council, to arrange an elimination—no, let's call it what it is—a murder. I did not become either knight or monk to be set such tasks. But then I thought it through, and believe me, Cousin, when I tell you that I thought it through at great length and on many occasions, and I came to an understanding of it from other points of view than that dictated by my own dislike. All of this, of course, long before I caught the smell of Rashid al-Din.

"There is far more at stake here than the life of one man. I understand that. What is really at hazard is the continuing existence of Christianity in the Holy Lands … and even should Richard's host prevail over Saladin's and uphold Christianity, the very form of that Christianity, its essence, will be disputed between rival factions of

Roman and Byzantine Christians just as bitterly as the true way of Islam is disputed between Sunni and Shi'a Muslims. Now, not being a Christian, that should concern me not at all, and it does not, except that our ancient Order requires the mantle of secrecy offered it by Roman Christianity, and most particularly by the Order of the Temple, in order to continue its sacred work. And as a loyal Brother of the Order and a student of its lore, I believe in the importance of that work and have sworn to do everything within my power to assist in its eventual completion, stripping a thousand-year-old veil of lies from the eyes of men and allowing them to see and understand the original Way to the Kingdom of God espoused by Jesus and his companions within the Jerusalem Assembly.

"To that end, I will deal with the Assassins or with anyone else capable of helping us achieve our aims. And that in turn means that I can bring myself to condone, if not to carry out, the murder of the Count of Tyre, because since the death of the Emperor Barbarossa, Conrad of Montferrat now represents the single greatest threat to Roman Christianity in Outremer. If he marries Isabella, even if he does not become King of Jerusalem in fact, he will entrench the Orthodox rites in this part of the world more strongly than ever before, and he will replace the Order of the Temple with the Teutonic Order, emasculating the Western knights, both Templars and Hospitallers, and depriving them of any voice in the future of the kingdom. And in doing that, in dispossessing the Temple, he will disrupt the workings of our Order and interrupt, conceivably for another millennium, the progress of our sacred mission. And of course, he *will* become King of Jerusalem as soon as he weds Isabella."

"Then there is naught for us to do but pray he falls to the *fatwa* before he marries her," Sinclair muttered.

"Perhaps. But as you say, Cousin, we can exercise no control over that. And Rashid al-Din has no interest in assisting with any designs of ours, am I correct?" He waited for Sinclair's nod, then added, "But answer me this: is it true that the Assassins see ritual slaughter of public officials in public places as a desirable means of spreading their own brand of terror?"

"It is."

"And is it true that it will be to Conrad's great advantage to consummate this marriage to Isabella just as soon as it can be arranged?"

"Yes. What are you suggesting?"

"Nothing yet. And when this wedding occurs, will it be a great gala event?"

"A royal wedding? Of course it will."

"Well then, tell me why you should not go to Rashid al-Din and inform him of what is happening with Conrad and his overwhelmingly ambitious plan to consolidate all of Christianity under himself as King of Jerusalem? And while you are there, why should you not offer to keep the imam apprised at all times of Conrad's movements and the development of his plans for the wedding? Thus informed, and when the time is right, Rashid would be able to send in his men to wreak the greatest possible havoc at the most propitious and appropriate moment, killing Conrad just as he is preparing to wed the Queen and take up the crown of Jerusalem. Now, *there* would be a statement of the power of the Assassin brotherhood, and it would fit our purposes to perfection."

"What d'you mean, to perfection?"

"Well, if this wedding does not take place, for any reason, well and good and we need not be concerned with any of this."

"But in that case Rashid al-Din will kill Conrad anyway."

"He probably will, but at least under those circumstances it will be his decision, not ours."

Alec sat staring at his cousin in unblinking awe, his right hand frozen in the act of rising to scratch at his nose, but then he allowed his hand to fall against his face, fingertips touching his lips, and shook his head. "That, Master St. Clair, is a stratagem worthy of a pope. It is inspired—utter, uncomplicated brilliance. Perfection!" He slapped his hand on his knees and surged to his feet, towering over André.

"Where are you going?"

"Back. Into the lion's den. I intend to go and ask that he see me now, immediately, for I have matters of grave import to share with him. He knows we are leaving in the morning and his curiosity will not permit him to let us depart without squeezing every single thing we know out of us. Wait here for me. I should not be long."

He was back in less than half an hour, and as he came he lobbed a magnificently gaudy dagger for André to catch. "It's yours, although the Old Man gave it to me in token of his high regard. I neglected to tell him that it was really you whom he now holds in such high regard. Enjoy the weapon, for you certainly earned it this night. The hilt is a stone called lapis lazuli and the metalwork is brass, not gold, but you could clean and butcher a full-grown camel with the blade and never dull it. That is a sheikh's weapon, my son. Wear it with pride. And now I am sure you must be as tired as I am, and we're to be on the road in the early morning, so let's find our bed rolls."

"I will, I will, but what did he say when you outlined your plan?"

"Nothing, not a word, but the miserable old sodomite actually smiled at me … one of the most frightening things I have ever seen. He listened rapt, and when I had finished he went and brought the dagger for me personally, giving it to me from his own hand. He liked your plan, Cousin. And now we control the reins. We have earned a sound sleep. Come."

"Gladly, but I cannot accept this." André held out the dagger, its blue and gold hilt extended towards Sinclair, but Alec crossed his arms over his chest, his fingers flat beneath his armpits. André frowned. "Come, it is yours by any argument, and as you say, it is a weapon fit for a sheikh. Why won't you take it?"

"Because it is not mine. You earned it with your wondrous idea. I merely passed the bait along to the Old Man. Besides, I have a dagger and I cherish it. See." He reached to the waistband at the small of his back and brought out a weapon far more beautiful than the one given him by Rashid al-Din. This was a magnificently ornate, sheathed dagger with a hooked blade, its hilt and gilded scabbard chased with silver filigree and studded with polished precious stones in red, green, and blue.

"I have never seen that before."

"Of course not. I keep it hidden, since otherwise I would have to forfeit it. Its very appearance makes a mockery of any vow of poverty and would excite the greed of anyone laying eyes on it. But I do not keep it for its monetary value, for in my eyes it has none. It once belonged to a young man called Arouf, who was brother to the wife of Ibn al-Farouch, my former captor. I found Arouf dead in the desert, after Hattin, and took the dagger from his body. Later, when I met al-Farouch, he recognized it, and later yet, when I became his prisoner, he took it from me. Then, once we had become friends and he set me free, he gave it back to me, as a memento of our time together, and I keep it in honor of that unexpectedly discovered friendship. So, keep you your dagger, and I will keep mine, both of them hidden from the eyes of acquisitive and avaricious men."

TEN

Within days of their return to duty, the cousins were separated, with the knowledge that they were likely to remain so until the next pieces of the developing offensive against the enemy were well in hand.

The unfortunate part of that was that no one could say how long that might take. The two Kings, Richard and Philip, were both laid low with *leonardia*, which the soldiery called scurvy. Richard's condition was far worse than the affliction visited upon Philip, and perhaps because he could see for once that he looked physically better and more attractive than his English rival, whose hair was falling out in clumps and whose teeth were rotting and visibly loosening, Philip fought off his own infection uncharacteristically and made frantic preparations to attack Acre with his own army and bring an end to the siege once and for all through his own unsupported efforts. The major portion of Richard's fleet, no longer under the command of Sir Robert de Sablé, was still locked in Tyre, unable to sail because of the troublesome and dangerous winds known as the Arsuf, and stranded there with them was more than half of Richard's army from Normandy. Philip wanted to press home his advantage and seize whatever glory he could in Acre while his rival was still sick and before these reinforcements could arrive from Tyre, and so he fought on alone, hammering relentlessly at the cornerstone of Acre's defenses, the Accursed Tower, while Richard was rumored—the entire campaign in Outremer appeared to run on rumors—to be yet abed but negotiating fruitlessly with Saladin's envoys over the terms of surrender for Acre.

However, according to a report that André passed on to Alec from Ibrahim towards the very end of June, Saladin was playing a game of his own and was consequently happy to buy time by whiling away days and weeks overseeing pointless comings and goings between envoys from both armies. The Sultan, it appeared, was daily awaiting the arrival of a fleet from Cairo and an army supposedly approaching overland from Baghdad, confident that the advent of either one would be sufficient to deflect and disarm Philip's army and its attacks on the walls of Acre. Alec took that information directly to his superior, Sir Robert de Sablé, Grand Master Elect of the Order of the Temple, only to have it set aside as unimportant in the grand scheme of things.

That night, after dining with his cousin for the first time in more than a week, Alec passed those tidings back to André as they sat atop the defensive rampart above the Trench, staring out over the calm emptiness of the desert beyond.

They had been disappointed on their arrival, for they had brought their arbalests along in hopes of finding something to shoot at. But the ground across from them that had been thronged with Saracen horsemen mere hours before lay empty and desolate, and their crossbows lay unused in the sand at their feet.

Now, piqued by what his cousin had said, St. Clair turned to look at him sidelong. "It's unimportant that we know what Saladin is thinking? That is insane."

"No, not so. I reacted that way, too, at first, but Sir Robert told me they already had that information and had planned accordingly. In the meantime, he said, he has larger fish to fry."

"Like what?"

"Cyprus."

"I don't follow you."

"I'm not surprised ... Richard wants to sell Cyprus to the Templars."

"To sell—? What kind of folly is that? Cyprus is a *place*, an island. You can't sell a place!"

"Of course you can, if it's yours and if you can command a worthwhile price. And you may remember, Richard made Cyprus his when he deposed the idiot Comnenus and took control of his so-called empire. And now he has changed his mind. He no longer wants the place and so he is looking to sell it to a suitable purchaser … the Order of the Temple."

"And why, in the name of anything resembling sanity, would he think the Templars might be even remotely interested in such a hare-brained idea?"

Alec Sinclair looked at his French cousin and raised his eyebrows high, rounding his eyes and pursing his lips comically. "Perhaps because he believes they are covetous of such a place. Perhaps because he has been a close friend of the new Grand Master for many years and he knows, because the Grand Master has told him, that the Order yearns for a stable, solid base of operations, far removed from interference by the kings and popes of Christendom and close enough to the Holy Land to serve as a launching area for future wars and campaigns. And perhaps because the coffers of his war chest are depleted and he knows the Order would be happy to pay a premium price for precisely such a place as he has to offer for sale … Think you any of those reasons might suffice?"

André shook his head in rueful wonder, as though surprised that he had allowed himself to be surprised. "And the negotiations are in hand as we speak?"

"No, they are complete. The agreement has been made, the sale concluded."

"I see. Well, I suppose it makes some kind of sense. What was the price, can you say?"

"Aye, I can tell you. But you can't tell anyone else. Agreed?" André nodded. "One hundred thousand gold pieces—Saracen bezants. Forty thousand initially, as a down payment, and annual payments of ten thousand for six years, once they have established their Rule there."

André whistled softly. "Richard did well … Forty thousand gold bezants is an admirable return on an investment less than three months old and that cost him nothing in the first place. And how long will it take the Temple to establish their Rule there, as you say?"

"Not long, it seems. They are prepared to move without loss of time. I have orders to sail for the island at once, to scout out a potential headquarters and report back to de Sablé. I will leave the day after tomorrow."

"Will you, by God? Where will you start? Will you visit Famagusta? If you do, I should like you to find my father's grave and tend to it for me. Will you do that?"

"Come, Cuz, you don't even need to ask that. Of course I will. And even if my travels don't take me there, I'll make the journey anyway, on my own. Rest assured of that. Now, what about you, what are you up to these days?"

André grinned. "Soldiering, what else? Ever since finding you, I've lost my special status. As long as I could claim to be the Official Seeker of Sir Alexander Sinclair, I was privileged to come and go as I pleased. Now that you're found and safe, I've become an ordinary grunt again, albeit a knighted grunt … I am now a plain Templar knight-at-arms, responsible for a forty-man squadron of sergeant brothers from Anjou, which means I am now permitted to rise for prayers throughout the nighttime hours, in addition to which, as a squadron leader, I am at liberty to conduct daily patrols of the sector of enemy territory facing, and sometimes almost encircling, our southeastern salient. But I have no time to be bored. Saladin's lads attack us every day, determined to breach the Trench, and sometimes it's all we can do to hold them off."

Sinclair cocked his head. "You said *Saladin's lads* … do you think of them that way? Without malice?"

"Without malice? I suppose I do, if and when I think of them at all. I think of them as simply being there, like the sand flies and the scorpions, part of this landscape. I certainly don't hate them as infidels or ravening, blood-drinking demon's spawn. As far as I have seen for myself, along with what you have told me, they are people much like ourselves, save that they adhere to different beliefs. They are men, like us, with problems of their own and tribulations we would recognize and acknowledge could we but see them. What made you ask me that?"

Alec grunted and stood up. "I don't know. Perhaps the hope of hearing you say what you said. Particularly the piece about not hating them. It's too easy to hate out here, and too many people are doing it, on both sides." He tightened the cinch about his waist and stretched up on his toes. "What's the difference between Jesus and Muhammad, Cuz, can you tell me?"

St. Clair grinned again. "No, I can't, but I have a feeling you are going to tell me."

"No, not I, for I don't know. That's too deep a conundrum for me. But even though I be not Christian in the proper sense, I would still support Jesus, as a man, for the difference between those two, it seems to me, lies rooted in power and the way, as men, they sought it. Jesus did not. He never did. He simply lived his life as he saw fit, and it was men, thereafter, who shaped him into the deity he has become. But Muhammad? Muhammad dealt in power from the outset, seeking to control men's minds and actions in the name of God. He might have been divinely and genuinely inspired by Allah, but that is beyond my ability to determine. All I can say, from my own viewpoint as an observer of men, is that I distrust mortal men who claim a personal relationship with God that requires them to tell others how to think and behave. And I find it enlightening that none of those men, be they sultans, emirs, caliphs, popes, cardinals, patriarchs, archbishops, or bishops, ever appears to be impoverished. And damnation, I am still hungry. Can you credit that?"

"You can't be. We ate but an hour ago. It's the excitement of thinking about your coming trip to Cyprus that is making you feel hungry."

"You might be right, Cousin, and mayhap you are, but I could eat something right now, nonetheless. Pick up your weapon there and let's walk and stretch our legs."

They had almost reached the point from which they had set out when Alec Sinclair stopped and handed his crossbow to André before digging his thumbs into his sides, below the edges of his cuirass, and arching his spine backward so that his shoulder blades came close to touching each other.

"Tomorrow will be the first day of July," he said with a grunt when he had finished. "I expect it to be anything but a boring month and I expect that much will happen while I am away in Cyprus. I almost wish I were not going."

"How long will you be gone, do you know?"

"No. It might take me a month to do what I have to do, so I'll be gone that long, at least, and perhaps even longer. I have no need to rush and there is no call for haste. Better to do the preparatory work thoroughly and make the correct decisions the first time around than to botch the assignment and be made to watch someone else being sent to clean up your mess and rectify your errors, would you not agree?"

"No argument from me."

Alec Sinclair looked up at the sky, then reached his hand out again for his arbalest, hefting it solidly and resting its shaft across his shoulder. "Look after yourself while I'm away, Cousin, and try not to get yourself killed. I'll look for you as soon as I come back, and I have no wish to find you laid up with the Hospitallers. They are our rivals, you know, and they grow smug whenever any of us has to place himself in their care. God knows we are glad to have them with us, but they can be irritatingly supercilious at times. Fare ye well, Cousin."

The two men embraced clumsily, bound in armor as they were, then went their separate ways, Sinclair returning to his quarters beside de Sablé's pavilion and the Templars' tent, and St. Clair to his own billet in the rows of tents that housed his squadron of sergeant brothers.

ON JULY THE EIGHTH, six days after Alec Sinclair's departure for Cyprus, eight of André's men were killed in a single encounter with a determined band of Saracen sappers. These men had evidently worked all night long, and without making a sound, to fill up a narrow section of the Trench with faggots—thick bundles of long stick-like bulrushes brought in from some great distance away, since there was no such growth to be found anywhere in the region surrounding Acre. They completed their task sometime before dawn, then lay in hiding on the ground beyond the Trench, concealed in plain view beneath their sand-colored cloaks, until after the guard had been changed just before daybreak. Then, when it was least expected, they attacked like *djinns*, leaping from concealment and charging afoot, in great numbers, to cross the narrow bridge they had built, while behind them their companions hurried to bring their horses over after them.

Their ruse almost succeeded, and their surprise would have been complete had it not been for two minor details that combined to confound them. One was that a young Turcopole, one of the lightly armored native levies trained to fight against the Saracen cavalry, had been unable to sleep, troubled by stomach cramps, and had gone walking in the predawn darkness, to stumble and fall to his knees at the very point where the newly built bridge of faggots reached his side of the Trench. Scarcely able to believe what he was seeing, he had raised the alarum immediately, attracting the attention of mounted Hospitallers who were passing on their way to an assigned patrol to the southward.

The Saracens attacked as soon as the Turcopole raised his alarum, but the Hospitallers were close enough to the bridge's end to reach it ahead of them and prevent a complete penetration of the Frankish position. It was a close-run thing, nonetheless, and the incursion swelled quickly into a major melee, with heavy casualties on both sides. St. Clair and his forty-man squadron had been heading out to the northward at the same time as the Hospitallers were heading south, but they heard the rising tumult at their backs and swung around to engage the enemy in a thundering charge. Afterwards, St. Clair would remember thinking that he had counted more than a hundred of the enemy on his side of the Trench as he arrived, some of them mounted, many more on foot, and that among the men on foot, Saracen sharpshooters were adding their own close-range missiles to the clouds of arrows and crossbow bolts being launched against the Franks from the far side of the Trench.

He saw his First Sergeant go down within moments of their arrival, killed by a heavy bolt that punched cleanly through him, armor and all, and sent him flying, and before he could even begin to react to that, two more of his men went down right in front of him, thrown over their horses' heads as the animals collapsed headlong. A hand reached up at him, thrusting a long, light lance, and he swept it away backhanded, then brought his long blade slashing down to cleave the thruster. Straight ahead, two mounted men converged on him, each of them swathed in the green robes of martyrdom, and because he could do nothing else he stood up in his stirrups, pulling his massive horse up onto its hind legs, its big, steel-shod hooves kicking lethally at the lighter animals approaching it. But even as the great beast reared, a man on foot ran in beneath its chest and stabbed it to the heart with a long spear, sending it toppling so that St. Clair barely avoided being crushed beneath it, kicking free of the stirrups and pushing himself nimbly backward, one hand thrusting against his heavy saddle as he vaulted like a man wearing nothing at all. But he was wearing more than ninety pounds of mail and armored plate, and when his heels struck the ground he fell backward, twisting violently sideways, and he barely managed to retain his grip on his sword hilt as the enormous weight of his dead horse crashed to earth beside him.

He rolled away desperately, knowing his two would-be killers were now looming over him, but only one of them pressed home an attack. André hacked desperately to parry a heavy, slashing blow that numbed his arm, then watched the glittering arc of the shining scimitar as it swung up again to finish him. But before the weapon could reach the top of its arc, there came a flashing blur and the thump of a crossbow bolt hitting meat, and the scimitar wielder vanished, smashed backward into the martyr's death he had come seeking.

Panting, almost sobbing, St. Clair lay still, gazing upward and unable to move for a moment. Around him, he could hear the cacophony of battle, the moans and grunts, curses and harrowing screams that always accompanied the clash of weapons and other sounds of strife, but for the time being he lay alone, catching his breath and wondering if he would be able to move when the time came for him to make the attempt. He tensed, raised his head slightly and looked around, unable to see anything at all on his right side because of the bulk of the dead horse, but then he grunted and half rolled, struggling first to a sitting position and thence to his feet, where he stood swaying slightly, flexing his fingers on the hilt of his sword. A spiked Saracen mace lay on the ground by his feet, and he stooped and picked it up in his left hand, holding it loosely and hefting it until he had the feel of it, lithe and springy yet pleasingly heavy in the wickedly spiked head. He sensed movement to his right and swung to see two of Allah's bearded Faithful come leaping towards him, dodging around obstacles as they raced to reach him, each trying to outdo the other. The sight filled him, surprisingly, with elation, and he drew a deep breath and felt himself grinning as he prepared to meet them.

The man on his right won the race, gripping his scimitar with both hands over his head and screaming Allah's name in exultation as he brought his blade down on the infidel's head, but André caught the blade on the upraised edge of his own, then clubbed him into oblivion with the mace in his left hand, before turning back and dropping to one knee to allow the second man to run directly against his extended sword and impale himself. As he felt the fellow's weight come to bear against his point, he thrust himself upright again and leaned into the blow, twisting his blade fiercely and then jerking it back and free before the man's flesh could close around it and imprison the steel.

He heard trumpets at his back and a rising thunder of hooves as more reinforcements arrived, shouting the names of Richard and Saint George, and suddenly the Saracens were in full flight, back across the makeshift bridge that had come close to breaching the Frankish lines. He looked back to the body of his warhorse, then ran as quickly as he could to snatch the arbalest and a quiver of bolts from the saddle horn where they had hung, but the crossbow had fallen beneath the animal and he could not budge it at all. By the time he straightened up again and headed towards the Trench, the fighting was all over. The last of the Saracens had retreated beyond the range of even the strongest arbalests, and someone at the front of the Hospitaller formation had already set the bridge ablaze with a bottle of Greek fire. Watching the roiling, viscous smoke and flames billowing from the Trench, St. Clair suddenly felt unutterably weary; the fear and exhilaration of battle were gone and in the aftermath, totally drained of energy and tension, he could happily have sunk down then and there to rest on the sand.

Instead, he set out to find his new second-in-command, whoever that might be now that his First Sergeant was dead. He found the man easily, the one nicknamed *Le Sanglier*, the Wild Boar, by his mates and who would have been naturally first in line for promotion in any case, and André set him to making a formal tally of the squadron's strength. That was when he discovered they had sustained eight fatalities, fully twenty percent of their complement, and ten injuries and wounds, one of which was serious enough to threaten to raise their losses to nine dead.

He accepted the tally without comment, then went, grim faced, to select a new mount from among the five that had survived the loss of their riders. He hauled himself into the saddle, surprised to discover that he had a deep ache in his right side, and that he could see dark columns of smoke staining the sky far to the south of Acre, seemingly beyond the sea. He instructed the Boar to have the others assemble and be prepared to set out on the patrol to which they had been assigned that day, then swung his horse around and cantered rearward, to where a small group of English knights sat staring southward at the smoke on the horizon.

"What's burning?" he asked as he rode up.

One of the knights nodded brusquely, recognizing him, and André remembered meeting him, too, in Richard's tent. "It would appear to be Haifa." The Englishman sounded completely uninterested, and shrugged. "Can't think of anything else it might be. It's on the far side of the bay, and there's nothing else between us and it, unless Saladin is burning his entire fleet at sea."

"Have we attacked Haifa?"

"God's entrails, no, certainly not. We have enough to deal with here, trying to topple Acre."

"Then who would burn Haifa? It could only be Saladin, but why would he destroy a town he holds secure?"

The English knight made a moue and shrugged disdainfully. "Who can say what goes on in the mind of a man like that? Perhaps he wants to keep it safe from us. Burning it down would certainly have that effect, would it not?"

St. Clair sat for a moment, absorbing that. "I think you are probably right, Deniston. Acre must be closer to collapse than we thought. Saladin must think we intend to move against Haifa the moment Acre falls. It is so close and it's a port, with deep water and safe anchorages, unfouled by wrecks. That means he must *know* Acre is going to collapse very soon—today, perhaps, or tomorrow."

"Oh, come now. How could he know that? We have the place sealed up tighter than a Cistercian nunnery. Nothing gets in, nothing gets out, including information … most particularly information. That's what a siege is all about."

St. Clair grinned. "Tell me, Lord Deniston, do you swim?"

"Swim? You mean in water?"

"Aye, like a fish. The Arabs do. There are swimmers coming out of and going into Acre every night that God sends. Believe me."

"Believe yourself," the English knight growled huffily, glancing at his companions to be sure they were witnessing his handling of this French idiot. "Never heard such nonsense. Swimming in and out, indeed. Hah!"

St. Clair could hardly admit that he had been assured that was so by a Shi'ite Assassin, so he merely shrugged, keeping his smile in place, and added, "Flying, too, in and out."

"Flying? *Flying?*" Again the appeal to his witnesses. "The fellow's mad."

"Not people, Deniston, birds. Pigeons. They send pigeons back and forth, bearing messages. Devout Muslim pigeons, I'm assured, who fly directly from mosque to mosque, minaret to minaret." He raised a warning finger. "Keep it in mind, and beware. Farewell." He turned and spurred away before any of the English knights could think of anything to say.

He made his way directly to where the remnants of his squadron sat waiting for him.

The Boar saluted him as he drew close. "All present, sir. Twenty-two sergeants fit for duty. Ten more in the care of the Hospitallers, one of them like to die, three to be kept in care, six more expected to return to duty within the day, after treatment."

André nodded in acknowledgment, his thoughts teeming. Reduced to barely half strength, his squadron was not, strictly speaking, capable of carrying out its patrol assignation for that day, for the rules were very clear concerning strength and numbers. All mounted expeditions must be in sufficient strength to discourage random attacks. A forty-man squadron was a deterrent to such attacks; a twenty-man force was not.

"We will return to quarters, Sergeant, and regroup. We are hard hit and too few in number now to ride out as we are without endangering our mounts. I'm sure you know by now that they are more valuable than we are. Every horse we lose damages our chances of victory. See to it, if you will, and send the squadron standard-bearer to accompany me. I will report to the field commandery and request replacements for the men we lost today. I shall need a list of the names of the dead, too, but not immediately, unless you have them ready. Do you?"

"In my head, sir, but not yet written down."

"Aye, well, be sure I receive a copy of the list when it is done ... before you go off duty for the day." The Boar saluted, and André turned away, pointing his horse in the direction of the distant field commandery.

There was great noise and activity around the enormous Templars' tent that housed the field commandery, with knights, not all of them Templars, scurrying in all directions. St. Clair knew that the scuffle that had engaged his own men, expensive and fiercely fought as it had been, had nonetheless been a minor squabble, incapable of generating this much activity. Whatever the cause, he was forced to wait in a line before he could talk to the senior Temple officer on duty. The man, a Poitevin called Angouleme, listened to his report and his request for more men, then wrote something down before looking up at André.

"Sufficient unto the day, Holy Scripture says. It sounds as though you and the Hospitallers performed well. It cost you dearly, but I have already heard that your people took down five for every one you lost. Nevertheless, half your force lost in one action is enough to justify a rest on a day such as this. Philip's own fortunes are proving little better than yours this day. Go you and order your men to stand down for the time being, but keep them close, against a sudden need. In the meantime, I'll send another squadron to make your patrol."

André saluted and turned to go, but then hesitated and turned back. "Pardon me, but did you say King Philip is in action as we speak?"

"Aye, against the Accursed Tower again. The engineers reported that it's fully undermined and should collapse at any moment, and so he mounted another assault to keep the enemy occupied. But he's taking heavy losses, I'm told. Next man, step forward."

St. Clair left the tent and found his standard-bearer waiting for him, and he sent the fellow back to their lines to tell the Boar to stand the men down for the remainder of the day. That done, he rode out seeking a vantage point where he could watch the French assault against the Accursed Tower, only to find that the action had already been disengaged, even though—or perhaps because—a large section of the tower's wall, some thirty feet wide, had collapsed into piles of rubble that were swarming with frantic defenders, looking for all the world, from where St. Clair sat watching, like a colony of ants whose nest had been severely damaged. He watched Philip returning to his pavilion, his progress visible even from more than a mile away, thanks to the prominence of his personal standard, with the royal lilies of France so unmistakably displayed.

Slightly disappointed to have missed the action, André sat high on his horse and let his gaze roam over the prospect in front of him until it came to rest on the pavilion of Richard of England, with its own unmistakable royal coat of arms. Richard was reportedly still sick, suffering from angry boils, falling hair, loose teeth, and rotting gums, yet supposedly deeply engaged, too, in the attempt to hammer out the terms of surrender for the garrison of Acre. André sniffed at that thought. The camp was awash with rumors and counter-rumors, but the most prominent among them was concerned with Richard and his attitude towards this surrender. Word had it that he was being adamant in refusing to discuss terms with the Saracens, merely laying down the law instead and demanding unconditional surrender, with the immediate return of all Frankish prisoners and the return of every possession, including not only the True Cross but all the towns and fortresses that had been seized from Christendom after Hattin.

If that were true—and knowing Richard, André was quite prepared to believe that it could be—then it was folly of the most extreme kind, since it left Saladin no room for retaining either status or dignity. Simply by acceding to such extreme demands, the Sultan would commit suicide, politically, religiously, and socially, and even St. Clair, newcomer though he was, could see the stupidity of asking him to do so. A man like Saladin would sooner die than live in dishonor such as Richard was thrusting upon him. He would never accept Richard's conditions.

Even as he thought that, André St. Clair knew he was exactly correct, and that Richard Plantagenet knew exactly what he was about in this matter. Richard was the Warrior King, the Shining Light of Christendom; he was the Lionhearted Monarch, England's Paladin and the Soldier of Salvation to Rome's Church; he would never settle for a mealy-mouthed, negotiated peace. Richard's personality demanded nothing less than total victory. He had bankrupted his new kingdom to pay for this war, and he intended to capture every shred of glory that might be available for the taking … and there would be little glory in accepting the chastened capitulation of a cowed infidel. Therefore the King was doing everything within his power to push the Sultan into committing all his strength to total war—a war Richard was convinced he could not lose.

So much, then, for honor and for Richard's commitment to his charges, André thought bitterly, certain now that his analysis was accurate. Beside the flaring light of the King's need for personal

glory and acclaim, the rights, lives, and expectations of all his countrymen and subjects were expendable, and he had the power, on all sides,
to do whatever he needed to do to achieve his ends. He would defy
Saladin to the death of the last man on either side.

Another movement caught his eye, too far away to identify, but
bright and unusual, a flash of feminine yellow against the high walls
of the royal pavilion. Berengaria? Or might it be Joanna? He thought
of both of them, seeing their eyes regarding him steadily in return,
and he smiled to himself, albeit nervously, wondering what they had
thought of his sudden and unexplained disappearance from Limassol.

Strange, he thought now, and not for the first time, that he had
not heard a single word from anyone in Richard's camp since that
day onward. He had spoken to de Sablé, it was true, but only very
briefly and of general things. De Sablé was far too preoccupied with
his many duties to have time for idle chatter over whether or not his
friend the King had been displeased with one of his lesser minions.
It was true, too, that he himself had made no attempt to contact his
liege lord since the King's arrival in Outremer. Some might call that
dereliction, but a small voice in the back of André's mind whispered
quietly and mutinously to him of loyalty and responsibilities. Sir
Henry St. Clair had given up everything to come out of his honorable retirement and place himself anew at the service of his King in
a strange land, struggling to learn new tasks and skills at an age
when most of his contemporaries had already died of old age, and
there was something lodged deep within André that insisted, with an
unrelenting pressure, that the responsibility lay with Richard to
acknowledge the loyal old man's death to his son in person. Until
that happened—and the truth surprised him because he had not articulated the thought before that moment—André knew he would make
no effort to approach the King. As for the two women, wife and
sister, he grimaced ruefully, half grin, half groan, thinking himself
well out of that situation, despite another small voice that muttered
mournfully in regretful undertones at the back of his awareness.

He grunted wordlessly, a sound born deep in his chest, then
sucked in a deep breath and attempted to empty his mind of such

thoughts, pulling hard on his reins and kneeing his horse around to return to his squadron, where, for the next few days, he worked to smother his own vague and confusing feelings of guilt over Richard and loyalty by driving and drilling his men hard and pitilessly.

But four days later, on the twelfth day of July, the city fell, and in the blink of an eye, it seemed, everything changed. The morale of the entire army took an upward leap, and suddenly everyone was enthusiastic again, eagerly seeking something concrete to do, so that they might be able to talk afterwards of what they had done at the fall of Acre.

André, wanting no part of any of that, found himself in the middle of it all regardless, relieved of his squadron-leader status and promoted to command a specially raised one-hundred-horse troop charged with keeping peace during the surrender. The day after the capitulation, he sat in attendance with his new comrades in arms as the defeated Arabs marched out of the city they had defended for so many months.

The crowd watching the evacuation was huge; every soldier in the Frankish armies who was not on duty that day turned out to watch the defeated enemy depart. But anyone expecting to see a ragtag, dispirited procession of shuffling miscreants was disappointed. The enemy emerged from the gates in a long column, walking with their heads high and their dignity wrapped around them so solidly that their mere appearance deprived the watching Franks of any wish to cheer or even jeer. Instead, they watched in profound silence, tinged with respect, and no man among them thought to offer insult to the departing enemy.

André St. Clair sat watching the exodus with something akin to pride glowing in his breast, for he knew that his cousin Alec would have been proud of the way these men accepted defeat and showed no regret or deference to their conquerors. When the last of them passed by, leaving none but hostages and prisoners behind for Richard's use, the officer commanding André's troop gave the prearranged signal, and the troop fell into place behind the Arab column in files of twenty-five mounted men, riding four abreast.

They accompanied their charges as far as the boundaries of their siege lines, then left them to make their own way into the desert, to wherever they might go.

"DOES ANYONE HAVE ANY IDEA why we are out here, sitting in the sun like this as though we were all idiots?"

Sitting at the head of his own squadron, two horse lengths ahead of its front rank, André St. Clair heard the question clearly—it had come from the extended triple rank of knights ahead of him—but he made no attempt to answer it or even to think about what the answer might be. His attention was dedicated to a matter that troubled him more personally. Something, some kind of creature, was crawling across the skin of his ribs beneath his right arm, and the slow itch of it was practically unbearable. Louse or beetle, he knew not what it was and cared less. His entire attention was focused upon the impossibility of scratching it, catching it, or interfering with its progress in any way, for it was separated from his clawing fingers by several layers of stinking clothing, fustian padding, chain mail, and an armored cuirass. He had not bathed in five weeks, and his stench was overpowering even to himself. Five weeks of unending desert patrols had achieved that, five weeks of strictly rationed water and the infuriating tedium of chasing phantom formations that remained uncatchable, were but seldom seen, and which sometimes attacked at nightfall and daybreak, inflicting casualties and then vanishing into the vast expanse of dunes. The men at his back, his own Red Squadron, were as sick of this existence as he was.

After a silence that seemed long in retrospect, one voice, also from in front of him, replied to the rhetorical question. "Because we *are* idiots, Brother. That should not surprise you. It is our calling. You know that. This is why we took vows of poverty, chastity, and obedience—purely so that we could sit out here in the desert sun, penniless, owning nothing, cooking in our own sweat, and obedient to the whims of some pitiless, demented whoreson whose task it is to dream up ways of testing our immortal souls. That's why you are out here with the rest of us ... you're a Templar."

"Silence!" André heard then. "I will not tolerate such talking in the ranks. Have you no shame? Remember who you are and where your duties lie. One more word like that from anyone and I will see the guilty man walled up for a few days, to contemplate the insults he is offering to God and to our sacred Order."

The speaker was Etienne de Troyes, and no man hearing him doubted for a moment that the notoriously humorless Marshal would do as he threatened. The internal disciplines and punishment exercised by the Temple for the mental purity and salvation of its brethren were designed as impediments to sin, intended to be savage, as a disincentive to waywardness, and it was not unusual for a disobedient or fractious brother to be walled up, quite literally bricked into a confined and lightless place, for a week or longer, supplied with no more than a bowl of water while he contemplated how he might achieve acceptance, reinstatement, and salvation.

A silent stillness settled over the assembled knights again. A horse whickered and stamped, setting off a series of similar reactions from other mounts, all of which had been standing in one place for far too long. The animal directly ahead of St. Clair raised its tail, and he watched emotionlessly as it evacuated a pile of dung to steam briefly in the sun. He leaned forward slightly to look to his left, to where the black-robed ranks of the Hospitallers occupied the other end of the Frankish line, and he wondered if they knew any more than his own people did about why they were all here. He had led his men out before daybreak with nothing but the order to march— no destination, no objective, which in itself was highly unusual— and they had marched until they reached this desolate place, where they had halted and drawn up in their battle formations.

The Hospitallers held the left of the line, on the lower slopes of the hill called Tel Aiyadida, which marked the easternmost boundary of the Christian advance. The Templars, as usual, manned the right, and the two extremities were joined by the various contingents of the lay forces, forming a front more than half a mile in expanse. Ahead of the line, stretching away to the southeast, the road to Nazareth was virtually invisible in the noonday glare, and to the left of that, rising in the middle distance, was another hill, the Tel

Keisan. There was no visible activity on the Tel Keisan, but it was enemy territory, securely held, the Templars knew, by Saladin's teeming and apparently inexhaustible regiments of black-robed Bedouin from Africa.

A trumpet sounded from the rear and was soon followed by the sound of galloping hooves as a messenger arrived with word that King Richard was approaching from the direction of Acre, accompanied by a large body of troops, and everyone present—in excess of twelve hundred mounted men—turned in their saddles to see the Lionheart arrive, anticipating that the large body of troops referred to would be the infantry they had left behind in Acre.

It was, yet it was not. The infantry was there, in strength, but they were there as guards for the huge column of Saracen prisoners that walked in their midst, roped together hand and foot, rank and file, and winding down through the dunes like an enormous snake. Richard rode in front, at the head of the snake, and he was in full blossom, riding the magnificent golden stallion that he had taken, had in fact stolen, from Isaac Comnenus. He was dressed resplendently as usual, in his finest, gilt-chased armor, over which he wore crimson, gold, and royal purple garments. Behind him thronged his personal retinue, a score and a half of peacocks and popinjays of all descriptions, including as always a number of celebrated knights and warriors whose manhood none could question without risk to life and limb. They rode some fifty paces ahead of the main bulk of their vanguard, sufficiently far in front to keep them relatively free of road dust other than that which they stirred up themselves in passing. Then, next in order, came an entire phalanx of Royal Guards, marching twelve abreast and led by a squad of drummers who set a steady, not too strenuous pace. Behind those, heavily guarded on both sides of their column, came the prisoners, their ankles tethered so that they could walk in a shuffle but could not stretch out into a stride.

Watching them emerging into view, André felt something formless shift in his belly, and glanced quickly towards the flanks of Tel Keisan, not knowing what he expected to see there, yet aware that something, some presentiment, was making him feel queasy. But the hillsides where he looked appeared to be empty of life and his unease deepened, for he knew that the opposite was true. The enemy was there. They were simply remaining out of sight. He swung back to look at the approaching column, trying to assess how many prisoners there were. The front was ten men wide, with two guards on each side, making a fourteen-man front, and he counted ten regular ranks behind the first before the movement and the clouds of dust defeated him. A thick haze hung over everything, stirred up by the passage of so many shuffling feet, and the moving ranks reached back into the opacity of the rising cloud until they became impossible to see. St. Clair's misgivings increased.

He turned his head and spoke to the knight sitting on his right, at the head of his own, Blue Squadron, a taciturn, humorless English knight whose real name André did not know because everyone referred to him, even in conversation with him, as Nose. There was good reason for the name, because whenever he was asked a question, even in French, he was most likely to respond, in English, "Who knows?" But in addition to that, his own nose was spectacularly misshapen, broken and bent beyond repair years before by a hard-swung club that should have brained him but missed.

"What is going on, Nose? And don't say 'who knows'? I've been on constant patrol these past five weeks and came in only last night, so I have no idea what's been happening around here. Why have they brought these prisoners all the way out here? Richard clearly has a purpose in mind for them. Do you have any idea what it might be? Have you heard any rumors? Anything at all?"

Nose looked back at him, then dipped his head. "They're the prisoners from Acre ... nigh on three thousand of 'em, taken at the fall of the city and held against Saladin's promise to free his prisoners—our men—and return the True Cross." He shrugged, spreading his hands. "That must be what this is all about. I can't think what else it might be. Saladin has been very quiet of late, making no great efforts to live up to his promises. But now he must be coming to meet us, to carry out the exchange of prisoners."

"Then why is there no sign of him? Why are we here alone?"

Nose grunted, deep in his throat. "Who knows? You'd best ask Richard that. Kings and sultans have ways of their own, I've noticed. They don't ask me for advice, and I don't offer any."

For the next half hour and more André sat and watched as the column wound down towards the center of the front line, and he took note of how even the veterans of the two monastic Orders joined in on the general chorus of acclaim and enthusiasm that greeted the advent of the English King. Richard was in fine form, showing no signs at all of his recent battle with scurvy and waving and smiling to everyone around him as he approached the line. When he arrived there, he drew his elaborate golden-hilted sword and brandished it above his head, and the line before him broke and opened up to allow him and his party to pass through. The sight of that caused a stir of anticipation among all the units making up the line of battle, for the prisoners, although still under heavy escort, were now theoretically beyond restraint and approaching the enemy lines, led by King Richard and drawing closer to freedom with every step they took. But nothing happened. The appearance of the column of prisoners evoked no visible response from the slopes of Tel Keisan, and André found himself wondering how far the captives would be permitted to go before they were stopped.

His unvoiced question was answered almost as soon as his mind asked it, for Richard, now approximately a hundred paces from where André sat watching, raised a hand above his head and made a circular signal before drawing off with his party to one side and making room for the phalanx of guards at his back to carry out what was clearly a set of orders drawn up earlier. The guards had stopped on a flat stretch of ground close to the midpoint between the two opposing hills, Tel Aiyadida and Tel Keisan, and now they split and wheeled, moving back and to both sides to flank the prisoners. As they did that, the other guards who had been marching on the captives' flanks began to usher them into formal lines and blocks, herding and pushing and counting heads until the front rank numbered one hundred men and there were ten men in each file, making a thousand men in all, each separated from his closest companion by two paces front and rear and an equal distance on each side. The sun glared down malevolently and there was not a sign of shelter or relief anywhere, and the assembled army sat, or stood, and waited, sweating, taking care not to lay bare skin against their armor. And in places, across the extent of the Frankish lines, a man would sway and fall, undone by the torturous heat.

When the block of men was complete, it looked impressive, St. Clair thought, still wondering why Richard was going to so much trouble here, and to what end, for there were still almost twice as many men again in the original column. But no one moved and nothing was said until the sergeants began shuffling the next ranks of prisoners into place to build a second block, also of a thousand men. Someone behind St. Clair, one of his own squadron, started to mutter something, but André twisted around in his seat and snarled at the man to shut up, being careful not to look and actually see who it had been. No one else spoke after that, and the time dragged slowly by, the misery growing with every moment that passed. And André St. Clair became increasingly aware that no slightest sign of Saladin or any other Saracen presence was being shown opposite them.

Some time later, when the prisoners had all been arranged into block formations, a senior sergeant passed the word along to the King, who sat pouting for a moment after receiving it. Then he nodded and sat upright in his saddle. He raised his long, brilliantly colored sword high above his head and swept it in another circular signal. Immediately, a corps of drummers marched smartly forward and began to rattle out a series of staccato beats. As the rhythm swelled, quadruple columns of crossbowmen jogged forward from the rear and took up position behind the prisoners. André knew, because he had worked on the composition of formations with his father, that each column of crossbowmen contained two hundred men, and he felt his shoulders start to grow rigid as he sensed what might happen next, but even as he saw the first bolts plunge silently into the backs of the bound and helpless prisoners, he was unable to believe what he was seeing.

The prisoners went down in swathes, like corn before the reapers' scythes. After the first few moments of suspense and uncertainty, the prisoners in the forward ranks realized what was happening behind them, and their fear and panic flared and spread like wildfire in a high wind, so that they broke and tried to run. But they could not run, because their legs were too close-shackled, so all they could do was stumble awkwardly and fall, screaming to Allah for succor.

To the left of the slaughter, sitting his horse with his entourage clustered behind him, Richard Plantagenet watched the massacre unfold, his face expressionless as though he were doing no more than watching a colony of bees being smoked into insensibility so that its honey could be harvested. Then, somewhere off to St. Clair's right, facing the carnage, someone among the Templars began to bang his sword rhythmically against his shield, twice with the hilt end and then once with the flat of the blade, creating a three-beat cadence to accompany his own chant of "By the *Cross*, by the *Cross*, by the *Cross* ..." The hammer-blow chant was picked up quickly by his neighbors to spread across the Templar ranks until it seemed everyone was shouting it, although not everyone was. André St. Clair's was not the only face dulled by consternation and disbelief among the Templar ranks that day, but they were a small minority. When the chant finally swelled to become intelligible to the watching King, Richard held his sword up over his head again, this time by the blade, so that the golden hilt became a symbol of the Cross being extolled by the Christian ranks, and the chant grew ever louder as the last of the Muslim prisoners were killed.

When it was over and the last man was dead, Richard signaled again, and his crossbowmen regrouped and trotted at the double step back to their original stations. After that the entire army wheeled about and returned to Acre, leaving the landscape strewn with enough murdered men to sate every vulture for miles around. André St. Clair rode among them, looking neither left nor right and making no attempt to speak to anyone, appalled to the very depth of his soul not merely with the magnitude of the sin he had witnessed but with the fact that its perpetrator was the same man who, a few years earlier, had reacted memorably with horror and outrage to the tidings that Saladin had executed a hundred prisoners after the Saracen victory at Hattin. But as the unmistakable sounds of jubilation and celebration began to burgeon around him on all sides, André could not continue to ignore what was happening around him, and he turned to stare, dead-eyed, at the spectacle of sober, solemn knights reeling like drunken men in the euphoria of having killed so many infidels for the greater glory of God.

"TWO THOUSAND AND SEVEN HUNDRED MEN, Alec. That's how many there were … Two thousand and seven hundred … More than that, truth be told … more than the seven hundred, but less than eight … Slaughtered like animals and left to bloat and rot in the desert sun."

"Hmm." Alec Sinclair kept his face free of expression and his voice toneless. "Well, once they're slaughtered, there's no place else out here to leave them, Cousin, during daylight hours at least. There's naught but the desert sunlight in which to bloat and rot. Not that I am trying to make light of any part of what you say. It is simply that the sane mind refuses to accept atrocities like that … What did you do while it was happening?"

"Nothing. I did nothing. I was … I can't say what I *was*, or what I was even thinking. I was numb, terrified, incredulous. But I am shamed to say I made no move to stop it."

Sinclair twisted his face into the semblance of a wry grin. "D'ye say so, Cousin? You were afraid to step forward and denounce the King of England as a murdering butcher, simply because he was surrounded by a few thousand of his rabid army, who were murdering thousands of other men with great enthusiasm? Tut, man, that's terrible."

His unformed smile vanished and he turned his head to look all around the place where they were sitting, an empty fire pit within fifteen paces of André's tent. The spot offered nothing of privacy, and a steady stream of knights and sergeants moved incessantly about it, coming and going on errands of all imaginable kinds. One man nodded to Alec in passing, recognizing him without evincing any untoward interest, and Alec returned the nod, muttering something unintelligible. He looked all around again, making sure they were not being particularly heeded, before he looked back at André, his face sober.

"It was the first thing I heard about when I stepped off the boat from Cyprus last night, and because the ship turned right around to return, the word will be in Cyprus the day after tomorrow. I heard the Bishop of Bayonne instruct the captain of the ship how to spread the glorious word on his return to Cyprus."

"What did you hear, what did he say?"

"That Richard had achieved a great moral victory over Saladin by executing the hostages being held against the Sultan's performance. That he had taught the infidel his proper place and chastised him sternly—and appropriately—for attempting to break his sworn agreement to return the True Cross. And I know that everyone else who heard the bishop speak of it believed it was a great victory and a much-needed moral lesson."

"It was murder, Alec—murder on a scale I could not have imagined. Pure, premeditated murder, merciless and mortally sinful. If there is indeed a Hell of fire and brimstone as the Christians believe, then Richard Plantagenet purchased himself a special place in the depths of it yesterday, for nothing in the tenets of Christian belief, no matter how distorted by priestly logic, could ever justify what that man did. That same man who swore piously and publicly, in the name of their living, merciful Christ, to return God's Holy Land to the people of the gentle Savior."

Alec Sinclair nodded. "Your liege lord is not as noble a figure as he would have the world believe, is he?"

"No, he is not ..."

"And now we have other important matters to discuss, but it must be elsewhere. There are far too many flapping ears hereabouts. Bring your arbalest and something to shoot at and we will find a place to practice our skills where no one can overhear us."

A short time later and a half mile removed from the crowded

confines of the encampment, St. Clair stuck a long spear into the ground, point first, at the foot of a dune. He had tied his sheathed dagger a head's length from the top of the shaft to form a crossbar, and suspended an old horse blanket over that, to suggest the size and shape of a tall, thin man, an impression heightened by the addition of a rusted, cloven old helmet to the butt of the spear. When he was satisfied with its appearance and sure that it would be recognized as a simple target from a distance, he remounted and rode back with Alec until a good hundred and twenty paces lay between them and it, and there they dismounted and unsaddled their horses before slipping their nose bags, each with a handful of oats, over the animals' heads. Only then, when the horses were looked after, did they unlimber their crossbows and walk towards the firing line Alec had dug into the sand with one heel.

Neither man had actually brought an arbalest with him, for the simple reason that the weapon was too powerful for such a casual exercise, since every bolt they fired from this close would vanish into the sand of the dune behind the target and be lost. Instead, they had brought smaller crossbows, less demanding in strength and power and more demanding in the skills they called for. Using these weapons, and from this distance, there was at least a possibility that the bolts they threw at the target would be recoverable. André fired the first shot, watching the flight of the missile critically, and when it fell short of the target he made a minor adjustment to his stance and tried again, grunting in satisfaction as he saw the quarrel hit this time and glance off the spear shaft.

His cousin acknowledged the shot, then took his own stance and did exactly the same thing, save that his second shaft glanced left off the target, rather than to the right as André's had.

"Very well, then," André said, holding his weapon tucked beneath one arm, "we're established. We have each hit the target and there appears to be no one watching us. And even if there were, no one could come close enough to us to overhear us, so may we talk now?"

"We may."

Sinclair turned, head down, and walked away to where his saddle lay on the side of a tiny hill of sand. He rested one booted foot on the cantle and propped the stirrup of the crossbow against his raised toes, crossing both his hands on the butt. André followed him quietly, merely watching and waiting, knowing that whatever his cousin might say next, it would not be inconsequential, nor would it be spontaneous.

"I sensed ..." Alec stopped, obviously considering his words. "I sensed a *reversal* in you today, Cousin, something that was not there today as it had been before, or perhaps more accurately, something that *was* there as it had never been before." André stood silent, waiting for the other to continue. He could tell that Alec was having difficulty with whatever he was trying to say, because his diction was far more precise, more painstaking than usual. His French was fluent and effortless, but the alienness of his Scots birth and back-ground came through in the way he articulated his words and vowels, speaking them crisply and clearly, yet in a way that no native of Gaul ever would.

"I have been out here in Outremer, perhaps, for too many years," Alec continued after a moment's additional thought. "I have grown used to living alone like an anchorite, away from other men, Christian men, if you understand what I am trying to say, and to conducting my own devotions in the way I was taught. In conse-quence of that, I have obviously not been exposed to the kind of changes that everyone who came over the sea with you appears to accept as commonplace. Not the kind of changes that one may point to and identify clearly. I suppose, really, that I am referring more to moral differences, to changes in perception and acceptance.

"Now that I am aware of them, I can see that most of them must have occurred since I left Scotland, and certainly since I left Christendom to come out here. They are changes of attitude, and of perception, more than anything else, I believe—changes in the way men look at things and *see* things nowadays." Again he stopped, shaking his head. "You plainly have no idea what I am ranting about here, and I can't blame you."

He sucked in and released a sigh, pinching the bridge of his nose. "Let me try another way. I am speaking here of the truths that you and I were taught by our brethren in the Order of Sion, when we were first Raised to the brotherhood—the truths that we were taught, unchanged since our forefathers fled Jerusalem twelve hundred years ago to escape the wrath of Rome and the false and Godless 'Truth' the Romans would impose upon them. And now here we are, you and I, more than a millennium later, back in our ancient home-land and still dealing with the wrath of Rome and the new, updated Roman version of truth. We swore oaths, all of us in the brother-hood, to do certain things, to observe certain conventions and to obey and sustain certain ancient laws that will enable us to carry out our duties and our tasks with honor at all times. And since the earliest days of our Order, those oaths and laws and promises have remained unchanged.

"But look now at our supposed exemplar, the Roman Church. *Nothing* is immutable therein, André. Nothing at all. Everything—every duty, every law, every obligation, every element of their credo—is negotiable and changeable, according to the will of whoever happens to be wielding the power at any given time. Look no further than the beginnings of this Order of the Temple, ninety years ago. Until then, for a thousand years, the mere idea of priests and monks killing other men had been anathema. But then—and granted, it was at our own brotherhood's suggestion—the priests perceived a way to effect great change in that, to their great benefit, as always, and it was a simple matter of rearranging a few priorities and repositioning certain criteria to conform to the will of God, as expressed to and interpreted by His priests. Nothing in the Roman Church, it seems obvious to me, is absolute ... Are you following me now?"

St. Clair nodded. "Aye, easily enough, but I have no idea where you are leading me."

A tiny smile cracked the seriousness of Sinclair's expression. "I have no idea, either, but I think it is time we both found somewhere new to go. Everything was brought into focus for me by the way you voiced your reaction to—your disgust over—the way Richard dealt with his Muslim prisoners."

St. Clair barely reacted to that, limiting his response to a minuscule headshake and keeping his voice low and calm. "Disgust is too small a word for what I felt. Nothing that I could possibly say could even come close to expressing what I want to say. I have the knowledge inside me, and someday, I know, it will spill out, purging and absolving me. Or so I hope. But between you and me let there be no misunderstandings and no lies. Richard did not 'deal with' his Muslim prisoners. He slaughtered them out of hand, and their blood is still thick and wet out on the killing ground. He murdered them by the thousand, and for no other reasons than to vent his spleen and show Saladin that he was angry and impatient with the Sultan's behavior."

"He is your liege lord, Cousin."

"No, Cousin, he is not. That status was forfeit, by his own design, when I became a Templar. You know that, because you had to forfeit your own liege in the same way. It was Richard's own idea that I should join the Temple, and he knew when he made the suggestion that it would result in losing my services and my fealty. That has come to pass. Richard Plantagenet can make no more claims on me. But even there he was being duplicitous, seeking to sway my father into joining his Great Venture … and not because he needed him. Sir Henry St. Clair had no great, vaulting skills that Richard of England could not have found elsewhere. No, the simple truth is that Richard dreamed up, or was given, or otherwise conceived the thought that Sir Henry St. Clair should go with him to war, as a perfect foil against the ever-present threat of having his own father's favorite factotum, William Marshall of England, thrust upon him as his Master-at-Arms. And once that thought was in his head, it became his will, and my father was powerless against it …"

Sinclair must have noticed the change in his expression. "What? What is it?"

St. Clair held up a hand to stem the questions. "It simply came to me that by the time Richard came with de Sablé to my father's house on that occasion, to talk the old man into going with him, he had already decided on a path. Robert de Sablé was already destined then to be Grand Master of the Temple, and Richard knew it. And if truth be told, it might come out that Richard was the author, somehow, of that nomination. It would certainly not surprise me. But even so ... If Richard knew that his friend Robert was to be the Grand Master, then he must have thought, too, being Richard, that he would be able to control the man, playing on his gratitude and his sense of obligation ... and that would mean, in turn, that Richard must have thought the entire Temple would fall, more or less without volition, into his grasp. If so, he misread his man badly, for Robert de Sablé will play the dupe to no man, be he pope, king, or emperor. He has been Grand Master of the Temple for less than three months and already his independence is manifestly obvious. But he is also a member of our ancient brotherhood, loyal to the core and honest and trustworthy to a fault, and that is something Richard will never even begin to suspect. He will never know where his dear friend's *true* loyalty is owed and paid. But that is of no help to us, here and now."

He stood chewing on his lower lip for a few moments before lowering himself to sit on the saddle by his feet. "So," he said then, looking up at Sinclair, "where do we go from here, you and I?"

Alec Sinclair laid his crossbow on the ground, then sat on his own saddle. "I have no idea, so I will be grateful for anything you might suggest."

"Hmm ... Well, speaking for myself, I have no wish to go anywhere near Richard or his armies. I might be content to hover on the outskirts of things for a while, but I doubt even that would satisfy me. What I really wish is that I were months and the breadth of seas removed from here, back in my home in Poitou, but that is plainly an impossibility. So in the meantime, I intend to immerse myself in my duties here, serving the Temple in whatever capacity is deemed to be suitable for me."

"And what happens when we return to fighting? What will you do then?"

André looked up in surprise. "I shall fight. What else would I do?"

"You see no contradiction there?"

"In fighting? How should I? I am a knight-at-arms. I've trained all my life to fight, as have you."

"Aye, mayhap, Cousin, but I have had ten more years to weigh the verities than you have."

"What verities? What is that supposed to mean?"

Alec Sinclair grunted, then grinned wryly. "I don't know, Cousin. I don't know what it was supposed to mean. It simply seemed strange to me that you could be so righteously angry over the slaughter of three thousand Muslims at one moment, and then at the very next be talking blithely about killing more of them. That, to me, is a contradiction."

"No, Alec, it is not. Yesterday was an atrocity—murder, pure and simple, the victims bound with ropes and then shot down. What I am speaking of, on the other hand, is warfare, cleanly waged, hand to hand."

"Infrequently, at best. More often from afar, with those things there." Alec nodded towards the crossbows they had come out here to use, and André shrugged.

"Perhaps so, but each side has an opportunity to win and emerge alive, if not unscathed."

"They still leave many people dead, to bloat and rot in the desert sun …"

St. Clair's eyes narrowed. "You are mocking me. Why?"

"Not mocking you, Cousin, not at all. Merely questioning the truth of what you appear to believe, because *I* believe that, at root, you don't believe it at all."

St. Clair pointed a finger at his cousin's face. "Even in your forested homeland, Cousin, that would be obscure and confusing." He reached behind him and pulled his saddlebags to where he could drape them across one knee, and then he dug in one of them and pulled out a cloth-covered bundle that he began to unwrap. "Sand grouse," he said. "Much like the grouse we have at home, save that they are even smaller. But I bribed a cook last night and purchased four of them for an outrageous price. Had I known you would be here today, I would have tried for eight. Here, have some. There's even some salt in the twist of silk cloth there."

They ate in contented silence for a while until Alec asked, "What think you of Philip of France? Will he recover from the disgrace of quitting the fight?"

André shook his head. "Philip will see no disgrace in what he did, and no one will question him. He rose from his sickbed and fought valiantly to bring down Acre at the Accursed Tower and was widely acclaimed for doing so, and within days of his final effort, Acre fell. Thereafter, he could state verifiably that his assault had been successful and his task completed. After that, he can argue, it was Richard who brought about all the troubles of the alliance, seizing the spoils of Acre, including captured lands, and refusing to share them with anyone, as though he alone was responsible for the two-year siege and the eventual fall of Acre. He offended not only Philip but even the Archduke of Austria, the last-surviving and most puissant vassal of Barbarossa in the Holy Land. Not to mention that he alienated the entire nobility of Outremer, whose lands had been confiscated in the aftermath of Hattin and were now won back to be confiscated yet again by the upstart newcomer from England. Philip will argue that Richard's arrogance and greed made the French Crown's continuing presence here in Outremer untenable, particularly in the light of Philip's extended and much-reported illness, with its attendant loss of hair and teeth. Bear in mind, he merely sailed away, almost alone. He did not simply pick up and flee. He left his army behind, to continue fighting under the Duke of Burgundy, and no one can complain about *that* choice of deputy … No, Philip will be treated as a hero by everyone who hears of his exploits without having to undergo the dubious pleasure of meeting or observing him."

Sinclair nodded, looking pensive. "And the underlying truth? Why did he really leave, André? Your own opinion."

"Greed, and politics. I believe he started planning his departure the day that Flanders was killed in front of Acre's walls, at the beginning of June."

"Flanders? Do you mean Jacques d'Avesnes, that Alsatian fellow? Was that his name?"

"No, d'Avesnes is a knight of Alsace, one of Flanders' vassals, and he is very much alive. I meant the Count of Flanders himself, and I do not think I have ever heard his full name, or if I did I have forgotten it. He was an amazing man, from all reports, prodigiously strong, powerfully engaging, and unforgettable to all who met him."

"What did he have to do with Philip, apart from being a neighbor and an ally?"

"Nothing, on the surface, but his unexpected death takes on enormous significance to Philip when you remember that he died without an heir. Flanders counted Artois and Vermandois among his holdings, and it is common knowledge where I come from that Philip has lusted after those territories—plus Flanders itself, with Alsace and the rest of Belgium to boot, all of them belonging to the Count—since he first mounted the French throne, nigh on a score of years ago. To have all those lands come open to dispute, and leaderless, while he was stuck out here must have galled him badly. That is why I believe he started making preparations to sail home the moment Flanders was killed ... and those preparations included his heroic, widely witnessed, and much-lauded assault on the Accursed Tower. I believe he planned and carried out all of those things well enough to ensure that he will arrive home almost as quickly as the tidings of the Count's unfortunate death, and the French Crown will move swiftly to secure the County of Flanders and maintain good order on France's northern boundaries thereafter. Philip may not be the world's greatest soldier, but he ranks highly among its most able administrators."

"Speaking of which," St. Clair added quietly, "I have not even asked you about your Cyprus duties. Those were administrative, were they not?"

"Aye, they were, after a fashion. I was to scout out and procure a suitable headquarters site for the people we will be sending in there to set up our operations on the island."

"I presume, when you say 'our' you are talking about the Temple ... or is the brotherhood involved in this?"

"No, not at all." Sinclair's denial was emphatic. "De Sablé and myself are the only two of the brotherhood involved at this stage, and I do not believe there are any plans to change that."

"So you found a suitable place?"

"I did—in one of the Comnenus castles, naturally enough, close by Nicosia. A preliminary occupation party of twenty knights and a company of sergeant brothers left to sail there yesterday. We passed them at sea on our way in, but we did not see them. Just as well, perhaps."

"Why so?"

"Because the bickering has already begun and I have no wish to be involved in any part of it. De Sablé doesn't, either, but he has little choice in the matter. He is Grand Master and it was he who made the sale possible, through his friendship with Richard. But he has specific instructions from the Chapter House on what needs to be done. Not *precisely* what needs to be done, but sufficiently close to be causing confusion already."

"I don't follow. I thought the Grand Master had complete power within the Order. Are you now telling me that is untrue? How do you know that?"

"I know it because de Sablé told me when I spoke with him this morning, on my return. The senior brethren expressed grave concerns about these latest developments, and he agreed to be guided by their consensus in this single instance. The Order has never had a secure, self-contained base of its own before, and the brethren are anxious to make no mistakes at the outset of such a momentous advance into unknown waters, for the potential could be enormous—far greater than many people have ever considered."

"How so?"

"Think about it, André. Think what is involved."

André shrugged, with one shoulder, as though to indicate his lack of interest. "I don't have to think about it. You've already told me: a free, self-sufficient base of operations, close enough to Outremer to provide a solid, versatile launching point for future endeavors, and far enough removed from Christendom to be free of the prying and interference of snooping kings and priests. I can understand why that would be attractive to the Order. Anyone could."

558 STANDARD OF HONOR

"Ah, but you are wrong. You see what I mean? You missed the import entirely."

André frowned slightly, then dipped his head in submission. "Very well then, enlighten me. What, exactly, did I miss?"

"The scope of it, Cousin. You see, you and I, as mere men, think in man-sized terms. But the Order perceives a greater opportunity here—not merely to establish a base of operations but to set up an entirely independent *state*! An island country of their own, defensible and governable, ruled by and answerable to the Temple alone. That is their vision, and they intend to make their dream a reality."

"By the living God! That is a grand scheme indeed, for the price of a hundred thousand gold bezants."

"They only set down forty thousand, bear in mind. The rest is payable in time to come."

"Aye, but still, that is … that is nigh on incomprehensible. And Robert de Sablé would rule it?"

"As Grand Master, aye, for as long as he holds the title. But I think Robert made a mistake at the outset, in agreeing to share any portion of his power as Grand Master, no matter how temporarily, even for such a grand scheme. I believe when he did that, he doomed the entire venture, because already too many mediocre men who should have no voice in such matters have differing opinions and are splitting into different camps. We now have factions, created almost overnight, with overt jealousies between them, and they are already squabbling over money. Besides—and I appear to be the only one aware of this—the Order itself has no respect for the Cypriots, with whom it must share the island. There is no thought of sharing. They are already talking about taxing them, brutally, and keeping them subservient to the wishes of the Order, but no one has said a single word about making any effort to befriend them or enlist their support or loyalty. And the place has only been in the Order's possession for a matter of weeks, not even a month. I swear, it is a venture doomed to failure, mark what I say." He stopped, noticing the set of André's head, and then sat up and turned to look where he was looking. "Someone coming, and not one of us."

Alec Sinclair stood up, raising a hand to shield his eyes against the sun's glare, and quickly located the shape of a man on a donkey, approaching along the crest of the dune on their left. He grunted and raised one hand high in the air. "It's Omar," he said. He lowered his hand, and the approaching figure, who was still far off but close enough for André to recognize him as the familiar old Palestinian who scraped a living as a water carrier, stopped and sat motionless for a count of ten, and then Alec raised his hand again, and the old man tugged at the donkey's reins, turning it around, and set off back in the direction from which he had come.

"What was that about?" André asked.

"A summons. I am to meet Ibrahim tonight at our place of stones. He has something for me, probably a message to pass along to de Sablé. D'you want to come with me?"

"Do I? Of course I do. But I don't understand what happened there. How did old Omar know where to find you, and how did he know you were you, from so far away?"

"There are not many places I could be, if you think about it. And he knew me by my clothes."

"Be serious, you lying Scots heathen, and tell me the truth," André exclaimed, for Alec Sinclair was dressed exactly as he himself was, identically to everyone else in the Templar community, in the white surcoat bearing the red cross of the fighting knights.

Sinclair grinned. "He knew me when I raised my hand in the air the first time. No one else would normally greet him that way. If they wanted him they would wave to him, or beckon him over. Then, when I lowered my hand, he counted to ten and I raised my arm again, confirming that I had understood his message, which is that Ibrahim will expect me tonight, or by noon tomorrow at the latest if I have difficulty tonight."

"And how did you understand the message? Tell me that."

His cousin made a moue, shrugging slightly. "The urgency is in the fact that Omar came out here to find me. Had it not been urgent, he would not have come but simply waited until we saw each other in the camp. The fact that he wore what he was wearing tells me that

Ibrahim has something to pass on to me from his people. Omar has two kufiya head coverings, one black, the other white. When he comes to me wearing the black, it is simply to inform me I must meet with Ibrahim as soon as it becomes convenient. When he binds the black kufiya in place with a white band, it denotes some urgency and requires a more prompt response. The white kufiya, on the other hand, means that the meeting is urgent, and the black binding holding it in place told me Ibrahim has a message to pass on. It is really very simple. The code was developed years ago. I'm told it goes all the way back to the days of the first Templars, to Hugh de Payens." He looked up at the sky, gauging the height of the sun.

"It's nigh on mid-afternoon. We had better return to camp right now. I will have to meet with de Sablé briefly, to inform him that we are going and that he should expect a communication from Rashid al-Din. While I'm doing that, you can requisition fresh horses for us and have them saddled, and pick up some oats for the nose bags— enough for three days, in case we run into any difficulties. We'll need three days' rations, too, against the same possibility."

"What about clothing? Will we wear armor or local dress?"

Alec Sinclair made the Islamic gesture of sala'am, touching breast and forehead in salutation. "One of the greatest advances made by the original forces who came here from Christendom long ago, before you and I were born, was the discovery that the people of these parts knew better than any newcomer ever could know what was best to wear in desert conditions. We will travel as locals and be undisturbed. When you are ready, bring everything to your tent and set up your squadron deputy to cover for you. I'll meet you there. No point in flaunting our preparations under the noses of my fellow staff officers." He glanced up at the sky again. "Let's say, in one hour."

André nodded. "Fine, but don't forget, you have to tell me what you found in Cyprus."

"You won't forget it. How then could I? We'll have plenty of time for that along the road." They set spurs to their horses at the same moment and struck out for camp, not even bothering to collect their makeshift target.

ANDRÉ ST. CLAIR RODE into the final phase of his life as a Temple knight with absolutely no anticipation of what lay ahead of him when he stepped into the stirrup and swung his leg across his horse's back, but as he would hear a thousand times in the life that lay ahead of him, it is not given to man to know the details of his destiny, and what is written may only be known when it has come to pass. What had been written for him before that afternoon had already come to pass, but he had not yet been informed of it. That task, the passing on of information and knowledge, had been given into the custody of his friend and cousin Alexander Sinclair.

It was close to the fourth hour of the afternoon by the time they left the camp behind them and struck out into the open waste of the desert. Six weeks had passed since the fall of Acre, and Saladin and his forces had withdrawn long since, southward towards Jerusalem and the cities along the coast, which meant that much of the danger of travel in the vicinity of Acre had been removed. Nevertheless, they rode in silence for the first few miles, each of them scanning the horizon from time to time simply to be sure that they were not being observed or followed. Then, after perhaps two hours of riding, and just as the sinking sun was approaching the last third of its daily journey down the arching sky, they breasted the highest of the dunes they had been traversing and saw, on the horizon ahead of them, the broken, serrated edge that marked the beginning of the field of boulders that surrounded their destination.

"You know," St. Clair said, breaking the silence that had held between them since they set out, "my mind has been returning to this place ever since the first time I saw it, because it reminded me of something, and I have just remembered what it is."

Alec twisted sideways in the saddle to look at him quizzically. "This place *reminded* you of something? You mean here among these dunes, or the rocks ahead of us?"

"Pardon me, I meant the boulders there. The field of stones."

"Aye, that's what I thought you might mean. Well, that surprises me, because I have never seen anything to resemble it before, and I

STANDARD OF HONOR

have been around for ten years longer than you have. What could it possibly remind you of?"

"Another place ... a field of stones."

"Tell me about it, this place. Where is it?"

"In France, to the south of Paris, just east of the main road to Orléans. It is a place called Fontainebleau, and I cannot remember how I came there, but I found myself there one day in a magnificent forest that stretched around me for leagues in all directions, and there in the midst of it, just as here, I found a field of giant stones like these, smooth and rounded boulders of a size to stagger the mind. Boulders everywhere, dwarfing puny humanity and towering all around in silence, merely *there*, to strike awe into the beholder ..."

"Just like this field here."

"Aye, but nothing like it, for the field of stones in France stands in the forest, so that everywhere, as far as the eye can see, the stones compete with trees, merely to be seen, though winning in most instances. There are no pathways there, no simple means of moving among or between the stones, save perhaps the occasional game trail, worn over hundreds of years by passing deer. And yet, among the deepest, largest, thickest groves of trees, there are glades to be found, and in one of those glades stands a cave ... a cavern very much like your cave here, in that it has been formed from clusters of great stones, piled one atop the other and eroded by weather and the local climes for thousands upon thousands of years. It is deep and dry, completely sheltered from the wind and rain. Very similar to your place here, yet utterly different."

Sinclair remained quiet for a spell after this outflow, then reined in his horse and looked thoughtfully at André. "We have established that Sharif Al-Qalanisi was your tutor in the Arabic tongue, as he was mine. But tell me, what else did he teach you? Did he lead you into the ways of philosophical thought?"

"Aye, he did. Do you have a reason for asking that, or was it merely a fortunate guess?"

"No guess, Cousin. This instance you have described is exactly the kind of mirror-image likeness that would have fascinated

Al-Qalanisi. Now what, think you, would he have asked of you, knowing that you have seen the parallel and recognized the paradox?"

"I am not sure I have recognized any paradox, Cousin."

"Nonsense, of course you have. Two fields of stones, identical each to the other in their content, yet set worlds apart in their appearance, the one in arid desert and the other in a forest of white-barked trees and pale green leaves, the one denying the very appearance of life in an eternity of lifeless sand, the other celebrating the driving thrust of life teeming around and between singular lumps and globules of stone like spores of moss among heaped piles of gravel. And between the two of these, you are the sole link. There is a message concealed there, somewhere. What think you Sharif Al-Qalanisi might have made of such a puzzle?"

St. Clair looked sideways at his cousin, tipping his head to one side. "I have no idea. Let me think about it for a while, and if I can respond to it at all, I will."

Sinclair made no response, and for the next while they plodded steadfastly and silently towards the looming line of boulders that marked the edge of the field of stones, but on the very edge of the area, before they could draw close enough to enter it, André St. Clair drew rein, and his cousin reined in beside him.

"I have had an astonishing thought," the younger cousin said, "one that might never have occurred to me had we not come here today, and had you not provoked me into thinking about matters I would never otherwise consider. Two fields of stones as you say, Cousin. Each radically different from the other, and yet each the same. The one, from my young manhood, from my youth, holds memories and echoes that resonate inside me, loudly enough to be painful. It appears rich and green, lush and full of promise. The other, an alien place that holds no images for me, no memories, no echoes, is a place of grays and dull, hard browns. Sere and lifeless, it is full of inert, obdurate stones and shriveled, dried-out remnants of what might, at one time, have been dreams worth the pursuing.

"On the one hand, my boyhood. In a green and pleasant land, bestrewed with promises and lushness. Plants grow everywhere I look, but all the plants are trees, with pallid, sickly leaves. No flowers, no edibles, and only trees … with roots all gnarled and dry, twisted and set in their growth, and surrounding, choking, covering nothing but stones, boulders that defy all pressures in their endurance.

"And on the other hand, my manhood, in a harsh and arid desert place, where boulders stand in profusion, as in France, but unobscured by growth, their surfaces wind-scoured and polished by the blowing sand. No flowers, no edibles, and not one twisted tree attempting to confine one standing stone within its roots.

"Two seeming truths, apparently similar. But only one is genuine."

A long silence elapsed before Alec Sinclair asked his question. "Which one?"

André St. Clair turned his head slightly to look him in the eye. "You tell me, Cousin, for I have no idea."

And both men laughed and kicked their horses into motion, riding in companionable silence once again. When next one of them broke the silence, it was again Alec Sinclair who spoke.

"We still have to decide what we intend to do next. Richard is planning to march south within the week, along the old coast road, to engage Saladin and take Jerusalem, defeating the Saracens once and for all. He has already made the dispositions for the line of battle—Templars in the vanguard with the Turcopoles in support, then Richard's native levies, his Bretons, Angevins, and Poitevins. The Normans and the English will come next, guarding the battle standard, and the French will form the rearguard, with the Hospitallers and the local Outremer forces supporting them. You and I have to decide upon a course of action for ourselves before that all begins."

"You're making no sense, Cousin. The Templars will form the vanguard, so that is where we will be."

They rode in silence again for a spell until Alec exploded, "Damnation, there's no other way to tell you this. It won't come out without being spat! When I was in Cyprus I made a journey to

Famagusta, to visit your father's grave, as I promised you I would. I found it without difficulty and prayed there for his soul to rest in peace, but when I returned to Limassol I heard a tale that I could not believe, and so I set out to investigate. There is a Jew there called Aaron bar Melel. Do you know of him?"

"No, I know no Jew of that or any other name, certainly not in Limassol. Should I?"

"Yes, you should. I was given his name by an associate—an agent of Rashid al-Din who has lived in Limassol for years, as a spy. He asked me about my own name and how it differed from the name St. Clair, with which he was familiar. When I explained that the former Master-at-Arms had been my uncle, the man became very excited and told me his version of the story of what happened to your father. When I refused to believe what he said, he told me how to find this man Aaron, and I went looking for him the very next day. He was not difficult to find ... Do you remember telling me about the purge being carried out against the Jews a few days before you left Limassol?"

"Aye, I remember. It cost me a last visit with my father."

"Aye. Well, this Aaron was one of the Jews being sought, along with his entire family, his wife, son, and daughter. I met his wife and saw his daughter. She is beautiful. His son is dead, killed during the purge. He was fourteen years old. But Aaron, his wife, Leah, and his daughter were rescued and concealed by a Frankish knight. The Jew named him, calling him Sir Henry St. Clair, Master-at-Arms to England. He rescued them before the troubles broke, according to Aaron, but I have no idea, because Aaron himself did not know, how your father found out about all that was about to happen in advance. Nor do I know what happened to the boy—but Sir Henry had them smuggled out of Limassol, to a fishing village farther along the coast where they remained until they heard that Richard had set out again to come here. At that point, they returned home to Limassol, to mourn their son and rebuild their lives.

"But someone informed upon your father directly to Richard at the time of the family's disappearance. Henry must have been seen doing what he did, or he was betrayed by one of the people he employed. Whoever reported it to Richard sank the blade in deep, then twisted it. It was done with absolute malice, and at a carefully chosen time, probably when he was drunk—Richard, I mean. He would have been furious to hear about your father's betrayal. Your father had already left for Famagusta by that time, and so Richard's bullyboys were sent up there to deal with him, with instructions to make whatever they did look like a random attack by guerrillas. And everyone believed that that is what befell your father and his two companions that night. But the killers talked about it in their cups when they returned to Limassol, and my Shi'ite associate overheard them. They were in his tavern at the time. An innkeeper soon learns to keep his mouth tight shut, and he knew of Sir Henry St. Clair only from hearsay—the man was King Richard's Master-at-Arms, after all—and so he said nothing to anyone until the matter of my name came up, at which point he told me what he knew."

He stopped there and waited for André to respond in some manner, but the younger man merely rode ahead like a man asleep in the saddle, his body adjusting naturally to the horse's gait. Having seen that his eyes were open, Sinclair assumed that he was listening, and continued. "I asked around, but I could not find out anything about the men that Suleiman described. That's my associate, Suleiman. I wasn't going to name him, but there is no harm done. Of course, they had all sailed away with Richard, so they had already been out here in Outremer for weeks by the time I landed in Cyprus." He spread his hands in a shrug. "Which means that there is no reasonable way for us to find out who they were. Their faces could be any among the hundred or so oafish lumps that hang about Richard constantly, waiting for instructions."

He looked away again. "I couldn't even find out if Richard sent them off deliberately or if they took it upon themselves to carry out his ill-stated wishes, the way his father's bullies did for Thomas à Becket in England. That would not be unlikely, for that incident appears to be one of Richard's favorite recollections of his father. He talks about it frequently, whenever he wishes to point out that it is inadvisable to cross a man of his background, so the murderers might well have acted on their own, in expectation of his pleasure and gratitude. But whether the one is true or the other, there's no doubt now that Richard knows both what he did and what he is guilty of. That's why you have heard no word from him since his arrival here. I doubt that he could look you in the eye."

That comment brought a response from St. Clair, spoken calmly, in matter-of-fact tones. "Oh, he could look me in the eye, Alec. Have no doubt of that. Richard Plantagenet could look me in the eye and smile at me and make me feel right welcome while my father's blood dripped from his hands. His self-love is so monstrous that he can now convince himself he is incapable of doing wrong.

"I truly loved this man, once, you know ... almost as dearly as I loved my father. He knighted me and I admired him greatly, seeing him as a paladin. But then, in tiny increments, one instance at a time, I began to see him as he truly is. All of the love and admiration, all the respect, all of the loyalty and duty that I had felt so privileged to owe him willingly for so many years began to turn to vinegar and ashes in my mouth, and my soul grew increasingly sick as more and more evidence of his perfidy and his unending selfishness became clear. And it all culminated with the obscenity of his destruction of the Saracen prisoners.

"After that, and what I suffered over it, even this information that he murdered my father, his most loyal servant, cannot move me to great passion. I believe it, but it does not surprise me in the slightest degree, and I think that were I to examine my own heart, I might even find that I suspected it—although I know I did not." André turned his eyes directly on his cousin. "I have mourned my father, and I have come to accept that he was murdered. To find out now that he was murdered by a spiteful, ungrateful friend makes little difference. Murder is murder."

St. Clair fell silent, and Alec Sinclair made no attempt to interrupt him, for he could see that there was more to come. And eventually André almost smiled as he said, "But I can understand now what you were attempting to say when you were muttering about our having to make up our minds as to what we must do next. Have you any ideas?"

"Aye, I have several. Go ahead. I'll follow you." They had reached the central area of the stone field, close by the pinnacle that marked the cavern's roof, and now St. Clair nudged his horse to the left, taking the half-hidden pathway to the sink hole that led down to the hidden entrance. Alec followed him, speaking to the back of his head as they moved forward.

"The first and most obvious option open to us, to both of us, is simply to disappear into the desert and live with our Shi'a allies. That should present no great difficulty on any front, since we have the Grand Master himself to assist us. He need simply claim a requirement for our services, as clandestine operatives, to be conducted beyond the perimeters of our regular encampments. And he would not even be required to lie, since he could never be asked about the Order that claims our loyalty along with his own. He would simply leave others to assume, which they surely would, that our duties lie in the service of the Temple. No one would ever think to doubt his judgment, for we both speak flawless and fluent Arabic and have the capability of mixing with Saracens without being seen for what we truly are."

"Aye, but were we to do that, we would be forced to live among Sinan's people. I do not think I could live that way, Alec. Can you imagine spending an entire lifetime with Rashid al-Din, with that scowling, hostile, humorless glare of his fixed upon your every move, and with the constant knowledge that even when you are not within his sight, he has a hundred or a dozen spies reporting to him on everything you say and do? No, pardon me, Cousin, but that suggestion leaves me lacking in enthusiasm. What else have you in mind?"

They had reached the sink hole, but neither man had made a move to dismount while they were talking of the Hashshashin. Now André stepped down from the saddle and Alec joined him, holding his horse's head by the halter.

"Well," Sinclair said, "we could desert and simply head into the desert to the south in search of my old friend and former captor, Ibn al-Farouch."

André turned to face him, one eyebrow raised in scorn. "Now there is a wonderful idea, brim-full of merit. I am surprised you were able to dream that one up so quickly, after the failure of your last notion. You are suggesting that we should surrender ourselves as prisoners and risk being slaughtered out of hand in swift reprisal for what we did to their brethren? That is simply a breathtaking idea."

"I am serious. And we would be in no danger. As emir, my friend Ibn has the power to protect us and give us sanctuary among his people. You would enjoy that, I think. He has a daughter, Fatama, who will be approaching fifteen years of age by now, and she is exquisite. You and she would like each other, I believe."

"Alec, I have taken vows, remember?"

"You could practice the same asceticism among the Saracens, Cousin, if that is what you wish. The emir has a brother who is very close to him, by name Yusuf, and Yusuf al-Farouch is a devout and learned man, yet also a man blessed with great wit and humor and compassion. He is a mullah, but a mullah unlike any other you might meet. You would enjoy him, too. So what say you, shall we seek out al-Farouch?"

St. Clair was staring at him wide eyed. "You are playing the fool here, are you not? Tell me, Alec, that you are jesting."

Alec Sinclair shrugged. "So I am jesting. I thought it might do you no harm to smile and indulge yourself in pleasant thoughts for a few moments. A fool can be a wondrously diverting person ... I also thought you might be less concerned than you were before with all this talk of vows and penalties and guilt and consequences were you able to laugh for a moment or two. It seems to me you have lost sight of the small fact that neither you nor I is Christian. And that is not a good fact to lose sight of, Cousin. You are starting to sound like a priest-ridden, guilt-tormented sinner, when what you really are is a privileged and enlightened Brother of the Order of Sion. Enough of guilt, Cuz. It is a meaningless concept."

"I was not thinking anything of guilt, Alec. I was far more

concerned with honor, and the way it vanishes out here like moisture on a flat stone lying in the sun."

"Ah, honor! Now there's a gold coin often gilded by people seeking to improve it. Tell me about honor, André. Tell me about how much of it you and I have seen practiced here and observed here, and— Here, look at this." Alec fumbled in his scrip and brought out a gold coin, holding it up to where André could see it and then flipping it up, end over end, to catch it in one clenched fist. "This is a golden bezant, stamped by the Sultan's coiner. I'll wager it that you cannot name me, here and now, a score of honest, truly honorable men among the army within which we march. There must be far more than a score of them among so many, but you must *name* me twenty such good men—men known to you in person. Starting now. And mind your feet while you are thinking of them." He turned and began to wend his way down the path that hugged the sides of the sink hole, and André followed him, deep in thought as he led his horse carefully behind him.

"Your coin is safe," he said when they were safely at the bottom. "I have thought hard, and I have named seven men—eight if I include Robert de Sablé, and why should I not? So, I can name eight, all of them known to me, and three of those are sergeant brothers of the Temple, honest and honorable but lacking in power or status. That shames me."

"That shames you? It is no fault of yours. Your honor is your own, as is the honor of each of the men you named. That's the wondrous thing about honor, Cousin. It lives within us and it sets its own standards for each of us, and each of us is constrained to live within its limits. Oh, you will hear me talk about the honor of the Temple, or the honor of their corps, or of the Order, but that is sheerest nonsense being put into words. *Things* cannot have honor. Only men have honor, and each man bears the burden of his own. And all of it comes down to conscience and to choices in the time of direst trial, to the point when each man must draw his own line in the sand and stand behind it. Your standard may not be the same as mine, Cousin, but in the world wherein no man may lie unto himself or

God, your honor is your own, it is your self, your soul, as mine is mine."

André St. Clair sucked in a long, deep breath. "Very well then," he said. "What is your next proposal?"

"I propose that we enter the cavern and deliver our greetings to Ibrahim. He must be waiting for us. Apart from that, I have no more proposals."

"I have, but only one."

"And what is that?"

"That we return to Acre and march southward with the army to Jerusalem. It is the most sensible thing to do, it seems to me, and while we are doing so, we will make time and opportunity to discuss our dilemma with Brother Justin, who has other tasks, now that his novices are all admitted to the Order as brothers. And, of course, with Master de Sablé. I meant to ask you this earlier, but have you any knowledge of how many of our brotherhood are here in Outremer, besides ourselves?"

"No, but there must be more of us."

"There are. Considerably more. I would guess at least two score, but little is done in the way of convocations, as far as I can see. We hold no Gatherings in Outremer, and that strikes me as being wrong, for pressure of other affairs should not affect the ongoing welfare of the brotherhood at large. So I will suggest to the Grand Master that he bend his mind to forming some kind of special chapter within the Temple's ranks, and to ensuring that its meetings be kept secret from the common fellowship. Would that please you? It should be easily achievable, and it would give us something upon which to focus for the remainder of this campaign, keeping our time and our minds focused on our true duties, free of the distractions of lesser things. What do you think of that idea?"

Alec Sinclair nodded his head once and then again, emphatically. "I like it. We return to Acre, talk to the Grand Master, march to Jerusalem with Richard's army, but reconstitute ourselves in the brotherhood along the route. That is an excellent idea. I knew you could think, Cousin, but now you have proved it. Now let us bid a good day to the formidable Ibrahim and take receipt of his dispatches."

Ibrahim, however, was not there. He had been there, and had waited for them for some time, but then, on a flat rock in the center of the cave where Alec could not fail to see it, he had left a letter written on a sheet of parchment, secured beneath one corner of a cage that held a pigeon. A leather tube of documents lay atop the cage. In his letter, he had explained that he had been there for an entire day and could wait no longer. The documents, he explained, were for the Frank *fidai*, or leader, the name used by the Hashshashin to denote the senior local representative of the Order of Sion, currently Robert de Sablé. Upon collecting the documents, Alec was asked to insert a bead into the tiny cylinder on the pigeon's leg and then to release the bird to fly home. André watched closely as Alec retrieved a tiny bright red bead from the lining of his scrip and dropped it into the tiny metal tube attached to the bird's leg.

"The red beads are used by and for me alone. I have a bag of them and always carry a few loose in my scrip. Ibrahim will know as soon as he sees this that I picked up his message safely and that all is well." He released the pigeon as soon as they left the cavern, and watched it fly until it vanished from sight, and then he turned to his cousin. "Now to Acre, and tomorrow, if God so wills it, we will strike south for Jerusalem, with Richard, and, with the blessing of Robert de Sablé, build our brotherhood to strength again in Outremer along the way. Lead on, Cousin."

ELEVEN

ndré St. Clair had cause to recall his cousin's observations concerning chastity and asceticism the following day, for before the army struck camp and marched out to the south, he found himself almost face to face with Richard's sister Joanna Plantagenet. The massive army had been astir since long hours before dawn, when the bells and trumpets of the King's Heralds had rousted everyone from their beds to begin preparing for what would be a long and wearisome day, Sunday, the twenty-fourth day of August 1191, the Feast Day of Saint Bartholomew. The prayers of matins had been set aside that day, because of the preparations for departure, but before dawn, notwithstanding that, the priests and bishops were everywhere celebrating Holy Mass, and the sound of chanted prayers reverberated on all sides, spilling over on each other from place to place and generating a sound that was like the buzz of an enormous beehive.

André, carrying his steel helm, and with his mailed hood unlaced to bare his head, had been making his way from crowd to crowd of worshippers, searching for Alec, and managing to look devout and intent as he deftly avoided stopping anywhere, but as he emerged into one area that had a higher concentration of torchlight than any other, it registered upon his awareness that the smell of incense was thicker here, the light stronger and the clothing of the celebrants, including no fewer than three officiating bishops, was of a much richer quality than anything he had seen before. He saw a concentration of clean and brilliant red-crossed white surcoats on his left and recognized Sir Robert de Sablé among them, unmistakable in his magnificent Grand Master's mantle of thick white woven wool with the plain black, equal-armed cross on front and rear. Alec Sinclair stood beside the Grand Master, and André began to swerve towards them, but he stopped abruptly when he saw the King standing on de Sablé's other side, and on Richard's left, the two Queens, Berengaria and Joanna Plantagenet, with their women clustered behind them.

Because of the angle from which he had begun to approach them, no one in the royal grouping had seen him moving, but something in the way he froze caught Joanna's attention, and she turned her head and looked right at him. André did not even have time to lower his head, and so he merely lowered his eyes, hoping that, from where she was, he would blend into the mass of faces behind him. He kept his eyes cast down for a count of five, highly conscious of how slowly time was passing, then looked up again to find her staring at him still, a slight frown marring the smoothness of her forehead. Willing himself then not to move a muscle or react in any way, knowing that if he did he would tighten her focus on him, he lowered his eyes again slowly and counted once again to five and then to ten, reciting to himself a litany of reasons why she should not be expected to recognize him: she had never seen him in the full Templar uniform, and when she had seen him, he had been clean shaven and his hair had been long and unkempt, befitting an unranked novice, whereas now his head was cropped short and he wore a heavy growth of beard. By his estimation, she was unlikely to remember him, but yet she plainly had recognized something about him, even if she had not placed him absolutely. He raised his eyes again, slowly, and felt a great surge of relief to see that she was no longer frowning at him, although she was still frowning, her eyes moving now over the other faces around him. He watched her then, willing her to look away, and soon she did, turning back towards the altar at the front. He decided he had best move away to stand in a different place on the fringe of the crowd, resolving to wait until later before speaking to Alec.

He did not leave immediately, however. Confident now that he had not been recognized and that Joanna would not be able to pick

him out among the crowd again, he eased himself up onto a nearby
stone and looked his fill upon the two Queens, neither one of whom,
it seemed to him, had suffered even slightly from the privations of
living in a military encampment. Berengaria in particular looked
superb; queenly and self-possessed, radiant and manifestly content,
she showed no slightest indication that she might be the wife of a
man whose complete disinterest in women was a matter for jest and
public commentary. Looking at her now, and noting the hectic flush
upon her cheeks, André fancied that he saw her glance sideways
towards a fine-looking young guardsman who stood vigilantly by
her side, approximately one step ahead of her, and he looked more
closely at the man, noting the stalwart, upright stance, the held head
high, and the defiant ardor with which his bearing proclaimed his
devotion to his duty as the Queen's Guard.

Amused, but not at all surprised, André moved his eyes to where
Joanna stood, as prominent as though she were alone, although
surrounded by a crowd. Joanna Plantagenet, he thought, not for the
first time, was a remarkable and attractive woman. It was plain to
see that she, too, was not lacking in physical affection or attention,
although try as he would, he could gain no inkling of who, if
anyone, among the crowd might be the recipient of her favors. He
found it surprisingly easy to smile at his own wonderings and to
accept and then dismiss the fact that he might have enjoyed those
charms. With one last, lingering look at the slim, upright figure, with
its thrusting breasts and closely draped waist and hips, he tilted
himself wryly towards asceticism, if not outright chastity, and
decided to make his way back to his own marshaling area.

With his thoughts thus busy on carnal matters, André had almost
forgotten about another gaze that he wished to avoid, and before he
stepped down from the stone he was perched on, he felt, more than
saw, the King's eyes fixed upon him. He would never know whether
the iciness in Richard's baleful stare was an expression of regal rancor
or of his own consciousness of having crossed and disappointed the
King—something his father had warned him never to do—in the
matter of Berengaria. Aware of some safety in the physical distance

between them, André held the King's gaze for a long moment, feeling courageous as he did so, yet simultaneously conscious of a deep dread, spawned by a nagging doubt about his responsibility to the man who was once his hero, in spite of everything he knew about him now.

It was Richard who looked away first, leaving André to rejoin his comrades with a sickening sense of having been irrevocably cast out, for better or for worse.

As soon as the Masses were concluded, camp-breaking stepped up to a frenzy as thousands of tents were laid out and uniformly folded before being loaded on the baggage train. The great siege engines had been dismantled and mounted on their transport plat-forms weeks earlier, after the surrender of the city, and armies of sappers and engineers had been busy for the previous few days manhandling them into position for the march to the south. They had then moved forward with them the day before, so that they were already several miles ahead of the army that would follow. There was much coming and going of traffic between the marshaling points and the Acre harbor, too, as barges pulled in to the piers to be heavily laden with foodstuffs and weaponry in preparation for the journey down the coastline, paralleling the army's line of advance along the ancient coast road built by the Roman legions before the time of the Caesars. But eventually everything was laden, the troops were drawn up in their formations, the last of the encampments were dismantled and the latrines filled in, and to a great, brazen rally of trumpets, the first ranks of the advancing host wheeled into place and struck out along the road to Jerusalem.

TWO DAYS LATER, after a slow and uneventful march in which they covered less than ten miles, marching in the cool of the morning and avoiding the sun in the afternoon, André St. Clair finally met with his cousin. He had decided to stay well away from Alec on the march and to leave it to his cousin to seek him out when he had time, for there was an ever-present danger of encountering Richard in the area surrounding the Templars' tent and de Sablé's own pavilion, and

André had no wish to court the possibility of a casual encounter with his former liege. He was unsure of how he might react on meeting his father's killer face to face, be he king or no. And so it was Alec who found him, sitting alone on the ground close by his tent and free, for the time being, from the presence of any of his squadron, his closest neighbors almost twenty feet away, a significant degree of privacy in the middle of an army that numbered tens of thousands.

"I brought wine," Alec said in lieu of greeting, lobbing a full skin into André's hastily outstretched hands and then looking around him in surprise. "Where's your squadron? Did you lose them?"

"No, but I lost patience with them. They're out there somewhere, drilling. I told my first sergeant, Le Sanglier, to have them set up butts and practice with their crossbows until dinnertime. It's been nigh on two weeks since last they practiced, and it seems like twice that long since I last had a moment to myself without their voices deafening me. Why is it, think you, that soldiers seem incapable of speaking quietly? Anyway, thank you for this. I won't even ask where you stole it from, but will drink straight to your good health." He unstoppered the wineskin and held it up to his mouth, then drank deeply before offering it back to Alec.

"Well," he continued eventually, "we are alone, so tell me, for my ears only, since you are the man with the inside information. Where are we going and what is our intent?"

"Arsuf is where we're headed. Have you ever heard of it?"

"No. Had you, before someone told you we were going there?"

"Yes, but solely because I went there once. It's an ancient port, about sixty-five miles south of Acre. And I said ancient, not merely old. The Greeks who built the place called it Apollonia. It's a walled town, too, not very large but easily defensible, with a sandstone fortress, now in ruins, on the landward side. It's one of the places Saladin's people captured after Hattin. Now Richard intends to take it back and use it as a base for his attack on Jaffa, another, larger port six miles to the south of Arsuf. Once he has those ports as safe harbors for his supply barges, he can then swing inland for the fifty-mile drive on Jerusalem."

"Hmm. And where is Saladin's army? Instinct tells me they may be protecting Jerusalem, but we are nowhere near there yet, so why would they bother, at this stage?"

"They are here. As you say, Jerusalem is in no danger at this point. Saladin is above us, up in those hills ahead and almost within view, watching our progress until he gauges that the time is right for an attack."

"What hills are those? With one sole exception, they do not appear to be too high."

"Nor are they. The high one is Mount Carmel."

"Now *that* is a name I have heard. Mount Carmel ... Is it close to where we are going?"

"Aye, it's right beside our destination."

"And you think Saladin will attack us from up there, from above?"

"Absolutely, but he won't wait until we reach Carmel. As soon as we penetrate the foothills, where the road rises and falls from crest to crest, he'll hit us with everything he has, but on a broad plane of attack—small groups of hardened attackers, plunging down out of the hills independently of each other, along the entire extended length of our line of march, hitting whatever they can hit, wherever they find it. They will swoop in, create as much damage and havoc as they can, then pull back out and flee before we can rally anything like a counterthrust."

"And is there nothing we can do to stop them?"

"Aye, we can turn tail and march back to Acre, but even so there will be no guarantee that they will not chase us. So we may just as well press forward."

"Faster, I hope, than we have been moving to this point?"

"No." Alec shook his head and almost smiled. "I find myself admiring Richard at times like this ... as a general, I mean, a strategist. I think he is inspired in this. He is restrained, cool headed, judicious, and clearly thinking far ahead. His policy of advancing slowly and in comfort is unimpeachable. March in the cool morning hours, rest in the long, hot afternoons, and thus remain unruffled and adaptable, untaxed by the heat and capable of responding quickly and strongly to anything the enemy might throw at us. If he continues to use tactics like these, he will have the edge on Saladin. Four miles a day, I know, seems deathly slow to men like us, accustomed as we are to riding everywhere, but you know as well as I do that an army's progress is tied to the speed of its slowest units, and in our case, the slowest units are our siege engines. We will be fortunate, I think, if we can maintain four miles a day with those. Were it not for the fact that this road was Roman-built and has been more or less maintained, our speed might well be cut in half. And yet we can't simply walk off and leave these devices behind us, lying at the side of the road, not without opening ourselves to the threat of having them used against us at some future date. So, we will keep forging forward and resisting the temptation to charge the enemy."

"Since when has charging and engaging the enemy been something to deplore?"

Alec Sinclair looked straight at his cousin without the slightest hint of raillery in his voice or his look. "Since Gerard de Ridefort led a Templar charge into total extinction at Hattin, four years ago. Since he lost his full force of a hundred and sixty Temple knights, plus a knot of Hospitallers, a mere month prior to that, charging downhill against four thousand Saracen horsemen at the Springs of Cresson. And since two thousand Frankish infantry went charging into death on the same day as de Ridefort's cavalry at Hattin. Every time we mount a charge against this enemy, we are overwhelmed and defeated, because Saladin's people know exactly how to counteract the superior advantages of our Christian horse. De Ridefort is dead now, and so are his tactics. You will see no more foolish charges mounted nowadays against a mobile, agile force of mounted bowmen." He stopped suddenly, cocking his head. "Listen. What was that?" The sound came again, a ripple of brazen trumpet notes. "Damnation, I thought that's what it was. Officers' call. I have to go."

He clambered to his feet and tossed the wineskin back to André. "Keep this. You'll need it. Tomorrow should be much like today, but we'll start climbing into the foothills the morning after that, and that's when the gnats will start to buzz down from the hills, so have your people ready. One of our staff members made the recommendation that crossbow units should march with their crossbows armed, ready for instant use, but his advice was disregarded. Personally, I think he was right, and if I were you, I'd have my people ride prepared for anything as soon as we enter the hill region. But as I said, that won't be until the day after tomorrow. I'll try to see you again before then." The trumpet call sounded again in the distance as he said that, and he brought his clenched fist to his breast in a salute. "That said, keep your head down in the interim. There's a sickness of Saracens out there."

ALEC SINCLAIR'S PREDICTION proved accurate. The next day, having covered another four miles without seeing a Saracen or being molested in any way, the army made camp just short of the foothills of Mount Carmel, and the morning after that, as they began to climb the slopes of the first hills, the attacks began and then continued throughout the day and into the night, creating a tension that kept everyone awake and fidgety, since there was never any warning of where the next attack would materialize. The enemy came down surprisingly quietly from the heights—and particularly so at night— in small, lightly armored, and maneuverable groups of thirty to forty bowmen mounted on wiry, sure-footed Yemeni horses. There was seldom any time to prepare for their assault, because they made so little noise before they swooped in to the attack, emerging from nowhere to create chaos and strike terror into the units they hit, charging and churning and killing and then withdrawing before the defenders had any real opportunity to rally and counterattack.

But it soon became apparent that the attacks were far from being as random and haphazard as they first seemed. Soon after the initial attacks on the first day of the campaign—for a coordinated campaign is exactly what these attacks turned out to be—a pattern began to emerge. As it solidified in the days that followed, it caused great consternation among the Franks, and most particularly so at Command level, where Richard and his increasingly frustrated allied commanders began to appreciate fully that, as things currently stood, they were effectively unable to counteract, or even to evade, the Saracens' design.

That design was simple, and its execution brilliantly effective. Any killing of Frankish knights or other personnel during the attacks was an incidental bonus. The primary target of every raid was each unit's stock of giant English, Flemish, and German warhorses, the massive destriers that bore the Frankish knights into battle. The Franks were outraged by the targeting of their defenseless animals, and their bishops and archbishops whipped themselves into a frenzy, brandishing bell, book, and candle as they called down death, eternal damnation, and appalling curses on the heads of the scurrilous infidels who would stoop to such deplorable depths of iniquity. But as Alec Sinclair pointed out to André the next time they were able to sit and talk, the Saracens were merely being practical, and admirable. Had he been in their place, he said, he hoped he would have been clever enough to identify the need that gave rise to their strategy and to have done the same thing. St. Clair had been hit by an arrow not half an hour earlier—it had glanced off the cuff of his mailed glove with no ill effect other than a momentary numbness in his hand—and had not expected to hear anyone on his side say anything like that, and he spoke right out.

"I know you admire our enemy, Cousin, but must you cheer for them? What, in God's name, is admirable about killing horses by the hundreds?"

"Everything, if it suits your needs. Show me your wrist. Can you grip your sword?"

"I can grip anything I need to grip. There's nothing wrong with my wrist, or my hand. It's my sense of outrage that's involved here."

"Pah! You're thinking about it as a horseman, André, and you have a weakness for fine horse flesh anyway. The Saracens would feel exactly the same way were we targeting their mounts. But look at it practically. The Saracens are confounded by our knights, even more today than they were four years ago at the time of Hattin, because our armor, both mail and plate, is stronger and heavier than ever before and improving all the time. Their arrows can no longer penetrate our mail most of the time—witness the strength of your own glove there—and our horses, our magnificent destriers and sumpters, make theirs look puny and ridiculous. Our individual beasts may be four and five times as large as theirs, and are themselves weapons, trained all their lives to kick out with steel-shod hooves on anything that comes close enough to kill or maim. Thus when we form ourselves in line, knee to knee, nothing can stand against us. That is the strength in us that, properly employed, they cannot defeat, or could not until now ...

"But now, I fear, they have finally seen that our greatest strength is our greatest weakness. Our horses, brought all the way across the sea from home, are irreplaceable. Each one, out here, is worth ten times its weight in gold because it would take that much and more to bring a new, fresh horse this far to replace one that dies. And each one that dies leaves a knight unhorsed and unable to function properly, for no man can fight adequately afoot, dressed as a Frankish knight in plate and mail. And in truth, no man can walk as a knight, in plate and mail, in the heat of the desert sun. It is not possible. Thus the logic in what the Saracens are doing now is faultless. By killing our horses, they can defeat us in the field, rendering us powerless to fight."

St. Clair had been sitting rigidly since Alec's diatribe began and now he was mute, his mouth slightly agape, his haunted eyes betraying that he understood the implications of everything Sinclair had said.

"Let your face sag a little, Cousin," Alec said. "The outlook is not as bleak as you seem to think ... I left you with more than half a wineskin when I last saw you. Did you drink it all?"

André shook his head, as though awakening from a light sleep. "The wine? No, I still have it. I do not often drink alone. Would you like some?"

"Oh no, not I. I merely wondered whether you might keep it until it dried up in the desert heat ... Of course I would like some. Where is it?"

"Wait." St. Clair went into his tent and emerged moments later, carrying the wineskin, and he tossed it to Alec, who held it up and hefted it before looking back at him in disbelief.

"You didn't drink a drop of it."

"No, and be thankful, for if I had, we would not be able to enjoy it now." He sat back down where he had been before and watched as Alec held the skin aloft and directed a jet of wine into his mouth without spilling a drop. "You said the outlook is not as bleak as it appears. What did you mean?"

Sinclair wiped his mouth with the back of one hand and tossed the skin back. "We know what they're up to now. That's what I meant. And that knowledge itself is part of our defense. So, beginning tomorrow they will find no more easy targets scattered in and around our camps. Instead, if they want to risk reaching our horses, they will have to infiltrate heavily guarded positions selected for their natural safety and difficulty of illegal access. And of those few who might get in to where the horses are on any given day or night, very few will escape alive. By the time we make camp tomorrow, everyone will know the new arrangements and adequate guard rosters will be put into effect. We have already chosen scouts who know what we need, and they will go out tomorrow morning, in teams of three and ahead of the various units, to find suitable holding stations."

"How many horses have we lost since this campaign began?"

"That depends on who you talk to. De Troyes believes the number to be around the one thousand mark. But de Troyes always sees the bleakest outlook on any prospect. I think he exaggerates. I would guess the number to be half of that, give or take a few score."

"Five to six hundred, then. That represents a vast herd of horses ... and a vast supply of meat, considering our shortage of fresh food, although in this heat meat spoils too quickly. "

"Oh, it's being eaten quickly enough. Some of the knights started selling the meat, and local warfare threatened to erupt, almost overnight, but Richard issued a proclamation saying that any knight who donated his horse meat to his own men would receive a replacement, free of charge."

"Sweet Jesu! That must have cost him prettily."

"Aye, no doubt, but it stopped the haggling, which could have grown ugly. Anyway, providing we can keep our remaining stock alive, we have no current shortage of horse flesh."

"Well, fodder and water are improving, I've noticed the land around us is changing, the vegetation growing lusher and greener."

"Aye, and as we round the flank of Carmel and come to the Plain of Sharon it will grow ever greener, with a profusion of water. It is marshland over there, and it is alive with wildlife, game of all kinds and giant beasts of prey. There are lions there as big as horses, and leopards the size of a man. It is beautiful. I was here once before, when first I came out here, long before Hattin, when the kingdom was flourishing, and it was a paradise. That's when I saw Arsuf."

"And you saw lions?"

Alec heard the awe in his cousin's voice and laughed. "Aye, I did, and one I will remember to my grave, a monstrous male, in full prime, with a huge black mane that rippled in the air as he walked. I heard him roar before I saw him, and the sound of it loosened my bowels. I've seen some wondrous beasts out there, beasts most men never see at all. Great birds that cannot fly but can outrun horses, and beautiful catlike creatures than can outrun those birds and are said to be the fastest animals on earth, and curious, repulsive creatures called hyenas that eat carrion and slink and shuffle in the night like skulking demons, yet have such mighty jaws that they can bite a grown man's face and crush his skull like any egg. I guarantee you will see some of those, for they swarm everywhere, even in daylight, and as long as this war endures and spawns dead men and horses, those things will thrive and prosper."

Several of André's senior sergeants had gathered around the two cousins, listening avidly, their eyes glistening. André looked over at the largest of them and grinned. "Did you hear that, Boar? Marshlands, and plentiful water. Hard to believe of this place, is it not?"

Alec spoke up again. "Hard to believe or not, it's true. But don't go thinking you might like to bathe in the waters there. Do you know what a crocodile is?"

André shook his head, but the man called Boar half raised a hand. "I do, I think? Isn't it a giant lizard of some kind?"

"Aye, that's exactly what it is. A giant serpent lizard that can grow to be the length of two tall men, with teeth the length of your fingers and jaws the length of your arm—jaws that will cut a man in half. I know not if it is true, but I have heard tell that the creatures cannot void their bodies' wastes as other creatures do, and so when they have eaten, be it a man or an animal, they lie paralyzed on the water's edge until the meal is digested, and other serpents crawl into their mouths and eat what remains in their stomachs. Thus, a man devoured by such a beast is eaten twice by serpents. Stay you clear of the water, friends."

"Enough, Cousin, you will have my officers unable to sleep tonight with such tales. Come, I will walk you back towards your tent. The rest of you, prepare for sleep, for by the time I return it will be curfew."

FIVE MORE DAYS passed by in slow and steady progress, and by the end of them the raids against the horses had all but stopped and the men had grown largely inured to seeing stretches of open water and strange, exotic creatures everywhere they looked. Morale and discipline among and within the various elements of the army was high, and a formless sense of anticipation was growing daily, nurtured by a constantly bubbling wellspring of rumor and hearsay: Saladin was massing his forces to attack them on the march; Saladin was concentrating his forces in the forest surrounding the town of Arsuf, where they were headed, and would set the woods afire as they approached; Saladin had gathered bowmen and countless wagonloads of arrows from all over his empire, sufficient to beggar the storms of arrows expended at Hattin, and intended to obliterate the Frankish advance beneath an unending rain of missiles. Whether or not any of the rumors were true, there could be no doubting the evidence of the marchers' own eyes, for Saladin's horsemen were visible everywhere, beyond bowshot and beyond easy reach, but there, and undaunted by the size of the Frankish army.

The army made camp that night on the coast, six miles north of Arsuf, near the mouth of a river and with a vast and impassable swamp at their back on the landward side, so that they settled down with more security and less fear of attack than usual, and André decided to go in search of his cousin, risking the possibility of coming face to face with Richard.

He saw no sign of the King, but found Alec sitting at a folding table, reading a document by the light of a four-branch candelabrum. Alec looked up, and his face split into a grin of welcome as he rose quickly to his feet and signed to a clerk at the table opposite him to gather up the parchment he had been reading. They were out in the open air after that within a matter of minutes, and as they walked swiftly away from the two great pavilions that dominated the center of the main encampment, André chuckled.

"You had my sergeants hanging on your words, Cousin, with your stories of the fabled crocodile, and I intended to ask you where you had heard such creature tales when next we met. But since then I have seen the things with my own eyes. I doubt that I have ever seen anything so evil looking as the sight of them sliding down the muddy riverbanks and gliding into the water. They are completely repulsive!"

"Aye, they are ugly, and they are frightening." Alec hesitated, teetering as he glanced about him, then pointed to their left. "Head over there, that way. I almost missed the way, but there is a quartermaster here who is hugely in my debt, for three enormous antelope shot by the roadside this morning and delivered to him fresh, from me, and it comes to me that he might have a spare bag of wine in his stores."

They found the quartermaster without difficulty, merely by following the smell of bread being baked by the ton in a massive array of portable clay ovens that were loaded and unloaded every day on the march, and he was profusely grateful for the services Alec had rendered to him. It turned out that not only did he have a spare bag of wine, he even had cups, a table, and two chairs in a small tent reserved for his own use, and no sooner had the two cousins sat down than he reappeared with a platter of fresh-baked bread and thick slices of cold meat.

When they had finished eating, Sinclair burped quietly and wiped the back of his hand across his mouth. "That was just what I needed," he murmured. "Now, what about you? Why did you come looking for me this afternoon?"

"Because I had nothing else to do and I felt like it. Why do you ask?"

"Curiosity." Sinclair wiped his mouth again, more carefully this time, and pinching the corners with finger and thumb to dislodge any errant particles of food. "Because when you arrived, I was just on the point of leaving to look for you. The document I was reading contained my own recollections of what had been said earlier at an officers' gathering. I have a task for you, should you be willing to accept it. I cannot order you to do it." He hesitated then, thinking about that, and shrugged. "Well, I suppose I could, but it would make no sense, for you would be under no obligation to proceed with it, once you were out of my sight."

"What is it? And before you tell me, tell me this. Is it achievable?"

"You mean, will it get you killed? Cousin, you are my entire family now that your father is dead. I have no wish to lose you. The task requires an Arabic speaker—someone who can move among the enemy without being detected and identified as one of us. We have many of them, most of them Arabs, but there is none of them whom I would care to trust with a task this … sensitive. I intended to do it myself, but de Sablé found out and forbade me. He has other plans for me tomorrow, it seems."

"Such as?"

"Commanding the Templar right."

"Good. Excellent. The man shows even more sound common sense than I would have expected. Tell me what you wish me to do."

"We are six miles from Arsuf. I need you to go and scout it out, to be absolutely sure that Saladin's people have not occupied it against us."

St. Clair frowned. "Why should that matter now? We have come all this way to attack the place. Are you telling me now that no one anticipated that it might be occupied? That defies belief."

"It does, and that is not what I am saying. What I am saying is that it now appears that things may change radically from what we had expected. For three days now, the enemy has been making broad and massive changes to his troop dispositions, and it all appeared to come together today in a series of open maneuvers that they did not even try to hide. Richard is now convinced that they intend to confront us tomorrow, nose to nose, and to try to provoke us into fighting on their terms. Saladin stands in sore need of a victory, for his credibility, and some say his discipline and control of his troops have all suffered badly since Acre fell ... and *because* Acre fell. So Richard believes we have come as far as Saladin can permit us to come without doing battle. That is why we are camped here tonight, with our backs to the swamp and safe against attack from there. It is also why the presence of the Saracen horsemen has become so visible all around us. Richard believes they will now press us increasingly and relentlessly until we give battle, no matter how unwilling we may be to play the Sultan's game. There is no doubt he is hoping to provoke us into committing the same folly that de Ridefort fell into so often, charging vainly against the drifting smoke of his mobile brigades. But Richard will have none of that, you wait and see. He will not be provoked. He intends to proceed with great caution from now on."

"I see. So what is the essence of this great caution Richard intends to exercise from now on?"

"Close-order, disciplined advance with no reaction to enemy provocation until Richard himself deems the time to be exactly right. The order of march will change immediately, split into five divisions."

"Divided how?"

"The Templars still hold the van, so there will be no great changes involved for us. But we will be joined by the division of Turcopoles, moved up from the center, which can only be to our advantage."

André nodded in agreement, for the Turcopoles were excellent troops, locally raised and trained in the same light, swift-moving cavalry techniques used by the Saracens. "And behind us?"

"Richard's liegemen from Aquitaine, Poitou, and Anjou, and his levies from Brittany. He has placed Guy in charge of those."

"Guy de Lusignan?"

"That's the man. Apparently his tactical skills are improving. Behind them, in the center, now come the Normans and the English, with the main battle standard. And then the French have the rearguard, with the Hospitallers in support and a motley collection of Syrian barons and their levies behind them. Henry of Champagne commands there, and he has Jacques d'Avesnes with him, so there is no lack of backbone in the rearguard."

"That is but four divisions. You said there were to be five."

"Aye, the fifth will be small but highly visible. Richard himself and Burgundy, supported by a hand-picked cadre of outstanding knights from all the various commands. They will be mobile, riding back and forth the entire length of the line of march, showing their faces and offering strength and support."

"So, if all this is true, why is there a need for anyone to go to Arsuf?"

"Because we have come sixty-two miles and have but six to go to reach our goal, and if we are forced to fight for every step from here onward, as Richard suspects we will be, then reaching Arsuf will take on a great significance, and the very last thing we will need or want is to arrive there and find the place strongly fortified against us. Hence the need to send someone there in advance, to assess the situation and report back to us. If the place is held and fortified already, we will accept that and make no secret of it. If it is not, on the other hand, we may then dispatch a special force to occupy it against our arrival, denying it to Saladin."

"When must I leave?"

"Ideally, you should leave immediately and spend the night between here and there, and you should take someone with you, someone you can trust. Do you know someone suitable?"

"Aye, you, but you can't come. Of all the others I would pick, none can speak Arabic and not a single one of them could pass for anything other than what he is, a Frank. So I will have to ride alone. But I am a big lad now, and it won't be the first time I have spread my blanket alone beneath the stars."

"You had better take one of them along with you anyway, for the first stage of the journey, at least, because you will want to transform yourself into a Saracen before you ride among them, and you will *not* want to go riding through the middle of this mob dressed as one of Allah's faithful. So you'll take your Arab clothing, weapons, and whatever else you need on a packhorse and change once you are safely out there. Do you have everything you need?"

"No, not here. I have my Arab clothing, but I left my Saracen weapons and armor with yours, in the cave among the stones."

"Hmm. See Conrad, the armorer. He will give you whatever you require, from the captured supplies."

"I will, but I won't need to take anyone out with me if I have a packhorse. I'll take an Arab mule with me. Then I can carry my own armor with me, for I'll tell you plain, I would not care to risk galloping back into camp here tomorrow, perhaps in the middle of a fight, dressed as a Muslim knight."

Alec Sinclair grimaced. "You have a point there. Very well, take the mule and carry your own gear. If you get caught with it, you'll already be in trouble, so it will make no difference."

"Pleasant thought ... I thank you for it. When will you want me to return?"

"Tomorrow, sometime after noon. That will give you time to settle down and examine the place closely in the morning, and then, if it is not already garrisoned, to sit tight and ensure that no concerted move is made to occupy it in the course of the morning. Of course, if you find it occupied, then all you need do is assess the strength of the garrison and make your way back to join us as soon as you can. You will not have as far to travel on the way back, and I can assure you that you will have no trouble finding us. Reaching us might be another thing entirely, but finding us should be very simple."

"Aye, I take your point. I had better be going, then."

"And on the topic that you brought up, of passing for other than what you are, make sure you take one of our Arabian horses when you go, and not a Belgian destrier."

"Well, my gratitude is overwhelming, Cousin. Had you not

thought of that, I might have ridden into the Saracens, all unsuspecting that I had betrayed myself. Sleep well tonight, and if you are brought to bay tomorrow, look after yourself. Farewell."

ANDRÉ ST. CLAIR LEANED forward, almost standing in his stirrups as he urged his horse silently to the last, steepest part of the ascent, and the uncomplaining mule surged up behind him. They had been climbing constantly for more than a mile towards the crest that now lay not a hundred paces ahead, and he looked along the ridge from side to side, watching for movement. Forming three-quarters of a circle like the rim of a broken bowl, the escarpment's edge was bare, sharply limned and clear of vegetation, and he wondered for a moment what had formed it, for beneath it the valley it contained did resemble a large bowl and he was perched high on the left edge of the break, the sea at his back, a mile below where he now sat, stretching hugely north and south, vanishing into a haze in both directions. He had no intention of climbing to the crest, and had come this high only because the terrain itself had dictated where he must go. His only interest now was in making the traverse, with his animals, from the narrow, precipitously sided ridge he was on to the sloping meadows on his left, where he intended to ride parallel to the crest, keeping below it, yet far above anyone who might be below him on the slopes.

Arsuf lay more than two miles behind him now, and it had been abandoned when he had reached it soon after dawn that morning, he and his horse the only living creatures within sight or sound. The ancient fortress with its sandstone walls was roofless and open to the weather, and he could see at first glance that no attempt had been made to secure it or to make it defensible again. He had remained there for four hours, nevertheless, obedient to his instructions, and at one point he had even ridden into the woods behind the town, aware that they stretched for miles, but remembering, too, the rumors that had whispered of ambush and destruction among the trees. He had traveled for more than a mile along a well-marked path before deciding that there was nothing in there and the rumors had been but rumors after all. Then, back on the town walls as the day wore on towards noon, it had become clear that if Saladin had any plans to man the fort, he had in all probability left it too late, for even at their normal rate of progress, less than one mile an hour, the Christian army would arrive by mid-afternoon at the latest. Unless, of course, it failed to arrive at all.

Confident then that he had done what had been asked of him, St. Clair had saddled up again and struck out northward, leading his pack mule towards the advancing army, and when he had reached the closest point to the slope that stretched up towards the high ridge, he had steered his mount off the road, to the right, and begun to climb.

He reined in now, with barely more than his own height between him and the top, and bent forward in the saddle, gentling his horse with the flat of his hand against its neck until it regained its normal breathing speed. He dismounted and led both animals, one at a time, across what proved to be a very narrow, steeply sloping, and treach-erous strip of ground that fell away into the deep ravine that edged the ridge, then remounted and made his way to the shoulder of ground ahead of him that masked his view of the valley below. The hillside ahead of him swept down gently for a hundred paces or so, then rose upward again to another, lower ridge, beyond which he could see nothing but sky. He prodded his horse forward gently to the other slope, and this time as he approached the crest he became aware of a sound, strange and unrecognizable, rising and falling in the distance. Curious, he spurred his horse more urgently, and it surged up to the top of the second ridge to show him a sight that took his breath away and left him staring open mouthed at the scene below him, with not a thought in his head of being seen.

A battle was being fought in the valley bottom, but even as he looked at it for the first time, trying to absorb the scope of it, he could see that there was something fundamentally lopsided about it. It took several moments for him to adjust to the new perspective, for now he was looking down from what felt like an immense height and everything appeared strange and different. Nevertheless, within a few moments he saw what it was, and understanding came to him in a flash, although it was a flash of disappointment. With a rising surge of disbelief he saw that Richard Plantagenet had blundered, for the first time in a lifetime of warfare.

It was clear that the Muslim troop movements he had identified that morning, with hundreds of riders moving far up on the high wooded slopes, had featured prominently in Saladin's attack, and that the first attack had come from there.

The Frankish army stood directly below St. Clair with their backs to the sea, and from where he sat he could not believe the closeness with which they were all jammed together, or the savagery with which Saladin's forces were attacking them from above, shooting arrows and crossbow bolts into the densely packed mass as quickly as they could launch and reload. So thick was the press down there that no aim was required from the heights above. Every missile fired, no matter how carelessly, found a target, and the raised shields of the Frankish knights formed a kind of roof against the downpour.

To St. Clair's right, the straight and narrow Roman road stretched back to the ground beside the swamp where Richard's army had spent the night, and he could see that it lay open, with no signs of trap or ambush to deter the Franks from retreating in that direction. On the other side, however, to the south, the roadway vanished into a tunnel of trees about half a mile from where the Franks had stopped their advance, and there were sufficient bodies, both human and equine, on the surface of the road to demonstrate that the Muslims had attacked from there, sweeping out of the tunnel and down through the woods above the road to stop Richard's army in its tracks.

Everything looked small and compact from where he sat, but André St. Clair knew that the Frankish host that looked so strangely small and cramped from his viewpoint was the largest foreign army ever assembled here since Roman times, and it was surrounded on three sides by a force that greatly outnumbered it. So closely were the Frankish troops packed that certain of the various contingents appeared as solid blocks of color, the most noticeable of those being the red-flecked white mass of the Templars on St. Clair's left, holding the vanguard which had now become the right of the line, and the solid, black-garbed mass of the Hospitallers of the rear-guard, now forming the left of the line. Between those were the blue and gold of the French knights, but it was the military orders of the Temple and the Hospital who stood out most significantly in the solid phalanges of color.

Richard had insisted from the outset of this drive from Acre to Jerusalem that he would not commit the same errors that had doomed his predecessors in their misadventures with Saladin. He had great respect for the Kurdish Sultan and he was determined that he would make no foolish or impulsive errors with his command that would present the Saracen leader with any undue advantage, and in Richard's eyes the greatest and most consistent weakness that the Frankish armies had demonstrated within recent years was their tendency to charge headlong against the enemy and consider the costs afterwards, when the appalling price had been paid and tallied. Richard was under no illusions about those tactics and their origins. They sprang directly from the stubborn, headstrong arrogance of the Templars and the Hospitallers, who simply refused to believe that there might ever be a circumstance in which they, with God so firmly on their side and in their prayers at all times, should even hesitate to engage the enemy tooth and nail. That the enemy knew exactly how to provoke those charges, and then how to avoid them and wreak havoc on the suicidal Christians as they charged past, appeared to have no significance to the senior field commanders of either Order. Their quest was for glory—their own personal glory first, and the greater glory of God incidentally.

Richard had been determined to curb that zeal, and had kept all of his subordinates on a tight leash. He had been fighting ruthless, determined, and ambitious enemies throughout his life, beginning in his boyhood, and there had been none of them whom he respected more than Saladin. And so he had insisted on a slow, steady progress from the moment he left Acre, keeping his knights tightly in check, in compact defensive formations that were, he believed, invulnerable to Muslim attack.

Now, however, from where St. Clair watched, it appeared that the King had held them in too tightly, for his cavalry forces were so densely compressed that they had no room to maneuver or even to regroup. Hemmed in on every side by their own infantry formations and under constant missile assault from the slopes above, they had no other option than to sit massed together, with the ground falling away at their backs towards the sea, and wait to be chopped down. Their armor was the finest in the world, and it rendered them all but invulnerable, but there were always weak spots in armor and accidental exposures to what was an incessant hail of arrows.

Then, even as he watched, St. Clair saw another phase of the attack develop as a solid phalanx of the black-clad desert nomads called Bedouin—he quickly estimated at least half a thousand—charged down from concealed positions high in the woods and launched a ferocious attack on the tightly compressed forces of the Hospitallers of the rearguard, on the far left of the Frankish line. Incredulous, St. Clair watched as the Hospital knights were squeezed even more tightly, something he would not have believed possible by that stage, and the protective lines of infantry fronting their formations swayed and buckled.

"Charge them! Break out, or you're all dead men!" He was shouting at the top of his voice, bellowing advice down to the beleaguered men who could neither hear nor see him, but even as he hurled down imprecations and exhortation, he could see that nothing was to be done. The scene was set for a bloodbath. The front line of the Bedouin charge approached the farthest edge of the rearguard formations and then the riders drew rein and leapt from their horses to charge in a solid block towards what they must have identified, for reasons of their own, as the weakest part of the opposing front. St. Clair could visualize their dark, feral faces as they swept forward, brandishing their fearsome scimitars. Of all the warriors of the Faithful, the Franks disliked and feared the Bedouin above all others.

He was not aware of having dismounted, but André was pulling at his clothes, ripping off the Arab garments until he stood clad only in the white lamb's wool loin wrapping of the Temple Knights. He crossed to the mule, moving slowly so as not to frighten the patient animal, and re-dressed himself as a Templar, complete with white, red-crossed surcoat, moving swiftly now that he had decided to die with his peers, and concentrating intently on wasting no time, not even to glance down at the scene below. Thus, engaged with the straps and lacings of his hauberk and cuirass, he missed the first few crucial moments of what next transpired down there, and it was only as he straightened up to slip his sword belt over his head and across his chest that he saw something had changed. Fully alert then, he stuffed his Muslim clothing and weaponry into the leather casings on the pack mule, then moved quickly to his horse and stepped up into the saddle, his eyes fixed on the scene below, to see a transformation that astounded him.

Whatever had occurred, he could clearly see that it had begun with the Hospitallers, for the knights had broken out there, surging through the defensive ranks of their own infantry to attack the Bedouin newcomers, most of whom were now afoot. But the breakout was not confined to the Hospitallers, for as St. Clair watched, rapt, the Frankish cavalry broke through all along their line in an irresistible rolling wave—and watching it occur he could think of no other term for it—that surged all the way to the right of the line and brought the Templars charging out and forward into the teeth of the enemy, who, judging from the way they buckled and recoiled from the assault, were obviously unprepared for anything of the kind. Even from as far away as St. Clair's viewpoint, it was clear that the tables had been unexpectedly and completely reversed.

The Saracens, so unmistakably jubilant and confident mere minutes earlier, were now reeling and eddying in confusion, unable to assert themselves in the face of what must have appeared to them as an absolute and unstemmable explosion of heavy cavalry. St. Clair had no knowledge of what had happened to the ranks of infantry between the knights and the Saracens, of whether they had been trampled in the charge or had managed to slip between the horsemen, but the Frankish forces rallied with every heartbeat. And then the Bedouin phalanx that had charged the rearguard simply shattered as the men broke and ran in all directions to escape the massive horses of the charging Hospitallers. But the Hospitallers permitted no escape. The fear and frustration they had been forced to undergo for so many hours resulted in an orgy of blood lust and slaughter. They slew men by the thousands in front of their positions as the madness spread southward to the right of the line and Saracens fled in utter panic and fear, leaving their Sultan impotent to stop them or even to try to rally them.

Now St. Clair could hear the difference in the sounds rising from below and he knew, from his eagle's-eye view, that he was witnessing the greatest rout in the history of the wars of the Latin Kingdom. The masses of cavalry were bunching up, pursuing the fleeing Saracens towards the edge of the forest in the south, but even so, before they could enter the forest proper, the leading ranks were stopped and began milling about, already starting to reform. He would learn later that it was Richard himself who stopped the pursuit, aware even then of past lessons learned through overzealous pursuit of fleeing enemies, and he would hear many accounts of Richard's personal heroism during the heaviest of the fighting following the breakout, none of which he would doubt for a moment. For the time being, however, he sat his horse alone up on the heights and watched the army reform and regroup along the road until he realized that they were about to march southward in good order to their intended destination of Arsuf. At that point, feeling uncharacteristically jubilant over the victory, he set spurs to his horse and set out down the hill, leading his mule, to rejoin his companions.

HALF AN HOUR LATER, frustrated and increasingly impatient, he was still far above the straggling army, headed in the wrong direction and unable to do anything about it. He had discovered the truth of the oldest adage among climbers—that it is far more difficult to climb down from a high elevation than it is to climb up there in the first place. The way the hillside fell away beneath him simply compelled him to keep moving northward, to his right. The alternative, to strike stubbornly southward and to his left, was simply too

dangerous to contemplate. The two animals he was leading left him
in no doubt about the folly of that, balking and refusing, stiff legged,
to go anywhere near the precipitous southern faces, and although he
was unaccustomed to noticing such things, he quickly came to see,
quite literally, that everything about this hillside sloped downward,
visibly, to the right. And so he gritted his teeth and concentrated on
picking his way along with great care, forcing himself to analyze all
that he could see going on below him, rather than allow himself to
grow more uselessly angry than he already was.

Someone, clearly, had made a decision to keep the main body of
the army moving southward along the road to Arsuf, and St. Clair
acknowledged to himself that whoever had been responsible—and
he presumed it was Richard himself—had made the correct choice,
for their current position was clearly untenable, an elongated,
cramped, and narrow stretch of hillside between the road itself and
the sea. After the pressures they had undergone in that same place,
he was unsurprised that they had no wish to remain there for a
moment longer than they had to, and so now almost the entire army,
regrouped and redisposed in clear formations, was winding steadily
along the road to the south, and progressing far more quickly than
they had since leaving Acre, secure in the knowledge that the
Saracens would not soon be returning to engage them.

The road, until it disappeared beneath the overarching trees at the
entrance to the forest, was crammed with marching men, and the
largest area of land between it and the sea had been converted into a
vast marshaling area where troop commanders and officers were
organizing units to join the exodus, falling into place behind the
passing ranks as space became available. The exercises were being
carried out efficiently, André could see, and the evacuation was
proceeding smoothly, but the single most significant and striking
thing that he could see as he drew steadily closer to the battlefield was
the extent of the casualties, and most particularly among the Saracens.

There appeared to be thousands of dead and wounded Muslim
soldiers everywhere he looked, and as he scanned them, seeing how
they had been mowed down in swaths, an image grew in his mind

from his boyhood, of a cornfield outside his father's home in Poitou, one remembered afternoon at harvest time, when everyone had stopped working to eat at noonday and the rows of corn, scythed but ungathered, not yet bound and stacked, had formed clear-cut patterns on the stubbled ground. He could see very few Frankish bodies among the casualties, which surprised him, for he was above the far left of the line now, the rearguard position of the Hospitallers, and their black-and-white colors were easy to spot from above, but it seemed to him that for every Hospitaller or other Frankish form he saw on the field, he could count ten or more Muslims.

He reached a stretch of hillside where, unusually, the lie of the land altered and he was able for a brief time to turn his mount and ride southward, back towards the battlefield. And then, quite suddenly, he was within hailing distance of the road below, where the lay brothers of the Hospital were fully occupied in doing what they did best, tending to the wounded. Several of the black-clad fighting monks, riding up and down in full uniform, were supervising the efforts of large, organized groups of infantry who were separating the living from the dead and the Christians from the Muslims, carrying the Frankish wounded to a cleared space by the roadside and the Muslims to a more distant spot, closer to the seashore. Down there, André could see, were more Hospital brothers, tending to the infidels as their brethren were tending to their own.

"You there! Templar! Stand where you are."

St. Clair reined in and saw that the speaker, or the shouter, was a Hospitaller, flanked by a pair of crossbowmen, each of whom was pointing a heavy arbalest uphill at him. He dropped the reins on his mount's neck and raised both hands above his head.

"Come down. Slowly."

André lowered his hands and nudged his horse forward and sideways, picking the easiest route down and highly aware of the arbalests pointed at him. The knight probably thought him a deserter or a coward who had sought refuge high up on the slopes to avoid being killed, and thinking that, he would have no compunction about giving the word to shoot St. Clair down without mercy. Finally, he reached the roadway and moved forward to face the Hospitaller.

"Who are you and what were you doing up there? And be careful what you say."

André made no attempt to smile or be engaging. "André St. Clair, and I was trying to get back to my unit. I was sent out last night by our Grand Master, de Sablé, to scout Arsuf and make sure it had not been occupied. He sent me because I speak Arabic and can pass for a Muslim. The clothing and weapons I wore out there are here, in the cases on the pack mule. Look, if you like."

"And was Arsuf occupied?"

"No, it was not. But it makes no difference now. Saladin's people will not stop running until they are far south of Arsuf."

"Hmm." The Hospitaller nodded towards the mule. "Show me what is in the cases."

Moments later, he sat frowning at the circular Saracen shield he was holding.

"Right. Well, I suppose I'm obliged to believe you, St. Clair, but I have to send you now to my superior, Sir Pierre St. Julien. You would have to do the same with me, were things reversed."

"I would. Where do I find him?"

The Hospitaller turned to the man on his right, who had long since put down his arbalest. "Take him to St. Julien." He glanced back at St. Clair. "God be with you, St. Clair, and good luck." He raised a hand briefly and swung away, already shouting at some of the men working nearby.

The knight called St. Julien accepted St. Clair even more quickly than the other had. As he was quickly checking the contents of André's packs, a group of men moved past them, carrying five wounded Hospitallers on improvised stretchers.

"How many men did you lose?" André asked him.

St. Julien twisted his mouth. "Not nearly as many as I thought we would. Our Grand Master went to argue with King Richard, begging him to turn us loose, but Richard refused. When the charge did break out, it was because one or two of our own knights had simply had enough, and out they went ... And everyone else went after them. It simply happened, and when it did, everyone joined in. I don't know about the rest of the line of battle, but I would be surprised if we lost more than half a hundred men—knights and foot soldiers both."

"You must have taken out ten men for every one you lost, then."

"Oh, more than that, for by the time we broke out, the men were beyond anger. They showed no mercy, gave no quarter. Everything that moved in front of them went down. Ah! They've found something over there. God speed, Sir Templar."

Thereafter, André St. Clair made his way along the road without being bothered again, and for the entire distance he was amazed at the disproportionate numbers of Muslim dead and wounded lining the road, with corpses piled in head-high heaps in many places. The crews whose task it was to clean up the carnage had nothing to say to him and little to each other. They were already listless and dull eyed, appalled into speechlessness by the awful, repetitive nature of the work they were doing and the condition of the mangled and dismembered bodies with which they had to deal, surrounded by the sounds and stenches of humanity in unspeakable distress. From time to time, he would pass a dead man who stood out as someone special by virtue of the clothing and insignia he wore, but for the most part, André was smitten by the sameness of it all and by the pathetic lack of dignity apparent in the heaped piles of discarded corpses. He had seen so many headless bodies and so many bodiless heads, arms, and legs that he thought he might never again be able to sit in a saddle and swing a sword, and it was while one such thought was passing through his head that something caught his attention from the corner of his eye, and he drew rein to look more closely.

But looking now at the carnage surrounding him, he could see nothing that struck him as being anomalous. There were living men among the fallen all around him; he could see some of them moving and he could hear their moans and cries, and somewhere almost beyond his hearing range, someone was screaming mindlessly, demented by pain. But whatever had caught his attention was no longer evident, and he dismissed it, gathering his reins to ride on.

He had traversed almost the entire line of battle by that time, and the cleanup crews had not yet reached this far. The section through which he was now riding had been the right of the line, occupied by the Templars and their supporting Turcopoles, and St. Clair had not realized before how closely the latter resembled the enemy they fought, for they were not uniformly equipped, and in many instances he could not tell, looking at the strewn bodies, which were which. But then, just as he began to turn away, he saw movement again, a flicker of bright yellow higher up than he had been looking before, just in front of the line of trees above him. He tensed, looking at it intently, knowing what it was but unable to say why it should be significant to him.

It was a Saracen unit flag, the equivalent of the colors carried by each of the Frankish formations, but whereas the Frankish troop divisions carried individual colors, each to its own, the Saracens bore only uniform yellow standards: large swallow-tailed banners on the end of long, supple poles, distinguished from each other by the varying devices used by each unit to identify itself and its leader. Now the banner moved again, not waved by the wind but stirred erratically, as though someone were moving against it, causing it to sway unevenly back and forth, and as it unfolded it displayed the device it bore, a number of black crescents, their leading edges facing right.

André felt his stomach lurch as he recalled the evening, months before, when Alec Sinclair had described the personal standard of his friend Ibn al-Farouch. "Remember," he had said, "if you find yourself outnumbered or in danger of defeat, don't go seeking death, for death achieves nothing but oblivion for fools. Go seeking life instead. Find the squadron with the five-moon pennant and surrender to its leader. That's Ibn. Tell him you know me, that I'm your cousin, and he'll find a comfortable chain to shackle you with."

Five black crescent moons, Sinclair had said, their leading edges facing right. The brief glance he had had of the pennant had been too short to count the number of crescents. He had seen only a cluster, perhaps five, but it might as easily have been six or seven, and he knew that he could not now ride away without satisfying his curiosity, so he turned his horse around and nudged it forward, up the hill to where the yellow banner now sagged motionless.

Among the bodies of slaughtered Arab and Christian horses, three dead Templars lay in plain view, their red-crossed, white-coated bodies intertwined and surrounded by Saracen corpses. He spurred his horse closer, examining the individual bodies of the knights, looking for men he knew, but he felt the hair stir on the back of his neck when he saw that the dead man atop the other two had not died by a Saracen scimitar but had been stabbed through the neck with a long, straight Christian sword. The blade was still in place, thrust clear through the chain-mail hood that covered the dead knight's head. The sole question in André St. Clair's mind was why, in a fight to the death against Saracens, a Christian knight would aim such a deliberate and lethal thrust at one of his brethren.

The knight had sunk to his knees and died there, his lifeblood drenching the front of his surcoat, and the men who lay beneath him, and the upthrust angle of the sword that killed him, had prevented him from falling forward. His heart beating fast now, André dismounted and stepped quickly to the kneeling knight. He pulled the head back and looked into the dead face. The man was an unknown. André pushed him firmly, so that he fell sideways and rolled off the bodies beneath him.

The next man lay face down on top of the man below him, covering his head and shoulders, but the man beneath had been the one who thrust the killing sword, for it had been torn from his hand by the weight of the falling corpse when André pushed it. He stooped and seized the second knight by the armholes of his cuirass and heaved him up, rolling him to see that, again, the fellow was unknown to him. He had been killed by crossbow bolts, three of which projected several inches from his breast. As he turned now to the third knight, André gave a whimpering, childlike cry and fell to his knees, his face crumpling as he stared between his outstretched hands into the dead face of his cousin Alec.

How long he knelt there, struck dumb, he would never be able to recollect afterwards, but he remained there, rocking slowly back and forth in agonized disbelief as he watched the slowly welling blood ooze from the grim rent in the armor over his cousin's left breast.

And only very, very slowly did it penetrate his awareness that dead men do not bleed.

When the realization did hit him, he whimpered again, and reached out with both hands to cup Alec's face, and as he did so, Alec's eyes opened.

"Cousin," Alec Sinclair whispered. "Where did you come from?"

André merely sat, hunched forward, gazing at his cousin's face, which was pallid and deeply graven with stark, blue-tinged lines. He knew he should say something, respond in some manner to his cousin's greeting, but his tongue felt frozen in his mouth.

"Where is al-Farouch?"

The strangeness of the question snapped St. Clair back to full cognizance, and his fingers tightened on his cousin's chin. "What did you say? Where is *who*?"

"Ibn al-Farouch. He was here but a short time ago. Where did he go?"

André sat back on his haunches but remained leaning forward, face to face with his cousin, his hand still grasping Sinclair's chin. "Alec, what are you talking about? Al-Farouch is not here."

"Of course he is. What is that, if not his?" André looked up, following the direction of Sinclair's gaze, and saw the yellow swallow-tailed pennant with its five black crescent moons.

"Quick, André, lift me up, quickly. Lift me up."

The urgency in Alec's voice provoked an instant response in St. Clair, and he rose immediately to kneel behind his cousin and grasp him carefully beneath the arms, cradling him as gently as he could. "How is that?" he asked. "Am I hurting you?"

"Aye, but not badly. I think I may be lying on top of al-Farouch, and if I am, he may not be able to breathe, so lift me up and move me to one side. Then I will need you to see to him—" Alec stopped, gasping for breath, but then continued. "Gently now, Cuz. Lift me straight up and step to your left. Can you do that?"

"Aye, I can manage that," St. Clair replied, but as he moved to straighten up, thrusting powerfully but steadily with his thighs against the deadweight of Alec's armored body, the agony of being moved, even thus slightly, ripped a tortured scream of protest from the wounded knight's throat. André froze before he could straighten completely, so that he was left crouching. Alec's weight seemed to increase in his arms and was growing insupportably heavier by the moment.

"Alec," he hissed, straining the words through his teeth. "Alec, can you hear me?"

There was no answer, and he knew his cousin had fainted from the pain. He tensed again, drew a deep breath and expelled it noisily, then inhaled again, sucking the air into his lungs as hard as he could, and straightened up quickly, lifting Alec as far as he could and then walking backward very carefully for two paces.

André lowered the unconscious knight to a flat piece of ground as gently as he could and then used his dagger to cut savagely through the straps and laces that held the riven armor in place. Grateful that his kinsman could feel nothing, he manhandled him remorselessly, turning him back and forth as he tore at the chain mail, clothing, lining, and bindings until he could see bare skin and the sluggish welling of blood from the wound in Alec's chest. Whatever had pierced the armor had been massive and sharp, and André guessed it had been a hard-swung battle-axe, for it had driven clean through both cuirass and chain-mail shirt, hammering individual links and pieces of metal into the gash it had made in Sinclair's chest. André prayed that the wound was not lethal, but he suspected that several of his cousin's ribs had been smashed, and he had no means of guessing at the extent of the damage Alec had sustained beneath that.

When he felt that he could do no more, he rose to his feet and peered back to the northward, looking for the distinctive black-and-white uniform of the Hospitallers, but none of them had yet come into sight, and so he knelt back down beside his cousin to find him conscious again. As soon as he came close enough, Alec grasped him by the forearm. His fingertips dug deep.

"Sweet Jesus, that hurt, Cousin. Did I pass out? I must have ... Was I right? Was Ibn beneath me?"

André St. Clair shook his head. "I don't know, Alec. I haven't had time to look. You were lying atop someone, a Saracen, but how would I know who he is?"

"An amulet, hanging from his neck on a silver chain. Heavy silver … Amulet is green … the Prophet's favorite color … Is there an amulet? Look and see."

André moved away and looked at the man who had been lying beneath Sinclair, but he had to reach out and search before he could find anything about the man's neck. A few moments was all it took, however, and he was kneeling by Sinclair again.

"Aye," he muttered. "A carved amulet of pale green stone, with a chain of heavy silver links."

"Jade, Cousin, it's called jade … Is he alive?"

"No, Cousin, he is not. I checked most carefully and I could find no pulse. Your friend is dead. What happened here?"

For a moment Alec Sinclair looked as though he might actually laugh, but then his breath caught in his throat and he grunted, clearly incapable of breathing as he struggled against the pain of his wounds. André felt the strength in his grip tighten then relax, still firm, but no longer panicked. "I saw him here, when we burst out. Could scarcely believe it." He paused, breathing hard, and André waited, making no attempt to rush him. "There he was, on foot and right in front of me, bleeding from the forehead so that he had to wipe the blood from his eyes with the back of his wrist. His horse, Wind Spirit, was dead beside him …" Another pause, filled with laborious breathing, and then, "He had a bare half dozen of his bodyguard still left around him, and as I saw him, one of our knights charged in to kill him, but he was careless and one of the bodyguards got him with a flung scimitar that took his head right off … And then I saw two or three more of our knights close in to finish Ibn. He wore nothing to mark him as an emir, but there was something about his bearing, as there always was, that set him ap—" The coughing spell broke unexpectedly, and for the next brief while André held Sinclair as his entire body convulsed in pain, racked with the ravages of coughing through a mouth suddenly filled with thick blood. Finally, when the fit subsided, André pressed him back onto the ground.

"Wait here, Alec. There are Hospitallers close by. I am going to find one and bring him back here." But when he tried to leave, he discovered that Alec had retained a firm grip on his wrist and would not let him go. Alec spat out a mouthful of blood and spoke again, his voice still strong but rattling in his throat.

"Don't fret about the Hospitallers, Cousin. They can do me no good. I'm finished. Now listen. Listen to me ... Will you listen to me?" André nodded, mute, and Sinclair continued. "You may hear people talk about me ... about what I did ... and they will probably make it sound shameful ... And perhaps it was. I simply don't know any more. I certainly did not set out to do it ... didn't know I would, or could, do such a thing. But there I was, and there was Ibn al-Farouch, about to be struck down ... I don't know what came over me, but suddenly he was down and on his knees, his sword gone, and I jumped down and was standing over him, seeking to defend him, I suppose ... perhaps to take him prisoner ... I know that was in my mind, that I could repay him for his kindnesses to me ...

"But no one wanted to take prisoners. Everyone was mad for blood. I tried to beat them back, our own knights, to claim him as my prisoner, but then one of our fellows struck at me, and suddenly I was fighting for my own life, against my own people. Two of them came at once, one with an axe, and he struck me, hard. The second one I finished with my sword. And then you came ... You say Ibn is dead?"

"Aye, Alec, he is."

"Bring me his amulet, will you?"

When he had it in his hand, he looked at it and grunted, wincing with pain, then held it out to André, who took it and weighed it wordlessly. "Do something for me, Cousin," Alec said in a hoarse whisper. "When all of this is over, will you find some way to send this back to Ibn's brother?" He caught his breath again, sharply, on an indrawn hiss. "Sweet Jesus, that hurts. But thank God, not too much ... His name is Yusuf. Yusuf al-Farouch ... he lives in a village near Nazareth." He stopped and held his breath for a long time before continuing. "The same Nazareth our Christian brethren tell us Jesus came from … It has an oasis … and they grow fine … fine dates there."

"I know. I remember you telling me so. The brother is a mullah, is he not?" He was looking at the amulet, and Alec did not answer immediately. "Alec? Yusuf is a …" But Alec's eyes were fixed and open, staring back at him unseeing.

"Brother? Are you well? May I assist you?" It seemed mere moments later, but as André looked up to see the black-robed Hospitaller standing over him, he knew that time had passed without his noting it. He glanced once again at Alec Sinclair, whose expression was unchanged, and then reached out one hand to the Hospitaller. "You can help me up, if you would. I fear I may have frozen here, for I have lost track of time." When he was on his feet again, he nodded his thanks to the Hospitaller and then indicated the still form on the ground. "This man was my kinsman and also my closest friend. He was my cousin, the son of my father's eldest brother. And I would like to bury him apart, I think. Perhaps down by the sea there, where his spirit might look out across the waters towards his home. Have you a shovel I might use?"

IT HAD TAKEN TWO JOURNEYS and several hours of backbreaking work to complete his self-appointed task, but now André St. Clair stood leaning on a long-handled shovel on a patch of firm sand several steps above the high-water mark that had been eroded over the years by the incoming Mediterranean tides. Before him at his feet lay a wide, deep grave, laboriously dug and wide enough to accommodate two bodies, side by side, and behind him lay the bodies of Sir Alexander Sinclair and his friend the Emir Ibn al-Farouch. He turned to where the bodies lay, then grasped Alec Sinclair beneath the shoulders and dragged him to lie along one side of the grave. Then he pulled al-Farouch to lie on the other. When they were both in place, he stood up and spoke to both of them, explaining how he would have enjoyed being able to treat them with more dignity, but that neither his honor nor their own would be besmirched by the means with which he, as a single man alone, was constrained to lay them down. He then bade them farewell in the name of the God they shared, albeit under different names, and when he had done so he went from side to side, rolling first Sinclair and then al-Farouch into the open grave. That done, it was the work of less than an hour to fill the grave again, tamping and tramping down the surface, then brushing it and scattering stones over it to conceal, as well as he was able, the fact that it was a grave and newly dug.

Finally, when his work was complete and the sun was close to setting, he sat down cross-legged at the foot of the grave and reached out to gather up the yellow piece of cloth that had been lying on the sand, pulling it towards him. It was the five-crescent pennant that had attracted his attention earlier that afternoon, and on it lay three objects. The first was the jade amulet that he had promised to send to the mullah Yusuf al-Farouch. The second was the magnificent dagger given to Alec Sinclair by Ibn al-Farouch, and the third was the emir's own dagger, which André had taken from its place at the small of Ibn's back, knowing he would find it there because Alec had told him, months earlier. Now, holding one of the sheathed daggers in each hand, he leaned forward and spoke conversationally, as though the two dead men at his feet could hear him perfectly well.

"Someone once read me a lesson from the Testament that said, 'Greater love hath no man than this, that a man lay down his life for his friends.' I always liked the thought of that, but now I wonder if the love could be any greater because the friend in question was an enemy. Be that as it may, my lord Sinclair, it is what you have done and your honor will not suffer by it. Nor will yours, Amir al-Farouch, from being loved in such a manner. And as you have said to me so often, Cousin, honor is all we have. It is the only attribute that keeps us separate from the beasts, and most especially from the beasts who masquerade as men ... But who will set the standard by which we govern honor when the men like you, the truly honorable men, are all gone? Another question that you posed and answered both. But is it one that you discussed with the emir? I wonder about that. For of course, the answer is immutable. We set our own standards, each of us, and each of us must cleave to his own distinctions.

"I never met you, Amir al-Farouch, but I wish I had. My cousin told me much about you and he painted you as a man of strictest honor. That makes you close to being unique, on either side of the gulf that divides your kind and ours. You are Muslim, Saracen, Arab, worshipper of the one, true God, whom you call Allah. This is your home, and Jerusalem is the Holy City of your Prophet, Muhammad, who ascended into Heaven from the Rock. Believing that, you believed, too, that you were privileged to fight in its defense, and you did so with great and unflagging honor. Your friend there, lying beside you, worships the same God, the One, the True, whom we call simply God. But his ancestors came, as did my own, from the self-same Holy City of Jerusalem. They were not Christian, but Jewish, and they called their God Jehovah, and His home, His temple, stood in Jerusalem, below where the Dome of the Rock now stands. And both of you have died in war, fighting against each other for possession of this sacred place. And for what? For honor? Whose honor? Certainly not God's or Allah's or Jehovah's, for the very thought of that is blasphemy. God has no need of man, and honor is a human attribute. For whose honor, then, are these wars waged? And how can there be honor in slaughtering people for possession of a sacred place?

"I can answer that for both of you. There is no honor in this war. There is no honor among kings and princes, popes and patriarchs, caliphs and viziers or whatever else you wish to name as titles. All of those are men, and all of them are venal, greedy, gross, and driven by base lusts for power. Ours is the task of fighting for their lusts, and like poor fools, we do it gladly, time and time again, answering the call to duty and lining up to die unnoticed by the very people who sent us out there.

"Well, my friends, I have buried you together, as you died together, and now I will leave you together. I received a warning yesterday, Cousin, to watch my back. I meant to talk to you about it last night, but you sent me to Arsuf. Then I would have told you of it tonight, but you died on me. So I will tell you now, and let you think more on honor.

"It seems that I was recognized some days ago by one of the men who killed my father. I was in close proximity to him and to his friends and he assumed, wrongly, that I was snooping for evidence against them. The man who told me was a man I had never seen, but it was clear he had difficulties of his own with these people, whoever they are. He would not give me names, but only said I should beware of 'Richard's bullyboys' as he called them, and watch my back because they were intent on killing me, to keep me quiet.

"In essence, Cousin, that does not inspire me to return to fight and die, killing good men like the emir here, either for Richard's personal ambitions or at Richard's instigation, so I know not where I'll go next, but I *will* undertake to see that the mullah Yusuf receives the emir's amulet. And so adieu, to both of you. I leave you wrapped there in your honor ... I will weep for you, Cousin Alec, and will rejoice at having known you. But not yet. Not yet. It is much too soon for that. But I will weep, for you, and for my father, and for all the fond fools dying all around us. God give them rest. Farewell."

Sir André St. Clair wrapped the two daggers and the emir's amulet in the yellow folds of al-Farouch's banner and stood up, stuffing the bundle inside his surcoat and then pulling his mantle about him against the evening chill as he went to where his horse and pack mule stood placidly grazing together. Lights were glimmering among the trees, where the Hospitallers had been working all afternoon to set up facilities to treat the wounded, and there was no shortage of people moving about, talking easily to each other now that the worst of the crisis was over and the cruelest excesses of the day had been set aside. He gathered up both sets of reins, for horse and mule, and led the animals slowly up the sloping rise to the old Roman road, where he mounted the Arab mare and turned northward, leading the mule.

"You are facing north, Brother. Arsuf lies south of here."

André turned and looked at the man who had spoken to him from the darkness beneath a neighboring tree. He was dressed in black from head to foot, and André smiled at him. "Are you a knight?"

"No, Brother, I am but a simple monk of the Hospital. I fight to keep men alive."

"And may you thrive and prosper at your craft, Brother. I am headed north, back towards Acre."

"Back to Acre? Will you not fight at Jerusalem?"

"No, Brother, I will not fight at Jerusalem, nor for Jerusalem. I am done with fighting. I intend to ride in search of a field of stones, in which to meditate and commune with my God. After that, when He and I have come to know each other better, who knows? I might even go and live among the Infidel. It can't be any more perilous than living where I do, among God's faithful zealots ..." He broke off and smiled at the expression on the tall monk's face, which he could now see clearly in the light of the rising moon. St. Clair took pity on him. "Forgive me, Brother," he said. "It has been a long day and I have far to travel in the coming years. Farewell, and God bless you."

Without another word he set spurs to his horse and trotted away, the mule in tow, and the monk stood staring after him, watching the tall, white-clad figure with the blood-red cross on its shoulders until he lost sight of it among the trees that lined the road.

FINIS

ACKNOWLEDGMENTS

In 2005, just as I was really getting into the nitty-gritty of researching this story, I received two books as gifts from really good friends: Sharan Newman sent me a French publication called *Les sites Templiers de France*—Templar Sites in France—by Jean-Luc Aubarbier and Michel Binet, published by Éditions Ouest-France, and Diana Gabaldon sent me a jewel of a book called *Arab Historians of the Crusades* by Francesco Gabrieli, the 1993 Barnes & Noble edition of the classic 1957 Italian compilation of Arab commentaries and insights into the Crusades "from the other side." Both books proved to be invaluable to me in the time that followed, allowing me to visualize connections and nuances that might never otherwise have occurred to me, and so I wish to express my gratitude to both donors.

It is truly astonishing how many books, articles, papers, and treatises there are out there on the Knights Templar, and a major part of deciding which materials to use for reference is the difficulty of being able to tell, at a glance, which are historically accurate, which are trustworthy, and which are purely speculative. Sometimes the distinctions are obvious, but I found myself traveling, on several occasions, in directions that I had never anticipated. Of course, as a writer of fiction, such tangential wanderings can be part and parcel of the voyage, and in this story of mine, I have borrowed from a few of them. By and large, however, I decided to rely upon respectability, and so restricted my later reading to works of generally accepted provenance. I thought, too, about including a bibliography here, then decided that it was much simpler to mention the half dozen wonderful books that I used most, mainly in keeping my story straight. They are:

The Knights Templar, Stephen Howarth, 1982, republished in 1993 by Barnes & Noble

Bible and Sword: England and Palestine from the Bronze Age to

Balfour, Barbara Tuchman, New York University Press, 1956, republished in 1984 by Ballantine Books

The New Knighthood: A History of the Order of the Temple, Malcolm Barber, Cambridge University Press, 1994

The Templars, Piers Paul Read, Phoenix Press, 2001

Warriors of God: Richard the Lionheart and Saladin in the Third Crusade, James Reston Jr., Anchor Books, 2001

The Templars: Knights of God, Edward Burman, Destiny Books, 1986

Once again, and as always, I am acutely aware of the debt of gratitude I owe to the Penguin Group production team. They are consistently dependable and reliable—not always exactly the same thing—and even when they are cracking the whip across my dilatory shoulders, they manage to do it subtly enough and with sufficient finesse and panache that my pain is lessened somehow by my admiration of the pink tissue paper they use to cover the metal barbs ... And among the Penguins, associated with them, are two paragons: Catherine Marjoribanks, my story editor, and Shaun Oakey, my astounding copy editor ... amazing people, both of them. To all, my thanks.

Jack Whyte is the author of the immensely popular Camulod series, a four-generation saga of the rise and fall of King Arthur, which has been translated into many languages. Born and raised in Scotland, he has lived for many years in Canada, working as an English teacher, a professional actor and singer, an advertising executive, and, always, a writer. Whyte now lives with his wife, Beverley, in British Columbia, where he is at work on a third novel in the Knights Templar trilogy. Visit his website at www.jackwhyte.com.